Curses of the Kingdom of Xixia

Curses of the Kingdom of Xixia
A Novel

XUE MO

Translated by
FAN PEN LI CHEN

EXCELSIOR
EDITIONS

Published by State University of New York Press, Albany

西夏咒, the Chinese original of *Curses of the Kingdom of Xixia*, was published in China © 2017 by Encyclopedia of China Publishing House / Xuemo Library Research Center. This translation is published by permission of the author.

Excelsior Editions is an imprint of State University of New York Press

For information, contact State University of New York Press, Albany, NY
www.sunypress.edu

Library of Congress Cataloging-in-Publication Data

Names: Mo, Xue, author. | Chen, Fan Pen Li, translator.
Title: Curses of the Kingdom of Xixia : a novel / Xue Mo, translated by
    Fan Pen Li Chen.
Description: Albany : State University of New York Press, [2023] | Series:
    Excelsior Editions
Identifiers: ISBN 9781438494951 (ebook) | ISBN 9781438494944 (pbk. : alk.
    paper)
Further information is available at the Library of Congress.

10 9 8 7 6 5 4 3 2 1

This translation is dedicated to my granddaughter,

Marcella Stonechen

Contents

Translator's Introduction

Curses of the Kingdom of Xixia presents a rich tapestry of the history, religion, and customs of a region of present-day northwestern China (including the provinces of Gansu, Ningxia, eastern Qinghai, northern Shaanxi, northeastern Xinjiang, Inner Mongolia, and southernmost Outer Mongolia) that once fostered a great Sino-Tibetan kingdom. During its heyday, the Xixia kingdom (pronounced *see-sia*; 1038–1227) rivaled the Song dynasty (960–1279) of China, and even invented its own graphic script. It boasted a cavalry so formidable that the Chinese paid tribute to Xixia to maintain peace. The Mongols, who ultimately conquered Xixia, called it the Tangut Empire. So complete was the Mongols' annihilation of the Xixia kingdom that its history and culture were practically lost to the world, until rediscovery by twentieth-century archaeologists.

The former Xixia kingdom and its people were absorbed into the Mongol Empire in 1227 and subsequently into the Mongol-ruled China of the Yuan dynasty (1279–1368). Xixia remained a part of China thereafter, through the subsequent Ming (1368–1644), Qing (1644–1911), the Republic of China (1911–1949), and the People's Republic of China (1949–present). Because Han Chinese (the main ethnic group of China) have entered the area since its conquest by the Mongols, it is now a region of mixed ethnicities, religions, and cultures—although the original Tanguts practiced a form of Tibetan Tantric Buddhism.

Xue Mo, the award-winning author of *Curses of the Kingdom of Xixia*, is renowned for his deep knowledge of the history, cultures, lore, and topography of this region. He is also an influential writer about Tantric Buddhism and spirituality and has a large following as a spiritual leader. Having spent ten years "shut-in" (voluntary confinement with a rigorous regime of meditation), the spiritual enlightenment he had attained purportedly enabled him to enter and engage with different realms of reality. Indeed, both his fantastic and mimetic realms are depicted in such graphic minutiae that it is as if he actually visited these places. He claimed to have seen the clownish tutelary god (many tutelary gods are clownish in traditional Chinese operas and rituals), a main narrator in the novel, straddling two mountain peaks with people disliked by the god passing through the valley under his crotch. Apparently, he and some local peasants are able to see the local deity, although most people can't.

Curses of the Kingdom of Xixia uses the discovery of "lost" manuscripts as a framing technique for presenting historical events and tales of the avatars of a local Tantric Buddhist goddess (Diamond Maiden Dakini; Vajrayogini; Snow Feather), a tutelary deity (Ajia), and a monk (Jasper), as well as people related to them, through different time and realms. Titled Nightmares; Crazy Ramblings of Ajia; Bodily Incarnations and Cause and Effects of the Dakini (translated as Tale of the Goddess); Family Instructions of Diamond Clan; True Records of the Curses; and Historical Mirror of Forgotten Events, the supposedly rediscovered manuscripts present seemingly unconnected stories. However, the same characters reappear in diverse disguises—not only in different historical periods but also in various spaces and dimensions. Snow Feather's mother, for example, appears in the guises of a female captive of a battle, a girl forced to bind her feet, and a woman forced into prostitution in a modern hotel of the region. Condemned despite the injustices forced upon her, her representations attest to women's plight throughout history as victims of their society and its prejudices.

The variety of locations covered in Curses include cities, villages, wilderness, mountain forests, and caves. The dimensions include worlds of the mundane, the ethereal, and dreams. Magical realism and mimesis coexist. Reality merges with illusion, the mundane with the supernatural; good and evil are shown to be two sides of the same coin.

Taking the readers through different historical periods and geographical and cultural spaces, Xue Mo reveals truths in Curses by blurring the distinction between good and evil, beauty and hideousness, reality and fiction, permanence and impermanence. One wonders whether the Barbarian Hag is a demonic cannibal, or might she be a Bodhisattva? Is she real or illusory (apparently, only Jasper is able to see her)? Hers is also the irony and tragedy of someone who becomes so addicted and inured to killing that she ends up slaying her own beloved son. Xue Mo also demonstrates the fleetingness of power by interjecting the "present" with future events, through juxtaposing the supreme arrogance of Braggart and the state priest with their eventual abject downfall.

The novel is also rife with religious lore and practices related to Tantric/Esoteric Buddhism, and local culture and customs. Xue Mo presents the tales behind iconographies in Tanka paintings of the goddess, such as the bull missing a leg and bears; and a portrayal of couple-cultivating (a Tibetan Buddhist cultivation through sexual union). Material culture of the region includes the crafting of ritual implements using human skin and skulls. Unusual Xixia and surviving customs include "riding the wooden donkey" (an excruciating punishment aimed at women); right of the state priest to a bride's first-night (*jus primae noctis*); celebrating double-suicide; belief in "walking water"; fear of the power of menstrual blood; and "Wearing Heaven's Headdress."

I first met Xue Mo in 2014 and was fascinated by the depth of his novel *Curses of the Kingdom of Xixia*. So I decided to translate it. Because this complex novel embraces history, literature, religion (Tantric Buddhist lore, local customs and beliefs), and is infused with local colloquial expressions and religious practices—it was a daunting translation project. During the summer of 2015, I went to Dongguan, Guangdong (where Xue Mo resided at the time), to discuss and clarify with him many of the novel's Tantric Buddhist concepts and colloquial terms. In 2017, I visited Liangzhou (present-day Wuwei), Gansu, where Xue Mo's son and spiritual followers took me to some of the sites mentioned in the novel. A few photos from that trip grace this book. I hope this translation of *Curses of the Kingdom of Xixia* will be as fascinating and inspiring for its readers as it has been for me.

Figure 1. Rebuilt city gate of Liangzhou (as inscribed on the gate), present day Wuwei. Author provided.

Figure 2. Qilian Mountain in the distance. Author provided.

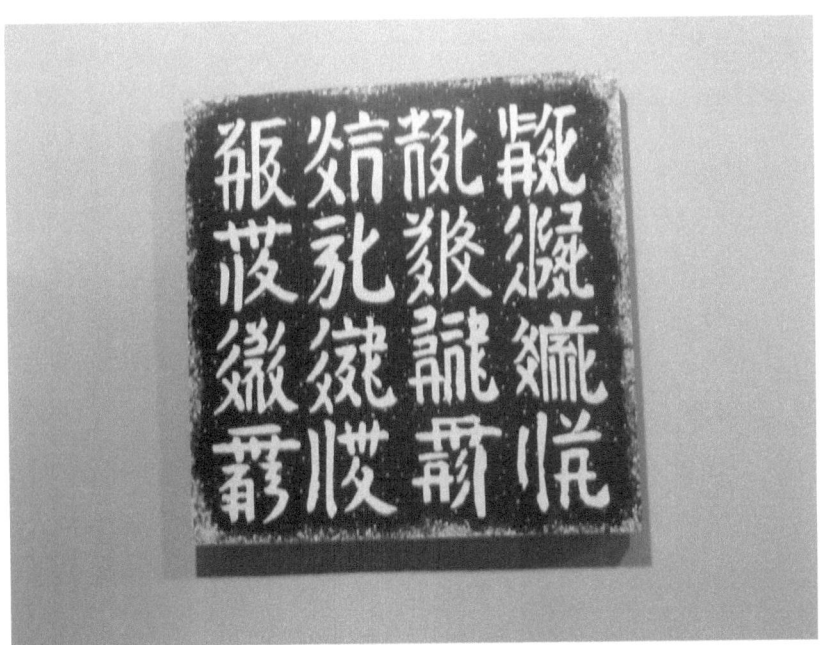

Figure 3. Tablet of Xixia writing at the Xixia Museum of Wuwei. Author provided.

Figure 4. Luoshen Monastery with the golden cupola-topped reliquary pagoda (originally built in 413 C.E.) which houses Kumarajiva's tongue. Author provided.

Figure 5. An erstwhile fortressed mansion. Author provided.

Figure 6. A traditional village house. Author provided.

Figure 7. Interior of the traditional house. Author provided.

Figure 8. Back lane of a traditional village. Author provided.

Figure 9. Backyard of a traditional house. Author provided.

Figure 10. The plan for the building of a Dakini Goddess Temple complex. Author provided.

Figure 11. The Diamond Maiden Cave was under reconstruction during 2017. Author provided.

Figure 12. The Dakini Goddess Temple complex was under construction and not open. Author provided.

Figure 13. The Dakini Goddess' relic was housed in an unassuming shrine at Chanshancun, a nearby village. The inscription on the elaborate bronze incense burner says "The Dakini Goddess Cave Monastery." Author provided.

Figure 14. The Dakini Goddess's relic and statue. Author provided.

Figure 15. Pine Surf Monastery. Author provided.

Figure 16. Photo of a picture of Monk Wu Naidan displayed at the monastery. Author provided.

Chapter 1

Origins of this Book

Majestically, you arrived riding on an elephant
    And tumbled into a womb;
Instantly, a blot of light emerged from the shivering universe
    Sneezing and swirling for thousands of years.

The Toad Cave

After you leave Chang'an, the largest city in western China, if you continue westward along the Silk Road, you will meet a Tang dynasty poet forever chanting this familiar lyric:

Where the Yellow River reaches the white clouds,
A lone city midst a mountain of ten-thousand feet.[1]

This lone city is called Liangzhou.

That mountain is, of course, the Qilian Mountain. The Huns[2] called it the Heavenly Mountain. A little over two thousand years ago, a man called Huo Qubing[3] caused the Huns to wail to the heavens, "Losing

---

1. This is the first couplet of "The Lyric of Liangzhou" by the Tang poet Wang Zhihuan (688–?).

2. The *Xiongnu* were a large confederation of Eurasian nomads who dominated the Asian Steppe from the late third century BCE to the late first century.

3. Huo Qubing (141–117 BCE) was a renowned general during Emperor Wu's (156–87 BCE) reign.

1

the Qilian Mountain, our livestock can no longer prosper; Losing the Rouge Mountain, our women will no longer have beauty!"

In front of the lone city is a desert known as Tenggeli. "Tenggeli" is an ancient Mongolian word. Just like "Qilian," it also means "Heaven."

Outside the lone city lies a mountain resembling a sleeping Buddha. Therein resides the Toad Cave.

One year, among the thick mist of vicissitude, Jasper's warbling voice glided down like a bird:

> Fattened are the rabbits of the great desert,
> Guiltily glide the black hawks.
> Camelthorns[4] cannot prick the camels,
> Greeness nourishes the thousand-year dream.
>   Look!
> Ajia, the guardian deity!
>   The mountains have aged, the waters have aged;
> The promised floor of the ocean
> Has become the world's highest peak!

Jasper is a protagonist of this book. He was thought to have been a monk who had broken his vows. The ludicrous romance between Jasper and Snow Feather brought fame to Toad Cave. This book is about them.

Toad Cave is a rock grotto. One day a yogi would come to the grotto; his hair as hoary as white snow, his face as pink as a peach. People called him Grandpa Jiu. I have already written about him in my *Mahamudra: Essence and Practice*.

He was my guru.

If you read *History of Buddhism in the Amdo Region*,[5] you'll find that grotto there. It has another name: Diamond Maiden[6] Cave.

So, Jasper announced:

> Wave your hand
> And go to the mountain!
> The mountain is so high

---

4. The botanical name for this desert plant is *alhagi sparsifolia*.

5. *Amdo zhengjiao shi* was written in 1865 by Brag-dgou-pa-dkon-mchog-bstan-pa-rab-rgyas (1801–?).

6. *Jin'gang haimu* is a goddess, also known as Vajrayogini.

That it reaches the sun.
The sun harbors Diamond Maiden Cave,
That cave is the melody of my life.

But, surprisingly, this world-famous grotto is hardly known to Liangzhou's own inhabitants.

The Mysterious Manuscripts

The Diamond Maiden Cave is a grotto in Xixia. It is one of the totemic guideposts of my life. My religious beliefs and creativity are all linked to it. You can find about all these in my *Mahamudra: Essence and Practice.*

Diamond Maiden is one of the deities of Tantric or Esoteric Buddhism. She is the main deity among the millions and millions of Dakini goddesses.[7] According to legend, there are two Diamond Maiden caves in China. One of them is in the province of Xinjiang; its exact location is no longer known. The other is in Liangzhou.

On a windy day, I entered Diamond Maiden Cave to perform a ritual offering. I used to go there every twenty-fifth day of each lunar month. We would worship by making offerings to the Dakini goddesses who had vowed to benefit all living beings.

These ritual offerings were equivalent to having a meal in the secular world, the only difference being that the guests were women who had completed their Buddhist practices. They were the Dakini goddesses. According to the ancestors, they existed in this world, either visibly or invisibly, in the millions and millions. Their leader was Diamond Maiden.

Countless ritual offerings had been performed in that cave of Xixia. According to records, such offerings were already made during the time of Empress Wu Zetian[8] of the Tang dynasty.[9] After that, during the Kingdom of Xixia[10] after the period of the Five Dynasties and Ten

---

7. *Kongxingmu*, literally, space-traveling goddesses.

8. Wu Zetian (624–705) was renowned as the only female emperor in Chinese history.

9. 618–907.

10. The Kingdom of Xixia (1038–1227) was established in northwestern China by the Dangxiang People. Its ruler called himself an emperor although it was actually a powerful kingdom of just one dynasty.

Kingdoms,[11] the cave became an even more renowned sacred site. Emperor Li Yuanhao of the Great Xia[12] was in the habit of conducting Buddhist rituals there; until one day, his son sliced the emperor's nose off.

What happened when I performed the ritual offering was different from the thousands and thousands of earlier offerings. Many strange events happened there. In this book, I will only mention the events not mentioned in my *Mahamudra: Essence and Practice*.

Everything started with a rock fall.

According to an old man surnamed Qiao, rocks fell several times in that cave. Once when the grotto was being repaired, a fella said, "Why repair such crap?" A huge rock tumbled down past his head and took his hat with it.

The same thing happened when we performed our ritual offering. Just as we were chanting the Offering Mantra to the point of forgetting ourselves, a rock plummeted and smashed a mud pagoda. There were many such pagodas in the cave, which were originally used to house the relics of venerable monks. However, this pagoda did not contain any relics. It housed a pile of manuscripts in both Chinese and Xixia writing. Most of its contents were written in Chinese, but Xixia writing was used for terms specific to certain periods that might have been misunderstood otherwise. I stayed indoors for three full months in order to decipher them. The experience was comparable to when Confucius was so absorbed by the music of Shao that he could not savor the taste of meat for three months. I even forgot where I was. Relying on the *Tangut-Chinese Timely Pearl in the Palm*,[13] I was finally able to make sense of the manuscripts.

Known as *The Curses of Xixia*, the collection consisted of eight manuscripts. The dates, authorship, paper, handwriting, and writing styles were all different. Possibly to prevent them from dispersion, they were bound with the kind of hemp thread used by Liangzhou women to stitch the soles of cloth shoes. The top manuscript was titled *Nightmares*. The scribbly writing that emerged truly resembled nightmares. The others

---

11. The period between the Tang (618–907) and the Song (960–1279) dynasties. The dates for the Five Dynasties are 907–960; those for the Ten Kingdoms are 891–979.

12. Li Yuanhao (1003–1048), originally known as Tuoba Yuanhao, was the founder of the Kingdom of Xixia.

13. *Fan Han heshi zhangzhongzhu* is an 1190 Tangut and Chinese dictionary, discovered in 1909 by a Russian explorer in Inner Mongolia.

were *Crazy Ramblings of Ajia; Tale of the Goddess;*[14] *Family Instructions of Diamond Clan; True Records of the Curses; Historical Mirror of Forgotten Events,* etc. They recorded events in a village named Diamond Clan, with emphasis on the spiritual journeys of a monk, or madman, named Jasper and a woman named Snow Feather. The manuscripts that followed *Nightmares* were mostly textual research of nightmares and provided me with more detailed information. I spent several years interpreting, clarifying, researching, and footnoting the seemingly confusing and antiquated language in order to present them to my readers in a style akin to a vernacular novel.

Because some contents of the manuscripts revealed modern concepts, I suspect that their final author or editor must have been of modern provenance. After conducting textual analyses and research concerning the possibilities—and based on facts such as the writer had to have been fluent in both Xixia and Chinese writings and also had the opportunity to build a mud pagoda inside the Diamond Maiden Cave—I eventually locked my gaze upon a man known as Indigent Monk, who had lived in seclusion for twenty years in Diamond Maiden Cave. Everyone in Liangzhou used to know Indigent Monk. Because the male protagonist in the manuscripts is called *Qiong* (Jasper), I suspect that the folks of Liangzhou confused the word for poverty, *qiong,* with Qiong (meaning Jasper, or fine jade). For twenty years, Indigent Monk wore what was known as a manure sweeper's cloak; that is, a cursorily washed rag from the garbage. It was said that Indigent Monk delighted in toying with writing, always writing and painting like crazy when he wasn't chanting sutras or doing meditation.

According to popular belief, Indigent Monk was also fluent in the Xixia script. A few prominent professors from Peking University arrived at Diamond Maiden Cave seven years after Indigent Monk disappeared and were shocked by what he'd scribbled on a cliff face within the cave. They were all poems written in Xixia script. Their caliber was said to rival that of Hanshan and Shide.[15]

Ten years before Indigent Monk disappeared, the folks of Liangzhou changed his appellation from Indigent Monk to Crazy Monk. For ten years, he roamed about as a madman. Opinions differed concerning his

---

14. *Kongxingmu yinghua yinyuan,* literally, "Karmic Cause and Effect of the Bodily Incarnation of the Dakini Goddess."

15. Two Buddhist monks of the Tang dynasty (618–907) known for their poems.

madness. Some thought he was really crazy. Certainly, his appearance supported this conclusion. His hair hadn't been cut for many years: it was long and resembled a horse's mane. His face was as black as a wok. The dirt and grime on his manure sweeper's cloak glistened. His long hair tangled messily in the wind and covered his face. He was in the habit of lying on the streets of Liangzhou, staring at the sky and muttering. He looked crazy indeed. Others, however, claimed that his madness was caused by his attaining ultimate enlightenment. It was said that when one attained the level of the Eight Bodhisattvas, the person would enter the stages of One-Entity Yoga and No Meditation.[16] At that point, polar opposites ceased to exist, and the mind no longer made distinctions. In terms of appearance, dirt and cleanliness became one. So, in the eyes of worldly beings, the person had become a madman. Quite a few such madmen existed in history. For example, the crazy practitioners of Tibet and Jigong[17] were all mad outwardly but had in fact attained exceptionally high levels of inner enlightenment.

I'm suspicious of both views but am more inclined to concur with the latter.

For more than ten years, I saw him sleeping on the streets. I became more convinced of the latter view when, during a certain winter, I saw his body on the snow enveloped by a layer of steam. So, I bought snacks to make an offering to him. He glanced at me coldly and said, "Shoo!" causing hearty laughter from onlookers. Embarrassed, I left the food by his side. "Get rid of it! That's where I sleep!" he yelled. "I'll put it there then." I said shame-facedly. Late that night, I passed by on my way back from a friend's place. The snacks were still in the corner where I left them. His snores thundered up to heaven. The snacks remained there for almost a week without being touched. And then some beggars ate them.

I sighed, "This is the noblest man in Liangzhou."

Later, during a moonless night, he taught me numerous essential ideas for cultivating the mind. I'm grateful for his assistance with the final steps in my eventual attainment of enlightenment. But I never dared to ask him about his past. He was something of a divine dragon, always showing its head but not its tail, just like Grandpa Jiu.

---

16. Ultimate stages in the Mahamudra system of Tantric Buddhism, they can also be translated as Non-Distinction Yoga and Non-Action Yoga.

17. Jigong (1133–1209) was a renowned Buddhist monk known for his crazy behavior.

I thought perhaps Indigent Monk was one of the manuscripts' authors. This was, of course, only conjecture. Diamond Maiden Cave frequently housed up to a hundred monks; it must have harbored some "dragons" and "tigers"[18] there.

I must emphasize that these manuscripts had a long history and contain such rich contents that they were a veritable treasure trove. I will only select from among them the single drop of water I need. They could not have been completed by just one person. For example, *Historical Mirror of Forgotten Events* began with the year Li Yuanhao ascended the throne as the Emperor of Xixia and continued without intermission until the end of the 1970s. *Crazy Ramblings of Ajia*, however, was recorded by a monk who successfully attained enlightenment through practicing the techniques of his own deity.[19] It was said he had attained the ability to interact with the Buddha and the Bodhisattvas face to face. It was said that the Tibetan guru, Tsongkhapa, also attained this ability; many of his writings were composed after he'd personally listened to the teachings of the Bodhisattva Manjusri. You can look up his biography if you don't believe me. It was said that that Tibetan monk was able to communicate with Ajia, the guardian deity of Liangzhou, and that he recorded faithfully what Ajia told him. Later, after I completed the practice of the Mahamudra, Ajia caught wind of my fame, looked me up, and became my best friend.

Origin of Diamond Clan

Most of the manuscripts mentioned the Diamond Clan. This seems to have been the name of a clan, but in fact it encompassed much more than that. It was symbolically rich as a fable and resembled a legendary kingdom. It had a clan head, clan militia, clan regulations, and a host of other unusual trappings. Judging from the manuscript, the dates for this Diamond Clan were also unclear. It seemed to have existed during the Xixia period; or it could have been the Republican period.[20] It could also have been any of the dynasties during the last thousand years.

---

18. Men of extraordinary abilities.

19. Known as *benzun fa*.

20. 1911–1949.

This might be just as well. Its ambiguity enables this book to represent massive chaos.

According to *Historical Mirror of Forgotten Events*, Diamond Clan's origin was an enigma.

An evening many years ago, an outsider came to Liangzhou with a wooden saddle on his back. No one knew where he came from, how he made a living, and what he carried on his back. His clothes were tattered, but he wasn't dispirited. When Grandpa Sun receded behind the mountains, he asked, "Where shall I live?" The folks of Liangzhou pointed to a mountain in the distance and said, "How about there?" So the man selected a slope, leveled it, and built a wooden cabin on it. Another day, a woman came; and then on another day, a few children arrived. They became a family. A year later, he bought a mountain slope in Liangzhou.

This was obviously not your ordinary outsider.

By the time the folks of Liangzhou recognized this, a year had passed. The outsider approached the regional official and bought the mountain slope. He then brought trees and stones and hired workers to build an enormous estate. This estate would later become a tourist attraction in Liangzhou. It was said that there was only one such fortified estate in the world.

Very soon, most of the surrounding land came to belong to the estate. No one else could pay as much as its owner could. No one knew where the silver, which seemed to always be pouring in, came from. People in the village even feared that if this continued, this outsider might even end up buying the entire region of Liangzhou. And then one day, a pack of horses pulling carriages arrived with the masters of the estate.

In this way, the ancestors of Diamond Clan arrived. No one knew from whence they came.

The folks of Liangzhou felt there was something imposing and intimidating about this estate. It occupied the top of the entire mountain. Anyone standing on the estate's parapets could see the naked rear-ends of women when they peed below. Since that time, there have been no more secrets in the villages. Everyone felt a pair of eyes watched behind their backs. Later, John, the missionary, summed up the feeling: the newcomers had taken the throne of God on High.

That estate was truly tall and massive. It was fifteen feet high. The walls were very thick. Even the gate was a foot thick. When it creaked shut, even flies could not enter. The courtyards and buildings were also designed with particular care so that they represent the Chinese characters, 一品當朝, meaning "First Rank at the Imperial Court."[21] The central axis represented the 一, the three courtyards formed the 品 character. Three cannon towers were built on the wall above the gate for archers and riflemen, which along with the courtyards formed the character 當. And the design of the entire fortress clearly represented the character 朝. The builder of the estate obviously had great ambitions for his family to attain eminence at the imperial court. But, one night, he suddenly vomited blood and died. The reason for his death was unclear.

Later, when the descendants of Diamond Clan increased in size, this estate became their public property, and it was named the Ancestral Hall. Diamond Monastery was part of the estate.

The Ancestral Hall was a sacred precinct for Diamond Clan. The founder's wooden saddle was placed on the offering table. Those traveling to distant lands used to carry a wooden saddle on their backs. Goods would be placed on the saddle, without which one's back would rot and flesh stink like that of smelly alpacas.

The saddle was worshipped in the Ancestral Hall, which barred females from entering. On the first and fifteenth nights of every month,[22] all the men of Diamond Clan would gather in the Ancestral Hall and perform a mysterious ritual. The Ancestral Hall was so large it was almost as big as a sutra hall. That wooden saddle and ancestral plaques were placed on the offering table. This saddle was the very one the old ancestor carried when he arrived at the village. It was, in fact, quite ordinary—the kind people used to carry heavy items, when traveling far, to prevent ruining the flesh on their backs. Jasper could see nothing divine about it, but he and his uncles still worshipped it. They called it "worshipping the Saddle God." Each person had to kneel and prostrate himself before it 108 times, after which he would sit quietly until a wooden mallet struck the third watch.[23] The men would then pretend they needed to leave to pee and slipped back into their own homes to cuddle their women's warm bodies, which had been left unused for half the night.

---

21. The first rank was the top rank of officialdom. They consisted of officials such as prime ministers and imperial tutors.

22. The lunar calendar was used traditionally.

23. The third watch referred to midnight.

It was like this every month.

Ever since Jasper was very little, his parents told him to observe the ritual. When it was performed, even Braggart, who was the least serious of them all, dared not act with abandon.

On the night before the twenty-fifth day of each month, the men would sleep apart from their wives at the third watch and get up at the fifth watch[24] to welcome the Diamond Deities, the Vajras.[25] The men would herd their cattle, sheep, camels, and horses in different directions, while chanting a mantra welcoming the deities. The five Vajras would arrive from five directions. From the east, the Guhyasamaja Vajra; from the south, the Havajra; from the west, the Mahamaya Vajra; from the north, the Yamantaka; and the center, the Heruka Cakrasamvara. These five Vajras represent the body, mouth, intention, merit, and career of the Buddha. The deceased ancestors said that everything Diamond Clan owned was bestowed upon them by these five deities.

Hence, Diamond Clan came to own up to a thousand mou[26] of arable land, the grass of the entire mountain for herding, and tens of thousands of livestock. It couldn't help but become wealthy.

At the beginning, family regulations stipulated that everyone had to work. The men worked the land and herded the animals; the women spun and wove. All the clothes worn by the villagers were made with the coarse cloths woven by the women.

This tradition lasted until the year Braggart became the clan head.

Braggart was frequently mentioned in the manuscripts. When he was young, he was fond of hunting with dog and hawk and toyed with the rifle and martial arts staff. His shooting skills were particularly impressive. He also had an extraordinary memory. Consequently, although he could not read, he was able to fortify his torrent speech with everything he'd heard. So people gave him the nickname of Braggart. He had served as a gunman for the rich families of Diamond Clan. In private, however, he frequently conducted a business that did not need capital. Later, he simply gathered his brotherhood companions and seized the properties of prominent local families and the Diamond Clan fortress. And then he turned around and appointed himself the clan head.

---

24. That is, four o'clock in the morning.

25. *Jingang*, meaning diamond, refers to Vajras, Buddhist deities who are the name-sake of Diamond Clan.

26. Each *mou* is 667 sq. meters.

During the decades when Braggart was clan head, whenever a child cried at night, the mother would scare him, saying, "Braggart is coming!" And the child would suck the mother's breast and hush up immediately.

The Girls from the Eggs

According to True Records of the Curses, "In the year 1004, on the twenty-fifth of the first month, five women in Diamond Clan gave birth to five eggs. When a particularly bright sun on a certain day shone on them, the eggs cracked and turned into five lotus flowers. Each flower bore a girl. Diamond Maiden was one of them." The births of these girls were also foretold in a book titled, Continuation to the Origins of the Heruka Cakrasamvara Vajra. It also prophesized the Diamond Maiden Cave of Liangzhou.

That year, the Khitans of the Liao dynasty[27] undertook a major southward expedition. Empress Dowager Xiao[28] and her son Yelü Longxu[29] personally led their army into the territories of the Chinese Song dynasty.[30] An old fellow named Kou Zhun[31] organized the resistance and ended up signing the famous Treaty of Chanyuan. Ever since then, the Song had to pay an annual tribute of ten thousand ounces of silver to the Khitans.

Emperor Zhao Heng's[32] face reddened from embarrassment.

Twenty-six years later, in the Arabian empire of the faraway West, an impotent emperor, in embarrassment, closed his eyes that had longed for a son. His dynasty would consequently disappear. The Caliphate would then change its system of inheritance from hereditary to electoral.

The water of the Yangzi disappearing eastward rolled,
Its crashing waves vanquishing all heroes.

---

27. 916–1125.

28. Empress Dowager Xiao (953–1009) was a famous politician and woman warrior of the Liao dynasty of the Khitans.

29. Yelü Longxu (r.983–1031) was the sixth emperor of the Liao dynasty.

30. 960–1279.

31. Kou Zhun (961–1023) was a minister at the Song court.

32. Third emperor of the Song dynasty, who reigned 997–1022.

In the following year, a new kingdom arose in western China. People called it Xixia. The Diamond Maiden Cave was eventually inhabited by the chief state priest of Xixia.

That year, the old man of history again chanted:

Verdant mountains remain,
But how many times will the red sun set?

And a children's ditty spread throughout Liangzhou:

In Qinchuan,[33] blood would immerse the wrists,
Only Liangzhou watches, leaning against a pillar.

When the old fellow Kuo Zhun, along with the group of Central Plains men he led, sweated in resisting the woman Xiao, the five girls lived peacefully not far from them. Having neither cares nor worries, they lived in obscurity. It was not until eight years later, on the night when the maidens left this world, that the villagers learned their names through dreams. They were Diamond Maiden, Treasure Maiden, Safflower Maiden, Success Maiden, and Buddha Maiden.

On that day, the Maidens again bought on credit from Butcher Zhang the inner organs of a pig to perform a ritual offering.

This offering was for a special ritual.

Practitioners would circle around the offerings and, while ringing 'diamond' bells and rattling hand drums, invite their gurus, their personal deities, and their Dakini protective goddesses. They would chant mantras, make offerings, and share a meal.

There were as many different types of ritual offerings as there were Buddhist deities. So how many Buddhist deities were there? According to Buddhist scriptures, they were even more numerous than the grains of sand in the River Ganges!

The type of ritual offering performed by the five girls was called the Diamond Dakini Goddess Offering. Nine hundred and eighty years later, I would learn how to perform this ritual from my guru.

That was also on the twenty-fifth day of the first lunar month.

During the thousand years thereafter, groups of travelers would continue to perform this ritual on that particular day.

---

33. These refer to the western Shaanxi, northern Gansu region.

This date has been considered the birthday of the Diamond Maidens.

Mantra Wheel

According to *True Records of Curses*, the five girls born from the eggs were very poor. They were like countless little girls in mountain villages.

This was, of course, based on local lore.

It was said they were so poor they couldn't afford to buy the food for the ritual offering.

This would be equivalent to girls who cannot afford to attend school during present times.

More than nine hundred years after their time, I got to know some little girls from the same village as the Diamond Maidens. They looked at me, a "visitor from beyond the sky," with eyes that seemed large because they were so scrawny. They laughed, grabbed the cheap candies from my hands, and greedily sucked the syrup on their soiled hands.

It was in this place of poverty that the Diamond Maidens grew without any cares. When a man called Butcher Zhang followed them, demanding money for the meat they'd bought on credit, they were only eight years old.

Butcher Zhang then had an extraordinary experience, similar to what I underwent a thousand years later.

They were performing a ritual offering.

Unfortunately, but luckily for Butcher Zhang, he didn't know it was a ritual offering. However, his ignorance was also a blessing in disguise.

It was said Butcher Zhang rushed up to them and screamed like innumerable creditors: "Give me the money!"

It was said Butcher Zhang was the last person one should owe money to. He would remember every penny owed to him, even after eight generations. Wolves are reincarnations of such avaricious beings.

But this was only according to legend.

As a consequence, I doubtlessly possess a wolf nature since I was Butcher Zhang in my previous incarnation.

A person I respected also had a wolf nature. He was something of an eccentric. In order to curse others, he searched arduously for the darkest curse.

That man never did find this curse. Therefore, he had no choice but to spit blood. He baked dry the black blood drops he spat and transformed them into words. People considered him an extremist.

Of course, normal humans who were not extremists wouldn't understand it was precisely this extremism that made him great. He rebelled against mediocrity. He created a "mantra wheel,"[34] out of all the black blood drops he spat, with which he resisted the influence of the mediocrity of the past thousand years.

The following explains the function and power of the "mantra wheel":

> Just as darkness approached, a horde of Goblin Dakini goddesses charged at Reluo,[35] with protruding teeth and dancing claws. Guru Reluo sat meditating and visualized a mantra wheel. The Goblin Dakini goddesses were not able to come near the mantra wheel, so they left. At midnight, another army of Worldly Dakini goddesses with blue faces and protruding teeth arrived. Displaying supernatural powers, they proceeded to attack him. But they too were unable to get close to the diamond mantra wheel and had to retreat. After midnight, the fierce Lion-Headed Dakini Goddess of incomparable power personally led numerous Wisdom Dakini goddesses to the space above Reluo's residence. Thunder roared and lightning sparked—a scene of mighty terror and fury. Instantly, Guru Reluo transformed himself into the ferocious Yamantaka.[36] He heaved a mighty roar, "Hum!" which resounded like the loud crash of a landslide and earthquake, shaking the Lion-Headed Dakini Goddess and her magical soldiers into a swoon, and causing them to drop to the ground. It took a while before they woke up. They then knelt before Guru Reluo's bed and begged for forgiveness . . .

In this scene, as recorded in the Buddhist biography *The Light of Yamantaka*, it was the mantra wheel that protected Guru Reluo.

You can find a similar scene in a very popular book among the Han Chinese. The difference between the two is that while in the former,

---

34. A circle in which a spell has been written.

35. Also known as Hot Luoduojizha Lotsawa and Geraud Lotsawa (1016–1198), he was a great guru of Tibetan Tantric Buddhism.

36. Also known as Vajrabhairava and Bhairava. He is the so-called Death Terminator.

Guru Reluo forgives his mediocre attackers; the Han Chinese screamed while spitting blood: "I will not forgive any of you!"

That book was titled *The Biography of Lu Xun*.[37]

After that person reached Nirvana (that is, passed away), many of the alien kinds he had cursed parroted that particular famous phrase of his. Most disgusting!

The Darkest Curse

According to *True Records of the Curses*, Jasper would not spit blood to create mantra wheels again.

The year that he left his study for the grotto, his guru transmitted to him several mantra wheels. He would chant a particular line when he did his mandatory daily yogic practice: "I promise to visualize the mantra wheel before the Vajradhara."

The guru transmitted to him different kinds of protective mantra wheels. These were the Diamond Mantra Wheel, the Raging Fire Mantra Wheel, the Lotus Flower Mantra Wheel, the Human Skull Mantra Wheel, among others. The Diamond Mantra Wheel represented the subjugation of demons, the Raging Fire Mantra Wheel represented wisdom, the Lotus Flower Mantra Wheel represented purity, and the Human Skull Mantra Wheel represented impermanence.

Later, he would use these mantra wheels to assist himself in resisting the polluting influence of evil.

But the most powerful mantra wheel transmitted by his guru was compassion.

The guru also transmitted to him the darkest curse in the world.

This darkest curse was also named "compassion."

The Light of Yamantaka provides evidence for this. Reluo, the guru of Tantric Buddhism, used the darkest curse to exterminate innumerable people who went against the tide of history.

Of course, this type of extermination had the typical characteristics of Esoteric Buddhism. Swords and spears were not necessary. Only a ritual was performed:

---

37. The famous early twentieth-century writer, Lu Xun (1881–1936) was revered as the nation's conscience and was highly critical of traditional China as well as of his contemporaries.

Having said this, he meditated and visualized the Yamantaka (Vajra) swinging the horns on the head of a bull. Thunder and lightning issued from the horns and burned Zhuqingba's estate into ashes. All the members of his family perished in the fire. Their souls were sent to the Buddhist realm of Manjusri.

Reluo built a mandala[38] and performed the Fiery Subjugation Ritual. His opponent also began to perform magic which caused such a great wind to blow that heaven and earth darkened, and sand and rocks flew like falling hail. The disciples of Reluo were so frightened that they knew not what to do. Reluo employed the Technique of Separation[39] to eliminate the power of the opponent's technique; and in a flash, the wind calmed and the sky cleared. People around Guru Reluo saw the towering fierce exterminator, Yamantaka, enter the body of the guru holding in his hand a human skull, which contained the one hundred and fifty-eight Buddha statues of "Veracity." ("Veracity" was the personal deity of Ritual Master Kun.) When Guru Reluo employed the Technique of Hooking the Soul, his disciples saw a sheep-like animal being drawn into the flour dough puppet used for the curse. Ritual Master Kun took ill and died suddenly the very day the ritual was performed. Again, Guru Reluo used the Technique of Transferring the Soul and discharged Ritual Master Kun's soul to the Buddhist realm of Manjusri.

Reluo used the Killing Technique by Hooking and nailed a "Diamond" wooden pin into the representative image of Langle. People around him saw the image tremble, struggle and bleed from its mouth and naval. Meanwhile, Langle felt out of sorts. He then lay down in bed and never got up again . . . Within a month, Langle and more than a hundred of his disciples died of the curse. Again Reluo sent the souls of all the deceased to the Buddhist realm of Manjusri.

The Manjusri mentioned in this book was the Bodhisattva Manjusri, known as the embodiment of the wisdom of Buddhist deities. Enabling those who were cursed to leave the temporary and illusory mortal world

---

38. *Tancheng*, literally means a ritual city. It represents the Buddhist realm.

39. This method separates the person from their protective deity.

for the eternal Buddhist realm, wouldn't this be a manifestation of great compassion through the use of a darkest curse?

Accordingly, a woman called Guanyin[40] sings the following in the same book:

> The five pollutions inundate the end of the world. People's minds have become cruel, violent, and unfathomable . . . Heterodoxy is creating evil karma, formidable might is needed to halt them . . . Those who had attained the power to perform the technique of salvation through killing should not retreat from the world . . . As for the barbaric, cruel, and violent populace, peaceful and civil teachings would hardly suffice. One should use techniques of wisdom and convenience. For such cases, even Buddhist deities will manifest fierce appearances.

These techniques were known as "Salvation Through Killing" in Esoteric Buddhism.

During a certain moment through the cycle of changes, a man known as Grandpa Jiu transmitted this technique to me. The one who transmitted another black curse to me was a spirit characterized by extremism.

The former "curses" sins; the latter brings about "salvation through the killing" of mediocrity.

Miracles

The *History of Buddhism in the Amdo Region* also records a miracle. When Butcher Zhang demanded money for the meat from the five girls, they actually flew away. This was a historical account. Histories are not novels.

So they flew away!

But Butcher Zhang was unaware that it was a miracle. This is characteristic of all those lacking in wisdom and blinded by profit. One or two leaves from a tree of profit will cause them to fail to see Mount Tai[41] right in front of them. Butcher Zhang's mind was thus totally consumed by the money owed to him. He was provoked by a certain

---

40. Goddess of Mercy, Avalokiteshvara.

41. One of the most famous mountain ranges in China.

type of emotion. I have also experienced this type of emotion frequently. When overcome with such an emotion, I could pounce upon anything, like a lion upon its prey.

Then a miracle happened.

True Records of Curses records numerous miracles frequently regarded as superstition by the ignorant. If you are interested, you can peruse the biographies of any of the gurus of Tantric Buddhism and find them full of such miracles. For example, the tenth Panchen Lama, who was the deputy head of the Standing Committee for the National People's Congress, was able to knead all sorts of stones as if they are mud. According to *Dalai Lamas of Tibet: Succession of Births* by the Indian author, Inder L. Malik, "Some officials serving under the Dalai Lama have eye witnessed some of the lama's mysterious, esoteric techniques. He could actually knead a stone like plaster." One day, the Panchen Lama made a gift of a piece of stone he had kneaded into the shape of a hand when he was eight years old, to Gong Tangcang, who would become the deputy chair of the Chinese People's Political Consultative Conference of the province of Gansu. When Guru Gong Tangcang's sutra expert saw it, he wrinkled his nose and said, "Who kneaded *tsampa* until it's so black?" He thought the stone was a piece of dough made of roasted barley flour!

The Flying Thief Snow Feather

Snow Feather is the protagonist of *Tale of the Goddess*. She was a legendary figure, a famous flying thief in Liangzhou, and a Dakini goddess.

According to this manuscript, Snow Feather was an incarnation of the Wisdom Dakini Goddess Niguma, who was a great Yogini guru of ancient India. She was the personification of Diamond Maiden. After she had completed the practice of Mahamudra, she attained the state of deathlessness through what was known as the Rainbow Body. Her Buddhist realm is historically known as the Sitavana Pure Land. According to the manuscript, Niguma had limitless kinds of incarnations. But simply put, there were five categories: bodily incarnation, speech incarnation, mind incarnation, merit incarnation, and career incarnation. According to Ajia, Snow Feather was Niguma's bodily incarnation.

There are many different opinions concerning Dakini goddesses. I have written about them in my *Mahamudra: Essence and Practice*. One can separate them simply into the Dakini goddesses who are beyond this world and those who are of this world, based on whether they are enlightened or not. Communication between the Buddhist realm and its practitioners is carried out by the Other-Worldly Dakini goddesses. The Worldly Dakini goddesses include those Yakshas and Non-Humans, etc., who have taken Buddhist vows to protect the dharma and those women who have attained achievement in their religious cultivation.

According to Ajia, Snow Feather was a Worldly Dakini Goddess before she was enlightened. After she attained enlightenment, she transformed into an Other-Worldly Dakini Goddess.

Snow Feather's tale used to be a topic the elders of Liangzhou told to chase away boredom. Her attractive image had always remained fresh in my life. Many, many years ago, when I was still wearing open-crotched pants, I already wished I could attain the martial arts skill of weightlessness that Snow Feather possessed. Back then, I would practice every day, sandbags on my legs and neck craned, and played on main roads like a naughty mule. I loved it most when it rained. Whenever the ground overflowed with water and was filled with mud, I would run barefoot like the wind on the roads: I never wore shoes when I was little since I had no shoes then. How clumsy the adults were in comparison! They would tread with utmost caution with their pants lifted but then slip and fall into muddy sows amidst roaring laughter of the onlookers. But I could run like the wind and fly east and west like the wind. In my mind, I *was* Snow Feather! That martial arts skill was, of course, only attained after arduous practice and inadvertent consumption of mud. Through practice, I figured out the secret to running through mud without slipping. The secret was to grab the ground with all ten toes. How I loved my toes back then! I used to fear constant use would wear them out. They became so tough I could even dart around comfortably in newly cut wheat fields. At first, the bottoms of my feet would bleed a little. But then they became as hard as hoofs.

Adoration of Snow Feather lent a legendary touch to my youth. I had always hoped I could train until my weightless skills would be "out of this world." I began practicing martial arts when I was ten, under the tutelage of He Wanyi, a famous martial artist in the city of Liangzhou. This martial artist was a disciple of Su Xiaowu, who was one of the ten martial arts instructors of Ma Buqing's[42] army. His martial arts

---

42. Ma Buqing (1901–1977) was a prominent warlord who controlled Qinghai during the Republican era.

abilities were comparable to those of Monk Stone, the abbot of Pine Surf Monastery. I had great regard for Monk Stone. But unfortunately, he passed away the year I was born. After predicting the forthcoming arrival of the Cultural Revolution[43] and telling his disciple, Wu Naidan, what to do, he crossed his legs and returned to the West[44] with style. I went to Pine Surf Monastery when I was sixteen, hoping to acquire his martial arts techniques from Wu Naidan. Who would have known that Wu Naidan was never interested in martial arts and consequently only learned Buddhist teachings from his master? I stayed overnight at that temple. That night I dreamt a short monk came to "bless and empower" me. An enormous swell of energy poured into the top of my head. The next morning, I related this dream to Wu. I thought Wu Naidan would compliment me on my good karma. But he only remarked coldly, "We Buddhists do not believe in ghosts and spirits."

My adoration of Snow Feather lasted until I was in my twenties. I practiced the techniques for weightlessness assiduously but was ultimately never able to take flight. The only accomplishment was that I finally could dart through houses and over rooftops. Back then, low houses and walls were no longer obstacles for me. As long as there were a few dents on the wall that my fingers could dig into, I could climb up in a jiffy. If I could be aided by first running a few steps, I could also travel sideways a few times before finding a way up.

I did not ultimately become Snow Feather, despite spending all those years training in the art of weightlessness. The skill only came in handy when I was in love, as the house of my present father-in-law was no obstacle for me at all. Whenever the fire of love burned inside me, I would don my night traveling cloak, just like Snow Feather did in the legends, and dart into the tightly closed courtyard of my father-in-law's place dozens of leagues[45] away. I would nudge my girlfriend with a hammer through the open window and wake her up from a deep sleep. My present wife would then slip out of bed and follow me to the fields where we'd chat the night away. Fortunately, back then romantic affairs were innocent, and nothing embarrassing happened. But later,

---

43. The Cultural Revolution (1966–1976) was a major sociopolitical movement. Religion and traditional culture were vehemently denounced, and attempts were made to extinguish them.

44. That is, the realm of the Buddha.

45. Each *li* is about a third of a kilometer in distance.

that experience became something my wife would use as an example to lecture me. Whenever I criticized our son for falling in love at an early age, my wife would pinch me secretly and say, "No matter how bad he is, he's not nudging anyone with a hammer!" And then I'd calm down. Every stage of life has its own tale.

It was probably after I turned twenty-five that I began to forget Snow Feather. I started to do creative writing and won some applause. My aspirations changed. I wanted to be a great writer rather than a flying man. So over the next ten years, I gradually became as fat as a pig. I was not darting through houses and over rooftops: in fact, I would pant like an ox just from walking upstairs. Then one year, when I was in the south, I met a woman who told me the story of her mother. That very instant I felt as if lightning struck me. Snow Feather of Liangzhou suddenly came back to life in my mind. She did not want to be a thief, but she was forced to by fate. There were many amazing events in her life—all incredible stuff. I wanted to write about them. Although this work would be totally different from what I have written before, I still wanted to write this novel. Friends who know my creativity all know that my novels gushed out of me involuntarily. I could not stop them; just as a mother cannot stop a baby from being born during childbirth, even if the fetus is deformed.

I can only take comfort in the fact that, like my earlier creations, this novel is a sincere outpouring of my innermost soul.

The Guardian Deity Ajia

In the folk beliefs of Liangzhou, Ajia was an old deity. He was a guardian deity of Liangzhou. He hailed from far off Xixia. It was said he was born in a grotto during the Xixia dynasty.

According to legend, Ajia was a Buddhist monk. But he fell in love with a local woman and was sent into exile for breaking his vows. After enduring all manner of tribulations, he eventually attained the Eight Worldly Techniques. At that point, he was subdued by the Yogini guru Niguma and joined the ranks of the guardian deities of Liangzhou. Historically, Liangzhou had numerous altercations with its surrounding regions. Ajia was supposed to have been of great assistance to his protectorate; accordingly, offerings to him never diminished during the last thousand years.

The legends regarding Ajia have been around forever and have long since seeped into the souls of the populace.

His story, and the journey of his soul, will be portrayed.

But within the manuscripts, Ajia was a confusing character. He appeared frequently throughout the manuscripts—sometimes as a narrator, sometimes as a protagonist, sometimes as an eyewitness, sometimes in Xixia, sometimes during the present. In any case, it was most bewildering. I don't even know whether all the Ajias refer to the same person.

Later, after I completed the practice of Mahamudra, a person who called himself Ajia came to visit me on account of my reputation. Thereby he became the main narrator of this book. The first story he told me was his own.

Chapter 2

The Iron Hawks of Xixia

Thereupon I searched for a thousand years
Along the long tunnel of time and space,
Taking Feng Menglong[1] with me
To perform all the tales of the pleasure quarters
And turn into a cuckoo bird[2] amidst morning rain's dusts.
One mouthful of blood after the other
Spat from my burnt, broken heart.

The Arrow that Fixed the Next Thousand Years

Those familiar with Xixia would invariably know of the fellow, Pan
Luozhi.[3] Look! He's pulling his bow into a circle, aimed at a swarthy
guy by the name of Li Jiqian.[4]

---

1. Feng Menglong (1574–1645) was a famous vernacular writer and poet of the late
Ming Dynasty.

2. The cuckoo bird was supposed to have sung until it spat blood.

3. Luo Panzhi (?–1004) was the leader of the Tibetans who resided in the Liangzhou
region. He cooperated with the Song emperor and killed Li Jiqian, the grandfather
of the future first emperor of Xixia.

4. Founder of the Kingdom of Xixia, Li Jiqian's (963–1004) father was an official
who served under the Song. Li rebelled against the Song and cooperated with the
Khitans, who bestowed upon him the title of King of the Xia, which would eventually become known as Xixia.

Ajia's story begins here. This is the earliest period covered in the manuscripts.

In Ajia's narrative, the result of that whistling arrow fixed the history of the next thousand years. The time was 1004; the location was the Tibetan Region of the Six Valleys. At that moment, Kou Zhun was wrestling with Empress Dowager Xiao of the Liao dynasty. Beads of sweat dripped from the whiskers of hoary old Kou. At that time, Liangzhou was inhabited by Tibetans and was known as Region of the Six Valleys; which referred to the six rivers that criss-crossed Liangzhou and brought everlasting freshness to its populace.

One evening when the setting sun was bloody red, Li Jiqian led a group of Dangxiang men and violently charged at Liangzhou. So, Pan Luozhi, who was guarding the city, said, "What's the fuss? I'll surrender—okay?" Li Jiqian replied, "Sure, sure!" without noticing the sneaky smirk on his opponent's face. As soon as he turned his back, the arrow we mentioned at the beginning of the chapter whistled toward him.

That Pan Luozhi was none other than Ajia's grandpa. Li Yuanhao, the grandson of Li Jiqian who was shot, would eventually become the emperor of Xixia.

I said, "No wonder you got to eat great fruits during that period!"

Ajia laughed and said, "Wasn't that the case!" And he began to tell his own story. His narrative was very disorganized and confusing. His forehead was covered with beads of sweat. At times he followed one thread, but at other times he'd start to talk about something else. And sometimes he didn't make complete sense. He tried hard to clarify things, but the words he used were, at times, obscure and difficult to understand.

"Is it okay to tell it this way?" he would ask timidly.

I'd beat my chest confidently and declare, "What are you afraid of? I've got me!"

I said,

I will use comet-like words
To overcome your language blocks.
I will use sky-like open-mindedness
To dissolve your accumulated hatred.
I will use the ink of darkest night
To record the experiences of your life.
I will use an ocean-like wisdom
To enlighten impermanence and induce compassion.

So Ajia laughed, "Look at you! Bullshit! Of course, you understand my story. But would the world understand your crazy talk?" I said, "I'm not bending to the world. The world will come to me!"

Look at you: Who do you think you are?

The Eternal Curse of Mankind

A calamity has fallen like a dark night.

Can you imagine a falling night? It is a large net, the world being the jumping fish within. It is a mouth full of blood swallowing a fluid made of red dust.[5] It is as fierce and invincible as death, as sturdy and indestructible as the void. These are the sensations of calamity.

The ravens of the Dangxiang people have arrived. I didn't know until later that those were the Iron Hawks.[6] I said, "Those horses were from your Liangzhou. Those big horses of yours were all over the world!" He said, "Don't use 'your' for Liangzhou, okay? Aren't you from Liangzhou too?" I laughed and said, "Well, not necessarily. Those born in Liangzhou are not necessarily of Liangzhou. They are first and foremost of mankind."

Let's continue with the Iron Hawks. How those enormous horses carried enormous men! And those enormous men wore enormous armor—that world-famous armor! According to the histories, the sky darkened when tens of thousands of Iron Hawks swarmed into the Region of the Six Valleys with their Xixia swords and divine bows. "How many people were killed?" I asked. "Don't know. The city moat overflowed with blood in any case," replied Ajia. That was when he made his escape. There was also Mom, and others who did not want to be killed.

> Yikes!
> Blood stains hung from the sky;
> Stench spilled over the earth;
> Flying birds were studded with arrows;
> Human heads as numerous as rolling sand.
> Run, Mom!

---

5. Red dust refers to the mortal world.

6. *Tieyaozi*, the heavily armored cavalry troops of the Xixia.

> Those heads of ours, once fallen,
> Could never be welded back on!

Yikes! We could run away from wind, we could run away from rain, but we couldn't run away from being chased. That Yuanhao sometimes took Zhao[7] as his surname, sometimes Li. But his resolve for revenge was as firm as the animal patterned rocks at the foothills of Mount Lotus Dragon. Mom said, "Dangxiang people are like that. Revenge is in their nature. If they don't exact revenge, they'd be too ashamed to face their ancestors." "Are you a Dangxiang?" I asked. "How would I know? It's been a thousand years. I can't be certain whether my ancestors hadn't been screwed by other ethnic groups. I don't belong to any ethnic group, but I'm also a part of all the groups. I'm a mongrel."

"You must be kidding!" I complained.

Ajia laughed, "In fact, you're a mongrel too! The books you write are also mongrels!"

The 'Iron Hawks' stormed in like a whirlwind. "Ah!" Screamed hundreds and thousands of people. Ajia shuddered on the city wall.

> The curved moon shone on the city wall,
> The moon rose from the wall to shine upon Liangzhou.
> In ten thousand homes of the seven leagues of Liangzhou
> Barbarians[8] play the lute, without realizing what's happening.

It was not possible for the lute to block the approaching Iron Hawks, who pulled their bows into circles, and arrows flew at us like sparrows. They cheered. They sang. A crowd of carousing ravens! But they all wore the wicked smile of the death god. This wicked smile was fixed in the histories.

> Look, Mom!
> Ravens of the death god arrived like night,
> A rain of blood sullied the sky!
> Don't be afraid—it's been like this for a thousand years.
> Though humans weren't born to be killed,

---

7. Zhao was the surname of the imperial family of the Song dynasty.

8. Northern non-Han Chinese were called *hu* barbarians.

But others are intent upon killing them!
Large may be your breasts, Mom,
Not enough to block the rain of arrows!

People on the city wall toppled over like tumbling bundles of wheat. The clamor shook heaven and earth. Blood gushed like the water fountains found later at the plaza of Liangzhou. Beautiful faces turned into haggard, yellow paper. Bodies trembled like leaves on a tree. Flowing tears turned into pouring rain and washed the blood stains on the city wall.

"Charge! Kill!" Hollered all the men.

Ever since humankind came into existence, such cries have never ceased. This must have been the eternal curse of humankind. Is it not so?

Stop trying to sound sophisticated! What then?

And then, the city was conquered. The army of the Li family searched the city to exterminate their grandfather's foes. The Iron Hawks had sharp noses; they could always sniff out the traces of Ajia.

The Divine Tree of Xixia

Didn't you want to start from the beginning? Well then, we'll begin with my three perilous experiences. Ajia smiled mysteriously.

I doubted his veracity. His words seemed to combine truth with lies, but I said, "Start talking! I'm all ears!" in any case.

Do you remember that big tree? That tree was considered divine by the folk of Liangzhou. One year, when they were paving a new highway, the tree being in the way, the city officials wanted it cut down. Several hundred citizens begged for its preservation. Eleven of them even threatened suicide. So ultimately it was saved. That's right. That was the one. Remember? Go take a look when you have the time. To this day, that tree still stands there peacefully in the middle of the highway. Every day, up to a hundred people kowtow to it. It is said that whenever a branch falls from the tree, someone in the village will die. Don't you remember? Yes, the tree I'm talking about was the grandpa of this tree.

The grandpa tree of Xixia was even bigger and older than this grandson tree of his. It was so old it had no teeth. Not only did it have no teeth, but it also had no heart nor lungs. Where the heart and lungs were originally now housed myself, my brothers, my mom and possibly a few others. I can no longer remember how many there were. There was a thousand-league-eye in the tree, which was in fact a hole formed from rot. From there, we could see Suzhou and Hezhou of Gansu a thousand leagues away. The carousing Iron Hawks were there too. They rode on naked women and carried screaming babies on the tips of their spears. I knew that fella Yuanhao had already occupied the entire Hexi. I'd seen him once in Liangzhou. He had a square face and large ears and walked like a sow. But people called it the gait of dragons and tigers.[9] Well, maybe so. He also had wolf eyes and an eagle hooked nose. The minute I saw his face, I knew that thousands of lives would be obliterated by him. I also knew that one day his nose would be sliced off by someone with an even faster dagger. Because that nose of his was extremely propitious—his imperial physiognomy was entirely based on that nose of his—once that nose died, then the rest of him would also die. I've heard him bellow, but I can't imitate his voice. No one can imitate his voice. It has been a thousand years, but I've never heard that sort of voice again. Yet I knew what that sound meant. It meant revenge!

Through the hole, I saw the vengeful Iron Hawks coming for us. Although Mom couldn't see them, she could feel them. Mom's large breasts heaved with fear. They were once filled with milk. They were also fondled by many men. The first man was Great-Grandpa. Mom was his concubine. When Great-Grandpa died, Grandpa inherited his properties. Later, Yuanhao killed Grandpa. Grandpa's brother, Second Grandpa, inherited his properties. And then, when Second Grandpa died, Dad inherited the properties. Mom made the calculations and concluded that I was seeded by Dad. But who knows? I truly don't know. I admit that I'm a bastard. So what if I'm a bastard? At least I own up to it, unlike those companions of yours. One minute they were "poor peasants," another minute they've become descendants of "aristocrats"![10] Shit! They fuck their own mouths!

Be more civilized!

Okay. Look—

The Iron Hawks have flown in! The sky of Liangzhou was laden with stinky clouds around a bloody sun. Horse hoofs stomped the ground like splattering rain. I believe that was when the earth in Liangzhou

---

9. Dragons are associated with emperors and tigers suggest prowess. This is obviously a flattering compliment for someone with imperial designs.

10. During the communist era, the status of "poor peasants" was safe and coveted. But the situation changed after the market economy prevailed since the 1980s, and China became capitalistic.

turned hard. Everyone says that good people won't stay in Liangzhou because its earth is so hard. Yes, the soil was packed solid by the iron hoofs: the iron hoofs of Yuanhao and the iron hoofs of Genghis Khan. After being stomped on thousands of times, the earth turned iron hard.

Let me go back to the Iron Hawks. Their metal armor clinked and clanged, making a racket that reached up to heaven. This racket was so loud that soon that old fella, Emperor of the Great Song, was unable to sleep any longer. Mom was also unable to sleep. She said, "Go to sleep, Ajia!" I said, "The Iron Hawks are here!"

"Where?"

"Ten leagues away!"

Mom sighed and said, "Fear has made you silly. Don't be afraid, Ajia. They don't expect us to hide in a tree."

"It's not true, Mom." I said, "They'll shoot at us—blood will gush out."

"You're being silly again!" Mom sighed.

After the time it would have taken to eat a meal, we really did hear the sound of the iron hoofs. This time, Mom turned pale. Through the thousand-league-eye, I saw Grandpa Sun laughing sneakily. I knew the reason he was laughing. That day, I'd peed in his direction. Mom said I shouldn't pee in the direction of Grandpa Sun, but I did it anyway. Grandpa Sun hated me now. As soon as he laughed, the Iron Hawks found out about the secret inside the tree. They waved their whips, spurred their horses on, and began to circle the tree. They didn't know the entrance to the tree trunk was under a bird's nest. The ravens on the tree were crowing. They were also defecating right onto the armor below. A man spat, pulled an arrow with his bow, and shot. The raven had sharp eyes, however. It shook its wings, and the arrow was diverted. Someday later, your guru will tell you, "That was not a raven. It was a great guardian deity." Ravens are dependents of Mahakala.

Look at that Iron Hawk! He turned red from embarrassment. Although he covered his face with his helmet, I could still tell he was red from embarrassment. He whipped his horse and galloped away. The others didn't try to shoot at the raven again. They must have thought there was something uncanny about the ravens. But they decided to shoot at the tree instead. "Aiya!" I cried. An arrow pierced through the tree trunk and shot right through the chest of my older brother.

A stream of blood gushed out of the hole created by the arrow. Fearing that the Iron Hawks would discover us from it, I reached out my hand to stop the flowing blood. But the sound of their hoofs had already receded into the distance.

So, of my brothers and I, only three of us were left. Mom's tears poured ceaselessly. They flowed from the hole created by the arrow and seeped into the earth below. Ever since then, the soil there became salty and alkaline.

"Can you be a little down to earth?" I asked.

The Feeling of Black Wind

Ajia laughed, "Don't play the sophistication card. Don't you see, I was just making up a story!" I wondered, *was it really just a story?*

Ajia continued: In that desert, many birds became our food, but the Iron Hawks were watching us. What they didn't know was that the Mongols were watching them. What the Mongols didn't realize was that, although no one in the mortal world was watching the iron cavalries of the Mongols, the god of death was smiling at them with an evil smirk. He was saying, "Who do you think you are? Even your great Khan[11] is not big enough to fill a gap in my teeth!"

Okay, we'll continue. The second calamity happened in the desert. It was the desert you always wrote about. The one called something like Tenggeli. Back then, there wasn't as much sand; the desert wasn't so big. It was even considered to be just the sandy beach of a lake!

The Iron Hawks began to circle us. That was the way the Mongols would hunt later. They would line up first, and then they'd make a large circle that they'd tighten. Wolves, foxes, hog badgers, etc., all kinds of animals would be chased into the middle. The great Khan would lead a group in first to shoot their round, and then the lesser chiefs, the chiliarchs and centurions, would take turns with their followers, killing until the sky was filled with the stench of blood. Those Iron Hawks also circled us like that.

I saw a wolf and a rabid badger with red eyes. The wolf had cubs with it, just as Mom had me with her. We arrived treading through the sand, which flared in the wind under our gait. Back then, I was always seeing wolves. They were the janitors of the land. They kept the land relatively clean by devouring all the rotten flesh. I harbor a lot of feelings

---

11. The Mongols called their chief "Khan."

for wolves, as many accomplished gurus eventually transformed themselves into wolves to perform ritual offerings at the Smasanam corpse forest burial grounds. But I developed this feeling much later. At the time, I was truly terrified by the approaching beasts. The wolves stuck out their long, salivating tongues, and made a bellowing sound. An arrow typically used by the Iron Hawks whistled by and shot the rump of a female wolf. The funniest sight was that of the badgers. Although they looked chubby, they could run like black bullets, appearing and disappearing among the rippling sand. I was both scared and amused. I heard Mom say, "Quick, Ajia!" I turned around. Both my younger brothers had disappeared. Mom pointed to a shallow hole she dug under a grove of willow trees. She told me to lie down there and close my eyes. I knew what she meant. As soon as I closed my eyes, I felt my body becoming heavy. Sand slipped into my collar like worms and coolly licked at my chest. I wanted to say, "Mom, don't bury me alive!" But I knew more sand was waiting like a thief for an opportunity. The minute I'd open my mouth, they'd steal into my mouth, advance into my throat and chest, and then swallow me up. They'd do that for sure. Besides, I knew that Mom would not bury me alive. Because when I opened my eyes slightly, I could see the incredibly blue sky. A large bloody cloud was rolling in the sky. *It's going to rain blood*, I thought.

A large shadow whizzed by, and then another. I couldn't hear anything, but I could feel the earth tremble. I sensed the black shadows of the Iron Hawks. It was the feeling of black wind. Have you ever seen black wind? That's right, it's like having the god of death blow into one's face. I don't care what you say, but I could hear the grinding of its teeth.

I didn't know how long it took. But gradually, the wind subsided. I shook my head to get rid of the sand and looked at the willow grove. A deadly silence. A silence that was ghastly. Mom had already climbed out from among the willow leaves. She was staring at a depression and crawling to it woodenly. I jumped up and crawled toward her. I shook her. She clenched her teeth to stifle any sound. I followed her line of vision and saw the bloody imprint of a hoof. I knew then why Mom was weeping. There was a protective talisman next to the imprint. It was my little brother's.

I said, "Were you going to say, 'Ever since then, the willows became red willow trees?'"

Ajia said, "How did you know?"

"Do you have anything new to say?" I asked.

God of Death's Big Hand

Of course I have! Just listen.

My remaining little brother died one evening. The Iron Hawks surrounded us again. I didn't know how the Iron Hawks could always smell us. We found out later. Their leader, Yuanhao, had a young servant who was always burning a mutton shoulder bone. Each time he burned one, the bone would say, "Look! There they are!" Do you know how to burn them?

"No!" I said.

Once, when we were just coming up to a herd of sheep, a red-beaked raven came and said, "Run, fast! The Iron Hawks are coming again!" Mom couldn't understand its speech, but she believed my translation. And then the shepherd killed a sheep quickly, gutted it, and buried it in the sand. He put my brother and me into the gutted sheep and sewed it up skillfully, leaving holes for us to breathe through. I could never forget the feeling. I think it must have felt like that in the womb—a combination of stench and stickiness. I concentrated on the small opening and breathed in and out through it. Life was like a sparrow, forever trying to fly away. But I said, "What are you running away for? Just stay put nicely." It was incredibly stuffy and dark in there, but I was still able to see the row of Iron Hawks. Welded to their horses, they approached very quietly, like the god of death.

That was when my younger brother was suffocated to death.

"How come you justly used a few dozen words for such a horrendous experience?" I asked.

That's because you exist. The world gave birth to you so you'd write about these experiences.

I remember it was autumn then. After that, we spent the winter in the desert.

Back then, where Diamond Clan would establish itself later, was only a lake. There was a lot of grass then, many mountains too. The grass was very tall—as tall as a man! That was the place that I, Mom, my little brother, and many people from the Six Valleys landed. Later, the place became a village, and the folks called it Diamond Clan.

There were many birds there: sand pheasants, wild ducks, turtle doves, and lots of others! We set traps using horsetail hair and placed them on the lake. That hair was like smoke, invisible to the birds. The openings of the traps were only as big as the heads of the birds so that when they dove into them, the harder they flew forward, the tighter the trap got. The birds didn't know to retreat backward.

Sometimes, taking a step backward will open up for one the expansive sea and sky.

I said, "Okay, okay! Stop talking about me. I've been going forward since I was born. I'd charge forward no matter what and ram a hole in the thickest wall!" Ajia laughed, "Aren't you worried you'd smash your head?" I said, "If I smash my head, I'll charge with my soul!"

The birds were like that. So, they became our food. Ajia smacked his lips.

Immediately, I smelled the pungent odor of burnt meat. That smell was just like the burnt sparrows I ate when I was little. I used to carry a ladder at night and lean it against a pile of hay. The sparrows had already exposed their nests when they went in and out during the day. I wobbled up the ladder and stuck my hand into the hay quietly. There was a hole in there. It was not a big hole. A warmth seeped from it from the sleeping family of sparrows. There were no snores. Sparrows did not snore. But they breathed. Their breath was a sort of silken wool that I could capture. My hand felt its way in, following the silken wool. Then, the mother sparrow would wake up. Like Ajia's mom when she saw the Iron Hawks, she'd chirp a few times in terror. Her family members would then clamor to hide. But that hand of mine had already grabbed their fate. No matter how they tried to hide, they could not escape fate. I took them back and threw them into the fire of the kitchen stove. In a short while, I would take out the eggs, tear off the feather that had burnt into clumps, and see the yellow meat. I'd tear apart the yellow meat, discard the innards, and take a bite. The delicious smoked flavor of the meat would exude from all of my pores.

So I knew exactly what Ajia was talking about.

"And then?" I asked.

Then, I entered Diamond Maiden Cave and became a Xixia monk. After experiencing many legendary tales, I became the protagonist of one of them.

Ajia said that back then the big hand of the god of death always loomed above our heads. We hid and hid. It wasn't until later we realized that that big hand wasn't only clutching at us, it was also after the Iron Hawks, and the Mongols, and the emperors who wore those yellow robes, and you.

And you, Xue Mo!

I shuddered. A dark cloud floated over my mind. I said, "Also Jasper, and Snow Feather, and all living beings."

My tears gushed.

Chapter 3

The Barbarian Hag

Tear off a roseate cloud to cover your face!
Don't let the ephemeral plant in your head!
    Don't you see—
At the edge of the sky, filled with yellow dust,
A sky-churning windstorm is rolling in.
Sideburns of cultivating ascetics in the grotto,
    Are overgrown with unkempt grass.

Wailing of the Hungry Ghosts

According to *Crazy Ramblings of Ajia*, Jasper finally reached Liangzhou after a lengthy trek.

We don't know when Jasper reached Liangzhou. The manuscript was very vague about this. Because Liangzhou, in Jasper's eyes, has become more than just a geographical concept. It had become a metaphor and ceased to belong to any specific period. It was just like using "once upon a time" in Buddhist scriptures to indicate a historical juncture. In the eyes of the wise, time is but an illusion.

But the moment Jasper entered Liangzhou, the metaphor reverted back to reality. Liangzhou was dead—a deserted shoal. It was the moment the demon of hunger was licking everything indiscriminately.

Chinese history was full of periods like this. Hunger was one of the nightmares of history.

Jasper crawled for a day and a night through the streets of Liang-zhou, and he snatched an eggplant lotus from the mouth of a dog. You know, dogs don't eat that stuff. But during times of starvation, even dogs change their nature. We don't know from which dirty gutter that dog found the eggplant lotus. But Ajia didn't think it was just an ordinary dog. It must have been an incarnation of the Dakini goddess, Niguma. As you will read later, in Lhasa there were always packs of dogs roaming the streets and circling a crazy woman. All those dogs were, in fact, Dakini goddesses.

These Dakini goddesses can be understood as goddesses from Beyond-the-World.

You must remember a man known as Guguruba, also known as Dog Guru. Incredibly ugly, he resembled a strange bird. He lived on Duron Island[1] in India. He was unable to find any woman willing to be his Mudra Mother, a companion for practicing couple-cultivation of Tantric Buddhism. But he was always followed by a female dog. It was said that female dog was also an incarnation of a Dakini goddess.

Hence, Ajia believed the black dog Jasper met must have been the incarnation of a Dakini goddess who brought Jasper the eggplant lotus to sustain his life.

Jasper swallowed the eggplant lotus, also known as "kohlrabi," in a few gulps and almost choked himself to death. Fortunately, he didn't die. Otherwise, the world would have had fewer amazing manuscripts.

Jasper came upon a strange scene. Suddenly, a procession of men and horses sauntered through the streets of Liangzhou one evening. The lead person was an old fellow, as thin as a sick bird yet exceptionally spirited. He beat a drum at the front. The drum sounded weak and muffled. More than a dozen men followed upon his heels, each bearing a sack on his shoulder. The sacks were not big. They were in fact quite slim. The men wobbled through the dead streets, yelling slogans as they proceeded. Curious, Jasper followed them. Upon arriving at a certain place, the group emptied the wheat in their sacks into a granary. Later Jasper found out that they were residents of Diamond Clan and here to pay their grain tax.

Jasper walked toward Diamond Maiden Cave. His path was strewn with corpses—mostly with thin legs, bulging bellies, and covered with green-headed flies the size of jujubes. The flies hummed and buzzed, like the German planes when they would later bomb London. They clamored frantically, licking the fluids of the corpses with outstretched tongues and sowing their seeds into the flowing, sticky juices. The sun also became

---

1. The Chinese transliteration, *dulong dao*, literally means "Poisonous Dragon Island."

crazed, pouring its flames onto the corpses with abandon. Now and then, the belly of one of the corpses exploded with an earth-shaking loud bang. The sky was strewn with hungry ghosts. Those who died such untimely deaths wailed throughout the nights. For without the guidance of the Black and White Anityas, they couldn't find their way to the court of Yama.

People are so strange, Jasper thought. *Why do they always want someone to lord over them?*

What Jasper didn't understand was that the folks of Liangzhou, who had been accustomed to being slaves, feared nothing more than becoming roaming ghosts after death. Their funerals mostly comprised the issuance of "passports" for the road to Hades. After going over the Golden Bridge, they'd go over the Silver Bridge and then the River Nai Bridge before they could report to the court of Yama. Yama would then deal with the deceased and dispatch them to their locations for reincarnation. They feared most the fate of becoming a roaming ghost. Which is to say, they feared their souls would roam the four directions without being under someone's control. Liangzhou, however, was filled with Great Strength Ghosts. Some have been worshipped as deities. They have great strengths and supernatural powers. They could do evil but also good. After being subdued by an eminent monk or a guru, they'd become protective deities.

Jasper thought, *Maybe the hungry ghosts wailed all night long because they didn't comprehend that the myriad manifestations are created by the mind and clung to the idea of hunger?*

According to folk legends, Jasper was born with the karmic gift of being able to communicate with and see spirits in another space. This didn't mean he had already completed his practices. His practices had nothing to do with this special ability. *Journey to the West* was chock full of demons possessing great supernatural powers but still incredibly stupid. Not an enviable lot. Martial arts novels also portray swordsmen who'd obtained true energies through unusual karmic circumstances. But when the energies couldn't be controlled, they'd dart in all directions and would in fact create tremendous suffering. Possessing the ability to see spirits was the same. Actually, possessing this ability before attaining enlightenment could be considered a form of kundalini syndrome.[2] It was a pain for Jasper to always see what he shouldn't see.

---

2. Kundalini syndrome refers to physical or psychological problems arising from qigong and spiritual practices.

The wailing of the hungry ghosts aggravated Jasper. Soon, he saw something strange. He saw an old ghost pleading with a ghost that looked like a clan militia. The old ghost said, "My lord, please let me leave so I can survive!" The clan militia said, "No! Hey, you can enter this village, but not leave! No one blackens Diamond Clan's face!"

Jasper thought in surprise, *Those ghosts of the clan militia are ferocious!*

He just realized the real reason behind the wailing of the hungry ghosts!

The Son-Expecting Hill

Ajia said the first person Jasper met at Diamond Clan was Barbarian Hag.

Barbarian Hag was staring with red eyes at the gradually approaching shadow in front of the setting sun. She had been like this for dozens of years. It was precisely because she'd been like this for dozens of years that no one wondered about her behavior. Many years ago, her son left the village to explore the world. He left with a camel caravan. He saw a white camel. That camel was tall and imposing, with belly hair stabbing the ground. When it bellowed, the mountain beyond the village trembled. The son said, "Mom, I want a white camel like that." Mom said, "When you grow up and make money, you can buy yourself one. I have no money!" The son said, "I'll make money then!" That night, he left with a camel caravan.

Camel caravans traveled at night. The road belonged to horses and carriages during the day and to camels at night. Barbarian Hag knew that she still did not guard her son well enough. The son said he would make a lot of money and take her away to enjoy the rest of her life. This her son told her in a dream. Barbarian Hag didn't like the dream, as only dead people communicated with the living through dreams; she was convinced her son wasn't dead.

Of course, he wasn't dead.

Therefore, Barbarian Hag hung around the village entrance awaiting her son's return. She always saw him treading the setting sun, sparkling sunlight spilling under his feet like flowing gold. She also always saw him this way in her dreams. When she was little, her dad told her that whoever dreamt of the color yellow would be rich. She dreamt of yellow color most of her life but got not even an iota of wealth. So she thought the dreams probably applied to her son. Surely that must have been the case. Her son must have made it rich in a faraway land. One day he'd return, treading the brilliant yellow sunlit road to fetch her so she could enjoy the rest of her life.

The son always approached like that but then disappeared before he got close. So Barbarian Hag always waited there. People in the village even called the hillock she sat on Son-Expecting Hill.

That particular evening, Barbarian Hag saw Jasper approach treading on sunlight. Except she knew Jasper was definitely not her son.

An indescribable stench engulfed the village. Jasper knew it was the corpses. On the river shoal, corpses lay one layer on top of the other. Sunlight licked at them gleefully. Now and then, one of them would explode with a loud bang. Most of them were devoured by wolves and no longer whole. It was said that people who died of hunger had very little flesh on them. But wolves loved the inner organs. So, the intestines that used to rumble from hunger ironically filled the wolves' stomachs, their fur glistening with a satiny, oily sheen. Those days of catastrophe were ironically the golden age for the wolves. They copulated and bred frantically. The valleys were densely studded with these wolves, which looked like tossed flax seeds from a distance. They never attacked the living as so many deceased were lined up for their enjoyment. They didn't even feel like looking at the living.

Jasper realized that a great calamity had befallen the place. Although he didn't know whether he could survive this calamity, he did not regret having come. He was getting closer and closer to the meaning of life after all.

Jasper saw Barbarian Hag on the hillock at the village entrance. He thought he should be happy since her existence meant the village wasn't completely dead. He smelled a strange odor. It was an indescribable smell. He realized later that was the odor of the god of death.

He saw Barbarian Hag staring at him the way a hungry man looked at food. Jasper thought this is the way a mother looks at her returning son and felt a kind of warmth. He asked, "Grandma, is this Diamond Clan?" Barbarian Hag stared at him at length before she nodded.

Jasper climbed up the hillock, composed himself, and looked at the village. The village was dilapidated. The sensation of dilapidation engulfed all the buildings in the village. But Jasper discovered something mystical: There was a Sanskrit symbol in the sky. It was the symbol in the heart of Diamond Maiden. Its existence signified that an incarnation of Diamond Maiden lived in the village. Look! That red Sanskrit word was smiling at him faintly.

He knew this village was his destination.

The Bloody Cellar

Barbarian Hag led Jasper into her house. She said, "People who traveled a long way should have a drink of water."

As soon as he entered the house, he was invaded by the stench of manure. He had to hold his breath. There was a pile of black cotton on the brick bed.[3] This must have been what the old grandma used to survive the winters. There was also a stand for a stove. The stand was made of wood, and the stove was made of mud bricks. Back then, few families used this setup. But there was no fire in it. The ashes and stove were cold and dead. A strange stench permeated the room. A wicked stench. Jasper knitted his eyebrows.

Barbarian Hag brought the water which Jasper took from her. He was truly thirsty. Water was a good thing. Whenever he felt starved, he'd drink water. After drinking a lot of water, he'd feel satiated. Moreover, he believed there was nutrition in water. People couldn't survive more than seven days without water. But if they drank water, then they could survive a few more days. This meant that water must contain some invisible good stuff. So he drank the water avariciously.

As he remembered it—that was when he fainted.

When he came to, Jasper found himself in a cellar surrounded by skeletons that were the source of the stench. Jasper felt his head aching. Obviously something had hit it. Barbarian Hag held a knife in her hand and was panting while staring at him. She swayed unsteadily. Red light shone from her eyes. Jasper realized the pain at the back of his head must have been caused by her.

After panting for a while, she charged at him, still swaying like a kite. Jasper grabbed her wrist, and Barbarian Hag let out an eerie screech. A rotten stench emanated from her mouth. Her toothless gums bulged from swelling. Jasper found out later that she must have accumulated too much heat from eating too much human flesh.

---

3. Brick beds are used in the north for sitting and sleeping. They can be heated underneath.

Barbarian Hag writhed violently a few times. But her violent writhing was but an unsubstantiated attempt. Jasper realized she was excessively weak. He pulled at her wrist and lifted her entire body.

Barbarian Hag screamed frantically with glaring eyes. This too was a soundless attempt looking more like huffing. Waves of horrible stench whistled and tumbled at him, and Jasper almost suffocated. He thought he was in a dream; everything seemed so vague. A ray of the setting sun shone into the entrance of the cellar and landed on the face of Barbarian Hag. A haggard and ugly face distorted by terror. Jasper later realized he himself must have been most terrifying. He also screamed. He screamed like this when he'd met hungry wolves in the Himalayan Mountains. He knew this scream must have been appalling too. Besides, it was deafening. His full-throated cry reverberated in the narrow cellar, wave after wave like a surging tide. He sensed the old woman struggling in vain but still trying to stab the knife into his throat. Her frustration must have been immense. He tossed her away ruthlessly as if he were tossing away a tattered sheepskin coat. Barbarian Hag gulped and fainted.

Jasper collapsed on the ground. He felt a barely perceptible pulsating pain in the back of his head. The woman's fall alarmed a pile of flies. Their humming engulfed him like a dream. Jasper also saw some freakish things like scorpions and geckos. He knew they were only illusions. Droves of wet, crawling insects gave him goosebumps. Later, he found out that the folks of Liangzhou called them "hemp shoe-bottoms." Bizarre insects with a strange name, these always appeared in damp places, like the underside of rocks and vats. No one knew how they managed to survive. At this moment, they were all staring at Jasper with lifted faces. They had probably never seen anyone like this "curly bearded guest"[4] with a prominent nose and deep-set eyes. This was the first of many gazes of amazement he would receive at Diamond Clan.

The corpses in the cellar must have continued to exude a stench, but Jasper could no longer smell it. One might say he no longer cared about the odor. He wasn't afraid of corpses. Before he received the Abhiseka,[5] he had cultivated the practice of visualizing skeletons. He would begin with visualizing the bones of the toes, one joint at a time, and gradually move upward to visualize the bones of the feet, the legs,

---

4. Curly Bearded Guest is the protagonist of a renowned Tang dynasty short story, "Biography of the Curly Bearded Guest" by Du Guangting (850–933).

5. A ritual that initiates a student into a particular Tantric deity practice.

the pelvis, the vertebrae, the ribs, and finally the skull, until his entire mind was full of skeletons. After that, he'd only see awkwardly stacked skeletons whenever he saw anyone. So he was not afraid of the corpses in the cellar. Although the skeletons were not clean and white—some had dried flesh, some had fresh flesh on them, most were rotten and stinky. He still wasn't afraid of them. Yet he was afraid of the red-eyed Barbarian Hag, although at the time he didn't know that was what people called her: for sure all the corpses were her food.

Jasper also saw bloodstains on the ground. The blood seeped through the ground. Dried blood curled up one layer after the other, and crackled when stepped on. The blood disclosed the origin of the corpses. They must have been killed by Barbarian Hag. She must have told them, travelers from afar need a drink of water and they followed her here and drank water. They had no inkling Barbarian Hag would lift a heavy, hardwood rolling pin behind them. Back then Barbarian Hag must have been stronger. She could kill or incapacitate them with one blow and then throw them into the cellar.

That must have been what happened. Jasper heaved a deep sigh and thought, when people turn bad, they become worse than anything else.

Barbarian Hag woke up. She stared at him with her red eyes. She crouched in a corner and looked tiny, somewhat like a strange bird. She then stretched out her bird claws and tried to grab a knife. It was a typical butcher's knife. It was pointed but dented in the middle, a sign that it had sliced a lot of flesh. Jasper shuddered. He stepped on the claw, picked up the knife, and put it into his own backpack. He thought that when he had the opportunity later he would perform a fire offering to release from purgatory the souls that had died from this knife. He saw all the skeletons smile, seemingly very happy.

He stepped onto the ladder to leave the cellar. The cellar was not deep. The ladder was not even three feet tall! Barbarian Hag charged at him, hoping to prevent him from leaving. He gave her a kick. Although it was not hard, the woman still fell a distance away and collapsed on the ground again like a tattered sheepskin. He heard a squeal from her throat that resembled a sigh and then her eyes rolled.

Above ground, Jasper realized the entrance to the cellar was directly behind the stool he sat on. A tattered hemp sack lay to one side. He then realized how all the possibly young lives died at the hands of Barbarian Hag. Once her trick worked, the bodies would fall into the cellar by themselves. Although the corpses on the river shoal could be used to relieve hunger before they rotted, there was no way Barbarian Hag would have been able to drag them to her own place. He felt delirious. The sun in the sky was deceitful, just a halo with faint light. Jasper touched his head, which still felt numb from the pain and heaved a heavy sigh.

There was dust everywhere in the house. There was a layer of something unrecognizable on the brick bed. Maybe they were chips from broken bones. Jasper didn't feel like scrutinizing them. He desperately wanted to lie down on the pile of cotton and sleep. He yawned broadly and felt sleepiness overcome him like a net. But he knew it was just the demon of sleep playing a trick. So he yelled *pei* ferociously. This was the famous Spell of Pei. It was one of the Three Essential Spells of the Striking Awl[6] that Grandpa Jiu transmitted to him. Whenever he uttered the curt "Pei" loudly, the demon of sleep would flee immediately.

He wanted to find something to eat in the house. But if there were anything to eat there, Barbarian Hag wouldn't have been sporting with her rolling pin. He had no choice but to leave the house and enter the village. The mud on the ground was very thick; it felt like walking on a cloud. He found a high spot, hoping to see a temple from there. Traveling monks invariably looked for temples whenever they reached a place. He finally saw some upturned eaves and walked toward them. A refreshing coolness filled his heart. It was like a lamb that had lost its way, finally locating its corral.

The old monk said, gratifyingly, "You're finally back!"

"Uncle,"[7] responded Jasper, "you didn't age. You look the same."

The old monk laughed and said, "Some parts aged, others didn't. Although the body has aged, the thing that knows the body has aged hasn't aged."

The old man was cooking poplar porridge. The smell was very familiar. Although he knew it tasted awful, his stomach still began to rumble violently. The old monk looked at him and handed him half a bowl of it without saying anything. Jasper slurped it and, unexpectedly, the entire sticky goo landed in his stomach. He felt he had swallowed a burning-red stone and screamed unwittingly.

After the pain died down a bit, he thought of Barbarian Hag. He was afraid she had died from his kick. If that was the case, then he

---

6. *Zuiji san yaojue* are methods for eliminating stubbornness or clinging to attachments.

7. *Jiujiu*, maternal uncle. He was the brother of Jasper's mother.

would have broken his vow against killing. He told his uncle about his experience. But the old monk only smiled mysteriously.

He said, "That Barbarian Hag died more than a month ago. I was the one who performed her funeral rites!"

The Snide Snickers

Jasper settled down at Diamond Monastery. All the monks in the world belonged to the same family, so they could stay at any temple they visited. This monastery, however, didn't look like a monastery anymore. The main Buddhist hall was dismantled, the beams were all used as firewood. The Buddhist statues were either rotten or falling apart: they were also baring their teeth and complaining. Furthermore, there were no offerings. When even the village was dying, who had the energy to support the monks? But it was still better at the temple than elsewhere because it had many poplar trees, the bark of which could be ground into flour and cooked into a goo. After that initial experience, Jasper was particularly careful when he ate that stuff, lest the entire content of the bowl end up in his belly in one gulp again.

The Ancestral Hall and the Diamond Monastery were in the same estate. It was more lively here than in the rest of the village. Braggart and his men came here frequently to discuss important matters. When that happened, they would bring a few pancakes or some other food for the monk. These were not offerings. They were meant to stuff the monk's mouth, lest it slip out that they were eating there on the sly. Braggart must not have been happy about his having to do this, which was probably one of the reasons Monk Wu was an object of his struggle sessions[8] later.

The estate was located at the highest point of the village, away from private homes. So, it was obviously a good place for Braggart and his men. There was only an old monk in the monastery. There used to be several hundred monks here, but after the religious prohibition, they'd all been sent home. The huge monastery had become conspicuously empty. If it weren't for frequent use of the place by Braggart and his men, the monastery would have been deadly silent.

---

8. The "struggle sessions" were held during the Cultural Revolution (1966–1976).

Jasper told many people about Barbarian Hag. But they all sniggered slyly and said she was dead. They all said her eyes were red before she died, and she was burned to death. But no one would say how. Jasper was somewhat suspicious of it all. Sometimes, he also suspected that his experience was a dream, but he would always see the old hag at the village entrance.

On a certain evening, Barbarian Hag took a beggar into her house. At the time, Diamond Clan was considered the wealthiest village in Liangzhou. Not a single man left Diamond Clan to beg for food elsewhere. All the beggars who wanted to survive rushed in from other places. Barbarian Hag gave Jasper a wicked glance and took the beggar into her house.

Jasper immediately went to the old monk and said, "Oh no, Barbarian Hag is going to kill someone again!" The old monk squinted his eyes, took a look at Jasper coldly, and said, "You have a problem with your eyes. As I've told you, she died a long time ago!" Of course Jasper didn't believe him. He flew to the entrance of the village and saw the shadow of the hag turning the corner. Jasper thought, *Saving one life is better than attaining seven levels of Buddhahood!* So he picked up a rock and ran to Barbarian Hag's home. Just as expected, the beggar was drinking water, and Barbarian Hag was just lifting her rolling pin. She seemed much stronger now than she was the last time. The beggar's brain might even splatter from her blow this time. Jasper threw the rock that whistled like a steam horn and smashed Barbarian Hag's bony foot. The room boomed. Barbarian Hag rolled her eyes and hollered, "Mind your own fucking business! This old lady of yours just want to help him!" The beggar also stared at him with anger. Jasper said, "Run! She's a cannibal!" The beggar stared at Barbarian Hag blankly. Barbarian Hag said, "He's crazy!" The beggar glared at him again. Jasper said, "Look!" He removed the sack that covered the cellar entrance and a terrifying stench wafted up at them.

Only then did the beggar believe him. He threw down the bowl and made his escape.

Jasper saw Barbarian Hag collapse onto the floor. She moaned, "I haven't eaten for three days!"

Jasper felt terrible.

When he left the house, he saw the beggar making his way toward the village. Strangely, however, he never saw him again.

The old monk watched him from a distance.

The story of Jasper and Snow Feather will now begin.

Chapter 4

Stealing Crops

Love is actually but a pale word,
Never comparable to the rain in your eyes,
Or the plum-blossom footprints
      Bit by bit
Causing the lonely sea of sand to clamor;
      The immense desert
      Without you, little fox,
Would really be deserted!

Chicken Feet Weed

Snow Feather's life was very dramatic. Before she completed her Buddhist practices, she was known as a flying thief. After she completed her practices, she was revered as a Dakini goddess.

Before she completed her practices, she was the most skillful flying thief in all of Liangzhou, capable of darting through houses and over rooftops as lightly as a bird feather. That's why she was named Feather. Normally, like rabbits who would never eat the grass near their burrows, she would never steal from the folks back home. But who would have thought that later she would infuriate the big shots and endure calamities thereafter.

Crazy Ramblings of Ajia records how she once stole crops. The identity of the narrator is rather vague, however. It could be Ajia or some youngster in the village.

Snow Feather left her house to search for chicken feet weed. Everyone in the village dug chicken feet weed, and of course, Snow Feather had to do the same. By now her notoriety had spread throughout Liangzhou, and she knew she shouldn't distance herself from the villagers. Outwardly, at least, she should do what everyone else did. Otherwise, it would be very difficult for her to survive in Liangzhou. Her past and her notoriety had already become huge obstacles in her life. People in the village looked at her differently. Of course she knew they also looked at her mother that way. It was a good thing her mom was blind and couldn't see the funny looks people gave her. Sometimes not having eyesight is a good thing.

The wild bitter endive in the village had already been picked. Snow Feather left her house. The ruins of this house without courtyard can still be found in a valley. I've visited there several times to commemorate Snow Feather. Of course, those visits could be considered as pilgrimages, since by the time I visited, she was already known as the incarnation of the Wisdom Dakini goddess, Niguma. Our chants during the ritual offerings on every twenty-fifth of the month contained information about her. The incredible tribulations she endured, comparable to the ordeals endured by Christ, later endowed her with an aura of holiness.

The odor of death permeated the air, the characteristics of which were the smells of charred matter. The odor of burnt matter was created by the scorching sun. The stench came from the rotting corpses. The valley below Snow Feather's home was always visited by wolves. They made an unrestrained sound that resembled the slurping of rice soup. Wolves always made that kind of noise when they ate meat. It was said wolf saliva could turn bones and flesh into a meat porridge-like rice soup. So the sound they made when they ate meat was one that suggested great relish. For those tormented by hunger, hearing that sound was worse than death. Snow Feather and her mother heard it every night.

The mud the cattle carts forced aside piled up a foot high, oozing on the roads of the village. Snow Feather labored arduously with each step she took. There were no more weeds nearby. They'd all been transformed into feces by the villagers' stomachs. Of course, the process was completed by sheep in some instances. Sheep were public property of the Ancestral Hall. No one had the right to transform them into feces. Snow Feather and other villagers had already picked all the bitter endives. They were the most delicious of all the edible weeds. Many years later, they would become highly sought after, expensive delicacies at markets.

Chicken feet weed looked like chicken feet. I've eaten it at Snow Feather's. Snow Feather had picked a whole basketful of it. Back then, Mom always told me not to visit Snow Feather. She said Snow Feather was a witch. And then Mom explained to me what a witch was. She said witches had long noses and loved to eat toads. As for the long nose characteristic, I found no evidence of it in Snow Feather. As for toad eating, however, I was in fact an accomplice as I've also eaten toads. When Snow Feather stuck the leg of a toad into my mouth, I thought it was the most delicious thing in the entire world.

Back then, I'd already eaten things much worse than toads. Take for example, the mold heads, the black stuff with a muddy, fishy taste that grew on wheat stalks. And for example, the chicken feet weeds. Snow Feather would parboil the weeds and dry them in the sun. The bright sun would caress the weeds that had turned black from boiling water and look at a tangled mass of cow manure. Later, whenever Mom described chicken feet weed, she'd use the term "cow manure."

I will never forget the Snow Feather who was drying chicken feet weed under the bright sun. She was extremely pretty, although she rarely smiled. She came like a waft of wind and left like one. I've always suspected she was a wisp of air. I was almost the only "person" who was close to her family. I put the word "person" in quotation marks because at the time I was not yet considered a person in the village. I was a mere child. Before marriage, a youth was not considered to be a person. This was one of the traditions of Liangzhou. No matter what age, even if he lived to be sixty, a childless bachelor would not have the right to lie in a coffin after death. His corpse would be dragged to the wilderness like a dead dog and be burned with wheat stalks. In the eyes of the villagers, he would only be a dead old child with no right to enjoy offerings. So, the fact that I wasn't considered a person gave me many privileges, including being able to visit an alien being like Snow Feather.

Snow Feather put the dried chicken feet weed next to her hand mill. That hand mill belonged to her household. When the villagers ground wheat flour, they used the communal water mill. Many of the foods at Snow Feather's home were prechewed by this hand mill. I used to see her mom sitting next to the mill and turning it round and round. And all sorts of flossy things would come out of it.

Snow Feather always ground the chicken feet weed herself. She would get me to stuff the weed into the hole of the mill with a wooden stick. I remember the weed being very prickly. It was the sort of plant that "bared fangs and brandished claws" even after it was dead. I kept on stuffing the weeds into the hole while Snow Feather turned the mill round and round. The weeds would moan, clamor, and groan until they became a flossy mass. The rumbling sound of the mill accompanied my childhood.

Snow Feather rarely smiled and was always extremely quiet. Only when she saw sweat flowing down my face did her eyes show a faint smile. That flash lightning moment was enough to turn my infatuated soul upside down. The harder I pushed the stick, the faster she turned the mill, until she broke out into a laugh and said, "Okay!" And then I would smile ingratiatingly with bared teeth. Back then, a reddish halo would cover her face, and her delicate nose would be covered with tiny pearl-beaded sweat.

At that time, her mom was already lying on the brick bed. She looked fatter. Later I found out she was, in fact, bloated. Many people in the village were bloated before they died. And then they were buried in the valley. When Snow Feather looked at her mom, her eyes showed great anxiety.

Snow Feather mixed the milled floss with water, made patties out of them, put them in a wok, and lit the fire. Without a word from her, I was already squatting next to the bellows of the stove. This was my favorite task. I can't remember how old I was then, but whenever my mom went to work in the fields, she would arrange for me to work the fire of the stove. She would specify the number of "boils." Each "boil" referred to having the water boiling until it almost spilled out of the wok.

I threw one handful of wheat stalks into the stove after another. I was very good at keeping the stove from smoking. The fire in the stove licked at my face. Snow Feather looked at me as if in deep thought. But I knew she wasn't looking at me. Her eyes were filled with purity and spirituality. This was her most beautiful moment. Later, when I painted a Tanka of the Wisdom Dakini Goddess, I based it on this memory. Experts said that, of all the Tankas I've made, this one reflected both form and spirit and was therefore incomparably beautiful.

Not only when I painted the Tanka, but even when I had to visualize my protective deity Buddha Mother in my religious practice later on, the image of Snow Feather would appear before my eyes. I truly wished to visualize the Buddha Mother according to her image in the Tanka, but if the Buddha Mother insisted on transforming herself into Snow

Feather, there was nothing I could do about it. This phenomenon was written into a poem by the sixth Dalai Lama, Karjam Saeji:[1]

> I meditate and practice until my dharma eyes are open,
> I pray for the three treasures to descend upon the spiritual altar.
> Visualizing the various saints, but where do I see them?
> Without invitation, the lover arrives on her own.

This poem could serve to reinforce the position Snow Feather occupied in my heart.

But when I was stoking the fire, I had no idea what the word "lover" meant. The older generation in Liangzhou used to refer to their lovers as "friends" and to visiting a lover as to "maintaining a friend." This was the more subtle way of referring to lovers. The forthright ones would call their lovers "female thief" or "male thief." This was the culture I was born into. But I never considered Snow Feather as my "female thief"; not when the villagers saw her as a flying thief, and not when she became a Dakini goddess later. Snow Feather was always Snow Feather to me. In my mind, she was always a moon hanging in the sky.

I pulled at the bellows energetically. The two leaves in it bellowed alternately, making a "pada, pada" sound. The wheat stalks in the stove glowed red. According to my mom, these embers were the best for cooking. That was when the flame and smoke had died down, leaving a layer of glowing, red ember with the finest heat. The ancestors of the village loved to heat themselves with embers. These ancestors were, of course, those who were dead but still hanging around. The other village kids and I used to light bonfires in front of our homes during wintry nights. I remember that the village was very cold. We would sing the ditty, "after midwinter, noses will freeze" and then charge toward the wonderful warmth. I would always heat myself greedily. One night, I suddenly discovered that all the people around the fire with me had no chins. I got so scared I rushed to Snow Feather's home, which was the closest. When I told her breathlessly about the strange chinless people, Snow Feather smiled. Her mother said, "Those are ghosts. Ghosts have no chins." She also told me how to distinguish ghosts, as when ghosts holler there would be no echo; ghosts didn't cast shadows under the light, and

---

1. His dates were 1683–1706.

ghosts were hoarse because they had no vocal cords, etc. Snow Feather said disapprovingly, "Ma! Don't scare him, okay?" Later I conveyed this knowledge to village kids younger than myself. Thereafter, whenever the villagers made a bonfire, they would only enjoy the flames; the embers were left for the ancestors and roaming ghosts.

The embers made a sizzling sound and licked the bottom of the wok with bluish tongues. The pot's bottom resembled a night sky studded with glittering stars. At first, the pot's bottom was black with patches of glittering stars. But gradually, more and more stars appeared. The large stars gave birth to small stars, and they all formed one big assembly. Then, the contents of the wok would make a sizzling sound. That sound was full of variations, exhibiting all five notes of the Chinese scale, and incomparably happy. Representing hope and happiness, it was one of the most beautiful songs of my childhood.

Steam spilled out of the lid gleefully. This was what my mom meant by one "boil." The steam washed Snow Feather's pretty face into an incomparably beautiful sight. Just then, Braggart suddenly appeared at the door. He must have seen the smoke from the chimney. During that period, few chimneys had smoke in the village. Whenever he saw a chimney exuding smoke, he would check to see if anyone had stolen crops. Braggart looked at me coldly, and then he looked at Snow Feather. His face gradually warmed up, having been washed by the steam. Snow Feather looked absolutely exquisite. I suspect it must have been his desire for that face, and the transformation of his sense of shame into anger, that made Braggart treat her so cruelly later on.

Snow Feather opened the lid suddenly without saying a word. Steam swooped out like thick smoke. I could never forget that muddy, fishy smell. That was the natural odor of chicken feet weeds. Even though there wasn't even a dreg in my stomach at that moment, I still couldn't stand that awful smell.

I sneezed fiercely at Braggart. I believe innumerable specks of spittle must've shot at him like the bullets of a machine gun. They whistled and cheered with elated sounds as if seeking mates. They collided and created metallic sounds like a flock of naughty robins. Braggart was pecked by them, like someone ending up with pockmarks from smallpox. I even suspected the psoriasis Braggart developed later was seeded by them. Years later, he used to squat curled up in the gully outside the valley to sun himself. Any scabby dog would be a hundred times more beautiful than he. Everyone said it was the result of bad karma. But I knew psoriasis was only one of the many things he deserved. By then, one of his karmic enemies had already reincarnated as one of his children. This was the child who accompanied him into the sunny gully. Ten years later, this child would grow into a strong man and hurl Braggart down to the ground like one would smash a toad. He and his dad were the two most notorious and depraved men in the history of Diamond Clan.

But Braggart was totally oblivious to the bullets of my sneeze. He was staring at Snow Feather with covetous desire. That's when I learned what covetous desire was. My aversion to Braggart lasted until I was middle-aged. That's why I'd never look at any woman that way.

Snow Feather was looking at the "cow manure" in the wok. It really was "cow manure." Everything made from chicken feet weed looked like cow manure, except the smell was even worse. All the villagers back then had eaten this 'cow manure' made from chicken feet weed. I could never forget that muddy, fishy taste. Mom said chicken feet weed saved my life.

Snow Feather picked up a broom and started to sweep the stove platform. This was equivalent to announcing that Braggart was not welcome. Braggart gave her a vicious look and left.

Snow Feather brought out the steamer basket and offered it to her mom. Mom grabbed one immediately and gawked.

Pounding on Mom's back lightly with her fists,[2] Snow Feather said, "Chew carefully, Ma!"

She knew that even this kind of food had become rare.

Mold Heads

I went to steal produce.

I left Snow Feather's home when she was gouging out her mom's feces. Snow Feather said, "Go out and play now. Come back later!" I knew what she was going to do. My mom used to do that a lot too. Whenever I was intensely constipated, Mom would have me take off my pants and used a stick to gouge it out of my asshole.

No matter how hard I tried to imagine Snow Feather doing it using a stick, I couldn't. Now you see Snow Feather's intelligence. By not allowing me to be present, she preserved for me only the most beautiful

---

2. This is considered to be a form of massage.

images of her in my memory. Of course she wouldn't let me see her holding a stick aimed at her mom's asshole the way future scientists would aim with a microscope, to gouge out, bit by bit, stuff harder than husks.

Of course, I couldn't imagine her doing it.

So I didn't.

I galloped to the fields like a wild horse. The fields were an expanse of green. Strange that there would be this expanse of green, which meant that even back then, there was good weather for crops.

I went to pick mold heads.

As I've mentioned before, mold heads were black delicacies that grew on wheat stalks. Members of the clan militia were in charge of guarding the crops. Sometimes they also came after the children who ate the mold heads. But usually, so long as the children didn't steal the ears of wheat, they left them alone. They announced that should they discover anyone picking wheat kernels even once, the person would never eat mold heads again in this life. They could tell because those who ate wheat kernels had green mouths; those who ate mold heads had black mouths. That blackness was a hundred times blacker than dog shit.

I went to pick mold heads.

It was said that mold heads was a sort of disease. Eating it was equivalent to ridding the plant of the disease. So Braggart said, "Okay. Let the motherfuckers feed their mouths. But should you find any sign of green in the mouth, then off with his tongue!" "Yes, we know!" Kuansan and the others responded, beating their chests. Aside from Snow Feather, I admired the clan militia the most. They all carried rifles on their backs and were as smart as excited braying donkeys.

There were very few people in the fields. Most of them had died. Half of the children had died. Half of them didn't have complete corpses. Some said they were eaten by wolves. I knew that more than half were consumed by people. I personally saw Mud Egg's mom slicing off Wuzi's thigh. And that evening, smoke issued from the chimney of Mud Egg's home. The delicious aroma went straight into one's brain and permeated throughout the village. You know, the most delicious and nutritious meat in the world is human flesh. Within days, a red gleam issued from the eyes of Mud Egg's mom, just like Braggart's old mountain dog that devoured corpses.

I crossed the corpse-studded valley and a sand bank then entered the wheat field. "Donkey-stinging hornets" charged at me in droves. They knew I wasn't a donkey, but they stung me anyway. My exposed skin was full of scars from them, which directly affected my ability to find a wife years later. The more beautiful ones didn't think I was attractive enough. How I hated those "donkey-stinging hornets"! I pulled some reeds, twisted them into a horsetail, and swung at the hornets. Those subjected to my reeds lay on the ground, writhing in pain. They thought I had no tail and couldn't fling them away the way cattle and horses did. But they didn't know those reeds were as strong as donkeys' tails. The hornets whipped by me screaming in pain, their bottoms convulsing. I knew they were struggling against death and wanted to fight back. They would strike back viciously. I knew their wicked intentions. So I stepped on them with my thickly calloused feet and crushed them into meat patties, with the clout of a mighty horse violating a lamb. You know, I was the kind of person who feared the strong but took advantage of the weak.

I feared Braggart the most. Although I've sneezed at him, I still feared him.

I saw him entering Snow Feather's home, carrying a cloth sack on his back. Many craned their necks and watched. Half of them were those lying in the gully with innards devoured by wolves. One of them hollered, "Fucking Braggart! You starved us, but now you take the public grain from the Ancestral Hall and go whoring!" Others chimed in, "Yay, yay! Let's go kill the fucking thing!" Another one hollered, "Fuck killing him, he's always making incense offerings—he has a protector god!" "Who's his protector god?" "A foreigner with a big beard, a fiend like the Ox Demon!"

I yelled at them, "Damn you! What do you know about Snow Feather? He can't even get to lick her!" A corpse with its belly devoured laughed heartily, "What do you know about Snow Feather, Boy? She was raised by a whore! What's a whore? A whore sells her cunt. She might be blind, but she's had more dick than you've had rice. She's had Western dick, Eastern foreigners'[3] dick, and some dick you couldn't even imagine!" I picked up a rock secretly and hurled it at him real hard while he prattled gleefully. As what was left of his intestines splattered, a throng of green-headed flies bolted with a loud hum and charged at me.

I waved with the reeds. After a few swishes, they were wailing for their mom and dad.

---

3. Eastern foreigners refer to the Japanese.

Suddenly, the group of starving ghosts stopped their commotion. They must have seen Braggart leaving the house dolefully. Snow Feather chased after him and threw the cloth sack at him. I thought it would strike him down. Who would have thought the sack flew as if it had wings and handed itself to Braggart gently? Braggart stuck out his tongue in embarrassment and then bared his teeth viciously. I suddenly realized he was a reincarnated wolf!

The starving ghosts laughed with gusto, as they rocked back and forth. One of them said, "Snow Feather's cunt must be gold-gilded!"

I smiled but didn't feel like dealing with those ghosts. I walked toward the wheat fields, which were welcoming me most heartily. The wheat stalks also knew that the mold heads were an infectious disease. So they lined up and shouted in unison, "Welcome, welcome! We heartily welcome you!" I loved their applause. The mold heads also stretched out their heads readily and said, "Pick me! Pick me!" I only wished I'd had twenty hands. I stuffed them into my mouth while I picked. My teeth also applauded gleefully. The muddy, fishy taste exploded through all the pores of my body.

I realized I no longer existed. I had turned into just a mouth and teeth. Mold heads flocked to me, one wave after another, surging ever higher. It was just like when Li Zicheng[4] entered the capital. Oh my God—my teeth couldn't chew fast enough. Clamor and agitation engulfed me. It was at that precise moment that I realized Snow Feather's place in my heart.

I suddenly thought of her.

I abruptly stopped the flood of mold heads from pouring into my mouth. What a momentous instant it was! I thought I should take some mold heads to Snow Feather! All the mold heads hollered, "Okay! Okay!" and surged into my pockets. Have you ever seen fish churning when a net is drawn? Yes, it was like that. They collided, laughed, and cheered. You have no idea how mighty I felt back then. There was only me and the jumping, cheering mold heads in the whole, wide world! They occupied all my pockets. So I tucked my tank top into my pants and let them pour into it. They were as excited as soldiers ready to depart for the front. I even forgot to notice Grandpa Sun hailing from the tip of the mountain, "Boy, I'm going down the mountain!"

---

4. The rebel leader, Li Zicheng (1606–1645) overthrew the Ming dynasty in 1644 and ruled over China briefly as the emperor of the short-lived Shun dynasty before his death a year later. He claimed Li Jiqian as his ancestor.

It wasn't until the sky turned the same color as the mold heads that I realized I should be returning home. The moaning of the starving ghosts filled the valley. They stretched out their bony hands and begged for the mold heads. I spat at them fiercely. Ghosts feared human saliva the most, you know. Then they all dispersed embarrassingly and watched me from a distance. Their saliva dripped as loudly as a waterfall. I felt sorry for them and tossed a handful of mold heads at them while yelling, "One will turn into ten; ten into a hundred; a hundred into a thousand; a thousand into ten thousand; ten thousand into as many as the sands of Ganges!" And then, mold heads filled the entire valley. The starving ghosts cheered and charged after them. They guzzled them down like an old sow gulping down noodle-cooking water.

The Sensation of Heaven

I swam like a fish through the valley filled with the stench of corpses and darted to Snow Feather's house. Her home was also as black as the mold heads. The night sky was filled with the noise of flowing water. It was, in fact, the chomping of the starving ghosts eating mold heads. I didn't feel like bothering with them. I knew they were a group of gluttonous ghosts. The ghost age of most of them was less than one year. Most of them had died last winter or this spring. A few of them were new ghosts. Some went to steal crops so they wouldn't become starving ghosts but ended up being shot by the clan militia. Mud Egg's dad was one of them. The iron bullets inside the gunpowder tore a large hole in his abdomen, exposing his palpating heart and squirming intestines. It was the clan regulation. Braggart said anyone caught stealing Ancestral Hall's public property deserved death. So he killed those who stole to make sure no one dared to steal. Mud Egg's dad moaned like an ox for three days and three nights before he stopped breathing. But his eyes wouldn't shut no matter what. There was nothing one could do. Cripple Big rubbed his hands to get them warm and covered those eyes for a long time, but they still wouldn't shut. So Cripple Big said, "Keep them open if you wish. What can you do anyway—even if they're as big as donkey's balls?" It was said that after Mud Egg's dad died the knife in their kitchen always made a chopping noise. The entire village could hear it. They all said, "Listen! That starving ghost is cooking!" But no one knew if the starving ghost had a single meal in the netherworld.

I called quietly, "Snow Feather! Snow Feather!"

Snow Feather opened the door holding a lit pine branch. The villagers used to use vegetable oil or mutton grease lamps. But even these rare items are no more, so they used pine branches from the mountain for light now. Snow Feather smiled, "Hey elf! Not in bed yet?" "I brought you mold heads!" I replied. "What mold heads?" "The delicious mold heads!"

I pulled out a lot of mold heads as I spoke. I said I didn't even have to pick them; they jumped into my pockets by themselves. They had to be much better than chicken feet weeds! I thought she would smile, that she would praise me, and stroke my head. Her hand was as soft as cotton. I loved it when she stroked my head. But she only gasped and reprimanded, "Why did you do such a thing?"

I said, "I picked 'mold heads.' They don't care. We always pick them." Snow Feather said, "What 'mold heads'? Look at them yourselves!" I saw the mold head's laugh. They laughed so hard, they buckled backward and forward. They laughed ceaselessly. And then gradually, they began to transform. They transformed into something fat and chubby. I finally recognized them: they were soybean pods!"

I cried in delight! In my childhood memory, soybeans gave the sensation of Heaven.

Snow Feather stiffened. I said, "Strange! How did mold heads change face?"

She latched the door and asked, "Did anyone see you?"

"No one but the dead ghosts in the valley," I responded.

Snow Feather heaved a sigh and then said, "Might just as well. We'll let Mom taste something delicious." She ladled out some water, stirred the pods in it cursorily, poured them into the wok, and lit the stove. A terrifying aroma exploded instantly. Her mom yapped, "Quick! Such an aroma—you want trouble?" I knew this aroma was a racing dog that would instantly announce to all in the village that Snow Feather's home was cooking something delicious! I saw Braggart sniffing with his nose. Red light glistened from his eyes. He stuck out his long tongue, dragged his long tail, and darted in this direction.

Mom said, "Quick! Burn some rubber outside!" Mom fished around and tossed over a broken tire. Snow Feather stuck the tire into the stove and presently pulled out a bright red tire with tiger-head-like flames.

I dragged the "fire tiger head" outside. As soon as I opened the door, a crowd of wizened heads craned in. I recognized them as the ones lying in the valley. I hissed fiercely, "Shoo! I gave you as much food as the sands of the Ganges! Are you still not satisfied?" But they just craned their necks and stared at the stove. And then, suddenly, they dispersed. It was because the "tiger head" had begun to spew its pungent, horrible smoke at them. That smoke transformed into snakes after snakes and gushed in the four directions. I knew they were seeking the avaricious noses of the villagers! Then the blue snakes caught up with the roaming aroma of the soybean pods and swallowed them into their bellies. What surprised me most was the franticness of the starving ghosts. They rushed off furiously, like an ox stung by donkey-stinging hornets. From this, I learned that burning rubber could ward off evil spirits. After that, I publicized this discovery to the world, and when the folks of Liangzhou expelled ghosts during their Vinegar Bomb ritual,[5] they would put a tire underneath a red hot stone. Later, since the villagers found the nasty smell too offensive, they eventually used human hair instead. That also worked. The ghosts squealed and screamed after smelling it too.

Mom heaved a sigh of relief. Snow Feather added a handful of wheat stalks into the fire. The soybean aroma spilled furiously from the wok. But they were swallowed by the snakes squirted out by my fire tiger heads. The snakes bred very fast. The sky over the village was filled with stinky, roaming snakes. They swallowed all the aroma. Quite a few in the valley died because such an aroma informed on them. They stole yam. The minute they boiled it in their wok, the aroma slipped out and found Braggart. Braggart pounced on them with fury along with the clan militia, smashed the wok that spread the aroma, and also beat its master until he became a dead donkey with a smashed saddle.

I lifted the tire and made circles with it in the courtyard. The tire sang a crazy song. Later I found out that what they sang was rock and roll!

Rock, rock, rock—rock until we come to grandma's bridge.[6]
Rock until the stars fall,
Rock until the dreams fall!

Suddenly, the ground turned over and crushed itself upon me. The rumbling of a flood poured into my ears.

---

5. *Dacudan*, an exorcist ritual found in northwestern China.

6. This is the first line of a very popular ditty. The other lines are different from the original folk song.

Snow Feather carried me into the house. The soybean pods were already ladled into bowls. Ma was eating them. Snow Feather said quietly, "Go ahead and eat!" She blew the light out softly.

I grabbed a handful and stuffed them into my mouth, pods and all, and then pulled out two green strings.

An indescribable aroma enveloped me.

Kuan San's Slaps

Ajia said, "Have you ever eaten boiled soybean pods? Of course I know you've had them before. But did you eat them after having starved for several months, not having had a morsel in your tummy all that time? And, also in the presence of a woman as beautiful as a celestial when you were eating them? And, while the light was off? And what you were eating was truly organic, without any chemical fertilizers to hasten their growth? And having all the starving ghosts gazing at you and drooling with saliva three feet long? . . . Now, you can understand what I tasted back then. It truly was the feel of being in Heaven. The aromatic soybeans I had missed forever, melted as soon as they entered my mouth. They cheered in delight, and danced all the way in the style of rock and roll toward every single pore of my body. They sang jubilantly. They danced. They were a horde of carousing savages. They made love in ecstasy. They were immersed in the great music of illusory bliss, just like what you and Snow Feather experienced after you'd attained enlightenment. The night sky reverberated with loud explosions of aroma. Rushes of blood bellowed like a flash flood. Hearts swelled like warring drums. You could even see the sniffing, cavern nostrils of the starving ghosts. They hollered, "So good! The smell is so good—it's in our brains!" although you knew that, in fact, their brains were already feed for wild dogs and wolves. Of course there were also the foxes, the badgers, the lynxes and what not. You can imagine all the beasts you can think of. The beasts were licking the aroma just like when they devoured the human brains. They produced the sound of cats licking wheat paste glue, or when adulterers copulated. Don't laugh! It's a sacrilege to laugh at this moment. I'm an unsullied spirit, you know!"

You must have been bored by my exaggerated descriptions. In fact, I didn't even convey one hundredth of the feeling. When we have nothing better to do someday, I'll make a point of just describing that feeling for you. Then, you'll see that I have an even greater imagination than the writers of the sensationalist literary style.

I could hear Snow Feather's wispy breathing. Only she breathed that way. Of course you've never touched her hand. It felt soft and boneless, as if it would melt. Only people who practiced inner kung fu, to the ultimate level, would be like that. Her breath was also soft and boneless. One might say it was as light as a cicada's wings. Your woman would be like that too later. But the breath of your woman was that of a human, whereas Snow Feather was a goddess: no, she, in fact, had the breath of an immortal. It was in that environment that I ate the soybean pods. Don't you think I had a taste of Heaven?

Maybe you already know what happened next.

Braggart kicked open the door with members of the clan militia. A huge beam of light covered us.

They didn't even knock. But even if they had knocked, there was no time for us to swallow the evidence in one gulp. Even if we could have swallowed the beans, they would have opened our stomachs to check. Believe it or not, they'd do anything! You know, Snow Feather's mom's past was incredibly complicated. There were many rumors, which according to hearsay, were true. But you must know that the most difficult thing to clarify in the world is women. Women's bodies and women's hearts are the most mysterious things. Of all the rumors, the only sup-ported by clear evidence was that she had worked in a hotel in Hexi. She and Braggart's older sister were sold to the brothel together. The latter contracted syphilis and was relieved of further suffering, but she had to continue to experience hell in the years to follow.

What kind of fate do you think Snow Feather could have?

You know, even without having a mother like that, she would still be a flying thief, an embarrassment. Here I'll tell you a famous legend from Liangzhou. The evening Snow Feather left Luoshi Monastery, she entered Pine Surf Monastery. There was a monk called Monk Stone at Pine Surf Monastery. By then, his fame had spread throughout Hexi. It was said his kung fu was the best in the world, none were better before him and possibly none thereafter, because the kung fu after his days became nothing but an exercise, like walking. Furthermore, according to contemporary scientific research, the health benefits of kung fu don't even compare to jogging. At that time, Monk Stone was incurably ill and on his last leg. The night we were eating soybeans, he was just talking to his disciple, Monk Wu Naidan, about the future. He said, "In the future, you will have to forebear everything, no matter what. Right now, you can still wear a cassock. But the day will come when you won't be able to wear an inch of red cloth." Monk Wu was doubtful. Of course he couldn't believe it. What would lamas wear if they didn't wear red cassocks? But later, he was indeed chased out of the monastery wearing a black outfit.

What I mean to say is: even without her mother, whose past was considered unclean by the villagers, Snow Feather couldn't have avoided her future fate. You know, what people call fate are those times in life where you have no choice.

We were seized and taken to the Ancestral Hall. The Ancestral Hall during this time didn't have ancestral plaques. There was just a row of stools the height of a Pekingese dog found in the city. A strange lamp exuded a dim yellowish light. That lamp had a large belly with three mouths. Each mouth held a ball of dim yellowish light. There used to be a gas light with a lampshade here. It would make a moaning sound and create a sparkly bright white light. However, Cripple Big touched it one night, and the shade turned into ashes. Ever since then, they had to use this "three mouthed raven" instead. Everyone in the village was there, with hazy, sleepy eyes. Their intestines rumbled from hunger, yet they were all very excited.

Snow Feather and her mother were hauled into the hall. I shouted furiously, "I picked the soybeans! I was the one!" But no one heeded me. I knew why they didn't heed me. I also knew it was the doing of those starving ghosts. They transformed the mold heads into soybean pods, so I ended up bringing real "bad luck"[7] to Snow Feather's place. Remember? At the time I hollered, "I brought mold heads, 'bad luck' to you!" According to the folks of Liangzhou, saying something like that would have been unpropitious. You know, this must have ruined their karma, as I truly brought bad luck to them. I realized that Braggart and the clan militia must have been watching me in secret. They and the starving ghosts were in cahoots in directing this conspiracy.

I screamed furiously, "I picked them! It was I!" You notice I said pick and not steal, which meant that the act was, in fact, unintentional. But I still felt somewhat guilty. Did you notice that the first line of this section said, "I went to steal produce." Maybe I went there to steal

---

7. *Meitou*, mold heads, also means bad luck.

intentionally? Don't ask me. I don't know. You know, sometimes I'm muddle-headed.

Snow Feather's face was pale, but her mom's was wooden. Having gone through so much, her mom always looked wooden. Maybe nothing in the world could scare her anymore.

Snow Feather should have exposed me. I thought, since I was only a child, no one would do much to me. The most I might get would be a good beating. Maybe by my mom and dad. Maybe by the villagers. It didn't matter. I wasn't old enough to have been branded a thief. But she refused to say so. I screamed furiously, but no one heeded me. I saw my mom glaring at me with cowlike eyes as large as the ends of roof tiles. She must have believed me. She knew that I would even die for Snow Feather. She could never forget the time I stole the golden toad grandpa had stolen from a shopkeeper, and gave it to Snow Feather. That toad was made of solid gold. When you poured water into its mouth, it would pee. I gave it to Snow Feather. Who would have expected her to give it back to my mom? What a beating I got from the sole of her shoe: my butt was blue for days! Of course my mom believed me. She came to me fiercely, snatched me like a hawk picking up a chick, twisted my arm, and stuffed a piece of cloth into my mouth. I suspected it was a stinky sock. Of course, it could also have been her head scarf. But it was for sure not her panties or bra. You know, the women of Liangzhou back then did not wear bras. When they nursed, their babies would grab their long, udder-like nipples. When it was too hot, my mom would bare her top and throw her foot-long breasts over her shoulders, and looked as if she was carrying two sullied bags of flesh on her back.

Braggart was the first one to speak, which he did using a harsh tone. The folks of Liangzhou called that manner of speaking "domineering with teeth." There was a harsh taste to it as the voice was squeezed out of the teeth. He said, "Did the shit-eater catch the shitter?" Later, Fatty Zang, who was in charge of education in the county would use the same line when he lectured his subordinates. And later than that, it became a catchphrase for all the officials of Liangzhou. I could tell the real meaning behind this. He was, in fact, reproaching Snow Feather for not appreciating his favors. The women started to babble. They obviously understood what Braggart was referring to. Before this, whenever they heard him say this, they would relax their legs, which were usually squeezed together ever so tightly. Fatty Zang's woman even used to visit

Braggart of her own will. She told people secretly that after she'd been done by Braggart, she now knew what being a woman was about. She even wanted to divorce Fatty Zang. But one disapproving shout from Braggart, and she immediately smiled in repentance.

Yeeya! Those were the days when passions flared and blazed.

Don't laugh!

As soon as Braggart uttered his last syllable, Kuan San jumped up. He clenched his teeth and gave Snow Feather and her mom a few brutal slaps. Snow Feather's mom toppled over immediately. Snow Feather wiped the blood from the corner of her mouth. She didn't help her mother up. She knew they'd hit her mom again the minute she was helped up.

Kuan San loved to hit people. No matter who was being "fixed" at the Ancestral Hall, he would be the first to do the hitting. Possessing neither a house nor any land, he joined Braggart in conducting the kind of business that needed no capital at Big Block Trough. Remember the place? "That was the village south of Yellow Sheep Town." Yes, that was the one. It was a deep trough next to a mountain slope. It was built up higher when the highway was built later. Before that, the penniless Kuan San and others watched for unaccompanied travelers, kitchen knives in hand. They would not rob groups since they had neither rifles nor daggers. Yes, you could call them destitute tyrants.

You must have seen *Les Miserables*. Remember the destitute, avaricious couple Cosette lived with? So you know there is no relationship between poverty and moral conduct.[8] Many indigent people in this world are evil. The folks of Liangzhou call them "destitute tyrants." The Niu Er chopped down by Yang Zhi in *The Water Margin*[9] was this kind of a person. Numerous such people existed in Liangzhou. During a certain historical period, you would invariably see a lot of them ganging up together like the destitute tyrants of Big Block Trough. Many fine sons and daughters of Liangzhou were hacked down and buried by them. But you shouldn't mind them. Although they were numerous and noisy, they were but fallen leaves on the ground. One waft from the wind of time, and they would disappear without a trace. What you'd face would be but a huge expanse of emptiness. Do you remember the line, "the vast

---

8. This statement is found in Communist literature, in which the poor were oppressed and upright, while the landlords were the tyrants.

9. Also known as *All Men are Brothers*, *The Water Margin* portrays Robin Hood–like bandits and is one of the most renowned traditional novels.

white mother earth is so clean"? If there are some footprints, aren't they just those few books of yours?

If it wasn't for you, Snow Feather would also have been buried by time.

Kuan San was someone one could never forget. Snow Feather couldn't forget him either. Years later, when she was practicing austerities in the cave below Qilian Mountain, she would perform a particular task every day. Yes, she would dissolve the sins of Braggart and Kuan San. This was in the "Eight Mantras for Cultivating the Mind." It said, "Losses I take willingly, the benefits I will donate." She would seize all the sins committed by Kuan San and the others and dissolve them using the technique of Empty Brightness. Furthermore, she conferred upon them the merits she had attained through practicing austerities. Later, Kuan San actually had a good ending. He was still able to noisily slurp up a whole basin of bread-soaked soup[10] at eighty-four, and exuded the energy of a three-year-old ox. The only problem with him was that he was always suspicious that his asthmatic eighty-two-year-old wife was having an affair with seventy-five-year-old Cripple Big. Every day he would scream, "Ah! Cripple Big is on the old witch's brick bed again—get the rascal!" And his daughters-in-law would say in surprise,

"Aren't you dead yet?!"

Kuan San slapped with a mighty punch. There'd be a good show whenever he showed up for someone's punishment in the Ancestral Hall. You know, Snow Feather was seen as something of a witch or spirit in the villagers' eyes. She had never been beaten before. So, even Braggart looked at Kuan San with approval. Since she was not the only one who received an "education" after having stolen produce, Snow Feather had to endure "taking a hit that will kill."

As I remember it: that was the first struggle session against Snow Feather and her mom, the most memorable of which were the slaps executed by Kuan San. By then, Snow Feather was already famous as a flying thief. For quite a while already, the police used to come after her whenever something was missing; and everyone would conclude flying thief Snow Feather had committed another infraction.

Soon after that, Snow Feather stole her first sheep. It was because her mom's legs became so swollen that she couldn't even step over a bump.

---

10. This is a typical local dish in western China in which an unleavened bread (known as *mo*) is broken into small pieces and soaked in soup.

Snow Feather knew her mom was going to die.

If she had known her mom was going to endure so much torture in the future, she might not have stolen the sheep. Ironically, her filial piety caused her mom to suffer the agony and shame that should never have been endured by any human.

The Shadowlike Martial Art of Weightlessness

The moon must have been hanging in the sky the night Snow Feather stole the sheep. That was her style. It was known that nights without the moon were perfect for killing, while windy nights were for arson. But those only applied to regular thieves. Snow Feather was a divine burglar. She always executed her deeds on moonlit nights. "Upright people do not commit deeds in the dark." No one could guard against something Snow Feather wanted to steal. Ajia related other incredulities she'd performed; such as, if her mother wanted to eat the meat buns of Lanzhou five hundred leagues away, Snow Feather would turn around, go there, and return in a flash. When she opened the steamers, steam issued from the buns! One day, Braggart saw Snow Feather on his way to the city of Liangzhou. He pretended not to have seen her, whipped his horse, and shot like an arrow toward the city a hundred leagues away. Who would have known that Snow Feather would be watching him from the city wall with a smirk on her face when he entered the city gate? That was when Braggart thought, *This type of person will have to be disciplined sooner or later!*

There were many stories like these about Snow Feather.

On that moonlit night, Snow Feather left her home. Viewed from the mountain slope, the village down below was dead—no human sound. The moon was luridly bright. Wind raged interminably. Snow Feather's mom wanted to eat a fat ram. Snow Feather had her eyes set on one by the Ancestral Hall. Although there were some in the village, they were privately owned, and Snow Feather never stole from the poor. She only wanted one belonging to the Ancestral Hall. It was the head ram, which had seeded many lambs. Whenever the sheep were herded, that horny ram would chase after the female sheep and force itself on them. Just like Braggart. Women he set his eyes on, never got to escape. One year, Braggart even wanted to claim the special right the lords of yore used to have; that is, the right to have the first nights of new brides.

In the past, the local lord would sleep with all the new brides for three nights. Later, this custom was abolished when a man called Zuo Zong-tang[11] came, waved his hand, and said, "There's no need!" That's when the custom finally ended. But Braggart was wicked and hoped to revive this special privilege. Ajia said, "If Braggart really did it, Snow Feather would have plucked his brain out."

Snow Feather came down the slope and floated toward the village noiselessly like the shadow of a ghost. According to *Tale of the Goddess*, her shifu-master was Grandpa Jiu, a man with great powers who had practiced austerities for more than twenty years in Diamond Cave. Grandpa Jiu was an expert martial artist. He specialized in the art of weightlessness, could walk on snow without leaving a trace, and could even become invisible! According to *Historical Mirror of Forgotten Events*, Grandpa Jiu used to do the women in the imperial palace when he was young. The lonely palace ladies would feel someone on top of them when they were half asleep, and this made them incredibly blissful. They all thought they were dreaming until a lot of babies were born. Thereupon, the emperor dispatched several tens of thousands of soldiers to surround the palace and jab with spears. The invisible Grandpa Jiu almost became a porcupine! At the time, Grandpa vowed that if he should outlive that experience, he would turn over a new leaf and take the tonsure. So, under the protection of the Bodhisattvas, Grandpa Jiu survived and eventually became a famous accomplished guru.

Of course, that was a legend.

Family Instructions of Diamond Clan also said that when Grandpa Jiu completed his practices and saw through the vanity of all things, the only "attachment" he was not able to "let go" of was martial arts. That was because he'd promised his martial arts master he would transmit the unique expertise he'd acquired. The words of a real man should never go back and forth like mill sluice gates operated by mules. One day, he went into isolation and began to practice a technique to ask his protective deity to bring him a disciple. He was in isolation for seven days. On the seventh day, Snow Feather's mom was weeding in the fields with her baby. Suddenly a wolf came and charged at the baby. Sharp-eyed and swift, Mom grabbed the infant like a tiger after prey. But the wolf did not leave. It watched them with wolverine eyes. Thereupon the

---

11. Zuo Zongtang (1812–1885) was a renowned nineteenth-century general. The dish, General Tso's chicken, was named after him, although it had nothing to do with him.

woman took off her head scarf and began to swing it above her head in circles. Everybody at Diamond Clan knew this technique for dealing with wolves. They believed that since wolves were the mountain god's[12] dogs, they possessed dog nature, which meant they were afraid of ropes rather than knives. Thinking the swinging head scarf was a rope, the wolf would stop pouncing forward. But it would not leave. It squinted its eyes and stared at the woman who yelled whenever she slowed down. The woman swung the scarf for so long that her arms were swollen, and her throat became hoarse. Finally, she saw someone appearing at the foot of the mountain. So she screamed, "Help!" But before she finished saying the word, the wolf pounced on her, seized Snow Feather from her bosom, and disappeared without a trace. Ajia said, "That was how the wolf brought Snow Feather to Grandpa Jiu in its mouth. And that was how she got to learn the martial art of weightlessness."

Look at her! She didn't look like a flesh-bodied person—she was clearly a wisp of smoke! That smoke wafted into the sheep corral and floated out with that 120-pound ram on her back, without leaving a single trace of footprint on the wall.

Based on this fact alone, Braggart was certain it must have been done by Snow Feather.

But you know that Ajia is a deity who enjoyed telling tall tales. If you believe him, you'd go deaf for three days!

Braggart's Double

Ajia said, "Snow Feather had plotted stealing the ram for a long while." He then told another story to prove this.

It was on a sunny midsummer's day. Several clumps of clouds floated on the mountain slope. Ajia added, "Of course, you know that they were really herds of sheep." Ajia loved to use metaphors to mystify deliberately. There's nothing you can do about this. The more uncultured, the more one tends to do this. "In what way am I uncultured?" he protested. I told him, "Who's talking about you? I was talking about the Ajia without culture. You are the Ajia with culture." Ajia was still displeased. He said, "Although there are many Ajias in this world, if you

---

12. The original refers to this deity as both the tutelary god (i.e., local protective god) and the mountain god.

mention Ajia when you talk to me, then you must mean me!"

It was a very hot day. You know, the hotter it got, the tighter the sheep flocked together. They'd squeeze together until they become a solid mass of wool. All the shepherd boys escaped to a shady spot. However, that lead ram was horny and began to chase after a female sheep. Normally, the shepherd boys would want the lead ram to chase after female sheep so its superior seed could be planted. Several of the large sheep in the village were seeded by the lead ram. Although that lead ram was not Braggart, it got to enjoy the privilege of the first nights with all the female sheep. All because it was the lead ram! The lead ram must be big, powerful, and preferably horny. For only a horny ram had zeal and loved to meddle in the affairs of the others; consequently, it was able to control all the misbehaving sheep that wanted to run around and not behave and also managed to win the throne of lead ram through emerging victorious against its opponents in the battles of the rams. There was only one rule in this world: the most formidable got to be the lord. Whenever it got excited, the lead ram would seduce a female sheep. Of course, the female sheep also wanted to be seduced by it. Look—a beautiful sheep had escaped from the mass. You know, it actually escaped voluntarily. If it hadn't escaped from the mass, then the lead ram wouldn't have been able to seduce it. This female sheep was most alluring. Its bleep was so charming it could melt an iron-hearted man into water, let alone the lead ram. So the lead ram chased after it ferociously. At this point, you must be thinking something was going to happen. You're right, something did happen, but it was not the rape of the female sheep by the lead ram. The story was in fact quite different.

Just as the horny ram was ready to pounce onto the beautiful female sheep, Snow Feather appeared out of nowhere. I didn't even see her walk or fly over, and she'd already grabbed the ram by its head and tackled it to the ground. The ram bleated, knowing what would happen to it next and hoped Braggart would rescue it! But Braggart was at Heavenly Girl's place at the time. He was just pressing himself onto Heavenly Girl's tits. He did hear head ram's bleating, but he thought it was Heavenly Girl's moaning. Suddenly, he covered his private parts and buckled over, screaming furiously. On the mountain slope, Snow Feather had just nabbed the ram's scrotum and began hitting it with a flat rock. The lead ram twisted its head frantically. This was called "hammering the ram" and was frequently done by the villagers. I saw the lead ram suddenly transform into Braggart and realized it must have been his double. Either that, or Braggart was its double. In any case, both of them were shrieking. Heavenly Girl was scared stiff. She fastened her clothes, which had been ripped apart by Braggart, to fetch help. By the time the doctor, Pockmarked Wang, rushed over, Braggart had already fainted from pain. It was said although Braggart wasn't impotent after that—that ram was gelded.

I've never told this story to anyone else. I'm not a gossipy type of deity, you know. However, no more large-sized sheep were produced in the village thereafter.

Because the lead ram was no longer horny, it fattened like a balloon until the night Snow Feather wafted over.

The day after the previous event, Braggart was infected with a sexual disease. A white sticky substance flowed from his private parts. He had a divination performed about it and was told someone used a talisman against him, and the person who placed the talisman and the person who stole the ram were one and the same. This was equivalent to telling Braggart that Snow Feather was the culprit.

Ever since then, Braggart considered Snow Feather his worst enemy.

Chapter 5

The Technique of Execution in *Nightmares*

It was as if a thousand years had gone by,
My parched soul continued to wait.
I wait for a waft of fresh breeze, to blow away my frustrations.
I wait for wisdom, to wash away the clouds of bewilderment.
I wait to sever the chains of birth, old age, illness and death,
I wait for the fresh greenness of life on the opposite bank.

Salvation through the Technique of Execution

The manuscript *Nightmares* begins with the Technique of Execution, which is also known as the "Killing Technique," and the "Subjugation Technique," etc. *True Records of the Curses* mentions four Techniques (Increasing; Extinguishing; Possessing; and Execution) for Increasing Longevity, Extinguishing the Star of Calamity, Possessing Love and Respect, and Subjugating Demon Armies. The Technique of Execution was used exclusively for subduing enemies. Guru Reluo, mentioned earlier, was an expert on the Technique of Execution, having executed many who went against the historical trends of the time. This form of execution, however, was not performed using daggers or rifles. Only a ritual was employed. And the soul of the deceased would receive salvation and be sent to the Pure Land.

Consequently, the Technique of Execution was also known as the Killing Technique.

The Killing Technique in *Nightmares* originated when the village's Butcher Zhang stole from Jasper's uncle. We know from *Annotated Collection of Nightmares* that, at the time, Uncle was invited by people outside the village to perform some rituals. Since it was far away, he didn't return for the night; so Butcher Zhang took the opportunity to steal stuff from the monk. According to *Annotated Collection of Nightmares*, this type of behavior was considered particularly unacceptable. It was said that those who stole from monks would end up in Hell. But since Butcher Zhang was a butcher, he wasn't bothered by such niceties as "the Karma of Sin"; otherwise, he wouldn't have been killing sentient beings, since the killing of sentient beings was equally sinful.

Nightmares' contents are very confusing. It is not clear whether the events transpired during the time of the Kingdom of Xixia or the present. It was also unclear whether it was a dream or reality. The contents and characters in the manuscript were also a self-contradictory chaotic mess. But according to the later *Family Instructions of Diamond Clan*, it still reflected many facts regarding Diamond Clan. The protagonist was Braggart, the father of the manuscript's author: I have never been able to find out through textual research whether he was related to "the clan head Braggart" of this book. He and Mom fought over their son, Jasper. Mom wanted him to take Buddhist vows and become a monk, but Dad wanted him to become a robber. Related to this story were other details, such as the death of Ajia, and the conflicts between two tribes, although the information was scattered and depicted like a nightmarish, confusing dream. Fortunately, there were a few other books that could be consulted, so that together they enabled us to get a glimpse of many rare sights.

I was never able to figure out the relationship between Jasper, Ajia, and Snow Feather of *Nightmares* and those in the other manuscripts. Although they have the same names, they seem to have experienced different life trajectories. For the sake of alleviating the problems of textual research and interpretation, I propose treating *Nightmares* as reflecting the existence of life "beyond form," somewhat contiguous with the "negative universe" referred to by scientists; that is, another aspect of this world's woven brocade.

I would like to add in passing that *Nightmares* was very difficult to read. In order to make it more acceptable, I've changed many of the unfamiliar words into colloquial language.

We will enter into the *Nightmares* below.

Butcher Zhang

The black wolf appeared again. Frozen atop the distant mountain, it looked like a black rock from a distance.

Jasper said, "Look at the wolf." Uncle said, "That's the mountain deity's dog." Jasper said, "It can tear many sheep to death." Uncle said, "The sheep are fated to be eaten by it. They owed it their lives from a previous incarnation."

Above the wolf, there was a large, black cloud, like the protective deity called Gong Bao in the Tankas. From a slit in the cloud, two bright balls of light shone forth like eyes. Jasper wanted to say, "Look, a protective deity!" But seeing how unhappy Uncle was, he heaved a deep sigh. The mountain was already very green. The grass and the trees were showing off their greenery with all their might. Mist seeped from the mountain and unfurled until one's heart was dyed green.

Jasper knew Uncle missed his wok painfully. That thief was simply too audacious. How could he steal something from the abbot of a monastery! This was the first time such a thing had ever happened!

That teapot was truly a great pot. It was so black and shiny it felt like a slippery fish. The tea it brewed had a strong taste. Even Dad had his eyes on it. He said, "I don't think much of any of your things except for that pot of yours, hee hee!" Uncle said, "Sure! It's yours once you take the tonsure!" Then Dad laughed and said, "No way you'll turn me into a monk!"

Dad was into conducting business without capital with those "brothers" of his. Whenever he wanted something, he'd gather his "brothers" and off they went. And then they'd have everything. Dad said, "Boy, don't listen to that old witch mother of yours. Those monks are the world's most useless things! They eat for free, drink for free, and cheat people's money—good for nothing. . . . Why not be like Dad? Boy, isn't Dad great?"

"No!" said Jasper.

Ever since he was old enough to understand, Mom told him, "Dad is no good. He makes himself happy from taking from others, but the others are crying!" At first, Jasper admired Dad. No one dared to bully him when they heard he was Braggart's son. Even the villagers did the same. Whenever they were bullied elsewhere, they'd say, "Hey, I'm Braggart's brother! You know, the Braggart of Diamond Clan!" The bully would then apologize and say, "Please forgive me! I had no eyes! Big men don't bicker with small men—please forgive me!"

Such was the immensity of Dad's fame!

But Mom said, "He's no good!" Uncle also said, "He's no good!" So Jasper too said he's no good.

"What's no good about me?" Dad rolled his eyes. "The world is full of pussies. That's why 'chiefs' and 'heads' take advantage of them. A weakling like you will be stomped to death! Follow me and you'll have wine, you'll have meat, you'll have silver, and lots of women! What's life about? Muddling through—that's what! If you're good, you muddle through. If you're lazy, you muddle through. One only lasts a few decades—why in vain? Follow me, Son!"

Uncle said, "Don't follow him!" Karmic retribution was definitely true. Uncle was always telling stories about karmic retribution. He took Buddhist vows and headed a monastery but got tired of it. So he built a cabin in the mountain and went there to practice austerities. Mom said Uncle had completed his practices. Jasper didn't know what that meant, but he knew Uncle must have been very good. The villagers always stuck up their thumb whenever Uncle was mentioned. Even then, his pot was stolen. Besides the pot, a few other items, such as the vajra scepter and the ritual bell, were also stolen. Uncle closed his eyes and meditated for a while. Then he said, "It was stolen by that Butcher Zhang." In Jasper's vague memory, he seemed to have been the person who demanded payment from the Diamond Maidens. But in the historical records, Butcher Zhang seemed to have lived during the Tang or the Xixia dynasty.

Jasper followed Uncle to Butcher Zhang's home to ask for the pot.

Dad said, "He deserved having it stolen! Who told monks to cheat the people out of food and drink?" But the villagers said, "This is one brazen thief! How can anyone steal from the guru?" Dad laughed heartily and said, "Gurus are just people. Would any thief dare to steal from me?" No one said yes.

Of course not! Dad had more than a hundred brothers under him. They had rifles, daggers, everything. Once he'd set his eyes on someone, one wave of his hand and the rifles and daggers would charge at the person like a swarm of bees. Who'd dare to steal from him?

The black wolf howled. Its voice pierced through the sky. It had done this for several days now. Only after seeing this wolf did Jasper realize black wolves existed in this world. He'd seen black foxes. There was a saying: "one thousand years white; ten thousand years black," meaning black foxes were fox spirits. But black wolves were rare. Their fur usually changed color with the land. When the land turned green, their hair would also turn green; when the land turned yellow, their hair would also turn yellow; when the land turned gray, their hair would also turn gray. Black wolves stuck out. If there was a hunter, then he'd aim his rifle at it, pull the trigger, and a fire snake would dart at it.

Butcher Zhang was an expert shooter. But he said, "That was a strange wolf. I shot five times and it was still there without a scratch. It must have been a wolf spirit." Hence, no one dared to shoot at it after that.

But how did Butcher Zhang end up stealing from the monk?

The shepherd boys on the slope clamored. The dogs also craned their necks and barked at the wolf. One of them said to Uncle, "You can do the Technique of Execution—why don't you execute the wolf?" Uncle said, "It's the mountain god's dog. What right do I have to execute it? Snow Feather, do you think it should be executed?" The girl said, "No. It was born to eat sheep. Let it eat a couple when it's hungry." That Snow Feather was as pretty and ethereal as an immortal. She had the air of Yue Opera performers.[1] Jasper liked her the most.

Uncle laughed heartily, "You're right. Whatever Heaven gave birth to has the right to survive. Have you seen Ajia?"

Snow Feather said, "I saw him just this morning. He always wears a frown. Guru—how come although both of you are monks, you are always happy, but he always frowns?"

Uncle said, "I've seen through everything, but he hasn't. He's always thinking about problems he shouldn't be thinking about."

Snow Feather looked at Jasper with her large eyes, "Come see me at noon. There's something very important." Jasper said, "That depends on whether I'll have time." Peeved, Snow Feather said, "Come even if you don't have time!" Uncle looked at him—hard to tell if he was smiling. "Go!" he said.

---

1. Yue Opera originated in Zhejiang during the early twentieth century and later took Shanghai by storm when the traditional all-male cast was transformed into an all-female cast, with female opera singers playing all the roles. It was characterized by elegance and gracefulness.

Jasper heaved a heavy sigh and let out all his repression. He squinted as he viewed the mountain. The wolf was gone and so was the mist in the valley. One could only see the jutting mountain rocks and the forest halfway up the mountain. Dad wanted him to marry Snow Feather, but he wanted to take Buddhist vows. Mom also wanted him to become a monk. Taking Buddhist vows was a good thing; it would enable him to escape the mortal world and avoid its problems. If he were to take a wife, then Dad would get him to join his business. Mom was not willing.

He should keep away from Snow Feather. Uncle said, "How much those people of the mortal world suffer! It's like having fallen into a house on fire! They are constantly rushing around for senseless things. You have to make a decision." Jasper heaved a deep sigh and said nothing.

Butcher Zhang was in the midst of forging a horseshoe. I can't tell whether he wore a Xixia outfit. His appearance was always vague in Jasper's nightmares. A woman tugged at the bellows furiously. The bellows panted; so did the woman. Flames darted up with the panting. When Butcher Zhang saw Uncle arrive, he seemed startled. But then he yanked out a piece of red hot iron, swung his mallet, and hammered it. Sparks flew in all directions.

Uncle looked at him with a smile. Jasper thought, *This Butcher Zhang doesn't look like a thief!*

When the banging stopped, Uncle said, "I don't want the other stuff. But that pot makes good tea. I don't want the other stuff."

Butcher Zhang stuck the grayish-black iron into the fire, wiped off the sweat, and said, "What are you talking about?"

Uncle said, "The sutra and the scepter are several hundred years old. They were used by Qiongpo Lama.[2] A while back, someone offered me several hundred ounces of silver, but I wasn't willing to sell them. The conch horn is also an antique. I don't want them. It's just that that pot makes good tea." Butcher Zhang jeered, "I didn't take anything."

Jasper thought, *He probably really stole them.*

Uncle said, "You didn't take them?"

Butcher Zhang said, "No, I didn't."

"Fine," said Uncle, "I'll go back then." And he turned around to leave.

---

2. Qiongpo Nanjiao (1086–twelfth century?), known in Tibetan as Mkhas Grub Khyung Po Rnal Byor. He was the founder of the Shangpa Kagyu Sect.

"Aren't you going to have some tea?" the woman asked.

Uncle did not respond to her. He said to Jasper, "Come to me tonight. I'll teach you the Technique of Execution."

Ajia's Questions

Braggart and his sworn brothers had procured several hundred sheep, horses, and cattle. When Jasper returned to the stockade, Braggart was in the midst of dividing them. Each sworn brother got one. The rest would be slaughtered and divided among the villagers. When he saw Uncle, Dad said, "Ha! I'm also practicing Buddha's Way!" Uncle laughed and said, "If you slice your own flesh and divide it among the people, then you'd be practicing Buddha's Way. You're doing robber's way!" Dad laughed loudly, "Listen, bullshit! What do you know? I'm practicing Heaven's Way! Rich people drink people's blood. When they're fattened up, I cut their flesh for the poor to relish to their hearts' content. So I'm practicing Heaven's Way!" Uncle said, "Heaven has its work; you've got yours. Just mind your own business. . . . Nothing I can do about you. Just don't corrupt the boy."

"What corruption? Look at yourself—you can't even keep your own pot! Kuan San, go get Butcher Zhang. We'll give him three hundred lashes to see if he'd admit to it or not? If I say he stole it, then he stole it . . . Ai, did he really steal it?"

"Keep out of my business." Uncle waved his hand, tugged at Jasper, and entered the mud house on the side. Mom was in the middle of swinging a Mani Prayer Wheel. Uncle said, "The boy shouldn't stay here any longer—he's being corrupted!" Mom sighed and said, "You're absolutely right. But the minute I mention it, he swings his dagger. He's determined to have the boy take after him."

"Don't worry, everyone has his own fate." Uncle fished out a few pieces of broken silver, put them on the table, and left. Dad's voice was heard from the courtyard, "Want me to send someone to search him?"

"There's no need!" said Uncle.

Jasper left the house. Uncle was already atop the hill, his cassock fluttering in the wind.

"Boy—come and eat some meat. Don't listen to the old devil. Karma my ass—shit! This meat didn't belong to the poor, it was from the rich. Wasted if we don't eat it!"

"Precisely!" said Kuan San, "Get drunk this morn if there's wine this morn; So what if we have to drink cold water tomorrow? One breath short and you're dead! Shit, live for a day and that's two half days!"

Jasper entered Mom's house without saying a word. The house was very small with just a brick bed and a mud stove. Mom would not eat the meat or use the things Dad had stolen. Aside from chanting sutras, she spun wool and made felt and things like that to exchange for food. Jasper lived with Mom.

Kuan San came in with a mutton leg and said, "Sister-in-Law, why be so inflexible? This meat didn't belong to the poor. Eat it!" Mom said coldly, "Don't corrupt my place." Jasper said, "Mom doesn't want it." Kuan San left, and they heard a woman's voice, "Forget her if she doesn't want it. What temple wouldn't take a pig's head? I'll take it if she doesn't!" "Sure, you can have it!" said Kuan San.

A mist came over Mom's eyes and then disappeared. Mom's eyes were deeply set and very dry. One couldn't see their bottom. Jasper scooped up some roasted flour, mixed it with tea, and handed it to Mom. Mom said, "You eat it—I'm not hungry." And then she put down the Mani Prayer Wheel, reached for a spindle, and began to spin.

Jasper left the house. A crowd was eating meat out there. A cooking pot was set up in the courtyard. Flames licked the pot and danced. Water bubbled and splattered. Jasper tried hard not to look at them. He was afraid they'd invite him over, so he walked past them very quickly. He heard Kuan San say, "The guys from Brilliant King Clan said they want revenge!" A woman said, "Who's afraid? Who doesn't have a dagger?" Many voices responded in agreement, "Yay!" "Who's afraid? A fallen head is just a bowl-sized scar!" "I'm only afraid they won't come!"

Jasper thought of Snow Feather. She was extremely pale. No one else in the region had such a pale face. Every time Jasper saw her, his heart would pound a few times. He didn't know why.

Grandpa Sun reached the midday point and was screaming with fury. Jasper felt agitated. Whenever he felt this way, he wanted to take Buddhist vows. He longed for the peacefulness of the monks. Uncle's little cabin was built in a peaceful valley. There was nothing there but the wind, the chirping of birds, and wild animals. As soon as he entered the cabin, the valley would cease to exist. He'd only hear Uncle's sutra chanting. Jasper spent his youth immersed in this sound. Lest he'd be corrupted by Dad, Mom sent him to Uncle's cabin as soon as he was old enough to know what was going on. Later, seeing how hard and lonely Mom's life was, Jasper began to visit home frequently in order to chat with Mom. Dad also took the opportunity to put his words in.

Dad told Uncle, "Dragon begets dragon, phoenix begets phoenix, the son of a rat knows how to dig holes. This son of mine is born to be a bandit. I warn you, I'll break the horns on your head if you try to make a monk out of him!"

Uncle laughed and said, "Is that so?"

Jasper's lips pressed into a smile. The mountain wind blew softly, and a tuft of his hair tumbled down. He wasn't sure how he felt about Dad. Mom said Dad was bad. But most of the villagers said he was good. The bandits banded together when Dad began conducting his "business." And then the robbers on the mountains no longer dared to "collect taxes." Besides, every now and then the villagers could partake of the meat dad "bestowed upon them as alms." Dad divided up the meat he robbed and called it the bestowal of alms. Ludicrous, whenever he thought of it.

But Jasper wanted quiet.

Ever since he was very little, he enjoyed watching Uncle's back as Uncle turned the pages of the sutra. There was also Ajia, Uncle's disciple who used to chant the sutras with him. Uncle's voice was sonorous, while Ajia's was high pitched. The two voices were a joy to listen to. When Uncle performed the induction ritual on Ajia, Jasper also participated. After that, Jasper also began to chant the sutras. When Dad found out about this, he was furious. He told Uncle, "Stop feeding that shit to my son. He was born to carry on my position!" Uncle was not angry. He merely asked, "Is that so?"

Jasper walked toward the forest. Because of the black wolf's appearance, few people visited the forest. The forest was gloomy and dark. There was a hole, which reached down more than ten meters to a rock-lined cell. Ajia discovered it accidentally. Jasper visited this place frequently. Uncle also knew about it. He decided an ascetic must have stayed there and told Ajia to go there to practice quiet meditation. Ajia took several dozen pounds of roasted flour, several blocks of tea, and then proceeded to live there.

Ajia was at the entrance of the cave staring at the sun. He looked pale and lazy. When he saw Jasper, he moved to one side so Jasper could sit by him. The birds in the forest were chirping, a breeze blew, the sun shouted loudly.

Ajia said, "I've been practicing, but I don't know what I'm practicing for? I became a monk when I was eight. It's been more than ten years. The more I practice, the more confused I am."

"What are you confused about?"

"At first, I only wanted to achieve enlightenment through practice. But then, I began to have doubts. Buddha said everything is impermanent and without the self. So, if I don't even exist, then what's the point of practicing anything?"

Jasper didn't know the answer, so he said, "Ask Uncle."

"I've asked him already. But he said to stop thinking and just keep on practicing the austerities. But I don't want to practice blindly." Ajia then turned to Jasper and said, "I want to find the Gonpo.³"

"Uncle said it's useless to learn too many dharma techniques. Better to practice one kind alone, and you'll attain perfection sooner," said Jasper.

"But . . . I have no faith in your uncle. I can't help it. Even though he's a recognized guru, I've been with him ever since I was little. I've seen him snore and wondered if gurus are supposed to snore? I've seen him pee and thought, do gurus pee too? I've also seen him lose his temper and seen his many problems. After a while, I lost confidence in him. I am thinking of looking up the Gonpo."

Of course it would be good to seek the Gonpo, thought Jasper. The fame of that Gonpo shook heaven and earth. He had thousands of disciples. It was said he had tremendous supernatural powers and had achieved a high level of attainment. But Jasper didn't say anything. He remembered that Uncle didn't like to talk about the Gonpo. Although Uncle didn't say anything about the Gonpo, Jasper could feel he didn't like the Gonpo.

"Or, was it because of the fact" Ajia continued, "that the guru couldn't answer my questions?" I asked him, "Where does one go after one finishes practicing a Technique?" He said, "The Pure Land." I asked, "If everything is impermanent, then would the Pure Land also be impermanent?" He said my views represent heterodoxy. I thought, *If the Pure Land is permanent, then the concept that everything is impermanent would not be correct. If the Pure Land is impermanent, then where would it be after one has completed the practices?*

---

3. *Gönpo* is a Buddhist term for accomplished gurus who are considered to be "worldly protectors."

"No one knows, no matter whom I ask." Ajia sighed, "I heard that even when Shakyamuni was a mortal, he didn't answer this question . . . I don't know the significance for practicing the austerities."

Ajia said, "If I don't practice the austerities, I don't know the purpose for living. But if I do practice the austerities, I can't think of the purpose for doing it."

Jasper laughed and said, "Forget about the significance, just keep on practicing. The significance for practicing lies within the act itself."

Ajia said, "No, if I don't know its significance, I'd rather not do it. If I don't know the reason for living, I'd rather not live."

"Does Uncle know about your way of thinking?"

"Yes. He said I've entered the demonic state."

The cave was not big. It was around three feet in circumference and would have been pitch dark if it weren't for the offering lamp. There must have been a crack somewhere in the cave because the lamp's flame flickered wildly, indicating a source of wind. But there was no sound at all. A Tanka was hanging on the wall of the cave. It was the portrait of Mahakala, Ajia's protective deity. Uncle had intended to transmit to him a Diamond Dharma Technique, such as the Heruka Cakrasamvara, or the Guhyasanaja Vajra, or the Yamantaka. But Ajia didn't want to acquire them. When asked what he wanted to acquire, he said, "Something that will protect me when I'm alive, and help me after death." So Uncle transmitted Mahakala to him. According to Ajia, it was extremely efficacious when he first began practicing the technique, and he felt wonderful. But then, gradually the feeling faded away.

"Why?"

"At first I had great faith in it, but gradually I began to have doubts."

Ajia became a monk at an early age. After he took the tonsure, he became Uncle's attendant. He used to always read whenever he had time. Uncle said, "You don't need to read a lot of books to reach enlightenment. Just select a technique and concentrate on practicing it. After you've completed it, you'll understand everything. Ajia, however, read the scriptures while he practiced. So gradually, the doubts increased, and he entered the demonic state.

He asked Uncle, "Didn't you say that once one completes the practice, he'll understand everything? How come you can't answer my questions?"

Uncle said, "That question was not even answered by Shakyamuni when he was a mortal."

"Does the fact that just because the Buddha didn't answer a question make not answering it right?" Ajia asked.

Uncle said he had entered a demonic state, and told him to recite the "Hundred Word Bright Spell" to eliminate the bad karma. Ajia recited it a hundred thousand times. But the doubts increased instead.

"I want to seek out the Gonpo," said Ajia.

Jasper said, "Would the Gonpo have the answer?"

"Of course he'd know. Otherwise, what kind of Gonpo would he be? I heard that his wisdom is as great as the sea!"

Jasper sat on a prayer mat. He usually sat on a prayer mat when he meditated. He hadn't slept since he was ten. When he got extremely sleepy, he would perform body kowtows. Uncle did the same for scores of years. Jasper thought it was strange that there were people in this world who never slept. Ajia said, "Many of us do this! Those who want to attain instant enlightenment always do this."

"It was said that the Gonpo understood Sanskrit since birth. But I don't believe it," said Ajia.

"Everybody says that."

"Does the fact that everybody says that make it true?" Ajia's eyes looked very bright. "But I still want to find him. Your uncle is the most famous guru here, but he can't dispel my doubts."

Jasper said, "You're just making trouble for yourself. Just do the practices and forget about their significance. I also wanted to find the significance of whatever, but then thought even the universe will eventually explode, so all significance will end up without any significance."

"That's why I practice the austerities, so I can find meaning within the meaningless. But ultimately, I can't find any significance. I left my parents, abandoned the joys and luxuries of the mortal world just for finding significance."

Jasper said, "There is no significance. The process of the experience is the significance."

Ajia smiled, "Your answer is better than your uncle's. He was always saying you possess inborn wisdom. I heard you were an egg when you were born. If so, then you'd be a Bodhisattva above the eighth realm. You'd better take the tonsure soon."

Jasper laughed and said, "But you've become even more troubled after you became monk, with your brain filled with questions on meaning and significance."

Ajia didn't say anything. The flame in the lamp suddenly became deadly quiet. After a long while, he said, "But I've been afraid of finding the Gonpo. What if he can't answer the questions either? That's what I fear the most. If such is the case . . . then I'm finished."

"At least," he continued, "right now, I can still look to the Gonpo. That in itself provides significance."

The Black Dragon Technique of Execution

Uncle was going to perform the Technique of Execution. It's a truly rare sight. Jasper went to see Snow Feather. But every time he saw her he felt ruffled. Wasn't sure why. He just felt so.

Snow Feather leaned against a pine tree and was whipping a branch of white thorn listlessly. She was extremely handsome; white where it should be white, and red where it should be red. Aside from the few freckles on her nose, she would have been considered perfect. One day, when Uncle was instructing Jasper about the technique of visualizing the Green Tara, he described the goddess as a beautiful sixteen-year-old girl. "Would she be like Snow Feather?" asked Jasper. Uncle smiled and said, "Okay—it'll be alright for you to visualize her." After that, Jasper visualized Snow Feather.

Maybe she's an incarnation of the Green Tara! thought Jasper.

Snow Feather didn't look at him. She squinted her eyes and stared into space, whipping the tree one stroke after the other, with a thorny branch. The tree forbore the whipping without saying a single word. Jasper thought, *That tree has cultivated a high level of endurance* and laughed.

"What's so funny—when I'm worried sick!" Snow Feather stamped her feet.

"What's there to worry about? There's nothing worse than death." Jasper smiled.

"But I do want to die! You know, that Kuan San lit a yak butter lamp outside our gate and has stayed there every day. I'm worried sick!"

Jasper shuddered but then laughed and said, "What are you afraid of? Just marry him!"

"Marry him? No way! He's a bully. He shows off just because he has some disgusting muscles."

Jasper felt flustered knowing the severity of her problem. Once someone lit a butter lamp three times at a woman's gate and stayed there, she would have to agree to his marriage proposal. Otherwise, he would continue to stay there forever.

"I'm going to become a nun unless you marry me. Kuan San is afraid of your dad."

Jasper said, however, "It's good to become a nun. I want to take the tonsure as well. But Dad said that if I become a monk, he'll beat Mom up every day. Dad wants me to get married so he can control me. Do you know that? He expects me to get married. If he hadn't expected me to get married, I would have married you. But since he expects me to get married, I want to take Buddhist vows."

"Why?"

"He wants me to take over his position."

Snow Feather laughed and said, "Then take the tonsure. I also want to join the monastery. Mom said nuns lead a hard life, but if Kuan San insists on marrying me, then she'd rather I become a nun. So long as my name is registered at a monastery, Kuan San can't force me."

So the two of them went to see Uncle. Uncle was the abbot, the Living Buddha of the monastery. Although he was not living at the monastery, he was still its abbot. There was a manager at the monastery who took care of managing the daily affairs. Whenever he needed advice, he would report to Uncle and get a "command arrow" from him for handling the affair. Usually, Uncle was too lazy to bother with mundane affairs.

Uncle's wood cabin was situated on a flat piece of land halfway up the mountain slope. It had two floors. The upstairs was a room for worship; the downstairs consisted of a bedroom and a kitchen. The slope was filled with flowers of different colors and styles swaying in the breeze. Jasper's childhood was immersed in the flowers.

Uncle was making Torma, a food made out of dough used as offering to the protective deity. Normally, Uncle made these in the morning. But it was almost evening now. When Jasper saw their triangular shape, he knew Uncle was preparing to perform the Technique of Execution. The shapes of the Torma differed based on the type of ritual technique to be performed. A square box-shaped Torma would be used for performing the Increase of Benefits; a semicircular Torma would be used for Placating; a round Torma would be used for Annihilating Disasters; these triangularly shaped Tormas were offerings for the Technique of Execution. It was said that Uncle was an expert in the Technique of Execution. But that was just a rumor. Jasper always saw Uncle performing this ritual, and he also always saw people dying in the nearby villages, but he had no idea whether they were "killed" by Uncle.

Jasper asked, "Is it worth performing the Killing Technique just for a few items?"

"Why not? The items are not the point. Once this is allowed to start, everyone will take advantage of us. It's unacceptable he'd take advantage even of me!"

Snow Feather said, "Then you should 'execute' Kuan San!" And she told him her own story. Uncle laughed and said, "That's a custom. It's not as if he's doing something evil! Furthermore, you need to have the karma for me to perform it. Without the karma, even I can't do anything about it. However, we can do what you had in mind and register you in the nunnery. You can either join the nunnery or practice the austerities at home. I'll get Gela to take care of the registration tonight . . . I'm going to chant a sutra now. Close your eyes and don't look."

The sound of Uncle chanting the sutra began, and the cabin was filled with a humming sound. This was a familiar sound that penetrated Jasper's soul, and he immediately entered into another state. It was a state of harmony and peace. Jasper delighted in this state. After having been immersed in mundane affairs, the soul would become a detached balloon, which floated up and down without being able to land. He would then long for this feeling of harmony and peace, a home for his soul. The reason Jasper read and chanted the sutra and mantras was precisely for building such a home for his soul.

Jasper thought, *The process of practicing was the significance for practicing; the process of living was the significance for living. But living was clearly a great illusion, full of impermanence which could exist or extinguish in a flash; consequently, its significance was also a great illusion.* The thought that he was living in a great illusion suddenly made him feel empty.

Snow Feather grabbed Jasper's hand all of a sudden and whispered, "Black dragons. . . . There are two huge black dragons. Shuu—it's terrifying." Jasper said, "Don't look!" He felt her soft little hand trembling and sweaty. His head swayed. A thick, dream-like feeling permeated his heart. It felt like a dream. Whenever this feeling appeared, he'd feel flustered, and everything would lose its meaning. He would then wonder: What's the point of living?

Jasper thought he'd been infected with that dreamlike feeling by Ajia. Before he met Ajia, he was too lazy to think about anything. He was as willing to endure being shamed as Mom was and as willing to flow along with karma as Uncle did. The days passed by easily after he practiced the rituals transmitted by Uncle, chanted the mantras, and recited the sutras. If it was not for the bursts of growth of his nails, he almost wouldn't notice the passing of time. Later, he met Ajia who was always full of different views and always asking "why." And imperceptibly, he also developed many "whys" in his own mind.

Uncle stopped chanting. He held up the Tormas and threw them onto the floor while chanting a spell. Shattered Tormas were strewn all over the ground.

Snow Feather was too scared to look at Uncle. Her face turned a bluish-white color as if she was frozen cold. Her body was also trembling almost imperceptibly. Uncle laughed. "You didn't steal a look, did you?" Jasper said, "No." Uncle said, "That's good. If you'd stolen a look, you'd contract dragon poison. Your body would become numb, and you'd turn into a leper."

Snow Feather's tears gushed out, "I feel numb—numb and bloated. I did steal a look and saw two black dragons eating the Tormas. They were as thick as a vat—scared me stiff."

Uncle laughed and said, "I told you not to look. Just as well—you'll get a taste of what leprosy is like."

Jasper had seen lepers before. Their bodies rotted, horrible fluids flowed from them, and then they would die. So he asked, "Is there a cure?"

Uncle said, "Yes—wash with my urine." He pulled out a chamber pot from underneath his bed.

As soon as she saw the stinky, yellowish fluid, Snow Feather wailed out loud.

Mom Was in the Wind

The mountain wind blew vehemently. The cabin trembled. A red light spilled from the mountain in the west, dying red even the chirping of the birds.

Mom came. She said, "We've got to let the boy take Buddhist vows soon. That robber[4] is liable to do anything. He could come up

---

4. The term she used to refer to her husband is *aidaohuo*, "a thing that deserves to be stabbed."

with something anytime and destroy the boy." Uncle replied, "Anything that can be destroyed is not a true dharma implement. If that's the case, it would be useless anyway for him to become a monk. How many cassock-wearing monks really practice the austerities?"

Mom said, "You're right." And she stared at Jasper with her dry, deep-set eyes.

Jasper said, "It really doesn't matter if one becomes a monk or not. The body can stay at home while the mind has taken the tonsure. Didn't Dad say he'd give you fifty lashes a day if I take Buddhist vows? I know he'd do it."

"It's not a problem," said Mom, "let him beat me! Son, Mom would be willing to have him beat me every day if you'd take the tonsure. I'll be used to it after ten days or half a month." She then said to Uncle, "Children can change when they grow older. They'll grow wild without a halter. Quite of few of that group of thieves were from good families. Take that Kuan San, he'd already recited the Mani Mantra[5] a hundred million times. Didn't he still end up as a robber?"

"You're right," said Uncle.

Mom continued, "And, when a child grows older, his mind will roam too. Once desire is there, the mind will grow wild. What I fear is that when that happens, he won't be able to control himself."

Jasper knew what Mom was talking about. What she meant was he was reaching puberty and would start desiring sex. Mom had always said, "Mortal world is a fiery hell." Jasper believed her. He could see how the world was a fiery hell from Mom's own experiences. Mom had endured too much suffering in her life. Uncle said, "The worst enemy for attainment is none other than women. So many 'ritual implements' were destroyed by women." Uncle said this to him ever since he was very young, so he believed it. So, other than visualizing his protective goddess, he tried not to think of women. Although he tried not to think of women, his body couldn't help it. Furthermore, he frequently felt attacks of the fiery, gushing force. Whenever that happened, he'd squeeze his crotch, and guide the heat to the bright spot, the bindu, at the top of the head.

---

5. *Mani zi* is the six-syllabled Sanskrit mantra: *Oṃ maṇi padme hūṃ*. The first word *om* is a sacred syllable found in Indian religions. The word *mani* means "jewel" or "bead," *padme* meaning the "lotus flower," the Buddhist sacred flower, while *hum* represents the spirit of enlightenment.

"How do you feel about it?" Mom asked Jasper, "Do you want to be a monk?"

Jasper looked at Uncle. Uncle was tipping a snuff bottle and pouring its yellow stuff into his palm. He then scooped up a little with his thumbnail, crammed it into one of his nostrils, breathed in forcefully, and sneezed loudly.

"You'll be whipped!" Jasper said.

Mom said, "Mom is not afraid of it. That robber has always tried to scare me with this. I'd be his prey if I'm always afraid of him. If you become a robber, what would I live for? . . . I've been fighting with him over you ever since you were little. He'd pull you to the west and I'd pull you to the east. Thank goodness for Uncle, and thank goodness for the Buddhist deities, my boy didn't turn bad. But he always scolded me that I made a tiger into a cat. He'd hoped our boy would inherit his position!"

Uncle laughed and said, "He thinks of it as a throne!" Jasper laughed too—only Dad would think that way!

Mom said, "Why don't we have his head shaved on the eighth of the Fourth Month? So it's settled. We've waited for a year already. If we wait any longer, he'll marry the boy off and the boy would have no choice."

"Okay," said Uncle.

Mom left. She drifted away in the wind. It was very dark except for the mountain path. Red clouds splashed over the western mountain, dyeing red the treetops. Mom was very thin. Her scrawny body shrank until it disappeared completely. Jasper wanted to weep. He wanted to tell Mom, *I don't want to be a monk.* Sometimes, taking the tonsure are gray words. A dazzling life would turn into a black-and-white photo once one becomes a monk. Sometimes, he thought there was nothing really wrong with being like Dad, who came and left with panache, so long as he maintained the baseline of not robbing the poor. Didn't you see how happily the poor smiled when Dad divided up the meat among them? That verve was so much more appealing than listening to the monks chant the sutra! But, as soon as this thought emerged, he'd tell himself, *That's absolutely wrong. Mom was right.*

Uncle said, "Your mom was right. Let's do it on the eighth of the Fourth Month." His words sounded like sleep talk.

The sky turned dark gradually. The wind whistled through the forest like the strange howls of nocturnal beasts. It was always like that at night. The sound resembled noise but also brought serenity. Engulfed in the whistling sounds was a magnificent quietness. Ever since he was little, that wind, that quietness and Uncle's chanting would drift toward him wave after wave until they melted into his dreams and his life.

Uncle lit a butter lamp, reached for a notebook, and wrote a few words in some empty space at the top of a page. He laughed and said, "That Snow Feather could be considered an enlightened person!" Jasper knew he was filling Snow Feather's name in the registry for the nuns. Quite a few families in the village had their daughters register as nuns before they reached puberty, lest unscrupulous men make trouble for them. Of course, this kind of registration was only titular. They could either enter the monastery or get married later, no one cared.

Suddenly, Uncle laughed. "That Butcher Zhang is bringing the pot." Jasper knew Uncle was always telling him about what would happen. "He wants to bring it back in secret. But it's too late. The ritual was already performed. The curse has already been activated. You know, that Technique of Execution is called the Black Dragon Technique of Execution. Do you want to learn it?"

"No," said Jasper. He thought no one had the right to take the life of another. When Uncle asked him why, that was what he said.

"But do you know that this 'Execution' is in fact an ultimate form of salvation? When teaching doesn't work for the wicked, then 'Execution' would be the only option. Once 'Executed,' he would be sent to Pure Land."

Jasper thought of what Ajia had said and asked, "What is Pure Land?" Uncle said, "Pure Land is Pure Land." As if he knew what Jasper would ask next, he added, "Don't hang around Ajia in the future. The fella is very smart, but his smartness is insignificant smartness."

Jasper wanted to say, "So his insignificant smartness managed to outwit your great wisdom." But he was afraid Uncle would take offense. But, truth be said, ever since he met Ajia, he always wondered where one would go after completing one's practices. Why even bother to work on practicing if one couldn't even answer this question?

Uncle said, "Go outside and take a look. Butcher Zhang is here."

Jasper went out of the door. The light inside also rushed outside with him. Sure enough, Butcher Zhang was just putting down a bag by the door. From the looks of it, he was intending to put it down and slip away. His face showed great embarrassment when he saw someone coming out of the door.

Uncle laughed and said, "Just leave the pot. I don't need the other stuff."

Without a word, Butcher Zhang turned around and threw himself into the wind.

Jasper was puzzled, "Didn't he refuse to admit he'd done it?"

Uncle replied, "The Tormas landed at his home. He got scared."

Chapter 6

Origin of the Flying Thief

How many destined romances have gone afar,
Only ill fate is close by;
Ill fate is good.
When Heaven endows one with great responsibilities,
It will always be there.

Snow Feather's Vow

Ajia's *Sleep Ramblings* records how Snow Feather's fame spread throughout Liangzhou. This story apparently happened before she stole the sheep. I've always suspected its credibility since it's not mentioned at all in *Tale of the Goddess*.

This tale by Ajia is very interesting. Ironically, after Snow Feather had subjugated a flying thief, she herself came to be recognized as a flying thief by the residents of Liangzhou.

Ajia began the story from the point after Snow Feather had left the mountain, upon finishing her training as a martial artist. He said when Snow Feather first left the mountain, she felt like a leaf tossed into an ocean. She had no way of escaping the constant sensation of helplessness and insecurity. She had very little memory of the human world. She could only remember the whistle of wind when the wolf carried her in its mouth and her mother's loud wailing. The latter, in particular, would frequently seep into her dreams. She remembered her mother as a beautiful young woman. But her memory was vague as to just how beautiful she was. Ajia used to describe to me Snow Feather's mom's charm in the past. That was one of the most memorable images of his memory.

After Snow Feather was taken by the wolf to the back of the mountain, Mom wept while she searched for her. During those ten-plus years, she combed through Liangzhou, which touched everyone. Of course, the one who found this the most touching was ultimately her own daughter. Ajia said that back then he used to always hear a hoarse and forlorn voice, resembling the weeping tune played by the three-stringed violin of the Xianxiao[1] performers. Whenever Snow Feather's mom saw a four-legged animal, such as a dog, Mom would chase after it and call her daughter's name—until all the animals, including wolves, would dart away as soon as they saw her. It was said that wolves did not ravage the places she visited. So, she was welcomed wherever she went. Although people did not welcome her with gongs and drums, they sincerely respected her. Therefore, she never lacked food. People would provide her with a bowl of food wherever she went. They'd listen to her complaints and sniffle along.

It was very easy for Snow Feather to find her mother, since there was no one in Liangzhou who did not know her. She effortlessly found the woman who was still calling for "Feather dear!" in a valley. She kowtowed to the woman in the dust and called her, "Mom!" She then discovered the old lady's eyes had become two shallow slits. She handed her the tiny belly protector she wore as a baby, which Grandpa Jiu gave her, and had Mom feel the scar on her back the kind wolf's teeth left unwittingly, as well as the protective talisman she had worn since birth. Thereupon, Mom hugged her and wailed, voicing her sorrow of being wronged in a manner that shook heaven and earth.

Ajia said, during that moment, Snow Feather vowed she would never leave Mom and would let her live the best life possible. Of course, in her mind, living the best life possible meant her Mom would be able to eat meat for the rest of her life.

It was precisely in order to keep this promise that Snow Feather would end up enduring inhumane miseries in the future.

---

1. A local form of performing art based on singing extemporaneously created ballads. Xianxiao literally means "the worthy and the filial."

The Nun Who Turned into a Rainbow

Ajia mentioned that the first place Snow Feather stayed at was Luoshen Monastery in Liangzhou. Back then, Luoshen Monastery was huge with many buildings from the Ming dynasty.[2] You must have heard about Kumarajiva's[3] famous tongue, which would not be incinerated when he was cremated. That's right: it was buried beneath the pagoda there, and that's why the monastery became a famous place for worship. This was already a place of devotion shortly after Buddhism was transmitted into China.[4] Snow Feather and her mother lived in a low room underneath the pagoda. A dumb old hag lived with them. No one realized that she had in fact already attained enlightenment. She seemed crazy and would laugh whenever she met someone—anyone except for Snow Feather. Whenever she saw Snow Feather she would weep and hug her the way a mother hugged a long-lost daughter. No one knew she had, in fact, attained the Rainbow Body. One night shortly after Snow Feather and her mother settled in, the abbot suddenly saw a blazing fire inside their room. The light shone throughout the city of Liangzhou, including the place you would inhabit later. That's right, the place you named Bright Mahamudra Studio.

Many people were awakened by the fiery light that night. They all cried, "Aiya! Shenluo Monastery's on fire!" They all rushed there, hoping to put out the fire to accumulate immeasurable merit. They hoped to use the cash of faith to exchange for rewards of mountain-like gold. Thus, you see their behavior was in fact a reflection of immense avarice. But you shouldn't complain about them. There are always many rocks but not much precious jade in the mountains—and many people but few gentlemen in the world. You're not that much better. You're only slightly more enlightened than the rest. Aren't you also stirred when you see beautiful women? So, don't laugh at others.

The crowd screamed, "Fire! Shenluo Monastery is on fire!" Crowds of Liangzhou's residents screamed while they pushed themselves toward the monastery, only to discover, however, that the light emitted from the plaza in front of the monastery. The flames soon vanished of their own accord. No one realized that the crazy nun, too, had vanished.

---

2. 1368–1644.

3. A Kuchean monk dated 334–413.

4. During the late Han dynasty (202 BCE–220), probably around the third century.

The type of practice cultivated by the monks at the time was Pure Land. They only knew to chant *A mi tuo fuo* and had no idea concerning the magnitude of the achievement attained by the crazy nun. It was truly a hundred times higher than even what I, Ajia, have attained. I asked him, "Is there anyone greater than you? Aren't you so great that you don't even need to shit? I thought you were a priceless treasure found only in Heaven!" Ajia laughed guiltily and said, "Look at you! You folks of Liangzhou are all the fucking same—including you!" I said, "Well, a boy raised by a wolf for three years can't change his wolf nature for the rest of his life. Especially when I've lived in Liangzhou for forty years! The only difference between me and the common folks of Liangzhou is I realize I possess wolf nature and examine my behavior every day, whereas they think they're the greatest in the world!" Ajia wrinkled his nose a couple of times and concluded, "Okay, okay! You talk more than you shit!"

But Snow Feather personally observed the process through which the nun transformed herself into light. Grandpa Jiu had told her about Rainbow Transformation. According to Grandpa Jiu, the corpses of some accomplished gurus would shrink gradually for several days after death. A barely visible rainbow would hover above the corpse until only its hair and fingernails remained after seven days. But instant transformation into light was rare. In this case, the normally crazy nun transformed into the statue of a Bodhisattva Guanyin on the offering table, a ball of red light emitting from her body. Snow Feather was enveloped by a strange heat that made her sweat after a short while. But the fiery light was like a balmy spring breeze, warm but not scorching hot. That fiery light wavered within Snow Feather the rest of her life. Later when she went to visit Grandpa Jiu, she told him about the event. Grandpa just commented offhandedly that the woman had completed her practices. As to what kind of practice she had completed—whether it was Rainbow Body or Illusory Body—Grandpa Jiu did not say. But Snow Feather was convinced that what the crazy nun accomplished was the Rainbow Body, since one day, years later, she saw that nun performing a ritual offering with a group of women at a location in Chong Mountain Range! They were consuming the fresh corpse of a young woman.

The Jade Flute from a Hundred Leagues Away

Different views existed as to Snow Feather's identity. Some people thought she was a lay person; others felt she was a nun, saying her adherence to

Grandpa Jiu was equivalent to leaving home for Buddhism since Grandpa Jiu was an old monk; while others claimed she became a nun at Luoshen Monastery, since she wouldn't have had the right to live there otherwise.

If she did indeed take the tonsure, then many of her actions clearly had violated Buddhist precepts. So, along with Jasper and Monk Wu, who were considered by the villagers as having transgressed Buddhist prohibitions, there are three Buddhists who violated the Sanga in this novel.

But in Ajia's tale, Snow Feather did not shave her head.

Snow Feather stayed at Luoshen Monastery for eight months. It was mostly uneventful. She basically performed the tasks of sweeping, cutting wood, and carrying water each day. Her mother, on the other hand, would sit in the corner of a south-facing wall and recite *Ah mi tuo fo*. Since monasteries did not allow unrelated people to reside there, Snow Feather had Mom invoke the name of the Buddha. She didn't expect her mother to become so addicted to it that aside from scolding her wayward daughter, she spent all her time reciting the name of the Buddha.

Those eight months were the most peaceful months of Snow Feather's entire life. If it were not for the following event, she might have been able to live out the rest of her life in leisure and peace.

The problem originated during an important Buddhist ritual performed at the monastery. It was a Water and Land Salvation Ritual, for beseeching blessings and preventing calamities. That particular ritual was the most famous event in Liangzhou's history. If Ajia hadn't told me about it, it might've been buried under the dust of age. So, to me, Ajia could be considered a meritorious agent for transmitting culture. Ajia remarked, "There's no need for such niceties—I am the guardian deity of Liangzhou, after all!"

It must've been a sunny day. Although there might've been a few glitteringly white clouds, it was very sunny. There was neither wind nor rain. Although occasionally a rain-laden cloud might pass by, it'd be too shy to rain. You know—oftentimes, even the sky can be a shameless flatterer—sometimes even worse than the officials of Liangzhou! When so many people were hoping for a sunny day, it'd be too embarrassed not to be sunny. The Water and Land Salvation Ritual performed during the day was quite successful. You know, success is an interesting word. Being successful meant there were no mishaps. So, according to this definition, it was successful throughout the day. But a small interlude occurred that night. It so happened that the highest provincial Buddhist priest wanted to listen to the tunes of Xiliang. Xiliang music was very famous of course—of great renown since as early as Xuanzong's[5] time during the Tang dynasty. Snow Feather must have been destined for fame that day. Now, one needs musical instruments to perform the tunes. They had all the instruments, except for the Qiang flute. Actually, it wasn't that there were no Qiang flutes there—a few could be found in the city of Liangzhou—but they were "mainland stuff." Do you know what "mainland stuff" means? It means they weren't good enough for the flutist, the best in the great Buddhist monastery of Ganzhou. His playing of the Qiang flute was famous throughout the world, which meant he was known to all the local musicians. Back then there were no televisions, etc., so there was no way that the common masses would've known about him. But of course, there was no need for them to know him. Even without knowing the famous line, "What need was there for the Qiang flute to resent the willows,"[6] they were able to give birth to, and raise, sons and grandsons just the same. And of course, it would've been useless for the commoners to know him anyway. Even if one generation knew about the person, another generation wouldn't have known about him anyway. So this business of saying someone was famous throughout the world was simply lying to oneself. If you want every generation of commoners to know about something, then you'd have to give them a reason for wanting to know. Look at me—I'm digressing again! What can I do? This is what happens when one is given an opportunity to speak after being silent for a thousand years. Although I, Ajia, am the guardian deity of Liangzhou, few people know about me.

So, the Gonpo wanted to listen to the music of Xiliang, but the orchestra was short of the required Qiang flute. The monastery's abbot searched throughout the city of Liangzhou but was only able to find a few broken ones in such poor shape they fell apart the minute the musician from Ganzhou tried them out. He said, "They won't do. Only my own jade flute will do. But unfortunately, I didn't bring it here with me. It's in the Big Buddha Monastery of Ganzhou." When everyone heard him, they didn't know what to do: the distance between Liangzhou and Ganzhou was five hundred leagues! They had no choice but to forget about the performance. That was when Snow Feather said, "Let me give it a try."

---

5. Also known as Tang Minghuang. He reigned from 712 to 756 and was one of the most famous emperors of China.

6. A line from "Lyrics of Liangzhou" by the Tang dynasty poet, Wang Zhihuan (688–742).

This was how Snow Feather gained instant fame in Liangzhou.

When Snow Feather left Luoshen Monastery, everyone thought she was going to find a flute within the city of Liangzhou. Who would have known that, within an hour, she would come back with the jade flute, which was as green as a green snake with a trace of blood-colored red at its lip. Later, this flute was collected by the Liangzhou Museum. After that, when some museum director retired, he refused to hand over the registration list of the museum collection, and the jade flute disappeared along with many other items in the collection. What seemed strange was that none of the numerous officials interfered. An old man named Pu Hua wrote a most compelling letter in complaint, but the matter remained as dead as a rock sunk in the ocean, not even a ripple was seen. Therefore, Ajia concluded he doubted the integrity of the officials of Liangzhou. I scolded him fiercely, "Just stick to your story—what fucking business was that of yours?"

The arrival of the flute saved Liangzhou's face. The highest priest thereupon donated five thousand ounces of silver to Luoshen Monastery, along with a golden top for its reliquary pagoda. It was said that this top was made of real gold, which shone most majestically. Because of this golden top, Luoshen Monastery became the most renowned monastery in Hexi. Its fame even exceeded that of Big Buddha Monastery of Ganzhou.

According to Ajia, the golden-topped pagoda was incomparably efficacious. Whoever prayed there invariably got what they prayed for. Then, Ajia looked around sneakily and whispered, "Do you know why Liangzhou never suffered from warfare? Look, the cavalry of Genghis Khan slaughtered the populace of forty countries—but the minute they entered Liangzhou, they were as tame as lambs. Why was that? When fierce battles raged between the Moslem and Han people during the Tongzhi reign[7] and rivers of blood flowed all around Liangzhou, why was this city alone unscathed? Why? Why did the entire country suffer frequent warfare, but Liangzhou alone never had a rebellion? Why?" He asked several other "whys" until I became annoyed and said, "Come out with it if you have a point!" Only then did Ajia say sneakily, "It was all on account of the reliquary pagoda with the golden top!" According to him, before Kumarajiva passed away, he said, "If my translations of the sutras are without mistakes, then my tongue will not char when

---

7. 1861–1875.

my body is cremated. If my tongue is not burnt, then build a reliquary pagoda in Liangzhou to worship it, and the city will never be ravaged by warfare henceforth!"

"Is that so? How come I've never heard of it?"

The Golden Cupola that Disappeared

Snow Feather, whose fame had by now spread throughout Liangzhou, must have discovered she now looked different in people's eyes. Having lived in the seclusion of a deep mountain since infancy, she had never been exposed to the evils of the mortal world. That was why Grandpa Jiu told her never to show off. But to save face for the populace of Liangzhou: she had forgotten this advice of her guru.

Snow Feather, ah, Snow Feather! You should have read my *Liangzhou and its People*!

Why did you become a rafter that stuck out?

See, people now looked at you differently. The fact that you could travel more than five hundred leagues within the time it took to eat a meal, climb over the tightly shut gate of the city of Ganzhou (as if walking on flat ground), and locate the Qiang flute the size of a tiny green snake from within some 110 rooms of Big Buddha Monastery: this meant for the others that no place was safe anymore in this huge city of Liangzhou!

Some folks have already moved their heirlooms to other places. Although the abbot no longer asked you to perform menial tasks, you could feel his respectful, cold distance. You suddenly saw Grandpa Jiu smiling at you.

You wanted to leave but could not bear to ruin the peaceful life your mom was enjoying.

One day, the highest priest had a golden cupola sent over. The reliquary pagoda with the golden cupola was incomparably attractive. You must have also sensed something inauspicious; you must have noticed signs of avarice in the eyes of some, among the throngs of visitors. You watched all the eyes carefully, even through the nights, and caused much suspicion on the part of the abbot. But one night, you were finally too tired. You dozed off for just a moment, and the golden cupola disappeared.

This was how you came to be considered a thief by the folks of Liangzhou.

They all assumed that only you could have nabbed a golden cupola from a pagoda more than thirty feet high without a ladder. Much as the compassionate abbot tried to dispel the rumors, they surged with ever-increasing ferocity.

This was the advantage of fame!

The Super Thief

The county dispatched "yamen runners," or policemen, who searched for many days. Of course, they didn't even find a single trace of the cupola. You know, most of those "yamen runners" were just bums—can't do anything but eat. How could they compare with a super thief? One who could take the golden cupola more than thirty feet high, like grabbing the dick in his own pants? You jeered at the "yamen runners" who came and left with bluster and pomp. You knew they were putting on a show to prove they weren't just food-holding leather bags, just clothes hangers. But you knew they were in fact nothing but food-holding leather bags and clothes hangers since there was no way this thief could be caught through their bluster. Who was the thief? This thief was a blue steel blade, created through forging hundreds of times, with thousands of times of hammering each round, while the yamen runners were just rusty iron scraps! This thief was a treasured broadsword capable of slicing through metal as if it were mud, while the yamen runners were but a tong used in a kitchen stove. This thief was bubbling, boiling water, while the yamen runners were but the crystals of dried urine. Ajia wanted to give many more metaphors, but I shouted and stopped him, "Enough! Aren't you just a minor guardian deity? You're just an ant pretending to be an animal by wearing a bridle-headstall!" Ajia sniggered, "Okay, okay! I won't rob your right to talk. In the future, you should stop robbing the philosophers of their right to talk too. You be a novelist and I'll be a guardian god!"

We now return to the yamen runners on horseback, who blustered with pomp for many days without finding a trace of the golden cupola. In a traditional novel, the county magistrate would invariably give the head of the yamen runners several lashes and set a date for catching the thief. The head of the yamen runners would then heave long and short sighs until his wife asked him why—and eventually all would work out. I also wanted to follow suit. But this kind of plot was as common as the churning maggots in the outhouses of Liangzhou. I would be condemned for following suit since Ajia was after all a deity—how could he be so totally devoid of imagination? So, I thought I could have the magistrate capture Snow Feather's mom. But then he said that this type of plot was like soy-braised pork: people have had enough of it too. I racked my brain until it hurt, but I couldn't think of something new. So, I decided to tell the truth. Sometimes the truth is the best.

In fact, just as I mentioned before, all the shouting of the yamen runners was a farce. They had to put up a show to get paid. Otherwise, the masses would complain. The dialect of Liangzhou sounds harsh, you know. Even when folks say sweet nothings, it sounds like bawling. Their cussing was a hundred times fiercer than the angry Asuras. The yamen runners swished their whips while riding and thought, *Heck—we've already tried hard enough!* They then let the horses gallop, swished the whips, and find an excuse to yell at anyone not quite to their liking, or anyone they've had problems with. That's what they were like.

The county magistrate was even less inclined to deal with the case. When he visited the monastery, the abbot served him a vegetarian meal without wine. This already had displeased him. And then he set his eyes on the abbot's golden Buddha and hinted at it by rubbing the smooth head of the statue. But the abbot bent his head—the tip of his nose toward his heart—and pretended not to understand the magistrate's hint. So the magistrate decided, "Do you think this attitude of yours could get me to find the golden cupola for you? You're a physician diagnosing the pulse from someone else's knee—you'll never get it!" He handed the golden Buddha to the abbot, scooped up some tobacco from his snuff bottle, sniffed, and sneezed emphatically.

What I described above was the truth.

Of course, this could also have been what should have happened at the time.

Thereafter, precisely because of this, although many folks suspected Snow Feather, the officers did not capture and interrogate her.

The abbot was as tense as if he were on fire. He knew that if the golden cupola could not be recovered, he would lose face. Besides, he wouldn't be able to face the highest priest either. So he had Snow Feather come to his room and asked in a whisper, "Are you really a super thief?"

Snow Feather laughed and said, "I have the powers of a super thief, but I am not a thief."

The abbot knelt before her and begged with tears, "Please save me!"

Snow Feather said, "Don't worry. I already know who the thief is."

Go, Go, Go, Just Keep on Going

Snow Feather could never forget that moonlit night. The moonlit nights of Liangzhou have always been famous. One of the eight famous sceneries of Liangzhou was the "Smooth Sands of a Moonlit Night."

The moonlit nights of Luoshen Monastery were also renowned. People said that if you sit quietly in the monastery's main hall, you could hear the 'shua, shua, shua' rainlike sounds of moonlight hitting its glazed roof tiles. When you walk out of the hall in amazement, you would see three strands of smoke wafting upward from the lake straight into the palace of the moon. The folks of Liangzhou referred to this as the "Three Heavenward Incense."

Since everyone already decided Snow Feather was the thief, the abbot was able to send her away politely. This gesture pleased everyone. Neither monks nor lay people wanted a super thief among them. It was said that Chai Shao, a brother-in-law of the Tang dynasty emperor, Li Shimin,[8] was an expert martial artist and could fly over roofs and travel along walls. Li Shimin exiled him to a location more than a thousand leagues away. When even an emperor feared such a person, how much less could we expect of the common people? So Snow Feather carried her mother on her back, and left in tears. When they crossed North Street she saw a crowd, she saw a crowd pointing at her and saying, "Look, the flying thief!"

As Snow Feather crossed the time and space of Liangzhou, and headed toward the wilderness, she must have been racked by deep emotions. She might have thought of her tragic future. Or maybe, she thought of nothing, like me. I never bothered thinking about the future.

---

8. Also known as Emperor Taizong of the Tang dynasty, Li Shimin reigned from 626 to 649.

I live in the present, without thinking about the past or the future. Later, a PhD at the University of Lanzhou termed it the "Realm of Clarity."

Snow Feather was probably like that. Otherwise, I wouldn't be able to explain her miraculous ending.

But even more possibly, she was very sad. When she left Luoshen Monastery, it had only been a few months since her entry into the human world. She had now tasted its treachery. When a child suddenly discovers how terrible the adult world is, he'd invariably feel like the sky has collapsed upon him. Many years ago, when a famous person in Liangzhou, whom I regarded as a divine being and guru, made me a victim, I also felt everything had turned gray. I felt like an invisible glass vessel separated my body and mind from the rest of the world and that I was exiled to Liangzhou by God. It was not until the light of wisdom shone from my mind-heart that the feeling finally dissipated.

Snow Feather must have been like this.

She must not have expected that her act of saving Liangzhou's face would create so much trouble for her. Ajia said, "She deserved it." I remember Ajia saying the same to me when I felt as wronged as Snow Feather did at that moment. Ajia was a worldly deity. In fact, you'll find all deities had worldly experiences when you study their tales. Having experience in worldly affairs was a prerequisite for people's acceptance of them as deities. They, of course, include the contemporary deities the government deems acceptable as objects of worship.

So, Snow Feather, you had no other option than to leave.

Snow Feather left, her mother on her back. Go, go, go, keep on going! They kept on going and walked past Flowing Water Alley. Everyone at Liangzhou knew that cunts were cheaper than unleavened bread in this alley. Prostitutes filled the alley, yelling, "Come here—it's cheaper!" whenever people approached.

Go, go, go, keep on going! They kept on going until they came to Shit Alley, filled with rural migrants whose job it was to collect night soil in the city. Night soil spilled out of people's doors into the alley—the name of the alley was later changed to Rain Pavilion Alley. Here a few red-eyed old men grumbled, "Such a pretty girl—why did she become a flying thief?"

Go, go, go, keep on going! They kept on going until they came to Sparrow Alley, thronged with sparrows and hawkers. A man raised an iron claw and said, "Flying thief—how about a flying claw?"

Finally, Snow Feather entered Pine Surf Monastery.

Pine Surf Monastery

Pine Surf Monastery had existed since that monk from Fengyang became an emperor.[9] It was always very small, with just a few monks. For ten generations, only one monk lived there.

When Snow Feather arrived at Pine Surf Monastery, its abbot was known as Monk Stone. Monk Stone was very famous, although he was only five feet tall. Everyone in Liangzhou at the time knew Monk Stone. He was the top martial arts expert.

Aside from martial arts, Monk Stone practiced mainly the Yamantaka Vajra and the Six Techniques of Niguma. He inherited these techniques from Ta'er Monastery and Rock Gate Monastery. This was the branch of Shangpa Kagyu that contained the teachings of Guru Tsongkhapa. Later, his disciple, Wu Naidan, inherited his position. And Wu Naidan taught the techniques to me. So, aside from the Five Vajras and the Mahamudra of the Shangpa Kagyu, I am also a direct inheritor of the Techniques of the Yamantaka and one of the inheritors of the Kalachakra. Ajia was willing to befriend me because of these facts. You know—even the deities of this world are snobbish.

Snow Feather didn't want to go to the monastery originally. But you must've known that the folks of Liangzhou were famous for snobbery. Let me give you an example as proof. There was a man by the name of Niu Jian who lived five leagues south of the city of Liangzhou. This man was incredibly intelligent, with a bellyful of essays. He wanted to go to the capital to take the civil service examinations but was destitute. One day, Niu Jian's mother slaughtered the only egg-laying hen in the household and used one of their doors as firewood to cook it to perfection. She intended to invite members of the clan to a meal and ask them for help. Who would have expected, however, that after extending invitations dozens of times, none would come to their home? So there she was weeping, when a man arrived and found out the cause of her sorrow. "I'll eat it, if they won't," said he. After he ate the hen and drank its broth, he sold his store for a hundred ounces of silver,

---

9. Zhu Yuanzhang (1928–1398) was the first emperor of the Ming dynasty.

which enabled Niu Jian to go to the capital and eventually become a Presented Scholar.[10] Niu Jian eventually served as governor general of Jiangnan and Jiangxi provinces and was very influential. The businessman who helped him was from Henan. Later, when Niu Jian served as viceroy of Henan, he was a Jiao Yulu[11] who toiled for the province and performed innumerable good deeds for its populace. That's why, although later many people condemned the populace of Henan, I still hold them in high esteem. My friend, Blind Immortal Jia Fushan, termed the folks of Liangzhou "horny peacocks that loved the rich and disdained the poor," whenever he mentioned them. He told many other stories that would make the deaf hear and the dumb speak, but we will not repeat them here.

When the snobbish populace of Liangzhou wouldn't allow a super thief like Snow Feather to make a home there, she was at the end of her rope. She looked around and saw nothing but desolation. The reeds were more than three feet tall; wild animals wailed. The area north of the city of Liangzhou was mostly swamp back then. Humans were scarce, while wild animals roamed. Skeletons of corpses were scattered everywhere, so were the wild dogs that gnawed on them. Snow Feather knew the wild dogs had their eyes on her blind mother. Although the mother was elderly, her flesh was at least fresh and ten times more delicious than dry bones. So the wild dogs followed them at a distance and waited for a chance to pounce. They must have considered Snow Feather a professional corpse-carrier.

So Snow Feather had no choice but to head for the lonely monastery nestled on the lake shore.

Monk Stone, who could predict the future, was already waiting for her. He pushed open the gate of the monastery before she opened her mouth. The creak of the gate ripped open the sky—so loud it shook me into a cold sweat!

"Aiya—scared me stiff!" Even the crickets by the gate woke up and shrieked.

---

10. Beginning in the late tenth century, the Chinese government bureaucracy was staffed predominantly by scholar-officials chosen through a civil examination system. The coveted highest degree, the *jinshi* (presented scholar), was awarded as the culmination of a three-stage process.

11. Jiao Yulu (1922–1964) was a symbol of the honest party cadre who devoted himself tirelessly to the Communist state.

By the Lake

Once Snow Feather got her mother settled in, she soaked some dried unleavened buns with hot water and fed her mother first before she ate some herself. While Pine Surf Monastery was short of money and monks, it had no shortage of dried buns. On the first and fifteenth day of each month, the populace of the surrounding region would arrive to worship and make a donation called "plate." Each plate consisted of fifteen unleavened buns. When Monk Stone received too many plates, he would break them into walnut-sized pieces and dry them on an unhinged door he placed on the beams of the temple. Whenever he did not feel like cooking, he boiled water and soaked some. Who would have thought that someone who ate mainly dried buns, like Monk Stone, would end up as strong as a stone pillar? Wonders never cease!

Many years later, after Monk Stone passed away, his disciple Wu Naidan inherited the tradition. He dried the buns and hung them from the beams. Whenever I used to "receive the techniques" from him there, I would look at the hanging buns and feel sorry for him. I would then leave him lots of money for vegetables. However, I discovered later that no matter how much money I left, Master Wu would still eat just dried buns. During the second half of his life, dried buns were his main staple. He would eventually build a large monastery using the donated money he'd saved.

This story will be relayed another time.

Now, after Snow Feather ate some soaked dry buns, she closed her eyes and took a short nap. As the night deepened, she settled Mom into bed and got ready to leave. Mom asked her where she was going. She said, "I'm going to take a bath." Mom said, "Why take a bath now?" And she replied, "If I don't wash myself right now, I'll never be clean." She then left the monastery. Ajia said, "She flew toward Luoshen Monastery like a wisp of smoke." He was very proud of using this metaphor. I said, "What are you so proud of? The word 'flew' isn't as good as the word, 'floated.'" So, Snow Feather floated toward Luoshen Monastery like a wisp of smoke. Truly, she could tread on snow without leaving a trace and was as fast as a flying bird.

Before she left, she borrowed a sickle from Monk Stone.

Snow Feather crouched among the reeds by the lake next to Luoshen Monastery. She heard the *shua, shua* sound created by moonlight hitting its glazed roof tiles. The stars laughed nonstop as if they had eaten "laughter fart." The abbot's snoring shook heaven and earth and filled every nook and cranny of the entire monastery. It was like this every night. Many people believed the abbot was reincarnated from a raccoon and that he chanted sutras even when he slept. This didn't affect the man from being an abbot. Ever since he'd memorized four volumes of the Agama Sutra, Buddha's words would pour forth whenever he opened his mouth. Nothing one can do about! He was a solid item. Like US dollars these days: solid everywhere! I heard even Lingyin Monastery of Hangzhou[12] came to invite him to lecture there. For him to stay at the tiny Luoshen Monastery was equivalent to having a great dragon reside in the shallows intended for shrimp. But the abbot said, "What can I do? I am a native of Liangzhou." Ajia wrinkled up his nose and said, "Listen to him! Full of himself—just like you!"

Snow Feather also heard other noises. Back then the folks of Liangzhou went to bed early. They entered the land of dreams soon after nightfall. Even the barking of the dogs sounded feeble and embarrassed. The night air clung vigorously to Snow Feather's vertebrae. The chill of the sandy ground gradually seeped into her soak-bun-filled belly. I wish I could say her belly was filled with mutton-soup-soaked buns, the kind found in Xi'an! The rumbling of her hungry intestines growled as forthrightly as farting. But you must also know that night travelers shouldn't stuff themselves, just as a traveling wolf wouldn't stuff itself with mutton. I will relay another story about a wolf that stuffed itself with mutton later.

I kept on wondering what else she must have heard. I thought of many other noises, but they were all the kinds that had already been written about by other novelists. So I said, "Okay, Snow Feather. Stop listening and start doing what you came to do!"

The Fire-Tending Scabby-Headed Monk

See, here comes the main story!

When the myriad music of the universe ceased to play, one heard an almost imperceptible sound all of a sudden. It was like a fart by the Moon—neither loud nor smelly. It was a sound that others might

---

12. Located in Zhejiang in southeastern China.

not have noticed, but Snow Feather did. A white shadow wafted by like a dream. It was vaguely transparent under the moon, as light as a butterfly and as blurry as steam. It tickled Snow Feather's nerves the way the hair of a beautiful woman might have done. Of course, it also tickled my nerves. If I had seen this shadow in the wilderness, I would certainly have thought it was a ghost. Maybe that's how ghost stories originated.

But I knew it couldn't have been a ghost. Ghosts couldn't enter monasteries since there was always the guardian deity, Ajia! The only time Ajia would allow ghosts to enter was when the monks were performing the Mengshan Alms-Giving Ritual. That was when all ghosts—fat ones, skinny ones, male ghosts, and female ghosts—would enter the monastery cautiously but self-righteously. Ajia loved to watch the shy female ghosts, although he would never admit to it. The ghosts of Liangzhou are just like the folks of Liangzhou. Ghosts are just like people. Oh, I forgot, Ajia was a deity, not a ghost. Please don't take offense, Ajia! However, there's almost no difference between ghosts and deities. Deities are but ghosts with power. What are you glaring at me for? You pick up a sieve and think you own the sky? If you're worshipped, then you are a god. But if you're not worshipped, then out you go with a sprinkle of vinegar! What do you think you are? Can you shit gold? Can you pee silver? Can you make me a section chief? I suggest you take it easy. We all know that you, Ajia, are no more than a poor ghost with power, with not even enough cash to fill a plate!

Let's continue to watch that shadow. That dreamlike shadow wafted around for a while and then floated toward where Snow Feather hid. I thought it had discovered Snow Feather. My heart pounded furiously; a thousand horses raced through my veins. I certainly could describe the feeling more intensely but don't want to put too much pressure on the hearts of my readers. So, let's make it short. Faster than I could talk, one heard a terrifying scream. If you want to hear what happened next, listen to the ensuing narrative.

That loud scream shocked the dark night of Shenluo Monastery and lasted for a thousand years. It lasted until after the great earthquake, which toppled its world-famous pagoda. Sometimes I wondered how this reliquary pagoda—that was not even able to protect itself—managed to defend Liangzhou from being ravaged by warfare? I couldn't help but be moved! It was willing to benefit others, without any consideration for itself. It was the Dr. Bethune[13] of pagodas! I had to force myself to suppress the surging clouds of suspicion, in order to set myself into a mode of piety. That was how I managed to win an old monk's fancy and got to hear Snow Feather's story.

That loud shriek also woke up all the monks and laymen. The abbot was the first one to rush over. But the sound of snoring in his room continued. I suspect he harbored thirty raccoons there to create that thundering snore. But that's just a guess. The continued snoring in the abbot's room has also been an unsolved historical mystery ever since.

The monks brought torches that shone on the scabby-headed monk in charge of the kitchen fire. I suspect he was not really scabby-headed, because I don't believe ugly people are necessarily evil. Although I look fine, I also harbor respect for those who are ugly. But Ajia swore the man was scabby-headed, so I said, "Sure! If you say he was scabby-headed, then scabby-headed he was."

That scabby-headed monk squealed ceaselessly. I knew his "lazy sinew" was cut. The "lazy sinew" referred to the Achilles tendon.

I also knew that his "lazy sinew" had been cut by Snow Feather's sickle. Having heard the story five hundred times already, I can't stop the details from pouring into my brain.

As for the scabby-headed monk's background, elderly folks of Liangzhou gave different versions. Some claimed he was an older disciple of Snow Feather's master, and his skills in martial arts were ten times greater than Snow Feather's. But I don't agree with this version, mainly because I've already written in this novel that Grandpa Jiu had a wolf bring him the infant Snow Feather so someone could inherit his skills. Claiming the existence of an older disciple right now would be tantamount to slapping my own mouth, so I undid his relationship to Grandpa Jiu even if he was, in fact, an older disciple. This tyrannical use of power as a writer reflects the fact that I have no real worldly power. There's nothing that you, Ajia, can do about it.

But I still appropriated aspects of Ajia's story that were of benefit to me. For example, according to him, even the Heavenly King wouldn't have been able to catch the scabby-headed monk, if his Achilles' heel hadn't been cut. This I believed. Otherwise, why would Snow Feather bother to use the sickle? It would otherwise have been equivalent to someone removing his pants to fart. According to legend, that monk

---

13. Henry Norman Bethune (1890–1939) is a famous Canadian surgeon, a selfless humanitarian, and the most renowned Canadian in China.

even regarded armies a million strong as nothing since he could fly in and out. This I also believed.

The abbot held up the torch and said smilingly, "Excellent! Excellent! We almost wronged Benefactress Snow Feather!"

Scabby-Headed Monk laughed and said, "I knew I'd be done in by her!"

That golden top was hidden by Scabby-Headed Monk in Luoshen Monastery's well. After chasing Snow Feather out of the monastery, the abbot arranged for the well to be searched the following day. Snow Feather had told him the golden top was in the well.

Guess how she knew?

After that, Scabby-Headed Monk was sent to the reform farm at Wangjing Stockade. He escaped one night, found himself a disciple, and taught him all his skills. After that, the disciple left the mountain, on a morning reeking with blood-filled light, to seek out Snow Feather for revenge. This obviously followed too mundanely a typical plotline. But Ajia clenched his teeth and said, "So what if it was typical? If someone had cut your Achilles' tendon, wouldn't you have sought revenge as well?"

I had to tell him, "What's the fuss? You're a god after all—be more gracious!"

Ajia said, during some historical moment, two people were looking for Snow Feather. The first was a monk who'd received a revelation. His guru told him to find Diamond Maiden Cave in Liangzhou. If he could rely on the Wisdom Dakini Goddess there, he could attain the ability to fly to Pure Land in mortal form. The other was Scabby-Headed Monk's disciple, together with a lama in a red cassock. It was said the lama's Killing Technique was incomparably powerful. He was able to exterminate whatever he wanted to destroy. One night, the lama performed a type of fire offering known as the Curse of Xixia. But strangely, it did not work that time. When he meditated on it, he saw an old man smiling at him in a mountain valley of Liangzhou. Curious about the phenomenon, he decided to trek a thousand leagues to Liangzhou in order to meet the man.

Seeing me looking puzzled, Ajia explained, "Every trade has its own people. Different expertises are like different mountains. Like you writers only understand literary stuff, performers only understand performance stuff. There are many other specialties that only its own people can understand; they'd be inscrutable to people outside of their fields!"

Ajia said, "Well, during the years of great changes, a man wearing tattered clothes was walking step by step toward Snow Feather."

Chapter 7

The Old Mountain Beyond the Horizon

The "Dream Chaser" transmitted by the wind
Formed a meandering snake;
The flower pistil
Blissfully kisses
This lonely heart.

Investigation

We will now relate the story of what happened after Snow Feather stole the sheep.

After Braggart began to suspect Snow Feather, he dispatched Kuan San to investigate.

Historical Mirror of Forgotten Events records the process.

Kuan San left the huge estate. The gate of the estate was very thick. It was made of cedar, a few feet thick, fortified with steel nails and wrapped in steel—most imposing and solid. Kuan San was the militia commander. Only he could use a fast-firing rifle called something like the Water Pente Rifle. The others used firelock rifles, which required being loaded with gunpowder and iron pellets. When the trigger was pulled, fire exploded from them. Their sound was horrendous, but the distance covered was short. The rifle Kuan San used made a high-pitched crack. He was a highly skilled shooter, who could hit anything he pointed at.

Braggart announced he wanted to "fix" Snow Feather to "put her in her place." The area hadn't had any thieves for dozens of years. Once a bad custom begins, there's no stopping it. But Braggart was also afraid of Snow Feather. If she could carry a ram weighing more than a hundred pounds on her back and charge through houses and over rooftops without leaving a trace, then she could also take Braggart's head without leaving a trace. Braggart touched his head before he promised Kuan San the emerald jade pipe mouthpiece. That was something Kuan San had his eyes on for quite a while.

"Sure, I'll investigate," said Kuan San.

Look! Kuan San was on his way to investigate. He took his rifle so he could shoot the birds he'd encounter. After walking more than a hundred paces, he'd already tied the heads of more than a dozen birds onto a braided grass rope. From a distance, it looked as if he'd grown a furry tail. There were many birds on the mountain, enough for him to shoot. He'd gotten a gunpowder specialist to make bullets for him, so he'd have enough no matter how often he shot.

The village oxcarts meandered along the mountain path and looked imposing from a distance. Village houses scattered throughout the valley and looked somewhat crowded. Viewed from the mountain slope, the courtyards looked like little mahjong tiles. Diamond Monastery was unexpectedly prominent. It was so named because it was the village landmark. Down along the large valley was another stockade. It also had a monastery in which the Brilliant King God[1] was worshipped. Consequently, their stockade was called Brilliant King Stockade, or Brilliant King Clan. The two stockades frequently fought about various secular matters, and Brilliant King Clan usually won. But a hundred years ago, a rule was made by the two clans that knives could be used but not rifles. Firelock rifles were strictly forbidden to prevent severe casualties. So, although Kuan San was an expert marksman, he couldn't shoot Brilliant King Clan folks the way he shot sparrows.

The Rifle Fired

Snow Feather's house was next to the cliff on the western side of the valley. She was cooking mutton when Kuan San entered. Her blind mother asked, "Little Feather. This sheep, did you really buy it?" Snow Feather said, "Just eat it. Why ask?" Mom said, "If you've stolen it, I'd die before I'd eat it."

---

1. Brilliant King God is a variant of Diamond God. Both are Vajra deities.

Kuan San entered the house.

Snow Feather had no courtyard. The slope was right outside the door, and one could see everything at a glance. Kuan San rarely visited. Snow Feather was very famous, so he didn't expect her to be so poor: other than a stove, kitchenware, and a few weapons, there was nothing in the one-room cabin. Just a few papercuts on the walls. They looked like small fish. A stream of warmth surged into my heart. Snow Feather, who lived in an arid region and was unable to raise fish, could only raise the little fishes in her heart on her walls. This detail manifested most poignantly Snow Feather's femininity. It was precisely this that brought warmth and associations about her for people, distinguishing her from the many Dakini goddesses who had never lived in the mortal world.

Without looking at Kuan San, Snow Feather kicked at a wood stump. Kuan San knew it was an invitation for him to sit down. Mom asked, "Who came in?"

Snow Feather said nothing.

Mom said, "No matter who you are, please persuade my girl to behave herself. Ever since she was old enough to understand, I've talked and talked to her, but she still became a flying thief. My tears flowed into a stream and my eyes became blind, but she still wouldn't change. Everyone needs to eat. If someone steals from you, you'd feel bad. If you steal from others, they'd feel the same."

Snow Feather looked at Kuan San, and left the house. Kuan San followed her. They came to the slope. Snow Feather said, "Mom is ill. She wanted to eat meat."

Kuan San said, "You've transgressed. Rabbits don't eat the grass around their burrow! He wants me to 'fix' you!"

"Based on what?"

Kuan San picked up a stone and threw it into the air. The rifle fired and the stone splattered.

"Based on this. Okay?"

Snow Feather looked at Kuan San who shook the rifle and laughed. "This rifle can fire continuously."

Snow Feather stiffened and was quiet for quite a while. And then she said, "If I die, what happens to my mom?"

"It shouldn't come to that," Kuan San said, "it was just a sheep, wasn't it? Maybe you just need to apologize. Go to Braggart's house tonight. Don't be afraid, you didn't kill anyone."

"Are you afraid?" Snow Feather pressed her lips together and smiled.

"What would I be afraid of?" Kuan San yawned.

"Don't worry. I don't kill." She said.

But Kuan San did wonder: How will that Braggart "fix" Snow Feather?

Stoning

Braggart made all the preparations before nightfall. Quite a few people had gathered in the courtyard, most of them being martial arts experts, more cold-hearted than regular citizens. Braggart thought, better to have cold-hearted people.

Braggart wanted Kuan San to wait there too, but the latter thought of Snow Feather's blind mother and said, "Look—it's okay if you don't give me the pipe mouthpiece. I'm busy tonight." Braggart laughed, took the mouthpiece, and tossed it to him. It was made of emerald jade. Braggart had exchanged eight bushels of barley for it.

"What if she doesn't come?"

"She wouldn't be Snow Feather if she doesn't come." Kuan San yawned. "But don't use the rifle. You can use anything else. Clan regulations. Use the rifle, you're in the wrong!" Kuan San thought, *Snow Feather, can't say I owe you!* He poured some snuff into his palm, scooped some up with a fingernail, and inhaled. A sneeze exploded. "See you," he said, "leave the rifle out, whatever you do! Better drink cold water than lose face!"

"I know! I know! Prepare the stones!" Braggart commanded.

When Snow Feather arrived, the top of Braggart's house was already filled with stones, and the group was ready. Cripple Big, Donkey Two, Jie Big, and Old Daddy-Nine were all waiting on the roof. A pale moon hung above the house. Braggart said, "Remember, throw the stones until she's dead! Stone thieves—the clan regulation said so. Don't be afraid!"

Cripple Big asked, "Can we use some other method?" Old Daddy-Nine said, "Yeah!" Jie Big said, "Maybe a good lashing?" Donkey Two laughed playfully and said, "Or we take turns and do her?"

Braggart roared, "Shut up! Pick up the stones!" The others looked at each other and obeyed. Donkey Two said, "Sure! Whatever you say!"

Snow Feather walked up the stone steps.

Snow Feather stood in the courtyard.

"My mom wanted to eat meat," she said.

"I had no time to get it elsewhere," she added.

Braggart roared, "This isn't just about a sheep. If you wanted to eat one, you could have asked me. How dare you pull the tiger's whiskers? Where's my face?"

Snow Feather stood in the courtyard without saying a word.

"You can take advantage of the rich, but this is the Ancestral Hall! If I don't 'fix' you, I'll have no face to be the clan head. . . . Don't blame me!" said Braggart.

Snow Feather said, "I came because Kuan San told me to apologize."

"I don't want you to apologize," Braggart sniggered. "What are you waiting for?" He roared toward his back, and black shadows flew toward Snow Feather. One couldn't see what Snow Feather did, but all the stones ended up on the ground.

"Are you really going to stone me?" she asked.

Secretly shocked, he ignored Snow Feather and said in a low voice, "Stone her now! You'll all die if she doesn't!"

The stones poured down like rain. One saw many Snow Feathers in the courtyard. After a while, she still stood there. "Do you really mean to take my life?" she asked.

"Faster! What are you waiting for?" Braggart hollered in utmost amazement.

They used all their energy to throw the stones. Soon, all the stones were gone. They thought she'd be meat sauce a long time ago, but one look showed she still stood at the same place. "Are you done?" She asked.

"Are you a ghost?" asked Cripple Big.

"I don't know myself." Snow Feather replied coldly. She turned around slowly and went out of the gate. Everyone on the roof shuddered.

After a long while, Braggart said, "It was that Kuan San's fault. We should have shot her!"

He instructed the militia to take their rifles if they had one, and off they charged to Snow Feather's home like a swarm of bees. The door was tightly shut. No one dared to enter it.

"Fire!" commanded Braggart.

Bursts of fire shot into the house. Before the gunpowder smoke subsided, they dashed into the house. But no one was there.

Braggart stamped his foot and said, "Now, there'll be no more peace!"

The Downhill Winds of Old Mountain

According to *The Crazy Rambling of Ajia*, Snow Feather entered Old Mountain carrying her aged mother on her back.

Old Mountain was very far, further than one's mind. Ajia always talked about Old Mountain, but he never explained to me why it was called "old." There's nothing I can do about it. Ajia was like that—he loved to mystify.

Historical Mirror of Forgotten Events contains records concerning Snow Feather's tale with which many folks in Liangzhou were familiar. But Ajia provided aspects of the story, for me, that Liangzhou's commoners didn't know. After I "entered" the Mahamudra, I was able to communicate with Ajia. Of course, you might instead consider it as nourishment I received from *Crazy Ramblings of Ajia*. For a long period, I couldn't distinguish dream from reality. I stayed indoors for almost three months when I translated *Crazy Ramblings of Ajia*. Just as Confucius was so absorbed with listening to the music of Shao that he couldn't savor the taste of meat, I similarly forgot where I was. In time, Ajia came to life for me.

Ajia's narratives were very good—they were much better than mine—even though I'm a writer and the legendary Ajia was a nobody. He wasn't even a farmer since he had no land, no agricultural implements, and no desire to work. Back then, no one would hire Ajia as a laborer. So he went to a wealthy household during mealtimes. Its manager would say, "Come and eat!" And Ajia would eat noisily and self-righteously. Later, Ajia became a butcher. And then because of special karma, he became a guardian god. But that will be the subject of another book.

Snow Feather's home was located halfway up a slope. It was an open-style house, meaning it had no courtyard. Ajia said, "Snow Feather didn't need to have a courtyard gate. No thief in Liangzhou dared to rob her." Who was Snow Feather? Snow Feather was a queen of thieves, a grandma of thieves, a totem looked up to by thieves. All the thieves claimed to be her disciples, although few had ever seen her. According to rumor, there were some who lusted after her beauty, but it was no more than lust. One night a bachelor visited her home. He tiptoed around, the tide in his heart surged and crashed, and the itch was unbearable. He was agitated and in a state of stupefaction. Just as he was dreaming of embracing the "warm jade and soft fragrance," he felt a numbness in his eyes, and his hands and feet became sore and weak. Realizing something had gone terribly awry, he covered his eyes and felt his way down the mountain. He never regained his sight. According to the doctor, Pockmarked Wang, his pupils were pierced by extremely fine, poisonous thorns. The man was a distant uncle of Braggart. According to Ajia's analysis, the acts of vengeance Braggart inflicted upon Snow Feather were probably related to this man's blindness. Good dogs always protect their owner. Bandits always protect their own group. Beware of its master when you hit a dog! Striking a member of Braggart's family was tantamount to slapping Braggart's face. But, the scope of Ajia's analyses was very limited, since he neglected another possibility: class struggle. However, we cannot expect a spirit soaked in a thousand years of traditional culture to have received the baptism of Marxism. Right?

Snow Feather went toward Old Mountain with her mother on her back. Old Mountain was Qilian Mountain. But it wasn't the outer part of Qilian Mountain. The mountain on the outside wasn't called Old Mountain; the one on the inside was the one known as Old Mountain. There were many wolves in Old Mountain. I went to Old Mountain with my father many years ago. The valley was filled with wolves, resembling scattered flaxseeds. I thought of the wolves, which looked like flaxseeds, whenever Ajia mentioned Old Mountain.

It was the dead of night by the time Snow Feather carried her mother into the mountain. The downhill wind brayed like a donkey. Maybe you've never heard a donkey bray. But don't worry, you'll know what it sounds like when you hear the downhill wind braying. There were times though when the downhill wind didn't bray; instead, it sounded like a woman's moaning. So, you need to distinguish carefully between when it brayed like a donkey, and when it moaned like a woman. The downhill wind was like a donkey's braying the day Snow Feather carried her old mother into Old Mountain. If Ajia said the wind sounded like a donkey braying, then it must have brayed like a donkey. He was, after all, the narrator. He was as powerful as God that particular evening.

The donkey-braying downhill wind gusted at Snow Feather furiously, hoping to blow her down into the valley. If she were blown down the valley by the wind, she would've been like the old ox that became a clump of meat after tumbling down the valley. Those days, old cattle frequently tumbled down the valley. While eating fresh young grass, they'd accidentally step on a stone. The stone would roll off, and the old ox would tumble downhill with a thundering crash. At that moment, the ox must have heard a loud bang but didn't yet realize it was the sound of their own fall. Old cattle were stupid like this. That's why Mom always said I was as stupid as an old ox. The old ox would begin to roll downhill before it realized the sound's source. At that moment, it would hear wind braying like a donkey, even on a windless day. By then the ox would wise up. It would be able to tell it was the wind braying, and not a donkey. The old ox would've felt fear then since cases of old cattle tumbling down the valley happened in the village every year. This meant it would've seen its companions tumble into the valley and would realize it was tumbling there too. It would also have known its result: that it would become a mass of meat. Its hide would be tattered, its breath would stop, and it would stare at the sky with white eyes. Snow Feather had eaten the meat of old cattle, which had tumbled down into the valley. She must've also known the result of such a tumble. But she still had to carry her aged mother into Old Mountain. Such was her fate. If you don't know what fate is, then consider the following carefully: when you must do something you don't want to do, that's fate.

Snow Feather knew her fate and heaved a heavy sigh. Fearing Mom would hear her sigh, the wind immediately rolled it up to the other side of the mountain and planted it into the heart of a man called Jasper. He would fall in love with Snow Feather in the future, although it would be an otherworldly love. So, lovesickness is a planted sigh. It was even less likely that Snow Feather would've expected someone to write about her many years later. Snow Feather thought that once she carried Old Ma into Old Mountain, no one would ever find her again. She turned around and glanced. The wind was most considerate. It had erased her footprints on the mountain slope immediately. Good. Since she entered the mountain to hide from her enemies, she wouldn't want her footprints to betray her!

Ajia said, "Snow Feather shouldn't have stolen the sheep that belonged to the Ancestral Hall. Rabbits don't eat the grass around their own burrow!" Ajia said, "Braggart had wanted to 'fix' Snow Feather for quite some time." Braggart used to leave the village from time to time. Whenever he left Diamond Clan's territory, people would ask him about Snow Feather. Braggart would then think, "Shit, she's even more famous than me!" It's been a while since he'd been thinking about "fixing" her. Who told her to be more famous than he? There was, in fact, nothing she could have done. If you should ever become more famous than your boss, then you'll have to be careful because someday your boss might want to "fix" you. There are many examples of this, both within and beyond this world.

Unable to understand this, however, Snow Feather was regretful the whole time she traveled. But she kept her regrets to herself. Being strong in character, she would never have submitted to defeat. She regretted having to alarm and move Old Ma, knowing how well the latter liked to live peacefully. But they had no choice but to go to Old Mountain. I frequently thought it would've been great if Snow Feather had a husband

and a child. Then she wouldn't have been lonely, even when she had to hide in the deepest part of Old Mountain. Ajia said, "Bullshit, would she be Snow Feather then? She didn't even have a friend! Too bad she didn't burst out of a rock instead of a regular birth. She wouldn't have to take care for an old mother then! If she didn't have her old mother, she could have flown far away a long time ago. Why would she stay in Liangzhou otherwise?" I kept wanting to say, "Could she fly away from her fate?" But I didn't say it. You must know that when I listened to Ajia tell this story, I was as naive as a child and would never say anything that sounded sophisticated.

Autumn had turned cold. I remember it was an autumn day. The downhill winds of autumn were stabbing and carried fallen leaves and the honking of wild geese. During that season, the long-necked wild geese were always flying south over the village. Ajia would stand on Diamond Maiden Mountain and yell loudly:

Long-necked geese, long-necked geese flying high,
I'll get you with a stick and chomp you grilled.

Ajia sang this ditty for many years without getting a wild goose even once. Later, he taught it to me.

Snow Feather also knew many ditties, but she was in no mood to chant them. Mom was grumbling again. "Girl, why don't you bury me alive so I won't be a burden to you?" Snow Feather wiped off her own sweat and said, "Ma, where do you want to go? Do you expect me to become someone even lower than pigs and dogs?" Mom responded with a sigh. Mom was always sighing. She was always using sighs to express her feelings. Mom resented that Snow Feather was a piece of iron she couldn't forge into steel. She wanted Snow Feather to live a peaceful life; but although the tiger didn't eat people, its bad name spread. Everyone in Diamond Clan knew Snow Feather was a flying thief. Who would be willing to help a flying thief? After starving for three days, Snow Feather stole her first sheep.

Snow Feather walked toward Old Mountain, swaying from side to side. She had great strength. Once, when someone tried to take advantage of her, she climbed up a tree with a stone roller under her arm. The roller weighed more than three hundred pounds, but Snow Feather still climbed up the tree like a huge swaying long-horned beetle. In my imagination, the person swaying in the wind toward Old Mountain did resemble a fat long-horned beetle. You must have seen the long-horned beetle before. It's a strange insect. Always gave me the creeps. Back then, during summer, I'd climb trees with Ajia to catch long-horned beetles. We'd carry a bag in one hand and grab long-horned beetles' backs with the other. The beetles would slink up and down with their backs hunched, hoping to escape their fate, but ultimately they all ended up where they were supposed to go, that is, they all ended up dead. Some I tossed down the necks of village women, who shrieked, squeezed them, hurled them down on the ground, and stomped them into green mush. Some we tied with a thread and let them pull until their legs fell off. Others were eaten by cocks. Cocks didn't like those beetles very much, but would eat them if they were starving. Snow Feather, who carried her mother into Old Mountain, was very similar to the long-horned beetles. She had no idea where she would end up. Just like me: I too don't know where I'd end up. Just like humankind: humans too have no idea where they'd end up.

Old Mountain was very deep. One year, I entered Old Mountain with a daypack. I walked for twenty days, until I saw the scattered-flaxseed-like wolves in the valley. Ajia told me, "The one you entered wasn't the real Old Mountain. You were able to keep on walking after seeing wolves. They won't eat you. Packs of wolves don't ambush sheep." I said, "I've also heard the ancestors say that. They all said packs of wolves don't attack sheep. But did the wolves know this? What if they were wolves without culture, who didn't know this fact, and ate me as a snack—what then?" Ajia said, "You have a point."

Snow Feather must've seen such packs of wolves. In those days, there were many wolves. Of course, there were also many other animals. When the wolves had other food, they wouldn't eat humans. Certainly, they must've wanted to, but they were Mountain God's dogs. The Mountain God told them, "You must not eat humans." The wolves would reply, "Sure, we won't eat them." So they stared at Snow Feather and didn't eat her, even when their drooling saliva was three feet long.

To Snow Feather, the wolves were like the Ancestral Hall's ram. She wasn't afraid of them. Ajia personally saw her tear a wolf into shreds, as easily as tearing up a rag. Rumor had it that Snow Feather practiced a martial arts form known as Iron Sand Palm. After thrusting and clenching her hands into a bag of metal sand for a thousand days, she could yank off a handful of flesh when she clawed anyone. All the villagers said so. Sometimes the women would say, "Play a trick for us,

Snow Feather." And she would grab a handful of mung beans, squeeze them once, and turn them into bean flour. Of course, she wasn't afraid of the wolves.

I didn't like this detail by Ajia because I was under the impression Snow Feather practiced a martial arts form known as the Vermilion Sand Palm. There was no way she would've practiced a clumsy martial arts style like the Iron Sand Palm because those who practiced it needed thickly calloused hands. Later, *Tale of the Goddess* stated the form practiced by Snow Feather was known as the Silk Palm. As with the Vermilion Sand Palm, it was based on cultivating one's inner force. Those who practiced the Silk Palm had such soft hands the palms felt as if they would melt. That was a pleasing thought. Although I've never had an opportunity to hold Snow Feather's hand, it should be okay to imagine it. I have nothing better to do in any case.

The wolves looked at Snow Feather. They didn't look at the old woman on her back; they knew the old one wouldn't have tasted good. Old women have no fat. They only have dry skin and bones. The other woman would've been delicious. Those firm legs, in particular, would've been nice and chewy, like sheep's eyeballs. But the wolves only smacked their lips. They thought, *Who told us to be the Guardian God's dogs?*

So it was, under the wolves' stare, that Snow Feather entered Old Mountain.

And into an astounding tale she entered.

Chapter 8

The Angry Ravens

The appointed date is distant and uncertain,
The long road like a night lasting a hundred years
Gradually disappeared like Halley's Comet.
In the wind behind my back,
I'll never see the flying long hair again.

The Procession of Wolves

Snow Feather had entered Old Mountain.

Old Mountain had already become quite humid. The cloud-cypress trees swayed self-consciously in the wind like young women carrying umbrellas. There were other trees, the names of which Snow Feather didn't know. She thought of them as pine and cypress trees. Not being a botanist, she didn't feel ashamed about not knowing their names. She only recognized the weeds and bushes, such as asters, stinky chrysanthemums, and hairy shrubs. These weeds made Old Mountain feel like Old Mountain. Old Mountain's characteristic damp stench invaded her nose. One sensed a wildness there that could only be found among untamed beasts. The wolves made a procession along her way and stared at her. This was the famous valley of wolves. It was said this was also where the old wolf king's den was located. Although Snow Feather kept reassuring herself that she wasn't afraid of them, she was still concerned. Of course, she wouldn't have been afraid of the wolves if Old Ma wasn't here. But with Old Ma on her back, she couldn't help but be worried.

Should the wolves really surround them, everyone knows what the result would be. So Snow Feather began to chant a spell Grandpa Jiu transmitted to her for restraining wild animals. She had already attained a small achievement by chanting it a hundred thousand times. One day, she saw a hungry tiger and chanted the spell. In a flash, the tiger yawned and became so incredibly drowsy it fell asleep in the shade and began to snore. Later, Snow Feather transmitted the spell to Ajia, who transmitted it to me. Although it was a spell for restraining wild beasts, it could also be used on humans. But it was only useful when used on lowly people. Later, whenever I came across a low person, I would chant the spell. But I had to imagine the person as a wild beast, or a pig, or a dog. Of course, this was an injustice to pigs and dogs, as lowly people are inferior to pigs or dogs.

Snow Feather chanted the spell while walking toward Old Mountain. All the wolves yawned, and their saliva took the opportunity to escape. The stench in the air grew stronger as Grandpa Sun receded in the distance. A turtle dove chirped furiously. Pheasants dragged their long tails and danced in the air. The marmots were the funniest. They stared with their glasslike eyes and called "*guada*" now and then. Snow Feather liked to listen to their calls. While they called, they would greet each other with their hands pressed together as if performing a divination! That's how they performed it. It's said they are reincarnated from Liu Bowen[1] of the Ming dynasty and, therefore, could foretell fortunes and disasters. Usually, marmots weren't so relaxed because the wolves would be watching. Usually, as soon as the marmots left their burrow, the wolves would kick up their hind legs, leap a beautiful arc in the air, and grab a marmot in its mouth as it landed. Marmots were fat and delicious. The taste of their meat was only second to human flesh. Although wolves preferred human flesh, the Tutelary God said, "See how the marmots are always burrowing holes all over me!" So the wolves said, "Okay! We'll eat them instead!"

The marmot's cries were monotonous and dry: "*guadada, guadada.*" The cuckoo's chirpings were also heard almost imperceptibly. But the wolves were silent. They were restrained by a mysterious power. This was the effect Snow Feather sought. If so many wolves howled loudly together, Mom would have wet her pants from fear. This was one of

---

1. Liu Bowen (1311–1375) was a military strategist, statesman, and poet who lived in the late Yuan and early Ming dynasties. Military strategists were also great diviners.

Mom's problems. Whenever she was scared, the murky yellow fluid would gush out uncontrollably. The stench of urine perpetually reeked their mud house.

Without averting her eyes, Snow Feather passed alongside a procession of wolves, yawning due to her spell. A suffocating stink emanated from each wolf's mouth. Wolves were unacquainted with toothbrushes, so dregs of decaying meat studded their teeth. After even one night of hunting, a horrible stench would explode in waves from their mouths. The mountain path, which wasn't a real road, would then feel like hell. Whenever Snow Feather thought she'd have to live here for the rest of her life, she was overcome by an ambiguous emotion. Of course she wanted to be a woman. But ever since she was very little, Grandpa Jiu told her sexual desire was the root of disaster. Grandpa Jiu talked from experience. He said if he hadn't lost too much primal energy when young, he would've been able to attain the Rainbow Body. What was the Rainbow Body? The Rainbow Body was a body resembling a rainbow in that it had form when seen but was nothing when touched. It had no birth and couldn't be extinguished. Heaven might age, and earth might become barren, but the Rainbow Body would be forever incorruptible. It was the real diamond-like body. Although many folks in Liangzhou cultivated the technique for achieving the diamond body, those able to attain the Rainbow Body were as rare as ivories in dogs' mouths. Snow Feather knew sexual desire was the root of disaster. Since that disastrous root impaired her guru, Snow Feather would surely keep her distance from it.

Regretfully, most of the techniques Grandpa Jiu transmitted to her were this-worldly, rather than otherworldly. Grandpa Jiu said, "Girl, you have to observe the Buddhist vows in order to practice the otherworldly techniques." Snow Feather said, "If I don't steal, my mom will starve to death. I'll learn them after I'm done taking care of Mom." Grandpa laughed and said, "What a talented disciple I have! So you can ensure you would die after someone else! The road to the netherworld doesn't distinguish the young from the old!" Later, it occurred to Snow Feather that maybe there was something in Grandpa Jiu's words.

However, Snow Feather, who already knew that sexual desire was the root of disaster, still felt desire, particularly in the dead of quiet nights after she had consumed mutton. That mysterious flame would start to lick at her belly until her blood boiled. When this happened, she would rise, put her clothes on, and go to the courtyard. The stars would laugh loudly. But the downhill winds would wrap around her and lick at her incessantly. Although they didn't extinguish the fire in her belly, it provided a different kind of comfort. She would then practice until daybreak all the martial arts forms her master had taught her. Later, she realized that the mysterious uncontrollable fire became the greatest incentive for her martial arts practice. Whenever she thought of Grandpa Jiu, who was unable to attain the Rainbow Body because of his sexual desires, she'd heave a heavy sigh and swallow her desire-filled saliva.

The Grandpa Mao Cave

Snow Feather walked toward a hidden place only Grandpa Jiu knew about. Grandpa Jiu had meditated there for three years. A practitioner named Mao had performed austerities here for twelve years and completed the Heruka Vajra Technique. It was said he practiced couple-cultivation with a girl for many years. According to her guru, Grandpa Mao would've only been able to attain the worldly version of the technique. That was when Snow Feather realized sex could not only be the root of disaster but also be of assistance in achieving great attainment.

The cave Grandpa Mao used exclusively for his twelve years' cultivation was located halfway up one of Old Mountain's peaks. The cave wasn't big. It was circular, about three feet in diameter, and had a level floor. Many years later, a writer also visited that cave. It was a naturally formed cave, with huge rocks piled upon each other—and it was exceptionally sturdy. The opening faced south so sunlight could come in at midday. The cave's floor was quite level, like the brick bed of a farmhouse. Buns made out of mud were buried inside the cave. When broken, you'd find grains of wheat in the mud buns. Because of their age, the grains would turn into ashes upon handling. I believe they were symbolic offerings. It was said great merit must be performed to attain the Rainbow Body. And the main technique for accumulating merit was through making offerings. Of course, there were many types of offerings: for example, the offering of broadcasting truths, the offering of expending wealth, the offering of endowing others with spiritual energy, etc. In that grotto, I clearly met the Snow Feather of that time. Of course, you might think of it as just a kind of feeling. I also carried on a conversation with her. Later I wrote our conversation into an essay, but it disappeared mysteriously. I thought maybe it was because Snow Feather didn't want others to disturb that sacred cave's peacefulness. It's just as well I lost that essay. Some things have to be tossed away.

Snow Feather swayed up the mountain. The slope was extremely steep and strewn with scattered stones. One misstep and she would have ended up like the valley-tumbling cattle. By the time I visited the mountain, the path was much easier to travel because water washing down the slope had widened the path over time. But it was still so steep I panted like an ox after every few steps. By the time I visited, there were no more trees on the mountain. Even Old Mountain's whiskers had been shaved off. Although it was still called Old Mountain, the name was no longer appropriate without the whiskers. The devastating results of deforestation continued until dozens of years later. The year I went up the mountain, I only saw foul punta grass. The wolves were also all gone. Only the ravens screamed "ga ga ga" ceaselessly. In my eyes, they were no longer birds. Everyone knew ravens were dependents of the great guardian deity, Mahakala. Of course, they also ate corpses: that was another technique for releasing souls from purgatory. When the ravens finish consuming the corpses, the deceased would enter Mahakala's Pure Land. Later, I found out that wolves could also release souls from purgatory. Sometimes their consumption of the corpses' flesh was equivalent to bringing the deceased to salvation. It was said that Dakini goddesses and accomplished gurus would sometimes transform themselves into wolves in order to eat the corpses. If you don't believe me, read Geraud Duo Jizha's biography.[2] He refused to eat a corpse when his guru told him to do so but tried some later. *Aiya*, it was incomparably wonderful, and he experienced the great bliss of attaining wisdom. There were many other such stories. But I don't want to be eaten by wolves. Do you?

Obviously Snow Feather didn't want to either. She wouldn't have chanted that spell otherwise. The wolves followed her in a swarm and gathered behind her. They were all yawning and spraying their stench up the mountain. Of course, the wolves didn't know that they had bad breath. They had no such self-awareness. But of course, I do, so I'd always hold my breath whenever I approached a girl, fearing the state of my own breath. Snow Feather felt as though the wolves' stench was drowning the mountain, but nothing could be done about it. Snow Feather was unaware of how lucky she was. Nowadays, if you wanted to smell that

---

2. His dates are 1016–1198.

kind of stench, you'd have to go to the zoo to kiss a wolf. And because they're now reared by humans, their bad breath has weakened considerably. Their stifling foul stench has also become a thing of the past. Alas!

Snow Feather lowered herself and squatted when she came to relatively flat ground. She set Mom down on a rock carefully. Mom asked, "Where are we?" Snow Feather said, "Grandpa Mao Mountain." That's how I found out the name of this mountain. That cave was the Diamond Maiden Cave. According to Cripple Big, the mountain was named after a Buddhist practitioner named Mao. After Grandpa Mao completed his practices, he left a footprint on a rock next to the cave. The imprint was three inches deep. He stepped on the rock as if he were stepping on tofu. I've seen the imprint. It was as clear-cut as if it were made with a mold.

According to legend, Grandpa Mao died after he had achieved completion. People in the village held a grand funeral for him and buried him. The following day, someone came back from the city of Liangzhou and said he saw Grandpa Mao performing *Xianxiao* songs on a street there. So everyone knew that Grandpa Mao had actually become immortal. Some meddlers dug open his grave and found no corpse in his pine-wood coffin. Only a hand shovel he used for digging herbs was there. Grandpa Jiu said Grandpa Mao had attained the Illusory Body. Snow Feather thought, *After I take care of Mom until she dies, I'll also perform austerities and attain the Illusory Body.*

Mom said, "I know Grandpa Mao. He was a good man." Snow Feather said, "Have you ever met him?" Mom said, "How would I have had such great fortune? Grandpa Mao became an immortal several generations ago! But I know the restraining spell you chanted was transmitted by Grandpa Mao. I've seen him in my dreams. I asked him to cure you so you won't be a thief anymore. But he said nothing—he just smiled. The Grandpa Mao in my dreams was always smiling. You know, although not all smiling people are good, the smiling Grandpa Mao was a good person."

Snow Feather smiled then. She squinted her eyes and looked into the distance. Although the distance was blocked by the mountain, she could still see it. True distance lies within the mind. If the mind is alive, then one can see what is beyond. There were many scenes in the distance. The best of them were able to accomplish the Illusory Body like Grandpa Mao. She wanted to marry a good man and had heard sexual desire won't be the root of disaster if she learned the technique for couple-cultivation. She wanted very much to ask Grandpa Jiu about couple-cultivation but was too embarrassed to do so. The moment she felt embarrassed, Grandpa Jiu would become a silent rock. Grandpa Jiu often turned into a rock. There was nothing she could do about it. If he wanted to become a rock, there was nothing Snow Feather could do.

Mom was still muttering about how good Grandpa Mao was. Mom was like that. She was always praising people who had nothing to do with her. The people she thought were good had never given a crap about her. Snow Feather was always giving her meat to eat, and meat soup to drink, enduring the stench of her urine and not getting married on account of her. But she never heard Mom say anything good about her. Snow Feather thought, *Well, she's my mom after all! Who cares whom Mom praises, so long as it makes her happy!* Snow Feather then thought, *Mom gave birth to me. There's no need to make Mom unhappy, just to exact a good word about myself.*

Snow Feather carried her mom up the mountain on her back again, the way she carried the rams she stole. Although their weight was similar, the feeling was totally different; because the rams were to be eaten, while Mom was the eater. When she carried the ram, she felt anticipation—the anticipation of a pot of delicious meat. Although Mom was against her stealing, her way of eating was very comforting to Snow Feather. Mom never lost her appetite because the meat was stolen; she would slurp the stewed meat as though she were slurping rice soup. Snow Feather preferred tougher meat that could be chewed but would cook the meat longer because Mom preferred meat that fell off the bones. Snow Feather wanted to share Mom's happiness and tribulations and thought: *How could she be considered a good daughter if she couldn't even eat thoroughly stewed meat with Mom?* Therefore, she also slurped the meat and soup with a thunderous din.

Snow Feather considered her alternatives for finding tasty meat for Mom to enjoy. First, she had to pick the right sheep. If Mom wanted to eat a tender one, Snow Feather would get a lamb. If Mom wanted a fat one, she would bring a gelded ram. She would always watch for many days before she would zoom in and take the sheep. Besides selecting the sheep, she also considered different ways of slaughtering them. Different slaughtering techniques would create different results. If she wanted the mutton to be extra nutritious, then she wouldn't drain its blood. She would gouge a large hole in the sheep's chest, reach her hand in to grab the pumping heart, and squeeze it hard. The sheep would then roll its eyes. The mutton produced in this way was red in color, and its soup was delicious with the blood's nutrition. But usually she would hang the sheep from the house beam and pour cold water into its mouth. After a few ladlefuls of water, the belly of the sheep would start to gurgle; and after a while, the sheep would pull up its tail and spurt out manure. At first the manure would be small solid pieces, but then it would become formless. After that it would resemble thin congee, until finally only yellow water would remain. Mom loved to eat the intestines. After this type of cleansing, the sheep's belly would be clean and ready for cooking after a vigorous wash.

Snow Feather thought that even with all this, Mom still had nothing good to say about her and was always complaining about her not behaving herself! But Snow Feather wasn't upset with Mom. No moms could ever be wrong in this world. If Mom wanted to scold her, then she'll let her do so.

Snow Feather found Grandpa Mao's cave and set Mom down first. Snow Feather was wary of barging into the cave because wolves also liked to live in caves. Besides wolves, foxes, badgers, bears, and other creatures also liked caves. Sure enough, she smelt a warm stench as soon as she reached the cave's entrance. It was the smell of bears, but there were no bears in sight. They were probably seeking food elsewhere. Of all the animals, the bears were best at making dens. They would neatly spread dry branches, reeds, furs, and feathers to make a very warm nest. But Snow Feather knew that bears were difficult to deal with. A bear could break a pine tree with just one swing of its paw. Of course, Snow Feather wouldn't have been afraid of bears if Mom wasn't with her. Although bears are strong, they are stupid. If she used martial arts on them, they'd be totally hopeless. But Mom was there! Even without being bitten or slapped by a bear, Mom would collapse just from hearing a bear's roar.

Snow Feather searched and searched until she finally saw the perfect location. Near the cave was a pine tree, split into a huge fork, filled with a giant bird's nest. A few ravens were quacking there. Snow Feather tied Mom onto her back and climbed up the tree. The tree trunk was very thick and without any side branches for six feet. But the notches in its rough bark were sufficient for the nimble Snow Feather to climb. Earlier, Grandpa Jiu had taught her Diamond Finger Kung Fu. Her fingers could dig into any little notch. She used to climb up to a roof rafter this way, and charge around the rooftop every morning like a big bird. This type of kung fu should have been practiced in the middle of the night when no one was around. But one day, she got up later and was seen by Cripple Big when she was charging around on the rooftop. Cripple Big gave a loud yell and bolted into the village like a crazy dog. So the villagers found out Snow Feather's secret. Braggart said, "Only flying thieves practice that kind of kung fu." Ever since then, no one in the village dared hire her to work for them again. After her mother complained of hunger for three days, she slipped down the hill and carried back her first sheep. As I remember it, that was her first offense.

The Ravens' Anger

Relying on Diamond Finger Kung Fu, Snow Feather climbed the tree. The shocked ravens shrieked, "*gaga.*" If you've never heard ravens cry, you'd never know how sickening it felt. If you want a taste of that feeling, pluck a bristle hair from a pig, and poke your urinary tract with it. Poke and poke, and you'll feel wave after wave of an unbearable itch spreading from the spot. You'll shiver and tremble. All your pores will tighten, and you'll feel as if you're gritting sand in your mouth. Of course, you may end up not feeling this way. There's nothing one can do about that. It only means you're insensitive. Sometimes, the sensations created by poking a pig's bristle at one's heart, and at one's heel, are different. But don't be disheartened, the ravens' cries are nothing but cries of ravens after all. No matter how insensitive you are, it won't influence your career, or your sexual climax. So just continue to read.

Snow Feather was afraid of hearing the ravens cry because she could sense their anger and protest. Of course, they understood that the birdlike humans were not big birds, that they weren't there as guests, and that they intended to take over the ravens' own home. Therefore, they sang like roaring winds, whinnying horses, and the bellowing Yellow River. They sang as they fanned their huge wings. Then Snow Feather felt a surging stream of air engulfing her, aiming to turn her into a valley-tumbling old ox—no, actually two cattle. But Snow Feather wasn't afraid. The wind wafted by the ravens' wings contained the smell of warmth and the strong odor of feathers, yet it was as comforting as a mother's embrace.

But Snow Feather's mother was frightened by the ravens' calls. She said, "Girl, listen to the ravens—they mean to fight to death!" Snow Feather said, "Even if the ravens fight to death, they are still but ravens.

What's there to fear? If we hadn't climbed up the tree, we'd be dead when the bears arrive." As soon as she finished the sentence, she heard the roar of a bear underneath. Snow Feather looked down and saw two huge bloody mouths exhaling a stench. A sticky white fluid ten times thicker than milk dripped from the corners of their mouths. Startled, Snow Feather drew in her breath. *If Mom and I were any slower, they would've ended up wearing bear-fur coats*, she thought. But her fingers never relaxed. In the past, Grandpa Jiu taught her how to make her mind remain as calm as a bright mirror, even under the most terrifying conditions. To achieve this, she had meditated for two years at the Diamond Maiden Cave. Of course, her meditation was different from that practiced by Grandpa Jiu. She practiced inner kung fu to increase her inner strength and stability. Grandpa Jiu, on the other hand, tried to attain the illustrious Rainbow Body. She didn't know how many years the guru had meditated. Although he never did attain the Rainbow Body, he did accomplish longevity. So, although he was hoary as snow, his energy never declined. Even the oldest person in the village had no idea as to Grandpa Jiu's age. Ajia said, "The old man was always drinking a longevity sweet dew from the Buddhist realm! One day, Snow Feather also wanted to try the longevity sweet dew. But Grandpa Jiu pointed to his chamber pot." Full of rust spots, the spout of the chamber pot was full of some sticky stuff. What made it even more unbearable for Snow Feather was the incomparably strange stench that always exuded from the spout. For several years, she smelled that strange odor. It is said that Snow Feather never did imbibe that urine. Ajia beat his chest and stomped his foot, saying, "What a pity! That was none other than sweet dew! It might've smelled stinky, but when imbibed, it would've turned incomparably delicious! One gulp, and your age would've been extended by at least a hundred." Ajia said that he'd been searching ever since he was a child, for maybe several kalpas now, to extend the limitations of age—to attain longevity. But he never did find Grandpa Jiu. You know, Grandpa Jiu existed in the Great Calm of Bright Illusory Void. His mind was like the sky. So naturally Ajia couldn't find Grandpa Jiu, who had no attachments. Ajia said, "Snow Feather was so foolish. How could she have missed such a great karmic opportunity?" But I thought, *Wasn't Ajia the guardian deity of Liangzhou? How could he have limits on his age? I suspect he was making it all up.*

With her mind as still as a bright mirror, Snow Feather looked at the two bears and knew they were a couple. They looked naively at the big birds on the tree. Snow Feather rather liked the bears' guileless look. She thought, *Wouldn't it be great if she had a couple of innocent sons like them?* As soon as she thought of this, she felt discouraged. Oftentimes thought is the origin of vexation. It's best not to think of anything. Get drunk today if there's wine today: Who cares if one has to drink cold water tomorrow? Getting through one day is equivalent to spending two half-days. This was how the folks of Liangzhou spent the last thousand years. Normally, it's much better when one doesn't think of anything. Just eat one's fill of mutton and feel lazily happy. But when one thinks of too many things, then the mind will betray itself right away.

So she shook her head and shook away all her desires. Clarity then occupied her brain. Although the bears continued to roar, she was too lazy to care about them, and just kept on climbing up. The ravens, on the other hand, became increasingly vicious. Their energetic wings whirled and whistled like an angry surf, and their cries turned into a tumbling waterfall. Their shrieks startled the mountain's other birds and animals, such that they also craned their necks and harmonized with them. Even Ajia was alarmed. Ajia said, "That must have been when Braggart became suspicious. The next day he organized a team of thirty strongmen and began a search that lasted forty-eight days."

Mom couldn't take the ruckus any longer. She said, "Girl, let's go down. Listen to them, how can they be ravens? They've got to be demon gods! We can't afford to provoke them!" Snow Feather said, "Ma, look—the bears are underneath waiting to eat us!" Then, Snow Feather tore the collar of her jacket and pulled out a ball of cotton with which she stuffed Mom's ears. The cotton stayed there for many years, until folks swallowed her body one day, and the cotton was defecated into the Bear Lying Gully later.

Seeing that the ruckus they created had no effect on Snow Feather, the ravens switched to another tactic. Immediately, Snow Feather felt a shower pouring down from the sky. When the first drop landed on her face, she instantly smelled something stinky. She wiped it with her hand and realized it was bird droppings once she saw the sticky black stuff. According to the folks of Liangzhou, people who had bird droppings land on them would have a year of bad luck. If it happens by accident, one would have to exorcize the evil influence by either having a monk chant a sutra or chant a sutra oneself as penance. Ajia said, "The easiest method is to spit immediately and draw a cross on the ground. Next, face the sun to inhale its essence and then exhale three times into the sky, visualizing while so doing that all misfortunes have been exhaled into the Realm of Illusions." Snow Feather knew about all these, but she had already carried her Old Ma a long distance away from the ground. So even if she had wanted to, she was unable to perform the ritual. She could only practice another technique Grandpa Jiu had taught her: which was to visualize the dirty, inauspicious bird droppings as ultimate sweet dew from the Buddhist realm that cleansed her sins! She closed her eyes. Hearing the whistling bird droppings that sounded like pouring rain, she realized the ravens had reached the end of their rope. She figured that they'd run out of tricks.

Bird droppings covered their bodies. An indescribable stench spread and formed a huge lake, which churned and surged in waves. Snow Feather felt she'd turned into a leaf. She vomited twice without throwing up anything. She then opened her eyes and found her shoulders totally covered with the sticky black and white substance that made her gag and coated her with the stench. A smoky drunkenness enveloped her head. She turned her head and saw Mom's face covered with bird droppings. The bears under the tree had fled some distance away. They must have found the bird droppings unsavory as well. At some point, mist rose on Old Mountain. Wave after wave of white fog drifted from the valley. The wolves' lingering howls surged like an ocean tide. The insects' chirping sounds turned into little spheroids. Fortunately, although the bird droppings were disgusting, once released, they couldn't be re-created anytime soon. Seeing that hard as the ravens tried, they could only squeeze out some stinky air, Snow Feather pressed her lips together and smiled. She then said loudly, "I thought you were tougher. How could those little droppings of yours be of avail to me?" I said to Ajia, "This doesn't accord with Snow Feather's character. She wouldn't have used such literary language as 'be of avail to me.'" Ajia laughed and said, "So you want her to say, 'You think you can fuck my cunt?'" I scolded him for using dirty language, and he sealed his lips.

Because of the heavy fog, one couldn't tell if Grandpa Sun had reached the West. But the ravens' shrieking made it feel like evening. You've probably heard the line of this lyric: "withered vines, old tree, ravens in the evening"? That's right, that was precisely the impression of that particular moment, except for the sensation of extreme peacefulness. As Snow Feather approached the nest, the ravens became increasingly wild. They shrieked until they became hoarse and squeezed until they had exhausted their droppings. Because they'd depleted all their tactics, they became angry out of embarrassment. A very thin raven charged at Snow Feather, flapped her head with its wings, and tickled her. The raven had obviously mistaken its own identity and thought of itself as a black eagle, with a muscle knot on its wing. A knock on the head from the wing of a black eagle could, of course, create a blue-and-black bump the size of a wine cup! What's a raven? "Aren't you just a raven? Snow Feather laughed sweetly. But Mom shouted, "Girl, the old bird is attacking me!" Sure enough, another black bird was aiming at her mouth this time. Greatly shocked, Snow Feather figured it wouldn't be good if it succeeded in attacking Mom's eyes. She'd heard birds like most to eat the eyeballs of animals. Ajia also liked to eat them. As a result, I always provided a few eyeballs whenever I made offerings to him. Aside from that, he also liked to eat the inner organs of animals. Although Ajia wouldn't grumble if I should forget to make offerings of them, but then he wouldn't work as hard at fulfilling my requests. "Isn't that so, Ajia?" Ajia turned red from embarrassment. He can swindle others with those tricks of his, but he can't deceive me. Actually, people and gods are the same. Those who partake of someone's food will speak well of the provider, and those who take from another will feel that he owes that donor. So long as your offerings are good, any god will help you.

The black birds charged at Snow Feather. But this time they picked the wrong target. Although her eyes were as bright as stars, they weren't created to feed ravens. Seeing a black dot hurl at her like the wind, Snow Feather freed her right hand and grabbed the bird in midair. She wanted to tear the bird to shreds to warn its companions, but her left hand was still holding on to a pine branch! Therefore, she opened her mouth and bit off its head with one bite. A moist warmth rushed into her mouth. As she was very thirsty, she took a few gulps. Mom asked, "What are you drinking?" She replied, "Blood of the old bird." Mom shuddered and said, "Forget it, I'm not having any." Having carried Mom for several hours already, Snow Feather was hungry. She hadn't intended to eat the bird, but her mouth couldn't be controlled. It crushed the bird's head and swallowed the pieces. Her intestines took the opportunity to growl loudly. She looked at the blood-spurting neck and opened her mouth wide. Her throat contracted actively—in a few gulps, that sticky fluid was sucked into her belly. A scorching heat rose from her abdomen, energy swelled into her limbs. But immediately after that, she vomited a few times without throwing up anything. I complained to Ajia, "This is not a nice description. It's destroyed the beautiful image of Snow

Feather. You can't ruin Snow Feather like that just because you yourself consume raw flesh with fur and blood." Ajia laughed weirdly. I'm quite certain he must have transferred his own experiences to Snow Feather.

Ajia said, "Well then, I'll do another version."

Ajia said, "Rationally, Snow Feather wanted to swallow the raven, but emotionally, she was unable to do so. Emotionally, she was unable to eat that black bird." The black bird struggled, creating tiny bubbles in the sticky black fluid. She wanted to throw the black bird toward the ravens; but the rational Snow Feather said, "Keep it. Mom hasn't eaten yet!" When she left, she brought the implements for making fire. She would grill the raven for Mom when she had the time. Although the taste wouldn't be comparable to thoroughly stewed mutton—one picks the firewood of whichever mountain one happened to land on—survival was their priority. She stuffed the writhing bird into her bosom, and readied herself for the ravens' next ambush. Little did she expect them to have flown high and far already, where they shrieked and circled in the sky. And in no time at all, they all darted into the clouds.

Snow Feather heaved a sigh of relief. She looked down again at the bears. They were staring at her adoringly, the way innocent girls worshipped their singer idols.

Rising Black Smoke

What Snow Feather didn't know was that when she and the ravens were fighting over their nest, Braggart had already led a group of people to her house and burned it. The rising smoke writhed like pythons, and its pine beams crackled like grilled fleas. This was equivalent to chasing Snow Feather out of Diamond Clan. Everyone heaved a sigh of relief. They all remembered that wintry evening, when Snow Feather begged at all the households with her mother on her back. Back then, who would have known she was the renowned flying thief of Liangzhou?

Ajia said, "There were a lot people who didn't know!" With a strange look, he asked me, "Do you know why she became a flying thief?" I said, "So she could feed her mother!" Ajia wrinkled his nose a few times and said, "You call yourself a writer? This was what everyone said. But let me tell you, Snow Feather stole for nothing else, except for one reason. What was it? I'm not going to tell you unless you submit to me." I laughed, "Submit to you? You are still rolling in the mire of life and death—why should I submit to you?" Ajia smiled embarrassingly and said, "Well then, I won't tell you the secret."

Infuriated, I said, "I, this old man of yours, don't care!"

No one expected the flying thief Snow Feather to end up living in a house on the slope of Diamond Clan's mountain. One day, Braggart went to the city and offered the whereabouts of Snow Feather to the police commissioner. The commissioner, however, waved his hand and said, "I know, I know, she's a righteous thief!" As to how she was righteous, he did not explain.

Consequently, many legends emerged in Liangzhou.

The most famous of them was the story about that golden cupola in Luoshen Monastery.

The Birds' Nest

Snow Feather finally climbed into the birds' nest, which looked small from afar, but was in fact quite large up close. She now realized why the ravens struggled so vigorously. It turned out there was a pile of eggs in there. Snow Feather was very happy. She said, "Ma, we have something delicious!" Mom didn't say anything. She just smacked her lips. Snow Feather moved all the eggs into a corner and undid the waistband that tied her mom. She then picked her up the way one would pick up a baby and placed her in the fork of the tree. She said, "Ma, the old birds were so smart! This nest is so solidly built—just like the hemp shoes you braid—each knot is perfectly hooked into the other." Mom said, "How you create evil karma! They were living here happily, until you seized their nest!" Snow Feather said, "Stay here for a few days first. Let me think of a way to get the bears' den." Mom sighed and said, "Why can't you live peacefully?" Snow Feather said, "Ma! I do want to live peacefully, but would people let me?"

Snow Feather tied Mom onto a fork of the tree. She picked a large sturdy fork, broke many large pine branches, and made a big nest that was based on the bird's nest. Fortunately, the treasure bag she brought had a lot of horsetail hair. By braiding and tying the branches together, the nest became large and sturdy. Even if Mom wanted to roll about, she would stay within the pine branch nest.

The small bird's nest would be used for storage.

Snow Feather broke a few eggs, told Mom to open her mouth, and poured them in. Mom hadn't had anything to drink all day. So she gulped them down as soon as the eggs entered her mouth. After having fed her a few of them, Snow Feather said, "Let's be frugal with them. Let me grill the old bird first." She struck the "fire sickle" and lit a cotton ignitor. She then plucked a handful of twigs, lit them, and left the large nest. When she reached a fork beneath, she broke some dry pine branches, lit them, took out the dead raven, and grilled it until the sky was filled with the smell of burnt feathers.

Mountain wind raged. The pine branches burnt quickly, and the bird feathers scorched into a clump. She tore off the clump of feather; the meat underneath was barely yellow. She bit into it, still streaked with blood. She had a mind to go back down the tree to continue grilling it, but the two big bears were crouched outside their cave. After witnessing the big nest-seizing fight, they realized these humans were still a threat to them and so continued to be vigilant. Snow Feather knew the bears' paws were sturdier than her brain. So she chomped on a piece of raven meat and swallowed it. A silky sensation slid down her throat. She climbed back up into the big nest and stuffed the bird into her Mom's hands, saying, "It's not very well cooked. Swallow whatever and make do right now, I'll cook it better for you tomorrow!" Mom took a bite and tried for quite a while to tear off a piece but had no success. So she said, "I ate the eggs and am not very hungry. You go ahead and eat it!"

After taking a few bites of the raven meat, she came out of the big nest and realized it was nightfall and getting dark. The downhill wind raged more fiercely. The fog disappeared, and the valley was filled with innumerable moving black dots. She realized they were wolves. She looked in the direction of home but could see no sign of it. Heavy sorrow filled her heart. She envied those who could live peacefully. But frequently, one can't control fate. Mom always said, "When the rock is too big, walk around it." Since the power of Braggart was as great as heaven, she had better avoid him. She didn't want to aggravate her existing problem and become a wanted criminal. Even though she was a flying thief, she had only stolen a few sheep—that was all. Mom had become the entirety of her existence. All she wanted was for Mom to eat and drink well during her remaining lifespan: that was all!

She discovered this was a good place with many wild animals. So long as there were wild animals, survival wouldn't be a problem. Although that big nest couldn't shelter them from wind and rain, it could serve as a temporary resting place. The cloth bag she hung on the tree's fork before she climbed up was swinging in the wind. It held a cooking pot, bowls, weapons, and other things in there. If she could think of a way to seize Diamond Maiden Cave, mother and daughter could conceivably live like immortals there—where there was no one who hated them or wanted to take advantage of them.

She heard the wolves howling—long howls. The sky darkened. One couldn't see any stars, so it must have been cloudy. The wind wasn't piercing, but still the tree shook. Fortunately, the nest was sturdily built. The location was also well chosen. Hard as the wind shook the tree, the nest remained intact. The only problem was that it was a bit too small. When she joined her mother there, neither of them could move. She wanted to build another nest. There was a section underneath the nest that had a fork with three branches. Although it was not as good as this first location, it was also very sturdy. She thought: *Let me build a nest there when I have more time.*

Before it got completely dark, she climbed down the tree to get the cloth bag containing her "household goods." She felt a little worried about them when she thought of the bears. There was no way the pot, bowls, and other things would survive a bear sitting on them. The iron cooking pot, in particular, was indispensable for her Mom with her poor teeth. After cooking for half a day in that pot, even the tart, sour raven meat would taste as good as rice soup. Snow Feather climbed the pine tree, put the cloth bag in one of its forks, and took out the steel dagger. She had a machete, but she'd thought it too heavy, and so buried it in Big Slope's dry sand. She now regretted not having brought it. Although the dagger was sharp, it wasn't as easy to use as a machete. Living in the lair of wild beasts, a machete would have helped embolden her.

Snow Feather stuffed the sharp dagger, wrapped in a leather sheath, into her bosom and pulled out a cable grip. She cut many branches, fastened them with rope, and made them into the shape of a nest. It was already dark. She thought she would make do for the night and continue the next day.

She entered Mom's nest again and heard her light snoring. Although she knew the nest was very sturdy, she nevertheless added a security rope around Mom's waist. She also took two sheepskins from the cloth bag, and covered Mom's upper body with one and her legs with the other. Then she returned to her own tree fork. This was when she discovered her mistake. She had several sheepskins at home. Although they weren't tanned, they were nevertheless sheepskins. But she'd only brought four of them. If she'd brought all twelve of them here, she could just throw them onto the tree fork right now and create the best accommodation in the whole world. But at the time, she just wanted to travel light and so buried them along with the machete. Fortunately, the sand there was dry, so she didn't have to worry about insects.

The sky had become completely dark. Clusters of green lights wavered in the valley. They were the eyes of wolves. There were also a few green lights at the entrance of Diamond Maiden Cave, so Snow Feather knew the bears weren't asleep either. They must have been watching the two bird-humans in the tree. The wind raged more fiercely. The moist odor, however, had disappeared; yet her stomach felt queasy. She knew it was caused by hunger. She was very tired. The mountain wind on her sweaty body was sickeningly chilly. A tremendous silence and clamor pervaded the dark night and "seasoned" her like soy sauce. She thought of an old man in an even more remote mountain. Of course she wouldn't dare call him an old man. He was her guru. Known as Grandpa Jiu, this man had many gurus himself. Each of the gurus had taught him a secret technique, and each told him to find a good disciple for that technique, lest it be buried with his coffin. It was said, Grandpa Jiu found several disciples. Monk Wu got his Black Dragon Execution Technique; a man known as Black Madman received the Dzogchen.[3] There was also a "Five Diamond Techniques of Niguma," part of a very complicated treelike system, the central trunk of which was the Bright Mahamudra. Grandpa Jiu regarded that technique as the pupils of his eyes. He eventually transmitted it to a monk of both superior learning and character. Many years later, it was transmitted to a writer. Needless to say, that writer was none other than me.

According to Grandpa Jiu's prediction, the writer would be the most powerful among all of his disciples. Through transmitting culture, he could spread truth to the Buddhist world, and those who would gain enlightenment through him would be as numerous as the stars. Ajia said, "Grandpa Jiu told me this personally." I believed him only partially. Ajia was originally only a Ghost of Great Strength. Because of his subjugation by Grandpa Jiu, he was transformed from being a local guardian god to

---

3. The highest technique in Esoteric Buddhism for attaining Buddhahood.

being a protective god of Shangpa Kagyu. This transformation is not to be underestimated, however. While the former was the equivalent of the Monkey King of the Flower and Fruit Mountain, the latter was equal to the Practitioner Sun who traveled west to obtain the scriptures.[4] While the former was just a spirit, the latter could obtain enlightenment. His position as a protective god of Shangpa Kagyu enabled Ajia to enjoy offerings aside from the local specialties of Liangzhou during the thousand years thereafter. Consequently, Ajia's closeness to me involved a certain amount of self-interest. Without my pen, very few people would know about him, which would mean those making offerings to him would be even more scarce. That's when you realize it's sometimes great to be a writer because writing gives you the right to speak; even spirits would sometimes want to ingratiate themselves with you. But I also wondered if the "writer" mentioned by Ajia, in fact, referred to Ajia himself. I've discovered that the Ajia who would merge with his characters when characterizing them, tended to show off purposely, in the pose of a real writer.

Sure enough, Ajia winked and said, "Grandpa Jiu once gave me a classic titled, *The White Lotus Sutra*. According to this sutra, a layman named Gyawa Pelwa will be born not long thereafter. His name was a transliteration from Tibetan. It referred to a man with wisdom resembling a rainbow across the sky, who would inherit culture, and proliferate and advance it with time. He would have great spiritual powers, great wisdom, and tremendous powers for subjugation. Whether heavenly beings above or beasts below, all would benefit from him. The sutra also said although Gyawa Pelwa would appear as a layman, he would also transmit holy teachings. Furthermore, he would be skilled at being artful and settling for what was convenient. Of all the pure practitioners, none wouldn't benefit from the dew of his techniques, and be blessed and empowered by his compassion, and thereby attain the holy way."

I assumed Ajia had thought of a different way of flattering me, since he obviously knew my ritual name. Unexpectedly, however, after he'd mentioned the prediction, he asked me shyly, "Could you train me to become a 'Gyawa Pelwa'?" I laughed until I was breathless.

---

4. The Monkey King in the renowned novel, *Journey to the West*, was the head of a group of monkeys before he was recruited to help Tripitaka obtain Buddhist scriptures from India.

Judging from the within-the-world value system, Snow Feather was the least accomplished of Grandpa Jiu's disciples, even though she was the most famous. Almost all the folks in Liangzhou knew of her. Almost all thieves, that is, "gentleman on the beam," adored her. In the eyes of the secular world, her fame was even greater than that of Grandpa Jiu since he always lived apart from the mortal world. Although he lost too much primal energy through dissipation during his younger days and consequently was never able to attain the Rainbow Body; but he, who had already completed the great attainment of longevity, was in no hurry. He wasn't in a hurry to die since he was always dissolving himself into a state of meditation for no one knew how many years. According to Grandpa Jiu, a Dakini Goddess predicted that one of his disciples would attain the Rainbow Body. As I remember, the day Snow Feather completed her practice of worldly kung fu, Grandpa Jiu was suddenly inspired to transmit to her the secrets for practicing the technique for attaining the Rainbow Body. When Snow Feather found out the technique of practice consisted of meditating perpetually like Grandpa Jiu, she said, "I don't want to learn it."

Grandpa Jiu asked in surprise, "Why not?" Many people exhausted ways of ingratiating themselves with him to learn this secret of his. But like a foolish person who's eaten an iron weight, his heart was hardened in his resolve against transmitting it. He would say, "Why would one pour a lion's milk into a chamber pot?"

And here Snow Feather actually refused to learn it?

Snow Feather said, "I need to take care of my mom." That was her only reason.

Grandpa Jiu said, "Your mom will eventually die." Snow Feather said, "It's the law of heaven that a daughter should take care of her mom."

Grandpa Jiu heaved a heavy sigh. He realized Snow Feather was the least selfish of all the people he'd ever met.

He said, "You've ruined your karma. You shouldn't have gone against your guru's advice."

And then he added, "It's okay to ruin one's karma. Karma is only karma. When one's heart changes, then karma will change anyway."

And he also said, "Someday you'll regret having refused this offer."

Sure enough, during a deep night when all was quiet, Snow Feather suddenly discovered a huge black hole called death staring at her. Grandpa Jiu knew she regretted it. But he said instead, "Go! Go find permanence! When you find it, I'll transmit the technique to you."

The Night Air as Cold as Sea Water

Snow Feather woke up in the middle of the night. The mountain wind fluttered her sheepskin. The night air, cold as seawater, seeped through her. Only the parts of her covered by the sheepskin weren't cold. She figured Mom must've also been cold, but Snow Feather didn't regret not bringing the other sheepskins. Often, if it's useless to regret, then one just shouldn't.

After one night, her eyes had gotten used to the darkness. Although there was no moon, she didn't feel it was all that dark. The sky to the east had a splash of lonely whiteness. Although the wind had died down, the quivering night air felt even more palpable. Wave after wave of noises wafted through the night air, most of them were discernible to her. The long howls that sounded like wailing were those of wolves. The ones sounding like beggars singing the *lianhualuo* tunes were those of marmots. The cries of foxes had a foxy charm, and those made by wild boars sounded simple-minded. But the most prominent of them was the ruckus of insects covering the entire night sky, like a tangled ball of mosquitoes and gnats. The mountain valley was a performance stage for all sorts of actors. The mountains were their audience with propped-up ears. It was a vague, gigantic impressionist painting, with light and dark patches. Indescribably magnificent! Snow Feather loved all this. She'd also enjoyed this type of life when she stayed at Grandpa Jiu's place. Grandpa Jiu called this "heavenly" music. Although Snow Feather hadn't read much, she understood that term. She knew that, aside from this term, nothing else could express the flavor of this sound. She used to miss her life in the mountain when she lived at Diamond Clan. Although it was arduous, it was free. It was tiring physically, but not mentally. The birds, the animals, and the insects, were much less complicated than people. After having lived for more than twenty years, she now realized that in this world, the best were people, and the worst were also people.

At some point, the stars emerged. The stars in the mountains hung low—one could reach out and pluck them. The entire night sky made a *huahua* sound to accompany the music of the various animals! Snow Feather was gradually melted by the sounds and turned into night air herself. This was a technique Grandpa Jiu taught her. It was called Sky Yogic Practice. She frequently turned herself into the sky.

She heard Mom moan. It was a very light sound, but Snow Feather still shuddered. She figured it must be too cold for Mom. She took her sheepskin and climbed into Mother's bird nest. The nest was filled with the familiar, warm scent of Mother. Mom always said that a woman constitutes the home. When one is little, home is wherever Mom is. When one grows up, home is wherever one's wife is. Now that Mom was in this bird nest, the nest had become home.

Mom continued to emit the smell of home among the already familiar homey odor. Mom must have been dreaming. She must have been dreaming of eating thoroughly stewed mutton. Sometimes she slurped, sometimes she smacked her lips, sometimes she chewed. Snow Feather thought, *I'll have to set a trap tomorrow to catch us a wild animal. I'll cook it until the meat falls off from the bones for Mom.* She covered her mother with the sheepskin.

Fighting the Bears

The next day it rained. The sheepskins were soaking wet, and Mom coughed continuously. Snow Feather dug up some wild ginger root and made tea with it to help Mom get rid of the cold. Then she thought, *It would be safer to live in a cave than in a tree. I've got to think of a way to get the bears to move.* That cave was originally hers—well, not really hers. But in terms of precedence, she did discover the cave first and had stayed there earlier for three years. According to custom, she would've been considered the cave's owner. So she wasn't being completely unreasonable in wanting the bears to move.

This shouldn't have been difficult, but Snow Feather wanted the bears to move voluntarily—without being harmed—which made it much more difficult. This cave was a superior dwelling. It was good for getting out of the heat in summer, and for hibernating in winter—of course, assuming Braggart and others wouldn't discover it. Why would the bears give up such a wonderful place easily? If not done properly, the bears could be so angered she would no longer be able to live in peace herself!

The bears also came out of the cave. They looked first at Snow Feather and then at the treehouse.

Snow Feather tested the direction of the wind and decided to get some reed grass to smoke them out. Hopefully, the bears would be sensible enough to move.

Once decided, she began to cook the black mountain goat she had trapped. She cooked an entire potful. She planned to cook the pieces in the pot, until the meat fell off the bones, for Mom. Mom liked stewed meat. For herself, however, she cut some meat into small pieces and skewered them with tree branches then barbequed them until the meat sizzled and the blood was almost cooked. This was a good way of eating. This way, one could live a long time in the mountain without eating greens and worry about getting scurvy. She believed the bears wouldn't move willingly, and she expected a fight. She wanted to eat as much as possible so she would have the strength to deal with the potential fight.

After eating the meat, Snow Feather collected a bundle of reed grass. She picked a location after calculating the direction of the wind and lit it. She then covered it with animal manure, so that it would only form smoke but not flare up and burn quickly. Thick smoke rolled straight into the bears' den and created a string of coughs sounding like those made by the elderly. And then, the male bear came out of the cave and roared at Snow Feather. It was a low rumble with a suppressed sense of anger, combined with a hint of pleading. Snow Feather could tell that the bear thought she'd created the smoke unintentionally. The bear was basically saying, "Hey, what do you think you're doing? Look, you're smoking me!"

Without heeding the bear, Snow Feather continued to feed reed grass into the fire. The smoke became increasingly dense. Thick plumes of smoke poured straight into the cave like a cork that was going to plug it up. Now, the female bear also came out of the cave. More congenial in character, the female bear just coughed. It did not roar. By now, the male bear could tell Snow Feather wasn't transgressing unintentionally and that it was an intentional provocation. After roaring a few times in a low voice and noticing how his opponent ignored it, the male bear charged at her. Snow Feather waited for the male bear to approach before she dodged lightly.

The bear swung at her continuously several times. Snow Feather only dodged; she didn't attack. After just a few rounds, she realized she'd had at least five opportunities to kill her opponent. In the past when Snow Feather killed a bear, she would stab its ear with a dagger. It would kill the bear instantly and also enable her to preserve the entire bearskin. She'd stab when the bear swung at her and missed. But this time, she didn't want to kill the bear so readily. Since she hadn't fought for quite a while now, she wanted some excitement. Although she'd experienced danger frequently in this wilderness, she still felt lonely and now wanted to practice with an opponent with whom she could have a contest of both intellect and strength. Just to pass time.

Snow Feather began to display her talents and fought with the bear, the way a cat played with a mouse. Maybe, it shouldn't have been considered a fight; it was more appropriately teasing. After swinging at the opponent in vain continuously, the bear became extremely angry. It swung at the little pine trees nearby and smashed several. The female bear only observed the fight. It did not join in.

After swinging in vain several times, the male bear became smarter. Realizing that this person wasn't easy to deal with, it ceased to make a fool of itself and simply breathed heavily. Snow Feathered added some reed grass to the fire again. But the wind changed its direction unexpectedly. Although the smoke was thick, it wafted in the opposite direction from the cave.

The female bear roared. The male bear then left Snow Feather and went into the cave. Snow Feather was in no hurry. The weather wasn't very cold in any case, and she was hoping to have some more fun with the bear.

When she climbed back up the tree, Mom said, "Don't seize their den. Go look somewhere else tomorrow and find another cave. Everyone would be the same, if you robbed their home, where would they go?" Snow Feather thought, *It might be just as well. Of course it would be good if I find another cave. If not, I can always deal with the bears later.*

The Midwifery Tale

One night several days later, the female bear howled all night. It howled most wretchedly. The male would come beneath the tree now and then and made a sound in a soft voice, as if it was pleading. Mom said, "Maybe the female bear is sick?"

When the sky was barely lit, they heard the male bear's guileless voice beneath the tree again. Snow Feather took a look and saw the bear watching her with its raised face, wearing an imploring expression. She said, "Let me see what this is about." Her Mom didn't stop her, she just said, "Be careful." Judging from its voice, the bear wasn't ill-willed. But she still took her dagger, just in case.

Seeing Snow Feather climb down the tree, the male bear cried out again and went straight to the cave. She could hear the female bear's piteous howls in the distance. Snow Feather entered the cave and smelled a strong odor of blood. There was a pool of blood on the ground, and the female bear was rolling in it. Snow Feather realized the female bear was having trouble giving birth. As soon as it saw her, it stopped rolling and stared at her with woeful eyes. Upon seeing those eyes of absolute purity, Snow Feather felt like crying. She thought, *Maybe it was a breach birth*. Many women in the village died of giving breech births. Everyone said they were killed by Bloody Ghosts. It was said those who died from childbirth would also turn into Bloody Ghosts seeking substitutes.

Snow Feather was very worried. Having never married and given birth, she knew nothing about midwifery; so she retreated from the cave. When the female bear saw her leave, she screamed very loudly, as if she had lost all hope. The male bear, on the other hand, pleaded with her in a low voice. She pointed to the tree and said, "Let me go find Mom." The bear seemed to have understood her and followed her like a guilty child.

Snow Feather climbed up the tree and told Mom about it. Mom said, "Try to turn the position of the fetus so that it's correct." Snow Feather said, "I don't know what position is correct and what's not." So Mom told her to carry her on her back to the cave. The male bear that followed them still looked terrified. Snow Feather discovered that bears actually had human emotions!

Although the male bear seemed to be docile, Snow Feather still feared it might change suddenly. Her heart beat like a drum. The cave wasn't large, so she wouldn't be able to use her martial arts skills the way she could outside. There wasn't even enough space for dodging in there. So it was really quite dangerous! She grasped the handle of the dagger tightly and was absolutely vigilant. But as soon as she saw the expression on the male bear's face, she felt herself rather despicable. The expression through the male bear's eyes was clearly that of a terminal patient looking at a divine physician!

The female bear moaned. Mom tried to feel its abdomen. Her stroking must have brought tremendous comfort to the bear, which lowered the sound of its cries. It cocked its ears to listen to the stroking. The male bear also stopped breathing. Snow Feather was very fond of its guileless look. She was even somewhat envious of the female bear.

After stroking for a while, Mom slowly moved the position of the fetus. Snow Feather took the opportunity to look at the cave. Bears are very good at fixing their homes. They cushioned their den with dry grass. Although the den was disheveled from the rolling of the female bear, one could still discern the work they'd done. Grandpa Jiu had always said,

"When you go to the wilderness, you have to learn from the animals. Animals know *fengshui* the best. The places they build their dens always comply with *fengshui* principles. They're always near a water source, away from evil winds, but with good air circulation." Grandpa Jiu used to say, "A staunch eagle wouldn't stand on a bent branch, a ferocious tiger wouldn't perch itself at a disadvantaged spot, a spiritual being wouldn't reside at a foul locality." Snow Feather thought, *Grandpa Jiu was right.*

After turning the fetus for a bit more, Mom patted the female bear's rump a few times, signifying for it to walk around. However, the female bear didn't move. The male bear roared at her; only then did she rise, tremoring. She was exhausted from the pain. She faltered and moaned as she walked. A stream of blood flowed to the ground. Mom smiled while panting. Judging from the looks of it, the position of the fetus was probably correctly turned!

The female bear's moaning became louder until she was yelling. Snow Feather's gums felt sore. The stench of blood whirled into her chest in waves. Her heart was filled with an incredible discomfort, so she walked out of the cave. Grandpa Sun had just risen to the treetops, and a thin layer of mist wafted in the valley. The few days in the mountain resembled many years. She had experienced many difficulties. The strange thing was, she always felt a pair of gloomy eyes staring at her from somewhere in the sky, which made her very uneasy.

The howling of the female bear became ever more intense. The male bear also roared. Snow Feather could sense joy in the latter's voice. As soon as she turned around, she saw a squirming mass landing on the ground.

The story of Snow Feather and her mother helping the bear give birth was very popular around Liangzhou. It was also recorded in *Historical Mirror of Forgotten Events.*

According to legend, the bears became Snow Feather's friends thereafter and helped her in various ways. This will be related later.

Practicing Kung Fu

The brightness in the east gradually thickened. A swath of red spread the way blood would in water. Rivulets of blood squirmed like roving snakes. After writhing three or four times, they twisted the white patch into a ball of red clouds. She remembered a morning when the sky was filled with rivulets of blood just like this one. That was the morning she offended Braggart.

It was time for her to practice her martial arts skills. She usually got up even earlier. During the summer, she trained during the hottest days, and during the winter, she trained during the coldest days. She would never stop moving and chanting.[5] Grandpa Jiu commented that she could really endure hardship. But the way she saw it, there was no hardship! She only felt joy, not hardship, when she practiced. As for hardship, she only felt it when she first began practicing. Later, the joy increased, and the hardship lessened until, gradually, there was no hardship—she only felt joy! She felt somewhat tired because she'd carried Mom on her back for quite a while the day before, so she got up a little later than usual. She was also delayed from relishing the heavenly music. She carried her treasure bag on her back and climbed down the pine tree. During the years she lived here in seclusion, she had leveled a piece of land on top of the mountain for practicing martial arts. That was where she headed.

The sounds of the beasts diminished. Those that sought food were satiated; those that sought mates were also satiated; those that needed to find release had also found satisfaction. The beasts should all take a rest now. Although green lights frequently appeared by the sides of the path, Snow Feather wasn't afraid. She knew the nature of wild animals. They also feared humans. As long as you didn't invade their territories, they would leave you alone. All the animals here had their own territories. The wolves had those that belonged to the wolves. Of course, the wolves' territories could also include small animals and insects, just as the officials of the human world would have subordinates. The masters of the territories would allow animals smaller than themselves to roam there. They would even refrain from eating the latter unless they were starving. Animals used their urine to mark their territories. Snow Feather remembered that the area she would pass through to get to the top of the mountain used to be within the domain of two pythons. Back then, she used to see them with their heads turned up to the sky during early morning or late evening. Each time they inhaled, the passing birds would inadvertently drop into their mouths. Fortunately, they did not harm humans. Whenever Snow Feather passed by their cave, they would stare

---

5. She would chant lyrics that served to remind her of the different moves.

at her with their red eyes. It was as if they had signed a friendly treaty with her; she and they passed through those years without threatening each other.

Snow Feather took a look when she passed by the pythons' cave. Although she couldn't see what was in there, she was still able to sense the familiar scent that only old friends would have. So she decided the pythons were still there. Snow Feather was very happy, although she did blame them for not doing a good job of guarding her cave for her by letting the bears make their lair there. But then she thought, *How would they have known you'd ever come back again!*

Snow Feather yelled "*hey!*" into the cave as a way of saying hello to them. The cave remained silent, however. She knew the pythons were lazy bums and were always too lazy to come out before Grandpa Sun's rays shone on their backs. But she knew they must've been aware of her presence. Pythons sleep with their heads on the ground and could detect any vibrations.

The east was much brighter now. She could vaguely see some animal dung at the top of the mountain but didn't feel like dealing with the matter. She just went through all the martial arts routines Grandpa Jiu had taught her. She liked most the Seven-Starred Mother and Son form and the Eight-Step-Turn form. These were the "gourd ladle" forms, meaning they were essential routines. The folks of Liangzhou had a saying, "If you know the Seven-Starred Mother and Son and the Eight-Step-Turn, you can fight throughout the world and never be blocked," but no one had ever seen what they looked like. The most popular forms in Liangzhou were mostly the Ten Rows of Hands, Separating-Hands and Eight-Quick-Ones, Six Harmonious Whips, among others Snow Feather was too lazy to learn. She preferred using more time to practice the martial arts form of weightlessness. She remembered how back then Grandpa Jiu would get her to dig a hole up to six feet deep and fill it with sand. Wearing an outfit filled with sand, and with sandbags fastened to her legs, she would stand in the sand pit, scoop out two handfuls of sand and then jump out of the pit. She would keep on scooping out sand and jumping out, until the pit began to deepen unnoticeably to a foot and then to three feet. Until finally, she could fly out of the six-foot-deep pit effortlessly. This was basic training. Later, Grandpa Jiu gave her a wooden sword and had her stab monkeys. She enjoyed chasing the monkeys among the pine trees all day, until soon after all the monkeys moved away. Although she did not intend to harm them, they all escaped without a trace from being embarrassed by their own clumsiness. And even later, the guru had her stab flying birds until she could do whatever she desired. Grandpa Jiu then said, "Okay. You've attained some accomplishment. Although it is not of a quintessential caliber, it could be considered a minor accomplishment. The master guides the disciple through the gate of expertise, but practicing it depends entirely on the individual. My job is done, the rest is up to you." Having said this, he made her promise not to commit evil, not to show off, and not to divulge the name of her guru—and then told her to leave the mountain.

Ajia said, "All the troubles Snow Feather had were probably due to the fact that she didn't keep her promise."

Chapter 9

The Monk Who Went on a Pilgrimage

Always lonely,
Always in a daze in my loneliness;
During my loneliness you did not come to my dreams.
In my lonely dreams, I was always traveling by myself.

The Princess in Her Dream

According to *Tale of the Goddess*, Snow Feather had already accomplished the technique of Dream Yoga by the time she carried her mother into Old Mountain. The Dream Yoga was an extremely profound type of Yogic practice. Once attained, one could avoid being deluded upon reaching purgatory—the realm one enters after death but before reincarnation— and achieve Buddhahood.

Back then, Snow Feather often dreamt of a monk who was born in Liangzhou but went on a pilgrimage to Nepal in the Himalayan Mountains after he took the tonsure. But there a holy man told him that Liangzhou was, in fact, the true holy land! Countless eminent monks wished only to go as pilgrims to Liangzhou. They included the likes of Kumarajiva, who abandoned the honor of being a prince and stayed in Liangzhou for more than ten years. Where else could you find such a holy land?

Ajia said, "The greatest accomplishment, attained by this monk from his pilgrimage, was the realization that his native home was the true holy land."

In the brightness of her dream during this particular night, Snow Feather discovered that the monk had crossed the Himalayas in search for her. Snow Feather could tell, from her dream, that those mountains were very high. She didn't know they were known as the "roof of the world." She just saw a sky filled with whiteness. It was her impression that the world was filled with red, the scarlet color of blood—white had become quite rare. Of course, that was just her impression. The Himalayan Mountains in her dream were filled with snow. Ajia said, "She could even feel in her dream the fresh coolness of the snowy-white mountains."

This was one of numerous dreams Snow Feather had.

Her numerous dreams resembled a lengthy story, performed in segments, as with a television series.

You knew, of course, that this would've been a simple matter for someone who'd accomplished the Dream Yoga.

Don't you also interpret dreams, create dreams, and visit the land of the Buddha through dreams? You would likely consider them dreams, until the day you discover that this world and this universe are just dreams. Whether reincarnation or Nirvana—they're fundamentally but dreams.

Snow Feather's dream began with a swath of red. She was meditating at the time. At the beginning, clarity infused everything, and then a lamp appeared. At first, the light was as small as a pea, but then it gradually expanded and shone on a beautiful princess. The princess's beauty was difficult to describe using words. You can't even find such a girl among the modern era's movie actresses. An actress might represent the princess's form, but not her spirit. Those who knew the princess would know, right away, that the actress was a sham.

For the same reason, I'm unable to describe Snow Feather's beauty. I'm unable to describe the elegance that exuded through her every pore.

The princess was sixteen years of age then. Later, you would always visualize the Dakini goddess as a sixteen-year-old. You know, for a girl, sixteen is the most wonderful age. It's the most beautiful time of a woman's life. Aside from her looks, the hormones of a sixteen-year-old are also at their peak. You realized later that Grandpa Jiu called hormones the primal energy, and working on the chakras and primal energy would become a part of your practices.

Snow Feather didn't even think it was a dream. I didn't believe it was either. Rather than a dream, I'd consider it a realm that appeared through meditation. But I have to call it a dream, otherwise readers might complain about my emphasis on the supernatural. Because we all dream, you might say; oh, I can dream that kind of dream too! Of course, you can dream. You can breathe too. But how can your breathing compare with Grandpa Jiu's breathing? How could your lifestyle be compared to the lifestyle of the sage Confucius? You may already know that your mind determines your lifestyle's value. I had to call it a dream. But you know Snow Feather's dream was actually a realm that appeared when she meditated. Let's just agree on this.

You know, I'm not worldly wise, but I must go along with the world. Someday when you see Diamond Maiden on a Tanka, you'll notice that half her hair stands straight up, while the other half lays down. The hair that lays down symbolizes her going along with the world. Then you'll realize that sometimes going along with the world is a manifestation of wisdom.

That's why I have to say, it was through a dream that Snow Feather saw the princess.

The beautiful princess had many suitors. They were, of course, all princes. A writer like you wouldn't have dared to woo the princess. Neither would I, even though people would, later on, worship me as Liangzhou's guardian deity. But the fact one is worshipped only means you receive what you deserve. Should you decide to become big-headed, the folks of Liangzhou would denounce you for being too full of yourself.

You must know that the most inauspicious thing in the world is the toad: the kind that wishes to consume the flesh of a swan. Don't you agree?

The princess's name was Huaman. For some, this name would boom thunderously. But it's okay if you've never heard of her name. I won't blame you for your ignorance since even the most experienced and knowledgeable ant wouldn't be cognizant of celestials' affairs. Besides, even if I thought you were ignorant, I'd have to praise you for your experience and knowledge. Having been born into this world, I've long since learned to go along with the world. If it weren't for this, I would have been without worshippers long ago.

It was said that Princess Huaman's beauty caused the deaths of many young men. Some died of lovesickness, while others died competing with her other admirers. There was even a rumor in Nepal at the time that those who died competing for her would end up in the Western Paradise. Ancient books were filled with such tales: you need not take them seriously. But everyone knew that Princess Huaman had an excellent pedigree and was of noble heritage. Her beauty had the characteristics of the exalted Lotus Dakini Goddess. Don't interrupt. I don't know what these characteristics were either. You know I don't gossip.

But I can vouch for her auspiciousness. Auspicious people in this world make one feel peaceful when you are with them, and one becomes blessed thereby. Soothsayers call this meeting a blessing-bringing person. Haven't you met many yourself? That princess was definitely such an honorable person because dying as a result of admiring her or through lovesickness for her, was far better than being a pig. It's true. You must have known that sometimes love is also a kind of faith. Therefore, if you truly believed that loving Princess Huaman and dying for her through a duel would take you to Paradise, then you would end up in Paradise after the opponent's sword pierced your chest. You should know that all religious techniques are created by the mind!

Let me give you an example to support this line of thinking. If you go for fifteen leagues south of the city of Liangzhou, you will see the ruins of a monastery. Within it, there's a pile of earth nine feet high and thirty feet in diameter. Buried in this pagoda was a man known in the historical records as Sakya Pandita. This man's scholarship was as great as heaven, his merit filled the earth, and his fame and distinction reached heaven and earth. Of course, you can emulate such a man if you would like. Even if you were a pig, if you could change your pig's mind into that of a Bodhisattva, then people would revere you as a Bodhisattva. Take Diamond Maiden as an example. She was a great goddess with a pig's head, called "Duoji Pamu" in Tibetan, meaning "Diamond Sow." The Han Chinese thought it sounded unflattering, and so took the pig part out of her name.

Let's continue to talk about the tomb stele mentioned above. There were many words on it without much content. The gist of it was that even if only a bird's wing touches the earth under this pagoda, this bird would find salvation after death and not fall onto evil paths. This is a stereotypical example of how mere contact can endow benefit. Therefore, I believe those who died for the princess were indeed blessed and fortunate.

Sorry about saying so much just to prove a simple concept.

Don't laugh at me; I'm very old after all. I've been through too many ups and downs. Although sometimes I appear as a youth, and sometimes as an old man, my mind is, in fact, full of wrinkles—like the large desert you wrote about.

I digress. Let's stop talking about how the pursuers wooed the princess, but speak instead of a certain day when the princess contracted a horrific disease called leprosy. The princess's flower-and-moon-like beauty was totally swallowed up by a type of germ.

Wasn't it frightening?

But don't sigh.

Very often it's hard to determine whether something is good or bad.

Like lingering clouds swept away by wind, all her suitors vanished.

This was, of course, quite natural. No one, including the princess' parents, wanted to be consumed by the leprosy germs. Therefore, the princess was locked up in a small house in a back garden; where an old man, who was completely covered except for his eyes, brought her food every day. One night, she dreamt of a woman who called herself Niguma. Don't laugh, I know she is your guru, and you often chant the Blessings of Niguma. I also know you frequently meet her in the Realm of Clarity. But right now, you can wipe that smirk off your face! I'm the God on High, and you have to listen quietly to my narration.

Niguma said, "Go! Go to Sitavana!"

Yes, that was the place you wrote about in your *Mahamudra: Essentials and Practice*, "One of the eight most famous corpse forests in India, that was where the locals abandoned the corpses. Corpses everywhere. Stench rose to the sky. Wild animals visited frequently."

As I remember it, you once said, "The corpse forest is the best place for self-cultivation. Here one can observe, very visually, the impermanence of life and develop the mindset of desiring detachment from the world." The red lights and green wines, the songs, dance, and new gadgets—such as television, internet, and the like—of modern society have occupied almost all the space and time in our lives. People have neither time nor interest to care about spirituality. They don't think of death, except when a friend or relative dies. Only then might they feel the impermanence of life and heave a sigh. But while sighing is easy, maintaining that frame of mind is very challenging. Before the sigh has been heaved completely, the mind has already wandered elsewhere. Even a mind that has attained some slight measure of enlightenment could be polluted by external objects. Like treasures wrapped in mud and pearls covered with dust, it would be difficult for their original sheen to shine through. That was why the ascetics of ancient India used to cultivate themselves in corpse forests in order to distance themselves from the din of society to face death.

Wasn't this what you'd said?

Therefore, the princess took leave of her parents and went to the corpse forest. Leprosy enabled her to see through illusion and allowed her to let go of the craving for the mortal world. At this location strewn with wild beasts and corpses, she performed body kowtows every day: the kind where the entire body prostrated itself to the ground. The woman she saw in her dream wavered continuously before her eyes. It was to this woman that she prostrated herself. Just as you would do later, the princess chanted the Blessings of Niguma, as she visualized the goddess. She prostrated her entire body and sincerely worshipped this totem of her heart.

She worshipped the goddess, in this way, for twelve years.

Then one day, at the height of seven tala trees, a secret Pure Land appeared.

Then, Niguma appeared above Sitavana. Her skin was golden purple. She held a hand drum in her right hand. Her left hand made a mudra gesture and held a skull, which contained the wisdom of great joy's sweet dew. Wearing ribbons and tassels, she was incomparably majestic. The princess wept for joy. Prostrating to the ground, she kowtowed and begged to be transmitted a technique for practice. Niguma said jokingly, "I am not Niguma. I am a flesh-eating Dakini goddess who wants to consume your flesh and skin. Are you afraid of me or not?" The princess said, "I would like to offer my entire body to the guru." Having said this, she threw the more than one thousand ounces of gold she was wearing to the sky as an offering to the guru and requested that Niguma initiate her to Five Golden Technique.

Niguma caught the gold, but threw it to the ground. The princess thought, *Why doesn't the guru care for my offering?* Knowing what she was thinking, Niguma landed on the ground and looked around with a smile. Then everything she glanced at turned into gold. The princess thought, *Is this an illusion or did the earth really turn into gold?* Niguma laughed and said, "Real gold is like this. Illusion is also like this. Reincarnation, Nirvana, all the techniques are nothing but illusions. Once you understand this principle, then everything in this world is gold. Why feel sorry for losing the paltry gold you offered?"

Again, the princess asked the guru to transmit to her a technique. Thereupon, Niguma looked up and down, and then at the four directions. Immediately, warrior gods and Dakini goddesses streamed in. In a flash, five Diamond Mandalas appeared in midair, in shining splendor, and incomparably majestic. All the necessary offerings were complete; everything anyone could have wished for was there. Within the mandala, five Vajras and their corresponding goddesses all appeared in the form of couples cultivating the wisdom of great joy through couple-cultivation. Sweet dew drizzled down like rain and dripped into the princess's mouth.

Twenty-four Dakini goddesses held hands and led the princess into the holy land. They sat in a circle in the mandala, and there Niguma transmitted to the princess the Couple-Cultivation Technique of the Five Vajras. After that, Cakrasamvara Vajra and the Dakini goddesses and warrior gods of the thirty-two holy lands arrived to participate in the celebration. They played music, danced, sang, and feasted—everything was most wonderful. Niguma said, "From now on, you will be a daughter to me. If you practice according to this technique, you will attain Buddhahood very soon. If you also disseminate this technique widely, you will benefit many who feel love and desire. Now, you can proceed to practice in seclusion. The twenty-four Dakini goddesses will escort you on your way." As she spoke, a rainbow extended to the ground, accompanied by heavenly music. Beautiful flowers showered from the sky. The Dakini goddesses sang beatific congratulatory chants, as they accompanied the princess to earth. Those chants of blessing were the Niguma Propitious Sutra mantras, which you would later recite whenever you did your Yogic practice.

To date, this secret realm still exists. Just like the land of Shambhala, only those with karmic affinity can see and reach it.

The secret Pure Land in which Niguma appeared was called Sitavana. It was also known as the second Buddhist realm.

Ajia said, "Don't laugh! I know you'll say I plagiarized your work. But you should know, maybe it's precisely through my quoting it, that it will have the opportunity to become known throughout the world."

During that historically significant moment, Niguma told Huaman that one of the latter's disciples would attain great achievement. He came from Liangzhou, and there he would return. There he would meet a Wisdom Dakini Goddess and attain enlightenment.

One day, the princess told the monk, "Go! Return to Liangzhou! The real holy land is your homeland. An incarnation of Diamond Maiden awaits you. After going through your souls' trials and tribulations, you will both attain instant enlightenment!"

Snow Feather knew he was the one fated to seek her.

The Monk's Choice

It was through Snow Feather's clear dream realm that the monk entered into this novel—through the rugged mountain paths.

Of course he also entered into history.

He was a thin monk. Because of arduous training, his face looked aged. Because he didn't use any body lotion, the skin on his face seemed somewhat rough. Although he would be a protagonist of this novel, he didn't have the handsome features of contemporary film heroes.

But there was something else that he had. He had an aura that only the faithful had. Nothing could mask that aura; not even poverty, suffering, and wealth could bury that particular trait of his. I once discovered that aura in the face of a foreign child, born in a manger.

When you've abandoned all the attachments in your life, then you will have that aura; for that's when you've transcended yourself.

The monk wore tattered clothes because he'd been traveling along the road for many years. The road was filled with wind, rain, and hail. Some evil spirits and demons didn't want him to approach Liangzhou. They didn't want the world to have another enlightened person. They hoped instead that the world would have more people who crave attachments so they could have more dependents. Therefore, they searched within the mortal world with wide-open eyes. Whenever they saw anyone with a mind to improve himself, they would employ all their strategies to destroy his faith.

The monk knew this.

Monks with a foundation in self-cultivation could even see the demons' wicked smirks and ingratiating smiles. The former to threaten, the latter to seduce. Most of the time, the demons' evil deeds were accomplished with the aid of nature—such as storms, ice, snow, scorching heat, and illnesses. It was said all monks have thirty-six major illnesses, seventy-two minor illnesses, and 108 trivial illnesses. Of course this was but a rumor. But you should know that while the power of the Daoist is only one foot high, that of the Demon is three feet high. There is no "free lunch" in this world. If you want to attain phenomenal achievement, then you need to endure phenomenal suffering. Mencius formulated this idea most cogently: "Therefore, when Heaven intends to give great responsibilities to a particular person, it would invariably first agonize his intentions, belabor his muscles and bones, induce hunger to his body and skin, make empty and tired his form, and problematize whatever he does; to thereby stimulate his mind, train his endurance, and advance from his shortcomings."

However, the monk never considered himself as having experienced any tribulations. He always thought he was enjoying himself. Of course, he wasn't putting on a show because undergoing tribulations was always the best aid for improving karma.

So, step after step, the monk approached Liangzhou.

Even while traveling, he visualized his own protective god. It was said he completed all the necessary chanting while traveling. You were like him in this respect, so you know what I'm talking about.

Therefore, I saw an auspicious cloud moving slowly toward Liangzhou.

I believe your success benefitted from your life experiences, which resembled a pilgrimage.

In fact, I can't tell the difference between you and the monk.

I don't know how many years the monk's trip lasted. Even he forgot how many himself. He only remembered that the day he left was the twenty-fifth day of a month. That day, many practitioners were performing an offering to Diamond Maiden. That day, Snow Feather, who was meditating, felt as if she were suddenly drunk. Her body was filled with a warm, great joy. She asked Grandpa Jiu the reason for this change, but he only smiled mysteriously.

That day, I also smiled mysteriously.

The choice made by a monk would determine his actions, and his actions would inform his fate.

Oh, look at me: here I'm prattling away again. Some blind critics would complain about my robbing the philosophers of their right to speak.

Of course, what they don't realize is that my speaking constitutes one of my actions, which together with my other actions would inform my fate.

Grandpa Jiu in Meditative State

Snow Feather went to visit Grandpa Jiu because something inauspicious happened. That morning, the offering water suddenly turned into blood when she was meditating.

Snow Feather boiled a lot of goat meat for Mom and took it up the tree along with its soup. It was enough to last Mom two days. She also put a lot of pungent herbs on the branches to prevent snakes from climbing up.

She then took care of the pythons and bid them to keep an eye on Mom instead of sleeping all the time. Snow Feather had gone to India with Grandpa Jiu in the past and had visited the Diamond Seat.[1] Many people raised pythons there and trained them to take care of their children. Like elephants, pythons were man's most faithful friends. So long as humans treated them as friends, they would be good friends.

And then, Snow Feather entered into the deep mountain.

The deep mountain was characterized by remoteness. The trees and grass were just like those in Old Mountain. But there were more wild animals and fog there; and it was more secluded. I thought Grandpa Jiu would have lived in a cave. But when I followed Snow Feather's footsteps to Grandpa Jiu's, I discovered he in fact lived in a wood cabin.

A cabin nestled itself at the densest part of the greenery. Of course, you couldn't tell it was a cabin because ivy covered its wood completely. The most fantastic thing was that a little bird there had been calling "Niguma" for the past two hundred years, according to local lore. So, when you hear "Niguma," you know you are close to Grandpa Jiu's.

One probably expected to see the place decorated with leather goods or woven carpets, like those you would later see in the bags of many living Buddhas. Grandpa's fame shook heaven and earth, so one expected his residence to have a luxurious appearance. But such was not the case at all. The house had only very simple kitchen utensils covered in dust and a huge cupboard. Grandpa Jiu's bedding was placed in a cupboard. The only reason I didn't call the cupboard a coffin was to prevent you from accusing me of mystifying things deliberately. But in fact, the cupboard *was* a coffin. Only it was bigger than a regular coffin and made of cedar wood. There were many cedar trees on the mountain, so it wouldn't have been difficult to make a coffin out of cedar. The coffin wasn't painted but was so shiny that it was smoother than a lacquered one. Based on this, I concluded it probably had a long history. No one knew how long Grandpa Jiu had lived. Many elderly folks in the village had heard of Grandpa Jiu since they were little. But of course, to them, Grandpa Jiu was only a symbol.

Grandpa Jiu was an ancient legend.

---

1. Name of the rock Buddha sat on when he became enlightened.

He was always meditating in the coffin. One day, he entered into a meditative state when he was boiling a yam. When he came out of the state, the yam was already covered with black, hairy mold. This was something Snow Feather always remembered. Back then, she thought Grandpa Jiu had died. She left the deep mountain and looked up an older disciple of Grandpa Jiu. The disciple laughed and said, "Go back and strike a singing-bowl next to his ear and he'll come back to life!" This was how Grandpa Jiu got to see the hairy yam. But he only said, "Stop meddling" and went back into the meditative state.

When she was in the mountains, Grandpa Jiu used to have her talk to the plants. Grandpa Jiu said one of his earlier disciples stayed there for twenty years and had become dumb by the time he left. So speaking to the plants became a daily ritual for Snow Feather. Later, she discovered that plants could also communicate with people. Whenever she talked to them, they would tremble in excitement. And the plants that listened to her speak grew particularly well. They would smile whenever they saw her.

Look at how all the plants smiled upon her arrival!

Snow Feather entered the cabin. Dust covered everything there. She knew Grandpa Jiu had entered a meditative state again. Grandpa Jiu sat in the coffin and had congealed into a rock. Bird droppings were piled on his head; or maybe a bird tried to make a nest on his head and eventually quit after many attempts. Grandpa Jiu's mudra-gestured hands were also covered in dust. She was afraid Grandpa Jiu was really dead, but she knew he wouldn't die. He was a yogi who had attained the ability to live forever. Only if he had become tired of the mortal world would he laugh and say, "Let me liberate myself!"

In fact, real liberation has nothing to do with death. When one has no attachments, then one is liberated. Snow Feather realized that. So, as someone worried about her mother, she knew she wasn't liberated. Even if she were to die right now, she still wouldn't be liberated. Death has nothing to do with liberation.

Grandpa Jiu said he wouldn't die just now. If he didn't want to die, no one could make him die. He said, "I carry the wind, rain, thunder and lightning with me. My life is up to me, not up to Heaven."

After cleaning off the bird droppings and dust on Grandpa Jiu, Snow Feather struck the singing bowl once, and then again. After quite a while, Grandpa Jiu's walnut shell–like eyelids began to squirm, causing the falling of much dust. He grumbled, "Water is blood, blood is water. What's the fuss?" Having said this, he closed his eyes again.

Snow Feather struck the singing bowl again. It wasn't until after a long while that Grandpa Jiu opened his eyes and said, "Just as well! Go, fetch my chamber pot!"

She brought over the rusty chamber pot, which was very light, as all the fluid in it had long evaporated.

Grandpa Jiu held it and began to shake it while he mumbled. After shaking for a while, the swishing sound of a fluid could be heard inside the chamber pot. Snow Feather wasn't surprised. In the past, she'd seen a person seeking longevity drink the fluid in Grandpa Jiu's chamber pot. The person had his fortune divined fifty times, and all said he wouldn't live past the thirteenth of the Fifth Month that year. So he came to seek help from Grandpa Jiu. Grandpa Jiu shook the chamber pot like this then and produced an amberlike fluid in the empty chamber pot, and the person drank it. You must have heard his story. When he was 133 years old, his daughter-in-law wouldn't give him food as she thought he was too old to be living. He took off his girdle when she was working in the fields and no one else was at home—and hung himself from a ladder. It was said he could otherwise have lived until 180. His ghost-spirit wouldn't dissipate after death, so the villagers would often see a white bearded old man weeping. Later, he was subjugated by Grandpa Jiu who made him a guardian deity of the village.

Snow Feather washed a bowl in the stream outside the door and handed it to Grandpa Jiu. An amber-like fluid flowed out of the chamber pot. It was quite thick. It was said that was, in fact, sweet dew.

I don't know whether Snow Feather drank it.

She stayed in the cabin for a day and a night.

It was said she also entered into a meditative state.

It was also said it was on account of the sweet dew's blessings that she didn't die from the tribulations she endured later.

The Greatest Ordeal

Through the brightness of a dream, Snow Feather saw the monk again. . . . He was walking barefoot along a mountain path all alone. His feet had rotted a long time ago, so that with each step, a bloody imprint was left on the ground. I knew he would bleed to death if he were to continue walking like this.

He was truly very weak and fragile.

He fell again and again. And he climbed up again and again. It was the kind of scene one saw in films.

Later, you would write in one of your essays, "No matter how long the road is under your feet, it would not exceed your stride."

The monk must've known this.

He must've been thinking, *If I keep on going like this, I will eventually reach Liangzhou.*

Even more likely, he wasn't thinking of anything at all. He just kept on traveling. Traveling was his ultimate goal.

For those who are enlightened, there is no place that isn't Liangzhou, no place that isn't the holy land. It was through the process of traveling that he realized his true self, one step after the other. Without the "traveling," he would've just been like any other youth; he would've labored like an ox and died like an ox. He would've been a fly that flew across the void without leaving a trace.

But he did travel in this way.

And so, he was able to transcend himself.

According to the legends, he met an elderly woman selling flatbread in a mountain valley. She held up a flatbread and said, "If you can answer my question, you'll get a piece of bread. I can also give you a pair of shoes."

She asked, "Didn't you people say there is no 'I' in all phenomena? If so, then who are you liberating?"

The monk replied, "The clarifications are in the Insight Sect."[2]

But the elderly woman snickered.

Again she asked, "You people say all is impermanent, then isn't the Nirvana you seek also impermanent? If it's impermanent, then why seek after it? If it's permanent, then would all phenomena still be impermanent?"

It was said the monk did not answer her question.

It was said although the monk wasn't able to give an answer, the old woman still gave him the flatbread. But the monk didn't accept it.

It was said the old woman was also called Barbarian Hag.

It was said the monk collapsed on the ground dejectedly. Suddenly, he no longer wanted to keep on going.

It was said that was the greatest ordeal of his life. It was more terrifying than the calamities of snow and wind; it was worse than even death.

---

2. *Weishizong* is a Buddhist sect.

It was said he lay in the valley for three days.

Within days, he had aged ten years. In the later Tankas about him, he was depicted with three wrinkles on his forehead. Ajia said, "Like your beard, his wrinkles had become his symbol."

Keep on Going: Herein Lies the Significance

Ajia said, "In the brightness of another of Snow Feather's dreams, the monk finally climbed out of the mountain valley."

The sky was a grayish haze. I should have said, "The sun was a black ball," but someone else had already said that.

Yes, the sun the monk saw was really a black ball. Everything had turned gray; everything had lost color and luster.

Truly, it was as if he'd become color blind. The feeling was a combination of disillusion and despair. You discovered that everything was staring at you coldly, without any emotions.

Later, many people thought the old woman was the incarnation of a demon. Even the monk had thought so. But to me, why couldn't she have been the incarnation of a Buddha?

She managed to rid the monk of his attachment to the significance of life.

When he climbed out of despair, the monk thought, *Whatever the significance, let me just keep on going!* All his strength relied on just this one notion.

He suddenly discovered the Nirvana he sought was also a kind of attachment, and the real significance of liberation was to eliminate all attachments.

Therefore he said, "I will go!"

To him, his life's goal was to keep on going. In other words, his "keeping on going" was the goal in and of itself and transcended his destination, Liangzhou. Of course, it also transcended Diamond Maiden Cave.

That was how the monk arrived at Liangzhou in Snow Feather's bright dream realm.

Back then, she didn't yet know they would walk into history together.

She was under the impression he had been walking since the inception of the Kingdom of Xixia. She had no idea when he'd arrived at Liangzhou, and didn't know whether he'd ever left Liangzhou.

The Tears That Poured Suddenly

Snow Feather took leave of Grandpa Jiu.

It's very difficult for me to describe her feelings. Just like one's inability to measure the sea's depth using a chopstick as a ruler, I'm unable to fathom what Snow Feather thought. I can only guess. I think her mind must have been like a cloudless sky and an ocean without any ripples. It must have been like that.

But she still had attachments. Often, attachments are a source of pain, but they are also a source of blessing.

In fact, many people's "having no attachments" constitutes the greatest attachment because they are attached to having no attachments; just like Jasper's attachment to Diamond Maiden Cave, your attachment to literature, and Snow Feather's attachment to her mom.

The only difference between you and others is the fact that, aside from those attachments, you "have no attachments." You use one attachment in place of all attachments; just as Shakyamuni used his attachment to "bring salvation to the multitude" in place of all other attachments.

Ajia said, "Your sole attachment became the motivation for your lives."

That particular day, the monk suddenly lost his motivation. When he lost his motivation, Snow Feather was meditating at Grandpa Jiu's place. In the realm of clarity, she suddenly understood the monk.

She suddenly wept. This had never happened before.

She also discovered a big ball of fire. But she thought this was the fire she had visualized. On this very day, Grandpa Jiu initiated her into the Couple-Cultivation Technique of the Five Vajras. The technique came from the Wisdom Dakini Goddess known as Niguma. Later, through the process of visualizing it for many years, I attained the Bright Mahamudra. The great fire of wisdom burned around the five Vajras. She thought flames that appeared in the realm of clarity were also a manifestation of the mind.

Yes, that fire was a manifestation of the mind. What isn't in this world?

Snow Feather also thought her sudden outburst of tears was a manifestation of compassion. This was also correct. When a person is suddenly filled with tears, he or she must have been moved by something. The act of being moved would invariably also induce the person to feel compassion.

Snow Feather also felt anxious. Consequently, she thought of Mother. She left the cabin without bidding farewell to Grandpa Jiu. According to local custom, one shouldn't kowtow to a guru when one takes leave of him. Otherwise, you would never see him again in this life.

She headed back in a rush.

Chapter 10

The Black Dragon Demons

The fated rebellion has miscarried,
The black house congealed like a tomb.
Is it Hell or Heaven?
                    Interpret it as you wish!
You, the infuriating witch!

The Men Who Guarded the Dam

Snow Feather's steps stirred up dust, which flew into the distance. You know it was the dust of history. It can blur people's vision. But through the eyes of the wise, they are as clear as the lines of one's palm.

Historical Mirror of Forgotten Events records several strange occurrences that affected Diamond Clan before Snow Feather carried her mother to Old Mountain: a cow gave birth to a *qilin*,[1] three sheep defeated a wolf, and other insignificant events. On the surface, they didn't seem to have anything to do with Snow Feather. But you know, oftentimes the sneeze of a mosquito can affect the dream of an old bear a thousand leagues away. Those events in the village, in fact, harbored the mysterious principles behind Snow Feather and her mother's destinies.

We choose here to relate the dispute between Diamond Clan and Brilliant King Clan.

The origin of the dispute was none other than water. Disputes about water had gone on for generations without a satisfying solution.

---

1. A lionlike mythical animal.

169

It was said that ever since humans lived on this land, water had been the main source of their quarrels.

A stream wound down from the snowy Qilian Mountain. It gathered the mountain springs and dazzled brilliantly in the midst of the mountain. When the water flowed into the territory of Diamond Clan, it passed through a natural opening. The men of Diamond Clan built a dam across the opening to reserve the water. After the water reached a certain height, they would use it to irrigate their land. Most of the land belonging to the village hung along the mountain slope and was dependent on rainwater. There would be a harvest when it rained; but when it didn't, the crops would be lost. Their land in the valley, however, could be irrigated, which meant they would be assured of that harvest, regardless of the weather. For that reason, that water source was the lifeblood of Diamond Clan villagers. It was also the lifeblood for Brilliant King Clan villagers.

As soon as Diamond Clan villagers dammed the embankment and waited patiently for the water to rise high enough for irrigation, Brilliant King Clan villagers would rush over like a swarm of bees, dig a hole in the embankment, and let the water splash straight down to their own parched crops. But the embankment hole couldn't be too large, otherwise many Brilliant King Clan villagers would end up as fish and shrimp. The size of the hole was not to exceed the Immortal Blocking Trough, a cliff that jutted out of the gorge. The dam was built against it. A cow spirit was known to roam at the bottom of the cliff. Sometimes, it would turn into a beautiful girl and carry on a romance with some handsome village youth.

Whenever Brilliant King Clan came to steal water, Kuan San would lead the villagers down the mountain to fight them. This was part of his job. The clan militia could participate, but they weren't allowed to use rifles. The clan militia of Brilliant King Clan militia also had rifles, which was also prohibited. This custom was similar to the rule that the military shouldn't get involved in civilian disputes.

The Brilliant King Clan villagers had already dug open the dam. The water poured down with a thundering roar. Villagers were all rubbing their fists while they waited for Kuan San, who stormed down the mountain slope like whirlwind, a straw of barley in his hand.

"Diamond! Diamond!" People roared. Of course they were hoping that the Diamond Vajra deities would protect them.

"Brilliant King! Brilliant King!" The villagers of Brilliant King Clan roared in response.

Kuan San burnt the straw of barley at the entrance to the village. All the villagers knelt down. They kowtowed first to the Saddle God and then prayed, "Heaven protect me, earth protect me, the five great Vajras protect me. Protect the front of my heart and protect the back of my heart; protect my nose and protect my eyes. Protect my ears so that wind cannot blow through them; protect my body so that it will be as hard as an iron staff." The protective deities of Diamond Clan were the Diamond Vajras, the protective deity of Brilliant King was Brilliant King Vidya-raja. It was customary for the two sides to pray to their own deities before fighting.

After praying, Kuan San roared, "Beat the mother-fuckers!" He grasped a spade and charged up to the dam. The villagers also raised an implement like a spade and swarmed up. Because of Kuan San's tremendous strength and fierce temperament, he was always in the vanguard. For this reason, each autumn, the clan would give him extra food as a subsidy.

Kuan San led the crowd, which charged toward the dam in a snake formation. According to the rule, both sides had to fight on the embankment whenever they fought about water. This way, no matter how many more people one side had over their opponent, they were unable to gain much advantage on the embankment itself. They always picked the strongest to guard the dam. When Diamond Clan villagers charged, they formed a snake formation so one assault would immediately be followed by another.

Kuan San charged into the crowd and smacked down two people. One fell into the water, while the other moaned on the dam.

"Diamond! Diamond!" the villagers of Diamond Clan roared together.

"Brilliant King! Brilliant King!" the villagers of Brilliant King Clan also roared.

Kuan San was so strong his spade swung as if it were blown by the wind and smacked opponents down off the embankment, one after another. He was allowed to smack but not to hack. In this armed confrontation, daggers and rifles were prohibited; they could only use agricultural implements. Moreover, they were not allowed to take lives. Should anyone die, then the opponent would be considered to have lost in principle. Once the law was involved, then the result would be devastating, since human life was priceless! There were exceptions, however. Should both sides suffer deaths, then the side with more deaths would be considered the winner.

Suddenly a man jumped out from the other side, bent over, and yanked a small tree from the embankment. He swung it at Kuan San, who immediately tumbled down the embankment. Without further pause, the man knocked ten more Diamond Clan villagers off the embankment.

"Cripple Big! Cripple Big!" Kuan San screamed from the bottom of the embankment.

Cripple Big led the assault with another group.

This time, the fight became a muddled warfare with the clamor of spades, shrieks, and curses merging into a whirlwind. Jasper knew that the one to lose would definitely be Diamond Clan with this kind of fighting. Whenever an opponent fell, another would fill his place. Brilliant King Clan had several thousand households, while Diamond Clan only had several hundred.

Sure enough, after fighting from morning to afternoon, all Diamond Clan villagers were moaning at the bottom of the embankment, while those from Brilliant King Clan were dancing amidst the thundering roar of the flowing water.

This was the scenario just about every time Diamond Clan defended the dam.

Why Doesn't Your Mom Die?

The folks of Brilliant King Clan retreated. Diamond Clan villagers were inconsolable. The water they'd dammed up for almost a month had been stolen. Most of those who tried to protect the dam were injured, to varying degrees. But the dam was still burrowed out by their opponents. This meant the villagers had to forget about irrigating their land for the next half a month, as it would take more than twenty days for the water to rise back to the needed level. But more frightening than that was the fact that even if the water could fill the dam, the folks of Brilliant King Clan would appear again.

It had been like this for the past several hundred years.

The village had no option but to present a lawsuit to the government. Such lawsuits had been delivered innumerable times in the past.

According to Donkey Two, whose job it was to stay in the city with the lawsuit, the lawsuit documents presented by Diamond Clan piled from the ground to the ceiling—but to no avail. Because Brilliant King Clan always presented even more litigation documents! The several hundred households of their village needed to have food too. Moreover, they had a document from their ancestors which, according to legend, was very beneficial to Brilliant King Clan. It clearly said, The water belonged to Brilliant King Clan. They were the Indigenous population. When they had a thousand households at their village, the land occupied by Diamond Clan was still wilderness, without the shadow of a single human being.

Diamond Clan conceded to the veracity of the above. So, although the county government dispatched officials to mediate between the two clans several times, this water problem remained as muddled as a tangled skein. Both clans needed to eat, after all!

All the villagers gathered at the Ancestral Hall. Kuan San said, "We've got to come up with a way to deal with this. The eight hundred mu^2 of irrigation land can't wait for the water." Jie Big said, "Remember that year when the fight for water was so fierce someone died on our side? Then we got some extra harvest. After that, only after we finished watering, we released some water to them."

Kuan San said, "Back then there was less irrigation land. But later, we cultivated a lot of the wilderness, and then there wasn't enough water. There's been less rain too, and snow has become rare. We've got to come up with something!"

"Yes! Yes!" They all sighed.

Braggart summoned a few elders and discussed for several nights. They decided that presenting lawsuits was a waste of time. If they wanted to win, they had to get Brilliant King Clan to lose in principle. There was only one way for them to lose in principle: that is, to have a death.

In the past, when the two clans fought, those crafty thieves of Brilliant King Clan were so blackhearted that they slew their opponents like chickens. But now when they fought over the water, they would be exceedingly cautious. They would only smack people's bottoms with their spades. How the folks of Diamond Clan wished one of their own would be killed! But the people of Brilliant King Clan made sure none of them died.

---

2. One *mu* is equivalent to one fifteenth of a hectare of land.

Braggart said, "We've got to come up with a way to deal with this!"

Who should we get to die? They wondered.

Braggart tried to put this hat of death on each of the villagers, but none of them fit well. Finally, he set his eyes upon Cripple Big's mom, a hag who was always complaining about being hungry. It was said she was demented.

So Kuan San went to see Cripple Big, who was transporting water with a camel at the time. He was responsible for transporting water for the Ancestral Hall and made leather goods in his spare time. Although he was crippled, he had skillful hands and was famous for crafting leather goods.

"Come over here, Cripple Big! We need to discuss something," said Kuan San.

Cripple Big was shocked. This Kuan San, who regarded him as cow dung, was now greeting him. Moreover, there was a smile on his face. Cripple Big's knees felt weak—he wanted to kowtow to him.

"Cripple Big, your mom, is she eighty already?"

"She's seventy-eight."

"Oh, how's she doing?"

"Not well. She has dementia—keeps on complaining about being hungry."

"You were great when we protected the dam. But the other side had more people so we couldn't win. We've got to come up with a way to deal with this!"

"Yes, we've got to come up with a way to deal with this!"

"But there's nothing better than having someone die. You know human life is priceless! Unless someone dies, no one cares. The county government doesn't really want to get involved either. Both the palm and the back of the hand belong to the same hand, right? We'll give it an excuse to be on our side."

Cripple Big felt confused. He didn't know officials needed any excuses to handle things.

"I've discussed it with the elders. We've got to have someone die. We thought and thought, and decided your mom is the most suitable candidate."

"What do you mean?"

"We've got to have a dead person and claim that the death was caused by the fight for water."

Cripple Big finally understood. Kuan San was grinning at him; Grandpa Sun was also grinning. Cripple Big mustered up all his energy to force up some phlegm. He forced and forced, and then spat it at Kuan San's face with all his might. Who would've thought part of the phlegm would fly straight at the protective talisman on Kuan San's chest? The talisman was an amberlike pendant with the image of his protective deity on it. People with status wore one.

"*Fuck your mom—why doesn't your mom go die?*" Cripple Big yanked the camel, turned away, and left.

Braggart's Eyes Were Icy

According to Ajia, Cripple Big was still furious when he returned home. He cussed using a horde of dirty words. Ajia said, "Liangzhou's dirty word vocabulary was the most comprehensive in the entire world, while that of Diamond Clan was the most comprehensive of those in Liangzhou, and that of Cripple Big was the most comprehensive of any in Diamond Clan. So Cripple Big got full satisfaction out of the cussing. However, he said most of the dirty words under his blanket. You must have known it was the tradition in Diamond Clan to kick when the door was closed and vent by farting under the cover of a blanket."

Cripple Big lived in the cart courtyard, next to the Ancestral Hall. The courtyard had many buildings back then. Half of them were for the draught animals; the other half were for storing grain. This used to be the carriage courtyard of a wealthy household. According to *Historical Mirror of Forgotten Events*, one year, the household's head angered a widow who came to protest when she was menstruating, and she sprinkled her blood at the courtyard entrance. Because of this, the wealthy household came to be ruined. Although in fact the collapse of the wealthy household was related to the household head's heart, the wise men of Diamond Clan still considered the menstrual blood as the cause for the household's downfall. You know the folks of Diamond Clan are like that.

For about five years, a hoary-headed old woman used to sun herself in the cart courtyard, which would later become famous. That was Cripple Big's mom. At the same time, another old woman was sunning herself somewhere else, a place called Diamond Monastery. That was Snow Feather's mom. The situation of the two old women seemed alike, but because they had very different children, they ended up differently in the folk beliefs of Liangzhou. Because the latter's uterus had harbored Snow Feather, she came to be worshipped as a Dakini goddess; while Cripple Big's mom became a byword for a wrongfully-dead ghost. The parents used to say when they lectured their children, "You think I'm Cripple Big's mom?"

This probably explains why the folks of Liangzhou wanted so desperately for their sons to become dragons. When you have a noble child, then you've got the funds to achieve nobility.

On that particular evening as recorded in Diamond Clan's history, Cripple Big returned home. Mom asked, "Savory Lad, you're back! Did you bring meat?" This was what his mom would ask every day. Cripple Big answered, "They said they'll divide the meat when a pig dies of disease. This time, I've got roasted yam."[3] Cripple Big fished out the roasted yam. His mom grabbed it immediately, took a bite, and swallowed it before she had time to chew. The readers who had eaten roasted yam could relate to what happened next: she choked.

Cripple Big said, "Go slower, go slower! No one will take it from you!" And Cripple Big pounded her back with his fist. He pounded it forcefully. This was the best method used in Liangzhou for dealing with choking. This method was subsequently transmitted to the rest of the world and came to be considered China's fifth-greatest discovery. The pounding made his mom's head wobble like waves. Mom's neck was broken; she was always napping with a drooping head. But no matter how old she was, she was after all Mom. Cripple Big thought, *Fuck you, Kuan San!*

To prevent his Mom from suffocating, Cripple Big grabbed the yam from her and fed her bit by bit. You know Cripple Big was known as a filial son. A filial son like this wouldn't want his mom to choke to death.

Mom mumbled as she ate, "That pig, when would it die?" This was her dream. She longed for the death of the clan pig, the way elderly ladies practicing the technique to reach the Pure Land, desired to see the Amida Buddha. In her memory, the only way to eat meat was for the pigs belonging to the clan to die, one after the other, from a plague. Based on this fact alone, we know she wasn't crazy.

Cripple Big's answer was very clever: "How would I know when it would die?"

---

3. *Sanyao.* The technical name for this root is *dioscorea opposita*.

"What if it doesn't die?" Mom stopped chewing and stared at Cripple Big.

Cripple Big thought, *That's right, what if it doesn't die*" But he said instead, "What wouldn't die in this world? Everything will die eventually!"

Mom believed him, and said, "Yes, everything will die eventually. That old thief, your dad, died a long time ago. This poor old mother of yours . . ." She opened her mouth, and Cripple Big quickly stuck a piece of yam into it.

Mom had had a really hard life. Cripple Big remembered when Mom used to cook for a wealthy household that she wouldn't wash her hands after she made dough there; so she could wash the flour off at home and cook the water to feed him. That was what he survived on.

Suddenly, he heard his name being called outside the door. He saw Braggart as soon as he went out. Braggart wore a black outfit, the collar of which flapped in the wind as if he were flying.

Braggart asked, "Did you spit on the image of the protective god?"

"I spat on Kuan San. He wanted my mom to die, so I spat on him. I said, 'Why doesn't your mom die?'"

Braggart said, "You've committed a crime! You know, you should be beheaded!" This shocked Cripple Big greatly. He remembered the soaring phlegm that landed on the protective talisman and became alarmed. He remembered how someone who had pissed in front of a protective god's image had his dick cut off by the villagers. He wanted to say something, but his throat was stuck all of a sudden. He had seen someone executed by rifle. The brain, when dipped with a steamed bun, was very tasty. It was just like eating beef marrow.

Braggart's eyes were very cold. He said, "Make arrangements for your mom. We're taking you to the city tomorrow. Alternatively, we can cut off your tongue. The image is stored in a safe. Your phlegm is on it. You can deny it, but they have instruments!"

Cripple Big shuddered.

Braggart said, "The rule was made by the ancestors. Anyone who spits on the protective god should die!" Braggart added emphatically, "No one can save you!"

Cripple Big shot a glance at the room and shuddered. He thought, *If I really went to prison, who will provide for Mom?*

Braggart yawned and said, "The gate of Yama's Hall is always open. It won't miss your mom. I have no time to chat. Look, it's fine with me if we deal with it within the clan. Since you're a fellow countryman, I'll have them make the knife extra sharp." Having said this, the flapping collars took Braggart away flying.

With gaping mouth, Cripple Big stared as Braggart departed into the distance. Only after a long while did he squat down, cover his face, and sob. He thought, *A devil must have come over me, why on earth did I spit at him?* For many decades, his knees would feel weak whenever he saw anyone of significance, but this time . . . Suddenly, he realized his act of spitting was not just in response to Kuan San's demand for his mom's death. He had, in fact, been harboring a strong desire to spit at people for a long while. That Kuan San was a mere toad who relied on the power of thunder. He had a sweet mouth but a thorny heart. Whenever Kuan San saw him, he would yell "Cripple Big, Cripple Big" without ever using his real name. Cripple Big had already accumulated a bellyful of explosives. But if Kuan San hadn't mentioned that demand concerning his Mom, those weak knees of his would never've been able to become strong. That Kuan San was as red and great as a louse on a menstruation belt! Even if Cripple Big could borrow someone else's guts, he wouldn't have dared spit on the man. But who told Kuan San to wish his mom dead? Cripple Big had nothing but Mom now. *Would he be considered human if he lets Mom die?*

Braggart had shrunken into a black spot in the valley. It looked like Cripple Big's heart at that moment. He wiped his tears and went back into the room. Mom was sucking the yam on her fingers. She asked, "Any more of that yam?" Cripple Big thought, *What a heartless Mom! Here her son was going to die, and she's asking for more yam!* But then he remembered she knew nothing of what Braggart had said. So he said, "No! Even those I had to roast on the sly!" But Mom's eyes continued to search Cripple Big. This was a habit of hers. Mom was already incapable of trusting anyone. Ever since the first day she married Cripple Big's dad, she'd been living a life of betrayal. Mom used to say: when her bridal sedan entered the gate, the room was complete with white felt, red woolen blankets, quilts, and the like. She thought she had truly married into a rich family, just as the matchmaker had described. Who would've known as soon as the ceremonies ended, the white felt flew away, the red blankets flew away, and the quilts also flew away. It turned out they were all there only to create a false impression. The next day, even the indigo homespun cotton outfit the bridegroom wore was stripped off. As Mom remembered, that was the beginning of her life of betrayals. Later, her old man with his crooked neck also smoked opium, gambled, visited widows, and did other things that made the villagers look askance behind her back. Until one day, someone broke his back and left him to die like a dog in a gully.

Cripple Big knew what Mom was thinking about, so he said, "Mom, I'm not Dad, I wouldn't lie to you!"

Mom uttered a contemptuous "humph" through her nose a couple of times, and said, "Dragons beget dragons, phoenixes beget phoenixes; the sons of rats know how to dig holes!"

Cripple Big knew Mom said that because he looked exactly like Dad. The folks of the village all said they were cast from the same mold. The minute she saw his face, she wouldn't trust him. There was nothing he could do about it. Cripple Big couldn't decide on the way he looked, so he was similarly unable to wipe away Mom's suspicions.

But the moment he thought of the next day, he couldn't help but shiver. He asked, "Mom, if I die, what would you do?" Mom said, "You won't die. Heaven doesn't kill grass without roots!" This was the wisest phrase Mom had ever said. Ajia said, "Based on this phrase alone, I knew the old woman was not crazy." Cripple Big asked, "What if I should die?" Mom yawned unexpectedly and said, "Don't you keep on trying to scare me! You're just like the old robber—he kept on threatening to die, but would never die!"

"But didn't Dad die after all?"

"That was later."

Cripple Big thought, Mom *doesn't believe me!* He sighed. How he wanted to embrace Mom and weep! But Mom didn't believe him. Soon, he didn't believe himself.

He suspected it was all a dream.

Maybe, it was in a dream that he spat on the image of the protective god.

Cripple Big's Shiver

As for what happened to Cripple Big that night, Ajia was very vague. He didn't know whether Cripple Big baked flatbread on the brick bed, or whether he still snored without a care in the world. It was obvious he wasn't clear about it. The giant eyes of history ignore the common folks, you know. No one pays close attention to what's on the minds of commoners. Even if the intensity of their internal struggles was no less severe than that of a war, histories would only remember wars and make heroes out of the creators of wars.

There was nothing one could do about this. Even Ajia couldn't help but follow suit.

Ajia's book only recorded the events of the following morning when Cripple Big went to the Ancestral Hall. Ajia said, "When Cripple Big arrived at the gate of the Ancestral Hall, even the village cattle carts came, and their thundering racket hurt his brain. You may have seen those big carts with wooden wheels, higher than three feet tall. The drivers would sit on the cart's shaft, and dream of having wives with large breasts." This was something out of a poem by the Gansu poet, Li Yunpeng.[4] Although Ajia was a god, he still had the bad habit of plagiarism.

The tone Ajia used was rather mysterious. He narrated mundane details as if he were illustrating a sexual romance. He said, "When Kuan San saw Cripple Big approach, he shouted, 'Hey, Cripple Big, you've really done it! How dare you spit on the protective god? You sure have guts!' Ajia said, "That was when Cripple Big believed he really did spit on the protective god."

His soul was scared up into the sky. *So it wasn't a dream after all?* he thought.

Ajia said, "Kuan San snuck up to Cripple Big quietly and whispered, 'You have my highest respect. I've also wanted to spit on the old thief myself for quite a while now, but I've always been a donkey's dung about my face. Here you wanted to spit, and you spat! The worst that could happen would be to have your tongue sliced off. But so what?!'"

Cripple Big acknowledged his comments absentmindedly and walked toward the animal shed as if he'd lost his soul. He untied the camel's reins, loaded the water buckets, and led the camel out of the gate. Unexpectedly, he heard Kuan San say, "The clan head said you don't have to do water today. Wait for him here!" He grabbed the reins from Cripple Big's hand, hollered at the camel, and left. Cripple Big rubbed his eyes and stuck his tongue out a few times. The strange thing was, he didn't feel terror. But he still felt as if he was in a dream.

Ajia said, "Normally, Cripple Big would have brought the camel halfway up the mountain slope by now, but today he had nothing to do. When he was busy, he'd always wished he could take a rest. But now

---

4. Born in 1937.

that he had nothing to do, he felt rather uneasy. The villagers were all doing their own thing—some hitching carts, others cleaning muck from the shed. Cripple Big, however, couldn't do what he should do."

It was only after enduring the most difficult hour of his life that he saw Braggart's body push itself sideways through the gate. The minute Cripple Big saw his domineering manner, he wanted to spit phlegm at him. There was no one more loathsome than Braggart in the entire Diamond Clan. In the past, Braggart was also so destitute he couldn't hold in his own pee. But later, he took advantage of his poverty, led a gang of bandits, robbed the rich, cheated the poor, and whacked with fury those who had been his benefactors. After several years of this, he became a big honcho. Look at the son of a bitch—he even walks like a domineering crab!

A few villagers went up to greet Braggart. Cripple Big wished they would spit at Braggart as well. But they only bent their waists. Cripple Big thought, *I should have spat at him a few times yesterday. Spitting once is spitting; spitting a dozen times is also spitting.* But once he thought of its potential outcome, he felt somewhat intimidated.

"Come here, Cripple Big!" shouted Braggart.

So Cripple Big bent his waist and went over. Ajia said, "Cripple Big really wanted to stick out his chest and belly, but he was accustomed to bending his waist before Braggart. He knew Braggart liked him like this. He was praised by the folks at Diamond Clan for being guileless. The fact that he could transport water to the Ancestral Hall, and roast yam for his mom now and then could all be attributable to the merit of this waist bending."

Cripple Big entered the Ancestral Hall and was greeted by several people on low stools there. Kuan San was squeezing a chamois and polishing his rifle. When others polished their rifles, they used cloths. But Kuan San used soft sheep hide that would create a sheen. Cripple Big also noticed the Doctor Pockmarked Wang pounding medicine there. He immediately became flustered because it was Pockmarked Wang who administered to the thief who had his hand chopped off last time.

They all looked at Cripple Big without saying a word. The silence crushed Cripple Big like a mountain. Cripple Big knelt down suddenly.

One person spoke, "Cripple Big, what did you do?"

Cripple Big did not dare to answer. He just kowtowed.

"Don't we obey rules anymore?" Another one asked.

Braggart said, "You don't obey rules, but the stockade does have rules. Although the rules are not made by the protective god, it might just as well have been. You're obviously tired of living in any case. I suggest you accept the clan punishment. The government will shoot you for sure. The clan punishment will be a bit painful. But bear with it. I've already had Pockmark prepare the medicine."

Kuan San put down the rifle and brought over a big cleaver. When he used it to hack a sheep for stewed mutton, he could hack it into lumps the size of fists with a few chops. Ajia said, "Look, Cripple Big was trembling."

Kuan San laughed out loud and said, "Look, Cripple Big, shall I slice off your tongue or chop off your claws? I'll do whatever you like. But, on account of our being fellow villagers, there's another way . . . Yesterday, do you remember what I told you?"

Cripple Big remembered what Kuan San had said. He thought, *How could I let my old Mom die?* He really wanted to say no, but the big cleaver in Kuan San's hand shone with an icy gleam that gagged him. You know, sometimes knives are more awesome than things like truth and ethics.

Braggart said, "Cripple Big, what are you staring at? Kowtow to the protective deity right away. Better drink water than lose face!"

Cripple Big took a look at Braggart and his cohorts. They were all looking at him. Tormenting Cripple Big had become a sport for Braggart, and also added excitement for Ajia. Just look at that Kuan San who was losing his patience. It was as if he resented the fact that Cripple Big was too stupid to recognize a favor. Ajia said, "If Cripple Big continued to hesitate, Kuan San would undoubtedly have swung the cleaver and hacked off those claws of Cripple Big's." Cripple Big shuddered. He then knelt down and kowtowed three times to the painting of the protective deity on the wall.

Cripple Big thought, *Mom! If I'm imprisoned or if I have my hands chopped off, you'd end up dead too! I can't be blamed.* But tears surged from his heart suddenly. Before he realized it, they spilled over his entire face and poured forth along with howls. "Mom!" he wailed.

"Who would have thought the guy would be so filial?" asked Ajia.

He Only Lied to Mom Once

Ajia's tone became serious, although he obviously wanted to joke around. But you know that not all subjects are conducive to lightheartedness. Ajia said, "Look, Cripple Big left home with his Mom on his back." Suddenly, night pierced right through his heart. Mom asked, "Is the meat thoroughly cooked?" Cripple Big said, while wiping his tears, "Sure, thoroughly cooked!" Ajia said, "This time he really lied to his mom." Earlier, as soon as he got home, he told Mom, "Mom! They cooked a pot of mutton in the village and told me to invite you there!" Mom said, "You're not lying to me, are you? You and your dad were always lying to me. I've been betrayed by the old thief my whole life. If you lie to me too, then there's no sense for me to live!"

Cripple Big said, "I'm not lying to you—no way am I lying to you! That mutton's been cooking for a whole night, even the bones are bare, the meat will melt on your tongue!" Mom swallowed a mouthful of saliva and said, "That's good! I've always dreamt of mutton so tasty one can die for. I reach out my hand—I reach and reach—but never get it. My arm stretched and stretched, the mutton always out of reach. Always just an inch away. I knew it was transformed from your dad. He cheated this old lady here my entire life! Don't you cheat me too!"

"No, I won't! Of course I won't!" Cripple Big wiped his nose and tossed the mucus onto the ground.

"I've never wanted anything in life: only a son who doesn't lie. My mom and dad lied, and the matchmaker lied: they all said they were marrying me to a rich family. Who would've known he was such a poor devil? The old thief always swindled money from me. He said he was going to do business, but off he went gambling the minute he left home. Not one honest word his entire life. So I thought at least my son wouldn't lie to me, right?"

"Yes. I don't lie!" Cripple Big took a big step and tripped; Mom danced on his back.

Kuan San was waiting by the roadside with a spade. He saw Cripple Big approaching and followed them. Cripple Big could feel a draft whooshing over his spine.

"Where?" asked Cripple Big.

"To the dam!" said Kuan San.

Realizing something unusual was going on, Cripple Big's mom asked, "Why are we going down the slope?"

"The meat is down there!"

"How come it's down there?"

"It's an offering for the river god."

Mom believed him. In the past, they used to get a few sheep, drain their blood into the river, skin them, chop them up and throw them into a pot to boil. The entire village went to eat it.

"Don't let the others grab them all first!" Mom said.

"They won't, they're waiting for you!"

Fires were lit by the mountain path along the way. The villagers were all tending the fires. Cripple Big thought, *Somebody must have leaked the news. So people knew where Mom was heading to right now.* Whenever someone died in the village and the coffin was being transported to the grave, people would light fires in front of their houses since fire could ward off evil and prevent the ghost's spirit from entering their gates. "But Mom is still alive!" Cripple Big was very angry. He wanted to stamp out the fires.

"Hey, Cripple Big!" the folks yelled.

"Hey, Kuan San!" the kids yelled.

Cripple Big felt happy now. The villagers were placing him on the same level as Kuan San, which had never happened before. Who was Kuan San? He was the favorite of the clan head. He was the leader of the clan militia. He, Cripple Big, however, was just a cripple, half of a complete person. Cripple Big felt a sense of glory among the smoke and fire along the road. He forgot the mother he was carrying to her demise.

"Great!" the folks yelled.

Cripple Big thought, *They must have known about everything to be yelling 'Great.' They've been taken advantage of by Brilliant King Clan for so many years they had to come up with a way to deal with it.* But he couldn't help but feel wronged for having to carry his mother to her death. He thought, *Was it a conspiracy against me?* But the sound of Kuan San's steps behind him prevented him from daring to think further along this line.

The flames by the path soared high into midair, looking mighty glorious both up close and from a distance, and tore away completely Cripple Big's sense of being wronged. He'd never been so celebrated in his entire life.

Mom asked, "Why are they lighting fires?"

"To worship the river god! They are all worshipping the river god!"

Mom was very happy. She said, "Savory Lad isn't like that old thief. I've never seen such fires! But I've eaten mutton. I ate mutton on my wedding day. The meat wasn't well cooked. But it was fine nevertheless, it was mutton after all. Is it really well cooked this time?"

"Really well cooked!" Cripple Big shook his body; Mom scooted up a couple of times.

"Savory Lad is so strong! When you shake, I feel like I'm going up to heaven!" Mom said happily.

The fires of the village gradually disappeared behind them. The dam's shadow began to loom large. As soon as the folks from Brilliant King Clan retreated, the villagers dammed the embankment again. Even though they knew their opponent would come and dig again, they couldn't rest in peace without blocking it. As Cripple Big walked along the embankment, his body swayed. He thought, *Why did I forget to ask Braggart back then to let Mom really get a meal of mutton?* If he'd asked, Braggart might have satisfied his request. But he forgot, and now it was too late. Mom was still hungry! He was muddle-headed when he got home in the afternoon. As soon as Mom asked about food, he replied, "I'll carry you on my back to eat meat tonight!" He thought, *I really should've let Mom enjoy a meal of meat.*

"How come there's no mutton?" Mom asked.

"They'll bring it in a little while."

Kuan San said, "Okay, okay, let's just do it here!"

Here was the battleground of the armed confrontation. It was a familiar spot to Cripple Big. Having carried Mom all this way, he was tired. The tiredness squeezed the misery out of him. Cripple Big wiped the sweat off his face and put Mom down. Mom stood unsteadily, looked around, and sniffed. She wanted very much to smell the aroma of mutton, but there was none. There were only the odors of mud, tadpoles, and a stench created by a mixture of other stuff.

"Where's the mutton?" Mom asked.

Kuan San said, "In a little while, the Dragon King will invite you to a feast!"

"What Dragon King?" Mom asked.

Kuan San said, "Let's just do it here!" He lifted up the spade, but Cripple Big stopped him and said, "Why not drown her!" Kuan San said, "A drowned corpse wouldn't look like it was hacked to death!" Cripple Big said, "Drown her first and then hack." Cripple Big wanted to say something to Mom, but he couldn't.

Mom realized something was wrong. She said, "Savory Lad, your dad lied to me my entire life, but you've never lied to me! I only came because I trusted you!"

"It's up to you!" Kuan San gave Mom a shove from the back, and she fell into the water like a black butterfly.

Cripple Big wanted to cry. He felt he should cry: he should cry "Mom!" loudly and then wail furiously. But he could do nothing, and he was unable to cry. He looked around at the dark night and felt that he was in a dream.

But a plopping sound emerged from the water. Kuan San lit a kerosene lamp and watched the black lump float and sink with water splashing around it. Cripple Big closed his eyes. He tried with all his might not to think that the black thing was Mom, but tears surged up all of a sudden. He wanted to say, "Mom, I didn't lie to you." But he knew Mom wouldn't have believed him.

The black thing squirmed and actually climbed up the bank. Kuan San gave it a kick and pushed it down. It climbed up again, and he gave it another kick. And then, he got tired of kicking. He swung the spade, and the black shadow was quiet.

"You can't blame me. They won't believe us without any injuries!" said Kuan San. He fished out the black lump with one hand and shone the light on it. Half of its head was gone. Its white porridge-like brain was pouring out. He mumbled, "So puny, worse than a sheep!"

Cripple Big saw Mom's remaining eye stare at him as if she couldn't believe that her son would lie to her. Ajia said, "Of course she didn't know her son, who had never lied before, only lied to her this once. But this once was enough to take her life."

Diamond Clan Could Raise Its Head Now

Ajia's tone began to get wound up. It was like a change of tempo in music. He said, "Look! Diamond Clan could raise its head now!" The villagers raised high the board of a door upon which Cripple Big's Mom was placed, and walked toward the territory of Brilliant King Clan. Cripple Big wore a funerary outfit and was followed by a crowd. They were quiet while they proceeded along the way until they reached Brilliant King Clan's territory, when they began to yell slogans. That was also when Cripple Big began to wail. He felt as if he were in a dream, but when he saw his mom clearly on the door board, he couldn't help but want to weep. The image of Mom scrambling in and out of the water kept on creeping into his mind.

"My dear Mom!" Cripple Big yelled as he wept.

Kuan San said, "Add 'Brilliant King Clan deserves death'!"

But Cripple Big wailed, "Kuan San deserves death!"

"No, no!" shouted Donkey Two, "It's Brilliant King Clan, not Kuan San!" Cripple Big tried very hard to correct himself. At first it was difficult, but after a while, it became natural. After yelling the slogan dozens of times, he even began to believe it was indeed Brilliant King Clan that had killed his mother. Certainly, when he thought about it carefully, *the real culprit was truly Brilliant King Clan. If they hadn't come to steal the water, who would've been willing to throw his own mother into the water?*

"My dear Mom! Brilliant King Clan deserves death!" Cripple Big wailed.

"Brilliant King Clan deserves death!" Jie Big and the others responded in chorus.

Old Daddy-Nine, however, laughed. The folks asked him: "What are you laughing at?" "How can you laugh when he's lost his mom?" Someone else said, "That's right! Everyone else hates Brilliant King Clan. We're all filled with anger. But here you are laughing instead! Could you be a spy for Brilliant King Clan?" Old Daddy-Nine would not respond to them, and he continued to laugh. Ajia said, "No one knew why he was laughing, but they all felt disturbed by it."

Cripple Big also felt disturbed. If it were someone else, he would've spat at the person. But Old Daddy-Nine had always been kind to him. So he ignored Old Daddy-Nine, raised his voice, and roared, "Brilliant King Clan deserves death!"

The moment he stopped roaring, he heard a piercing cry. He turned around to take a look and saw it was none other than Old Daddy-Nine, wailing loudly with tears and mucus streaming down his face. Although he was laughing a moment ago, he was now wailing. One rarely heard Old Daddy-Nine cry. So some folks said, "Old Daddy-Nine has gone mad from old age!" Just as they were still feeling shocked, he stopped crying and laughed ominously again.

Along the way, all the folks of Brilliant King Clan stuck their heads out to watch. Then one of them yelled, "Oh no! Someone has died!" Thereupon, nervousness wafted through the depths of Brilliant King Clan like a wind. Seeing them so, Cripple Big wailed even more feverishly, and Jie Big also roared even more emphatically.

The center of Brilliant King Clan was also its Ancestral Hall. You know, back then the center of all the villages was the Ancestral Hall. Many people had already gathered in the Ancestral Hall, craning their necks to watch the source of the wailing. They were also very nervous. They never doubted the deceased was killed by one of their own, since one of the precepts of Vajras, the deities worshipped by Diamond Clan, was not to lie. Brilliant King Clan had a larger population, and there was no preventing one of their more reckless ones from committing such a deed. They did wonder, however, why the opponent waited until now to settle the debt? So one of them asked this question.

Thereupon Kuan San roared, "We, your elders, just found out. The corpse was soaking in the water!" Ajia said, "You know, lies tend to sound more convincing than truths. That fact established, the lips of all the folks of Brilliant King Clan were sealed. No one dared to pose another question."

Ajia said, "The crowd gradually increased in size, but all their faces appeared sullen. Human life was priceless after all! Now that someone had died, they were in the wrong in principle. Even without considering right or wrong, it was sickening enough just to see the corpse on a door board with its white mess of brain matter. Cripple Big had covered Mom's face with a piece of paper, but the wind blew it away in no time. According to their custom, the deceased shouldn't be exposed to sunlight. But since the bloody corpse was able to subjugate all the villagers of Brilliant King Clan, he conveniently forgot all about the custom. When he thought how Mom had suffered throughout her entire life and wasn't even able to possess a wholesome body after death, Cripple Big couldn't help but wail loudly. The villagers of Brilliant King Clan also became aggrieved upon hearing his wailing."

Seeing this rare sight of Brilliant King Clan behaving themselves, Kuan San and the others were most pleased.

Ajia said, "Now that the affair involved human life, which was priceless, the county government had to get involved. Those of Diamond Clan heaved a sigh. For many years, they had hoped to get the county government involved and bring justice to their side."

But Old Daddy-Nine leaned against a small tree and cried. His crying was very loud. Even louder than Cripple Big's.

The Round Stone Pile

Historical Mirror of Forgotten Events records in detail the court proceedings and depositions from both sides. Now, one never knew when Brilliant

King Clan might make a comeback. When that happens, then the records would become primary evidence.

The corpse was exposed to scorching sun for three days in front of the Brilliant King Clan Ancestral Hall. The prominent figures of both clans and a county official negotiated in the hall. Locked in stalemate, neither side was willing to relent. In terms of clout, Brilliant King Clan was obviously more powerful. But since they'd killed someone, they had lost in principle. So Diamond Clan could insist with the might of steel teeth and iron mouths. Because of the fact that Diamond Clan was situated at a higher location, the water had to collect for more than twenty days before they could irrigate their land. They wanted to legalize the dam and build a sluice so that when the clans needed to irrigate, they would open the sluice and keep the dam intact. This was key to Diamond Clan's ability to irrigate, and it wouldn't prevent Brilliant King Clan from irrigating, so the latter agreed to it after mediation by the county official.

This was a tremendous victory. Ajia said, "Cripple Big's mom didn't die in vain!"

The next step involved the number of days each clan would be allotted for irrigation. Brilliant King Clan had ten times the amount of land that Diamond Clan had, so they requested ten times the amount of time for irrigation. This was a fair proposition. However, three days of irrigation per month could hardly satisfy the needs of Diamond Clan. The fact that Diamond Clan suffered a death meant it wasn't possible for the treaty to be fair. It had to be lopsided: Who told you, Brilliant King Clan, to kill someone?

This argument lasted three days with no results. But everyone left the entrance to the Ancestral Hall because the corpse was green and bloated, and it was exuding a putrid fluid. Green-headed flies congregated, followed by maggots that covered the corpse and began to spread. The stench whistled and spun. Unable to withstand the stench, the heads of the two clans moved their location for negotiation. Kuan San gestured with his eyes, and Jie Big and Old Daddy-Nine immediately stuffed cilantro into their nostrils and followed the heels of the clan heads. The corpse followed wherever the heads of the clans went. The unbearable stink permeated Brilliant King Clan's territory. Many people couldn't stop vomiting. Even more disgusting were the maggots which had no qualms. They formed a flood that spread wherever they felt like spreading. Maggots could be found at the base of everyone's walls.

They all cried, "Disgusting! Disgusting!"

The heads of Brilliant King Clan began to concede. They agreed to give the opponent water for four days and nights.

No, said Braggart, this wasn't even enough to feed the cats. Ajia said, "Although Braggart sounded harsh, he was actually delighted inwardly by the sign that the opponent was willing to negotiate. The water from a day and night could in fact irrigate several hundred *mu* of land!"

"It's too stinky! Too stinky!" the folks of Brilliant King Clan gathered to complain to the negotiators.

The heads of Brilliant King Clan conceded again, "We'll give you five days and nights."

"No!" Braggart and his men had steel teeth and iron mouths. "It's got to be at least ten days and nights!"

"Ten days and nights?" They cried in disbelief. "What insatiable lions! You have so little irrigation land. And you've also got arable mountain slopes that only need one good douse of rain. We'll have to stab our throats! You get meat, but at least give us some broth! At most, we'll give you six days and nights. Even for this, we'll have to abandon a lot of our land."

"No! No!" cried Braggart and his men, "we'll take this lawsuit to the capital!"

According to Ajia, at first the county official was just making useless, ambiguous comments, the way someone uses thin mud to smooth over an already smooth wall. He could've played this game until both sides became exhausted, but that stench was truly unbearable. That stench was different from other stink. It was a stench only found in rotten corpses. He'd already thrown up five times. Any more vomiting, and he'd probably throw up the bitter fluid of his bile. So he was forced to speak up.

"I say seven days! We'll make it seven days. The government also had a meeting concerning this—seven days it is. Brilliant King Clan will get twenty-three days. No more yelling!"

"Not days, it's days and nights," corrected Braggart.

"You're right. Seven days and nights," said the deputy county mayor. "It was studied by the county government."

Since the county government had already met and made the decision, there was nothing the heads of Brilliant King Clan could say. They just sucked in air between their teeth for a while before they said, "Okay, that's it! No more! Any more arguments, we'll pay for the life with another life and fend for the family of the person willing to die!"

Braggart said, "You can't say that—the most valuable thing in the world is human life!" Ajia said, "Based on this sentence alone, Braggart could join the ranks of superior politicians."

Then the deputy county mayor had his secretary write a document. The two clan heads put their fingerprints on it while he served as the witness.

Those of Diamond Clan returned home in euphoria. According to the deputy county mayor, the corpse was so stinky it should have been buried wherever right away. But Braggart said, "No way, this is evidence! We'll take it home, put it on the dam, and erect a stone pile on top of it!"

Ajia said, "Later, when Jasper returned to the village, he saw the circular stone pile at Diamond Clan's dam and thought it was an *e'bo*[5] for sacrificing to the mountain god!"

---

5. Known as "obo" in Mongolian, this is a heap of stones or wood piled on top of a mountain or highlands for performing sacrificial rituals.

Chapter 11

The Crunching of Fava Beans
in the Dead of Night

It was said that the comet grew a tail again.
That broomstick
Must have been your flipping, flying long hair.
Can you sweep up all the spit in the sky?
This world,
Why is there never a swath of Pure Land?

The Bears' Return of Favor

Tale of the Goddess records the beautiful sunny afternoon before Snow Feather met with calamity. Grandpa Sun smiled happily in the sky. There was neither mist nor cloud. The snowy mountain in the distance loomed down, filling her heart with crispness. The air was full of the bright laugh of sunshine.

Mom said, "Today is such a fine day! Carry me down there, I should walk around some. If I don't walk, I won't have legs anymore!" Mom pounded on her legs. Mom always sat cross-legged. She strictly followed the rule of sitting cross-legged when she recited Buddha's name. Snow Feather thought that the crux of cultivation lay in the mind rather than the legs. But then decided, "Let Mom be! Mom should be able to do whatever she pleased." She grabbed a sheepskin, carried Mom on her back, and climbed down the tree.

The valley was one large expanse of brilliance. Sunlight spread all over like a thick layer of gold and sang loudly and happily. The leaves danced. Haloes of light collided in the sky, creating goldlike tinkling jingles that harmonized with the birds' chirping. The bear cubs ran over clumsily when they saw Snow Feather climb down and started to nudge her with their heads. Snow Feather was touched by their show of affection. She hadn't been as intimate with Mom for many years now. The bear cubs grunted lovingly. Snow Feather thought that their parents must have told them about how Mom helped with their births. Having stayed a long time in Old Mountain, she realized that animals have their own languages. They could communicate among themselves and tell each other stories. They could also transmit their own culture and pass along their own wisdom. Mother bear watched Snow Feather's mom from a distance and looked very pleased. It wasn't clear where the male bear had gone. Ever since the female bear gave birth, the main job of the male bear was to seek food. Since bears eat both vegetarian and nonvegetarian foods, seeking a meal wasn't a difficult task. But on a moonlit night, Snow Feather actually saw the male bear worship the moon. Grandpa Jiu had said animals could also do self-cultivation. Their practice consisted of worshipping the moon. As they worshipped, their animal nature would gradually vanish, until they could transcend themselves and possess supernatural powers. Snow Feather had seen foxes worship the moon, but she never expected bears to do it too. Of course, she never expected this self-cultivating bear would someday be embroidered into Tankas by her believers and revered as a protector of the Dakini Goddess.

It was warm during the day but chilly at night in Old Mountain. As soon as Grandpa Sun descended behind the mountain, cold winds would whirl around. Snow Feather got some animal hide but could barely fend off the cold. She thought, *This isn't sufficient long term.* She had to think of something! The bear cubs soon grew chubby and were always playing by the cave entrance. Although it was a good cave, Snow Feather didn't have the heart to nab it from them. Her mother's eyes were covered with a film. It was said the bile of bears could melt it. A sticky fluid would start to flow from the eyes, and after a few days, the eyes would regain sight. Although this smacked of quackery, she knew the bile of bears was good for curing eye diseases. Who would've thought that, when she mentioned it to Mom, Snow Feather got an earful from her, who said, "This old lady here deserves to be blind, don't you ever scheme against the bears!"

When Mom said this, Snow Feather's face turned red.

After Mom helped the bear give birth, the bears became their best friends and always placed animals they'd caught under the tree. Once, they even got a deer. It was hard to imagine how such clumsy bears managed to catch the expert runner. The bear couple must have expended much strength and effort. Snow Feather was very touched. Although she didn't intend to take their bear bile to cure her mom's eyes, her face still turned red. She felt the thought itself was an insult to bearkind.

The bear cubs' show of affection greatly moved Snow Feather. Although they were small, she still swayed when nudged by them. Snow Feather carried Mom in her arms to more level ground, lay down the sheepskin, and had Mom lie on it. The little bears cuddled in her mom's bosom and nudged her with their hairy heads. Mom was happy and amused!

Suddenly, they heard the roar of an animal nearby. It was the male bear. It was fast approaching and carrying an animal on his back. The bear cubs rushed over in delight. Snow Feather thought of something, and her face flushed suddenly. Mom said, "Look at how they enjoy themselves!" The bear cubs stood up and played with their father. The male bear grunted in a low voice, sounding a bit grumpy, but also as though it was teasing them.

The father and sons sported affectionately for a while before they entered the cave. It was then that Snow Feather discovered the male bear was in fact carrying a wolf. The wolf's head was smashed—it must have been crushed by the bear's paw. The male bear tossed the wolf in front of her and looked at her with his black eyes. She understood what he meant. The wolf was a present for her. She knew wolf meat tasted terrible, but obviously the bear didn't know that. But Mom needed a wolfskin blanket. The downhill wind was ever stronger at night and was always swirling around the bird nests. Nothing could've been better than a wolfskin blanket. Her heart felt warm. *Animals are much better than humans*, she thought. *Animals always return favors, while, more often than not, humans return favors with enmity.* She stripped the wolf, cut a piece of meat, and gave it to the bear cubs. The bear cubs barely had teeth and weren't yet strong. They tore at the meat for quite a while and created muddy lumps out of it.

Mom said, "Don't throw away the meat! Although it tastes awful, it's good for curing stomach chills." Snow Feather nodded. She then cut some, which she threw into the pythons' cave, as well as the bears' cave, before she cooked the rest.

Snow Feather had eaten wolf meat before. Wolves from different places had different flavors. The best tasted like dog meat, except with a heady, muddy zing to it. Others tasted quite awful—like sawdust. The wolf the bear caught had a muddy taste to it, somewhat like the dog meat found at Diamond Clan. Mom had stomach chills and was frequently uncomfortable, so she ate more of it.

Snow Feather mixed some mud, which she smeared onto the inside of the wolfskin. Wolfskin had to be tanned, or else it would be infested by worms. But tanning required technical expertise; besides, there was no way of getting the necessary ingredients. She had no option but to use the traditional method employed by villagers, which meant smearing it with mud several times and then exposing it to the sun. When all the hide's grease was drawn off by the mud, then it was barely usable.

Mom said, "My eyes are always twitching these days. Wonder what's happening in the village? I'm worried about your uncle. He's old, and the harvest was bad. I wonder how he's managing? Find some time to look in on him. Don't make a big deal of it, just look in on him. You can take some of this wolf meat with you. Although it tastes awful, it's still meat!"

Snow Feather got her mother settled in, took some wolf meat, and headed down the mountain. Although the weather was getting chilly, the grass was still a lush green. The snowy mountain in the distance glinted. The snow on top never melted, but the snow on the mountainside would turn into the rivers that watered Liangzhou. They were historically known as the Valley Waters. They included the Stone Sheep River, Pricking Wood River, and West Camp River; they constituted the lifeline of the entire Liangzhou. Diamond Clan was one of the beneficiaries of the Valley Waters. When the tabs were tallied, however, it was clear that while they benefited from the water, every generation also suffered untimely deaths because of it. Much as water provided for Diamond Clan, it also caused the villagers to suffer the miseries of armed conflict.

There were also paths in Old Mountain, but what were known as paths were just spaces among boulders that could barely accommodate one's feet. The roadside weeds were taller than the travelers. Snakes infested the weeds. But they shouldn't be referred to as snakes: they were known as little dragons. The little dragons weren't afraid of humans. Many years ago, they loved to go to Snow Feather's home. She used to find a coiled sleeping snake whenever she opened a flour cupboard or a rice chest. Mom would have Snow Feather light incense, kneel down, and pray, "Little dragon! If you came from the mountain, please return to the mountain. If you came from the waters, please return to the waters. This humble place of ours cannot accommodate an honorable guest like you. Please leave!" After praying thus a few times, the snake would slither onto a plate. Snow Feather would then take the plate to an area rarely visited by humans, put it down, and kowtow to it. The snake would slowly slither away and disappear among the weeds. She remembered being very young at the time. Those days brought back warm memories.

Unconsciously, she grew up and experienced many other things. Never again had she delighted in this particular childhood amusement.

The Familiar Stench

After leaving the mountain, what greeted Snow Feather was a familiar sight during any period of starvation, a recurring historical cycle that had become inescapable nightmares of humankind.

It was obvious there had been great changes outside of Old Mountain. The gullies were littered with sinister piles of scattered bones. A pack of wolves was gnawing on any with shreds of meat left on them. When they saw Snow Feather approach, they snarled instead of fleeing. She brought out her lasso, a nylon rope six feet long with a two-kilo weight at its end. She'd adapted it from the stick the villagers used to control dogs. Wolves were the dogs of the mountain god. They feared ropes. As soon as the wolves saw the coiled rope in her hands, their smile turned into whimpers.

There was a certain smell, the kind Mom used to refer to as "dead kitchen stoves with cold ashes." In other words, everything in sight lacked life. There was not a single sign of human life; everything smelled of death. Even Grandpa Sun lacked color, brightness, and vivacity; it was barely performing its job.

She did a rough calculation. It didn't seem like she'd been in the mountain for more than a few days, but it must've been many months. Seven days in a grotto would be equivalent to a thousand years in the mortal world!

The last time she entered the mountain, Grandpa Jiu transmitted to her Niguma's Mahamudra yogi classic, "Technique for Transforming the World into an Illusion." According to Grandpa Jiu, "Thoughts constitute one's mind. Knowing your mind makes transformation possible. By day, you should cultivate transforming the illusory body, and by night, cultivate your dreams. When one studies the self through the six roots[1] and its corresponding six dusts,[2] then the self will attain illusory nature. Once one has attained illusory-nature but is visible, then there is no difference between illusions and manifestations. Being visible without the self is the same as transforming the world into an illusion. If you practice this technique of creating an illusory world, you will eliminate attachments and the making of distinctions, and thereby enter into a deep state of meditation." Snow Feather practiced this technique. Gradually, she was able to dissolve the various physical manifestations into illusions and feel as though she were dream-walking when she traveled.

It was quite a distance to Diamond Clan after Snow Feather left Old Mountain. There was no sign of inhabitants in the settlements along the way. The land was strewn with terrible remnants of corpses, torn apart by dogs and wolves. Ghastly winds made the stench whistle and whirl. The mountain was full of drifting vengeful souls and roaming ghosts who wailed the way witches did when they summoned the souls. Their cries of hunger filled heaven and earth. Snow Feather chanted spells to help release their souls from purgatory. But most souls clung to their exposed corpses in the wilderness. Generous as heavenly rain might have been, it couldn't nurture the grass without roots. Awesome as Snow Feather was, she couldn't bring salvation to those without the karma for it. So she concluded, *fine, if you want to stand guard over your corpses, you go ahead!*

Suddenly she saw someone peeling the fine bark off an elm. The trunk of the tree was already stripped bare. Only the branches had some fine bark left, and he was scraping it carefully into a dish. He looked terribly emaciated and resembled a hungry ghost, swaying so badly whenever he moved that he probably wouldn't last long. Snow Feather cut off a piece of wolf meat and handed it to him. His eyes sparkled

---

1. In Buddhism, the six roots refer to the eyes, the ears, the nose, the tongue, the body, and one's intention.

2. The six dusts refer to sex, sound, smell, taste, touch, and method.

upon seeing the meat. He grabbed it and sank his teeth into it, his head shaking from side to side, like a wild dog tearing at an ox's sinew.

Snow Feather asked, "What happened?"

She asked several times, but the man ignored her. He concentrated on tearing off the meat. Only after he'd managed to swallow a few mouthfuls did he reply, "Dead, dead, almost all dead and gone!" "What's Diamond Clan like?" "Don't know. They all say Diamond Clan is doing well. But people have gone in, and no one has come out. People say those who went in were cooked and eaten." Snow Feather didn't feel like asking any more questions. She just said, "What nonsense! The folks of Diamond Clan aren't cannibals!"

Snow Feather heaved a heavy sigh. She knew that given the misery along the way, Diamond Clan was bound to be no better.

By the afternoon, she finally saw the entrance to Diamond Clan. Kuan San and others were beating someone up. The person wailed, "Why can't I leave to survive?" Kuan San said, "Don't you leave! We'll die together if it comes to that!" And they dragged him back into the village.

Snow Feather took a side path into the village and went up Screen-Wall Hill. The village was also full of "cold ashes and dead stoves." The gully was full of corpses, with a stench that choked the sky. The dark gullies swarmed with squirming black spots like flaxseeds. Hard to tell whether they were wolves or wild dogs.

Seeing no villagers, she followed the ridge down into the village. Uncle lived at the foot of a large hill. They didn't visit each other much. She had the impression Uncle was heartless and lacked goodness. Although people called him Degree-Holder Ho,[3] he was in fact as quarrelsome as a fighting cock. Sometimes, when he didn't have enough to eat, he'd visit Snow Feather's house. Uncle loved to eat yam noodles with vinegar sauce. Her mom would cool the noodles with water and dress them with vinegar sauce. Uncle would take the bowl and fill the room with thundering slurp. But although he ate their food, he had no qualms about cursing her mom in front of the villagers, denouncing her as a disgrace to the family. Mom, however, was always worried about Uncle. After all, he was her only relative; even if one were to break a bone, the muscles would be connected. Whenever Snow Feather complained about Uncle, Mom

---

3. *Xiucai*, also known as holder of the licentiate or bachelor's degree, the lowest of the three degrees in Imperial China.

would say, "Uncle is your flesh and blood.[4] Without him, where would you be?" Fortunately, Uncle was kind to Snow Feather. Even if she were to ask him for a star, he would think of a way to pluck it.

The stench became increasingly strong: it was truly an evil stench. Snow Feather held her breath as she walked. She remembered the terrible things the villagers did. She didn't want to deal with them, or even to think about them. Grandpa Jiu said she didn't have enough compassion and urged her to have more. In her daily visualization practice, she was always expatiating sins and beseeching blessings for the people, but her people didn't seem to include any of the villagers. She couldn't help but feel a surge of anger whenever she thought of those who'd put Mom through so much torment. Grandpa Jiu said, "What you need to exterminate the most is rage. Remember, that's a fire which can scorch your forest of merit and virtue!"

The gate of Uncle's household was shut tight. Snow Feather didn't need to knock. She slipped the latch and the gate opened. Third-Turner was sunning himself in the courtyard and greeted her with a smile. His inner organs no longer had any support and drooped down to create a protruding belly. But his smile was still radiant. He yelled happily, "Mom, Older Sister is here!" After a long while, Aunt came out. Her face was so bloated that her eyes were but narrow slits. She uttered an "Mm" as a form of greeting and let Snow Feather into the house. There was a layer of dust in the room. It probably had not been dusted for many days. Uncle was lying on the brick bed. When he saw Snow Feather enter, he struggled to raise himself into a sitting position. He didn't say anything; but to Snow Feather, his silence spoke volumes. She thought, *The trouble she caused last time might've had repercussions for him.* Although he was educated, his poverty—along with his wife's well-known wanton behavior—made him a person no one respected in the village. It was said that Aunt would loosen the sash of her pants for any man in the village. When the men had nothing better to do, they'd discuss their experiences with Aunt at the corner of the southern village wall. It was also said Aunt had the habit of beating Uncle up. She would push frail Uncle onto the ground, sit her mill-like buttocks on top of him, and reduce him to howling and wailing. Aunt had her good points though. She was a tremendous worker. During harvest time

---

4. *Gutou zhu'er*, literally, the master of your bones, refers to the maternal uncle in northwestern China.

in the autumn, Braggart would point to the ripened wheat and say, "Three 'works' for reaping one *mu* of the field." In other words, one could earn three days' pay for reaping one *mu* of wheat. Aunt could scythe from the afternoon until the next morning to harvest one and a half *mu* of wheat—which meant she could earn four and a half days' wages, in just a day and night. She made more from this than anyone else in the village. It was on account of her that when the wages were tallied in the autumn, Uncle was able to carry home from the Ancestral Hall about enough food for more than half a year.

Uncle dragged himself up. He didn't ask any questions, which was, of course, fine with Snow Feather. She didn't want to tell him where she was staying, either. She brought out the wolf meat, and the three boys pounced on her. Aunt slapped them away. They fell and bawled, but their hollering sounded more like gasping. There was, in fact, no sound. *They're really starved*, thought Snow Feather. She took out a dagger, cut a few slices of wolf meat, and gave them to the boys. Third-Turner gulped down his own slice, grabbed his elder brother's, and zipped away like wind. Number Two bawled, and Snow Feather cut another slice for him.

"How disgraceful!" sighed Aunt.

Snow Feather said nothing. She didn't like Aunt. Aunt's face was very bloated. Snow Feather found her disgusting because she was always seducing debauched fellows into coming to her house when Uncle wasn't around. Once, during Chinese New Year, Snow Feather's mom bid her to go visit Uncle. As soon as she entered the house, she saw strange men crouched on the brick bed. The Aunt was flirting with them and totally ignored Snow Feather. Ever since then, Snow Feather rarely visited Uncle's home.

Snow Feather asked Uncle, "Why have so many people in the village died? Isn't there grain in the storehouse?"

"Those are reserves in case of war," said Uncle. "Braggart has the clan militia guarding them! People died in most village households. Quite a few families had everyone die. Any longer, the entire village will be finished." Aunt said, "If we have to die, then everyone should be dead!" Her eyes gleamed with hatred. Snow Feather shuddered. She felt Aunt had somehow changed. Although Aunt had been lascivious in the past, she'd never exuded such menacing coldness. *Hatred can make people evil*, thought Snow Feather.

Snow Feather fed Uncle a piece of wolf meat. Uncle munched on it. His eye sockets were sunken and dry, and his eyes looked glazed.

After munching for a long while, Uncle said, "We're finished. There's no way we can last till winter!"

Snow Feather said, "Although the wheat hasn't ripened, there are ears on them. Why not steal some to eat?" "Don't talk nonsense!" Aunt looked around nervously, "Don't you know anyone caught 'stealing crops' gets beaten to death? The corpses in the gully—some died of starvation, others were beaten to death."

Uncle said, "Girl, get some water and cook the meat thoroughly. I have trouble chewing it!" Snow Feather nodded and went outside to get some hay. She then took the lid off the wok and found that hairy green mold had already grown in it. A familiar stench rushed to her nose. She turned around and saw Aunt staring at her wickedly. She immediately took a spatula and scooped out the green hair. Only then did she realize the stench came from a few pieces of meat . . . "That's strange, where did this meat come from?" "The monk brought us some mutton," explained Uncle. She stifled her disgust and scooped the stinky sticky stuff into a broken basin. Unexpectedly, a finger suddenly jumped into her vision; its shining nail was laughing at her!

Aunt giggled embarrassingly and said, "We had to find some way to survive!"

Snow Feather tried not to throw up. She washed out the wok, added water to it, and boiled the wolf meat. She kept on feeling Aunt's eyes sweeping over her, but she dared not turn her head around because the woman's expression reminded her of a hungry ghost looking at steamed buns. She felt weird, fed the stove fire, and walked into the courtyard. Their boys were watching the wok from a distance. She thought, *Kids are kids, they'll brighten up as soon as there's a bit of food in their stomachs.* Suddenly, she saw Third-Turner sneaking a peek at her. To her surprise, his expression was exactly the same as that of Aunt's. She couldn't help but shudder.

The smoke rose straight up into the sky from the chimney, and then scattered down. The courtyard became hazier. Snow Feather felt that the smoke had a conspiratorial smell because it so stealthily enveloped her. Her dreamlike feeling became ever more intense.

Snow Feather carried another bundle of wheat straw into the house. Uncle asked, "Is she okay?" Uncle always used "she" instead of "older sister" when referring to her mother. Snow Feather responded with a *hmm*. She fed the fire a few times, and steam poured out of the wok.

Flames radiated from the stove fire. As soon as she saw the firelight, Snow Feather felt like laughing at herself. She was truly overly sensitive. Sure enough, as soon as she thought this way, she only saw gratefulness in Aunt's eyes, although Aunt said nothing. Aunt was a strong-willed woman. Of course, she didn't want Snow Feather to see such a humiliating sight. These days, everyone was in the same boat, Snow Feather had a mind to tell her. But she knew this would embarrass Aunt. So she thought she better not say anything.

After it had cooked awhile, Snow Feather poked at the wolf meat with chopsticks. It felt much softer. She fished out a piece, tore it into long shreds, and poured hot broth over it. She then asked where the salt was. "We haven't tasted salt for more than half a year already," replied Aunt. Snow Feather brought over a bowl to Uncle to feed him. He drank a few mouthfuls of the broth first. Snow Feather suddenly felt sorry for Uncle. Because she saw the shadow of her mom in his face, she felt something warm soar in her heart. She picked up some wolf meat with chopsticks and fed it to Uncle. Suddenly she heard a thundering slurping and realized it was Aunt drinking broth out of a ladle. The boys rushed at her. But one push from Aunt, and they all tumbled back outside. But none of them cried. They crawled back up and stared at their parents' mouths. Snow Feather felt a sniffle in her nose.

After Uncle ate half a bowl, Snow Feather said, "That's enough, you don't want to get sick from overeating." She took the bowl and called the boys who rushed over happily. She fed them a spoonful each at a time. *I should have brought more wolf meat,* she thought.

Aunt said, "Girl, don't leave. It's dark out there. There's something I want to tell you."

Snow Feather took a look at the brick bed, covered with a layer of dust, and frowned. She said, "No thanks, Mom will miss me." Actually, when she set out, Mom had told her to come back tomorrow if it got too late. She wasn't to travel at night under any circumstances. Snow Feather was also reluctant to travel at night. Her scalp tingled from the thought of the corpses along the way, but she was also scared of the brick bed at Uncle's home.

Uncle said, "Stay. I'll tell you about your mom. I may be in another world anytime now."

So Snow Feather decided, "Okay, I'll make do for the night!"

The Row of Heads Along the Brick Bed

The wan moonlight seeped through the plastic-covered window and shone on the row of heads along the brick bed.

Aunt took Third-Turner to the inner room, which had a wheat straw-covered brick bed. Aunt and Third-Turner rolled in the straw. Snow Feather felt somewhat guilty.

Uncle's voice sounded hollow. It was as if he were talking in his sleep. Uncle was telling her the story about her mom. Snow Feather had heard some of it before. For instance, Mom had told her so many people had died that their heads rolled like rocks on a shoal. Mom said that the cavalry delighted in chopping people's heads off. They spurred their horses and screamed as they approached. Mom ran and ran as if she were in a nightmare, but the dense pattering of the hoofs also caught up with her from behind in that nightmare. Heads flew off, one after the other. They screamed in terror as they spun through the air with gaping mouths, which were hoping to bite the wielders of the broad knives. But they ended up with only mouthfuls of sand and stones. Then they were hung from the horses' rumps and became just notes listed in someone's merit ledger.

Uncle said, "Your mom ran and ran but couldn't outrun the nightmare. The broad knives swished. Later, after the heads of all the men around her had flown off, the women were chased into a big courtyard. Your mom's future husband was among the men who guffawed maliciously."

"That was how Mom became a captive," sighed Uncle.

Mom never told her what happened to her next.

All the villagers knew, but Snow Feather did not.

Snow Feather knew Mom didn't want to reopen the old wound.

"That's all," said Uncle. And the house was quiet.

The wan moonlight shone into the room, and onto the row of heads along the brick bed.

Snow Feather felt as if she were in a dream.

The Resounding Cutting Knife

The sound of chomping on roasted fava beans came from the inner room. It sounded creepy in the dead of night. Snow Feather was not sleepy. The hollow sound of Uncle's words was still echoing in her head.

The moon shone on her Uncle's face. He was smacking his lips and consuming the moonlight, which must have been delicious as Uncle looked very content, although the smacking sound was quite loud and gave off a strange smell. The boys were all asleep. But Snow Feather felt as if they were looking at her through the slits of their eyes. The ruckus of squabbling wolves and dogs could be heard in the distance, rowdy and loud.

Aunt was still crunching loudly on fava beans. "Where on earth did she get them from? It's been a long while since I've had fava beans." Snow Feather remembered she was able to taste roasted fava beans only after the clan distributed bonuses. It was so tasty. Her mouth watered from hearing Aunt crunching on them.

She's so greedy, Snow Feather thought, she ate them all herself and didn't even give Uncle any.

Suddenly, she heard Aunt call out, "Snow Feather . . . Snow Feather." Aunt would feel embarrassed had she known I was listening to her. So she didn't respond.

There was a rustle in the inner room and then the pattering of footsteps out of that room. Curious as to what was happening, Snow Feather squinted and peeked. Much to her surprise, what Aunt was putting into her own mouth looked like someone's finger in the moonlight. Snow Feather's heart quickened. Aunt wafted slowly toward the boys. She opened her mouth and blew at their faces. She drew in a long breath and breathed out very slowly. Snow Feather recognized this as the practice of transferring one's own essence to one's children. Sometimes, when a child in the village had become too sick to eat, his mother would exhale onto him, when he was fast asleep, to transfer her essence to the child. Sometimes people who collapsed in the desert could also prolong their lives by inhaling each other's breath. *Aunt is a loving mother after all*, thought Snow Feather.

After breathing on her boys for a while, Aunt returned to the inner room but then came straight outside. In the moonlight, her face looked white and somewhat sinister. It was no longer bloated and in fact seemed quite attractive. No wonder the village men were glued to her—she was a beauty after all! She was surprised at the sinister way Aunt looked at her and suddenly realized Aunt had a pestle for smashing ginger in her hand. The sharp pestle shone like a blue burning ball of will-o'-the-wisp. Snow Feather had seen will-o'-the wisps before. The light was blue, and its flames licked the sky like flying camel hair in the wind. Aunt walked over slowly, as quietly as a shadow. Uncle had stopped smacking. He must've eaten enough moonlight. The moonlight continued to waft through the window in waves, bringing a feeling of maliciousness. Aunt's eyes also gleamed with a strange blue color. Snow Feather was not afraid of Aunt, but she did fear the strange blue gleam. She held her breath and told herself not to be scared. She moved her fingers a little, found them moving easily, and felt assured.

Aunt's silhouette appeared enormous, but Snow Feather knew it was because she was lying down herself. If she were standing, Aunt would have been of a normal size. *Why did Aunt do this?* she wondered. The answer became obvious. She could see hesitation written all over Aunt's face. She must have been struggling with herself. She knew Aunt didn't like her, but Aunt was her aunt after all. Besides, she came in order to bring wolf meat to them. She heard Uncle turn to another side in the bed and realized he was awake. She heard him say, "Are you really going to do it?" Aunt didn't say anything, and Uncle was silent. *I wish Uncle hadn't woken up,* thought Snow Feather, "if he weren't awake, I'd still have an uncle." But now that he woke up, she would never have an uncle again. She then heard Uncle say, "Don't let the girl suffer. At least he still remembered she was his niece. She then thought, *Why didn't it occur to them that she might not be asleep?* That was when she discovered a rope around her neck. Uncle held one end while the three boys held the other. They held their breath and were ready to pull hard should they find her awake. *So the three boys are also hopeless,* thought Snow Feather. This was when she realized Aunt must have been breathing at the boys to wake them up.

Aunt lifted the pestle. She lifted it very high and held her breath so she could concentrate her strength. Her eyes were wide open and very large. Snow Feather remembered how her face was so bloated that the eyes were just slits! So it seemed everything was done to confuse her. Suddenly, some strange faces appeared in the dark, and they were all laughing at her. Snow Feather knew they had all died under Aunt's ginger-smashing pestle. No wonder so many people died in the other households. Yet only one child died at Uncle's. It suddenly dawned on her that the deceased men must have been Aunt's lovers. They entered the court of the netherworld after being coaxed into her bed, and were pounded by the swishing ginger-smashing pestle. They were all lascivious ghosts and stared at her with lewd eyes. They were either looking for a substitute, or waiting for her to enter their world before they'd rape her. After she realized this, many more of them appeared with pestles in hand. Snow Feather found herself surrounded.

Aunt's pestle came down slowly and created a draft. What would have been considered fast normally became slow motion in Snow Feather's eyes, the way a video is played back at slow speed; and the draft bellowed like angry waves. The men egged her on, baring their yellow teeth and spraying stench. Their bloodstained eyes were wide open. They knew that Snow Feather was awake and winked at Aunt to warn her. But Aunt ignored them and flung down the pestle. Snow Feather could easily have grabbed Aunt's wrist, twisted it, and broken it. She knew that the wrist would have snapped like split firewood and filled the room with the sound of a raven's shriek. The rope around her neck tightened in readiness and trembled like a python filled with energy. Snow Feather could feel the excitement and nervousness of the rope pullers. They salivated for the tender flesh of her virginal body, tired of eating the tough flesh of old men. They salivated for this tender flesh that presented itself to them, not caring that she was their niece and cousin. To them, she was only delicious meat. Her breasts were as delicate and tender as camel humps; her hands and feet were as firm as bear's paws. Her fat was as aromatic as butter, and her tongue was indescribably wonderful. If they could only add some condiments, such as the "thirteen spices," then the flavor would be even more incredible. Snow Feather could even see their mouths dripping with fat while chewing her flesh and Aunt crunching on her fingers like roasted fava beans. Aunt's face shone with incomparable beauty. Her sexy lips exuded such sensual charm that the lascivious ghosts drooled even more. They sang softly and danced slowly, for the loyal souls through the limitless expanse of the sky.

The pestle was still falling in slow motion, the draft it created filled the sky. Eerie blue lights darted everywhere like rats grinding their teeth in the wilderness. Uncle's heart pounded like a flood. When the pestle was about to kiss Snow Feather's head, Aunt shouted in a low voice, "Die, you!" Aunt waited for the type of sound created by the pestle. In the past, whether the sound was dull or crisp, loud or muffled, high or low, depended on where the pestle landed. If it sounded like a splash, it meant that the target was either a fat person, or that the pestle landed directly on the nose, causing mucus to splash all over the pestle normally used for smashing ginger: this was, of course, quite disgusting. If, however, the sound created was a sharp and happy crash, then either the target was lean, or the pestle landed directly on the forehead. But if the force crushed the forehead, then brain matter would splatter, and heavenly food would be wasted. You should know the brain is the most nutritious part of the human body. It and the eyeballs were Third-Turner's favorites. Whenever steam poured out of the wok in full force, he would rush there first, stick in his thumb and first and middle fingers, and gouge out the eyeballs and the big glob of flesh around them. Eyeballs were black, but what covered them was grayish white and extremely tasty. Except the fluid around the eyeballs was somewhat bitter, but the delicious flavor would drown the bitterness, just like the sun always dispersed dark clouds. Aunt was hoping to hear a sharp sound since her husband told her not to let the girl suffer. She was a kind woman after all and didn't want her own niece to suffer too much. She'd hoped the pestle would strike Snow Feather's forehead or temple. A direct hit at those locations would either knock out or kill the person. Familiar with all the tricks of the trade like a professional executioner, of course, a sharp sound was what Aunt hoped to hear.

To her surprise, what she heard was a dull thud. From the feel of it, it was as if she had struck Snow Feather's belly. She was obviously shocked, except Snow Feather was unable to see her expression clearly in the moonlit night.

To Aunt's surprise, Snow Feather was staring at her. She didn't know where the pestle had landed. It felt like it landed on the pillow. But Snow Feather's head was on the pillow.

Aunt screeched eerily. She no longer worried about waking anyone up. She swung the pestle continuously like a madwoman, but every time it seemed to land on the pillow, although the pillow was evidently tucked under Snow Feather's head!

Aunt finally ran out of steam.

She threw down the pestle, ran into the kitchen, and rushed back with a cleaver. She screamed, "What are you waiting for? Do you think you'll live if you let her leave?" Judging from her tone, she was no longer just thinking about food but about destroying the evidence of the deed.

The cleaver swished piercingly. It was hard to believe that the aunt who had seemed so weak during the day could swing the cleaver like heavy rain. It must have been the training she attained from chopping meat for dumpling fillings. But strangely, what the cleaver struck was still the pillow. The hay in the pillow flew out and darted around the room like dragonflies.

"Pull the rope," Aunt screamed.

Snow Feather felt the rope around her neck tighten. Fearing they would succeed if she moved any slower, she gave it a swift tug and left for the courtyard. Snow Feather was so quick about it that by the time she had gotten to the courtyard Aunt was still chopping at the pillow.

Since Uncle and his boys still hung on, they were all in the courtyard with her. Snow Feather felt disgusted with them, so she swung the rope, and they and the rope became a swinging mallet. The swinging mallet felt very light, however. *They are truly starved*, she thought.

Aunt flung down the cleaver and wailed, "Girl! We want to live too!"

As soon as she cried out, Uncle and the boys released their hands and scattered off like crows.

The boys also wept. A black shadow rolled toward Snow Feather and knelt in front of her. It was Uncle.

Uncle bawled like a baby.

Origin of the Devastating Calamity

According to *Tale of the Goddess*, it was only midnight when Snow Feather left Uncle's home. Her heart felt unusually still; it was as if heaven had collapsed and the earth had sunk. Grandpa Jiu called that sensation "enlightenment." Did it mean, then, that she had become enlightened? Utter shock shrouded her. Uncle kowtowed to her and begged her not to blabber. He would utterly lose face, he said, "Everyone in the village was doing it." This was how all the beggars who entered the village became their food, although no one talked about it. It was okay if people had guessed it, but not for people to hear about it, much less to see it. Since Snow Feather had both heard and seen it, they'd all die should she tell the authorities about them.

Snow Feather left Uncle's house without saying anything.

The wan moon shone on the lonely white village. She recognized that queer stench. All the woks in the village cooked fingers. They were all children's fingers. She remembered how children's bones were the most numerous in the gully. Many of them were grayish white as though they'd been cooked. She thought perhaps the officials weren't aware of the situation. She should go to the city of Liangzhou the following day to report this. Their lives would be saved when the relief grains arrived.

Although the moonlight was bright, it turned pitch dark after she walked ten paces. The shock at Uncle's lessened the terror of darkness. In the past, she'd meditated at 108 locations of demonic terror. It was said the shock induced by them resembled enlightenment. Such being the case, her feelings this instant must have been a type of enlightenment. Everything blurred like an illusion. Mountains, rivers, and earth had all turned into shadows. She remembered traveling to all sorts of places in search of locations of demonic terror. But there was no comparison between the shock of those places and what she was feeling now. So, her "flesh and blood" was the true demonic terror! Everything appeared different now.

She had a mind to return to Old Mountain, but then decided that since she was already out here, she might as well make a trip to Liangzhou and report the starvation problem at Diamond Clan to the authorities. She was going to tell them about the cannibalism but then decided against it when she thought of her mom. Then she thought, *I don't have to say who was eating humans. I don't have to name anyone and implicate Uncle.*

Although the moonlight made it easier to travel, it had the disadvantage of showing her all the twisted corpses on the ground. Most hadn't a single scrap of flesh remaining. It wasn't clear whether wolves or humans consumed them. All the same, they were eaten. It was said when Zhang Xianzhong[5] occupied Sichuan, he killed the locals to feed his men. When all the Sichuanese were slaughtered, he'd kill his own men and horses. He had several million men, but when the founder of the Qing dynasty caught up with him, he'd already killed more than half of them. One arrow shot by the Qing, and his heart was pierced. So, the members of Uncle's household were not the only cannibals.

Snow Feather tried her best not to look at the corpses along the way. Green lights kept appearing. Snow Feather knew they were foxes and wolves rather than ghosts. Ajia said, "The foxes and wolves were in seventh heaven those days, with a glut of gourmet food. Consequently, they had no interest in attacking live people." Snow Feather wrapped around her waist a lasso with a dart at the end. One tug at the lasso, and the dart would fly off.

---

5. Zhang Xianzhong (1606–1647) was the leader of a peasant revolt from Yan'an, Shaanxi Province. He conquered Sichuan in the 17th century. His rule in Sichuan was brief, however, and he was killed by the invading Manchu army of the Qing dynasty (1644–1911).

Ajia said, "That night Snow Feather was not scared. She was just in total shock. Shock is even more emotionally charged than fear, you know. Fear only applies to the moment, while shock is attached to the past, present and future." Ajia's narrative tends to be self-contradictory. According to him, Snow Feather brought meat buns at Lanzhou several hundred leagues away in the amount of time it took to drink a cup of tea, but now he's claiming it took her half a night to get to the city of Liangzhou. Let's just not worry about that—he could explain it as her desire to travel slowly. He could come up with many excuses: I don't feel like exposing him.

Ajia said that the folks at the county seat were holding an assembly when Snow Feather reached the city of Lianzhou. A high official was making a speech. He was awesome and pompous. "The land in the region of Hexi was larger than the three islands of Great Britain," he claimed. So his speaking at Hexi was equivalent to speaking in Great Britain, which was also equivalent to speaking to the world. Ajia said this particular official was one of the greatest celebrities of his time. There were many other celebrities at the time—some even got written into poetry. "Such poets were sinners against the common folks," said Ajia. "Those they praised in poetry were the criminal ringleaders who caused the starvations. They were cheerleaders—none of them met a good end." Ajia said, "When a small butcher grew to be a big thug through the rooting of cheerleaders, the thug's butcher-knife will ultimately aim at those cheerleaders themselves."

I yelled at Ajia, "Stop screwing around! Continue with how the world got turned upside down!"

Snow Feather was thirsty and hungry. She stayed to one side, not daring to interrupt the self-righteous high official. She'd report the problem after the assembly. "The wait saved her," said Ajia, "otherwise she would not have lived to attain Buddhahood."

Suddenly, Snow Feather heard a terrifying scream, "Lord An, people are eating people!"

The person said exactly what Snow Feather had intended to say. A few people charged at him to cover his mouth, but he still managed to voice a lot of what Snow Feather had in mind. Snow Feather assumed the high official surnamed An would immediately dispatch relief, or at least order an investigation. But Lord An hollered at him for starting a rumor and for bringing shame to the folks of Liangzhou.

"Shoot him! Shoot him!" roared the high official.

Someone timidly said, "Of course he deserves to die, Lord An. But can we go through the legal process?"

"I am the law!" hollered Lord An, "shoot him! Shoot him!"

A rifle fired. Snow Feather was tongue tied.

"Back then, heads and corpses hung from the trees along the several hundred leagues between Liangzhou and Ganzhou," said Ajia. "Some starved to death, others were shot."

After that, Snow Feather returned to Old Mountain. She left Old Mountain again later. It was another night with wan light. She floated to the clan granary like a spirit.

This was the origin of the disaster she would encounter.

Chapter 12

The Crime

Along the long tunnel of space and time
　　　Approaching from Xixia,
The cavern wind harbors gossips from a thousand years,
　　　Wave after wave.
A black rope snickered in the darkness,
A skinny spirit danced in the wind;
At the end of the cold draft lies a cavern,
The cavern is a jealous witch.

The Monk Who Broke His Vow

That autumn Jasper was still a Buddhist monk who adhered strictly to his vows. He observed them as he guarded his own eyes. He couldn't have imagined that someday he would be considered, by others, as a wayward monk.

For years, his story was used as a negative example in lectures on celibacy at numerous monasteries. However, years later, his meeting with Snow Feather would become a sacred event. According to the local beliefs at Diamond Clan, he was an incarnation of the Vajra, Heruka Cakrasamvara. Rather than a wayward monk, he was known instead as the couple-cultivation partner of a Diamond Maiden incarnation. To date, tens of thousands of pilgrims still pay homage to the site where they completed their couple cultivation and reached Buddhahood.

That autumn Jasper began the journey of his destiny with the aid of *Tangut-Chinese Timely Pearl in the Palm*. Some say that Jasper was from

213

the distant Himalayan Mountains and had assiduously performed religious practices for many years in the snowy mountains. Others say Jasper lived in isolation for many years in Diamond Maiden Cave, through which he gained tremendous wisdom. He may even have authored *Tale of the Goddess*. My own research indicates he was at least a key person in the promulgation of the myth related to Diamond Maiden Cave.

On a desolate cold autumn day, the first book Jasper opened was *Crazy Ramblings of Ajia*.

Ajia's memories, which crossed space and time, provided tremendous inspiration to the authors of those manuscripts. It was said that the authors could also transcend space and time and meet with the aged but lively Ajia at numerous historical junctures. Of course, this was only based on hearsay.

That was when Jasper dispelled the mist of history and yelled, "Come out, Ajia!"

The Bloody Mess

In this narrative by Ajia, Butcher Zhang was still demanding payment from the girls in the cave during the Xixia dynasty. His hairy mouth gaped—the way Braggart would many years later—at the tears of the frail girls. Another typical scenario that had continued for a thousand years. Unlike those girls, however, the later women could not fly away. Only their words and tears could. After their tears flew for a while, some of them would say, "Let me die!" And flying away from this mortal world of red dust became their wish.

But the "butcher" would holler with his gaping hairy mouth, "I won't let you go, even if you die!"

Butcher Zhang must have been like that too.

When he saw the girls fly into the air, he grabbed one of them frantically.

"Your life or money!" Wasn't that what he hollered?

The girl's flying body stayed there for three hundred years.

History of Buddhism in the Amdo Region has a record about it:

. . . The Diamond Maiden Monastery, which was known as the Toad Cave, was not listed among the four monasteries of Liangzhou. An eight-year-old girl used to buy organ meat from a Butcher Zhang there. One day, when the butcher demanded payment, he chased after her and saw five girls performing a ritual offering. Furious that he hadn't received payment, the butcher grabbed the lead girl around the waist and flew up with her. Because of him, her body did not leave the mortal world. Later, people covered her with a thin layer of embalming incense. The four other girls flew into the sky. In this way, the butcher received enlightenment. To this day, there continues the custom of offering sacrifices to him by butchers. In the past, red sweet dew used to flow from the private parts of the girl's embalmed body on auspicious days. And then, one of King Huoer's consorts said, "What a disgrace for womankind!" and used gold to plug up her cervix. Subsequently, an inauspicious event ensued. Guru Manlong remarked, "She used to be eight feet above the ground, now she is only one hand span from the ground."

Note, in the historical book referenced above, the girl who remained behind stayed eight feet above the ground.

It also specified that she was suspended in midair.

This happened on the twenty-fifth day of the twelfth month of the lunar calendar of 1011.

That year, before the skeletons of Wang Xiaobo and Li Shun[1] had rotted, all the common folks of the Great Song dynasty had to tighten their belts. They looked gaunt, and their sweat poured like rain. But they dared not slacken for a single moment because the central government had issued a proclamation announcing the need to deliver the "annual tributary silver" to the Khitans of the Great Liao dynasty. A literary man known as Liu Sanbian[2] racked his brain to compose lyrics. Soon, the lewd songs of his "at the willow bank, morning wind, waning moon" would resonate throughout the central plains.

Meanwhile, the pope in Rome, thousands of leagues away, was also increasingly strapped for funds and began to dream of an eastward "punitive" expedition. Dozens of years later, the crusaders would enter

---

1. Wang Xiaobo and Li Shun instigated a rebellion in Sichuan that lasted from 993–995.

2. Also known as Liu Yong (ca. 984–ca.1053), Liu Sanbian was the most prolific lyric writer of the Song dynasty.

Jerusalem, crush the heads of the babies there and open their bellies to get the coins hidden within, sending some seventy to eighty thousand Moslems to Heaven.

The mortal world of that period harbored numerous other bloody events.

Three hundred years later, a man named Sa Ban would enter the cave. By then, the Xixia Kingdom had already become bubbles in the pool of blood. Those with military clout were the descendants of Genghis Khan.

Aside from the Diamond Maiden who stayed in the mortal world, the bodies of the other four all flew to the Buddhist realm.

A Bloodstained History

"Butcher Zhang attained salvation the very moment he grabbed hold of the girl," said Ajia. He was thereby able to leave the mortal world and enter Pure Land.

That was how he left his body in the sensual world, along with the girl who was suspended in midair for three hundred years. Nine hundred years later, I would discover the body of the butcher in a mud pagoda.

The cave retained its glory in the Xixia Kingdom. According to excavated materials, at least one state priest of the Xixia had resided there. Although during the long period thereafter Diamond Maiden Cave hosted many pilgrims, its heyday was long gone.

On a certain day during the seventies of the twentieth century, some peasants of Liangzhou rediscovered Diamond Maiden Cave. Until then, it had been sealed up for several hundred years by time and by the mountain.

At the same time, they also discovered up to a hundred Xixia artifacts. History didn't forget Xixia just because time flowed past the Yuan, Ming, and Qing dynasties. Up to a hundred Xixia manuscripts were stuffed into plastic rucksacks by illiterate peasants.

According to specialists, any single item would have been priceless because the history of Xixia had been mostly obscured by blood.

According to the histories, during the summer and autumn of 1226, Genghis Khan seized Suzhou, Ganzhou, Xiliang, and Lingzhou. He also surrounded Zhongxingfu, the capital of Xixia. During the summer of 1227, the last ruler of Xixia surrendered, and Xixia ceased to exist. Genghis Khan died of illness that year in his palace at Pure Water County.

The Glorious Merits of War

According to *Historical Mirror of Forgotten Events*: Xixia's enemy selected the tactic of slaughtering the entire population in order to exterminate the Dangxiang people. Those who wagged their tails and begged for mercy survived. But the tenacious ones dissolved into pools of blood overnight. Their documents were burnt, their land was occupied, the men were slaughtered, and the women were sold. Those lucky enough to escape the butcher's knife either fled to distant wildernesses or changed their names and identities. It was said that those surnamed Dang were the descendants of the Dangxiang people. They used Dang in memory of their ethnicity. Some changed their family name to Li in honor of their ancestor, Li Yuanhao.[3]

These people finally dissolved in a pool of blood.

Genghis Khan died during that same year. It was rumored he died from a poisoned arrow. This "favorite of Heaven," renowned for his shooting skills, ultimately died from an arrow wound.

After that, Kublai Khan,[4] founder of the Yuan dynasty, died. And then Ögödei Khan,[5] Taizhong of the Yuan dynasty, died. After that, Köden,[6] the Prince of Xiliang, also died. As a result, the invincible Mongol warriors ultimately also became piles of bones after a hundred some years. They occupied the largest expanse of territory in the world, using taut bows and sturdy arrows. They guffawed boisterously as they leveled fortified cities. They even fought their way to Moscow; the Russians called them "God's whip for punishing humankind." But the forces of impermanence didn't forget them. Their ending was ultimately the

---

3. Ironically, the surname Li was bestowed as a favor from an emperor of the Tang dynasty to Li Yuanhao, as Li was the imperial surname of the Tang.

4. Kublai Khan (1215–1294) was Genghis Khan's grandson and the conqueror of China. He became the founding emperor of Yuan dynasty.

5. Ögödei Khan (1186–1241) was the third son and successor of Genghis Khan.

6. Köden (?–1251) was Ögödei's son.

same as that of the beautiful Snow Feather, who left nothing but a skull from her temporary residence in this world. The only difference between the Mongols and Snow Feather was that I made the skull of the latter into an exemplary object as a warning to myself, while the sinful bones of the Mongol warriors were tossed away in some garbage-filled corner.

"The glorious 'merits of war' in the histories are but stupendous 'crimes!'" said Jasper.

The Helpless Tears

According to *Crazy Ramblings of Ajia*, most of the heroes who engaged in battles would suddenly realize, on their last breath, that they possessed absolutely nothing.

They were not able to take with them the coins and beautiful women. Their descendants could only temporarily safekeep the mountains of gold and prodigious power. Someday, the gold and power would also change hands.

They would discover that they possessed nothing but the eight feet of yellow earth that covered their corpses.

"In fact, they did possess one more thing," said Jasper, "they had sins."

The huge territories they occupied were ultimately conquered by others. The countless beauties they possessed in the end turned into polluted bones. And the mountains of gold and silver would also vanish without a trace.

But the sins would become maggots that would stick to their bones.

Jasper said, "Later, some dung maggots among humans glorified the crimes with an even more disgusting phrase. They called it: 'heroism'!"

A piece of filthy blood-stained cloth was waved like a flag for thousands of years.

Hidden behind the disgusting word were lakes of blood, mountains of bones, and torrents of tears from orphans and widows that flowed like the Yellow River.

History books show people cheering when minor thugs tested their butcher knives on the heads of common folks. In the ever-increasing waves of applause, the thug would grow into a tyrant. But the ludicrous unalterable truth was the fact that the tyrant, eyes reddened from killing, would ultimately brandish his butcher knife at the cheerleaders themselves!

The magnificent tyrants were experts at scheming: they schemed against heaven, they schemed against earth, they schemed against their companions, and they schemed against the common folks. The only thing they were unable to scheme against was their own death.

Everything crimes beget will ultimately vanish, except the crimes themselves.

"Through the endless changes during the past thousand years," said Jasper. He saw the women of Xixia wail helplessly in the dead of night, with vapid tearful eyes."

When the galloping iron hoofs of the Mongol cavalry thundered over their heads, they could only weep helplessly. Of course, the men were, on the other hand, mighty: they have swords, they have rifles. Later, they would also have missiles and atomic weapons. But the women only had tears.

Suddenly, Jasper wept aloud.

"Before the helpless tears of the women, heroism is nothing but crimes!" he said.

The Ultimate Light

There was a passage in *Crazy Ramblings of Ajia* that smacked of contemporary relevance. I suspect it was penned by the Indigent Monk. It went roughly as follows:

> The most dreadful human behavior is not massacre, but its praise. Just open the histories and you'll find that those worshipped were the very people who killed their own kind. The more they killed, the more likely they will be recognized as heroes, such as Napoleon, Alexander the Great, Genghis Khan, Zeng Guofan,[7] etc. They signify the downfall of the human race. They also represent the crimes of the historians and literary men who participated in the process.

---

7. 1811–1872, Zeng Guofan was an eminent Han Chinese official, military general, and devout Confucian scholar of the late Qing dynasty. For his military accomplishments, he was made a baturu (a Manchu official title for rewarding military prowess), decorated with a yellow riding-jacket, rewarded with the rank and title of marquis of the first class and the right to wear the double-eyed peacock's feather.

Lured by cravings and fortified by power, the killer will proceed to commit massacres. When people cannot stop the atrocities, they will endure the suffering of their destiny. But one must understand that massacres are crimes that should be castigated, and not praised. Praising them is even more condemnable than the act itself since while his crimes will eventually cease with the killer's demise, the "praises" could be transmitted to our descendants as an embodiment of culture; and the genes of sin will be planted into the souls of humankind. In the wake of suitable weather, the seeds of sin will germinate, take root, and flower, producing thereby even more lethal butchers.

Consequently, works that praise butchers are malignant tumors for the soul. We have to eradicate them. We must tell everyone in no uncertain terms that the powerful invaders praised for more than a thousand years are not heroes. They are in fact butchers and representations of sinfulness. The real heroes are figures such as Gandhi, Christ, Mencius, and Confucius who disseminated love among humans and in histories. They are the ones deserving of praise and applause.

When our books are filled with praise for bloody crimes, our hearts will change, just as one stops smelling stench after an extended stay at a fish market. When a stench persists for a thousand years, human souls will invariably be affected. The habituated sin will evolve into a collective subconsciousness. Like the "scab-eating addiction," the evolution of a 'taste' will ultimately cause an already deviated soul to become even less humane.

You don't believe me, do you? Well, just open a history book and count the names of those who truly loved and brought light to people. Butchers and tyrants have been presented as heroes. Even a talent like Beethoven considered Napoleon a hero and praised him with music. His Symphony No. 3 in E-flat Major Op.55 was originally named "Eroica" (Heroic Symphony) in homage to Napoleon, before the latter declared himself an emperor. The fact was: Whether Napoleon became an emperor or was just an administrator, his greatest achievements lay in invasions and massacres. Yet, to the world he was a hero. Wasn't this the downfall and lament of humanity?

Li Bai,[8] our immortal of poetry was similarly unable to free himself from vulgarity. A swordsman he praised was able to "kill a person every ten paces; travel for a thousand leagues without stopping." But ultimately Li Bai's fame rested on his sensibilities, reflected in lines such as "the pure wind misted in the six directions, distantly beyond all reach." That the beauty of the latter could overcome the shortcomings of the former made him the great Li Bai.

But few are clear-headed. From Ban Chao[9] known for "tossing away his brush to join the army," to Lu You[10] known for deciding to "mount a horse to strike down the crazy barbarians," to others of the Ming and Qing dynasties, and those of contemporary times, the craving of literary men to "bestow titles" upon 'heroes' buried their inborn conscience, and neglected compassion to all living beings. When a people or the entire world praises "genocide in disguise," the calamities that will befall humankind will never cease.

Almost all national heroes are in fact practitioners of genocide. Aroused by literary lines such as "let me drink the blood of the Huns when thirsty, and consume the flesh of the barbarians when hungry,"[11] they have all lost their rationality. They all want to take over other tribes' territories, to massacre other tribes' peoples, to become emperors and enslave other humans.

Consequently, to this day people sing the praises of Xue Rengui,[12] who fought and slew people all over China. History

---

8. Li Bai (701–760) was a Chinese poet acclaimed as a genius and romantic figure who took traditional poetic forms to new heights.

9. *Ban Chao* (32–102) was a Chinese general, explorer, and diplomat of the Han dynasty.

10. Lu You (1125–1210) was a prominent poet of the Song dynasty.

11. These are lines by the famous Song dynasty patriot, Yue Fei (1103–1142) in his lyric, "Manjianghong."

12. Xue Rengui (614–683) was one of the most famous Chinese generals during the early Tang dynasty, due to references to him in popular literature.

lamented Yue Wumiu's[13] failure in achieving his ambitions. Zhuge Liang,[14] who was disposed to combat, has been praised as a man of wisdom; while Liu Shan,[15] who abdicated the throne because he could not bear to see his people lose their lives, came to be known as "the inept weakling." Duke Xiang of Song[16] who insisted on "humanity and righteousness" has even been ridiculed for several thousand years. The world is congested with literature that acclaims butcheries and their butchers. This 'crime' was passed down from generation to generation until it became the latest craze, and wars and combat filled this small planet of ours. The butchers rose from pools of blood one after the other, laughing boisterously, surrounded by heaven-storming cheers.

How dreadful!

We can neither influence the powerful nor eliminate their crimes. Compared to them, our pens are puny. But we can control our pens and make them the voices of conscience. One faint voice will, of course, be drowned by the clamors of the time, but when tens of thousands voice themselves in unison, they may wake up some of the souls enveloped by the nightmare. They may open their eyes and holler in a way that would benefit humankind. When one generation after the other holler in this way, more people will eventually understand the meaning of sin.

Frequently, the cheerleaders of the butchers are even worse than the butchers themselves, for it is precisely through the clamor of the cheerleaders that the small butchers grow into looming tyrants. However, the tyrant may end up swing-

---

13. Also known as Yue Fei (1103–1142), he is best known for leading Southern Song forces in the wars during the twelfth century between the Southern Song and the Jurchen-ruled Jin dynasty in northern China, before being put to death by the Southern Song government in 1142.

14. Zhuge Liang (181–234) was a chancellor of the state of Shu Han during the Three Kingdoms period.

15. Liu Shan (207–271) was the second and last emperor of the state of Shu Han during the Three Kingdoms period.

16. Duke Xiang of Song (d. 637 BCE) was the ruler of the state of Song during the Spring and Autumn Period.

ing his increasingly crazy butcher knife at the heads of the cheerleaders.

Our culture should not be a culture of such cheerleaders, as history has shown that those who sang the praises of the sinners ultimately became their victims.

When facing all the butcher knives of history, we should express ourselves resoundingly, hysterically, and on pain of persecution, "Those are sins!"

Should people yell thus generation after generation, one day humankind would blush from embarrassment when reading past histories for having considered bloodshed as rouge.

Then, they would say, "Come! Let's toss this crime-filled rag into the gutter and rewrite history!"

The rewritten history would invariably contain a supreme brightness that benefits humankind.

Chapter 13

The "Buddhist Head-Shaving Ritual" in *Nightmares*

I burned one sandalwood incense stick after the other
       To inquire after my fate;
The smile of the Buddha was inscrutable,
I could only turn the pages of the divination book.
Hints in the oracles
       You considered them too hot,
       I thought they were too cold;
Just like the two of us right now
       You are forever evading,
While I am always questioning.

The Enemy

We now continue with *Nightmares*.

Nightmares may be difficult to follow for less focused readers since it does not follow our reading habits. While at times it's as lucid as a painting, at other times it's massively chaotic, which is why it's named *Nightmares*. To wise readers, *Nightmares* could be exhilarating since it provides refreshing vistas.

Let's first enter a certain morning of *Nightmares*.

Gela came to fetch Uncle that morning, saying the clan head had invited him there to discuss the issue of fighting the enemy. Gela was the housekeeper of Diamond Monastery and the most powerful person there.

Uncle snickered, "Fighting what? It's a cat biting a dick under the same quilt!¹" But he had Jasper accompany him there anyway.

It was a gorgeous day, sunshine sparkled like gold. The light breeze was refreshing and soothing. The green of trees, the green of grass, spilled over. "But on such a beautiful day, people will discuss fighting," Jasper shook his head.

Some psychologists claim dreams have no color; since the section of the brain controlling color would be dormant then. But this nightmare had a golden sunlight. The author frequently dreams in color. So this did not seem strange.

Some records in *Nightmares* differ from those found in *Historical Mirror of Forgotten Events*. According to the latter, Brilliant King Clan was Indigenous, while Diamond Clan arrived later. According to *Nightmares*, however, the two clans were originally brothers. The mountain used to belong to two brothers, with a Mani rock pile in the valley as their border. The older brother occupied the south, and his descendants were known as the Southern Branch Clan, while the younger brother had the northern part—his clan was called the Northern Branch Clan. Both grew to be large clans. In terms of population, the southern branch was fewer in number, but in terms of power, they were on equal footing. At first they bickered over religious beliefs. The northern branch decided that everything was "real," while the southern branch decided that everything was "illusory." The gods they worshipped also differed; one worshipped Diamond King, while the other worshipped Brilliant King. They eventually came to be known as Diamond Clan and Brilliant King Clan. The two clans insisted on their own views and quarreled incessantly. Unable to win through speech, they resorted to physical combat. Later, the arguments extended to grasslands, the water source, religion, and so on. Battles and bloodshed continued unrelentingly for several hundred years.

The wealthy household Braggart had robbed in the previous chapter of *Nightmares* was that of Brilliant King Clan. In his eyes, the borderline between the north and south was not as important as that between the rich and the poor. The poor were by definition good, while the rich were evil.

"Even the pee of the poor is cleaner than the milk of the rich!" he said.

---

1. They really should coexist.

The stories in *Nightmares* concerning folks like Jasper and Snow Feather were also different from those found in *Tale of the Goddess*. One scholar attributed the difference to the fact that *Nightmares* originated in Jasper's subconscious and surfaced in the form of nightmares. Another felt the difference was because the events might have been distorted memories of what had happened during an earlier part of Jasper's life before the beginning of our story. But a scholar who believed in mysticism decided that *Nightmares* occurred in a transcendental space. One might term this space a "negative universe," one that corresponded to the real space we live in, something like the virtual reality on the web in its being both real and unreal. The same folks who existed in real space also populated that space: folks such as Braggart, Kuan San, Uncle, Grandpa Jiu. At once tangible and illusory, it was most fascinating.

Regarding the various points of view above, the author offers no comment.

In the "Head-Shaving Ritual" section of *Nightmares*, Kuan San fell in love with Snow Feather and lit an oil lamp at her front door. Not wanting to marry him, Snow Feather had herself registered at a nunnery so she could avoid numerous problems associated with the mundane world.

So, as soon as Kuan San asked about Snow Feather, Uncle said, "She was registered at the nunnery a while back. Look before you leap next time, lest you become a fart-chasing fly!" Kuan San laughed in embarrassment, "What a pity a beauty like that would end up with dark oil lamps and old Buddhas. What a bummer!"

Jasper said, "Better than having an ox eating a rose!" Uncle laughed heartily.

Kuan San then said, "Jasper, why don't you marry her? The gal is a rare beauty. One look at her the soul flies away! I heard you want to become a monk. Forget about that—what's so good about being a monk? Boring!" Seeing Uncle looking at him, he changed his tone and said, "If you really want to be a monk, then be a high priest like your uncle, one with merit and virtue!"

"But I'm not a high priest. I'm just a believer without merit and virtue," replied Uncle.

People had already gathered on the grassy area in front of Diamond Monastery. The clan head was hollering. Grandpa Jiu was playing a game using sheep bones with a group of kids. A kid cheated, and Grandpa Jiu wailed. This Grandpa Jiu looked like a beggar and was in the habit of either crying or laughing—or saying ridiculous things like a madman.

Everyone took advantage of him except for Uncle, who treated him with respect. A blond foreigner was watching the game on the side. His name was John. He had arrived a few years ago as a missionary. He had been beaten a few times but did not leave. To the villagers, he was the same kind of trash as Grandpa Jiu.

The clan head waved to Uncle when he saw him from a distance. Uncle waved back and sat down far away. The clan head had someone invite him over, but Uncle refused to budge. It was a formality that had to be performed. In actual fact, the clan head preferred keeping him at a distance and so left him alone. Jasper knew Uncle wasn't interested in such matters, or even in showing up. But fighting the enemy concerned the entire clan; and as someone maintained by Diamond Clan, he had to come. Diamond Clan lost during the previous fights because Brilliant King Clan was more heavily populated. Several members of Diamond Clan were injured—one of them was seriously wounded and died of tetanus. Fortunately, Braggart would lead a band to nab more than a hundred sheep from the opponent now and then and thereby save face for Diamond Clan.

Grandpa Jiu seized a sheep shoulder bone and made off with it. A few kids ran after him. Unsteady on his feet, the crazy old man stumbled and fell on his face. Blood trickled out of his mouth, and he wailed. Everyone looked at him, instead of at the clan head, and laughed. Infuriated, the clan head roared at them, and the kids scattered. But Grandpa Jiu bawled incessantly.

Kuan San went over, gave him a good kick, and shouted, "What are you crying for?" Grandpa Jiu's wailing, however, became ever louder and pierced into the clouds.

"Oh, misery! Misery!" He screamed as he wept.

"What misery?" someone asked.

Grandpa Jiu wiped the mucus from his nose and yelled, "The sea of misery knows no bounds!"

"Let's start the meeting!" the head of the clan roared. Kuan San took a few men with him. They stuffed a handful of grass into Grandpa Jiu's mouth to stifle his hollering and dragged him away into the distance. Grandpa Jiu spat out the grass and left, all the while waving his hands and feet, and wailing. Instead of diminishing in intensity as he left, his voice increased in vigor with each bawl and pierced right through people's hearts.

John said, "Yes, we are all brothers. We have to love each other!" Having lived there for a few years, his local dialect had become quite good, "Love your enemies!"

Kuan San screamed, "Fuck your love! One more word from you and we'll stuff you with grass too!" The foreigner drew a cross and smiled warmly.

All the families had to prepare weapons according to the clan head's instructions. Each family had to bring a rifle—the shortage of rifles was the main problem last time. Each person was required to have a stone-throwing slingshot. Sometimes slingshots were even more convenient to use than rifles. Machetes and cudgels had to be made ready. Plus, each family was required to donate two silver dollars for lodging a lawsuit at the county seat. Lawsuits had been going on for several hundred years. Sometimes they won; sometimes we won. The results were entirely dependent on the amount of silver spent. Everyone knew the lawsuit was a farce, but there was no choice. The government's soldiers would assist whoever won.

One would have expected Braggart to lead the attack. But according to him, dogs shouldn't fight dogs. He was of the conviction that the poor should all be friends. Since some of the enemy were poor, attacking them was not good. However, he was most avid when it came to attacking the rich of Brilliant King Clan. He frequently assaulted them without prodding and basked in glory from doing so.

John came over and told Uncle, "You should do something about this, Master Wu. We are all brothers."

Uncle laughed and said, "Do you want me to be a madman too? One crazy one should be enough." He then added, "The one who was nailed to the cross was the same."

John sighed, "Precisely. If your thoughts are a year ahead of the others, you'd be called a vanguard. If you are five years ahead, you'd be a saint; but ten years ahead, you'd be a madman. A hundred years ahead, you'd be called a demon for sure!"

Uncle said, "I've read that Bible of yours. That man was also a Bodhisattva. I would only say this to you when we're alone. If there's anyone else around, I'll say that you preach heresy."

"Why?" asked John.

"That's what everyone expects me to say—if I don't want to be a demon. I know about the universal love you preach, we call it compassion . . . but I can't say that. How many people have you converted?"

John forced a smile and said, "Three."

"Not bad." Uncle sighed, "It's not easy to preach here. Whatever possessed you to do this?"

Kuan San shouted from a distance, "Master Wu—what are you saying to the demon?"

Uncle said in a low voice, "See, if I continue to talk to you, I'll become a demon too!" He then replied loudly, "Demons are living beings too. I'm bringing him salvation." John left without saying a word.

Grandpa Jiu's voice continued to explode, "Oh, misery! Misery!"

The Demon in the Mind

Jasper could not help but feel somewhat choked as he watched John depart. He had heard John proselytize and knew it was about doing good deeds, enduring shame, and giving. But somehow he'd been regarded as a demon. He asked Uncle about it, and Uncle said, "Sometimes, demons would pretend to be saints."

He'd wondered why Uncle said that.

Now he realized Uncle had no choice.

Cripple Big approached and said to Jasper, "Your dad wants you." Jasper looked at Uncle who asked, "Is it important?"

"Yes."

Uncle said, "The myriad demons reside in the mind. Go, Jasper!"

So Jasper followed Cripple Big back to the stockade.

The stockade was built atop a mountain, with cliffs on three sides and protected by stone walls. A pathway with stone-hewn stairs wound itself onto the other side and was usually guarded. Since the stockade was quite large, the men who wanted to live there permanently could move there with their families. Mother had wanted to move out of the stockade several times, but Father did not allow it, fearing the enemy would kidnap his family to blackmail him.

Jasper pulled a face when he saw Dad. Braggart turned to the woman beside him and said, "Look at him—this kid of mine is just like a girl! Ai! A tiger father raised a sick cat!" "One never knows—once a cat tastes fish, it can be fiercer than a tiger!" the woman laughed.

"You may be right!" Braggart also laughed.

"Kid, "said Braggart, "I can't let you loaf around anymore. Any longer and I'll have no descendants!" "That's right. You've managed this stockade for decades already—you can't let some outsider take over! We can see the kid is a coward, but he can be trained. Just look at Kuan San. So well behaved at the beginning—what a tiger he is now!" added the woman.

Kuan San laughed and said, "My mind was lassoed back then. The kid's the same." He turned to Jasper and said, "Don't believe in that dogshit! It's a nightmare. Once you enter, it's hard to wake up. You struggle and struggle with all your might. But once you wake up, you see it was just a dream! In the dream, you don't know."

"I never believed that shit. I don't believe someone could be up inside this blue sky. I don't believe when I kill an ant, its soul would come after me. I don't believe some old monk's mumbling can prevent disasters. That other day, Uncle's face got bloated like a pan. I told him, if you're good at chanting the sutras, show me! If the bloating disappears right away, I'll become a monk!" said Braggart.

"Did it disappear?" asked the woman.

"The fuck it did! His head was as big as a pan for half a month before the bloating disappeared. I said, how can you prevent other people's disasters if you can't even prevent your own?"

Jasper wanted to say, "Uncle was dissipating everyone's karmic sins through the bloating! He would visualize the illnesses and sins of all living beings and absorb them into his own body every night." Aside from the bloating, Uncle had all sorts of other ailments as well.

Cripple Big didn't say anything. He just chuckled.

Braggart continued, "Monks cheat when they are alive, and they cheat after they're dead. When alive, they cheat people into giving them good food and drinks. No stopping after they're dead. Damn them! Sooner or later I'll fix them. Kuan San, would you dare rob the monasteries? lots of treasure there!"

"Of course I dare! Why stop once started—you can only go to Hell once anyway!"

"Fuck going to Hell!" said Braggart, "I don't believe there's a Hell under the ground. The monks invented that to cheat people. Who'd feed them if they don't scare people?"

Jasper said, "If there's nothing important, I'm leaving." He was used to hearing Braggart talk this way. After a while, he began to wonder if Hell did indeed exist. If it did, then these sorts of people should have been sent there a long time ago.

"Don't leave yet." Braggart turned to the woman and said, "Get him to change his mind to become a monk—have you ever heard of anything more stupid? Jasper, go with her!"

Jasper took a look at the woman and recognized her as the famous Heavenly Girl. She had performed the "Heavenly Worship Ritual," which basically meant she was married to Heaven and didn't have to marry anyone. It also meant she could sleep with anyone she wished; so she often made headlines. Women cursed her, but they also feared her; men cussed her, but they also wanted to bed her. She was a frequent guest at the stockade.

Braggart said, "See if you can make a man out of the kid."

Kuan San laughed and said, "A piece of cake for her!"

Realizing Dad's scheme, Jasper tried to escape. But someone blocked the door and grabbed him by the waist.

"Mommy! Mommy!" yelled Jasper.

The person said, "Stop calling. She moved out already—this morning." Jasper wailed.

"What's with the crying?" said Kuan San, "You won't stop smiling after this."

"Yay! We couldn't wait for it back then!"

Jasper was tossed into a tiny room.

The Rebellion

"Don't cry," said the woman as she stroked Jasper's face with her hand. Jasper turned wooden and let her stroke him. The woman felt the woodenness and stopped. She wanted him to make a fuss, but he became wooden. *It's not good to be wooden,* she thought.

She began to unfasten her buttons. She unfastened her buttons very slowly while watching Jasper. Knowing crying was useless, he stopped crying. Mom's eyes blinked in the corner of the room. *I'm not afraid,* he thought, *Mom's here!*

The woman's clothes flung open like a butterfly, scattered on the ground and exposed her body. She was very thin. Her breasts drooped, and her bones bulged. The bones twisted and grated loudly. Jasper saw her blood throb furiously. He was very thirsty. *How did Father procure such a woman?* he wondered.

He was surprised by his own calmness. He remembered Uncle's words and began to scrutinize all the polluted aspects of the woman—the mucus in her nose, the blood in her body, the feces in her belly—until they became lucid. Seeing him smile, the woman asked, "What are you smiling about?" Jasper replied, "There's mucus in your nose, blood in your body, and feces in your belly." The woman laughed and said, "Indeed?" She embraced him and kissed him forcefully.

Jasper felt a strange smell rush at him and felt like laughing. He rubbed his mouth and thought of Snow Feather unexpectedly. Would she taste so vapid?

The woman continued to smile and began to twist her body violently. "Go! Go!" Kuan San cheered her on outside the room.

Jasper looked up at the ceiling, which was unexpectedly filled with stars. One star was chasing furiously after another. The one being chased tried to escape frantically. *How come the stars are like this too?* he thought.

The woman reeked of sweat. All the pores of her body expanded, and a strange fragrance filled the room. Her body began to shine, and her skin became smooth. The skinny breasts pumped up too. Jasper thought it all very strange. The fragrance was now surrounding him and inundating him.

Mom's eyes disappeared unexpectedly.

"Mom!" Jasper cried.

"I'm your mom," said the woman as she panted. Her face had already transformed into a full moon. Jasper thought, *How scary, how did her face become a silver platter?* And then he wondered, *Where have I seen this face before?*

Kuan San's laughter resounded again. He wished he could hear Father laugh. He knew Father's laughter would be the cold water that could wake him up. Father obviously also knew that, so he purposely refrained. He heard the woman whine like a sheep, and his heart felt tickled. Jasper saw a herd of sheep bleating and thought, *Are they the ones that Dad kidnapped?*

"Take your clothes off!" said the woman.

She had transformed entirely into a beauty with a melon-shaped face, willow eyebrows, white teeth, and red lips, and was looking at him smilingly. Her body exuded an intoxicating fragrance. He thought, *She's even more beautiful than the Dakini goddesses!* He remembered Ajia saying enlightenment could be attained more quickly through "being intimate" with a Dakini.

The woman reached out her hand and loosened his girdle. She must have possessed some sort of magical power because he would have resisted otherwise. But he did not: he felt lazy, and his blood was boiling. The woman was the same. Flames of fire dragons darted about her body.

"My boy!" he heard Mom's cry.

It was Mom's voice. Jasper looked around but did not see her eyes. Yet he saw Dad hiding in the ceiling and staring at him stealthily. Snow Feather was there. Strange, how come Snow Feather was there too? Uncle was reciting the sutra furiously in isolation. The resounding beating of the singing bowl overcame him in waves.

"No!" said Jasper.

But his clothes had already slipped onto the floor on their own. Jasper did not take them off, and the woman didn't take them off him either; they slipped off by themselves. They were traitors. There are too many traitors in this world, and Jasper felt he had also become one. His mouth had rebelled, his heart had rebelled, and his hands had also rebelled. "Mom! Please save me!"

The woman's hand was a fish swimming on his body. Jasper wanted to say, *No! No!* but he was unable to utter any words. He took a deep breath and thought he'd chant a mantra. But the mantra had already slipped away to some unknown place. *Traitor!* he thought.

"Come!" said the woman.

She squeezed his genitals continuously. Jasper thought, *I won't!* Suddenly he really wanted to take the tonsure. He thought it would be much better to become an ordained monk. *Yes, it would be much better.* But his hands swam away from him and began stroking the woman's neck.

Everything had rebelled! he thought.

Head Shaving

He couldn't remember when Mom entered the room. He only remembered a gust of wind, and suddenly Mom was there. The woman suddenly screamed, turned into a snake, and slipped away through a corner. The corner of the walls had no holes, but that was where the woman had slipped away.

"The hussy!" Braggart could do nothing but sigh.

Jasper rushed out of the stockade with his hands over his face. Two Dakini goddesses propped up his arms, and flying wheels propelled him under his feet. The earth receded rapidly underneath him and wind bellowed past his ears. His heart rammed onto the ground, and thirst transformed into a whirlwind that churned in his heart. *Did I break the vow?* he wondered. As soon as he thought he'd broken the Buddhist precept, he wept. Uncle had told him that a broken pot could never be repaired. *I've become a broken pot!* he thought.

A thick forest approached him. He had already arrived outside Ajia's cave. Ajia was chanting sutras in the cave. He was protected by a Vajra fire curtain next to him. This was the fire curtain he created through visualization when he meditated. It was said when one could visualize this very distinctly, no demon could enter the cave. Jasper thought, *Didn't you say you feared nothing? Why visualize the fire-curtain then?* He remembered he hadn't visualized a fire curtain when the woman approached him, knowing well that it could not have blocked women. Then he thought, *If the fire-curtain cannot even block women, can it really block demons?*

"Ajia! Ajia!" he called.

The Dakini goddesses flew away like two birds, the flapping of their wings reverberating throughout the valley. Jasper knew they were afraid of Ajia's stench from not having bathed for a long time. Ajia loved to eat garlic too. He would chant the spell, "*Gaka gagaga ah*" every time he ate garlic, but the stench was still overpowering. Jasper called out to the birds in the distance, "Were you afraid?" Then he lowered his head and thought, *I've become a broken pot.* Sorrow came over him.

Ajia was chanting a spell. A wheel with a spell was located in his heart. Light flashed in and out of the wheel, thereby benefiting all living beings. Knowing he would not come out of the cave at the moment, Jasper lay down on the grass and watched the white clouds. One cloud gave birth to another, until the entire sky was filled with clouds. Jasper thought, *That was a mother cloud, since only mothers could give birth. But then, where was the male cloud?* He let his eyes roam afar, and searched; but he lost himself instead.

"Wake up!" said Ajia.

Ajia stared at him with a wooden face. Jasper said, "I've become a broken pot." Ajia said, "Don't be ridiculous!" "I've really become a broken pot!" Jasper wanted to weep. He squeezed his eyes really hard but not a single teardrop. Even the eyes have mutinied! When he wanted to be strong, tears would surge. But now that he wanted to show weakness, the tears hid somewhere far—further away than his mind.

"You've slept a long time—so long you've become a pig!" said Ajia.

"But I didn't sleep!" said Jasper. He explained Dad's evil deed and that he had become a broken pot. Ajia laughed and said, "Nonsense, you've been sleeping here all along! More than a day—you've gone nowhere!" Jasper lowered his head and saw the scratch mark left by the woman's fingernails. The dazzling bright red mark was sniggering at him! So he said, "Look—gouged by the woman!" Ajia said, "Obviously made by tree branches. Didn't you fall when I gave you a shove?" Jasper asked, "Did I fall?" Ajia said, "You didn't fall?"

Jasper looked at Ajia earnestly. When he saw Ajia wasn't joking, he said, "Oh, I see. It was a dream." But then he wondered if he was in a dream right now. He took Ajia's hand. Ajia was very thin; his hand was very bony.

Ajia led him out of the cave. Jasper thought, *But I was undoubtedly outside the cave!* Yet, he still felt Ajia leading him out of the cave. The cave was deep and seemed never-ending. There was neither wind nor light. He could only feel claws tearing at him. "Where are we going?" asked Jasper. Ajia replied, "I don't know where we're going either. This is a path without a destination. No destination, no meaning, nothing."

Jasper thought, *Is a path without destination, a path?*

"Of course it's still a path," said Ajia, "only paths without destinations are real paths."

A light emerged from the end of the cave like the top of a stick of incense on a moonlit night, indistinctly enlarging itself. Once up close, they realized it was an oil lamp. The face of an old monk seeped out of the lamp's haze. He looked like Uncle. His unfathomable eyes were as bright as chilly stars. Suddenly, Jasper felt scared. He screamed, "Ajia!" There was no response. He turned around and saw the grayish small path scurry into the distance like a snake.

"Ajia! Ajia!"

Even Ajia has rebelled! thought Jasper.

"Shave your head and be ordained!" said the old monk.

Jasper was under the impression that this was how he became ordained as a monk.

The Leader

Jasper strained himself to open his eyes to look at Mom. Mom was moaning on the brick bed. Mom's moaning sounded like chanting. She had just been whipped by Dad. Ever since Jasper became an ordained monk, Mom received a whipping every day. Dad was very good at whipping: it would hurt like crazy but leave no scars. Mom said the scars were in her heart where blood flowed. Mom said, "The heart is made to hold blood. Blood flows in and out of it. The more blood flows through it, the more vigorous it becomes!" As she said this, her face lit up brightly.

Mom got up to cook for Jasper. Mom's mud cabin was located in the gully. It was a temporary shack built by hunters. Mom lived there after she moved out of the stockade. "It was a close call," Mom told him, "If I'd arrived any later, that woman would have ruined you!" Jasper was shocked and thought, *Wasn't that a dream?* "Of course it was a dream," said Mom, "but everything is a dream in this world! Don't you know? Mom can also enter into your dreams." Jasper asked, "Are we dreaming now?" Mom said, "Of course we are."

Grandpa Sun was shining brightly in the sky; the grass in the gully buckled over from laughing. Jasper thought, *Mom's really good at joking!*

Mom cooked the tea and added milk and sugar to it. Jasper asked, "Mom, where did you get the money from?" Mom said, "I exchanged a pair of turquoise earrings for them." Jasper said, "I have a few ounces of silver." "Keep them. You'll have a long way to go. You have to go on a pilgrimage. Pilgrimages are hard, but everyone has to go on one eventually. You've lived in vain if you don't go on a pilgrimage." Jasper asked, "Where should I go?" Mom said, "I don't know either. But the ancestors said the holy land's in Nepal. You'll reach it after crossing many, many snowy mountains. I heard many pilgrims died there. Mom would hate to let you go, but how can you be Mom's son if you don't go on a pilgrimage?" A holy radiance lit up Mom's face. Strange, Mom got beaten and now has a holy glow. Mom laughed. She said, "The holy glow came from the beating. Without being beaten, there would not be the holy glow."

Mom's really good at joking, thought Jasper.

Mom pulled out a sutra and handed it to Jasper. She said, "Take it with you. It was from your Uncle. He's been snatched by your father to be a horse-mounting stool. Actually, it doesn't really matter if you take this with you. But you should never lose the sutra in your heart!"

Jasper knew what Mom said was crazy since Uncle had just ordained him and shaved his head. He stroked his head and felt a handful of hair. He was shocked—didn't Uncle just shave the head? Mom laughed, "Hair grows fast!" And then she added, "Seven days in a cave is a thousand years in the mortal world! Your heart is always in the cave, so of course you won't feel time fly."

"What a bummer!" said Jasper.

"Why?"

"People who feel a day is like a year, feel their lives are long. But with me, a moment is like years of their time. So even a hundred years would be a blip in time with me. What a bummer!" Mom laughed before he finished. Mom's laughter sounded like Snow Feather's. She said, "Those who lived to a hundred haven't lived. Those who lived an instant do not live in vain. Go, Son, follow your path!"

Jasper left and was greeted by Snow Feather who was waiting for him with a horse. Outfitted in the attire of a Buddhist nun, she also had her hair shorn. Snow Feather said, "That Kuan San won't leave me alone. He kept on saying that my registration was nominal, so I ordained for real. Let's go!"

"Where are we going?"

"I don't know either. There are so many paths in this world. We can go anywhere we want!"

Mom came out, stuffed a packet of yak butter in his jacket and said, "Go! Paths are created by walking. There are no paths if you don't go!" Snow Feather followed Jasper onto the horse. Mom slapped the horse's rump. The horse neighed loudly and flew!

As soon as they turned the corner, they came upon Kuan San who was striking a gong feverishly. People gathered amidst the ruckus, rifles and knives in hand. Jasper knew they were on their way to fight the enemy. *No way am I going with them!* thought Jasper. But Snow Feather said, "There's nothing wrong with watching the excitement. We're not doing anything anyway." Jasper thought, *Snow Feather has gone mad! Bullets shower like rain during combat—one can even die from it!* But he was kidnapped by the horse that charged straight at the crowd.

"The leader's here! The leader's here!" cheered the people.

Jasper looked around confoundedly.

Kuan San scampered over and knelt down to offer him a crown studded with feathers. Jasper turned and looked, but Snow Feather had disappeared. She was hiding in a gully and snickering; she looked like "Heavenly Girl."

"Hurray! Hurray! The leader! The leader!" cheered the people.

Jasper said, "You must have made a mistake, Kuan San!"

Kuan San said, "There's no mistake. The oracle said that the leader would arrive riding on a golden camel."

"Who pronounced the oracle?"

"Your father, of course!" said Kuan San.

Jasper stepped on someone's back and dismounted the camel. He thought, *How did the horse turn into a camel?* The golden light of the camel dazzled him. The person who served as his footstep stood up and turned out to have been Uncle. Uncle had grown old and wrinkled. Jasper said, "Uncle, how come you became a horse-mounting stool?" "Wrong," said Uncle, "I'm a camel-mounting stool, not a horse-mounting stool. But if you want to call me a horse-mounting stool, then a horse-mounting stool I am. You are the leader after all!"

Braggart was laughing on a high mountain. His laughter pierced heaven and earth, but no one heard him. Everyone was hollering at the top of their lungs until they turned hoarse: "Long live the leader! Long live the leader!"

Jasper felt his head and found the crown there. He thought, *So, I'm really their leader! But, then, who was the ordained monk?*

A mist swept from the mountain and enveloped everyone. Jasper knew that was in fact Father's laughter. *Who would have known Father had this kind of power?* he thought.

But Grandpa Jiu screamed from a distance, "It's not real! Not real!"

Braggart shouted, "What's not real? You're not real!"

Grandpa Jiu hollered, "You're right, I'm also not real!"

Kuan San went over and gave him a good kick, "Since you're not real, then why holler?" Grandpa Jiu took a tumble and scampered into the distance like a monkey.

Jasper ascended the ruler's platform. Braggart was smiling sneakily. Jasper thought, *Isn't he the leader?* Braggart laughed and said, "You are the leader now. You were brought here by the golden camel. It didn't bring me!" The camel stretched out its neck and howled. Seeing Jasper watching, it bared its golden teeth uncannily.

I've been taken! thought Jasper.

He remembered what Uncle had said once about fighting the enemy. He said whenever they fought the enemy, one person took the blame for all the crimes. That person was blamed for all the deaths and injuries. Are they playing this game with me now?

Jasper searched for Uncle and found him crawling on the ground. A person stepped on his back to mount a horse. "Uncle, how come you became a mounting stool?" Uncle turned to him baring a mouthful of white teeth, "If I don't go to Hell, who would?"

"Charge! Charge!" the men on the horses screamed.

Jasper thought, *So be it! Since I'm already on the battlefield, I might as well be a warrior!* He raised the leader's broadsword. Strangely, the broadsword had been waiting for him for quite a while now and was ready to charge. But he then thought, *I hope the enemy will get out of the way—the bloodshed is bound to be horrendous!*

The enemy charged at him like a mountain peak. It was on a wide expanse of grassland reeking with the stench of blood. *No wonder, the land is soaked in blood!* thought Jasper.

"Run, you people!" Jasper screamed at the enemy.

The folks of Brilliant King Clan roared in laughter, "You should be the one to run! Look!"

Jasper turned around and saw no one behind him. A few dandelions swayed among the yellow grass. He thought, *Strange, was my horse so fast they couldn't follow me?*

"They couldn't follow you?" a skinny guy yelled, "they're all dead!"

"All dead?"

"All dead and reborn. Born and dead again countless times. Why don't you just do your tricks?"

Jasper yawned loudly and thought, *What a bummer! Were we fighting the enemy? How come the enemies are here but everyone has run away!*

"Do your tricks!" the voice of the skinny guy had become barely audible.

Jasper did a headstand on the horse, which galloped like the wind. He then swung his body along the stirrup and yanked up all the dandelions. The cheers clamored like a mountain.

"Bravo!" Braggart's cries were also heard.

This should be enough—one should never overdo a good thing! thought Jasper. He tugged at the bridle and the horse stopped. The enemies surrounded him in excitement. The skinny guy said, "I've never seen such great tricks! Take off your hat!"

Jasper doffed his hat, and a piece of silver flew toward it. Suddenly, silver rained from the sky like hail. Fortunately, the hat was so large that none of the pieces fell onto the ground.

"Enough! Enough!" cried Jasper.

"If you say enough, then it's enough!" The skinny guy whistled, and the crowd dispersed.

Jasper felt very tired.

Leprosy

The butcher arrived. He knew that Uncle's spell had taken effect because he had contracted the dragon disease, which was also known as leprosy. He said, "Didn't I return the wok to you?" Uncle laughed and said, "It was too late. The ritual was already done." "Can you take it back?" "No. Spilt water cannot be taken back."

The butcher asked, "Is there a cure?"

"Yes, there's a cure." Uncle pointed to his chamber pot, "Wash it with this urine."

The butcher sniggered sarcastically, "Do you know why I stole from you?" Uncle said, "Yes. Because you hate me. Whenever you were striking the iron, you were in fact striking at a monk's head." The butcher said, "I'm glad that you know. My dad is still suffering in Hell. He comes to my dreams every night and tells me. Hell didn't exist when he didn't know there was a Hell. But with you talking about Hell all the time, Hell came to exist for him. How I hate you!"

Jasper pointed to the chamber pot, "Are you not going to wash yourself?"

"No! I'd rather rot to death than wash myself with that!" He tore off a piece of his own rotten flesh and swallowed it. He then glared at Uncle and left.

"No, I won't wash myself in it! I'd rather rot to death than washing in it!" He hollered outside.

Feeling sorry for him, Jasper stuck his head out of the bedcover and asked, "Is there any other way?"

Uncle said, "Yes. He can repent. Do you think he would repent?"

Jasper jumped out of bed and went outside. The butcher had already reached the phallic symbol at the bottom of the mountain. The phallic symbol was a huge rock that resembled the male organ and had been worshipped by the villagers for a thousand years. There was an altar next to the phallic rock with a pile of human heads. The butcher yanked off his own rotten flesh and fed the pieces to the heads, which opened their mouths and smacked their lips with relish.

"Hey! There's another cure!" said Jasper.

"I know," laughed the butcher sardonically, "forget about getting old me to repent! He should be the one to repent!"

Jasper sighed, returned to the house, and saw Uncle repenting. He thought, *That butcher was hopeless.*

Uncle said, "You shouldn't have slaughtered."

Jasper said, "But I didn't slaughter!"

"If you hadn't slaughtered, where did all the heads come from?"

Knowing he was referring to the heads on the altar, he said, "That was strange, where indeed did they come from?"

"Everyone said you killed them. I didn't believe them but that's what they said. When everyone says so, the person who doesn't believe it, is crazy."

Jasper now remembered being a leader, but wasn't that just a dream?

"A sexual transgression in a dream is still a transgression. Don't you know that the woman is pregnant with your child? That's what everyone says. I didn't believe it, but that's what everyone says." Uncle took a whiff of snuff and sneezed.

"Does the fact that everyone says something make it right?"

"Of course. Whether something is right or not depends on how many people say it."

"What if the speakers are all crazy?"

"It would still be right because the standard of madmen would be used."

"What if the leader is mad?"

"Then what he says would be even more right, because he is the leader."

"Now I understand," said Jasper. He left the cabin to look for Ajia. Ajia was waiting for him by the road. He said, "How foolish! What's with whether something is right or not? There's no right or wrong in this world!"

"Is something right just because there's no right or wrong?"

"Yes!" Grandpa Jiu popped out from the back of a tree.

Mother's Destiny

Jasper accompanied Mother to the stockade for her to receive Father's whipping. This was her daily routine. Mother said, "He wants to arouse your anger. The moment you become angry, he wins. To him, anger is part of manhood. But all evils originate in anger."

Jasper understood this.

Jasper said, "I want to be angry, but I can't because I know this is all a farce. Although you bear pain from his beating, I know none of this is in fact real."

Mom said happily, "You finally understood!"

Many people greeted them along the way. They all knew that Mom bore beatings on account of Jasper's taking the tonsure. They called her "Goddess Tara."[2] Jasper wondered if it was the "White Tara" or the "Green Tara" but didn't feel like asking. Whether white or green, she was a Goddess Tara in any case. Mom didn't care about any of it. To her, enduring pain in order for her son to avoid an evil path was worthwhile. It was her duty as a mother. It was her destiny to nurture the fetus of her son with her blood and essence, to raise him with her milk, and to use her own suffering to help him attain his goal.

Many people had moved to the stockade. Constant attacks on the enemy created fear of enemy reprisals. As a result, more and more bandits were now in the stockade. Jasper knew that all the bandits in the world made a living from killing, without whom Father's stockade would have been empty.

"Hey!" Kuan San greeted them. He looked quite mighty with all the decorative pendants hanging around his neck. The pendants were sundried penises he had sliced off of enemies. It was believed the enemies' sexual prowess would thus transfer to him. The women of the stockade squealed when he fucked them every night. But Braggart was not interested in doing this. He was the director of the show.

"Jasper, your beloved lives right here! Just take off your cassock, step on it, and you'll be able to marry her."

Jasper thought, *Taking off the cassock from the body is easy, but what about the one in the mind?*

Mom said, "Don't listen to him. Let him say whatever. He wants to arouse your anger! There's nothing he can do if you don't get angry."

Kuan San said, "Your son is fucking awesome! He hacked at the enemy like cutting melons. Look at how mighty he is!" He pointed at Jasper.

Jasper lowered his head and discovered a garland of dried flesh resembling carrots around his neck too. He took it off, tossed it at Kuan San, and told Mom, "They accused me wrongly!"

"Accused you wrongly?" laughed Kuan San, "you can deny my accusation, but can you deny the accusation of a thousand people? A man owns up to his own actions!"

---

2. *Dumu* is also known as Doro Buddha. Some believe she is an incarnation of Avalokiteshvara. The literal meaning of *dumu* is "the mother who brings salvation."

"Don't worry if they all accuse you wrongly, Son." Mom patted his back and added, "the mind of a saint remains pure even if he'd committed a mortal sin."

Jasper thought, *Even Mom thought I killed!* He felt Kuan San putting the garland of dried flesh back onto his neck again but didn't feel like doing anything about it this time. *Even Mom accuses me wrongly!* he thought.

"Pure?" Kuan San laughed, "What symbolizes purity? Is it the mind? Is it action? If it's the mind, then no one is pure in this world! So it has to be action. Cultivation cultivates the behavior. The way this son of yours behaves, he became a demon a long time ago!"

Mom smiled and said, "He's my son even if he's a demon." She lowered her head and comforted him, "He's my son even if he's a demon. A mother does not reject an ugly son."

Teary from frustration, Jasper thought, *What does Mom think I've turned into?* And then he began to doubt himself. *Have I really become a demon?*

Dad was waiting at the entrance with a snake-whip in hand. He laughed from a distance, "So you're on time!" Mom said, "I, this old lady of yours, keep my word!" She turned to Jasper and whispered, "Don't take it seriously. It's just a farce."

Jasper knew this farce had been performed for more than a thousand years and gazed at the stockade lazily. Everyone was busy doing something in the stockade; some pounding sesame seeds, some eating fish entrails, some lapping at dog food. Jasper was very surprised. He remembered the stockade being filled with bandits, so why were they performing the tasks of saints? Then he heard someone holler, "It's all the same. Bandits are saints and saints are bandits!"

A roar of laughter.

Father's snake-whip cracked and whistled. Scarlet blood flowed to his feet. Jasper knew this was Mother's blood. Strange—didn't she say there'd be no wounds? He turned around and saw Father whipping at a sheepskin. The blood was from the sheepskin.

A voice called out, "A lamb! A lamb!"

Jasper shuddered. The blood gurgled and sounded like a lullaby. Mom used to sing it to him when he was little. But he discovered that Snow Feather was the one singing it now.

Snow Feather said, "Your dad wants to marry me—aren't you mad? He said he did everything just to make you angry. No anger, no sin. Without sin, you wouldn't be a man!"

Jasper wanted to say, "Who said I'm not a man?" He rattled the rosary bead of penises on his chest and wanted to defend himself. Unexpectedly, he saw Kuan San, who was close by, smiling at him.

"Aren't you mad?" asked Snow Feather.

Jasper shook his head. He knew it was a dream; what's there to be mad about? Father shouted, "Who said you're dreaming? Look at how your mom is beaten! How can you not be mad? Are you human?" Sure enough, Mom was under the whip. The clothes on her back had already been licked off by the whip. Scarlet streaks laughed at Jasper.

Maybe it's not a dream after all! he thought.

He pinched his cheek and felt an intense pain. The sun was screaming in the sky. The person who was pounding sesame seeds stopped and looked at Jasper with a smile. Something black flowed out of his pestle. Jasper realized that they were not sesame seeds; they were in fact ants.

"I'm bringing salvation to them," said the man.

Jasper couldn't help but laugh out loud. He thought, *Fancy a bandit saying something like this?* Embarrassed, the man changed his tune, "They are bringing salvation to me."

That's more like it, thought Jasper.

Mom was all smiles as she approached him. Her face shone with a holy radiance. She said, "It's done! Let's go!" Jasper asked, "Did it hurt?"

Mom said, "Yes, but I'm happy to do it." She then added, "Moms are born to suffer, to suffer for her son. Without suffering, I wouldn't be Mom!"

Jasper felt like crying all of a sudden.

Braggart grabbed Snow Feather unexpectedly. Snow Feather looked at Jasper cheerfully and said, "Be angry!"

"No way!" said Jasper.

Suddenly Braggart grew huge like a massive roller and crushed Jasper into a piece of paper.

Chapter 14

Monk Wu's Sheep Hearts

In that tube of fate,
Sometimes I was a Zhang, sometimes a Li,
      Sometimes male, sometimes female,
      Like wind, my soul
      Came and went, drifting;
My parched cries were streaked with blood.
      The summit of the nine heavens
Is filled with imprints of my searching eyes.

He Gouged Out Five Hearts

Jasper found out that the old priest went out every night. The old priest was known as Monk Wu. But Jasper called him Uncle.

Monk Wu always went to the gully by himself. White bones were strewn across the ground. At first, Braggart would arrange for Jie Big, Old Daddy-Nine, and the like to carry and bury the corpses. He would subsidize two pounds of grain for each corpse carried and three additional pounds for burying it. Kuan San always manipulated the situation to favor himself and went alone. Tough and strong, he'd jog to the gully with the corpse on his back. Too lazy to dig a pit, he would dig a hole under a cliff, throw the corpse into it and hack above it with a spade so that the earth would cascade down and bury the corpse.

At first, there weren't many deaths. So Kuan San basically monopolized the job and even hoped for more deaths. But gradually, as more and more died, he brought Jie Big and Old Daddy-Nine along. And then so many people died that the subsidy from the clan decreased to two pounds of grains for burying each corpse; and the grains were the cheaper varieties. So the men would simply dump the corpses anywhere a depression could be found, toss the corpse into it, and sprinkle a few shovelfuls of earth on it. Whether they sprinkled earth on it or not in fact made no difference, since none of the bodies would remain whole by the next day anyway. The corpses had hardly any flesh on them since they all died of starvation. What the wolves could eat were the intestines. Strangely, however, the chest and thighs of the corpses showed signs of being carved. Jasper could tell they were done by humans.

Jasper had had a taste of a corpse, although he wasn't sure whether it would be considered a corpse. He had performed ascetic practice for two years in a corpse forest. It was where corpses were dumped and the best place for religious cultivation; as immateriality and impermanence would dash into the mind on their own, without requiring visualization. Then you'd no longer have attachments and cling to the mortal world. You'd feel an intense sense of detachment. That sense of detachment, along with truth and the Buddha mind, constitute the three fundamentals for enlightenment. Before Jasper met his guru, he had sought long and arduously. He had crossed snowy mountains, traversed swamps, and entered forests in search of a famous guru named Huaman. One day, he met her in a corpse forest eating a newly dumped corpse. She pointed to its leg and told him to eat it too. He found out later that she was testing his faith, but he didn't realize it at the time. Disgust overcame him, so he hesitated for just an instant, and the guru disappeared. Seeing some leftover juice on the ground, he dipped a finger into it and savored an indescribably delicious flavor when it barely touched his tongue. At that very moment, he felt himself filled with great joy and became enlightened. Later, he suspected it was a dream. He always felt he was dreaming. Oftentimes he couldn't tell the difference between dream and reality; so his sense of attachment subsequently diminished.

He secretly followed Monk Wu out of the monastery. Monk Wu went to the gully next to the monastery. After midnight, Kuan San and his men dragged over a few corpses. It was a family of three children and two adults. Kuan San and his men dumped them and left. Jasper wanted to ask them to bury the corpses but didn't feel like speaking. He rarely talked to the villagers, who considered him an alien and were critical of him. Whenever he approached them, they would clam up and give him an odd stare. Before he'd say anything, they would holler, "Barbarian

Hag died a long time ago!" Even if Jasper wanted to say something else, they'd holler at him like this. So he dared not talk to them anymore. But Monk Wu was willing to converse with him, so he expressed his desire to bury the dead children. Monk Wu said, "Let's leave them lying there. It serves to blacken the party." Jasper didn't understand what he meant but didn't feel like asking.

Monk Wu went straight to the gully. He picked up a rock to chase away the dogs and then sat down cross-legged. Immediately, something bright shone in the sky over the corpses, brilliantly and majestically. Jasper could tell it was a mandala. Although it was not the mandala of Cakrasamvara Vajra, he was sure it was a mandala. Monk Wu yelled, "Hey!" and a few streams of light entered the mandala. Jasper knew he was bringing salvation to the souls of the deceased. He didn't expect Monk Wu's skill to be so great that he could create such a distinct mandala.

After some sutra chanting, Monk Wu fished out a dagger. Jasper recognized it as the one he brought back from the home of Barbarian Hag. It was in his backpack. Monk Wu must have taken it at some point. Monk Wu's cassock rustled loudly from the mountain wind. He stretched himself and bent down. A few quick strokes, and a black object was on the tip of the dagger. Jasper's heart throbbed violently. He felt his chest and thought, *Maybe someday he'll gouge out this heart of mine too!* He remembered how recently he would sometimes discover some meat among the cooked wild greens. Monk Wu always felt the need to explain it, "Mutton heart." *Maybe what he ate was human heart*, he thought.

In no time at all, Monk Wu had gouged out five hearts, which he placed into a plastic bag. And then he messaged his own lower back by pounding it and asked, "Were you scared stiff from this?" Jasper knew he'd been discovered. His mind drew a blank.

Monk Wu shook the bag and said, "These are but food. One has to survive. Can't waste these treasures from the human bodies. Let's go!" He left without waiting for Jasper.

The night had become totally dark. A gust of mountain wind pierced through his bones.

The kitchen stove was already lit when Jasper entered the gate of the monastery. He proceeded to the kitchen directly as he was usually the one in charge of feeding the stove whenever they cooked. He sat on a stack of hay. Soon, the bottom of the wok turned red. Monk Wu had already chopped the meat, which splattered violently as soon as they were put into the wok. Monk Wu placed a lid on the wok quickly. He said, "Make sure the lid is on when you stir-fry the hearts. Otherwise, they'll all end up on the ground!" Indeed, the meat splattered in the wok and banged at the lid. Monk Wu lifted the lid just enough to insert his chopsticks, and chopped meat would escape through the crack now and then. Jasper smelled an incredibly delicious aroma. He thought the fact that it smelled good was an unforgivable sin.

What he couldn't understand was why the hearts kept on bouncing.

After stir-frying for a while, Monk Wu poured the pile of black things into a bowl. He asked, "Do you want some?"

"No." said Jasper.

"Me neither. Let's go to the home of the Degree-Holder. They would not survive the night otherwise. . . . This is truly the best mutton."

The Thick Darkness

The dead of night had reached its peak; the road was almost totally blurred. One could only feel the way. Jasper stumbled along. Monk Wu's cassock rustled loudly in the wind. The aroma wafted joyfully and charged straight into his mind. He felt somewhat disgusted.

The stench of the rotting corpses stained the night and formed various shapes and colors. The wind was green, the blood was red, and the stench of the corpses was puslike. Fear became lightning that threatened to strike now and then. The village in the dead of night looked deader than ever. Because there was no oil for the lamps, the village was completely drowned by a thick darkness. There were many sniggering faces in the darkness. They were all those of children. Jasper always dreamt of children sniggering and snarling at him. Knowing they were but ghosts, he clobbered them to death. But the moment he stopped hitting them, they would open their eyes and snigger at him again. He was always dreaming such dreams and waking up utterly tired. He thought these must have been nightmares. He felt he was surrounded by sniggering and snarling children who snuck up on him and pinched him. But as soon as he noticed them, they disappeared into the night.

The road gradually turned white and twisted itself as it hastened into the distance, very much like the khata scarf,[1] which would appear

---

1. A white Tibetan ceremonial scarf.

when he practiced visualization. Such a khatalike road, which led to Pure Land, frequently appeared in his soul. Whenever he was unreservedly devout, he would proceed slowly along the road amidst the heaven-stirring chanting of mantras. Dakini goddesses would dance inside rainbow lights and sing songs derived from antiquity. It was said they were transmitted a thousand years ago by Niguma, the founder of a religious sect who learned them from a Buddhist realm. Jasper grew up with these songs.

The barking of wild dogs could be heard nearby. They were tearing at something. They must have been fighting over the corpses. Occasionally, he also heard the howling of wolves. But there were no human sounds. There was neither light nor voices in the village. Death was everywhere, no one knew whether he would live until the next day. Jasper also wondered. Even before this outbreak of starvation, he had wondered what death was. Death was just the cessation of breathing. When the exhaled breath could not be inhaled, then the person would die. Death was, in fact, as simple as that. But this was rational. When death really threatened the villagers so closely, Jasper could not help being enveloped by a sense of hopelessness.

They entered Degree-Holder Ho's home. Monk Wu lit the lantern he brought himself. The light chased away the darkness. Degree-Holder Ho was lying on a brick bed. Others lay beside him. The god of death was already smiling at them. Their legs were mere skin and bones. The children's bellies were bloated like balloons. Without nutrition, there was no support for the inner organs, which drooped down to the belly and created a watermelon out of it. Their death was imminent. However, the eyes of the woman shone as she looked at Monk Wu. Monk Wu brought out the stir-fried meat and said, "Mutton heart, it was an offering." The eyes of Degree-Holder Ho also shone, but his hands were too weak to move. Monk Wu grabbed a handful of meat and fed it to him bit by bit. A boy stared at the meat with wooden eyes. Presently, a stream of saliva drooled from a corner of his mouth. Just as Jasper was wondering about it, the boy's head cocked to one side, and he collapsed on the brick bed. Jasper knew that he'd died. Later on, Jasper would see many others die of starvation. They would all drool before they'd cock their heads and stop breathing.

After feeding a few pieces to Degree-Holder Ho, Monk Wu said, "Enough!" And he began to feed a child. The child smacked his lips woodenly. Jasper was reminded of the corpses he saw earlier and felt his stomach churn. He forced himself not to watch the look of avarice on the boy's face, so he turned to look at Ho's wife. By now the most beautiful and sensuous woman in the village also resembled a skeleton. She stretched out her clawlike hand very slowly. She stretched and stretched until she finally grabbed hold of some meat. But as she contracted the hand, the meat fell off between her fingers. So she looked at Monk Wu. Thereupon Monk Wu fed her some that she chewed sluggishly.

It was clear to Jasper that, without the food, this family would not have lasted more than a few days.

After feeding them for a while, Monk Wu said, "Enough! they shouldn't eat much. People can die from overeating after starving too long." But Degree-Holder Ho continued to look at him with longing and panted. Monk Wu wrapped the meat carefully and put it back into the plastic bag. He blew out the light in the lantern and walked toward another home.

All the survivors had consumed the mutton hearts brought by Monk Wu.

The Familiar Sound of Sobbing

Back then, there were already some corpses strewn along the gully. They obviously died of starvation. Although there was grain in the village, Braggart said they were reserves in case of major warfare. War reserves made an incredibly legitimate excuse. Although some food was distributed later, it was only enough for a few months. The days of the rest of the year seemed so long that people wished they could club Grandpa Sun down the mountain sooner!

Back then, only Braggart and the clan militia headed by Kuan San had grains to eat. They had to stand guard and prevent potential sabotage by Brilliant King Clan. But most of their energy was spent on blocking the villagers from escaping, to beg for food elsewhere, and bring shame upon Diamond Clan. Back then Braggart's fame spread throughout Liangzhou. Whenever Diamond Clan was mentioned, people would say, "Sure—of course we know about that Braggart of Diamond Clan! When people were dying everywhere in Liangzhou, only Diamond Clan had no deaths!" This was of course due to the good work of the clan militia. They guarded the entrance of the village and only allowed entry. At first, some tried to escape. But later no one had the energy to leave even if they could. But the clan militia continued to keep vigilant surveillance over the slightest movement at the entrance.

Jasper went to dig for mountain yam on a piece of land. That ground had been dug countless times, but those with any energy left would still give it a try; and with luck, might find a piece of yam larger than a walnut. This was not the poplar goo that one could swallow in a single gulp—although even poplar bark had disappeared—nor the chicken feet weed that stank of mud. This was *bona fide* food! When he felt starved, Jasper would go to that piece of land. Just like people leaving for Xikou during famine, it had come to represent a distant but hopeful dream.

The yam was planted on a mountain slope. When the rain was timely, the entire slope would be filled with yam leaves dotted with blue or white flowers smiling happily in the wind. The yam of Diamond Clan was very famous, as evidenced by the saying, "The turnips of Hongxiang, the garlic of Jiahe; the flax of Haizang Monastery rivals button-hook thread; the mountain yams of Diamond Clan are powdery and tasty." Come spring, donkeys would arrive from all over, carrying grain to exchange for the seed yams of Diamond Clan. A distant dream now, but that used to be the most festive time of the year.

Jasper left the monastery and approached the yam farm. Death still enveloped the village: no sign of life. The absence of smoke in chimneys had become normal. Hence, the issuance of smoke would have been abnormal. It was through such an abnormality that Braggart was able to discover Snow Feather's supposed theft of crops.

The corpses continued to exude a pungent stench. It was said that rotten corpses stank worse than anything else in the world. Only "deadly stench" might describe it—a truly nauseating stench. Who would have expected the once flirtatious, adorable bodies to become such objects of stench? Realization of this fact may help one to become less attached to earthly things. Jasper realized why the practitioners of India preferred the corpse forests. Everything there demonstrated the unpredictability of life.

The sight of living beings had become a rarity. Those alive were all lying at home, for they believed that only death at home constituted a good ending. According to the custom of Liangzhou, those who died outside would not be allowed to return home. Those who died in the wilderness became roaming ghosts and were not accepted by King Yama of Hades. So those facing death had no option but to lie on their brick beds to await the inevitable.

At length Jasper saw a living person. The thing slinking up and down in a bend of the gully was, in fact, a person with a blanket draped over his shoulders. At close range, Jasper recognized him as the famous Big-Bellied-Fellow of Diamond Clan, famous for being able to consume more than three pounds of cured meat at a setting. He frequently squabbled with other villagers. He had tremendous strength just like the "furless tiger" Niu Er of *Men of the Marshes*, so everyone called him Niu Er. That Niu Er was lapping at something on the ground like a dog. Jasper suddenly felt nauseated. It was a pool of vomit with undigested chunks of carrot and mountain yam on the ground! Lest Niu Er would feel embarrassed by his presence, Jasper left quietly.

Jasper noticed his footsteps had become silent. He wondered if he had turned into a ghost. He could always see that Barbarian Hag at the entrance to the village waiting for beggars coming to Diamond Clan. Its fame as a wealthy village had always attracted beggars. They would arrive confidently; but none were ever seen leaving. There must have been other reasons than the efforts of the clan militia. Jasper did not feel like pursuing this line any further.

His body was wracked by an indescribable frailty exemplified by two facts: one was that he wasn't even able to kill the lice in his clothes. No matter how hard he pinched them, he was unable to pop them; he eventually had to rely on his teeth to do it. The second was that he couldn't even step over the small stones on his pathway. He was no longer able to lift his incredibly heavy legs. Fortunately, he had a shadow, which provided the sole evidence that he was still alive.

The land that grew mountain yams had been turned over innumerable times. Jasper knew it was unlikely he would be pleasantly surprised; still, he found a stick and began digging. His hands had no strength. The stick looked like it was moving, but in fact it was not. Jasper heaved a sigh. He knew that even if anything were buried in the soil, he wouldn't have the energy to dig it out. Moreover, even if he had the energy, what he'd gain wouldn't match the energy spent.

So he tossed the stick away and lay down on the mountain slope instead.

The sky was gray. It was cloudless. Grandpa Sun was lively and bright, but the sky was still gray. It was not just the sky, but everything appeared gray from his being enveloped by the aura of death. He thought prisoners condemned to death also must have felt this way before execution. So must those suffering terminal illnesses. The aura of death had already woven a gray gauze separating him from the rest of the world and made him a lonely island. Unexpectedly, however, he wasn't scared. It wasn't so much his not being afraid as his not having the energy to be afraid. His mind also became dull, and his thoughts were stuffed by woodenness.

However, he felt unreconciled by having to die so young. He used to regard death as a star in the furthest distance. But now death was approaching ever closer and was smiling at him ever so affectionately. Any moment now, a corner of his mouth might drool, and then his head would cock to one side, and he would plunge into another world. *How would he feel then?* he wondered.

He also pondered the question of where he would go when the time came. *Would he still be known as Jasper then? Would he really see Hell[2] then?* It was said that the human form was the most precious of all living forms. According to a parable, there was a wooden lifesaver in the eastern ocean and a sea turtle that emerged out of the water once every five hundred years. The probability for the turtle's head to enter the lifesaver was greater than for it to transform into a human. *If this was true*, Jasper wondered, *then would he still be human in the next life?*

He also thought of the meaning of life. Although he was human in this life, there was no evidence of it. More often than not, within the time span of a nap, the world would change into something else; without a trace of the past or hint of the future. Everything could change within an instant and become illusory. Jasper thought of how Ajia frequently had nightmares and was unable to distinguish dreams from reality. He suddenly understood Ajia. Just then, he heard Ajia's laughter. *Am I about to die?* he wondered.

Suddenly, a black shadow flashed by. A cloth bag tumbled on the ground. He looked around. There was no one.

Opening the drawstring of the bag, he was overcome by the aroma of grain. Too weak to wonder further, he took a handful of the uncooked grain and stuffed it into his mouth. Immediately, the fragrance peculiar to grain enveloped him.

Jasper heard the familiar sound of a sob.

Not daring to eat too much, he pulled the drawstring of the bag after consuming the handful. He could feel the nutrients of the grain

---

2. The court of Hell is where the fate of the deceased would be decided.

cheering in his body: sometimes like charging vanguard soldiers, sometimes like exploding fireworks, sometimes like a scattered school of fish. They bawled so loudly that heaven and earth shook. They screamed "charge" and "kill" until they were hoarse. They were a band of porcupines dancing disco.

Gradually Jasper regained some energy.

He proceeded back to the monastery and remembered that Monk Wu had already collapsed on the brick bed from hunger. The "mutton hearts" had become ever scarcer since people would now charge at the recently disposed-of corpses before waiting until it was dark. They no longer worried about what others might say; survival had trumped face saving. Cannibalism had become a public affair. Everyone in the village was familiar with Xianxiao performances. They all knew that during the end of the Ming dynasty,[3] Zhang Xianzhong[4] butchered his soldiers as army provisions. So, whenever there was a new corpse, anyone with an iota of strength would pounce on it and gouge out either its heart or its legs. Only after that would wolves get to clean up the battlefield. By the time Monk Wu got there at night, even the bones had been chomped down by the wolves. The poplar trees in the monastery had no bark left; chicken feet weed had become even more of a rarity. Monk Wu used a hand mill to grind the cob of corn that resembled flour and had a tinge of sweetness to it. It tasted much better than chicken feet weed but caused constipation. They had to help each other during bowel movements by gouging out the feces with a stick. When he faced the aged buttocks of Monk Wu, the ugliness that assaulted Jasper embarrassed him. *There goes the last trace of civility*, he thought.

On his way back to the monastery, Jasper ran into Niu Er, who was already dead with his blanket collapsed next to him. That pool of vomit obviously failed to save his life. *Such is life*, thought Jasper. He wondered if Niu Er would have inflicted so much pain upon others if he had known of this ending?

Back at the monastery, Monk Wu had already lit the kitchen stove and was cooking "dumb wheat." The folks of Liangzhou referred to boiled grain as "dumb wheat" to distinguish this method of cooking from roasting by dry-stir-frying which would cause the grain to pop. "Some-

---

3. 1368–1644.

4. Nicknamed Yellow Tiger, Zhang Xianzhong (1606–1647) was the leader of a peasant revolt from Yan'an, Shaanxi Province and later conquered Sichuan in the seventeenth century before he was crushed by the Manchus of the Qing dynasty (1644–1911).

one left a small bag of grain by the gate of the monastery," said Monk Wu.

It was said that all the households in the village received a small bag of grain by their door. But no one knew who brought them.

The Plumes of Chimney Smoke

Suddenly, smoke appeared in the village. Numerous plumes of smoke rose straight up into the sky in an orderly fashion—a most unusual sight!

Just imagine the sight of a mountain valley studded with low, mud houses scattered along the creases of the slopes, panting lifelessly. The wan Grandpa Sun shone on the grimy village. The plumes of smoke were the only sign of life. On a windless day, they would rise straight up into the sky; and a young boy reeking with the smell of milk would be singing underneath one of them in a high-pitched voice, "The smoke in the chimney rises straight up to heaven. The water in the Yellow River washes the red rug. When the red carpet tears, Girl Number Seven dances!" That boy was me. When the smoke reached maximum height, it would slowly scatter downward and envelope the village in a hazy dream. Many years had passed, but that dreamy feeling lingered in my heart.

Usually, the most beautiful moment of the rising smoke was during the evening when Grandpa Sun was gentle and moist. But to Jasper, the Grandpa Sun of that particular evening wasn't red. It was rather a gloomy white. "That was quite true," said Ajia, "the world back then didn't look like the normal world; it was more like Hell." He said. "Hell felt like a wan moon, where everything was shadowy and indistinct. Although I've been to the netherworld, the soup of oblivion which I had to drink upon departure obliterated my memory!" I can't stand Ajia's "show-offish" tone, but there's nothing I can do.

So Jasper ate the "dumb wheat" at the monastery. It had been many days since he had tasted real grain. Monk Wu chewed a few mouthfuls perfunctorily and then sat down with his rosary beads. Extremely skilled at meditating, he could eat very little and sit for a month without eating or drinking anything. When he meditated in isolation during his earlier days, Monk Wu had stayed in a mountain cave for a year with just a bag of grain, making his daily consumption less than a mere few ounces. But Monk Wu was preoccupied recently. Worried about the villagers, he would chant the *Auspicious Sutra of Niguma* whenever he had the time. He prayed for the quick passing of this calamity.

Chapter 15

The Captured Flying Thief

On the tomb base of what is known as the 'soul,'
   Is a black tombstone.
I will die beneath the black tombstone.
    I wish to transform into a butterfly
To flutter to a tune of the *Liang Zhu* tale[1]
In the midst of the lonely graves.
But in the end you turned into a cricket instead
Spreading your wings by the withering grass of the wilderness
And chanted alone under the waning moon in the morning wind . . .

The Volley of Shots that Protected the Crops

According to *Tale of the Goddess*, a "wind ring" appeared around the moon the night Snow Feather was captured. It was supposed to have been a windy night, but strangely there was no wind. Later, Ajia would explain the phenomenon as a forecast of the calamity that would befall her. Imagine a huge ring whirling incessantly around the moon like a flying saucer, emanating an aura of mystery.

That absolutely normal moonlit night would, however, become a turning point for Snow Feather's destiny.

---

1. The story of Liang Shanbo and Zhu Yingtai, also known as *The Butterfly Lovers*, is a most popular Chinese folktale of two star-crossed lovers who were united as butterflies after death.

"That night, she again floated toward the village granary like a spirit," said Ajia.

I've always wondered if Ajia had fabricated a slipshod tale. Many people couldn't believe Braggart guarded the grain and let the villagers starve to death. But my aged Dad provided proof for the veracity of Ajia's story. When Dad told me his version of the tale, Braggart was still alive. Based on our relationship, Braggart would've been considered a paternal uncle of mine. He would sun himself at a corner of the southern wall every day. Skin and bones, he resembled a sick monkey and looked like an opium addict. Father also suspected that he smoked opium, but there was no proof. Then, a villager indeed discovered opium poppies in Braggart's backyard and reported it to the police station. The station quickly dispatched a policeman there, and Braggart was fined two thousand *yuan*.

According to Father, Braggart performed innumerable evil deeds during his life, yet he got to live out the natural span of life. The high official who was even worse also got to enjoy life until its natural end, contrary to expectations. There was nothing one could do about it. It was after Braggart seized Grandpa and put him through a "struggle session"[2] that he developed choking disease. Thereafter, Dad considered Braggart a mortal enemy, the one who killed his father. Later, during a *qingsuan* session,[3] Dad took the opportunity to give Braggart's legs a few vigorous hacks with a pickaxe handle. Braggart squealed for half a day like a knifed pig. "Braggart had no conscience," said Father, "he had the grain, but would not let people have it. He starved more than half the villagers."

Dad also talked about Snow Feather. But he talked about her as he would have any other girl in the village since he didn't believe in ghosts and spirits. He did take us to pay our respects to the ancestors on the thirtieth of the Twelfth Month and kowtow to Grandpa and Grandma's grave before saying, "Let's go, ancestors! Let's go celebrate the New Year!" But come the fifth of the First Month, he would dip a brush in vinegar and chase them out of the door by sprinkling the vinegar. Hence, when Dad talked about Snow Feather, he spoke about her the way he would have about anyone.

Mom also talked about Snow Feather, but she was a Buddhist.

---

2. Struggle sessions were a form of public humiliation practiced during the Cultural Revolution (1966–1976).

3. A session held to "expose and criticize" select people. At this point, Braggart must have fallen from power.

Whenever Mom mentioned Snow Feather, she would join her palms and show utmost respect. To her, Snow Feather was the Bodhisattva Guanyin. She would always add "the Dakini Goddess" before she mentioned the name "Snow Feather." What Mom and Dad had told me proved that at least half of Ajia's story was true.

But Ajia swore to its veracity, beat his chest, and said, "What do you mean half of it was true? It was entirely true!" "What's with all the swearing, idiot? Anything in a novel could have been true! I believe in everything you said!"

That moonlit night Ajia described was a gloomy one. Snow Feather was greeted by a wilderness filled with wronged souls. They were all wailing that they shouldn't have died, and it was all Braggart's fault. After Snow Feather's trip to Liangzhou, however, she realized that Braggart was not the only one at fault. But no matter who was responsible, no one could make the ghosts human again. They all died unnatural deaths. Although they were all destined to live until a ripe old age, they all ended up dead before the *li* "established" age (thirty), the *buhuo* "with full self-confidence" age (forty), and the *chuiji* "before the topknot" age (childhood). Without King Yama's dispatching the Black and White Anityas and the Horse and Bullheaded Demons to fetch the souls of the deceased, these ghosts were unable to find their way to King Yama's court in Hell. So they became a flock of lost, roaming ghosts. Like willow catkins hovering in the wind, they had no control. Unable to reach either heaven or earth, they suffered hunger and cold and had no means of livelihood. They could not see the sun of the mortal world as they had no sight. Grandpa Sun belonged to the humans but not to the ghosts. When they died, no one placed a guidance lamp above their heads; therefore they now had to grope among the stones to cross rivers during the long, dark nights. They were a flock of ravens with their eyes covered. They were a drove of headless flies. They suffered pain and felt hopeless. They sang a mournful song, "Go, go, go, and keep on going; go until the ninth of the Ninth Month!" They had no sun, no one to greet them. They screamed as they walked, "Where did my life go? Where's my life?" They all knew they had only one life; and once gone, it was gone forever. They were all seeking the life that had slipped away from their throats. They said, "The road is long and distant, but seek for it I will, from above and below."[4] They said, "The enduring Heaven and earth

---

4. This is line 97 of "Lisao," a poem by Qu Yuan (343–278 BCE).

will have an end, but this lingering sorrow will be everlasting."[5] They wished for more starvations in the world so they could find substitutes for themselves and be reborn. They were the most heartless of all the ghosts. Hatred had blinded their minds and consciences. They exhaled at Grandpa Sun, whom they couldn't see, hoping their grievance could transform into a dark cloud to shade the sun and strengthen the camp of the starved. They spoke evil words. They said, "Since I'm already dead, you can't threaten me with death anymore!" They said, "If people do not fear death, how can one threaten them with death?"[6] Ajia's saliva sputtered and drooled as he harangued. I said, "Enough! You're too much for your readers!"

It was on a moonlit night like this that Snow Feather wafted toward the granary of the village for the eighth time. Her last seven trips resulted in the issuing of smoke from the stoves in the village. "You exist today because of her," he said. "If it weren't for her, your mom and dad would have been long gone. Where would you be today?" He made many other comments like this I didn't feel like arguing with him over. I knew that all those who became deities felt self-righteous. Ajia, too, felt one of his sentences was worth ten thousand words.

"Shit!" said Ajia. Although militiamen were on night duty, no one believed anyone would steal the grain. Back then, many died from the rifles of those protecting the crops. The pockmarks on your grandpa's face were made by the shots from one of them. You remember seeing a pockmarked old man when you were three years old? His outstretched palm had jellybeans for you. You used to yell, "Grandpa, jellybeans! Grandpa, jellybeans!" You passed through your childhood eating Grandpa's jellybeans without knowing Grandpa died many years ago. You noticed the shining pockmarks on his face and told your dad about the grandpa who gave you jellybeans. Remember how your dad's face changed? He'd heard that those who ate food from the netherworld would die instantly. So he scooped up a ladleful of night soil to pour down your throat. You were very smart—a clever imp you were even when you were little—you immediately said, "Dad, I lied!" Your dad heaved a sigh of relief, and you continued to eat Grandpa's jellybeans. Grandpa's pockmarks were as bright as the sun to you, but you didn't know they were formed by

---

5. This is the last line of "Song of Everlasting Sorrow," a poem by Bai Juyi (772–846).

6. This is from chapter 74 of *Daodejing* attributed to Laozi (571–531 BCE), the putative founder of Daoism.

the rifle pellets of the crop-protecting militia. When the volley of iron pellets whistled from the steel muzzles of the rifle, they first formed a red line, and then they collided with each other and cheered like the wronged souls in the mountains. They performed disco dances: they were a flock of dancing elves; and then they transformed from the red line into a broom. Your grandpa immediately covered his eyes with his elbows. The iron pellets pierced through his tattered cotton jacket and bit into his bony elbows until they were dripping with thick blood. You didn't know, but he would've been blinded if it weren't for his elbows protecting his eyes. As it was, he only became pockmarked. If he'd been blinded, he wouldn't have been able to recognize you as his grandson and give you jellybeans. And because of the jellybeans, a sweet memory was added to your childhood.

You know, the crop-protecting iron shots not only attacked eyes, they also pierced chests. If the latter had happened, then the person wouldn't just be blind. See the eight ghosts who danced with the most abandon among the wronged souls? They felt that they deserved death the least. They were suddenly sent to the court of the netherworld by iron shots, while they were at their most robust. No, I was wrong: it was not the court of the netherworld, it was just the netherworld. They didn't have the right to enter the court of the netherworld. You know, those who died of unnatural deaths didn't have the right to enter it. They were just roaming ghosts. They wailed throughout the nights, not realizing that being roaming ghosts, they were in fact much freer than humans. You know, having been the least free of all, they were afraid of freedom. They had become donkeys hitched for so long that they couldn't survive without a harness. Only when the mind became free could one sing to freedom!

"So you know about the Age of Enlightenment in the West?"

Therefore, no one dared to steal the crops thereafter. It went without saying that no one dared to drool over the war-reserve grains either.

But Snow Feather wafted into the granary.

The Granary and its Seal

Historical Mirror of Forgotten Events describes the storeroom in detail. It was a very large room the size of a sports field with many granaries in it. What did the granary look like? Imagine a room with four walls, without a ceiling, or doors, or windows. No, it also had a bottom with a hole, a chute. The chute was more than a foot above ground to prevent moisture from the ground from entering the granary and ruining the grain. The walls of the granary were lower than the walls of the room and contained the war-reserve provisions. Also, the ceiling of the storeroom had a skylight for releasing moisture. I suspect that Snow Feather entered and left through this skylight. But one could never be sure. Maybe she had perfected some technique, such as traveling through the earth?

Normally three guards were on night duty. They lived in a separate room. Two of them were in charge of the keys, while one person had custody of the seal. The seal was carved out of wood and had patterns or Chinese characters. The person in charge of the seal would level the wheat and press the seal into it to create a pattern. This seal was equivalent to an official seal and was not to be duplicated without permission. So, the guards who had the keys didn't have the seal, and the one with the seal didn't have the keys; and kept each other in check.

Braggart had neither the keys nor the seal. According to hearsay, Braggart was not only mean to his fellow clansmen; he was also cruel to his own kin. During the years he presided over the village as the clan head, three corpses left his home. His dad and two of his children died of starvation. This became the main reason he was not beaten to death later. A few years after the starvation event, the county government organized a meeting among the villagers due to the tremendous number of deaths; but they still elected Braggart as the clan head. They all concluded that during times of bad harvest, none of them could have been as deadly impartial as Braggart. Many years later, when the practice of corruption spread like wildfire, the fact that three corpses emerged from Braggart's home became an ever-popular topic of conversation, and he ended up as a positive example.

"Snow Feather entered the storeroom through the skylight and slid down a rope ladder," said Ajia. The rats in the storeroom scampered, singing songs of their own kind. As I remember it, there were also some bats, which all the folks of Diamond Clan knew were transformed from rats. Aside from wheat, the granary also stored vegetable oil. When the rats consumed the oil, they would itch in the back for forty-nine days, after which a feather would grow where it itched. Then the feather would multiply until it eventually became a wing. Just as the carp turned into dragons after jumping over a dragon gate, rats transformed themselves into bats based on the power of the oil. I knew rats and bats belonged to different species but didn't want to discredit Ajia's power of imagination. You know, science obliterated the power of human imagination.

Snow Feather must have heard the flapping of the bats' wings, but she wasn't really scared in her capacity as a thief at the time. Everyone has five *yang* evil energies, but thieves have six of them. Let me tell you something—if you're out during the dead of night and start to feel your scalp tingle and your pores expand, then most likely there's a ghost next to you. But don't be afraid—just steal something nearby. Even a wooden stick. And you'll have an extra *yang* evil energy because of the theft, and you won't have to be scared of the ghost anymore. Her possession of six *yang* evil energies helps explain why Snow Feather could travel through deserted graveyards on such dark nights and was not scared by the malicious laughter of malevolent ghosts.

But Snow Feather knew the black bats were staring at her sneakily. Although they didn't eat grain, they loved darkness. She was always dreaming of bats these days, which was a bad omen. But she suspected she dreamt of them because she saw them in the storeroom. She wasn't bothered by the rustling noise created by the bats. She knew the sound existed outside the mind; and what really bothered her was in her mind. So, she got rid of the rustling sound from her mind.

She stepped gingerly over the equipment for the draught animals, such as the hemp harnesses and rubber cartwheels. In fact, she could have walked with heavier steps, as the guards on night duty were sleeping in the small side room. They were sleeping like dead pigs the previous times she visited. Since the imprints of the seals were exactly the way they had been, maybe they hadn't discovered the theft. They had no idea Snow Feather copied the pattern of the seal and carved it herself. They could have discovered the loss, based on the obvious lowering of the level of the wheat. But if the rats had created a hole at the bottom, the level of wheat in the granary would also have lowered. But then, the imprint of the seal would have been disturbed at the top. In the case that the seal imprint had not been tampered with, yet the level of wheat had become lower, then the night duty guards must have been in cahoots with each other in executing the theft.

What Snow Feather didn't know was that the guards had already been given more than a dozen "cunt boards" by Braggart. "Cunt boards" was a popular colloquial expression in Liangzhou to refer to slaps on the face. The guards bawled for their moms and dads, protesting their innocence. They searched and searched until they finally found some unusual signs in the skylight.

Snow Feather approached a granary slowly. Of course she was too smart to steal from the same granary all the time. She stole from a different one each time. She would put her bag on the wheat and dig it out with her delicate but calloused hands, one handful at a time. When the bag was nearly full, she would weigh it with her hands before tying it up. And then she would level the wheat the way it was and use the seal she had carved on it. She had visited eight times before this and had stolen from eight granaries.

You must have found out later it was Braggart who discovered the traces. He then braided almost invisible horsetail hair into a pattern and placed it in the granary. When the chimneys in the village issued smoke inexplicably and everyone smelled the aroma of grain that they'd missed for so long, naturally Braggart found out about the mysterious bags of grain at the entrance of all the homes. He obviously realized that such a beautiful job could only have been performed by Snow Feather.

Therefore, Snow Feather discovered that the skylight was suddenly blocked.

A voice roared outside of the storeroom, "Put your hands into the cat hole!"

The Ancestral Hall

Snow Feather was escorted into the Ancestral Hall, which had handled many cases of thievery during the several hundred years of its existence. There was an extremely tall white poplar outside the hall. The inside of the hall was lit by a few lamps with three wicks made of cotton and soaked in vegetable oil. Each cotton wick was topped by a light the size of a fava bean. The clansmen who had eaten the grain stolen by Snow Feather now had enough energy to denounce her.

To this day, I don't know why Braggart did not send Snow Feather to the official court. If he had, she most likely would have been executed by firing squad under the tyranny of County Magistrate An. If this had happened, then she would've been no more than a "flying thief" to the villagers. Therefore I realized the utmost importance of "understanding."

To those who did not "understand," Snow Feather was just any person; but for those who "understood," she was a Dakini goddess. Hence the ancients had said, "If I hear the Way in the morning, I could die without regret in the evening."

Perhaps Braggart was hoping to use Snow Feather to establish his own power. Perhaps he didn't want her to die too easily; or, even more likely, he wanted to play a game of cat and mouse.

"There's no need for you to dwell on this—why be so petty?"

The weak, yellow hues of three-wicked lamps lit the Ancestral Hall. More ghosts than humans arrived. The ghosts came for entertainment for lack of anything to do. Although fortified by the nourishment of the stolen grain, people still preferred to rest on their brick beds. It was only after much berating by the militiamen that a few skin and bones came to the Ancestral Hall.

I don't feel like repeating the words they used to denounce Snow Feather. You can describe it however you want. A wire pierced through her wrists. She must have put her hands into the cat hole as she was bidden. Although by then there were no more cats since they had all become food for the villagers, but the cat holes remained. Braggart and his men tied her jade-like, delicate hands with a rope before they dared to open the door and pierce her wrists with wire. Snow Feather's face was pale. Ajia described the scene with a trembling voice.

"I don't want to describe Snow Feather's suffering in minutia," said Ajia. After her wrists were shackled by the wires, the night duty guards gave her a good round of slapping, returning the "cunt boards" they'd received from Braggart on her account. Snow Feather's face was swollen and black and blue, and her hair was disheveled. She looked like a female ghost in a horror film.

The other villagers did not beat her. Although the grain Snow Feather sent them gave them enough energy to beat her, they refrained from swinging their claws. They just said, "That's enough! That beating was enough!"

When the guards were too fatigued to strike any more, Braggart stared at Snow Feather with a sinister look and said with clenched teeth, "You get to choose. We can send you to the court at the city of Liangzhou, or we can break your legs according to clan rules."

Snow Feather gave it a quick thought and replied, "Break my legs!"

A Difficult Task

The folks realized soon that leg-breaking was easier said than done. None of the villagers had enough energy to lift a rock that could break her legs. If you remember how the starving Jasper was not even able to squish a louse or step over a stone, you'd realize what a heroic feat it would have been for someone to smash a leg with a large rock. Of course there were still militiamen who had enough energy to carry rifles. But they all made a show of being coy, and none of these men were willing to lift a rock and smash Snow Feather's legs. That was when we realized that people hadn't lost all conscience.

Braggart had to yell, "Kuan San, you do it!"

Kuan San's face turned red as he looked around. He then disappeared into the darkness and came back in a flash carrying a round rock that looked exactly like a head, complete with eyes and eyebrows. One didn't know whether it was a rock that turned into a head, or a head that transformed into a rock. Kuan San said, "I brought it—who will throw it?" Braggart said, "You!" Kuan San said, "I'm not throwing!" Braggart asked, "Why?" Kuan San said, "I've proposed to her, and she refused me. If I did throw, then people will think I'm using it to pay back. So I won't do it!" Braggart pointed to Cripple Big and said, "You do it!" Not daring to look at the villagers, Cripple Big struggled to pick up the rock. Of course he wasn't pretending. He heaved, intending to lift the rock above his head to throw it down forcefully the way he broke firewood. Finally getting the rock to his chest after much difficulty, he suddenly tossed it aside and said, "Someone else do it—I can't bear it!" Braggart's finger pointed to one after the other. Jie Big, Donkey Second, and the others bowed their heads one after the other. "That must have been the most moving scene of that era," said Ajia.

Braggart cussed furiously, "Shit eaters! You shit eaters!" He went over and lifted the rock himself. The muscles on his face bulged, indicating exertion. He was also skin and bones, not stout. He lifted the rock and walked toward Snow Feather slowly. She sat on a mud stairway and waited woodenly for the falling rock.

The folks closed their eyes. The muscles on their faces were also bulging as they tried to prevent themselves from collapsing. The lamp wicks seemed to gust madly like raging wind, or panting tigers, or even gasping lions during orgasm. The heady aroma of vegetable oil infused the air. It must have also contained nutrition, as the folks opened their mouths wide and inhaled the oily air emphatically. They dreaded the sound but waited for it. After the sound, there'd be red blood and white bone marrow on the ground, and bone chips would splatter all the corners of the room. Should a sharp chip pierce into a person's eye, he'd scream wretchedly, and a bitter fluid would splash from his eyeball as brilliantly as fireworks during the Lantern Festival. After a few days, his eye would either wither into a sunken pit, or a glass flower would emerge in the eyeball.

They all waited for the sound.

The sound should be a splitting crack, like breaking dry firewood, in which case more bone chips would splatter. But more likely a heavier thud would be produced since Snow Feather's legs were muscular, judging from their robustness when she walked. Those were obviously a sexy pair of legs. Unfortunately, the men were already castrated by starvation then and were no longer able to enjoy civilized life with women. During those two years, there wasn't a single birth in the village. It was not clear if the women had no more eggs, or the men had no more sperm. Hence, the lack of appreciation for those well-formed sexy legs of hers.

I'm not sure what Snow Feather's state of mind was when she waited for the landing of the rock, as she had a wooden face. Maybe she was very peaceful; like a dead donkey with no fear of being gnawed by the wolves, or a dead pig with no fear of being scorched by boiling water. I prefer to see her, however, as practicing humiliation endurance then. You may have heard the story of the immortal who endured humiliation. Smiling calmly, he allowed a tyrant to continuously abuse his physical body. But Snow Feather did not smile. If she had smiled, many folks would have deemed her arrogant and picked up rocks to crush her legs. You know, the folks of Liangzhou detested nothing more than seeing others better than themselves, even if it was just their attitude. I could understand Snow Feather's woodenness during that moment; being wooden was the best expression for that instant. Screaming or smiling would be out of character for her. Art supersedes life, you know.

I desperately wanted to imagine Braggart's expression then, but my brain refused to comply and what appeared in it was always the image of his aged self. He would squat in a corner of the southern wall like a sick orangutan, clear mucus dripping down his nose and smiling ingratiatingly at passersby. His backbone was broken by his youngest son. There was something mysterious about the birth of that son. Braggart's woman had been sterile for many years but then became pregnant unexpectedly. The night the child was born, a loud bang was heard south of the village where half of a mud slope crashed down. My dad had said, "Listen to that—something strange is going to happen!" That night, Braggart's woman gave birth to his youngest son. "This lad was a reincarnated creditor," said Ajia. He was so brave and strong that at ten he'd beat Braggart until the dad bawled. One evening, the son tried to throw Braggart up to the second floor but missed and broke the dad's back. Ever since then, Braggart crouched in the corner like a skinny orangutan, and became a landmark spectacle of my native home. You now might understand why it was impossible for me to think of Braggart as a ferocious being. This also means that my power of imagination has room for improvement.

However, I was able to imagine the sound when the rock fell. I thought that the rock must have whistled the way falling bombs did in films. Although I knew that a round rock wouldn't have whistled that way, I felt it had to sound like that to do justice to Snow Feather and to prevent my being labeled a mediocre writer.

I could also add a scream, but you must know that Snow Feather wouldn't have screamed. Her forehead could be studded with pearl-like sweat, amberlike blood could flow from the corners of her mouth, chips of her bones could splatter like shrapnel, but she would not scream. At the most, she might have uttered a *hm*. But I'm not inclined to describe that sound, you know.

When people finally opened their eyes, they found Braggart grimacing instead.

"Heck!" he said, "I don't want a bad name either! We'll crush her with carts tomorrow!"

That rock was still rolling in a corner.

Kuan San's Love Proposal

According to *Historical Mirror of Forgotten Events*, many events transpired at the Ancestral Hall that night, and several characters might have been the hero. The heroine was, of course, Snow Feather. As for who the hero was, Braggart, Kuan San, and Cripple Big have all been suggested.

Crazy Ramblings of Ajia, however, favored Kuan San as its choice.

"Kuan San slipped into the Ancestral Hall stealthily," said Ajia. Three of the four on night duty were already asleep. One version claimed

that Kuan San made sure they were soused. I doubted this since I wondered how there could have been any liquor during that time. But Ajia
said, "Yes, there was! It was the terrible kind that made the head feel
like a rat burrowed a hole in it when he got drunk!"

Snow Feather was locked up in the Ancestral Hall. You might
have seen that type of building before, the kind with four beams, eight
pillars, and curved eaves. This was where Diamond Clan worshipped
their ancestors and housed the ancestral tablets on an altar. Filial sons
and grandsons used to kowtow to them on the first and fifteenth of each
lunar month in order to please the ancestors. The folks of Liangzhou
believed the deceased became gods with powers living humans did not
possess. They could enable their descendants to become rich officials.
But no one knew why Diamond Clan never produced any high officials.
It was said the reason lay in the fact that the descendants had failed
to place the graves of the ancestors at propitious locations that could
attract the essence of heaven and earth. So, although the ancestors had
become gods, their powers were limited since they were but minor ghosts
and spirits, unable to be of assistance even if they'd wanted to. But it
was even more likely that the ancestors were, in fact, displeased with
the descendants. Consequently, delighting the ancestors was even more
important than worshipping the Buddhas, which elevated the position
of the Ancestral Hall to an incomparably high level.

The Ancestral Hall and Diamond Monastery were the most solid
buildings in the village. When the big earthquake of 1927 struck, all the
houses in Liangzhou collapsed. But only the walls of the Hall crumbled;
its four beams and eight pillars remained intact. Because Snow Feather
was tried in the Ancestral Hall, it became a sacred place years later. A
conspicuous tablet inscribed with "The Dakini Goddess Snow Feather"
etc. would be placed on the altar, and many practitioners would arrive to
pay homage to her. It was said that those with sincere hearts could feel
the blessings of the Dakini Goddess. I've slept there several nights. At
night, I only heard some sobbing as if the mice were holding a funeral.

Ajia expended a lot of saliva in narrating the story of Snow Feather
in the Ancestral Hall. You must know that the less cultured a person is,
the more he feels a need to show off. I know that this statement will
offend Ajia. But much as I love Ajia, I am even more partial to truth.
I can't very well deny my conscience just to please a local deity.

So it was in an atmosphere created by the intentional exaggerations
of Ajia that Kuan San entered the story. We could hear his heartbeat: the

kind imbued with desire. Who would have thought this kind of heartbeat existed during that particular time? "The other three on night duty were either asleep or drunk," said Ajia. It didn't matter which, so long as you knew Kuan San had an arena for performing. I prefer to think that the others were drunk because only through their total inebriation could the following episode be possible. Kuan San slipped in quietly. He shot a stealthy glance at his companions who were either drunk or asleep and woke Snow Feather up by shaking her lightly.

He wanted to break the wires that pierced her wrists but feared that she would knead him into noodles without the shackles. He took out a black lump—it was opium. You know, everyone at Diamond Clan had some of this illegal stuff. Judging from this alone, Ajia decided Kuan San came prepared. Kuan San scorched the black stuff using fire tongs, which he burnt with a lamp until they glowed red. He then put one end of a rolled a piece of paper into her mouth. A wisp of white smoke wafted into her mouth. It swam gleefully toward her wrist and swallowed the pain. This was a realistic detail. We could see Snow Feather heave a sigh of relief and then gaze at the night sky with squinted eyes. She seemed to be looking at everything and not looking at anything at all. This was her most beautiful expression, the one that would be captured in the Tankas about her in the future. People would have different inter-pretations concerning this expression. For example, you could say she had merged her various manifestations into illusions; or that her eyes were filled with compassion for those without karmic affinity with her, as well as for those who believed in her; or that she was showing love for all sentient beings, etc. But what was certain was the pain must have been incredibly excruciating—otherwise she wouldn't have inhaled the smoke.

Kuan San waited for her to look more relaxed before he said what he came to say. He said, so long as she agreed, he would escape with her to wherever she wished. They could fly up to the nine heavens to embrace the moon, or dive down the five oceans to catch turtles. He was willing to be her slave the rest of his life. She could ride on him, beat him, scold him—even call him a son of a bitch. He would treat her so well that if he should kiss her, he would worry that she might melt away; if he were to hold her, he would worry that she might fall. She could sit on his head and shit and pee on him. Ajia's saliva sprayed and spattered as he repeated Kuan San's words. He became so worked up he pretended I was Snow Feather. During the climax of the declarations, his face turned so red he resembled an old cock who'd consumed three catties of sorghum liquor. "Enough! Enough!" I said, "I got your point—so Kuan San was proposing to Snow Feather. So long as she was willing, they could run away from Diamond Clan to the ends of the earth or the most remote recess of a mountain, where no one would break those incomparably sexy legs of hers! Correct?"

"You are so smart!" said Ajia.

"What did Snow Feather say?"

"She didn't say anything."

"Did she spit at him?"

"No."

She just sat there fixedly, as if she were already in a Tanka.

Chapter 16

The Dharma-Protecting Divine Bullock

It was an unexpected gust of wind
  A bit of sand
  A glimmer of hope
The bellow of desolate west wind
Was the anticipation I nurtured for a thousand years;
But the sandstorm blew away the laurel in your eyes
  Hence the lotus flower fell into decay.
There was the shrill of a cicada on the lotus leaf
  Woefully, the cold cicada
Sang a song on a lofty and rare love.

The Bullock's Thoughts

Tale of the Goddess explains the origin of the Dharma-Protecting Divine Bullock depicted in her Tanka.

On that day, everyone who was still alive at Diamond Clan went to the courtyard next to the Ancestral Hall where the farm carts were stationed. Ajia said, "It was doubtful Snow Feather would escape her destiny this time. I thought the clan members should all kneel down and beg Braggart to forgive her. But no one said anything. They all knew that indulging her in this case would mean that even the rats in the granaries would've become food for the people, let alone the grains."

The courtyard housed the granaries, the corral was for the draught animals, and the haystacks were there. Back then, most of the assets of the clan were housed here.

Braggart selected an oxcart—the kind with wooden wheels as tall as a man. The wooden wheels were formed by nailing together bent pieces of hardwood. The wheels were attached to a wooden shaft, with metal lynchpin strips that looked like strips of gold. On a blood-colored evening, Grandpa found a pile of such golden strips. At first he thought it was a large ball of fire. But upon closer examination, he was greeted by the gleam of a pile of golden strips. He gave them to the elderly manager of the courtyard to use on the ox carts. But the manager sold them instead and used the proceeds to buy several acres of land and build the present huge courtyard. Later, the manager was so frightened by rumors about these strips that he drowned himself in a pit of fermenting flax. Grandpa wept until his neck muscle was torn, blaming himself for the manager's death since the latter would not have jumped into the flax pit if it weren't for the golden strips he'd received. After that, Grandpa took to caring for the draught animals at the courtyard.

Grandpa always spoke about the lively but bloody scene that had transpired in the courtyard. He was convinced that the only difference between animals and humans was their different outer layer. The basis for this conclusion was the tale of the dharma-protecting divine bullock.

The most robust bullock was harnessed onto a cart under Braggart's bidding. Although people were frail back then, the beasts were amply fattened by the grass in the wilderness. At first the bullock thought they had intended for him to haul manure. The bullock was always hauling manure. Although the cart was very tall, the amount of manure it could hold was quite limited: some twenty scoops with a large spade filled it. It was as easy for the bullock to pull such a cart as it was for a donkey dropping to withstand a wheat stalk. It saw no problem at all. It took a look at the cart filled with cow manure and laughed. It thought, *Why are there so many people here just to watch me haul manure?* It concluded that people were dense and then allowed them to harness the cart to him obediently. He felt the wooden yoke on his neck and a cord fastened around his belly. Then he felt a flash of pain in his nostrils signaling a command.

The bullock began to move obediently. The cart groaned. The courtyard was filled with holes created by hoofs after rainfall, which bit at the wheels and caused them to jolt. This was a fair world: while the wheels crushed the holes, the holes were also biting the wheels.

The bullock soon realized that for some reason his excruciatingly painful nose ring was pulling him toward a woman. The intelligent bullock immediately remembered a certain morning when the red sun sparked with golden rays. The bullock liked the sun, as there would be no windstorms when it was sunny. During windstorms, sand would pierce its eyes and nose. Having sand in its nose was not a problem—one big sneeze and they were gone. Of course, it would have to sneeze when humans weren't around, lest its mucus spray upon them—then they'd retaliate with the whip. What bothered the bullock was the sand in its eyes. Unlike the camel, it did not have long eyelashes to protect it.

It was on that sunny day that the bullock received a full beating. The driver lashed at its back until it turned into a bloody mat using a whip fashioned from the hide of its grandfather. The reason was quite simple. A boy had climbed onto the manure cart. The bullock didn't like the boy since he kept poking its anus with thorn grass,[1] causing extreme discomfort. It wasn't so bad when the grass hit dead center; the worst that might happen then would be for the grass to gather some inopportune manure. But when it missed the mark, then the grass would pierce the bullock's flesh like a leech bite and create a most distressing irritation. So when that brat climbed onto the cart, the bullock began purposely treading on bumpy ground. It had intended to just scare the kid, not expecting he would fall right off the cart! What was worse was the fact that the bullock was unable to halt the moving wheels that very instant. Of course you know what followed—the kid's legs got crushed!

The bullock just realized that its nose ring was now being tugged so it would do exactly that.

The bullock couldn't understand it, as what happened to the kid had always been the one regret of its life! After the boy screamed his way to the city and later returned, he was never again called by his own name. All the kids screamed, "Cripple Big! Cripple Big!" whenever they saw him. The kids called him "big" because he was of an older generation. "Big" referred to one's "uncle." Jie Big and Cripple Big both belonged to the same generation of most of the kids' uncles. Back then, Cripple Big became the greatest source of entertainment for the kids of Diamond Clan. When they had nothing better to do, the kids would proceed to the home of Cripple Big. They would first quietly ascertain that he was at home and then yell in unison, "Cripple Big! Cripple Big!" Cripple Big would then wobble out to chase after them. And the kids would

---

1. The botanical name for *jiji* is *achnatherum splendens*.

dash away like the wind while yelling "Cripple Big!" There was no way that Cripple Big could have caught up with them, but the crazy clods of earth in his hands would dart off like birds and explode behind them. Of all my childhood memories, the one I regret most was teasing Cripple Big. Many years later, I saw the aged Cripple Big at a river bend and expressed my apologies to him then. I didn't think he would remember me; but, unexpectedly, he said, "Aren't you Chen Danian's son?" Of course he didn't know that my other name was Xue Mo.

The bullock realized that people wanted to make the woman into another Cripple Big!

Anger consumed it. The bullock tossed its head, and the person holding the reins flew off like a kite. It had a mind to gore the man with its horns but knew that would've been too much for the man. If it should kill the man, the villagers would undoubtedly clamor for the bullock's life. It knew the villagers considered the animals that gored humans to death as ill-omened. Having turned into a drove of lice crazy from starvation, they longed for an excuse to kill the bullock in order to drink its blood, eat its meat, and tan its hide to make whips to lash its own kind.

I just don't want the woman to become crippled! thought the bullock.

Shadows of a whip flashed. The bullock's back was flogged. An explosion of pain. The humans were teaching him a lesson. The rein was tightened ruthlessly a few times. The bullock felt as if its nostrils were being ripped apart. This was equivalent to their saying, "Are you going to be obedient? If not, I'll flog again!"

Fearing its nostrils would be ripped apart, the bullock didn't shake its head again. Almost subdued, it proceeded forward with the cart. The potholes chomped at the wheels. Manure dust crept out of the cracks under the cart and was scattered by gusts of wind. Everyone was looking at the bullock with bated breath. *The woman must have done something wrong.* The bullock had rarely seen the woman before. She was prettier than the village women who were either as fat as the thunder god's hammer or as thin as a monkey. This woman, however, was neither fat nor thin. Blind Immortal Jia would have described her thus: "With white teeth and red lips, her face was as beautiful as a plum blossom. Her gait was as beautiful as a willow branch swaying in the spring breeze." Blind Immortal Jia used to sing Xianxiao stories at the Ancestral Hall. The bullock enjoyed listening to them too. If it weren't for the fact that someone was grabbing the woman's hand, she would certainly walk like a swaying willow branch. They were always holding struggle sessions against people at the Ancestral Hall. But then the bullock thought, *Would an Ancestral Hall that didn't hold struggle sessions be considered an Ancestral Hall?* In any case, this was the first time an oxcart would be drawn over a woman's legs as the result of a struggle session. The bullock shook its head emphatically and shot a glance at the villagers. It wondered if the person who gave the command was drunk and wished to find from the expressions of the onlookers a reason for not obeying. But anticipation was written over all their faces. They were all obviously waiting for the result of its submission.

The world has gone berserk! thought the bullock.

The bullock lugged the cart as commanded by the pull on the nose ring. The cart rumbled and bumped along. The woman gradually looked bigger. To the bullock, humans always looked large: unlike dogs, which regarded humans as small. The folks in the village always compared people who looked down on others to dogs. Cattle were obedient animals that even looked up to children and obeyed them when they pulled the reins. The woman was staring at the bullock, but it couldn't tell how she felt from the way she looked. The bullock, however, knew she was afraid. *There's nothing one can do—anyone would be scared about becoming a Cripple Big. But if her legs are broken by the oxcart, then the kids won't be calling her Cripple Big, they'll call her Cripple Auntie instead. It'll be something terrible in any case.* The bullock could see her limp like Cripple Big. *There was something funny about a woman who "walked as beautifully as a willow branch swaying in the spring breeze" turn into Cripple Big.* The bullock could not bear to do it now. It was suddenly reminded of what Blind Immortal Jia said when he sang one of the Xianxiao stories. According to him, cattle were reincarnations of Bodhisattvas. They served the multitude when they were alive, and they offered all their parts after they die. Blind Immortal Jia urged people not to eat beef. The shaman priests in the village also refused to eat beef, believing they wouldn't be able to ascend to Heaven if they ate it. But they always used cattle hide to make drums and beat on them when they performed rituals to subjugate demons. So the villagers concluded, the shaman priests vented their frustrations over not eating beef by beating on the drums. Many folks in the village still ate beef, nevertheless. But the bullock could tell from her smell that the woman didn't eat beef. It didn't know that the woman did indeed observe the injunction against eating beef, and that to her, cattle were truly Bodhisattvas. Of course she wouldn't consume the flesh of Bodhisattvas. The bullock realized all this in a flash. I don't know how it understood all this. Maybe this was karmic wisdom accumulated from a previous existence. *The woman and I love each other*, thought the bullock. *I can't possibly make her into a Cripple Auntie!* The bullock shook its head emphatically.

The oxcart continued toward the woman as before, calmly and unswervingly. It saw its companions poke their heads out of the sheds. Unexpectedly, a calf mooed loudly, as if it also knew what was going on. Its voice protracted and lingered. Although later we found out that this happened by pure coincidence: the calf was simply hungry for milk. As the calf explained later, "How did I know where the oxcart was heading?" But often this is how things evolve in this world. Sometimes events of absolutely no significance became significant. The bullock was moved by the calf's mooing and felt that even a calf had a sense of righteousness. So, it became even more confident in its resolve.

The cart approached ever closer to the extended legs. Its wheels sounded heavy and heartless. The bullock saw the woman's pale face and smiled sneakily. Only the corners of its mouth drew upward almost imperceptibly, as if it was regurgitating. It shot a glance at the villagers, hoping to see an inkling of sympathy on their faces. But he only saw woodenness and anticipation. A few women closed their eyes, unable to bear watching the scene. For the bullock, this was the most moving sight.

The bullock had just stepped over the woman. This meant that the wheels were about to crush the legs, which would break with either a crisp or a dull sound. Either way, red and white stuff would splatter everywhere. The villagers loved to imbibe the white stuff. The bullock saw Braggart drink its dad's bone marrow. The butcher had originally intended to consume it. He hammered at it repeatedly and made more than ten white indentations before Dad's incomparably hard leg bone broke. Soft, white stuff poked its head out of the crack. The butcher reached out with his hairy mouth and was just about to suck at it, when Braggart nabbed the bone and said, "You're as strong as a bull yourself, what do you need this for?" So saying, Braggart slurped down a few mouthfuls. Old Dad's bones were rich with marrow since it was the strongest bullock in the village. But even the mightiest would eventually age. The night Old Dad left, he shed tears knowing it was his turn to go. The afternoon before, clan's men were pointing at him because of his age. Old Dad wished he weren't old and went to an oxcart on his own. But Old Dad couldn't even pull an empty cart by then. So the clan's men pointed at him and said, "It's ready for the cooking pot!" The bullock remembered well all the details of the day Old Dad was slaughtered. It was neither cloudy nor sunny. The butcher hauled Old Dad by the nose ring into the courtyard, its eyes brimming with tears. Old Dad looked at its son, and then at the villagers. Suddenly, it knelt down with tearful eyes. The bullock mooed angrily, knowing well Old Dad's hard work and merits: the numerous superior breeds it seeded and the countless hours of work it did. But Old Dad still ended up being slaughtered. Bullock could not bear to even remember the scene, but the villagers were completely indifferent. A woman said, "Look! This bull can weep!" A man responded, "It's become a spirit, a spirit! Better slaughter it right away!" After that, the white marrow ended up in Braggart's mouth. The soft, white matter was always squirming before the bullock's eyes.

Would the woman's marrow be like Dad's? wondered the bullock.

The calf mooed loudly, as if it needed to pee but had a urinary tract that was welded shut. Bullock wondered if it had a karmic affiliation with the woman from a previous existence: it smiled slightly, looking as if it was regurgitating. Knowing the wheels were about to crush the woman's legs, it inhaled forcefully, mustered its might, and yanked ferociously to one side. The wheels creaked. The speed was well controlled; any faster the cart shaft might have cracked. The nose felt a sharp pain; the reins had already slipped out of the driver's hand. There was an explosion of cussing.

The cussing made the bullock change its mind. It had intended to just change the direction of the oxcart; but the cussing reminded it that they will make him do it again and that it wouldn't be so easy the next time around. The human would pull at its nose ring and whip not only its back but also its face. Whipping the face was known as performing the head-wrapping whip. It was used specifically on those animals that were recalcitrant. The bite of swishing whips on the hairless parts of the face was more painful than being hacked by a knife. The bullock had experienced the head-wrapping whip many times after it refused to work for the heartless humankind, after observing Dad in the stewing pot. The most terrifying lash was that made of musk deer hide, which was the softest, the most refined, and the loudest. Although the sound was crisp, it could rip through the toughest cattle hide. A black-and-white cow was blinded by the head-wrapping whip. The bullock knew that this swerving aside would invariably result in a full lashing; and then the nose ring would pull it back to the woman until the cart crushed the soft, white marrow from her legs.

Fuck—being headless only means having a scar the size of a bowl. I'm revolting! thought the bullock.

In fact, the "mutiny" by the bullock was based on staging a "shock."

Mooing loudly, it began to dance crazily while pulling the manure-filled oxcart. Its eyes glared like bronze bells, its nostrils flared, and its calf muscles bulged with energy. The oxcart jolted up and down. The scattering manure caught by the wind covered the clan's men. The bullock saw women dashing toward the corners of the courtyard with gaping mouths. It found their flustered looks on their faces encouraging. A few men were charging at it, needless to say, with whips. Without the whips they would have been just like the women. The manure whizzed as it fell to the ground. Bullock knew the tomblike, bulging pile had become as flat as the Gobi Desert. The narrow doors around the courtyard receded from the cart. The wind howled and women shrieked. A tightness on the back could be felt—must have been the kisses of a whip. It wasn't painful though; it must not have been the work of a professional. The drivers were the lashing experts. One strike unleashed by one of them on a weight scale would dislodge five hundred catties[2] of weights. The bullock had tasted it once and was on the ground after one lash. There must have been a magical force in the whip. . . . A few more lashes—two of them were quite painful, must have been the work of a driver. Robust, but not that bad, nevertheless. Lashes on the back were not a problem; as the back was thick and furry, studded with callouses from the yoke. It was more worried about the head-wrapping lashes. As if the thought had reminded the humans, a flurry of head-wrapping lashes enveloped its face, followed by an explosion of pain. It now regretted having thought of the head-wrapping lashes. But they weren't so bad in any case. They didn't hurt as much as they used to. Must have been the starvation. Many humans would steal into the shed and dig through the hay hoping to find some fodder but were as successful as trying to use a cold fart to light dead ashes. It had been a while since the bullock had tasted fodder itself. *Starvation was good,* thought the bullock, *it made the head-wrapping lashes less painful.*

People waved their arms in front the bullock to get it to stop. *Heck with them!* It charged at those trying to block it and wanted desperately

---

2. One catty is equivalent to five hundred grams, a little over a pound.

to gore the fucking lot. After this display of "shock," its bullish temper was aroused, and it was no longer afraid of goring humans. It had only gored a human once before. Years earlier, a boy made a sport of poking the bullock's penis with a whip while it was drinking water. *What an unbearable humiliation!* That kid was the son of the driver who always whipped the bullock's dad. *What an immense disgrace!* Blood surged and drowned its sense of reason. It charged at the kid and swung its horns, intending to scare him. Who would have expected the kid to collapse from the shock and fall right onto a horn that took off one of his ears! The bullock panicked and ran, but the driver caught up with it nevertheless and struck it down at the courtyard gate with one lash. It would have lost its life if its keeper hadn't intervened. The impression made by that lash was so profound that it never dared to gore humans again. During this instant, however, it wanted to display all the powers of its horns, but it was shackled by the shaft of the cart.

The cart felt ever lighter, as manure poured out each time it turned a sharp corner. The courtyard was hazy from the cart's flying dust and earth. Everyone took cover in the corners of courtyard, except for the few swishing whips that were exhibiting their might. The woman, however, stayed put. The bullock noticed two men fairly close to the woman holding the ends of an almost invisible wire that pierced through her wrists. This was how the ancestors fixed flying thieves. The bullock concluded that the wire was the equivalent of its own nose ring. *The humans were always so smart; they always thought of ways to inflict injury on others.*

The oxcart had already turned three and half circles around the courtyard. The bullock did not turn round and round on the spot lest its cumbersome body might touch the wire shackling the woman's wrists. A knock from it would invariably tear her wrists, just as a vigorous tug on its nose ring would rip apart its nose. The pain would have been insufferable. The bullock didn't want her to suffer such agony.

Thereupon the bullock looked around. Although the head-wrapping lashes rained down even more, it was still able to discover a way out through them. The humans had negligently left the courtyard gate wide open. A few of them stood there to enjoy the spectacle. "*Best to escape,*" thought the bullock, "*Of the thirty-six tactics, escape is the best.*"[3] Fearing that the thought would remind those with the whips, the bullock shot

---

3. This refers to *Sun Zi's* (544–496 BCE) famous *Art of War*.

a stealthy glance at them. Their faces contorted with anger and hatred. *I didn't do anything to you*, thought the bullock, *I just didn't want to make a woman into a Cripple Auntie, that's all! Do I deserve so much hatred? Humans are the most irrational of all beings*, it concluded. But it didn't feel like bothering itself about that. Should they figure out its intention, they could close the gate in a matter of seconds and block its mode of escape. Hence, the fourth time it approached the gate, it switched its routine and charged outside. The shaft of the cart creaked. Although it didn't break, it must have suffered an internal injury.

People at the gate scattered. The bullock felt one of the axles gouge the door frame. The cart jolted. The door frame was very clever, however. Fearing the entire frame would collapse—in which case it would no longer be a door frame and would have lost the entire battle—it gave up a large chunk of its wood the way a gecko would discard its tail to survive. The bullock immediately felt the pulling easier.

As very little manure was left in the oxcart, its speed was faster. Originally, the bullock had schemed staging a fake "shock," but after all that happened, the "shock" seemed real now. The mud on the road splashed. There were few people but a lot of wind. Much of the wind was created by the bullock itself. That it knew. The bullock felt so poetic that if it could write poems, it would have written something like "I wish I could travel, riding on the wind."[4] But being a bull, it lacked the ability to express its emotions poetically. That's why it was ridiculed in expressions such as "playing music to an ox" to refer to presenting something refined to an unappreciative receiver.

The wind howled. The mud splattered like clouds to the edge of the sky. The bullock looked like it was riding on a cloud. It thought of the Demon King Bullock,[5] the divinity worshipped by all cattle for more than a thousand years. All the cattle wanted to be a Demon King Bullock, just as all monkeys wanted to be a Monkey King,[6] and all humans wanted to be a Genghis Khan. Although they were but dreams, humans could become great through realizing their dreams. So did cattle. What

---

4. This is a line from the lyric, "Shuidiao getou" by Su Shi (1037–1107), a renowned Song dynasty statesman, poet, calligrapher, and painter.

5. Niu Mowang, a powerful demon in the popular traditional novel, *Journey to the West*, originally published in 1592.

6. The Monkey King, Sun Wukong, is a protagonist of the above novel.

distinguished the bullock from other cattle was the result of his thoughts and actions on this very day.

Shouts tailgated it. The bullock could see the dots formed by those chasing after it without turning its head. *I'm not scared of them. Oxen are raised by eating grass, not by human's shouts. Let them shout—I, the bullock, am not scared!* Judging from the sound of the oxcart, it had been empty for quite a while now. The planks lining the cart clanked with a hollow resonance. Some of the nails must have gone loose—the planks were performing clapper talk.[7] Back then, shows used to be performed in the courtyard, so the bullock had heard clapper talk and loved the rhythms of the clappers. The cart was falling apart. Without the damned cart, it would have flown into the clouds already. Sure enough, a plank fell and clanked on the ground. The bullock felt like it was in Heaven.

The bullock dashed toward the wilderness. *Best to go to the wilderness to make the cart fall apart.* People were always discarding coal ashes onto the roads in the village to fill the potholes. But deep treads made by wheels on rainy days filled the path outside the village. Once baked hard by the sun, each of these treads was anathema for the planks of the cart. The even louder clanking they created sent a pleasurable vibration to the bullock. The bumpy mountain path also brought pain to its hoofs, as if the potholes intended to tear them apart. Maybe the potholes knew the hoofs were delicious and so gnawed at them. Although extremely uncomfortable, it didn't really bother the bullock which was born to travel. Any path would do. If there was no path, then a road could be created from traveling on it. The bullock had no fear. Of course it knew that fear would have been useless and thought, *Why be scared if it's useless to fear?*

That was the happiest journey the bullock ever undertook. The excitement reached a climax. The bullock was no longer satisfied with galloping on the pathway, even though more planks fell. It wanted to shake free of the yoke that required even more jolting. Suddenly, it swerved abruptly into a field next to the pathway. The bullock didn't realize that its speed would create a tremendous torque—it didn't even know the word "torque." By the time it realized something was amiss, the heavy cart was hurtling downward and the bullock was tumbling down into the gully along with it.

---

7. *Kuaiban* is a form of narrative singing accompanied by clappers.

The Transcendent Broken Leg

According to *Crazy Ramblings of Ajia*, the bullock returned to the courtyard a couple of hours later. No one lashed it again. It shivered; its muscles quivered. It had intended to break the shaft but broke its own leg instead. This was truly a case of someone who had planted flowers intentionally but got none, yet planted willow branches unintentionally and created a grove of willow trees! The soft, white marrow oozed down to the ground from the broken leg. Some men lapped at it like dogs.

Although the bullock might have broken its leg unintentionally, this act became part of a myth after Snow Feather became a goddess. People claimed that the bullock was divine and that it would rather break its own leg rather than those of the Dakini goddess. That's why there's an ox in the left bottom corner of her Tanka and it received people's offerings as a protective deity. Of course the villagers couldn't forget the hair-raising scene. Something else they couldn't forget was that Braggart gave permission to a butcher to stab the bullock's neck when it was obvious that the animal would not survive. Its blood and beef were the most delicious foods in people's memory. Objectively speaking, its beef was one of the foods that saved the villagers of Diamond Clan then, just like the "mutton" stir-fried by Monk Wu and the grain stolen by Snow Feather.

Historical Mirror of Forgotten Events also includes another detail: when the bullock returned to the courtyard, all the draught animals gave heartrending howls. It was as if they were pleading and screaming. It was not clear if their bawling was directed at the bullock or at Snow Feather. The truth of the matter was that no one was able to hitch another ox onto a cart that day. The clan's men used whips and rods on them to no avail and finally had to give up. The bellowing of the cattle and donkeys came to be known as one of the mystical events that had occurred in Diamond Clan. It was not until Snow Feather was deified that folks of the older generation realized the draught animals knew her true origin.

Crazy Ramblings of Ajia claims that the bullock broke its leg intentionally. "Your narrative above was not correct," said Ajia. According to him, the bullock's leg did not break when it tumbled down the gully. The bullock hauled the cart for a while after they had rolled down the gully. The bullock couldn't have traveled if it had a broken leg. Ajia's version is corroborated by *Historical Mirror of Forgotten Events*, which notes that the bullock ran some distance with the cart after they had tumbled down the gully. Later, Cripple Big was supposed to have found half of the bullock's leg in a crack in the ground. This certainly would have made the bullock into an accomplished hero. *Tale of the Goddess* affirms Ajia's version. After Snow Feather became a goddess, Diamond Clan built a temple for her. The statue of a protective divine bullock was placed in one of the side buildings. The difference between it and normal oxen was that one of its front legs was chopped off in the middle. The missing half of the leg was held in place by the hoof of the other front leg and used as a weapon, the way Indra used a vajra scepter.

When all the cattle and donkeys bawled that afternoon, all the villagers thought Snow Feather would now get to keep her legs.

But in her Tankas, Snow Feather's left leg was always slightly shorter than her right. One has to scrutinize it to notice since most Dakini goddesses in Tankas bend one of their legs, which reflects one of the many symbolisms portrayed. The straight leg symbolizes Fundamental Concentration and not entering life and death; the bent leg symbolizes not entering Nirvana in order to bring beneficence to the multitude. In some, the heel of the bent leg of the Dakini goddess touches the crotch to symbolize double-cultivation.[8] Snow Feather's Tanka is the same. The most obvious difference between her legs and those of the others is the addition of a bracelet on each to symbolize this particular tribulation she endured.

So the bullock's broken leg brought transcendence to itself but did not prevent Snow Feather from having to endure the calamity.

This became the most forceful reason behind people's despising Braggart later.

Crazy Ramblings of Ajia narrated the details.

The Rumbling of the Oxcart

According to *Crazy Ramblings of Ajia*, Braggart lugged an oxcart amidst the angry bawling of the draught animals. He picked an oxcart because the edge of oxcart wheels was braced with an iron frame. Besides, the narrow wheels made leg crushing easier. A horse cart had rubber wheels and was so much wider that when filled with manure it would weigh several tons. The legs would be chopped clean off if one of them were

---

8. Religious cultivation through a special form of sexual activity.

used. Braggart apparently did not intend for that to happen. Ajia felt that he was not entirely without conscience. "Although Braggart was mean," said Ajia, "he did do it out of fairness." This conclusion was based on the fact that Braggart had his third son's hand chopped off after the latter stole someone's fruit. When he became old years later and was beaten until black and blue in the face by his youngest son, the son without a hand was the one who supported him. The handless son acquired old books from the recycling depot and sold them on the ground in the city of Liangzhou. It was from his rundown secondhand book stand that I obtained numerous renowned Chinese and foreign rare books.

Braggart interpreted the bawling of the animals as a form of protest and was infuriated. He regarded himself as the emperor at Diamond Clan. He used the head-wrapping lash on the beasts to discipline them. His expertise was only second to that of the drivers. Regarding all those being whipped as mortal enemies, his whip lashed resoundingly, its shadows flashing in midair like lightning. The fur on the heads of the beasts flung off like flying leeches. In effect a seal, the whip soon sealed the mouths of all the beasts. But although he was able to seal them for the time being, he could not seal them permanently. That very night, all the animals bawled again. The horses' neighing, the cattle's mooing, and the donkeys' braying wove into innumerable long worms that floated out of the cart courtyard and surged toward Liangzhou like a river in a valley. They echoed on Qilian Mountain, sometimes like a Long Snake Military Formation, sometimes like an Eight Gated Golden Lock Military Formation; sometimes intense, sometimes mournful, sometimes resounding, sometimes melancholy; sometimes reaching straight up to the ninth heaven to seize the moon; and sometimes right down the five oceans to capture a turtle. It lasted for three nights, scaring the crap out of so many folks that impressions of maps were created on their mud brick beds.

"I thought you'd never shut up!" Braggart said through clenched teeth when the beasts finally let up.

He turned red from anger. "If the beasts hadn't bawled," said Ajia, "Braggart might not have been so angry. If he weren't so angry, he might have let Snow Feather go. You see, his fury was caused by anger!" "What you're saying is irresponsible," I said, "you're basically blaming the animals for Snow Feather's broken legs." Ajia knew he was wrong; but being as hard and stubborn as the beak of a well-cooked duck, he said, "I was creating fiction. Are you novelists the only ones allowed to create fiction?" I said, "But this type of fiction is vicious. It's equivalent to framing the animals!" He had to smile guiltily after hearing out my righteous indignation.

Braggart threw down the whip. He gave a shout, and the militiamen immediately took over the oxcart. There must have been at least ten other oxcarts in the village, aside from the one the bullock destroyed. Flames rise high when many people gather twigs. Collective strength is immense. Two men hauled the cart shafts. They heaved because the shaft was made of a heavy, hard wood. Their faces were pale. If their stomachs were full, their faces would have flushed scarlet red as though painted with pig's blood. But as you know, few people could flush red back then. "Right, never mind the color of their faces, just continue with the story!" The oxcart clanged as it was lugged from the edge of the courtyard to the center. Everyone could tell what Braggart intended to do. Yes, he wanted people to pull the cart to break Snow Feather's legs. He knew well that people would do what the animals wouldn't do. He was a smart one, no wonder he was the clan head!

Braggart designated two militiamen to pull the shafts and two to push the cart. I thought he was going to fill the cart with manure again. But he waved his hand and hollered, "Get on the cart!" He was beckoning the women, who approached obediently. Why didn't he summon the men? Well, this was where his cleverness was obvious! He must have realized that while the men might have pitied the lovely woman, the women were probably filled with hatred and jealousy for Snow Feather. You know, the women were like the men of Liangzhou: they couldn't stand anyone better than themselves! They were jealous of anyone prettier, anyone better dressed, or anyone who lived better lives. Just think, everyone had seven cavities in the face and two in the lower body, but why should you be prettier? Why should you be more famous? Why should you be the one to give and not they? Why should you be able to enter the granary as if walking on level ground, when they're afraid just from looking at it? So, women began to climb into the oxcart under Braggart's direction. At first seven of them got on. But then Braggart said, "No! No! Get off!" He then had the men carry ten stone rollers into the cart. It was the kind used for rolling wheat. After the autumn harvest each year, the clan's men would spread the wheat on the threshing ground—like what your mom did when she made crepes. The young men would hitch the rollers onto draught animals and roll over the wheat to thresh its grains from the stalks. Yes, those were the rollers. How heavy you ask? Not heavy, really. Each one was probably around two hundred catties. Braggart then had seven or eight women get on and sit on the rollers. Why? Did you forget? Wasn't your novel *Hunting Ground* about having widows clean the reservoir during the rain-praying ritual? Why? Right—widows were inauspicious, even more so the pregnant ones; those menstruating were as lethal as atomic bombs! Braggart suspected that Snow Feather knew black magic. Like a dog that gnawned at a train due to its lack of scientific knowledge, Braggart considered Snow Feather's martial arts skills as black magic. *Even if you were to perform black magic*, he thought, "*you wouldn't be able to block ten rollers and seven atomic bomb–like widows!* He looked around and appeared as full of might as when a bullock looked at the cows.

And then, he hollered, "Start!"

The resounding "start" was so awe inspiring and vicious that he sounded even more Japanese than the Japanese themselves. Too bad no one was able to transmit the scene online. Braggart would have been shoved to the ground and stomped on right away.

The oxcart "started," and its iron wheels rolled. The widows screamed. One of them said that the rollers were going to roll off. Sure enough, the rollers were grumbling angrily and shouting, "Get off, widows! Get off!" The villagers knew that the rollers were manifestations of the highly venerable White Tiger Constellation. Even at the threshing ground, women weren't allowed to sit on the rollers. Any roller sat on by a woman will keep on losing its umbilical cord. What's the roller's umbilical cord you ask? Well, it's the wooden rod on the roller. The other consequence was only known by the woman who sat on the roller. Henceforth, a sticky substance would flow from her private parts. Should you lack peace at night, then just set a roller straight up in a corner of your courtyard, and your household will enjoy peace and health thereafter. Should you have angered Lord Heaven unwittingly and fear its punishment, what should you do? Well, don't be scared. The worst punishment Lord Heaven can perform is to have Heaven fall on you. Don't be scared: just erect a roller in your courtyard, and the roller will become a Heaven-propping pillar. Sure, Lord Heaven, go ahead and let your home collapse on me; but see if you can shove this roller first! Of course he can't because you can also place a soiled menstrual pad on the roller. One look at it, and Lord Heaven's head would swell into a basin! Let alone getting close, just a glance would cause him to disgorge his inner organs! Should the menstrual pad happen to assail his nostrils, then, *aiya*, he might as well forget about ever being a Lord Heaven again because he could pollute the heavenly palaces. The celestial beings would not permit someone polluted by the scent of a menstrual pad to serve as Lord Heaven. In the worst case scenario, he might even lose the ability to ascend Heaven ever again. But most likely, he would have to stay by your gate temporarily and serve as your door guardian for the night. If one couldn't find a menstrual pad—since the women of Diamond Clan did not use pads—then you could find a pair of soiled menstrual panties, the power of which was ten times that of pads. Along with the stone rollers, you could create havoc in Heaven the way Monkey did in *Journey to the West*. So, the White Tiger Constellation rollers—do you think they would let widows sit on them? They screamed furiously while they tried to overturn in protest.

Seeing the struggling of the rollers, Braggart hollered, "Get off for now!" And the widows got off. Braggart then had an animal feeder bring a coil of rope made of twisted grass.[9] Why did he order a rope made of grass? Well, such a rope was none other than a Black Dragon. You, the ferocious White Tiger, might claim yourself all powerful and can fight Lord Heaven by holding menstrual panties and induce fear even in Lord Heaven, but I, Braggart, have no fear of you! Aren't you nothing more than a White Tiger? Well, I will get a Black Dragon to fight you, the White Tiger! Blind Immortal Jia was always singing the Xianxiao tale of *The Eastern Expedition of Xue Rengui*. Everyone knew that the White Tiger Constellation Xue Rengui was the mortal enemy of the Black Dragon Constellation Gai Suwen. If you, the White Tiger roller, wants to rebel, then I will use the Black Dragon rope to bind you. Sure enough, the Black Dragon was so incredibly powerful that a few wraps around the rollers, and the White Tiger laid down the flag and stilled the drums in submission without a further fart.

Braggart tied the Black Dragon a few more times around the rollers and gave them a shake. *Even if you want to roll around now, you'd be flies trying to chase away farts*, he thought. He wanted to get the women back on but then thought, *Let's try this first. If this doesn't break her legs, we'll employ the widow atomic bombs!*

The cart proceeded, ensuing his pronouncement of "Start" again. The rollers hit against each other and made a low but crisp sound. It was a gritty noise. Everyone present felt that they were chomping

---

9. The Latin name for jijicao is *achnatherum splendens*.

sand. But the White Tiger Constellations had ceased their earlier angry protestations. They were just groaning as if they were comforting each other and saying, "Forget about fighting that Braggart now! A magistrate is not as powerful as a local manager. We'll let him show off for a few days and then smash his feet when we get the opportunity later!" Sure enough, when Braggart came to watch people threshing wheat the following year, the umbilical cord of a roller suddenly fell off, and the unshackled roller flew at him at an angle. If it were not for the hay, Braggart's feet would have turned into pancakes. He screamed for ten days without ever suspecting that this was premeditated by the rollers the year before.

The oxcart rumbled forward like an unstoppable approaching train. To ensure instant success, a militiaman even placed a brick under Snow Feather's legs. But a swing with one of her legs, and the brick slid three feet away.

I have no idea what Snow Feather's facial expression was at the time. I heard that her face was scarred by the punches from the night guards. Originally her hair was disheveled, but I heard she smoothed it with her fingers. I also heard that she wanted to wash off the blood stains on her face, but the request was refused by Braggart. He obviously wanted her to appear as a disheveled ghost before the villagers. Snow Feather had no choice but to moisten her headscarf with saliva and barely cleaned her face with it. Thus, her appearance was relatively appealing. Years later, the elderly folks of the village would still click their tongues and lament about how she was the most "human-like" woman they'd ever seen. The description, "human-like" was the most complimentary phrase used by the folks of Liangzhou.

It was said that Snow Feather remained calm when the wheels approached. Now, although people cannot choose their fate, they can choose their attitude. Indeed, the villagers grumbled about her calmness that day. It was a true peacefulness, a calmness that transcended material existence, a detachment that showed an unperturbedness by neither flattery nor insult.

As I remembered it, the resonance of the oxcart's wheels was slow and heavy. The stone rollers in the cart chomped at each other like rumbling thunder. I also heard the bated breaths of many of the folks. The repressed air currents in their chests created a tsunami-like bellow. Cells lived and died constantly, creating a thunderous noise with the magnitude of a tide. I could clearly see everyone die and reborn in a flash. Listen to the tremendous explosions of the cells in their bodies! Sometimes they resembled grenades and sometimes firecrackers in metal drums. Because the grenades were constantly suppressing the noise of the firecrackers, one heard mostly the explosions. In between the explosions, there was a sound resembling rubber balls that emerged from deep water. Those were the newborn cells. Their births weren't accompanied by the convulsive pains humans experienced during birth. They simply gurgled continuously out of the water. You may have seen springs with constantly emerging bubbles. Cells are like that. In a flash, many newborn cells would replace the dead ones; which means that the villagers, during that moment, were no longer their original selves. Once you realize this, you could eliminate many attachments.

Within that short while, most of Braggart's cells were displaced; the only item that was not displaced was his anger. The hatred in his heart prevented him from seeing the nature of things. He had no idea that years later he would lose his title as the clan head. He could not see that a dozen years later he would come down with illness and moan in bed for many years. His heart of anger would be of no help to him then. He would be even less likely to realize that one day he would wither like a wind-parched sheepskin and that one evening, his favorite youngest son would break his back! He was muddled by his present power. The rumbling oxcart stupefied him. He probably had no idea that, when he would be buried in a pit like a dead dog by his sons many years later, the fierce look he had on his face at that moment would be imprinted in the memories of many villagers. That fierce expression, along with his other evil actions, informed the evidence of his existence.

"I don't understand why those with some temporary power can't see that the power will eventually disappear?" said Ajia.

"Stop trying to sound sophisticated—continue with your story!" I said.

The wheels rolled as powerfully and unstoppably as death, sounding like rumbling thunder. The men pulling the cart panted. I was under the impression that they were sweating. The picture of sweat-laden men pushing the cart would have made for a more exciting scene, but they didn't sweat. According to scientific calculation, they'd have to exert themselves for about half an hour before they would sweat. The distance in the courtyard only required a few minutes. But it was a prolonged and unforgettable journey. The cart's wheels were closing in on Snow Feather, who still exhibited no sign of terror. I thought she should have begged for forgiveness, but then she would no longer be Snow Feather. There was no way I could imagine her cherry lips yell for help.

I only saw the rim of the wheels skim the ground. At a certain moment, I was even unable to hear anything. I had no thoughts, neither good nor evil, and I saw my original self. I was stunned. My mind resembled a cloudless sky, or even more so it resembled a sea without any ripples. I finally realized why Dakini Goddess Maji La told her disciples to select locations of evil to cultivate themselves; the moment one felt totally stunned was the most opportune moment for attaining enlightenment. Of course, this is what I've concluded. But because I've never attained enlightenment myself, I continue to hold the thankless position of a guardian god during a wide expanse of time and space.

The nail-studded wheels finally made contact with Snow Feather's legs. But I was totally stuck in the realm of being stunned. I don't know whether the villagers screamed, whether some of them covered their eyes, and whether some sighed? You know, I'm afraid of making baseless assertions. The string of questions about the villagers was merely an attempt at validating their humanity. If there was no sign of conscience in Diamond Clan, then these people would be nothing but animals. No, animals would've been ten thousand times better!

I also had no idea if Snow Feather had screamed in terror. I do not want to have her scream in terror. I could see her bite her lip and I saw her face turn from pale white, to green, to black. I thought she would faint. But she did not. She wanted to stand up—she could've if she had a stick. But you know her standing up might've angered Braggart. So, better stay lying down! However, she would've lost her life if blood continued to flow.

I felt so flustered I was totally out of my wits.

A dark red blood gushed under the cart. There was also soft white matter, the bone marrow, supposedly the essence of the human body. It was said that a hundred catties of grain would transform into a drop of blood, a thousand drops of blood would engender a drop of sperm, and a thousand drops of sperm would engender a drop of bone marrow. If such was the case, then the bone marrow in the cart courtyard must have wasted lots of grain. Don't think that I salivated over the bone marrow—I'm a divinity after all! Although I am a protective deity, and have always been offered blood-wine when the folks of Liangzhou worshipped me, they'd take a cock to a threshold, chop its head clean off, and let its blood drip into a bowl. The Daoist priests[10] claimed that blood sacrifices were necessary for the ritual, but the truth of the matter was they all really wanted to eat headless cocks. They'd eat and eat and take the rest home for the wife and children. So don't take me for a gluttonous deity—I'm not. Although I hadn't attained enlightenment, my conscience was not annihilated by greed! When I saw the red and white fluids ooze out of her legs, my heart shivered like autumn wind blowing at some donkey's ears.

I tried to "borrow" some of Snow Feather's pain. I have that power, you know. I tried a bit and transferred some of it—probably about 10 percent. Guess how painful it was? Well, let me tell you—I fainted from it! You should know that the worst of all pains is the kind that went all the way into the bone marrow! That pain truly stabbed deep into the bone marrow! See how I shiver from just remembering it now! Suddenly, I felt a hatred for Braggart. Why inflict so much agony upon another human being? Ever since then, I harbored the desire to punish him. Although the process posed some difficulties, since he did not believe in the existence of deities, I was constantly looking for an opportunity to give the donkey a lesson. An opportunity finally presented itself. One day when he was groping toward a widow's home, I led him to a fresh pile of shit left by a child and had him step right into it. Was that disgusting or not?

Something happened at this moment that more or less salvaged the reputation of Diamond Clan. It showed that humanity still existed there. It was the animal feeder, your grandpa. He carried Snow Feather in his arms and ran out of the cart courtyard. Since the punishment was already executed by then, no one gave another loud fart. I saw a strange expression on Braggart's face. I thought he either harbored regrets or was feeling bad. You know how badly I wished that he'd had a conscience. Judging from his expression, he seemed to know where the animal feeder went. And of course, you knew he went to Diamond Clan Monastery, which had the best medicine for wounds.

There was one more detail. I forgot to say whether the cart's wheels chopped Snow Feather's legs clean off, or whether they just broke them. I didn't ask but figured it must've been the latter, as her legs were shorter; but the bottom halves were still there later on. But you'd also know

---

10. These refer to non-Buddhist priests who could be Daoists or local shaman priests.

that without the few inches, she could never be a flying thief again. The children in the village, however, never did call her Cripple Auntie.

"That afternoon," added Ajia, "the divine form of the bullock with the broken leg had already floated up to Heaven and saw the entire episode clearly. Although its broken leg did not save Snow Feather from the torture, it harbored no regrets. It was precisely the result of its behavior that enabled what would have been a normal bullock to become part of a Tanka."

The Symbolisms in the Tanka

According to *Tale of the Goddess*, Monk Wu was chanting a sutra when Snow Feather was carried into Diamond Clan Monastery by the animal feeder. His voice resonated through his entire chest and abdomen and was most sonorous. Monk Wu was practicing the Technique of Extinguishing by treating the starvation as a calamity and attempting to extinguish it. Little would he know that worse was yet to happen not long thereafter.

At that moment, he heard, "Hurry, Master Wu, save her!"

Monk Wu said "*aiya*," jumped out of his seat and told Jasper, "Hurry, go get the 'white medicine'!" Jasper brought the "white medicine" from Yunnan.[11] Monk Wu mixed some with water and had Snow Feather swallow it. He then had Jasper go to the backyard to pluck some white thorn hemp[12] where lots of it grew. Jasper tore off the thorns quickly and rubbed the branches between his palms a few times. A green juice oozed out, which was applied to the wounds. Monk Wu then set the bones—God knows how he set them. Monk Wu's orthopedic skills were supposed to have been the best in Liangzhou. His least-accomplished disciple was the most famous orthopedic doctor in Liangzhou Hospital. I suspect that Snow Feather's bones were broken rather than crushed. That must have been it, otherwise I can't imagine how Monk Wu could have pieced together bones that were smashed to smithereens. I'm sure readers would have misgivings concerning what even I have trouble imagining. So I'm inclined to lessen the damage. Although the fact

11. The *baiyao*, "white medicine," of Yunnan is the most famous Chinese medicine for treating wounds.

12. The Latin name for *baicima* is *nitraria retusa*.

remains, however, Heaven knows what the legs would have been like after a cartload of stone rollers had gone over them.

According to Ajia, it took Monk Wu a couple of hours to set the bones. Jasper's application of plaster was one of the funniest sights he'd ever seen. Not knowing how easily plaster set, Jasper wasted a lot. Fortunately, plaster was plentiful in the monastery, as Monk Wu was always creating statues of Dakini goddesses out of it. He had a bronze mold. You just need to press mixed plaster into the mold; and within moments, a Dakini goddess would be born. He had two types of molds, one for a red Dakini goddess and one for a white Dakini goddess. The red Dakini goddess was a red-colored statue of a naked woman in a "bow-and-arrow" pose, with the left leg bent like a bow and the right leg straight like an arrow. Wearing a necklace of human skulls, she drank the blood of a demon from a bowl made out of a human skull, which she held in her left hand. The naked white Dakini goddess had her legs bent toward her back like those of an acrobat on a lotus flower. All the decorations on the Dakini goddesses were symbolic. For example, the demon's blood symbolized the Sweet Dew of Great Bliss, the lotus flower symbolized uncorrupted purity. Monk Wu had Jasper cast statues of the Dakini goddesses every day. He said, "Each time you make a Dakini goddess, an extra one will be there to bring you salvation in purgatory." This was the same type of thing the elderly ladies in the village would say: that for every "*ah mi tuo fo*" one recited, one would receive a golden pea in the afterlife. Jasper knew this was based on "power technique" rather than truth. Strictly speaking, this type of view did not accord with the core of their religion. It became a form of trade, just like the businesses of this world. Jasper continued to make plaster casts of the Dakini goddesses nevertheless, as folks inside and beyond the village were wont to "invite" the Dakini goddesses home to worship them. *One can never judge anything definitively*, thought Jasper, *plaster is plaster on its own. But used on a wounded leg, it becomes a medicine; used to make a Dakini goddess, however, it becomes sacred. Hard to say which of those constituted the original nature of plaster.*

Historical Mirror of Forgotten Events records much hearsay concerning Snow Feather's wounded leg. According to hearsay, the process of treating her leg was complicated and that she was treated in the city of Liangzhou. Also that in the dead of a certain night, Monk Wu had a horse carry Snow Feather to Old Mountain and sought Grandpa Jiu.

But they were all based on hearsay. *Family Instructions of Diamond Clan* proved that an animal feeder did lead a horse to the monastery on a certain night. Some villagers eyewitnessed the event. Back then, the feeders had the right to use the animals.

But *Crazy Ramblings of Ajia* claims that the person riding the horse was not Snow Feather—it was in fact Jasper.

Chapter 17

The "Gonpo" in *Nightmares*

The sutra says, when the mind is pure then the Buddhist realm is pure,
But that is only what the sutra says.
Too mysterious are the words of the sutra,
But not mysterious enough to rid your smile.
The rosary beads in the hand are always clamoring—
A bodhi seed, a drop of dew;
       What they reflect
Are always your world.

The Gonpo

We continue to enter Jasper's nightmares, the contents of which were derived from the book, *Nightmares*.

It was obvious that when Jasper wrote this portion, he no longer distinguished dream from reality and would become confused now and then. The situation vaguely reminds one of when Balzac wrote *Old Goriot*—fusing dreams with reality—although the analogy barely holds since Ajia always believed that what Jasper entered was, in fact, another time and space. Seeing my puzzled look, Ajia explained, "You know about memory, right? When a memory is short, we call it memory. But when it is long—by long I mean it has exceeded the limitations of one's bodily existence—then it has a different name. It would be called 'past life.'"

Knowing well what a muddle-headed deity Ajia was, I never expected to hear anything that made sense from him.

What I couldn't grasp was the relationship between Ajia the narrator and the Ajia in *Nightmares*.

One evening in *Nightmares*, the character Ajia pulled a long face. Like Snow Feather, he'd been searching for permanence. But ever since he could understand things, the guru had told him there was no permanence in the world.

"I've got to find the Gonpo. He will save the world," said Ajia. "That Gonpo, has he transcended the ways of the world?" asked Jasper. "He should have," responded Ajia, "everyone says that he had gone beyond the worldly. They all say that. I hope he's transcended the world. Only then would your father have no power over us. However, sometimes when everyone claims something, it could actually be wrong."

"So, you're saying that the Gonpo . . ."

"Don't speak nonsense! You can defile anyone but the Gonpo. We have nothing left except for the Gonpo. If the Gonpo is gone, then everything is gone. Life with nothing left is terrifying."

Jasper shuddered.

"I've never seen the Gonpo," continued Ajia, "but I've met the Khenpo.[1] I didn't like him. Otherwise, I would have looked for the Gonpo a long time ago." Jasper didn't feel like listening to his nonsense, so he stared at the pine trees in the mountain. The pine trees stared back at him. "As soon as that Khenpo saw me," continued Ajia, "he called me daddy and said that I was his father in a previous existence. I fear nothing worse than being called 'daddy.' Whenever that happens in a crowded place, I'd shudder from fear."

Jasper laughed and said, "I'm the opposite. What I fear the most is to have to call someone daddy."

"It's in fact the same!" sighed Ajia, "we're both pathetic . . . How about the two of us go to seek the Gonpo?"

"Don't you have a guru already? And Uncle treats you so well!"

"But I have no faith in him. Why? Because he always snores, always farts, always wipes his nose. I have no faith in him. I've recited the mantra a hundred million times but there's no enlightenment. None whatsoever! Faith is the mother for attaining merit and virtue. Without faith, there's nothing I can do . . . I keep on wondering how a guru would be snoring and farting?" Ajia looked very troubled.

"What if the Gonpo is the same?" Jasper could not help laughing.

---

1. Buddhist scholar.

"This is what I'm afraid of! Right now, at least I have a dream. I'm afraid that if my dream of the Gonpo is gone, then I'd have nothing to live for!"

What is my dream? wondered Jasper.

Butcher's voice wafted over from the distance, "I'd rather die than repent!"

Rescue

"Idiot!" said Uncle.

"They all say Butcher was reincarnated from a wolf," he told John. John smiled.

"Everyone knew I put a curse on him. I was hoping it would be dispelled. But he won't listen. I'm not worried about his death; I'm worried about his family. His wife and kids all depend on him to live. They're really pitiable!" said Uncle.

"You want to save him?" asked John, "You want to save his body or his soul?"

"It's the same. Saving the body must start with saving the soul. Without soul, the body is meaningless. He won't wash with urine or repent. What's to be done?" sighed Uncle.

Uncle is troubled, thought Jasper. *Would an accomplished guru be troubled?* he wondered. *Maybe there's a reason for Ajia's lack of faith in him?*

"What reason? It's heresy!" said Uncle, "Stop mixing with him again. What's accomplishment? Accomplishment is great greed, great anger, and great stupidity! To attain sainthood from being a common mortal, use great greed! To slay even personal attachments, use great anger! To do what you know you shouldn't do, use great stupidity! Don't you know, being troubled leads to Buddhahood?"

John continued, "There's a way and it works. But I don't know whether he'd accept it."

"What way?"

"Love."

"It's the same," laughed Uncle, "repentance is love; love is repentance. The words are different, but the meaning is the same. But, you can give it a try." He then told Jasper to take the Christian priest to the butcher.

Jasper led John down the mountain path. They saw the butcher and a group of people yelling. Kuan San's loud voice resounded like the roaring of an ox. "Evil man!" he roared, "who's ever heard of a guru putting a curse on someone?"

The butcher yanked rotten flesh from his body as he railed, "Swindler!" Seeing John approach, he hissed at him dismissively, as if chasing away a dog, "Shoo, shoo! You want me to love my enemy? I'd rather die!"

"See, it's hopeless!" John spread his palms.

The Black Wolf

Protected by night, the black wolf charged down the mountain.

As soon as the sun set, a huge silhouette of the wolf's head hung on the sky-screen. *Are you going to devour heaven?* wondered Jasper, "be careful lest your stomach explodes!" Kuan San said, "Someone must have stolen the wolf's puppy and buried it in Diamond Clan's corral. The wolf can smell it and has come in revenge!" Ajia said, "Nonsense! The wolf is the result of all the killing. Just look at all the people you've killed! The karma gathered and gathered until it became a black wolf. Sooner or later, it'll come after your life. Look—it's coming!"

As the black wolf charged down the mountain, it peed on its way on the ninety-foot phallic symbol at the village entrance. This represented the worst offense to the villagers. The folks kowtowed and prayed to the totem every morning. Childless women would mix some of its earth with water and drink it to ensure giving birth to a fat baby. The totem had consequently become dilapidated. But even a dilapidated totem was a totem. And having a totem was better than having none. How could the black wolf pee on this sacred object? Simply intolerable!

Thereupon, the butcher swung his rusty knife and charged at it. He wanted to take his rifle along, but it had been taken by Goodie Wang to subdue evil. Even a rusty knife was a knife; the butcher was filled with courage. According to hearsay, the others were so scared stiff that their pee formed a torrential river. But that was just hearsay. The truth of the matter was that the butcher was the most courageous among them, which was why he became a butcher. Unfortunately, the brave butcher was unable to find the black wolf. Some claimed the butcher's murderous aura was so overwhelming the wolf hid from him. Others claimed that both the butcher and the wolf were looking for each other, but they did not meet. Nothing one could do about that.

The black wolf crossed over mountains and vales, and charged with stench. All the gates of the stockade were tightly shut. Bandits guarded themselves with strong fortress gates. But the paltry domestic animals owned by the unfortunate commoners were all attacked by the wolf. The ground was strewn with sheep corpses, and the wailing of the tribe shook heaven.

"Where the hell is the butcher?" shouted Braggart in the stockade, "such a showoff but totally useless when he's needed!"

The butcher was just feeling frustrated over not being able to find what everyone else seemed to have seen. After hearing Braggart's comment, he bellowed, "How about you? Why don't you go kill it? You brag like an ocean, but can't do shit work!"

"Ha!" Braggart laughed, "Gentlemen like me move the mouth, not the hand!"

When the villagers heard them, they all wept and wailed, "We're finished! The brave one can't find the wolf. The one who can find the wolf is too scared!"

Jasper asked Uncle, "Why don't you execute the wolf by performing the Execution Technique?" "I have no karmic affinity with the wolf," said Uncle. "What is karmic affinity?" asked Jasper. "Karmic affinity is karmic affinity," replied Uncle.

The wolf howled the entire night. The sheep which were not already dead, shivered.

Ajia said, "That wolf is in fact not wolf. It's your enemy. Your enemy's totem is wolf. You've killed too many when you led the group against your enemy. It's come to seek revenge!"

Jasper said, "You also think I did it?" "Who else, if not you?" asked Ajia.

Jasper thought, *If even Ajia says that I did it, I must have done it.* And then he asked, "Why didn't the wolf come after me?" Ajia said, "It was looking for the butcher." Jasper asked, "Why couldn't they meet?" Ajia replied, "Because the butcher has leprosy."

The Protective Gods

The wolf disappeared the moment the sun rose. The sheep which had collapsed from fear climbed up, blinked their bleary eyes and went to graze.

An obviously pregnant Heavenly Girl arrived. Uncle was in the midst of chanting the sutra; the water in the pure-water bowl vibrated from the resonance of his voice. Jasper was performing the juniper-burning ritual. He would set fire to the juniper branches and sprinkle roasted flour, white sugar, and yak butter on them, for the protective gods who loved yak butter. Now that Uncle had served as a horse-mounting stool, his benefactors diminished noticeably since no one wanted to give offerings to a horse-mounting stool. Within days, they were out of yak butter. Thereupon the protective gods clamored, "How can you not give us any yak butter and still expect us to protect you?" Uncle said, "Look—I don't have any either!" "That's your problem—but we've got to have some!" they clamored.

"There's really nothing I can do," said Uncle, "I can't be a beggar, can I?" The gods clamored, "Why not? If you could be a horse-mounting stool, why not a beggar too?" "Any more shouting from you, I won't ask you to protect me any longer!" "That's not up to you either. We have to protect you—it's our responsibility!" "To protect me as a horse-mounting stool?" "Yes, to protect you as a horse-mounting stool!"

Uncle sighed and turned to Jasper, "Go take my snuff bottle to Goodie Wang's home and exchange it for yak butter. My dick will turn numb from all their hollering!"

"Be more civilized—how can you talk about the gods this way?"

"Isn't it enough that I'm getting yak butter for you?"

When Jasper arrived at Goodie Wang's, the latter said, "I can only give you ten catties of butter for this snuff bottle. Bring your guru's string of agate rosary beads if you want more—I'll give him eighteen catties for that."

Jasper came back and put some butter on the burning juniper branches angrily. He then turned to the gods, "Why don't you punish Goodie Wang?" "How can you encourage us to perform an evil deed? How can we punish a good man?"

This was when the woman came up the slope.

The woman said, "Jasper, how can you ignore me? When you used me, you were full of sweet nothings. But the minute you're done, you pulled up your pants and made yourself scarce. You have to respect the Buddha even if you have no respect for the monk. You have to consider the child even if you have no regard for its mother. This baby in my belly is your own flesh and blood!"

Jasper became teary-eyed from frustration, "What are you talking about? I didn't even touch you!"

"You didn't touch me, but I did touch you! It doesn't matter who touched who—the baby belongs to both of us!"

Uncle laughed and said, "She's right. You can't ignore this, Jasper."

"I didn't do anything—I didn't even take my clothes off!"

"True, you didn't take your clothes off, but the clothes took themselves off!" laughed the woman.

A protective god chimed in, "Own up to it, Jasper! A man owns up to his own deeds!"

"I really didn't touch her," said Jasper, "according to Ajia, the rod has to enter the lotus flower to make a baby."

Uncle chided, "Don't listen to Ajia. The fella is getting worse and worse. He won't even listen to me. Why believe what he says?"

"But what he said is true!"

"When someone is in the right, then what he says is right. When he's not in the right, nothing he says is right." Uncle rubbed his nose. He was addicted to snuff, but he didn't have the snuff bottle anymore. "Although I don't have snuff, I speak the truth. That Ajia is full of lies!"

A protective god said, "Even when I had no yak butter, I continued to protect him as a horse-mounting stool. If it weren't for me, his back would have been crushed a long time ago."

"It still hurts some even now!" Uncle swayed his waist.

"Didn't you sway your waist like your Uncle, Jasper?" asked the woman.

Jasper tried hard to remember, but his mind pulled a blank. Seeing the protective gods glare at him, he thought, *Maybe I did make the baby.* He couldn't help feeling pleasantly surprised by the fact that he could create a human being.

Uncle said, "At least you touched her. Many who were not even touched got pregnant anyway."

"Precisely," said the woman, "five women are ready to give birth in the village. They all say that the children are Jasper's."

"Now, this is complete nonsense!" said Jasper.

"How can five people all speak nonsense?" said a protective god. "It's no longer nonsense when three people say the same thing! Isn't there a saying that three makes a tiger? Well, five makes them whatever they want to be!"

"I can't do anything if you won't own up to it," laughed the woman. Suddenly, she lowered her head and turned to Jasper, "The baby is in fact your Dad's. But if you won't own up to it, who would?" She looked like she was whispering but the voice resonated like a torrential flood.

The protective gods suppressed their laughter and pretended not to hear it.

An Auspicious Omen

The five women did give birth. They gave birth to five eggs the next morning. The women said, "We heard Jasper was also born from an egg." He would not admit to it, however. It went against the nature of things.

The sun rose and sunlight shone on the eggs that cracked into lotus flowers and harbored a girl in each.

Everyone said this was an auspicious omen. Birth from an egg was a manifestation of those who had attained Eighth Place Buddhahood.[2] The shell protected them from blood pollution, and they were not attached to the uterus. Everyone said so, such that in time it became a historical fact.

Grandpa Jiu took a great liking to the girls. He bathed them and did all sorts of what others would have considered dirty jobs for them. "Now I have playmates!" He was very happy. He rattled a hand drum that guided the girls out of the uterus.

As Jasper remembered it, his life slipped by with the rattling of Grandpa Jiu's hand drum. He looked troubled when he said, "It must have been magic. I'm sure of it. He'd rattle the drum for a while and a year would pass by; he'd rattle it some more and another year would slip by. This was how several years slipped away in a flash." Ajia said, "You wouldn't have done anything anyway."

It was in the pounding resonance of the drum that Braggart grew mighty. He extended the fence of the stockade to an infinite distance and built it to an infinite height. All the villagers moved into the stockade. This assertion was suspicious because it was equivalent to alleging that all the villagers had turned into bandits. But to their enemy, this was actually correct. After numerous frantic plundering attacks, the stockade became ever larger, until it was almost a city. There were only two exceptions to this phenomenon. One was the black wolf that could

---

2. *Badi pusa* have reached a place of no worries or attachments.

appear whenever it wanted to, regardless of the height of the fence. Ajia trembled from fear and often hid in the far reaches of a mountain cave, where he recited the heart sutra and visualized a fire curtain. Even then, the shadow of the black wolf would dart at him and shield his clear sky.

"I tried to escape. I tried with all my might. I'd feel that I'd escaped from it. But the minute I turned around, it would be following me at the same distance," said Ajia.

"Was it a dream?" queried Jasper.

"No, not a dream. I couldn't see the wolf, but I could feel it. Feel it ready to pounce on me and devour me. If it did devour me, that would have been the end of it. But it wouldn't devour me. It was a hanging sword that wouldn't fall!"

Jasper asked, "Who'd believe something like that?" Ajia said, "Ignoramuses wouldn't believe it, but wise men would." Jasper queried, "How many wise men are there in this world?" Ajia responded, "Can't be many, otherwise, they wouldn't be called wise men."

Everyone said that Uncle was a wise man.

The other popularly recognized wise man was the Gonpo.

The Gonpo was different from Uncle. Uncle was a real monk. But when counterfeits flood the market there's no space for real goods. Even those of his own tribe disowned him and used him as a horse-mounting stool. Excepting him, all the other monks turned secular. Dad threatened them with a knife and told them to take off their pants and "marry" the widows in the stockade. Braggart said, "Don't despise them. They are family members of martyrs. Their husbands died in glory in order to protect your happiness. It's an honor to fuck them . . . Look, you can turn secular, or you can become a horse-mounting stool!" So the monks who did not wish to become horse-mounting stools embraced the martyrs' women and made many babies. Thereupon, the tribe's population expanded and its might increased.

Uncle was the only one who refused to submit. He would rather be a horse-mounting stool. Within days, a thick callous formed on his back like a camel's. One night, a skinny guy from Brilliant King Clan stole into Uncle's cabin. He was dispatched there by the enemy. He said, "Local goods are not valued locally. You should come to us. We all know what an accomplished guru you are—there's only one like you every five hundred years!" Uncle replied, "I'm getting on in years. And I miss that snuff bottle of mine. I want to redeem it from Goodie Wang when there's more yak butter someday. There's nothing more that Goodie

Wang wants than seeing me leave!" The skinny guy said, "Look, you can come over anytime you want. We welcome you to 'renounce the darkness and seek the light'!" Uncle said, "I don't know what's darkness and what's light. To me, darkness is light; light is darkness!"

That Gonpo, however, was above the two clans. It was said he built an estate in the mountain between the stockades of Diamond Clan and Brilliant King. It was an incomparably luxurious estate, totally hidden in the woods. It was said tens of thousands of accomplished masters live there. They have attained "increasing benefits," "eliminating calamities," "possessing compassion," and "ability to subjugate," and had incomparable powers. But it was all based on hearsay. Fortunately, both sides were in awe of the hearsay. The more it was based on hearsay, the more mysterious it seemed. So both sides announced, "We welcome the Gonpo's men to come anytime they wish to come, and ask for any offerings they wish to have."

So, every first or fifteenth of the month, the Gonpo would dispatch someone to stand on a mountain rock that resembled a hooked nose and yell, "Yak butter!" or "Roasted flour!" Then yak butter and roasted flour would flow unstoppably up the mountain like water.

Ajia said, "I've got to find the Gonpo. Otherwise, I'll starve to death!" His supplies were provided by Uncle. It used to be twenty catties of roasted barley flour, eight catties of firewood, and one catty of yak butter; but now they've been reduced to half. Ajia said, "In the future, he wants me to fend for myself! What am I going to do? Have you ever seen a guru like this? He snores, he wipes his nose, and he gives me no food!" Jasper said, "Even those were picked out from the gaps in his teeth! He only had water for himself! Everything is under 'reform.' No one is allowed to give food to a horse-mounting stool. Anyone who did, would become a horse-mounting stool himself. He could only plant some barley on the kitchen platform. How much do you think he can reap from a tiny space like that?"

"I heard," said Ajia, "at the Gonpo's place, yak butter formed a sea and roast flour piled into a mountain. Smoked meat rolled around like the fleas on a pig! But what I fear the most is that the Gonpo also snores!"

"He's the Gonpo even if he snores."

"But whenever I hear snoring, I'd think, how can he bring salvation to all beings if he can't even control his own snoring? I know, to you, the snores are not snores—they are sutra chanting."

"I never said that!" Jasper suppressed a smile.

Jasper also wanted to seek the Gonpo. According to Mom, Uncle's cabin was to be converted into a breeding station soon. They lost many horses from the forays against the enemy, so Dad procured a horse of good breeding from beyond the mountains and set his eyes on this cabin. Jasper asked her, "Does he still whip you?" "What a strange question!" Mom said. "Does it mean that you're not Mom if you don't get flogged?" "Of course! I see you've become smarter. Would he be Dad if he didn't beat people up?"

Jasper asked, "Where's Snow Feather?

Mom said, "She escaped to the Gonpo's a long time along. She also left something for you!" Mom fished out a paper wrap and opened it. There was a scorpion in it.

"I understand," said Jasper.

That night, he and Ajia escaped from the village.

The Escape

The night they escaped was a moonlit night. The black wolf hadn't appeared for quite a while now. Life in the village seemed somewhat boring. On account of the numerous men and horses he had, Braggart assumed the position of the stockade chief. As stockade chief, he was in the process of planning another attack on the enemy. He said, "Men are born to attack the enemy—what's the purpose of life otherwise?" He took the stallion into Uncle's cabin resolutely, saying, "I've set my eyes on this place for quite a while now, but haven't found an excuse for taking it." Uncle said, "Do you need an excuse to do something?" Braggart laughed and said, "Of course I do! It doesn't look proper without an excuse. One is a scoundrel without a good excuse, but with a good excuse, one becomes a politician! Where's Jasper?"

"He left to look for the Gonpo."

Unexpectedly, Braggart laughed while saying, "I don't believe that there is a Gonpo. How stupid—he won't find what he wants. I was hoping he'd inherit my position! But, fine if he doesn't, someone is pregnant with his baby. I didn't believe it. But everyone said so. So I said, fine by me! Even if it's not his, I'll consider it his. Even if it's a bastard, I'll consider it his. I was a bastard myself!" He laughed boisterously.

Jasper shot a glance at Ajia and felt ashamed. He thought, *If what Dad said got spread around, it would be a great disgrace. Dad could be a bandit but not a bastard. His being a bastard would disgrace Grandma!*

Ajia hacked at the thick birch saplings with a machete. They were even sturdier than a fence. This was the road to the Gonpo's. The more difficult the path, the more valuable it would appear to be. Ajia wiped his sweat, looked at the wan moon and said, "Fortunately, the black wolf is not here." Jasper laughed and said, "How come I feel like we're in its mouth?" Ajia agreed, "Me too!"

The further they proceeded, the denser the birch saplings became; until they looked like a woven mat. They heard a rustle in front and surprisingly found Grandpa Jiu pulling the birch saplings together and weaving them into barriers. Jasper screamed, "Hey, what do you think you're doing?" Grandpa Jiu laughed and said, "I don't know what I'm doing either!" Ajia said, "Let him!" And he sat down panting.

"You got me! You got me!" Grandpa Jiu clapped his hands and left the mountain, the soles of his shoes clapping at the soles of his feet.

"Let's call it a day, I'm dead tired!" said Ajia, "Let's sleep for a while. There's nothing I fear more than having a snake go in my ass, or my ears . . ." Jasper said, "Stuff your ass with a sock. Leave the face. People will laugh if you're worried about your face now!" After a long day of activities, they dozed off.

Joining the Band

The warm sun kissed his face. Jasper woke up. Ajia was snoring thunderously. Ajia, who hated it when others snored, was by no means any less mighty when it came to snoring himself. Jasper thought, *How come people can always see the thorn on someone else's hand, but not see the log in their own eye?* Ajia's snoring was by far louder than Uncle's. Jasper wanted to laugh, but then noticed that they'd already arrived at a strange place. The mountains resembled a row of sleeping elephants, each biting the buttock of the one in front and created a huge valley. Many square tiles dotted the valley randomly. Upon scrutiny, they were one-room cabins. Jasper recognized them as rooms used for religious practice. The humming sound of sutra chanting emerged from them.

Is this the Gonpo's territory? Jasper wondered.

He leapt up. A mountain stream splashed down from somewhere, and glistened. A flock of little birds was singing. Jasper could tell they were singing in praise of the Gonpo. He kicked the sole of Ajia's foot and screamed, "Get up! The Gonpo is here!"

Ajia rubbed his eyes, yawned, and said "What's with the yelling? I knew it already!"

Jasper looked behind him. Two stockades loomed right before him. The one in the south was Diamond Clan Stockade, the one in the north was Brilliant King Stockade. Jasper thought, *When we were thinking of the Gonpo in the stockade, he seemed to be at the edge of the sky. But here it looks like they were within a few feet!*

Ajia said, "Of course. He received offerings, but you made the offerings."

At that moment, the door of one of the tiny cabins opened. A monk emerged from it. He asked, "Are you joining the band or dropping by?" Jasper thought, *What's he talking about? What's joining the band?* But Ajia replied, "Joining the band."

"That's good," said the man, "we don't have spare room for those passing through. Each hole has a turnip, there's no extra hole. But the mountain is big, the forest is dense. We can manage if you plan to join the band. Did you bring your housewares?"

"What housewares?" asked Jasper.

"Knives and axes are good. You've got to have a saw. Of course, the most important houseware is your heart. The heart contains myriad things. But the heart must be prepared. Only the heart that is prepared is a heart." A string of bright rosary beads dangled from the monk's neck, glaring in its brilliance.

Ajia said, "What's with all the preparations? Isn't our arrival here preparation enough?"

The old monk wrinkled his nose a couple of times, "What are you talking about—

maggots and ants come here too. Are they supposed to be prepared? Look, if you want to stay, then quit being a smart aleck. Otherwise, go the hell back!"

Jasper looked back. It was a bluff behind him, and he realized that they had been climbing a cliff all night. Cloud and mist wafted over the cliff face, which appeared bottomless. He felt dizzy. He looked at Ajia who was glaring at the old monk. He said, "Ajia, there's no returning. Since we're here already, let's just make-do." The old monk smiled and said, "Precisely. It's easier to embark on a pirate ship than to leave it." Jasper laughed and thought, *He's a funny one! What's with "joining the band" and "embarking on a pirate ship"—why didn't he choose some better-sounding words?* Then he thought, *We might as well stay.* But Ajia plopped himself down on the grass and said, "I'm here to perform religious practices, not to be bullied. I want to see the Gonpo!" The old monk sniggered, "Do you think a brat like you will get to see the Gonpo? Even I, a Khenpo, hardly ever get to see him. How much dried shit have you lapped up yet?"

Ajia looked at the old monk with bewilderment and was just going to ask a question when someone spoke underneath his buttocks, "You're hurting me!" He looked down and saw a writhing snake. Jasper said, "Strange—snakes can talk here." The old monk said, "What's so strange about this? If it had human skin, it would be just like you!"

Ajia laughed and said, "I know who you are! You were one of the Gonpo's disciples. You must have bad-mouthed him and got transformed into a snake!" The snake shot a terrified glance at Ajia, writhed violently to free itself from underneath his buttock, and shot into the grass.

"You decide for yourselves." The old monk yawned and entered the cabin. In a flash, the sound of snoring boomed. Ajia frowned and said, "This snore is at least as loud as your uncle's." Jasper said, "Your snores are even louder! All humans snore—there's nothing to it. What makes a person human is the heart, not the snoring."

Ajia laughed out loud, "How can you say that I snore? Simply ridiculous! I've never slept since I was old enough to know what was going on!"

Halo

Jasper and Ajia borrowed an axe, felled several dozen trees and built two cabins for cultivation along a gully. Ajia continued to practice the Mahakala Technique that Uncle taught him. He wanted to ask the Gonpo to transmit to him a Diamond Technique, but he didn't know where to find the Gonpo. The others he asked were equally clueless. He asked the old monk who said, "There's no need to ask since all the techniques you've learned were transmitted by the Gonpo. The Gonpo assumes innumerable transformations. All the gurus who transmitted different techniques were manifestations of the Gonpo." Ajia asked, "What did I come here for, then?" "How do I know what you came here for?" The old monk was very angry because Ajia's snoring prevented him from sleeping at night.

Ajia said, "I want to see the Gonpo."

The old monk said, "Go ahead! If you don't mind wasting your energy, then go ahead!"

So Ajia took Jasper along to look for the Gonpo. The mountain and wilderness were strewn with isolation buildings, each housing a practitioner. But none of them spoke. Jasper knew that they were all observing the vow to keep silent. Anyone who spoke during isolation would bring infinite bad karma upon himself. Heedless of the fact, however, Ajia shouted, "Gonpo! Gonpo!" His voice traveled forth in one wave after the after, and echoed back into countless "Gonpos"!

"What's with all the yelling?" A head stuck out of one of the isolation rooms and snarled at Ajia.

"Where's the Gonpo?" asked Ajia.

"In the heart!" The man glared at Ajia and tucked in his head. Ajia grumbled, "What diffidence!" He turned to Jasper and said, "I can see that they all lack self-confidence." Jasper said, "It's good to have an empty heart,[3] one can't put anything into a heart that is not empty."

They held hands to boost each other's courage and continued their search along the gully. All the isolation cabins were exactly the same, as if they were produced from the same mold. Furthermore, they were strewn about the entire wilderness, all the way to the horizon. Jasper thought, *Who would have known it's so huge here—maybe ten thousand people here!* Ajia said, "It's got to be more than ten thousand—maybe infinite! I don't think we'll find the Gonpo even after nightfall." Jasper said, "Fine if we can't find him. Some things are better not found!" "Precisely! I remember once hearing a thunderous rumbling noise, shooking heaven and earth. Up close it turned out to have been produced by a drum the size of a palm. The sound was deafening, but the drum was unimpressive." "What's your point?" "Nothing."

A huge sutra hall stood prominently on a piece of leveled ground in the middle of the mountain. It was white. A humming sound emerged from it. Jasper went toward it and came upon a red gate. Through its

---

3. *Xinxu*, literally, empty heart, usually refers to a heart that has a guilty conscience, or is timid, or lacking in self-confidence.

crack, he saw a group of people chanting inside. He smiled and said, "The Gonpo must be here!" But Ajia said uneasily, "Not necessarily." He leaned on the gate with his shoulder and pushed with all his might. It creaked open. All the sutra chanters turned their heads around—the rows of gaping mouths opened and then closed. "Where's the Gonpo?" shouted Ajia.

The crowd roared with laughter. One of them said, "Another madman!" Ajia said, "I'm not mad. Where's the Gonpo?" A fat priest came up and said, "What are you yelling for? You're disturbing people's practice . . . Forget about looking for the Gonpo. You won't be able to find him. If the Gonpo wants to see you, he'll appear before you. If he doesn't want to see you, you'll never find him!"

Ajia looked at Jasper and smiled, "We've come in vain!"

"What are you talking about?" said the fat one. "Knowing this fact made your trip worthwhile. Now go home and perform your practices well."

Jasper tugged at Ajia and turned around. He tried painstakingly to find the way back. But the grass had somehow shot up to a tremendous height. Their footprints were all gone, and the isolation rooms hid in the grass as if they were playing hide-and-seek. The sun had slanted itself westward and was rimmed by a huge halo. Ajia said, "I'm afraid it's going to be windy tomorrow." "A good thing too! This place gives me the creeps. The wind will clear it up." "Too much wind will even blow away tents." "No problem. We live in cabins." "Sometimes cabins will turn into tents. You can't control them."

Thereupon, Jasper felt unsure of himself, and said no more. He turned around toward the way they came.

The insects were singing in praise of the Gonpo. The sun took this opportunity to slip away behind the mountain. A huge mouth began to swallow up the sky. The valley and its weeds melted into liquid and flowed into the mysterious mouth.

Jasper called, "Ajia!"

But Ajia had disappeared.

Jasper looked around, but Ajia was nowhere to be seen. Everything had vanished.

Wishing to find the Gonpo, Jasper had instead lost his friend. Even worse, he could never find his way home again.

In the dream, Kuan San seeped out of the darkness and drifted over slowly. Picking up Jasper's feet as one would a bird, he tossed him into a birdcage.

Millstone

Jasper proceeded in the darkness. He dared not move fast lest he fall off the cliff. That Ajia was still nowhere in sight. To vanish like that—there was something mysterious about this Ajia! The wind began to howl. The halo that rimmed Grandpa Sun had turned into a wind that harbored numerous shadowy tunes. He wasn't so much bothered by that as he was by the disappearance of his "home." A journey without a destination was the most terrifying type, one never knew where one was heading to.

Jasper sighed sorrowfully.

A night bird shrieked. Jasper said, "Don't scream—I know you're not Ajia!" Suddenly, the ground began to twist. It shot forward carrying Jasper. Jasper said, "Road, ah, road—where are you taking me?" The road said, "I'm taking you where you're going!" "You've kidnapped me then!" The road laughed and said, "Nonsense! I can't exist without you—so who's kidnapping whom?" "Up to you then! Sooner or later you'll get tired!" And then he thought, *Better to have a road than none.* But then it occurred to him, *Not having a road is not a problem either. One can just sit quietly if there's no road.*

A lamp was lit. Jasper was very happy. He suddenly found himself in his village. Not that he could see anything; it was the sense of a familiar feeling. A sound of yelling shot from a house into his ears. Jasper realized that he was indeed in the village, as it was obviously the voice of Snow Feather's mom. The house also emerged from the dark night gradually with an eerie light. Sure enough, it was Snow Feather's mom.

Snow Feather's maternal grandfather was moving a millstone with his son; his head was covered in sweat, and he was panting breathlessly. The father and son heaved and ho'd while Snow Feather's mom twisted underneath the millstone. Jasper shot into the room and shocked the father and son. "Save me, Jasper!" cried Snow Feather's mom.

"It's none of your business!" panted the old man.

Taking advantage of the interruption, Snow Feather's mom pulled out her bloodied feet and said, "How cruel of you, Dad! How can you do this to me just for a few *mou* of land!" The old man said, "Blame yourself! I can't stand being poor anymore!" He lifted his robe as he spoke and shouted, "Look! I can't even afford pants!"

Jasper could not help but laugh. Snow Feather's uncle also laughed. Snow Feather's mom, however, cried, "What are you laughing for? Look at my feet!" The old man said, "What's there to look at? Who told you not to bind your feet? They want small feet. Come, Sonny!" The father and son crushed her feet with the millstone again.

Snow Feather's mom snickered, "Dad, just for those few *mou* of land!"

Dad said, "I can't stand being poor anymore! The eldest girl was exchanged for a draught animal, the second girl was for a big cart, you for land. I want to enjoy a few days as a rich man!"

Snow Feather's mom said, "Go ahead, Dad!" She stretched her feet toward the millstone.

"I'll die!" screamed Snow Feather's mom.

Jasper rushed over and took away the millstone. The soles of the feet had already been broken into halves with the toes bent under. Covered in cold sweat, Snow Feather's mom said, "So these are the three-inch lotus feet,[4] right?"

"Butcher! Butcher!" screamed Jasper.

The old man grabbed Jasper's collar and said, "If you hadn't said I was a butcher, I wouldn't have known I was one. But now I know I am indeed a butcher. Damn you! Get lost!" He gave a shake and Jasper was tossed out of the house into the dead of night like dust.

Someone snickered in the night. It was Ajia.

Jasper thought, *This had to be a dream. Look, Snow Feather's mom was even younger than I!*

Creating Gods

Ajia said, "Maybe the man I saw was really the Gonpo."

"What did he look like?" "I couldn't tell. They were debating about a scripture." "Which scripture?" "They were all talking nonsense. They debated and debated until finally, the Gonpo decided on the winner."

"Was there a winner?" asked Jasper.

"Yes. I asked: why did the Gonpo make the decision? They said that it was because he was the Gonpo. I then asked: who decided on the designation of the Gonpo? They said, the Gonpo was decided by the Buddha. I then asked: who decided who should be the Buddha? They said, the Buddha is decided by the mind. So I said, why the rigamarole—

---

4. Euphemism for bound feet.

from now on, why not let the mind make the decision? As soon as I said that, they all came at me with daggers to kill me. I had to escape."

Jasper laughed and said, "They must have thought you'd entered a demonic state. What happened next?"

"After that, I hid in a Bodhi tree and debated with them. I craned my neck and told them I would die content if I should lose the debate. I debated with them for eighteen days before I won."

Jasper laughed and thought this Ajia was bullshitting again—here he'd been away for just a while and he claims he'd debated for eighteen days. But he didn't want to uncover him.

Ajia said, "I went through all the sutra halls to debate the scriptures with them, until they were all speechless. They then called me a demon." "What did the Gonpo say?" "They said they were carrying out the biddings of the Gonpo. But I never saw the Gonpo. I thought I saw him, but then didn't really see him. I don't know whether he was tall or short, fat or thin, broad or narrow. But they said they were carrying out the orders of the Gonpo. Listen, they're coming!"

Sure enough, torches surrounded them from all sides. The shouts shook heaven and earth. Jasper turned pale and said, "You've created a calamity. The Gonpo is not to be doubted. How could you say what you did when they've only got the one Gonpo left?" Ajia said, "I thought theof truth about the Gonpo was the same as mine."

Jasper tugged at Ajia and ran in the dark. The road was unexpectedly even—whatever happened to the jaggedness just now? He remembered how the road ran furiously with him on it a moment ago. The jaggedness must have been leveled by that. The torches formed a sea of fire behind them. *This Gonpo certainly has many pious disciples!* thought Jasper.

Ajia said, "I now know that the Gonpo must snore."

"Why?"

"It's a feeling."

After running for a while, Ajia began to weep. Ajia's wailing resembled the howling of a wolf. It was a lingering sound coupled with a sense of hopelessness. "What are you crying for?" rebuked Jasper. "I used to have a Gonpo in my heart, but now I've got nothing. How am I going to survive without a Gonpo? I should have a Gonpo to help me travel through this long dark night! But I don't have a Gonpo anymore!" sobbed Ajia. "You didn't even see the real Gonpo. You don't even know what he looked like!"

Ajia wept. "Faith constitutes the real Gonpo. Without faith, there is no Gonpo. I know the Gonpo vanished the moment I doubted him. Such a long journey through the dark, and I don't have the protection of a Gonpo anymore!"

A voice hollered among the torches behind them, "Stop chasing him away! That would be too easy on him. Better to let him wail!"

"That's right!" said the torches in unison, "let him wail!" And they stopped the chase.

Ajia wiped his tears and screamed, "I'm not going to wail if that's what you want!"

A voice shot over, "Why not? You don't have a Gonpo anymore!"

Ajia said, "Sooner or later, I'll create a new Gonpo!"

"He's finished!" an old hoarse voice said, "He knows the Gonpo can be created. He's finished!"

"He's finished! He's finished!" everyone roared in unison.

Greatly shocked, Ajia collapsed on the ground and wailed.

After a long while, he sobbed spasmodically, "The old robber was right. Those who know that gods can be created can't create gods!"

Chapter 18

The Old Mountain

Along the lingering tunnel of time and space,
      I seek assiduously.
I experienced the bustling glories of the Han and the Tang,
I bathed in the mists and rains of the Ming and the Qing,
      The skiff of life,
Drifts forever among life and death.
The gale of time gusts vehemently,
      Blowing away each of my bodies,
But it cannot nab the search by my soul.

Garbage

According to *Crazy Ramblings of Ajia*, the most brilliant people in Chinese history perished under the sinful butcher knife of the Yuan dynasty.

These people were the ancestors of Diamond Clan.

Back then, Liangzhou was a region of the Xixia Kingdom. It was said that it resembled a secondary capital. In terms of culture, however, Liangzhou occupied an irreplaceable position.

The people of Xixia created a most splendid civilization. They had their own writing system, their own culture, and all manner of things bearing the imprint of the words, "Great Xia." But they did not possess an even more barbaric butcher knife than the Yuan.

It has been a thousand years since their existence. Who weeps for them? Who has ever denounced the crime of burying that brilliant civilization?

Echoing in the space above the world is nothing but a sigh—that there's too little information. What the Xixia left were countless enigmas. The people known as the Dangxiang were so dignified they did not even deign to leave behind a single book.

There's a stele in the Temple of Literature in Liangzhou. It is considered a national treasure. Its content is presented in two different writings: the Han Chinese writing and the Xixia writing. Known as the Xixia Stele, this is said to be the best preserved stele of its type in the country.

Yet, a plastic woven bag next to the Diamond Maiden Cave was stuffed full of this type of national treasure.

One day an official arrived. The tall elderly man who had treasured the contents of the bag for several years asked the official, "Are they of any use?" "No!" replied the official. Therefore, these bits of "garbage" were tossed into fire, and flames obliterated the history effortlessly. Later, an expert found the remains of one of the items in the wilderness. He screamed, "A national treasure!"

It was a manuscript by the state priest of the Xixia Kingdom!

Karma

The manuscript by the state priest of Xixia, along with countless other treasures, was buried by an earthquake several hundred years ago.

They waited quietly for karma or a historical opportunity.

On a certain day during the twentieth century, Jasper and Snow Feather will knock at a door together.

Before this, they experienced life in the mundane world, just like the spiritual rock at the Nonsensical Cliff of the Great Wilderness Mountain.

That is the story Ajia will recite.

The Jujube Red Steed

According to *Tale of the Goddess*, the day after Snow Feather's injury, Jasper left the village on a horse. He was blocked by the militiamen at its entrance. Jasper said Snow Feather had a fever and that she'd die if he didn't get medicine for her from the city of Liangzhou. He was not lying. Getting medication was indeed one of the goals of his trip. But he had another purpose, which was to enter Old Mountain—to find Grandpa Jiu and to fetch Snow Feather's mom. He packed the more than one catty of beef he'd received from the clan, the result of the bullock's self-sacrifice.

The militiamen said, "Go quickly and come back right away!" So Jasper sped the horse and went straight for the city of Liangzhou.

The horse Jasper rode was the best one at Diamond Clan. It was the one used for pulling the official carriage and was the color of dark red jujube. It came from the Shandan horse farm and was of superior breed and genes. I grew up on a jujube red horse. Father had me herd a horse since I was seven. I would herd the red jujube horse and a most frisky black donkey by a lake. The red jujube horse had a huge rump, and I would lie backward on the horse's back, belly down with my head on its rump. It was even more comfortable than the Simmons mattress I used later. The bell on the horse's neck rang monotonously. The horse would sneeze loudly, swing its tail, and splash the mud in the gutters with hoofs larger than bowls. The horse's belly was covered with dots of mud. I suspected it splattered the mud on purpose, as gadflies were always circling around its belly and biting it. Most of the time, the horse got rid of the gadflies using its tail. Sometimes, however, it would jump up furiously, although it took care not to jolt me from its back. That was when I knew gadflies must have bitten an important part of the horse (yes, the genitals, the most vulnerable part of the horse). Should a bee sting you there, you'd suffer too. Although long, the horse's tail was not able to reach that area. I would get off the horse then and bend my head to look. Sure enough, several gadflies would be reveling right there. I would pluck the bloodsuckers lightly. No need to use force—a light squeeze would produce a handful of blood. If I should squash harder, blood would splatter onto my face. It must have really hurt the horse for so much blood to have been sucked from that particular location. Later, whenever I saw the women in the village clutch their husbands' genitals when a couple fought, I'd suspect they learned the trick from the gadflies. So it was that companion of mine that Jasper rode to the city of Liangzhou. The jujube red horse "dug" holes. This was a graphic way that the folks of Diamond Clan described the galloping of horses. This was when riding on horseback was the most steady and comfortable. The front hoofs "dug" into the ground and created potholes. The back of the horse arched up and down like distant mountains. Jasper felt like he was riding among the clouds. I also loved that kind of sensation—

such a great sensation. One day, the sensation floated toward my belly wave after wave and created a scorching fire there. Immediately, I was immersed in an indescribable sense of pleasure. That was the first time I found out that such pleasure existed for humans. Later, I was always riding in my dreams. Each time, the sheet was soiled once again. The folks of Diamond Clan called this phenomenon "horse galloping," truly a most apt representation for wet dreams.

Jasper arrived at the city of Liangzhou, galloping as if he rode on clouds. He looked for Monk Wu's most "unaccomplished" disciple, who stayed at the northern end. Back then, grain was still being supplied to the residents of the city. Although they were also hungry, they were in Heaven when compared with rural peasants. In a small clinic, Jasper found a man merely three feet tall. Although hunchbacked, the fame of this person was greater than Heaven. The man had several people in the clinic. He had them lying face down on a bed. One could hear a *gaba gaba* sound, and they'd smile. Jasper told him about Monk Wu's business. Greatly alarmed, the man immediately took Jasper to the hospital across from the clinic to obtain the best medicine. Jasper said later that, to that person, Monk Wu was the equivalent of a heavenly deity.

After leaving the city, Jasper proceeded to Old Mountain.

Snow Feather's Instructions

Snow Feather's instructions to Jasper are recorded in detail in *Tale of the Goddess*.

When you enter Old Mountain, you will see three roads. Take the one on the right. Proceed for a little over ten leagues, and you'll see six side roads. Choose the third one on the left—there's a pine tree that looks like a big umbrella. You'll find an intestine-like narrow path on the left, or southern, side of the pine tree. Once you get there, put on your boots and smear tobacco soot over them as there are many snakes and poisonous leeches there. There's no need to fear the snakes, they'll slip away as soon as they smell the tobacco soot. But the leeches are a real problem. Wear your sheepskin jacket inside out, fasten the waist cord, and tie up your sleeves and leggings so they can't enter your body. When you feel a sharp sting on bare skin, you'll know you're being stung by a leech. You'll see half of a leech inside your flesh. Don't pull at it. If you pull at it forcefully, you'll break the leech into halves and the remaining half will bore into the skin. Give it a sharp slap. The leech will contract from the pain and come out of the flesh. If convenient, you could also dribble warm urine onto the leeches. They are cold blooded, so your urine would feel like boiling water to them. Travel along the narrow path until you see on your left (which is north), a forest—a very dense forest. You'll see many animals in the gully that look like flaxseeds. Those are the wolves. Don't be scared. When wolves are numerous, they don't attack sheep. If you ignore them, they'll also ignore you. In the unlikely event that they surround you, chant the protective spell to ask the mountain god to restrain his dogs. Don't repeat the spell too many times. Just recite it seven times, more than that and the mountain god's head will burst from pain. Be sure not to race the horse when you see the packs of wolves. Just travel slowly. They'll chase after you the minute you start to run. Don't look around on the horse, particularly not at the wolves. Just treat them like rocks. However, take my lasso with dart to embolden yourself. In the unlikely event—and only in the very unlikely event—the wolves surround you, then you can swing the lasso in circles. But don't lash at them either. Since wolves are the mountain god's dogs, they have dog nature. They are afraid of ropes and flying dust. You won't have trouble crossing the gully this way.

Once you've crossed the gully, you will see a white poplar tree that was was struck by lightning. A fox that had become a spirit used to live there. It was struck by lightning one night. The tree is very conspicuous, with its top half totally burnt. Don't go too close to it. A couple of wild boars now live there. Don't be afraid of them. The male boar is blind, and the female is also very old. If you don't bother them, they'll say "*zuzong youling*, the ancestors are efficacious." Go around the poplar and proceed along the reeds to the south. Be careful though, and tread only on the stones. There are a lot of stones—just make sure that you don't tread on the mud outside the path. The most important thing you have to be careful of there is your horse because there's the skeleton of a horse in the swamp. If you don't want to frighten your horse, tie it up first, and then snap off a sapling and use it to shatter the skeleton. Make sure you smash the bones; they provoke the horse the most. Don't go right up to the horse skeleton—just hit it with the stick from a distance. Be careful that you don't use too much force and end up not being able to restrain your own body. There may be snakes in the horse skeleton, or maybe not. Just be careful. If you'd like, you can smear some tobacco soot on the stick; there's a lot of tobacco soot in Monk Wu's pipe. Actually, why don't you take the pipe with you? If there is a snake, then stretch out the pipe and let it bite the pipe. And then you can give the mouthpiece a forceful blow. The snake will get drunk from the tobacco dreg blown out of the pipe. If you want to eat snake meat, then take it by the tail and shake it hard a few times to break its bones. You can skin it next; be careful it doesn't bite you. Sometimes snakes that look dead can still bite. Best cut off the snake's head with a knife. But be careful with this too. Best throw it far away using a stick because a severed snake head can also bite. After this, you can untie the horse without further worries. Horses are very smart; it will know to tread on the stones.

After you cross the swamp, you'll find yourself in a deep depression that looks like a belly button. You'll see the tops of many mountains bowing to you; some will look like badgers, some like reclining elephants, and others like pythons. There seem to be many mountain paths there, but don't take them whatever you do. These paths don't lead anywhere. You'll end up going around in circles and never get out of there. Just choose the mountain that looks like a screen wall. Don't go up the mountain. Just go along the gully at its foot. The gully is filled with red rocks like rust. The red color is, in fact, rust. The rocks are very heavy. According to the forecast of Grandpa Jiu, who has prodigious powers, an iron mine will be established here. By then, Old Mountain will be just like a city; there will be no more wolves and very few snakes. Strange people of all sorts will populate the valley. After growing and multiplying for some years, those people will one day vanish with the mountain. According to hearsay they were annihilated by a type of bomb they created themselves. But that is something that will happen in the relatively distant future.

Go along the gully strewn with red rocks for about eight leagues until you come to a mountain pass. The place is filled with animal drop-pings and overgrown grass. Don't worry about treading on the droppings. Although they stink, they are the cleanest stuff in the world. You'll want to hold your breath. But if you don't, many of your karmic hindrances[1] will dissipate then. Proceed without any fear. Although the pass is nar-row, it's wide enough for the horse to pass through. Once you cross the pass, you'll find a large open area. The grass there is very green and the

---

1. That is, karmic consequences that stand in the way of enlightenment.

water quite clear. You'll see an inconspicuous tent on the grassland. In the tent, you'll find a large wooden box that is, in fact, a coffin. You'll see a white-haired old man. His body looks dirty but has a mysterious fragrance. That is the vow-fragrance found only on those who observe all the Buddhist vows. This fragrance comes from the dharma-protecting heavenly being. You cannot see the heavenly being, but the heavenly being can see you.

You should kneel and kowtow to the old man. Just kowtow three times. And then tell him that you were sent there by Snow Feather who begs him for the pill of sweet dew. He will give it to you for sure. After he hands the pill to you, kneel down again, and do not rise. Because you are saving his disciple, you are helping him indirectly. In other words, he owes you. He will give you anything you ask. Of course, he will scold you. But don't rise even if he scolds you. You have to ask him for a technique. He will ask you which technique you want, and you will say that you only want the Bright Mahamudra. That was the technique the great sage Khyungpo Nalijor procured from India, after experiencing thousands of tribulations and dangers. Once you acquire that technique, obtaining release will be as easy as taking a candy from your own pocket.

The Horse Chomping on Hay at Night

So Jasper entered Old Mountain.

There were medicinal herbs in Old Mountain. The herbs in Old Mountain were the best. The real Old Mountain was in fact quite far away. It was already evening by the time Jasper left the city of Liang-zhou. He dared not enter Old Mountain in the evening. Even though horses had "night eyes," he was still afraid of entering it at night. Night belonged to the ghosts and spirits. He didn't want to enter the world of the ghosts and spirits. The halolike scars that looked like eyes on the front legs of the horses were their "night eyes." They would become effective once night approached. The folks of Diamond Clan all knew that if a horse begin to puff and salivate and refuse to proceed, then it had seen a ghost. There was nothing that ghosts fear more than saliva. Knowing that, horses would spit at the ghosts when they saw them. Although it was only evening, the horse was already sneezing and spitting. Jasper knew the place was filled with ghosts that had starved to death. Everyone at Diamond Clan knew the newly deceased would stay in purgatory for forty-nine days, reincarnating in seven days at the earliest and taking as long as forty-nine days at the latest. But there were also some wronged ghosts that had been roaming the village for more than a hundred years. Ajia said one became a wronged ghost when the sense of injustice felt by the deceased was so overwhelming that it could not dissipate. Those were the malicious ghosts. The power of malicious ghosts was immense. For example, Dou E was able to induce drought in her native land for three years.[2] Some malicious ghosts could be subdued by eminent priests and become dharma-protecting deities. According to Ajia, the guru Padma Sambhava[3] had subjugated many malicious ghosts who offered him their heart spells that could control them and made Buddhist vows. But Jasper was not able to subdue the ghosts who had starved to death. Sometimes they were in front of the horse; sometimes they went behind it. The horse was so afraid of them that it pursed its lips and spat continuously, spraying thousands of drops of saliva like a mist sprayer. To the ghosts, each drop was a bullet!

Jasper stayed at an empty home. The brick bed in the outer room had a quilt. He did not look at the inner room. There were many homes like this along the way. With all its members dead, they were, in fact, no longer homes. The ones who died earlier were in fact better off because they would be buried by those who died later and avoid having their bones exposed to the sun. It was said that those whose bones were exposed to the sun would turn into spirits. Jasper wanted to find a lit-up home, but he only saw corpses and bones along the way. No light could be seen. He visited several homes, but none had any residents. So he complied with fate and stayed in one of them. Jasper lay down on the brick bed with his clothes on. Wheat hay lined the bed. All the brick beds he saw in the village were lined with hay; the better-off ones used woven mats; the even better ones were lined with bed planks; the best ones were lined with rugs. If the entire household had died, any rug would have invariably been seized by others. Hay was fine—better to be indoors than outside. *I only need to lie down for a night—I'll head for Old Mountain bright and early next morning,* thought Jasper. According

2. Dou E is the protagonist of a renowned Yuan play by the name of "Injustices Done to Dou E."

3. Also known as the Lotus-born.

to the way Snow Feather had planned it, he should arrive there by noon, if he left early and all went well. Jasper pulled the horse into the room to have a living being there to boost his courage. He gave some hay to the horse. Normally, the hay fed to horses was chopped up using a guillotine chopper, but the horse was not fussy right now. Horses are an easygoing type of animal. It will eat hay that is not chopped up.

Have you ever listened to a horse chomping on hay in the dead of night? Well, in pitch darkness, you would find the crunch of the horse's teeth grinding the hay very monotonous but also quite charming. It was as if it had arrived from distant high antiquity—unadorned and lingering. The sound would bring a peaceful feeling. Jasper was thinking of a terrible ghost story, but as soon as he was immersed in the sound of the horse's chomping—ah, a feeling of peace wafted toward him. Like a wisp of mist, feelings of peace floated over slowly, scattered in waves and enveloped you. Your body and mind entered peacefulness. The peaceful Jasper wanted to look at the stars. If he had slept on the roof, he would have been able to see the stars. He wanted to see the stars through the window in the room. He thought if he could see stars, then tomorrow would be a fine day. He hoped the next day would be a fine day since Snow Feather also arranged for him to visit her mom. He remembered the kindly elderly woman. It must have been very scary for a blind old woman to stay in an old forest in a deep mountain. Snow Feather wanted him to bring her mom to the monastery. Since she had already been punished, there was nothing more to be afraid of. She felt calmer. It wasn't a bad thing after all.

There was a wan moon outside the window. With the wan moon shining on the window, the window also appeared pale. Phantoms seemed to appear in the room. Jasper looked at the horse; and the horse also looked at him, both thinking it was a good thing the other was there to prevent himself/itself from being lonely. Jasper became half-conscious in the midst of the horse chomping on hay in the dead of night.

He dreamt he was lying in a room lined with hay. A horse was spreading the noise of chomping on hay. He dreamt of a wan moon shining on the window. Phantoms seemed to appear in the room. A woman with her hair loose came out of the inner room, wearing clothes that had been bleached white by Grandpa Sun. Her clothes were torn and tattered. The woman sighed sorrowfully and stared at him eerily. After staring for a while, she approached him quietly, stretched out a hand, and rubbed Jasper's belly furiously. Jasper felt a stabbing cold on his belly and screamed. Shocked, the woman charged into the inner room. Jasper who was now awake heard the horse sneezing. Everything in the room looked exactly the same as in the dream, and his belly felt frozen. But there was no woman. Greatly puzzled, he got up and suspected that someone was in the inner room. A beam of light streamed down from the skylight directly onto the brick bed there. Sure enough, a woman was sleeping on the bed and wore the same faded and tattered clothes as in the dream. Moonlight shone on her face. Jasper's heart missed a beat: the woman's face was already rotten and gave off a sharp stench. Jasper almost screamed.

He shuddered and left the house with the horse. He was afraid the woman would chase after them. He'd heard that if sunlight or moonlight shone on a corpse for long enough, the corpse would become a spirit. In which case, it would possess unlimited power and no longer be a mere corpse. Many years ago, a disaster occurred in the village. At midnight every night, a large swarthy fellow riding on a tiger would kill people at the riverbank, brandishing a broadsword as large as a door. Jasper heard that those who tried to block that fellow were routed and their blood formed a river. And then, Monk Wu performed a technique to subjugate him. The technique he practiced was the Yamantaka Fire Offering Execution Technique. He put himself in isolation and performed the technique for seven days, before he finally subdued the demon. Monk Wu led the villagers to a bird's nest in the mountain gully where they found a dead child with a small knife in its hand astride a dead cat. Because the corpse was on a tree, it was not eaten by wolves, snakes, tigers, or leopards. Furthermore, having absorbed the essences of heaven and earth and touched a metal weapon, it was able to become a spirit. Jasper had heard that when the villagers chopped the dead youngster in half, scarlet blood flowed from his corpse. Such spirits were always appearing in the village—it was said that many of them became yakshas, malevolent spirits.

Jasper rode by letting the horse go wherever it wanted. It occurred to him that the woman must have meant to remind him about the chill with good intentions, so he would not catch a cold. When he told Monk Wu about the dream later, the monk thought so too. Jasper then regretted having left the place. He thought how woeful it must have been for the woman, if her good intentions resulted in driving him away!

The horse was heading in the direction of Old Mountain. Jasper decided against sleeping some more. Since he didn't know how long he had slept, he had no idea as to the time. He thought he would go to the entrance of Old Mountain in any case. If it was still dark then, he would gather some twigs to build a fire and proceed into the mountain as soon as the east turned white. So, he managed to save time this way quite unexpectedly.

A wolf howled in the distance, and the ears of the horse perked up. This was how horses signify alertness and indicated that the horse didn't like the sound. It also used its perked-up ears to remind Jasper to be careful and that the direction they were heading had many wolves and wasn't pleasant. Jasper patted the horse's neck, which was equivalent to saying, "What are you afraid of, coward?" Thereupon, the horse relaxed its nervous ears in embarrassment.

He must not have slept very long, because the sky looked the same when he reached the entrance of Old Mountain. Fortunately, Monk Wu told him to take along some matches. He gathered some twigs and grass, and lit a fire. He then chose a grassy patch and tied the reins around a large rock nearby. Although the horse was a military horse, it was nevertheless a horse and could misbehave. When I was young, I once herded a black-maned horse from our team. It pretended to be well-behaved, so I was fooled into wrapping the reins around its neck. Who would have known that the minute I turned away, it escaped to the Huangcheng Grassland several hundred leagues away. Dad followed the imprint of its hoofs for ten days before he found it at the grassland where it was born and raised. From then on, whenever I herded it again, I would tie its reins on one of its front hoofs. The distance between its head and hoof was no more than two feet, so it could only bend its head and eat grass. Should it decide to escape, it could only do so at a wobbly gallop like Cripple Big. Consequently, Jasper would not dare to be lax. He wrapped the reins around a rock.

The minute the fire was lit, night became gentle. What fire brought for humans was not only gentleness but also a sense of security, as wild animals feared fire. He had heard that ghosts were also afraid of fire. Whenever Jasper returned home from a long trip when he was young, Mom would invariably build a fire in front of the gate and have him jump over it, as oftentimes unclean stuff might follow one home. Diamond Clan referred to wronged ghosts as "the unclean ones." Having one follow you home would be as unlucky as having an owl in the house. Should the wronged ghost seek a substitute, someone would die in the home the same way it died. If it was the ghost of someone who died from hanging, then a member of your household would commit suicide by hanging. If it was someone who died from bleeding, then someone in the household would die from bleeding. And so on. If you suddenly felt like committing suicide, then an unclean one must have followed you home. You'll have to say to yourself, "The myriad techniques depend on knowledge; salvation and release depend on the mind. Leave if you wish, why find a substitute?" You'll stop wanting to commit suicide the minute you say the above. If the ghost you met has the potential for enlightenment, he might even become enlightened through understanding the words; in which case, you've essentially brought him salvation. More often than not, however, the wronged ghost merely wanted some spending money. You should then just burn some mock money to dispatch it. Hence, fire was the best thing. However, it is said that although ghosts fear fire, they are only deterred by fires with flames. When only a fire's embers remain, ghosts would gather around it to warm themselves. So Jasper gathered more twigs to build a roaring fire, lest he invite in a horde of starving ghosts.

The horse's chomping on grass in the dead of night resounded again. Horses are the best of animals. It would have been lonely for Jasper if he'd had to travel at night without the horse. Jasper shoved the fire toward the horse but not too close, lest the smoke bother it. Gradually, sleep overcame him. So he moved toward the horse and drifted away.

When the brightness of a dream gradually expanded, Jasper found himself in another nightmare.

Chapter 19

The "Nirvana" of *Nightmares*

I shouted and shouted until I was hoarse,
But only dead silence was the reply.
        Among the vast sea of humans,
Yet I am unable to scoop up,
        The seeking pupils of my eyes.
By my ears, only the whistling of the autumnal wind,
Before my eyes, only the footprints of impermanence.

Territory

In Jasper's nightmare, the folks of Brilliant King Clan arrived, walking along the stream and yelling in unison. That stream used to belong to both clans. But later, Brilliant King Clan, which had a larger population, said the spring belonged to them. The crowd roared in unison, the noise shook heaven and earth, and the spring became theirs.

Unfortunately, they lived downstream. Although the water flowed downward, the spring originated upstream. So the folks of Diamond Clan planted trees by the stream; they built a mill with a house over it and a water wheel next to it. When the water turned the wheel, the mill would crank and grind.

In the nightmare, Cripple Big was in charge of the mill. A bachelor, he and his aged mother were dependent on each other. Cripple Big was a dutiful son. Whenever people came to use the mill and gave him food, he would leave the thick porridge for Mom and slurp the thin part himself. He was quite robust, nevertheless.

331

The folks of Brilliant King Clan swarmed upstream. They pulled up the trees, dismantled the bridge, and hollered, "This is our territory! You can't plant trees and build bridges here!"

And then they shouted at Cripple Big, "You can't put a mill here either!"

Several dozen men wrapped palm fibers around the millstone a few times, pulled together in unison, and demolished the mill. A burst of dust soared.

Cripple Big wailed, "Fuck your grandma! You expect me to eat wind?"

Someone came up and said, "Eat this!" He waved his hand and sand filled Cripple Big's mouth.

The villagers looked on from the mountain, cursing and hollering. But no one dared to go down the mountain. Those from Brilliant King Clan were also afraid of going up the mountain. The pile of stones on the mountain was perched to charge down. They'd never seen the folks of Brilliant King Clan so united and ominous. They also knew that the opponents wished to enrage and goad them to go down the mountain in order to take advantage of a free fight.

"Are you all dead?" Cripple Big twisted his neck up the mountain and hollered.

"When a rock is too big, we have walk around it!" replied Braggart.

"Kuan San! Kuan San!" yelled Cripple Big.

Kuan San stuck his head out of the stockade and laughed, "What are you shouting for? A gentleman does not stand under a collapsing wall!"

"You, a gentleman!" The folks of Brilliant King Clan roared in laughter. They poured oil on the planks in the mill and set fire to them. Flames shot up. The young trees that the villagers had so painstakingly planted were also snapped and thrown into the fire.

However, Grandpa Jiu was laughing, "You're digging your own grave!" Jasper understood what he meant. Many years later, a massive mudslide would overrun Brilliant King Clan and fix the impermanent village into relative permanence.

"Let's dig up everything!" one of them shouted. They lifted their spades and turned over the fields that the folks of Diamond Clan had created next to the stream. The green saplings turned into mud.

Jasper shouted, "Don't waste them! You can have them when they are ready for harvest!"

Braggart said, "Sonny—be careful you break that tongue of yours! You can't say anything like that—you're not the head of the clan!"

"This is wasting a gift from Heaven!" said Jasper.

"Go ahead and bury them," hollered Cripple Big, "we'll complain to the Gonpo!"

The folks of Brilliant King Clan burst out laughing. One of them said, "Don't you know? We are here by the Gonpo's order! We do whatever his Reverence bids!"

"Crap! It's all crap!" shouted Braggart. He then turned around to the villagers and whispered, "What are we going to do if they dig at the dam? That's all the water we've got. If they destroy the dam, we won't even have enough water for drinking, let alone irrigating the fields!"

Before he finished his sentence, the folks of Brilliant King Clan had already begun to hack at the dam. The splashing of water became increasingly louder.

"Stop!" Braggart said, "The rule was established by the county government. You might want to drown yourselves, but you can't let us die from drought!"

"What rule?" one of the opponents said, "rules are made by people, so they can be changed by people!"

Another continued, "Even the reverent Gonpo is always changing his commands. Suddenly something is white; suddenly it's black. It all depends on his mood—he's the Gonpo after all!"

"Furthermore," continued someone else, "he gave the order to destroy the dam!"

Grandpa Jiu laughed, "Everything is the Gonpo's order—what a Gonpo!"

Cripple Big wailed. Jasper said, "Don't cry. Let them break the dam. They break it, we'll repair it! Let them destroy the mill. They destroy it, we'll rebuild it!"

The folks of Brilliant King Clan shouted, "We'll destroy them again and again!"

Jasper also hollered, "We'll repair them again and again!" He turned around to the villagers and said, "Such is life!"

The Plague

According to *True Records of the Curses*, the plague began with a black sheep. The sheep turned to its side and twisted its body into a figure eight. Eyes staring, it suddenly jumped a few times, fell onto the ground, convulsed a few times, and then died.

Kuan San said, "Wow! This sheep danced!" He took it and skinned it in no time. Although he could not bleed it, he nevertheless cooked it up in a large pot and let some big fellas eat it. The men's heads steamed from the sweat.

Mom told Jasper, "Don't eat it—I won't let you eat the meat of dead animals." "All the meat we ate was from animals that died!" laughed Jasper. "I meant animals that died on their own," Mom laughed and added.

The big fellas yelled, "Yum! Yum!"

Mom said, "Eat up then!"

In the evening, the manager of Diamond Monastery came and said, "Strange! Many of the sheep at the monastery also died. They died the same way!" Mom said, "In the past, many also died this way. Medicines were useless." "And then?" asked the manager. "And then, there were no more sheep."

A terrible situation.

But the manager said, "Terrible, but there's worse. You know Ajia is going around talking nonsense. It's heresy. He says the Gonpo also snores, the Gonpo has to be validated by the Buddha, the Buddha has to be validated by the heart. So everything is validated by the heart . . . He's making everyone nervous."

"What's wrong with that?" asked Mom.

"Everything! Everyone has a heart. If all you need is validation by the heart, what do we need the Gonpo for? If this gets around, then the world will be a mess. Do you know that a few young monks at Diamond Clan have begun to disobey the guru?"

"This Ajia . . ." Mom wanted to say something but sighed instead.

Jasper knew Ajia has been visiting people lately and talking a lot. This is what happens when one is out of one's wits. Jasper left, intending to find Ajia and persuade him to stop telling the truth.

"This Ajia is worse than the plague. He's a flood and a fierce beast—this is what the Gonpo said." Jasper heard the manager saying this as he left. He thought, *That Gonpo is certainly all knowing. There's been barely a sign.*

"Of course he's all knowing. Look!" Ajia pointed to a grove of swaying flowers on the slope, "Even the flowers are spies. That tree," he pointed to a cedar tree, "is also a spy. They may look naive, but the minute you turn around, they'll betray you."

"I believe you," said Jasper. "Sometimes even the heart can betray you."

"That which betrays is not one's heart—it's one's consciousness. The heart is that which can discover the betrayal." Ajia squinted, shot a glance at the clouds and said, "I know my crime is so great that I'll die without burial. Do you remember a few years ago when that young man said the sky had nothing but air and ended up being burned alive? How can the sky be nothing but air? Should that be the case, where would Heaven be?"

"Heaven is in the heart," said Jasper.

"Be careful. If someone hears this, you'll also become a flood and a fierce beast too! Everyone needs a Heaven, a real Heaven that resides among the white clouds. If you say it's in the heart, then they'd feel their Heaven is gone. Without Heaven, there's no paradise, and the Gonpo would lose his job. Look!" He pointed to a row of crosses. "They've just been crucified."

"You're allowed to do anything but think," said Ajia.

Jasper wasn't sure he understood.

"I finally found out who the Gonpo is. He's an old monk from somewhere else, an ordinary monk who didn't say much. It's hard to figure out the depth of people who say little, so he appeared sophisticated. One day he came here. Someone said he's a Gonpo from elsewhere and invited him to take the seat of honor. So he began to think that he was a Gonpo himself. All the people around him called him "Gonpo." After people called him Gonpo for a thousand—or ten thousand—times, he became a Gonpo. Once he became a Gonpo, then those who needed a Gonpo sought after him to depend on him. Some believed in him; others feigned flattery. Gradually they formed a group. They swindled food and drinks out of people, basked in the glory of the Gonpo, and performed elaborate Buddhist rites. . . . After that, he became a veritable Gonpo."

"Did he have the powers of a Gonpo?"

"Of course he does. Once he became a Gonpo, then he had the powers of a Gonpo. When everyone needs a Gonpo, then he will have the powers of a Gonpo. There was a monk at Diamond Monastery who always saw a Gonpo during meditation, sparkling with golden light. One day, I told him, get some dust from *The Great Buddhist Sutra*, mix it with water, and wash your eyes with it before you look at the Gonpo again. At first, the image was still that of a dignified Buddha, but gradually, the golden light disappeared, the characteristics of the thirty-two sages vanished along with the eighty traits of beauty. All he saw was a wrinkled old monk wearing a soiled robe. That was when he realized that the Gonpo was the impersonation of a malicious ghost!"

"What happened next?"

"After that, he died. Some say he committed suicide. But who knows? Those who know the truth can't live out their natural span of life. Hey, I know you are listening—but I'm not scared of you!" Ajia hollered at the flowers. A mysterious titter was transmitted by the wind.

"It'll be my turn next," said Ajia.

"Are you scared?"

"Of course," replied Ajia. "Death is a huge black hole—it's bottomless—that's why I want to live. I know life is illusory, like a fly traveling through the void leaving no trace. But I still want to rebel against the illusion. So I did my best to practice, to learn, to discover, to create—all to hopefully create something relatively permanent in this void. But I know it's all useless. Many years later, even the universe will explode. Then, all the relatively permanent things will vanish permanently in the void. All existence will become a huge void. That's why I'm both afraid and unafraid. What makes me afraid is evidence that I've lived."

Ajia smiled bitterly. He suddenly became haggard.

"I'm a firefly," Ajia coughed lightly, "although I know I can't change the world, I still try to give off my own light."

"You've become thinner," said Jasper.

"That's because I'm spending my life's energy. Right now, all my thoughts come from the depth of my life. All the philosophers use their lives to light their thoughts. Those who write books, transform their lives into books. Those who lecture transform their lives into speech. Those who act transform their lives into action. At the same time they manifest their own worth, their lives are also spent. But these will become the only existence in the void. This is the reason for living. Look at me . . ."

Ajia was pale and haggard, but a holy light shone on his face. "I'm going underground. They've begun to search for me. I'm not afraid of them, but I'm still going down there. It's not that I'm afraid of death, but I want to live in order to shine some more light. However, my fate will follow me no matter what!"

He entered a cave in the ground as he spoke.

Man Under the Ground

The plague was spreading. Sheep corpses were scattered all over the slope like snow. Even some of the large draught animals fell. Because Uncle had gone on a pilgrimage, the villagers asked the manager of Diamond

Monastery to submit a request to the mountain deity on their behalf. They wanted the deity to dispatch a wolf deity to get rid of the plague. Three days later, the black wolf began howling on the mountaintop. But the domestic animals continued to die in droves.

Someone said, "We should go ask the Gonpo about it!"

Everyone else said, "How come we hadn't thought of it?" They immediately prepared offerings and had the manager take them to the Gonpo for assistance. When the manager returned that night, all the villagers surrounded him. Wanting to know what the Gonpo looked like, Jasper squeezed to the front and asked, "What does the Gonpo look like?" The manager laughed and said, "How would I know what he looks like? But I did get his edict." Jasper asked, "So you didn't see the Gonpo?" "How would I get to see him? He was in isolation. A red string connected him to the outside." "Which cave?" "How would I know?" Jasper thought it very strange. He wanted to find out the origin of the edict; but seeing how everyone was looking at him askance and knowing they must have thought it unseemly for him to question the existence of the Gonpo, he zipped his mouth discreetly.

"The Gonpo said someone put a curse on them," said the manager.

Everyone clamored, "No wonder they are dying in droves!" "No wonder the wolf god couldn't drive away the plague demon!"

"Who put on the curse?"

"The Gonpo didn't say. But the Khenpo performed a divination which said that it was an underground person."

"An underground person?" said someone. "Maybe it's a ghost!"

Jasper thought of Ajia immediately. His heart throttled and he slipped away when no one was watching. He went to the well in the backyard and said to the well, "Ajia—someone is after you. Leave!" The well transmitted his voice to Ajia in the distance. Bubbles welled up. Ajia's voice burst out of the bubbles, "How can I escape fate?"

Jasper sighed. He lifted his head and saw a raven on a tree snickering at him. Jasper knew that it had heard their conversation, so he hollered, "I don't care if you've heard—you can't find him!"

The raven quacked and flew away.

The Red-Beaked Raven

Grandpa Jiu was playing with sheep shoulder bones, with five little girls. One of the girls cheated and Grandpa Jiu wailed.

Mom came over and said to Jasper, "Remember, when I die, be sure that you don't find anyone else. Just get that Grandpa Jiu and give this to him." Mom took off a necklace of turquoise stones, "No, present it as an offering and ask him to perform the salvation rites for me."

"What are you saying this for?"

"Remember, this is of utmost importance!" Mom said. "He's mad—it's so . . ." said Jasper. "Don't speak nonsense!" continued Mom, "When I was twenty years old, I knew he was a real monk; at thirty, I knew that he had attained the Way; at forty, I knew he was a guru of great accomplishments; at fifty, I knew he'd already become a Buddha."

Unexpectedly, Grandpa Jiu turned around and spoke to Mom, "You won't die—your inner organs are all there! Right, Jasper?"

Jasper stuck out his tongue secretly. He was beginning to believe what Mom had just said. Once, he suddenly noticed that someone in the village had no inner organs. The person's abdomen was as empty as a stove chamber. The person died shortly after. Since then, Jasper knew someone would die whenever he saw a person without inner organs. So he asked Grandpa Jiu, "Can you also see if people have inner organs?" "No, I can't. But I can tell that you can!" laughed Grandpa Jiu.

Jasper turned to Mom and said, "He's right. You have all your inner organs. You won't die." Mom smiled. She put the turquoise necklace around his neck and said, "Don't forget what Mom said."

Jasper remembered that Ajia not only had inner organs, but they emitted a light not found in others. So he thought with a sense of relief, "He won't die!"

The villagers had already begun to dig for the underground man. Some went down the wells, some dug into the ground, some searched the mountain caves—what a mess! The Gonpo dispatched two men to assist the villagers. They called themselves monks but wore regular clothes. During the day, they performed divination and fixed the area for the search. But at night, they would slip into the home of the "Heavenly Girl" and fill the village with lascivious screams. But no one dared to fart about it since they were the Gonpo's men.

The next day, they said, "Look for the red-beaked ravens!"

So the villagers followed the red-beaked ravens, a type of raven with red beaks. No one knew where they came from. Jasper suspected they were sent by the Gonpo. They were the Gonpo's spies, like the flowers on the mountain. He remembered a raven overhearing when he was warning Ajia at the well. *Although that wasn't a red-beaked raven, it was a raven, nevertheless. Could it betray Ajia?*

Grandpa Jiu said, "Who told him to give his body as alms? What an idiot. Why give his body as alms just now? The moment he gives his body, the red-beaked raven will go for his flesh. It'll be a wonder if he's not found!"

Although Grandpa Jiu was talking to himself, Jasper knew what he was talking about. That technique of giving one's body as alms was something Ajia practiced frequently. During the practice, he would invite over all the wronged ghosts, the parents of the Six Paths,[1] and all living beings of the Buddhist realm. He would cut off his own head and transform it into a huge alms bowl. And then slice off in turn his eyes, ears, nose, tongue, body, etc., place them into the alms bowl, transform them into sweet dew, and offer it to the multitude. Of course, this was all done through visualization. It was through such visualizations that Ajia transformed from being a minor monk into Ajia. All his wisdom was derived from that almsgiving.

"Everyone says that Heaven will exterminate those who do not fend for themselves. But he gives away even his own body and mind. How absolutely unfilial![2] And they call me mad? Talk about a real madman!" Grandpa Jiu babbled on, his disheveled hair burning in the wind.

Jasper said, "Mom said that you are some guru of great achievement. I don't believe it, but Mom does. You should save Ajia!"

"Are they going to kill your mom?" Grandpa Jiu rolled his eyes.

"No! They're going to kill Ajia." Jasper was sweating from anxiety.

"Does Ajia believe in me?"

"No, he doesn't."

"Well, then I can't save him. Those who believe in the Gonpo, can be saved by the Gonpo. Those who believe in me can be saved by me. Those who don't believe in anyone, can't be saved by anyone!"

"There's no way to save him then?"

"Not necessarily. Unless he believes in himself—it's called self-belief. But he lost faith in himself a long time ago. He believes in fate. The

---

1. The Six Paths consist of those of humans, heaven, Asura malevolent spirits, beasts, Hell, and starving ghosts.

2. According to Confucianism, which upholds the ideal of filial piety, one derived one's body from the parents; hence, any harm done to the body was considered unfilial.

snake of fate has already swallowed his faith." Grandpa Jiu left singing, "My shoes are tattered, my hat is tattered, the cassock I'm wearing is tattered."

Jasper said, "You're not Jigong,[3] so why are you singing this song?"

"Who said that I'm not Jigong? I'm whoever I want to be!" hollered Granpa Jiu.

Jasper then thought, *This song won't be around until a few hundred years later, how come he knows it?*

Placing a Curse

The villagers found the cave by following the red-beaked ravens that sought after the flesh. A huge alms bowl hovered in the sky above the cave. The bowl was filled with all manner of stuff transformed from Ajia's flesh. The gluttonous red-beaked ravens were all there, and the villagers followed them.

"Hey! Come out of there—you who placed the curse!" one of them shouted.

"Come out of there!" the crowd roared.

Jasper screamed, "Don't come out! They'll kill you!"

Kuan San shoved him aside, "Leave! How can you help an outsider? Your family's sheep are all dead, and you're still helping him?"

Jasper said, "Ajia didn't place a curse. He's always practicing the giving of his body as alms. How can someone, practicing this, place a curse?" Someone laughed, "Listen to the boy! Do you think anyone practicing a death technique won't place a curse? Hey, could all the animals die if he didn't practice a death technique?"

"Come out! Come out—practitioner of Death Technique!" hollered Cripple Big. Jasper thought, *Slaves are sometimes even more vicious than masters!*

Ajia came out of the cave lazily. Having squatted in darkness for so long, he now tumbled into darkness under sunlight. He rubbed his eyes. His rosary beads swung side to side. Fearing that the villagers would get him, Jasper stood in front of Ajia and yelled, "Ajia would not place a curse!"

---

3. Ji Gong (1130–1207) was a Chan/Zen Buddhist monk known for performing crazy acts.

Kuan San said, "Would the Gonpo wrong him?" Cripple Big said, "Even we wouldn't wrong him, much less the Gonpo!" Another continued, "If the Gonpo said that he placed the curse, then he placed the curse. He placed the curse even if he didn't."

Ajia could gradually see the people before him. Kuan San went up, gave him a good kick, and said, "Fiend! You've killed ten thousand sheep! Fucking die ten thousand times, you'll still owe!" Someone said, "If he can't pay this life, there's always the next!"

Ajia asked nonchalantly, "Whatever the Gonpo said was his business. Do you also think I placed the curse?"

"This is what the Gonpo thought. If the Gonpo thought so, then we also think so," one of them answered.

Ajia shot a glance at Jasper and smiled bitterly, "Just look at this—to think I wanted to transform myself into light and illuminate them!" Kuan San said, "Why not illuminate yourself!" Cripple Big said, "Yeah! If you can't save yourself, how can you save others?" Another added, "If you're rolling in dung, how can you make others clean?"

"Maybe," said Ajia, "you're right. Did the Gonpo really say I did it?"

"Yes, of course he did! How would we know if he didn't? Even if we know you're wronged, once the Gonpo said so, we'll have to wrong you!" said Cripple Big.

A hoarse, aged voice wafted over, "Cripple Big—how can you say something like this? If you continue, you'll become an Ajia too!" Jasper turned around. Everyone also turned in surprise, but no one knew who spoke.

"Die! Die!" quacked the raven.

Ajia told Jasper, "I'm not afraid to die. Jasper, even if I die, I won't be dead. I'll continue to illuminate them."

"Crap! You're full of crap!" someone shouted.

Ajia turned around to face the crowd and said, "Since you accuse me of placing a curse, then I'll do one!" He yanked at his rosary beads with both hands; the beads scattered, "I swear as a Dharma-Protecting deity of Xixia—when I die, I will transform into a malevolent ghost and exact revenge!"

Kuan San wanted to charge at him and cover his mouth, but Ajia's curse was already placed. It was said that the power of this curse came from Xixia.

"Revenge! Revenge!" the black bird quacked. This was when Jasper realized this black bird was not a raven but a parrot. He suspected this was the one that had leaked Ajia's secret and shook his head in annoyance.

The Seed of Fire

Ajia was lashed a thousand times. His back turned to mush. Ajia groaned but continued to curse. Although the villagers cheered, they shivered within. Ajia's curses rolled like stones in their hearts.

"Revenge! Revenge!" shouted Ajia.

"Slice off his tongue!" the others said.

A flick of the knife, a piece of flesh popped out of Ajia's mouth. The parrot flew over, snatched it, and downed it in one gulp.

"Revenge! Revenge!" the parrot also shouted.

Ajia's mouth was filled with blood. He could no longer speak, but his eyes continued to release black curses causing people to shudder. The big tree outside the Ancestral Hall withered all of a sudden. This tree had been around for a hundred years and was the pride of the village; yet it died. The manager said, "This is bad. One rat can ruin a whole pot of soup. One person places a curse, everyone loses peace!" However, a voice was heard, "If no one places curses, everyone would sleep like dead hogs. What's so great about that?" This was not a familiar voice. They searched but couldn't tell who had said it. Jasper looked at the parrot, which turned its head and ignored everyone.

In the midst of the ruckus, an elderly man arrived. His hair and beard were hoary white, but his eyes were shining black. He said, "I'm from Brilliant King Clan. We heard you're executing someone who places curses. The clan head asked me to come. He said we'll take him if you don't want him. We need someone who can curse; everyone is falling asleep."

The clan head asked the villagers, "Shall we give him to them?"

"No!" shouted the villagers. "We are for anything that the enemy is against. If they want him, we'll keep him!"

The old man laughed. "You're actually helping him by not giving him to us. If you give him to us, he'll just be a cripple. But if you refuse, he'll accomplish accumulating merit!"

"What merit?" asked the clan head.

The old man said, "Don't you see how all the philosophers became famous once they became martyrs? For example, Socrates, and Christ—

they all exchanged immediate death for perpetual life. I'm doing this as a favor for you. Besides, this Ajia released another type of curse, aside from cursing the cattle and sheep. This other type of curse is really terrifying. But we need the curse. Look, everyone is falling asleep. We'll rot on our own without the sting of a gadfly."

"We don't understand what you're saying," said Kuan San, "But one thing for sure—we won't give whatever you want. He's doomed to die."

The old man laughed out loud and said, "I was just trying my best, knowing it wouldn't have worked anyway. Although this Ajia looks weak, his mind is in fact a seed for fire. I was just hoping to preserve some seed of fire for the world. Nothing I can do if you insist on killing him. Fortunately, we've still got parrots in this world. Hey!" he shouted. The parrot flew over and landed on his shoulder. "So long as the parrot remains, Ajia's words won't die even if he dies. If his words don't die, then he won't die!"

Kuan San, "Why listen to the crap? Get the hell out of here!"

The old man laughed out loud and left.

Tears pouring down his face, Ajia followed the old man with his eyes.

Jasper thought he had seen the man before. He didn't think that he was from Brilliant King Clan. *Is he a transformation of Grandpa Jiu?* he wondered.

Although Ajia's back had turned to mush, the villagers were still not willing to let him go. Jasper knew they intended to kill him. Although he knew the villagers would consider his words as farts, he nevertheless begged, "I beg of you, please release Ajia! Look, he already got what he deserved!"

"Release him?" laughed Goodie Wang. This Goodie was the most benevolent person in the village. But good people can be even worse than evil people when they turn malicious. Jasper saw some compassion in the eyes of many but only malice in Goodie. Jasper knew that he was trying to use malice to prove his goodness.

Goodie Wang said, "This is no ordinary human being. He is a demon, and demons have to be subjugated! Last time, I almost lost faith in the Gonpo because of what he said. Horrible! Simply intolerable!"

Jasper said, "How can faith be real faith if you can be persuaded otherwise?"

"Of course it's real faith!" said Goodie Wang. "Everything can be persuaded! People with no faith, will have faith from listening to people talk and talk about faith. Truth that didn't exist will exist when people talk and talk about the truth. He didn't place the curse, but people kept on saying he did—then he did. He didn't deserve death, but people kept on saying he did, so he does!"

Kuan San yelled, "What's all the bullshit? Whose side are you on? Stop the bullshit! Should he die or not?"

"Of course he should!" said Goodie Wang. "Who else is there? We all need a scapegoat! Who told you to save the human race, Ajia? All those who want to save the human race should die!"

Jasper was confused. He didn't know whether this Goodie was good or evil. These words were loaded. Jasper looked at the poor Ajia and thought, *I've got to think of a way to save him!*

Jasper dashed to the stockade to see Braggart. Only Braggart could save Ajia now. Unexpectedly, Braggart was building a fire that just got lit. Smoke soared from it. Some people were shoveling yak butter onto the firewood.

"What's this for?" asked Jasper.

"To worship Heaven," answered Braggart. He was rather surprised, as his son hadn't spoken to him for many days. So he asked, "What's up?"

Jasper gulped and asked, "Can you save Ajia?"

Braggart looked around and said, "I was just going to save him!" He turned to Kuan San and said, "Go! Take a few men and bring Ajia here!"

Jasper went with Kuan San and the others to look for Ajia. But he had disappeared. There was a bundle of thorns on top of the mountain. Ajia's moaning could be heard from the bundle. Jasper yelled, "Ajia's in there!" Kuan San folded his arms and looked relaxed. Seeing how anxious Jasper was, he smiled and said, "Kid, in a while you'll see I'm being compassionate. Don't you know sometimes cruelty is the greatest compassion?"

What kind of logic is that? thought Jasper.

As they spoke, the villagers had already lifted the bundle and tossed it down the mountain. A black dot tumbled down, sometimes bumping up, sometimes falling down. Ajia's cries became barely audible. Jasper then remembered that Ajia no longer had a tongue, but even someone without a tongue could yell. "Ajia will die!" screamed Jasper. He remembered that in the past, only the worst criminals were punished this way. He thought, *Why do the villagers hate Ajia so much?*

Suddenly, Jasper understood. The villagers had always hated Ajia because he was so different from them. Even if there was no plague, no edict from the Gonpo, Ajia wouldn't have been allowed to live for long. Who told Ajia to be Ajia? This village didn't need someone with a clear head. Then he thought, *Could all the sheep that died also hate Ajia? Why did they pick this particular moment to die and create so much hatred for Ajia?* Surprisingly, all the corpses of the sheep on the slopes in the wilderness revived and were bleating!

So, thought Jasper, *all swindlers—they all pretended to be dead so Ajia would suffer!*

That Kuan San had already run down the mountain. He carried Ajia and dashed up again like wind.

Jasper thought, *Dad was Dad after all! Blood is thicker than water—he'll do me the favor!*

Illumination

When Jasper rushed over, Ajia was already put on a rack over the fire. He was still alive and was writhing in the fire. When he heard Jasper's scream, Kuan San dashed over and held back Jasper. Braggart smiled from a distance and said, "Don't meddle, Son! I'm dressing his wounds!" Jasper knew Dad's trick. He'd sound like honey but harbor a dagger in his heart. So he hollered, "What did Ajia ever do to you? They hated him because they feared him. Why do you get mixed up in it?" Braggart laughed and said, "I'm dressing his wounds!" He took a shovel and tossed a few chunks of yak butter into the fire as he spoke.

Jasper squatted down and wept. There was really no one who could save Ajia in this world. Ajia will die for sure. The roaring fire burned explosively. It must have been the oil in Ajia's body. *Could such a thin body like Ajia's have any fat?* Jasper wondered.

Braggart announced loudly, "Didn't he want to illuminate others? Now, he can really do it!"

Jasper opened his eyes. It was already dark, and the fire indeed illuminated the sky. The crowd below the mountain was watching the fire seriously. Ajia had already left the bonfire. He was squatting on top of the flagpole of the stockade and smiling at Jasper.

Jasper now believed Dad was really dressing Ajia's wounds. But then he thought, *What kind of dressing is this?*

Then he heard Dad holler, "Crush the bones and mix it with the hog feed!"

Chapter 20

The Pilgrimage

I died again and again, and was born again and again,
　　　　Playing a dazzling variety of roles.
　　　　Life and death, continuing perpetually;
Sometimes a cow, sometimes a horse, sometimes a pig,
　　　　But unable to free myself from the millstone of fate.
　　　　No one could tell me
The way out for the soul.

The Leech Gully

At some point, the horse suddenly sneezed loudly. Jasper saw the horse staring at him with its blue eyes. He told the horse, "I had another nightmare." The horse shook its head and smiled. Horses just sway their jaws when they smile. It said, "Don't worry, I often have nightmares too!" The horse said it in its mind, but Jasper understood it anyway. "In my nightmares, I would go back to when I was a colt. I was a prince among the horses then, a red horse prince. White horse princes[1] were not popular on the military horse farm you know—red horse princes were the most sought after. Many fillies chased after me, but I was only interested in one beautiful filly. She was the most exquisite being. The two of us sported as we galloped through the grassland. The earth darted underneath our hoofs, and wind raised our manes. We were swifter than

---

1. *Baima wangzi* (White horse prince), usually refers to princes riding on white horses in Western fairytales.

347

clouds and nimbler than butterflies. We looked forward to the future. My dream was to sire a flock of ponies with her. All the colts would be as strong as me, while all the fillies would be beautiful as her. Before I realized my dream, however, they put a rope around my neck and gouged out those eggs of mine that used to jiggle whenever I galloped. Thus I became a gelded horse. I've been in a nightmare ever since. No one could understand my suffering. Actually, no—one person could have. His name was Sima Qian. You can read his letter to his friend, Ren An."[2]

Jasper patted the horse's neck and said, "My nightmares are different from yours. Yours are physical, but mine are spiritual. When your body vanishes, your nightmares will vanish. But mine are different. I can't get away from the nightmares when I'm alive, and they won't end after I die."

The horse sighed, "It's the same, it's really the same! Physical nightmares frequently transform into spiritual nightmares. Don't you see how the souls of the starving ghosts continue to wail, although their bodies suffered from hunger?" It sneezed emphatically as it spoke.

Jasper opened his eyes. The horse was staring at him earnestly. He suspected that the conversation he just had was conducted through a dream, so he smiled.

The fire's embers had already burned out. Jasper's throat felt a bit scratchy—maybe he'd caught a cold. He looked around, but didn't see any ghosts. *The east was already bright. I'd better be on my way!* he thought. He usually started out shortly before daybreak whenever he traveled. Loosening the reins, he mounted the horse and proceeded through the entrance to Old Mountain. He pulled out the darted lasso Snow Feather had given him to boost his courage. She bid him not to lose it because Mom would only follow him back to the village after touching it. Aside from that, it also had many other uses.

Jasper told the horse, "Let's go, Brother! Let's not talk about nightmares anymore. We can't free ourselves from them anyway!" The horse was as quiet as Sha Wujing[3] as it carried Jasper.

---

2. Sima Qian (145 BCE–90) was a famous historian of the Han dynasty and was considered the father of Chinese historiography for his monumental work, *Records of the Grand Historian*. He was castrated at the command of Emperor Wudi (r.141–87 BCE) for defending a general and subsequently decided to live on to finish writing the history rather than committing suicide as was expected of a gentleman scholar. His "Letter to Ren An" expounded his suffering and explained the reasons for his resolve.

3. Also known as Sandy, Sha Wujing is one of Tripitaka's disciples in the Ming novel, *Journey to the West*.

The sky had become brighter. There were no rosy clouds in the east, which was good, as it might rain if clouds were to burn there. Although Jasper was not worried about losing his way, he didn't like rain, particularly when he traveled. The splattering rain always affected his mood. He gulped down some food and thought of Snow Feather. A warm sensation stirred in his heart.

The air in Old Mountain was very humid. Fog rolled in from a valley close by. The horse's hoofs made a crisp clattering sound on the stones of the mountain path. Birds chirped in the mist. *Nature is so beautiful!* thought Jasper, *It continues to be lovely, regardless of all the starvations and deaths among the people.* As he thought of the situation in the village, he felt as though he had entered Heaven.

Sure enough, there were six small pathways leading from the main road on the right. One of them was filled with wild chrysanthemums as large as the sunflowers in the village. Most of them were yellow. Many bees buzzed. *Aren't bees not supposed to be able to fly in fog?* thought Jasper. One can never tell about a lot of things, but then he thought maybe it was something he'd imagined. Another pathway was filled with mountain peaches. The peaches were only as large as the thumb. If it were springtime, red peach flowers would have covered the path! Mountain peaches are sour and tart—not at all tasty. But if you crack open its pit and roast the kernel, then you can make a very tasty tea with it. Some monkeys were fighting over the mountain peaches. They were too involved in their squabble to notice Jasper approaching on horse. Jasper entered the third pathway on the left. Ordinary trees and weeds grew there, and fog-drenched stones lay about the ground haphazardly. Jasper saw the huge pine tree, which gave him the feeling of seeing Mother. It was an aged tree. There's a saying: thousand-year-old pine; ten-thousand-year-old cypress. This pine was probably at least a thousand years old! A group of squirrels made a ruckus in the tree.

Jasper picked some pine nuts. *Why didn't the villagers come to Old Mountain to forage for food?* he wondered. *If the militiamen weren't blocking the village entrance, maybe the villagers would come to the mountain and find food.* But then he thought, *maybe many people never thought of going to the mountain because they've been tied to their land all their lives and never thought there was a way out of their problems beyond their land.* Suddenly, he thought of all the corpses he'd seen along the road to Old Mountain. He realized they must have intended to go to Old Mountain but starved to death along the way. *They must have been waiting for relief from the government, until they gave up hope and tried to find help on their own. But by then, it was too late. They were no longer sufficiently fit to travel the distance required. Perhaps some of them did make it to Old Mountain but were struggling at death's door in some cave, having eaten wild animals or already been eaten by them.*

Jasper remembered Monk Wu suggesting to someone about going to Old Mountain. "Old Mountain?" said the person, "I've no intention of filling some wolf's stomach!" Later, he ended up filling some wolf or dog's stomach anyway. Jasper knew that, for those who had never gone to Old Mountain, the mountain was a terrifying nightmare. They had no idea how romantic the wild chrysanthemums were!

Jasper heaved a long sigh and thought, *The minds of the starving ghosts died before their bodies did!*

Jasper thought of how Genghis Khan, in the histories, annihilated forty countries and chopped off more heads than the sands of Tenggeli Desert. *But what if he hadn't killed all those people?* He knew that even if Genghis hadn't killed them, they would have been long dead anyway. *The world would have been the same whether they were killed or not. How? It would have been the same in that everything in the present would vanish without any trace like flowing water!* He thought of how the village hadn't changed much, despite all the deaths. *Those people would have died sooner or later, and they'd still be buried by a thick layer of yellow earth without leaving any trace.* As soon as he thought of this, he felt choked by a strong sensation that drowned everything. He suspected he'd fallen into another nightmare. Sometimes he couldn't tell whether he was dreaming or awake. This happened frequently.

Jasper said, "Horsie, let's go!"

The horse said, "Am I not already going?"

Jasper saw an intestine twisting and racing forward. It was gray and looked like a snake scurrying away. It twisted so furiously that it toppled the weeds and stones whichever way. Jasper thought this was probably the intestine-like narrow path Snow Feather had mentioned. He took out the tobacco soot he'd collected. He had gone all over the village and scooped out the soot from dozens of pipes using a grass reed. The pipes were of different shapes and calibers. Some were made from sheep hoofs; some were from the wings of black eagles and welded from brass water pipes. After swallowing countless puffs of tobacco, the pipes had gathered a lot of soot. This tobacco soot was even more unsavory than human turd. A taste of it, and the eyes would smart with tears. If you don't want to live anymore, just consume half a catty of the stuff: it's guaranteed to be more effective than poison! When Jasper was collecting the tobacco soot, many of the pipes hadn't been used for quite a while already, so it was mostly dried soot that he'd obtained. He mixed it with water after he got back and didn't think leeches would be particular about it. Monk Wu only sniffed snuff, but he had a two-foot-long brass pipe to offer to benefactors who brought him offerings. Jasper took it with him.

According to Snow Feather, Jasper should have worn a sheepskin jacket inside out. But he didn't wear a sheepskin jacket. If he were going to Old Mountain directly, it would have been fine for him to wear it. But he was heading to the city of Liangzhou first. If he were to enter the city on horseback wearing an old sheepskin jacket, he would have been a laughingstock for the folks on the streets. What he didn't realize was the fact that he would suffer greatly for this error later.

Jasper said, "Horsie, Horsie—run with all your might! Don't let the leeches catch up with us! Be fast but don't trip. If you trip, I'll be thrown into a nest of snakes!" The horse intoned softly.

Jasper smeared the tobacco soot on his felt boots. He was wearing Monk Wu's robe, the sleeves and waist of which he'd tied. He couldn't bear to smear tobacco soot on the robe and thought, *The leeches can't be faster than the horse, can they?*

He gave the horse's belly a squeeze with his legs, and the jujube-red horse galloped.

At first the path was quite wide, but as they proceeded, the cliffs began to press upon it. There were many weeds and vines on the mountain. The vines twisted and crisscrossed above the path, and all manner of weeds poked at it. Jasper thought the path didn't even qualify as a pathway. Stones sometimes bolted under the horse's hoofs as they stepped on the rubble. Dampness, with the stench of decay, assaulted him. He wasn't sure whether leeches had the ability to hear, but he could see many wriggly things poking out of the leaves. Fortunately, the horse was very fast, but a rustle could be heard behind his back. He turned his head and saw a drove of leeches scurrying forward like a torrential flood. The horse's neck was already covered with black dots. They had already begun to suck its blood. Their bodies arched up and down: one could tell that they were squirming to enter the horse's flesh. Jasper shuddered. He then slapped them with his hand. The leeches that were struck wriggled their bodies and the heads that had entered the horse's flesh so laboriously pulled out. They screamed wretchedly and tumbled down its neck.

Jasper noticed a torrent of leeches in front of them as well. The vibrations of their sound or movement must have transmitted to the leeches news of the arrival of food. They wriggled excitedly. The ones in front welcomed them, while those behind pursued them. They roared like rumbling blood. Jasper couldn't tell whether it was the leeches or his own heart. He slapped furiously. Immensely grateful, the horse galloped swiftly and steadily. Jasper noticed that the leeches on the horse came from above. They rained down from the vines above, seizing the precise moment when the jujube red horse passed underneath them in order to forage for food. Jasper discovered volleys of leeches both in front and behind them. He also felt a rustle on himself and looked down. Sure enough, his robe was covered with countless arching leeches looking for entrances to his body! His boots were actually quite clean, indicating that tobacco soot was indeed their nemesis. He quickly grasped his boots and then wiped his hands over his robe. The areas he smeared showed their original cloth. The leeches continued to carouse in the areas he didn't smear.

Suddenly, he felt an itch on the back of his hands. Some leeches were already sucking at his hands. He felt a pain. He grasped his boot immediately and rubbed the back of his hands. The leeches rolled off instantly, as if they'd been scalded.

The horse neighed loudly. Jasper knew it was asking for help. He smeared tobacco soot on its neck. As he smeared, he slipped his boots out of the stirrups and rubbed the boots against the horse's belly. The touch felt unusual as the horse's belly was already covered with leeches. His boots turned red immediately. He knew it was the horse's blood. *If we continue like this*, he thought, *The horse will bleed to death . . . But, I'll do my best. I'll do whatever I can!*

However, very soon, he was unable to take care of even himself!

The leeches on Jasper figured out a way to deal with him. They adopted the warfare technique of well-drilling and began drilling right into his robe. They arched their bodies as they bit into his robe, and the heads of some were already inside it. These were the stupid leeches. The smart ones roamed his body until they discovered his weakest spot, which was his neck. This was first discovered by the leeches that landed on his neck by accident. Although Jasper had worn a scarf, it had been loosened by all the activities quite a while back. Several leeches had already begun their attack and were sucking the first draft of blood. Jasper felt an itchy pain. The ambush of the leeches was quite gentle.

Oftentimes, you wouldn't even notice that they've begun to suck your blood. If you were absolutely still, you would of course immediately notice the strange objects on your skin. But if you were active or nervous, you basically wouldn't feel the gradual flowing of your blood into the leeches' stomachs. Of course you'd feel some pain, but it would be an itchy rather than jabbing pain. When Jasper was helping the horse, he was unaware that at least a dozen leeches had already entered his neck. One of them bit a main artery. The blood happily offered itself to the leech, even without being sucked by it!

Jasper found out later that the pathway he'd entered was called Leech Gully. Many years later, it would become known throughout the world because of Xue Mo's book.

Jasper rubbed his neck and grabbed a handful of soft things. The long ones were as long as a foot. They looked like earthworms but had flat heads that resembled those of cobras. Jasper was terrified of such things. He screamed loudly and flung them away. It was then that he realized that these soft things had roamed to his chest. He regretted not smearing his neck with tobacco soot earlier. Although having sticky tobacco soot on the skin felt no better than being stung by leeches, at least tobacco soot did not suck one's blood and was not so disgusting. He fished out the plastic bag carrying the tobacco soot. There was very little left. Too lazy to use his hand, he wiped his neck with the plastic bag, but could do nothing about the leeches that had already entered his body.

He felt an itchy pain throughout his body. It was as if a leech had bored into every single pore. His stomach churned just thinking about the repulsive soft worms indulging themselves on his body. He felt like throwing up.

A skeleton came into sight. It must have belonged to some animal the blood of which had been sucked dry by the leeches. The horse knocked against it, and the skeleton crashed down with a clatter. Gradually, more and more bones appeared. They were mostly the skeletons of small animals, but then there was actually a human skeleton. It leaned against the side of the path and looked terrified. *If people had told others about the perils of Leech Gully*, thought Jasper, *no one would have dared to enter Old Mountain. This was truly more horrifying than hunger!*

The torrent of leeches continued to rain, but it gradually became lighter. The deluge of leeches continued to surge behind them, but those blocking them in front had lessened. *Maybe we're approaching the end*, thought Jasper. He felt an itchy pain over his entire body. The itch was even worse than pain as it reminded him of the squirming leeches. The part of his neck devoured by the leeches continued to bleed. The tackiness on his chest felt very uncomfortable and blood seeped through his collar. He only hoped the horse would not lose its footing. Should they let the surging torrent of leeches behind them catch up with them, the blood in his body would not have been enough to nourish them. *Although leeches are tiny things,* he thought, *they can be horrendous once they gather into a drove!*

Suddenly, Jasper heard an explosive boom. It was like the eruption of a mountain deluge, the trembling of all the leaves in a forest, and the hissing of thousands of snakes. It was as if the sound originated in his body, but his body clearly felt enveloped by the sound. He then felt that the horse had turned into a leaf and was floating on the ocean of the sound. He never did figure out what it was. Later, when he asked Monk Wu about it, the monk replied that it was probably the sound of terror. Jasper was not satisfied with this answer. Monk Wu then explained, "In other words, the sound came from the bottom of your heart." Jasper just smiled.

However, physical pain prevented him from wondering further as to the origin of the sound. Pain pierced his entire body, from the surface into the deep layers. He felt thousands of sharp mouths gnawing at him. Although he knew leeches had no claws, he felt as though they were tearing at him with thousands of claws. They sucked his blood as they chomped on his flesh and smacked their lips with satisfaction. Jasper thought he was going to collapse.

Just as inexplicable as the disappearance of petrifying plagues, the torrent of leeches vanished suddenly. Jasper breathed a sigh of relief and realized he had already escaped the leeches' territory. He had arrived at a relatively arid area. Looking back, the swarming leeches had stopped advancing. They swarmed together and formed a mountain of leeches. Realizing that that mountain had almost buried him, Jasper gasped.

After galloping for a while, he saw sunlight among the mountains. Jasper finally heaved a sigh of relief. He dismounted and discovered more than a hundred leeches on the horse with most of their bodies in the horse's flesh. Jasper slapped at them furiously. More than half of them contracted their bodies after being beaten. They didn't retreat voluntarily; it was a natural reaction to pain. Leeches were highly flexible. They could stretch to a foot or contract into a mere inch. When hurt, they would contract naturally and emerge from the horse's skin. But there were a dozen very stubborn leeches that clung to the flesh shamelessly, even after being slapped several times. They belonged to the type that would not repent unto death. They sank their teeth into the horse's flesh and refused to give in. Their bodies were still squirming; they were obviously still sucking its blood. Jasper remembered the other method Snow Feather taught him: to douse them with warm urine. Sure enough, the minute urine touched them, they dropped in a flurry.

After taking care of the leeches on the horse, Jasper took off his clothes and slapped at the dozen or so leeches on his chest and legs. But he couldn't see his back. He thought, *If urine can get rid of leeches, then the horse's tongue should be able to lick off the leeches too, since the temperature of the horse's tongue is comparable to that of urine. If urine feels like boiling water to the cold-blooded leeches, then the horse's tongue would be a slab of red hot iron!* So Jasper said, "Come, Brother, lick off the horrible worms for me!" The horse said, "Sure! We brothers look out for each other!" It stuck out its tongue and began licking. Very soothing. After licking for quite a while, the horse neighed softly. Jasper smiled and patted its neck.

The Old Wolf That Clacked Its Teeth

According to *The Ramblings of Ajia*, Jasper entered the forest.

Jasper did not see packs of wolves resembling flax seeds in the gully. He only saw an old wolf; it was an ugly old wolf with dangling nipples indicating that it was nursing cubs. It had a long scar on its face, which must have been the result of a past fight. It seemed to have a limp; and upon closer examination, Jasper discovered its front paws had no toes. Monk Wu had said that this type of injured wolf was the cream of wolfkind. It must have had rich experiences combating humans. Why didn't it stay with a pack? Hard to say. Maybe it was the loner type, or maybe it left the pack because it was ashamed of being old and ugly.

Monk Wu had said that packs of wolves did not attack sheep unless provoked. The wolves of Qilian Mountain tended to be better behaved. They would observe the rules of the mountain gods the way Buddhists adhered to their vows. But sometimes the occasional flying thief—Jasper thought of the villagers' deprecation of Snow Feather as a flying thief, and smiled—being of thief nature, would be up to no good when others were not present. Maybe this old wolf belonged to that category. Even more likely, it was chased out of the pack for this reason. Jasper suddenly became nervous. He had never confronted a wolf before. He was very scared of wolves. The horse's shoulder was also quivering. He knew that the horse was also very nervous.

The old wolf glared at Jasper coldly. This served as further proof of the old wolf's slyness and ferocity. Villagers always talked about wolves. They said wolves were afraid of staring at humans. They feared nothing more than confronting humans face to face. Even the most vicious wolf would avoid staring directly at the eyes of humans for any length of time. This wolf, however, was an unusual exception. Its eyes were very cloudy and seemed inscrutable because of the haziness. It was through this impenetrability that its ferocity seeped through, chillingly and eerily. Jasper felt the leaves trembling in confusion around him, and an uncanny wind whirled in to envelop him. He suddenly realized that the wolf was trying to crush his willpower. It obviously had no idea about his background and would not attack rashly before taking his measure. It used its eyes as a fierce weapon. Their contest had already begun the moment the wolf and human began staring at each other.

Jasper felt cold sweat on his back. He remembered the game he used to play with his guru's other disciples: eye-staring. You could manifest all sorts of expressions with the eyes, such as anger or playfulness. The use of different facial expressions was allowed. But the minute the opponent diverted his eyes or smiled was when you won. Jasper thought the wolf was also playing this game. This insight made him relax somewhat. But then he realized this wasn't just a game: this was a gamble of life or death. Immediately he reminded himself of this fact. Who would have thought this reminder would make him even more nervous?

The eyes of the old wolf sent wave after wave of currents, which whizzed and charged at his eyes. He thought of the legendary Great Technique of Capturing the Soul. He had heard that this technique did indeed exist. An experienced yogi master could use the power of a spell and his own concentration to guide your heartbeat to resonate with his. When the resonance reached a certain limit, you could die from it. *Is the wolf also playing this trick?* Jasper tried to fathom the mind of the wolf through its eyes, but the haze drowned out everything. He was reminded of the Gonpo in his nightmare, whose mysteriousness increased due to the lack of clarity. Jasper felt his eyes smart; he hadn't blinked for a long while now. He was afraid that the opponent would take advantage of his blinking to charge at him and attack his throat. His eyelids were being weighed down by a thousand catties. He could even discern a snigger in the eyes of the old wolf. *It must have discovered my nervousness*, he thought.

The old wolf's pupils were yellow: the color of yellow earth. Jasper suddenly thought of the Spell of the Mountain God. According to Snow Feather, that spell should not be recited too many times—seven should suffice. So Jasper recited it seven times, while watching the wolf to see its reaction. The wolf shook its head and closed its eyes for a bit. Jasper also took the opportunity to blink a few times. And then the wolf suddenly opened its mouth wide enough to stuff a watermelon in there. The corner of its mouth reached its ears: that mouth was a veritable basin of blood! The wolf opened its mouth a few times as if yawning and then snapped it shut. The teeth clacked and looked like they were snapping at air, or imitating people clacking their teeth. Monk Wu used to clack his teeth every morning. He'd been doing it for dozens of years. Later, when he left the world for Niguma's Sitavana Pure Land, he still had a mouthful of good teeth. The old wolf also had superior teeth, with elongated canines. Its tongue was also very long. Little hooks studded wolves' tongues. He had heard that bones would dissolve into water when wolf saliva dripped on them. Of course, Jasper did not believe such ridiculous notions. Even so, he was shocked by the hugeness of the wolf's mouth. Given the opportunity, it could easily snap off his head. He had never before seen a wolf of this size. A tingling numbness rose from the soles of his feet.

Jasper pulled out Snow Feather's lasso-dart. The lasso was tied in such a way that its dart would bolt with one fling. The problem was, it was easy to toss but hard to withdraw. Not recognizing its handler, the dart might well dig a bloody hole into the operator when withdrawn. He now regretted not having learned some martial arts. He had given up numerous opportunities to do so. He had thought, *What was so good about martial arts? When one dies, his martial art skills vanish with him. Martial arts worldly skills. They are impermanent. I want to learn something permanent!* He had thought that rather than wasting time and effort practicing martial arts, he would be better off performing body kowtows and accumulating some merit. But at this juncture, he truly had regrets. He thought that if Snow Feather had encountered something like this, she would invariably be more resourceful than he. But the lasso still boosted his courage—the minute he brought it out, the wolf stopped snapping its teeth. It looked first at the lasso and then at Jasper. And then it cracked its mouth, as if smiling. Jasper realized the wolf knew he didn't know how to use the lasso and turned red from embarrassment.

The horse also stared at the wolf, its neck continued to quiver. Horses could make any part of their bodies quiver voluntarily. They could do this on any part that a gadfly landed on. Jasper realized that the quivering areas were those attacked by leeches. *So, thought Jasper, the horse wasn't really afraid after all!*

The horse stared at the wolf quietly, indicating that it was an experienced war horse. If it were a noisy frightened donkey, it would be kicking and braying right now, exposing the extent of its abilities, and proving how shallow it was. Seeing the stability of the horse, Jasper felt embarrassed by his own fear. Monk Wu had always said, "That which causes fear is not some outside object, it's one's inability to control one's own mind." Thereupon Jasper took a deep breath. He remembered what the guru taught him about dealing with outside appearances. There was a time when different sights would appear whenever he meditated. Sometimes it would be a Buddha, sometimes a demon, sometimes Heaven, sometimes Hell—sometimes pleasing, sometimes terrifying. The guru said, "Be it a Buddha or a demon, Heaven or Hell, they are all manifestations of the mind." And he told Jasper to destroy everything, be it a Buddha or a demon, Heaven or Hell. Only the clarity and consciousness of his mind should be preserved. Jasper thought, *Why don't I treat the wolf as a manifestation during meditation?* As soon as he thought of that, his sense of fear lessened.

The old wolf began clacking his teeth again. Its saliva dripped like a waterfall. Jasper looked at its belly, which resembled an empty bag and concluded that this was a hungry wolf. Its nipples were elongated and red, like those of an old sow. Jasper seemed to see a pack of wolf cubs wailing in some mountain valley. A strange emotion surged in his heart. *This old wolf is a mother after all*, he thought. Suddenly, he recalled how the Buddha sacrificed himself to feed a tiger and cut his own flesh to feed a hawk. When he thought of such tales, he used to think he could perform such deeds as well. But now that he met the wolf, he realized he was very far from being a Buddha. He couldn't even consider letting the wolf take a bite of him, or cut a piece of flesh to give as alms. This thought caused an enormous attack of shame, and the sense of fear vanished.

Ajia said, "Suddenly, Jasper became immensely compassionate." He thought, *I am truly just an ordinary being after all!* He said later that if the wolf had charged at him at that moment, he probably would not have resisted because he had suddenly lost the will to fight. Tears blocked his vision. By the time he wiped away his tears, the wolf was long gone. It was as if the wolf had never existed. Ajia said, "It was Jasper's great sense of compassion that saved him." He didn't know that the wolf wasn't just an old wolf—it could have been a wolf spirit. Jasper couldn't have been able to harm it, even if he had a gun. No one in the world could have matched its powers, if it had decided to strike. However, during that very instant, Jasper acquired the most powerful armor in the world, which was compassion.

Jasper finally found the tent.

He felt like he was dreaming. The sky was covered with stars that roamed like fireflies. Wasn't it obviously daytime? He saw the sun, but the moon and the stars surrounded it. He suspected it was a hallucination.

Jasper entered the tent and discovered it had in fact draped over a wood cabin. A young girl looked at Jasper coldly. He did not see Grandpa Jiu or the coffin Snow Feather mentioned. The house was tidy and spotless, without a single speck of dust. It was no wonder since such unsoiled grassland should not have had any grime. Jasper thought the girl looked familiar but didn't know where he might have met her. This was a very common feeling. At the risk of being accused of plagiarizing *Dream of the Red Chamber*,[4] I can't ignore the reality of Jasper's feeling, just because of fear of people's suspicions.

Jasper was afraid of staring at the girl. He only asked hesitantly, "Is Grandpa Jiu here?"

The girl answered, "I don't know who Grandpa Jiu is."

Jasper told her about Snow Feather. The girl snickered, "She's full of trouble!"

She said, "I don't know about sweet dew . . . But I've got a pound of black beans here. You can take them back!"

Jasper remembered what Snow Feather told him about begging for a technique, so he knelt down. The girl seemed to find it amusing. She said, "Do you really think I can perform the empowering Abhisheka ritual? If you really believe in me, then I'll perform it for you!" So saying, she touched his head with her foot lightly.

"You can now thank me for the favor!" she said.

---

4. Authored by Cao Xueqin (1715–1763), *Dream of the Red Chamber* is a traditional Chinese novel. In this novel, when the main hero Jia Baoyu meets Lin Daiyu, one of the main heroines, he claimed he had met her before but didn't know where.

The Other Side of the Swamp

After he left the tent, Jasper remembered Snow Feather had said her mom was on the other side of the swamp.

When he passed by the white poplar tree that had been struck by lightning, Jasper found in front of it two piles of bones. Judging from the shape, he could tell they were the wild boars' skulls. So the wild boars had already died! When Snow Feather mentioned them, she had said they were still alive. But now, even their flesh had been gnawed clean by other animals. Jasper felt like he was in a dream.

A cloud of green flies buzzed above the bones. Jasper even smelled a stench, along with the odor of mold characteristic of deep mountains. The reek of dampness was very strong. All the withered branches and fallen leaves had rotted. All manner of worms and insects poked their heads out to stare at him, startled by the sight of such a strange animal here. Jasper and the insects were shocked by each other. He thought it was funny. The horse sneezed, and Jasper realized his own ridiculousness.

He saw the swamp. He snapped off a tree sapling and began looking for the horse skeleton because Snow Feather had said it would aggravate the horse. The swamp was expansive, so he could see into the far distance. But he only saw a badger struggling in the mud. There was no horse skeleton. He did find a pile of powdery stuff he recognized as bones, decomposed by microbes. *Maybe these are the horse skeletons Snow Feather mentioned*, he thought. There was no need to break them; they had already disintegrated. The swamp didn't look like a swamp. If it weren't for the lightning-struck popular tree, Jasper would have wondered if he'd taken a wrong path.

Jasper discovered a tent across from the swamp. He knew it was just a feeling, but oftentimes, feelings are even more accurate than sight. The struggling of the badger was quite obvious. Mud and water splattered and plopped. Jasper realized the treachery of the swamp from the mud. It was obviously trying its best to appear calm to seduce him to enter it. The badger was tricked by it. Its footprints were at first solid and then gradually became shallower, until they entered the mud where the badger got trapped.

Unexpectedly, shale lined what looked like a pathway. Maybe this was what Snow Feather referred to as "the path." *Let's give it try*, thought Jasper. He held the reins and walked on the shale. The horse followed him silently. It was truly a fine horse. The shale was more solid than he had expected. There was a sense of firmness when the hoofs tread on it. Jasper proceeded, feeling each step. After traveling awhile, he decided the swamp was trying to confuse him intentionally. There was a skeleton right in front of him. It had sunk into the mud from the belly down, yet its top half was the same color as the swamp. *No wonder one couldn't see the swamp!* Jasper thought it was probably from a feral horse, but then there was nothing one could do if one's domesticated horse were to fall in. The horse must have known what Jasper was thinking. It neighed loudly. He knew it was scared.

Jasper stopped and looked at the badger. Mud had surged up to its neck. Its body had already been swallowed by the swamp. Lifting its head, the badger screamed: its voice was piercing. The more it struggled, the faster it sank. In a flash, its head disappeared. There was just the bubbling mud.

Jasper was covered in cold sweat from viewing the badger's dramatic demise. He wanted to retreat but felt embarrassed. So he asked the horse, "Why don't you decide? If you want to proceed, then neigh three times; if you don't want to proceed, then neigh once." The horse shot a loaded glance at him and neighed twice. The horse had kicked the ball back to his court: he realized this was one highly experienced old horse.

Jasper took a few more steps and heard the sound of wetness under his feet. Bubbles emerged there. He knew the shale could withstand his weight but not the horse's. So he said, "Horsie, let's go back! I'm afraid you'll sink. If you do, I have no way of saving you! You don't belong to me—you are the property of the Ancestral Hall. Let's go back!" The horse could tell his dignified speech was really to mask his own fear and laziness. But it said nothing. People are like that; the horse was used to it.

Jasper thought, *Should I look for another path?* He left the swamp and walked toward a slope.

He heard the chirping of myriad birds. He never realized that such a place existed in this world. Although he could hear the chirping of various birds, he still felt drowned in a sensation of clarity. The horse's hooves seemed indistinct; the stones they struck flew down the valley. Jasper could see the sky through the crown of the trees. Not a cloud in the sky, but then he thought this was just how his soul perceived it. He had longed for this sense of clarity in the haze of his past. Quite unexpectedly, it came to him today.

The mountain path was lined by huge rocks fractured by evil winds since antiquity. Dark and looming, they seemed as hard as granite but had begun to break into pieces. Sunlight shone on the path that twisted like a khata scarf. He thought of the Diamond Maiden Technique taught to him by Guru Huaman. In this practice, he was to visualize a khata through meditation and see it drift all the way to Niguma's Sitavana Pure Land. According to the guru, Niguma was a true manifestation of the Diamond Maiden. The sky would be strewn with rainbow-like heavenly flowers, with twenty-four Dakini goddesses chanting the Blessings of Niguma! Dazed, Jasper felt he was practicing the Technique. He wondered, *Aren't the myriad birds chanting Dakini goddesses?*

The mountain path became increasingly steep. The horse was also straining itself. Jasper dismounted. Although the ground felt solid, he still felt the sensation of sleepwalking in a void. He seemed to see two rolling black balls while in this daze. Upon focusing, he saw two bear cubs rolling around. The horse neighed softly; it was reminding Jasper! Jasper knew their presence meant adult bears would be close by. Sure enough, as soon as the horse stood still, a large bear wobbled out of a cave.

Jasper finally noticed the large bird's nest in the tree. *Snow Feather was very fortunate to have been able to perform her practice in such an abode,* he thought.

Jasper yelled, "Auntie Ho!"

By the time he finished calling, the bear had already charged at him with a roar. The horse reared on its hind legs. Jasper felt a powerful force pushing him off the horse, and the ground hit his buttocks ferociously. His head boomed, the wind whistled past his ears, and rocks snapped at them ferociously. His tumble finally ended inside a depression on the steep slope. Jasper looked down and broke into a cold sweat; he would have continued tumbling down if it weren't for the depression!

The jujube red horse neighed loudly. *Oh no!* he thought, *the horse will be eaten by the bear!*

Although he knew the danger above, Jasper continued to climb back up. Surprisingly, the horse and the bear were having a standoff. The horse's long mane fluttered in the wind. It had the grandeur of a male lion. The bear charged at it, waving its two front paws. The horse turned its rump toward the bear and kicked his hind legs at the bear's head. The bear ducked, and the hoofs got its shoulders. The bear roared and took a tumble. Jasper never thought that the horse could be so impressive. He had heard that bears' paws were extremely powerful: they could crush the heads of draught animals. A villager had encountered a bear once. One fling of the bear's paw, and the man's face was taken off.

In the legends of Diamond Clan, bears were even more terrifying than wolves.

As he climbed back up, the bear charged again, swinging its paws. The horse continued to greet it with his hind hoofs. Having suffered from their kick, however, the bear was aware of their power and was careful not to get close. It circled the horse, hoping to attack frontally or from the horse's side. The horse was experienced and always faced the bear with its rear. The bear resembled an Eight Trigrams Boxing expert, and the horse was a veritable Tai Chi master!

The bear flung its paws a few times, but was always greeted with kicks from the horse. The bear was very smart; as soon as the horse began to kick, it would retreat. The horse, however, was not as calculating—it would kick whenever the bear advanced. There was a standoff for a while, neither could do anything to its opponent.

Jasper couldn't help but be worried. He knew the horse could only deal with one bear. Should the two cubs or another big bear join in, then the horse would lose for sure.

Speak of the devil, sure enough another large bear arrived on the mountain. The horse also noticed this problem and changed its tactic to one that took advantage of its own agility and speed. It began to roam the relatively level slope. This became a situation of two bears chasing after a horse.

Jasper was very anxious, fearing the horse would escape. Without the horse, the bears would undoubtedly come after him. With his paltry abilities, he would collapse just from a bear's sneeze. He decided he'd pretend to die should the horse run away. He'd heard that bears didn't eat dead people. And then he wondered, *Was Snow Feather's mom already eaten by the bears?*

There was no indication the horse would run away. It was just that the standoff had now become a chase. This was actually more advantageous to the horse, as it was wont to gallop. Its rump would always face its opponents now, and it could kick if necessary. The bear that just arrived wasn't aware of the power of iron hoofs but learned to keep its distance after one kick.

Jasper sweated profusely as he screamed, "Auntie Ho! Auntie Ho!" *If she was already eaten by the bears, how sad it would be for Snow Feather,* he thought.

Suddenly, a hoary head poked out of the large bird nest and asked, "Who is it?"

Delighted, Jasper yelled, "It's me, Auntie Ho! Snow Feather sent me here to fetch you."

"I thought it was some bad person!" Then she hollered. When the bears heard her, they stopped the chase and gazed most reverently.

The horse galloped toward Jasper, completely soaked in sweat. Jasper patted its neck and said, "You are truly a loyal friend!" The horse neighed softly.

He climbed up into the big bird nest. He felt as if he'd journeyed for several centuries and felt an odd fatigue. After eating some wolf meat Snow Feather's mom gave him, he collapsed on the sheepskin, and his eyes closed involuntarily.

A familiar feeling ambushed him.

He felt as if he'd seen the holy land. At the same time, he also felt as if he'd entered another nightmare.

Chapter 21

Chicken Feather Notices

That flute reverberated again,
In the winds of the Third Month.
Serenely swallowed the crimson lips.
    It had been a hundred years
        On the island blanketed with peach flowers,
Forever kissing ecstatically.

An Incident That Startled Liangzhou

According to *Historical Mirror of Forgotten Events*, the reason behind an incident that startled all of Liangzhou was apparently hunger. But *Family Instructions of Diamond Clan* viewed hunger as only the ignitor—the dynamite lay elsewhere.

That morning, Jasper heard three soft taps on his door. He was in the midst of practicing Inner Fire Meditation, a special type of Buddhist meditation. Controlling his life energy and visualizing fire within his chest, Jasper began to feel warmth, indicating the fire he visualized had already created real heat. Jasper could pass through the winter on a snowy mountain wearing only a cotton outfit. The Inner Fire Meditation Jasper practiced was also transmitted by Niguma. Niguma's Inner Fire Meditation was exceedingly powerful. It was said when she started an inner fire, she could melt the snow of an entire mountain. Jasper heard the knock just as he felt a delightful warmth rising up from the energy nodes of his midsection.

He came out of his meditation and opened the door. Snow Feather's house had been burned down; so after her mom was brought back, the two of them stayed in one of the monastery's side rooms. Besides Jasper, Monk Wu, Snow Feather, and her mom, the monastery also housed Old Daddy-Nine who looked after the Ancestral Hall. Monk Wu had registered with the government, but Jasper hadn't. So Jasper was considered a guest monk. But he thought, *So be it! There's no need to be so serious about all this. One is a guest since birth. Everything in this mundane world is sufficient to fulfill the temporary needs of the guest. Nothing is worth quibbling about.*

Jasper saw a "chicken feather notice" there with the words: "Go to the storehouse to get grain this morning." He had heard Monk Wu talk about chicken feather notices before. In the past, a fellow by the name of Qi Feiqing[1] managed to gather several thousand residents of Liangzhou to smash a police building using this method. According to Monk Wu, the advantage of this method was secrecy. No one knew who the instigator was. He'd heard that anyone who didn't go when he saw this notice would have his house burned down.

Jasper took the notice to Monk Wu and found him staring blankly at the same notice in his hand. Monk Wu said Snow Feather and her mom also received a notice. These chicken feather notices became a mystery in Liangzhou. No one knew who had sent them. There were many theories concerning this, but no one could prove the veracity of any of them.

Jasper and Monk Wu went to the storehouse in the cart courtyard and saw many villagers scrambling over the grain. The guards were tied up—their mouths stuffed with cattle wool, and their eyes covered by the eye-coverings used on donkeys cranking mills. They looked very funny.

The gate of the storehouse had been smashed open quite a while ago. Although the gate could have been pried open easily by lifting the axle from its hole using a rod, this had not happened. It was obvious the lock had been smashed by an eight-pound hammer. But when the lock couldn't be broken, the entire lock was pulled off. Obviously, whoever did it wanted to complicate the incident by making it a robbery rather than mere thievery.

Jasper's head throbbed—robbing war-reserve grain is a grave criminal offence!

---

1. Qi Feiqing was the leader of a secret society by the name of Gelaohui, who in 1908 led a renowned peasant rebellion in the Hexi region of northwestern China.

Members of the clan were hauling grain. Although the folks of Liangzhou were cowards, they knew a crowd could get away with breaking the law. They knew should Heaven collapse, the tall ones would hold it up! All the clansmen tried their best to haul grain home—not only haul it home but hide it. The worst that could happen was death. They could die of hunger or be shot—of the two, the former was less comfortable!

Because of the limited space in the storehouse, the granaries were dismantled. Grain poured down all over the floor. As more granaries were destroyed, grain flowed outside the storehouse like water. Jasper couldn't believe there was this much food in the village. *What a crime that so many people starved to death when there was this much food!* Monk Wu also shook his head and sighed.

Due to their frailty, people could haul very little. Some greedy ones actually fell backward from the weight on their backs. The smart ones would carry very little and make several trips, the way rats hauled grain in a storehouse. Grain poured out through the storehouse gate and flowed toward the Ancestral Hall. Most rats made their nests in holes beneath the storehouse and could drown from this deluge of grain. So they fled in all directions, squeaking piercingly. These fat rats made people salivate. Rats had disappeared from the village's homes a long time ago. Even the rat holes on the riverbanks had been completely dug out. Jasper had eaten a grilled yellow rat once—so tasty! The meat was grilled until golden—one bite and the delicious aroma went right up into his brain! People claim that one rat was comparable to three chickens. They were absolutely right about that. If the villagers had known there were so many rats in the storehouse, they wouldn't have died from starvation so complacently.

The largest rats were larger than raccoons and had bulging bodies. When they scampered, their claws reverberated on the floor. Some people tossed away their bags in order to chase the rats. The huge rats were slow, but the people were even slower. Fortunately, there were many people. When a rat turned a corner, a person would crush it with his foot and squeeze out its soft entrails.

Although those rats were tasty, because people had grain, even large rats were allowed to wobble away slowly.

The sun was already high, but Braggart was nowhere to be seen. Maybe no one reported it to him. Many of those hauling grain were actually militiamen! The moment they lay down their rifles, they became commoners—just as Japanese devils became Japanese people as soon as they put down their weapons. Jasper, however, was always opposed to this line of thinking. He felt it wasn't enough to merely lay down one's rifle; one also had to lay down the rifle in one's heart.

There was no loud voice. No one wanted to say anything provocative. If everyone hauled the grain, everyone deserved beheading. But should one person decide to scream something like "Let's rob! Let's do it!"—the nature of the situation would be different. He would become the leading culprit. All the folks of Liangzhou knew this. To them, horses are too fast, cattle are too slow; it's best to ride a donkey and be neither. Ajia said, "In Liangzhou, the rafter that sticks out is the first to rot; the bird that sticks out its head is the one shot." The officials of Liangzhou were in the habit of running their eyes over their subordinates regularly. The minute they discovered someone with their head stuck out, they'd smack the head and make this person bend at his waist. It was the same with the residents of Liangzhou. The minute someone stuck his head out, they would become a shooting target. Even if he didn't bring a disaster upon himself, he'd lose a layer of skin!

Ajia said, "The calamity Monk Wu later encountered was also due to the fact that he stood above the crowd." "Look," Monk Wu tugged at Jasper and said quietly, "Let's go! We won't take any."

Jasper knew what Monk Wu meant. Monk Wu had taken Buddhist vows. So had he. Monk Wu had always said, "I'd rather die of hunger than break my vows!"

He saw people staring at them in amazement. Jasper knew they had already angered the masses. When the masses wanted to commit cannibalism, he and Monk Wu wanted to save people. When the masses robbed grain, they wanted to keep their vows. Suddenly, Jasper saw hatred in the eyes of the masses. He realized when everyone was corrupt, anyone wanting to remain pure would become a public enemy.

He would discover later how severely the villagers hated Monk Wu.

Dying Civilly or Militarily

The day the storehouse was robbed, more people died in the village. Although they knew starved people shouldn't eat a lot, they couldn't resist the grain's allure. If you've never suffered hunger, you wouldn't know about the power of that allure. For example, imagine a strong young man who hadn't seen a woman for ten years. When this man was out of his wits from carnal desire, he suddenly saw a voluptuous naked girl—no, a young woman, a mature young woman. How great do you think her allure would be for him? Well, even that allure would not be as great as that of grain for starving ghosts.

Their intestines had stuck together from not having seen food for a long time. It sent out invisible hooks to rake in food from the throat into the stomach. It raked in a lot of cooked wheat kernels. Large balls of wheat kernels entered the stomach and the now paper-thin intestine that was no longer able to contract and relax. What do you think would be the result? Yes, at first the intestine would be blocked. It'd look like a small snake that swallowed a big rat. You could see a large bulge in the narrow intestine. The bulge could move neither up nor down, neither to the front nor the back, until the intestine broke.

This was known as "dying civilly."

There were also those who "died martially." Continue to imagine the stomach that had shrunk to the size of a fist. It had lost all elasticity and become as thin as a cicada's wings and as crisp as a dried leaf. Suddenly, bandits arrived from the esophagus, baring their fangs and brandishing their claws. Expanding rapidly without the slightest scruple, they danced and caroused like someone had stirred a nest of scorpions with a stick. Their reinforcements never faltered, and they swelled rapidly like mad mosquitoes. What would be the result? That's right, the stomach became a landmine. In no time, the stomach would shatter and reduce the life into smithereens.

All the deceased this time "died martially." They screamed as soon as the food entered their stomachs. Before the screams ended, they had already expired.

No one expected this to happen.

But there was no time for Diamond Clan to snivel and sob. A few police cars entered the village the following day. The folks of Diamond Clan called police cars "oh-ah cars" based on the sound they made. In the past, when these cars entered the village, a group of kids would chase after them yelling, the way a donkey dying of thirst chased after a water cart. But this time, the village was unusually quiet. One could call it dead quiet. No one was surprised by this sudden arrival of excitement. No one showed astonishment at the horde of uniforms brought by the cars. They all knew the arrival was related to the storehouse robbery. But no one cared.

No one even cared about the god of death who'd been roaming the village and appearing frequently.

All the villagers were taken to the Ancestral Hall. There was some grain in old cloth bags. Some grain was buried by clansmen in places only they knew. They would not tell even if you beat them to death. They would rather go through instant death by a bullet than suffer lingering death from starvation, which was equivalent to being killed by a tiny knife and small rope. The clansmen pulled wooden faces and harbored wooden hearts. They were as wooden as the Jews who were being herded into gas chambers. They pretended to be the most reverent and obedient humankind, without any scolding by the policemen. They were as scrawny as bedframes and chicken bones. They were skin and bones. They were a flock of lonely souls who'd been starved for a thousand years and were just released from the necropolis. They moved mechanically. Would they fear the police if they didn't even fear death?

Once again, the Ancestral Hall began to be filled with commotion. All those who were alive had become suspects. One could say they were already criminals; since aside from the monk, Jasper and those who could no longer move—the majority of them had stolen grain. Although the storehouse gate was open, anyone who had taken grain was considered to have committed robbery. This was obvious. Everyone admitted to the crime readily. Some even hoped to be taken by the police right away so that they could eat a few proper meals. But the interrogation lasted several days. The policemen wanted to find the person who had delivered the chicken feather notices. They began with those they suspected of associating with secret societies and religious sects, as such notices were characteristic of those groups. So they concentrated on the elderly, as some of them had been members of the Yiguandao religious sect and the Gelaohui secret society. The delivery of chicken feather notices in Liangzhou during the end of the Qing dynasty was carried out by Gelaohui. But most of Gelaohui's members had already starved to death. The few who hadn't wouldn't have had the energy to deliver the notices, even if they'd wished to. Most of them were as dry as mummies and had to be carried to this meeting. To accuse them of committing the crime would've been equivalent to having someone with obviously good eyes speak like a blind man.

The police interrogated each and every one of them. It was said delivery of the notices was even more serious than the storehouse robbery; while robbery was a penal crime, the chicken feather notices were a political conspiracy. If it could instigate the robbery of a small storehouse, then it could also instigate the robbery of a large storehouse.

If they could scheme the robbery of one, then they could scheme a thousand or ten thousand, and even large-scale banditry or rebellion. It was said that all of Liangzhou felt as if it were facing the imminent arrival of a great enemy. This feeling of "the imminent arrival of a great enemy" came at a most opportune time, as the starving residents of some counties had already begun planning the siege of the large storehouses in their county seats. One of them had already put into action their plan. But the minute they lifted their cudgels to attack the storehouse gate, several were shot dead by the police, who were already there waiting.

The interrogation period provided the few days when Diamond Clan folks of that period ate the best. Having no time to grind the wheat into flour, they boiled the kernels whole and ate them. The investigators didn't want anyone to die of starvation during their investigation in the village. Only suspects could have the boiled wheat. Those who were excluded as suspects—such as children—didn't have the right to enjoy such treatment. Consequently, children who didn't know where their parents had hidden the stolen goods wailed and begged to be considered criminals. At first, some suspects actually died from overeating. The police then restricted the amount of boiled wheat distributed and also controlled the proportion between the wheat kernels and water: a spoonful of water to half a spoonful of wheat. Only then did fewer people die from overeating.

As things became clearer, they also became more muddled. It was clear which people had participated in the robbery. Like lice on a bald head, they all admitted to guilt without the use of corporal punishment. What was unclear was who had plotted the incident.

Finally, the interrogation had to end. The villagers were dissatisfied by police's sloppy handling of the business. They all begged for more interrogation—they thought it would be best to be interrogated until harvest time. Upon seeing the uselessness of their begging, many women wept. Suddenly, the Ancestral Hall was filled with bawling. They all wanted to eat the boiled wheat until doomsday. The police didn't know whether to laugh or cry.

They couldn't imprison all the folks of Diamond Clan, but they still needed to justify themselves to their superiors. Otherwise, what if people instigated such mass activities again? So the "oh-ah cars" took away eight men and two women. They were the first to arrive to take the grain and so could be considered the leaders. If they didn't have to leave Diamond Clan, the villagers would have envied them, since they would get to eat some more boiled wheat. But the minute they heard that these people were being taken to the city, no one wanted to fight for a spot since they all feared unfamiliar places. So the police took the ten clan members to the city. A little over a month later, news came from the city of Liangzhou that of these ten clan members, three were to be executed, two got life imprisonment, and the others received five- to ten-year sentences.

It was said Diamond Clan dispatched representatives who rode in a cart to the assembly to observe the execution. Each participant was subsidized two catties of roasted wheat. The horse cart departed the night before, rocked for a whole night, and finally reached the assembly around ten the following morning. Much to their surprise, all ten clan members had gained weight. The only problem was that one of the members to be shot pooped his pants when the verdict was announced. This fact immediately destroyed any envy representatives had for the criminals.

The representatives repeatedly portrayed details concerning the execution. According to them, few people were there, possibly because of the prevalence of starvation. The villagers were regaled with the entire scene, as they stood on the cart. They said that as soon as the shots rang out, the brain matter of two of the three splashed into the sky and then came down, splattering over the ground like whitish glue. What a waste of a heavenly treasure—it could've been dipped with steamed buns and eaten! What then? Then, all three kicked their legs a few times like slaughtered chickens; heaved a heavy sigh, and their feet trembled a few times like a scalded grasshopper's hind legs. And then they were completely still. All the representatives concluded that the people died even more quickly than chickens. Sometimes a headless chicken would run for quite a while, splattering the whole courtyard with blood before it died. But people—people would just kick their legs a few times.

The representatives also talked about the other prisoners who were present. It was said most of them were unable to keep their shit from splattering. A sticky yellow stuff flowed out of their pants, but there wasn't any stench. Maybe their sense of smell was blown away by the rifles' bang. And then the other prisoners collapsed to the ground.

It was said Snow Feather was the only one who remained standing after the shots, although her legs were still in casts.

The representatives also said Snow Feather was saved by her broken legs. If it weren't for her broken legs, she would undoubtedly have been designated as the best candidate for delivering the chicken feather notices. No one would've believed she hadn't done it. Even if she hadn't done it, the folks of Diamond Clan would've selected her as the culprit. Back then, anyone selected by the clan as the thief would have been deemed the thief. "The eyes of the masses are discerning and bright!"[2] If that were the case, then she would certainly have been shot. But when the head of the police saw her injured legs, she was the first one he crossed off the list.

She was imprisoned because she had stolen grain previously. It was a case of pulling out mud along with the turnip. Questioning during the interrogation eventually dug up the previous event. So she was arrested as a thief. But because of the bloodiness of her leg crushing, people were reluctant to broadcast her case unlimitedly "over the internet." She would've been shot otherwise.

Snow Feather in the Realm of Clarity

Many years later, I went to Wangjing Stockade, which was located on the outskirts of the Tenggeli Desert. Although Snow Feather's verdict was life imprisonment, she was only incarcerated there for five years. Many major events occurred after that, and Liangzhou became "toasted wheat kernels in a roasting pan." Even if Snow Feather had wanted to stay there, it wasn't up to her. *Tale of the Goddess* contained a "Chronicle of Snow Feather's Life." But there was no information for those five years. Since no one was able to provide her activities for those years, they were vaguely described as "she treated prison as a ritual space." It was said she was famous at the prison farm since she performed superbly all the tasks given. Later, this became significant proof of her accomplishment in cultivation.

I saw the expansive semidesert, strewn with undistinguished rocks and arid weeds. It looked black and was consequently also known as the Black Gobi. Occasionally, one would find tufts of hairlike stuff on the rocks. These are the hair lichen, *facai*. Years later, the hair lichen would become a coveted delicacy in southern China because *facai* sounds like *facai* ("get rich"). What impressed me the most were the numerous grave pits there. At least a thousand years old and loaded with sacrificial artifacts, those graves became popular sites for grave robbers. It was said many local peasants became rich from grave robbing. The proliferation of such legends encouraged avarice in people.

---

2. This is a popular Chinese Communist saying.

Local peasants had no idea a person named Snow Feather had been there. As I've said, Snow Feather was destined to be famous throughout China but little known in Liangzhou. Although five years of her life were spent in that desert, no one really cared. What people later discussed with relish was the stolen cultural relics. Their minds were crammed with avarice.

I sat quietly in the desert where Snow Feather had herded sheep and felt the wind from the depth of the desert. The desert wind whispered softly to me tales of this shepherdess. I believe Snow Feather must have experienced the cleansing of her soul during those five years. From a historian's point of view, those years represented the watershed of her life.

At that moment, I was sitting in the Black Gobi. I let go of my consciousness, and melted into the profound azure sky. I could feel myself dissolved by the air. Not a sound, except the wind, a crisp fresh wind, without any dregs of dust or mundaneness. Gradually, it dissolved me.

I saw Snow Feather walking out of a sturdy gate, herding a flock of sheep. One could discern a slight limp in her legs. The sheep's bleating wafted in the wind. That sound was best for curing souls' wounds. I don't know if Snow Feather had ever felt suffering—I couldn't tell from her calm and transcendent face. She brandished a whip that sounded like water, which resonated with my heart. I didn't know how I could approach this girl.

I believe herding sheep in the desert can help one's soul settle into clarity. If you lie on the sand and look at the cloudless sky, you will feel the clear brightness dissolve you, and your consciousness will resemble the void. It is said that Sky Yoga is practiced by staring this way at the sky. It is said the enlightened heart is like a vast cloudless sky and an ocean without ripples. So you released your heart, so the desert wind could blow away its dust, and the azure sky could wash away the triteness in your soul. At its hottest, you even saw lizards roaming the sands happily, their feet gliding over the sand and creating the splashing sound of a flood. You saw a sheep glaring at them. They communicated through a language of souls. You may have heard the content of their conversation, but you were not able to describe it. So you smiled reservedly. Yes—this smile was even closer than words for what was expressed.

You heard the insects chirping exuberantly. You could understand their language and realized they were singing in praise of Grandpa Sun! They sang, "You've given us life, you've given us light! We are happy; we dance! We are lucky living creatures!"

You saw Snow Feather smile in the breeze, although you've rarely seen her smile. She narrowed her eyes and was intoxicated by the insects' singing. She might have forgotten many things. You wanted to ask her if she still remembered the man named Jasper. But then you decided to leave her alone. Her smile, after all, was as rare as the appearance of the Northern Dipper stars in broad daylight!

You could only see Snow Feather in the realm of clarity. She always existed in that clarity where the two of you communicated with each other. You communicated wordlessly—you savored her clarity through your own clarity. You could feel her smile and see her look at the whole world, everyone except you. She propped up her chin with one of her hands while the wind furled her hair. The sheep were a blur in her vision, like a thousand-year-old painting that had been damaged by water. *Everything must have looked like this to her,* you thought. "Yes," you said.

You've always felt she was "freeze-framed" like this in the desert at Wangjing Stockade, with the specks of sheep as her ritual implements. This was how Snow Feather entered the history of your soul.

The Niguma you would later see in your visualization practice was Snow Feather. You were constantly searching for her. You sought her in one crowd after another but in vain. You'd hoped to find her among the multitudes. This became the most important search of your life. Your heart was filled with passion and great joy. The writing that flowed out of your great joy was referred to by a woman as "divine."

This became the source of your lifelong passion. You could exist without worldly women but not without Snow Feather. Hence, your world became devoid of people—everything seemed profound as if in a wilderness but always waxing limitless poetic.

At that moment, you wished you could approach the Snow Feather in the desert of Wangjing Stockade and enter her line of vision, her clarity. You took big strides and walked faster and faster. You felt as if you had traveled your entire life, yet you discovered that she always remained the same distance away. She was always underneath the white clouds with the cloudlike flock of sheep. The gentlest Gobi Desert breeze was whispering to her. You seemed to understand what it said, but you knew it was no more than "seemed."

You couldn't imagine the rifle, shackles, and guard that should have been there because you knew in her mind they wouldn't have existed. You knew when things didn't exist in one's mind that they ceased to exist in one's life. You knew everything was a manifestation of one's mind.

Although you thought of the various sufferings she had endured there, what floated before your eyes was Snow Feather in the realm of clarity. You were unable to imagine her any other way. The cloudlike flock of sheep, which had roamed for the past thousand years, sometimes floated east and sometimes west, much like the wind. Like the murmurs of the wind, their gentle bleating formed inerasable traces on your heart.

You walked toward her steadily, approaching her realm of clarity. You saw the powders of red dust hurled up by the gale of antiquity. They exploded like fireworks next to her. You prefer to consider them as flowers scattered by heavenly beings, since this informs a propitious image. Just like when you perform your daily visualization of being blessed by the Dakini Goddess, you also saw Snow Feather listening among the shower of flowers. Your gait was light but steady. You knew it would be very difficult to get close to her, but you persevered. You saw dancing limbs, the enchanting fragrance of reed chrysanthemums.[3] There were also gazelles that stared at you with blurry eyes. You wanted to say, *Be close to me, oh Dakini Goddess of my fate!*

You saw Snow Feather turn around and look at you—Wang Luobing's[4] melody greeted you. A glistening flash—you knew it was the laughter of a bayonet in the sunlight. But you shook your head and got rid of that unpleasant image. You could follow Snow Feather's squinting eyes and look at the horizon. Through her deep blue pupils, you finally saw her hopes.

However, what you now saw was a sky of yellow dust, which you knew would follow her like her shadow. A dark halo was approaching from the distance.

You saw her cracking a full smile.

You said, "Come! Let's go for a ride!"

---

3. *Huangmaochai*, Artemisia desertorum.

4. Wang Luobing (1913–1996) was a renowned Chinese songwriter who specialized in creating Mandarin-language songs based on the music and culture of ethnic minorities in western China. The specific song referred to here is "In the Far Away Place," which describes a beautiful shepherdess.

Chapter 22

The Vanished Water of Xixia

Fated tears dropped in the autumnal wind
    Water-like autumnal wind;
The myriad autumnal waters cannot wash heart's frustrations.
Let the tears bring them out then
And transform them into a dry, cracked evening.

The Entirety of Mankind

Ajia's story appeared again within that pile of manuscripts.

According to one of them, Ajia entered Diamond Maiden Cave and became a monk, after he had escaped from the Iron Hawks.

This Ajia seemed to have been the Ajia of Xixia. I have no idea as to his relationship with the Ajias mentioned in other manuscripts.

According to this manuscript, Ajia was very dedicated and continually engaged in self-cultivation in isolation. He always stayed in the Cave and meditated away from the mundane world. Impressed with the young man, an elderly man at the foot of the mountain had his daughter send food to Ajia. Ajia ate once a day during midday. The daughter brought food to him once a day.

The tale harbors many hidden inscrutabilities that await development and hold innumerable possibilities.

I smiled mysteriously. Ajia looked at me furtively.

I asked, "Ajia—was that monk really Ajia?"

He said, "Idiot—why be so dumb! To the wise, Ajia was Jasper, and Jasper was Ajia. He and you, Xue Mo, are one and the same!"

"Oh, I see! If I am the moon, then they are its reflection in a pool."

"Of course! All of Ajia's tales happened in your life. You are also a heretic, a deluge, and a fierce beast to the worms in corpses. You have also met food-bringing girls who helped you with their lives. So, to you womankind represents great mothers. They are beings who live for dreams."

Yes. In this life of yours, women move you the most.

The mustard seed contains Mount Sumeru.[1] Little you and I contain the entirety of Jasper, Ajia, and numerous humankind.

The Notes of the Qiang Flute

On this day, the Snow Feather of Xixia entered a Xixia cave.

Water vanished in her home. Two vats filled with water vanished mysteriously. The vats didn't leak, but the water had vanished. This was known as "traveling-water." This does not refer to ravage by fire. "Traveling-water" is "traveling-water." This water had been traveling for a thousand years.

Traveling-water was inauspicious.

After the water vanished, a family could die from the lack of it.

The only way to dispel the misfortune after such an incident was to find water. You can't find it through a river or in a well. You have to go to Gobi Desert and walk around. You have to walk and walk until you find a hole dug by a cattle hoof that is filled with clear water. Bring back the water in cupped hands, have everyone in the family drink a drop of it, and the calamity will disappear. This was known as "finding-water."

Look—the girl had gone to find water. She left the tree-hidden village. Back then, the land was covered with green grass, and the mountains were overgrown with trees. The folks back then didn't destroy plant cover because they all believed in shamans. The shamans said, "All living beings have souls. Don't harm the grass and the trees!" Science refuted that belief a thousand years later, and the folks then said, "Oh! There's no problem with cutting the trees and burning the grass!" So, the mountains became bald. But so what? Who cares what will happen a thousand years later?

---

1. Mount Meru/Sumeru is a sacred mountain with five peaks in Hindu, Jain and Buddhist cosmology and is considered to be the center of all the physical, metaphysical, and spiritual universes.

The girl looked very much like Snow Feather. Her pretty figure in a Xixia outfit entered your historical vision. You knew she was performing a play. The stage, which was formed by heaven and earth, was huge. Throngs of people wore their costumes and throngs of people arrived. But you didn't care about them. You were only concerned about the moment you would enter the stage. You wished you could freeze the scene, but you knew nothing can stay impermanent in this world. Everyone was a performer; everyone was here for but an instant; everyone was as ephemeral as a rainbow; everyone would vanish like lightning. So quit sighing! Even the one who sighs is nothing more than a dew under scorching sun.

Just watch the girl and see her proceed along the tiny, wet path. The path was moist and clean because of the light rain on the previous day. Her gait was poetic, and you could discern a smile between her eyebrows. The traveling-water seemed to have been a game played by providence.

There must've been other people at Diamond Clan during Xixia, with names unfamiliar to you. You were not interested in them, however. I don't blame you for being finicky. Only a few people really lived during any period, others simply accompanied them. Wasn't it so? You can open that book called history and find that only a few ordinary names stood out during the five thousand years of Chinese history.

All the other living beings were swallowed by impermanence and left not a single trace. This would've happened to this girl too, but for the fact that I can access past lives! Like a salmon struggling upstream, I traveled through the lingering tunnel of time and space. I searched and searched, until I finally found you skipping along the path.

I knew you were on your way to find the water. Girl, why don't I call you Snow Feather—I have also been finding-water myself, but I'm unable to find the greenness that fills heaven and earth. I will continue to search for it, nevertheless. *Can you read me, Snow Feather?* I kept on thinking, *Even if I just find a drop of water each day during the great eon, I will eventually water my soul into a lush green!*

The girl of Xixia—were you also like me? I understand your loneliness. I know that to seek in a cave the size of heaven and earth was insignificant. But you are not inconsequential. So long as a pine seed is lodged in your soul, it will grow and grow until it reaches heaven one day.

Your gait was light but steady, like all those who entered history. My dear girl, how I wish I could enter your time and space to accompany you! But your shadowy figure was fuzzy and indistinct. You'd vanish as soon as I lose concentration. The sandstorms of this world are too strong; too many noises clamor, trying to soil the mirror of my soul. I can only watch you quietly and feel your helplessness. I so wanted to see your companions too. But I know they'd vanished a long time ago. They of yesterday have already transformed into the dusts of today.

You left the village and walked toward the desert. Why was the desert black? They all say violent wind was responsible for it. But I knew it was the "glory" of being dyed by blood. Ajia was playing a flute in the black desert. I knew this was the Qiang flute. The music of this flute had been playing for a thousand years to accompany the lyrics of Liangzhou. Never mind him! That lunatic was even worse than impermanence. I could never find out his background.

You stepped to the music of the Qiang flute. Or maybe the music was accompanying you. Why don't you accompany each other and proceed? Don't stop walking. The water you're bound to find is smiling secretly at some location within heaven and earth!

I couldn't tell how long you'd searched; oftentimes, a thousand years are but a flash of time. I couldn't tell how far you'd traveled either; oftentimes, a thousand leagues are but a single thought. I only knew you'd searched sincerely for the medicine for cooling. Did you want to cure anxieties of the soul?

A bit of coolness seeped from a misty void. I saw it—it was indeed the water you'd been seeking. It wasn't in a hole created by a cattle hoof. It was in a depression made by a camel's paw. Instead of reflecting the sun, it reflected a white fox. Of course, you knew it too had searched a long while for this.

A voice wafted from the distance, "Kill it—it's drinking your life-line!" The voice sounded like Ajia's. I began to feel disdain for him. But Ajia said he'd never screamed and that it was my own voice.

Really? You must have also seen that pool of coolness. So, did you also see the fox that was dying of thirst? You just stared at it, dumbfounded. The fox's long tongue lapped, and the pool of coolness gradually disappeared.

I heard your sigh. You said, "Lap it up, fox! At least someone got to drink it!"

But I saw clearly that your moist lips suddenly became parched and transformed from the shape of a rose to that of a dried mountain yam. The anxieties of your soul had begun to rise within your body and fermented into liquid fire. They flowed like a rising tide. They bellowed with indistinct dry cackles. You knew they were a flock of inferior people. Don't be scared—impermanence was roaming your way like a python. It was like the lingering music of Ajia's flute.

The Gonpo's Rose

A messenger of the Gonpo sent over a rose. It was a black rose. Only the Gonpo had this particular variety of rose. Ajia finally realized that the calamity of the traveling-water had arrived.

Mom just spread to the wind news of your impending marriage. She had already visited the Gonpo to select an auspicious date. This was the regulation. The regulations of Xixia, the Great Xia, were more stringent than anywhere else. By then, Yuanhao had already promulgated the practice of the shaven head. Just like the rulers of the Qing dynasty later, men were ordered to have their heads shaven. All the men sported brilliantly reflecting heads. Grandpa Sun complained, "Damn—they're even brighter than I!"

Yuanhao also established many other regulations. Most of them were swallowed by history, but a few remained and managed to enter Ajia's diary later. Ajia said, "How come it's my diary? It should be our diary." I said, "Sure! Sure! It belongs to the lot of you, if you want." Ajia snickered and said, "You're so shallow! No one wrote this book. It already existed between heaven and earth. You, I, and he, are just outlets for it."

Sure—let's go back to the regulation!

The regulation was that all the brides of Xixia had to offer themselves to the state priest before their marriage, since the state priest was the Gonpo. According to *Affairs of the Black Tartars*, "It was the custom of Xixia for everyone but the ruler to revere the state priest. All the girls had to be offered to the state priest before they could wed."

Now I understand, Ajia.

So Mom tried to console the girl.

Mom said, "What are you weeping for? Don't you know it's the regulation?" The girl's tears gushed, "Does that make it right?" Mom said, "But everyone does it!" The girl said, "Does everyone do it make it right?" Mom said, "The hole will get poked anyway—who cares by whom? Didn't you hear the emperor say that it's called offering your body? You'll accumulate unlimited merit!" The daughter said, "I don't want the merit. I just want to live my own way." Mom said, "But he's the Gonpo after all—many people wish they could do it!" The daughter said, "The Gonpo is an old bloke. His hair is white; his skin sags; the corners of his eyes have gum. I've even seen him pick his nose—so disgusting! His throat has phlegm when he chants the sutras. He's just like the old blokes in the village. I don't want to do it."

Mom said, "At first no one was willing, but then everyone gets used to the idea. He's the Gonpo after all!"

Knowing that protest would get you nowhere, you just wept. That regulation had made everyone weep. All regulations bite, but one could always cry. Fortunately, one always had enough tears. So you let go of yourself and allowed them to cleanse the sob in your heart. The music of the Qiang flute was mournful—it must've been weeping as well. Let them flow then! Let them flow until the earth had aged and heaven had become desolate. Should they gather into a pool, consider it to be the found water! Have Mom drink some, have Dad drink some. Let everyone who wanted to drink some, so that no one would die from traveling-water!

The blurry image of the fox was now in focus. You saw it stare at you blankly through your teary eyes. I knew it had been searching for a mate for a thousand years. All the villagers knew. Don't underestimate that body of white fur. Without attaining merit for a thousand years, it would've been nothing more than an animal. But its snowy white fur showed that it had become a celestial!

The celestial came and left through your teary eyes. You could come and go as you please—this was your home originally. But where was my home? My home is filled with regulations. But I can't find myself in any of the regulations.

One regulation was smiling, however. Ajia's journal made a detailed record of that regulation. Many girls who refused to accept the black rose followed it instead.

Listen! A group of daughters were singing, "Let's die together, without coveting life. Let's lie together, as always!"

The Bloody Sun of Xixia

The girl of Xixia held the hand of the Xixia Ajia and left the Xixia cave. It was a strange day. The sun rose from the east that morning as usual. Yet it was as large as the spoke of a wheel and as red as fresh blood but without any brightness. This signaled bad luck to the folks of Xixia. Many people noticed this inauspicious event. They looked at each other in alarm in the palace of Xixia, but its ruler continued to talk and laugh as if nothing was amiss. As I remembered it, this occurred on the first day of the New Year. Yes, the first day of the New Year of Xixia was the same as our first day of the New Year. The fact that this happened on the first day of the New Year was a bad omen. They predicted, as accurately as a strategist could have after an event had already happened, that the demise of a notorious leader was approaching.

The name of this wicked man was Yuanhao. He had eight wives, all with strange names. The most lascivious of them was called Lady Mozang. When her husband was beheaded by Yuanhao and the entire clan was to be exterminated, Lady Mozang hid in a monastery and had her head shaved to become a nun. Yuanhao saw her one day. Her beautiful, sexy face seduced Yuanhao into a drunken stupor. The rest was history, and you're familiar with what happened. The woman's older brother seized the army's command tally. One day, Yuanhao snatched the Crown Prince's consort and thereby enraged his own son. The fellow flashed the command tally before the Crown Prince and said, "Go! Go kill him—I'll help you! Who's ever heard of a dad like that!" So the Crown Prince brandished his sword and chopped off Yuanhao's nose.

Was it that simple?

Yes. Great historical events frequently originated in something insignificant.

However, evil consequences always originate in evil. Yuanhao's lifelong sword brandishing naturally attracted a sword!

The two of you shot a glance at the dark, bloody sun and left the cave. A gully several dozens of feet deep stretched in front of the cave and meandered westward. I've climbed up this gully once. It was rocky and misty. I knew the gully was connected to Old Mountain but had no idea what was connected to Old Mountain thereafter. You seemed powerless. You knew the human body was a treasure, the best implement for cultivation. But the woman pulled you along, and you couldn't say no.

Leave! Leave the shadow of the black rose and go into the unknown. The unknown may be a place of happiness. Happiness is a distant word. You could feel her exhilaration. Women are like that. If you hadn't met her, you'd have followed the rule. But now, she no longer wanted to live unhappily. A flock of ravens approached, squawking loudly. You could tell that they were applauding you. They were accomplices to the conspiracy. Did you have your eyes set on the flesh of the two young bodies? You spiteful ravens!

Corroded rocks crushed under your feet. They used to be granite and as hard and sturdy as iron. But wind throughout the ages stripped them down. Just like this, nothing escapes the tongue of impermanence. It licks and licks until the world is changed.

You hobbled inside the impermanence while I watched the shadows of your backs. My pen feels edgy. But don't worry, the worst pen is still a pen. I finally understand your tale, but I'm not moved as I've already seen too many tears and too much bloodshed. Have you ever seen one's heels? They used to be as soft and delicate as a virgin's breasts. But later, they'd be scoured by the rocks of time until covered by thick calluses. My heart is like that. Although that's my own story, I won't weep about it.

I watched in silence his departing back, and that of yours, the woman of Xixia. I know you hailed from Loulan, a place once as prosperous as paradise, but ultimately buried by wind and sand. So must have Xixia. Your back would leave Xixia, leave the Ming and Qing dynasties, and enter some evening during the Republican period. But there was one thing you would never be able to leave, and that was your fate to suffer.

I don't know why you must suffer or why your fate didn't change during the past thousand years. Your back was sometimes round and chubby, sometimes thin and slim. But your sense of helplessness in the face of all the suffering was fixed despite the changes. Also the tears—the wind of time blew and blew but was unable to blow away the tears in your eyes. I was always inquiring. I inquired of the old man who controlled fate, but he never gave me a straight answer.

The blood in the sun gradually diminished and seeped into the earth. Stench spread throughout the land. That was the blood of the men of Xixia. The blood preferred to flow. So let it flow—it was willing. But I'm more concerned about your tears, fragile woman. Why did you knit your eyebrows when you should be smiling, with your shell-like teeth on your flowerlike face? The whirling teardrops on your eyelashes seeped into the parched land and turned it a glaring scarlet color. *Am I right, woman—my mother and wife, life after life?*

The gully stretched in the midst of your helplessness like the writhing body of a python. I heard you sing. I don't know the name of the song, but I can feel its content. There was no sorrow in the song; just goodness. This was also a Xixia regulation. Of all its regulations, this was the only beautiful one. This regulation smiled in Ajia's journal.

According to this regulation, double-suicide by lovers was considered an act of virtue.

I also understand it as an act of virtue. There's nothing better than dying with one's lover in this world. When I leave Xixia and enter the cities of the twenty-first century, I can no longer find a girl who follows one to death. Ladies have become hussies; they clamor for fame and fortune but no longer harbor love in their hearts.

I envy you. You! Yes, you—you and she embraced and accompanied each other in Xixia, till death would you part.

Your backs stopped moving. I see you embrace each other. A natural bed spread in the valley. It was quite ordinary looking, an exceptionally smooth rock. You stared at each other. I saw you smile like flowers. You took out two white silk scarves, knotted them into joined loops, and placed them around our necks. We smiled and tightened gradually. We heard the beating of heavenly drums. A group of beautiful little girls appeared in the gully, singing:

> Night is the cassock of this life,
> The cliff is the cave of our past lives.

Poetic Corpses

Don't ask me where I went. Back then, the concept of Heaven hadn't existed there yet. Back then, they called it the holy land of Sitavana. Sitavana was Niguma's Pure Land. People say that it was a mysterious realm that would appear ordinary to the living but exquisitely beautiful to the deceased. Sitavana is occupied by Dakini goddesses who sing and dance happily without any cares. Their world is filled with sweet dew from the distant Buddha's realm. One gulp of this sweet dew would enable one to live a century longer.

You can read my *Black Wolves of Xixia* for stories on Sitavana. Like my *Sacrifice to the Vast Desert, Hunting Ground,* and *White Tiger Fort,* they are songs of my fate.

There's also a type of mysterious realm called the Dakini holy land. There are twenty-four of them hidden in the corners of the earth, some above ground, some underground. The main deity of these holy lands is Diamond Maiden. They are my best friends and frequently invite me to be their guest. I gulp down the sweet dew of great bliss, and perpetually bathe in brightness. Sitavana is connected to the various holy lands by innumerable rainbows. If you have the will, you can reach those beautiful realms.

In fact, my mind is also a holy land. Twenty-four large energy paths connect themselves to the site of the soul, each being a time tunnel. Each night, twenty-four Dakini goddesses melt into our minds and bodies through these paths of light to purify us. They swallow up avarice, dissipate stupidity, and annihilate the emotion called anger by snipping it in the bud. Thereby, I distance myself from beastliness and approach the holy land. The day my life ends, the Dakini goddesses will summon, "Come to us! You, who honor your promise!"

That's when you will realize where I went.

Mom and Dad also knew where we went. They didn't weep. Several dozen men with shaven pates found us in embrace in the rarely visited gully. Still devoid of brightness, the wan sun hung in the sky. Sunlight couldn't reach our wedding bed. According to the Xixia custom, the deceased were not allowed to be exposed to sunlight. It was believed that corpses could become spirits from borrowing sunlight.

"Did you borrow the sun's energy, Ajia?"

"Don't you bring me into this! I'm a permanent deity, not a ghost!" screams Ajia in fury.

I see you snicker—I know you want to say there's nothing permanent in this world. But don't say it, Ajia also knows it. He'd seen too many examples of impermanence during the past thousand years. You and I are the same. We die and then are reborn, and then die again. Sometimes we have this surname; sometimes we have that personal name. But we could never break away from the essence of fate.

"What essence?" you asked.

"Stupidity! We went from the stupidity of Xixia, to the stupidity of the Yuan dynasty, and then to the stupidity of the Ming and Qing dynasties. How I wish I can become enlightened, my dear wife!"

Thereupon you wept. You wept in the midst of your parents' laughter. You're an intelligent girl. You know what I meant. What one fears is not death; one fears the loss of wisdom by wallowing in the mundaneness of life.

They lifted our poetic corpses and wrapped them in bolts of brilliantly colored silks. I yelled, "There's no need to waste them! What's the use of dressing up putrid leather bags?" But you liked the colors and smiled sweetly upon seeing the silks. You were particular to pink, as it was the color worn by brides. You considered the corpse-wrapping cloths as your bridal gown.

"You've gone mad again, dear wife!"

"It's okay to be mad," you said, "beauty that is mad is still beauty. How can the ugliness of life compare with the beauty of death? Don't you see how the cesspool of the living stinks with overwhelming stench, while the withered flowers still offer beauty?" "I won't argue with you. I'll let you feel good on this fine day."

The parents wrap us again in a white rug. This is also the rule. You're not willing. You don't want the colorful silks covered, but you know it's the rule. What are rules? Rules are also fate. Don't defy it—there's no need to worry too much for those corpses. Let them mess with them as they wish!

They sing as they carry us outside the village. Suddenly, many people gather on the road. Many posts line the road. They make sheds out of them and serve wine and meat within. Folks drink as they sing Xixia songs. They are seeing us off! This is the most glorious moment of your life. In the past, you were a shy rose blooming quietly. But now, I am wind, you are sand; we will cling to each other to the end of the world.

You could die from envying us, dear fox!

But why are you still weeping? Could it be an attachment to this mundane world? What's so good about the mundane world? There's too much unpleasantness in the mundane world: birth, aging, illness and death, resentment and hatred, not getting what one seeks, leaving one's beloved. There are also many rules for killing others. You don't understand why there're so many rules? One should be able to live well, be happy and without worries. I'll tell you: the rules were established by the few whose intention it was to seize. Rules were just like the iron cavalries of Xixia who brandished their broadswords to seize the Great Song.

You must have heard the wailing—wailing originated in the Great Song. People there are stupid. They always wail when someone dies, unlike us in Xixia. We sing, enjoy ourselves and laugh! We of the Great Xia revere those who die in war and despise those who die of illness. To the folks of Xixia, those who die for love are martyrs. We rebelled against a rule. So why weep?

I know you are weeping because of your past. If you knew you were going to die so young, you'd have had more fun! I'm beginning to think that way too. There's no way that cave I stayed at could compare with your vivacious body. But I was always greeted by impermanence.

That impermanence was always screaming within my fate like maggots attached to a bone.

I did ultimately agree with you. I discovered the burden of the flesh and relished the joys of the flesh. These bodies wrapped in silks and white rug no longer manifest the liveliness they possessed when they were in the cave. Back then, you caroused vivaciously. Your body delighted in mine; my soul comforted yours. Even the memory of that dissolution of the flesh and soul brings back the feeling of ecstasy! But now, you are just a waft of light breeze, the essence of which I can no longer capture. Where is your flower-pistil tongue? Where is your lubricated water lily? Your breasts and fragrance too have all become an icy-cold past.

The lively folks in the wooden sheds are sending away two cold corpses.

Let's leave! We have no choice but to leave and proceed toward the unknown. I don't know if we will ever reach the holy land. The mouths of Sadgatih, the Six Karmic Paths, are wide open and sucking furiously. We are but helpless, floating kites. We fly and fly, controlled by the karma that has accompanied us for a thousand years.

Where is the end of this infinite journey? Where is our ultimate destiny? We can't endure too much suffering; we are but a young couple. Our goal was to enjoy love without the wind, the rain, the Gonpo, and the Iron Hawks. We just wanted to embrace till death in a quiet village.

Was that considered too much of a luxury?

We've finally arrived at the grave. It might be just as well—if we couldn't age together in embrace, then we might as well die! At least we died in embrace. The villagers have already built the scaffold. This sturdy scaffold is our wedding bed.

Slowly, they lifted us, neither too high nor too fast. They lifted us the way rosy clouds embrace radiant water lilies. They lifted us without too much force or violence, lest they awake us from our deep slumber. The distant mountains have become more distinct. A breeze wafts gently; the robust scent of spring. That Yuanhao had also died. He died among his own rules. Yet, heaven and earth lost no charm due to his death. They, in fact, look brighter.

Smile—woman of Xixia—and hold my hand! Although we are wrapped in silks, the sky is imprinted in your eyes. I hear you laugh. Although that laughter is intermingled with tears, it's nevertheless laughter. I hear the furious squawking of the ravens. They're still singing that song:

"Let's die together, without coveting life. Let's lie together, as always."

The folks in the sheds drink liquor according to custom. They are playing the finger-guessing drinking game. The loud yelling of this game has continued. Even after a thousand years, Liangzhou is still filled with this noise. They're sincerely happy. Everyone knows theirs is a permanent wedding. The couple on the scaffold would remain each other's one and only forever.

Drink up! This liquor is homebrew. It's a bit sour and bitter, but it's still liquor. All liquors can cause inebriation. Once inebriated, heaven and earth would vanish. I finally realize the reason the folks of Liangzhou drank. It has been a liquor capital ever since it was established as a prefecture during the Han dynasty. You twitch your mouth—I know you dislike drunkards. But they need a reason for living. Unlike you and me, they don't care about spirituality. But don't forget, the search for spirituality is the worst addiction. Once addicted, you'll never have peace.

The curtain of evening pulls over the valley; Grandpa Sun yawns. People's voices are hoarse. They've been sated with liquor and meat and have sung their fill. They lift up their torches. The scaffold carrying us lies in wait quietly. Do you see the white fox? It's on the mountain, staring at you silently.

The fire has been lit. The wind crackles. In my memory, the fire was really lit. The folks of Xixia are dancing and shouting. I want to hear what was said, but it was obscured by a bellowing that filled heaven and earth.

"Did they really burn you, Ajia?"

"Don't worry if it was real or not. Reality is fictional; fiction is real. Why is that blockhead of yours always fixing things?"

"Fine, Ajia—whatever!"

Chapter 23

The Broken Shoes on the Monastery Gate

No one during the evening;
In an evening with no one,
        The mind is a fortress.
The pale corpse-wrapping dispelled the dream,
The lonely path is a karma without resolution.

The Red Flag Flapped in the Wind

According to *Crazy Ramblings of Ajia*, Diamond Clan began the New Life Movement[1] shortly after Snow Feather was imprisoned. No one knew where the name came from. That's what Braggart called it.

The nature of many terms in this world are basically the same. They are formulated to manipulate the minds.

There are many Braggarts in this world who can always come up with all sorts of terms, each being an excuse to torment. What such terms manifest is, in fact, the avarice of the Braggarts.

At the beginning, Braggart only aimed at the issue of public morality. This was the easiest way to invite accomplices, as public morality had been emphasized for thousands of years, even though standards shifted

---

1. The New Life Movement was a civic education movement promulgated by Jiang Jieshi (Chiang Kai-shek; 1887–1975) in 1934. Everything in this chapter, however, makes references to terms ("public censure assemblies," "bad lot," "fixing," "exposure," "struggle against," "creating damage") used during the Cultural Revolution of 1966–1976.

according to people's inclinations. Therefore, civil cases were judged and punishment administered according to sumptuary rules at the Ancestral Hall. Examples include the seizing of petty thieves and unfilial sons. After being soundly whipped with willow branches, they'd slaughter their own chickens and sheep and invite revered clan members to dine on them. They'd then perform public repentance and vow to never infringe again.

But later, a change took place since the Braggarts were always growing. Evil in one's heart is a seed that sprouts, flowers, and bears fruit, once given appropriate soil, water and light. Hence, Braggart grew rapidly. Processing public morality cases no longer satisfied his ever-expanding greed.

It was said the type of greed most difficult to control is the greed for power. This is the reason behind the prevalence of Braggarts among humankind.

It was also said, on the Diamond Clan stage, Braggart's performance was so brilliant he surpassed all others before him.

The cause of the change was actually quite simple: during the trial of one of the cases, a petty thief mentioned Snow Feather's mom and that she had been sold to Hexi Hotel. So what was Hexi Hotel? It was a famous brothel in Liangzhou! After much probing, public morality cases even more serious than theft emerged, and Diamond Clan was brimming with excitement.

Public morality cases used to be tried in the village school since menstruating women would offend the ancestors' spirits in the Ancestral Hall. According to the beliefs of Diamond Clan, women's blood during menstruation was as lethal to the ghosts and spirits as poisonous gases and biological weapons were to humans. Aside from preventing pollution of the sacred ancestoral site, holding such events at the village school also served to educate the village children. So children grew up watching the games played by adults, and their passion for them would be ten times that of their ancestors by the time they became adults.

Later, displeased by the eminence enjoyed by the ancestors, Braggart took advantage of new trends and began to destroy the old to establish the new. He annihilated the gods, the Buddhist deities, and the ancestors—and even tossed the ancestral tablets into a river. After bobbing on the water for more than ten days and seeing their "filial sons and grandsons" still unrepentant, the ancestors took advantage of water released at the dam and moved to Brilliant King Clan, one and all. The folks of Brilliant King Clan were relatively attached to tradition and were careful not to be rash about all the ancestral tablets that had rushed over. Although many of them had been involved in quarrels with the folks of Brilliant King in the past, they were now spirits rather than humans. The bulging tombs had dissipated all the debts incurred in the human world; the living do not resent the wrongs of the deceased. Moreover, some of them were also their own ancestors, proving the hearsay that Diamond and Brilliant King Clans had a shared ancestry. A few elderly members of the latter fished out the ancestral tablets surreptitiously and worshipped them in secret rooms. Many years later, Diamond Clan perished in a great flood, while Brilliant King Clan prospered for more than a hundred years. Some people concluded that Brilliant King Clan was protected by the ancestors. By the same token, the annihilation of Diamond Clan was attributed to their overwhelming lack of respect for the ancestors.

The Ancestral Hall, without ancestral tablets, gradually displaced the village school and became the most crowded and exciting place at Diamond Clan. A tall dunce hat was placed on the head of Snow Feather's mom. The villagers hollered slogans indistinctly. One couldn't really make out what they were hollering about, but they hollered. They had the right to holler whatever—you had to just listen without questioning. But you knew whatever they were hollering was by no means songs of praises, nothing like "long live the whatever." Don't even bother to ask about the reason for the struggle session. Struggle sessions didn't need reasons, just as the singing of praises needed no reason. The reason used was, essentially, a sentence for punishment. That sentence was fabricated according to someone's whim and was just words of a drunkard and a fart in a dream. For example, this was the way someone cussed at Snow Feather's mom: "Okay for you to be taken and sold there—nothing you could do! But you let the men of Brilliant King fuck you! The holes of Diamond Clan's women should never be poked by Brilliant King men!" The voices in the village were very nasty.

Jasper could not forget the way Diamond Clan denounced Snow Feather's mom. The one thing they couldn't endure was the fact that she had clients from Brilliant King Clan. Since all men from Brilliant King Clan deserved death, anyone contaminated by Brilliant King Clan's sperms should also die. You may have seen a urinal. No matter how clean the pot is, once it's contaminated by urine, it stinks of urine. How can women who'd served as urinals for Brilliant King men not stink of their urine?

All those deemed problematic in terms of public morality were herded to the riverbank. This was also the graveyard where more corpses had been dumped than any other place during the past hundred years. Ghosts roamed there. Normally, people would be too scared to go there. The public censure assemblies were held there precisely to help rid the villagers' fear. It was the same as inviting people to a banquet when new houses were built. The human aura of the crowd was used to purge any evil influences. Everyone at Diamond Clan participated that day since Braggart would censure anyone who refused to attend. Some from nearby villages also arrived to watch the excitement. One could consider it a packed crowd. It was a clear day with a light breeze, just enough to flap the banner embroidered with the Diamond Clan emblem. The villagers sang the Diamond Clan anthem off key. But an off key song was still a song. They sang enthusiastically. If the entire clan was off key, then it would not be considered off key; just as if everyone on earth had gone mad, then no one would know he himself was mad. Jasper always felt as though he were in a dream.

Those days, Jasper always saw Ajia jumping up and down, blabbing nonsense with righteous indignation. But Jasper didn't feel like heeding him. He even felt contempt for this kind of god. Although they were supposed to be dharma-protecting deities, they never really punished the wicked. They just received offerings and worship, without purging evil from the mundane world. Ajia, however, snickered and said, "Why blame me? The evil was created by people, so it has to be endured by people. This is the natural order of things, you know. Of course, I will not call this karmic retribution—but how about calling it getting one's just deserts? The one who sows the seed gets to taste the fruit."

Monk Wu was also seized. Most things in the monastery had been smashed, including the Vajra scepter and bells. Even the Buddhist statues were shattered. When Kuan San smashed the Buddhist statues, the statues said nothing. So Braggart said, "We were all cheated! These things couldn't even save themselves, how could they save us?" Many people then joined in and accused Monk Wu of being a swindler. After much calculation, they decided the monastery had cheated them out of thousands of catties of yak butter, as well as many other things. So they began to treat Monk Wu the same way Braggart treated him. Aside from public censure, Monk Wu had to participate in voluntary labor for Diamond Clan to repay the many years of swindling food and drinks from the people. It was surely the case of a "delicacy" that was hard to digest!

On the day of the "public censure assembly," the folks herded the "bad lot"—so named by Braggart—to the graveyard. Braggart's intention was obvious; those beaten to death could be buried right there and then without having to haul off the corpses. Braggart was very enthusiastic during the public censure assembly. He wanted to use his enthusiasm to mask his crime of having starved so many people. The villagers were too lazy to investigate the matter. The ones who really wanted the matter investigated were the starving ghosts; but they could no longer do so. It was said they'd all turned into evil ghosts to demand Braggart's life, but they were all dispersed by Braggart's flames. The evil aura of wicked people is most powerful. That's why people say ghosts fear the wicked. So the starving ghosts waited patiently for the day when Braggart's evil aura would diminish. They eventually got their wish. The day Braggart reached eighty, the starving ghosts stuck to him, and he became perpetually hungry. "I'm so hungry—so hungry!" The village resounded with his howling. He always gulped down food ravenously and thunderously. But no matter how much he ate, he couldn't prevent the hunger that attacked him like whirlwind. Until one moonlit night, he lay on his stomach next to a pool by the village and ravenously slurped down the mud mixed with reeds, saying, "What great noodles you made, dear in-laws!" He ate like this for an entire night, until purple mud seeped out of his ears.

Braggart and the others made ready the birch saplings. These were the most flexible whips that grew in the wild. They whistled when brandished. During the first few years of the "public censure assemblies," the birch saplings invariably resounded throughout the meeting place. The militiamen brandished these whips and lashed furiously. Braggart presided over the meetings with a crooked mouth. The story about his crooked mouth circulated around the village for many years and constituted the only proof for the existence of gods and spirits during that era. When they tore down the temple of the god, Lord Guan, Braggart bellowed at the god the way he hollered at the Buddhist deities. Braggart was as imposing as the mountains and rivers. The Buddhist deities made no retort and never hit back. But Lord Guan was infuriated. Braggart slapped him once, and he gave him back three. So Braggart's mouth became crooked, and his face bloated into a pumpkin. Lord Guan intended to go after his life, but Ajia intervened and said, "Let him go! Give him a break since he and I are fellow countrymen!"

With his mouth crooked and face swollen, Braggart cut a most impressive figure. The crooked mouth expressed unequivocally the villagers' hatred for the "bad lots," and the swollen face created an awe-inspiring charisma that almost superseded Kuan San, who always administered thundering slaps during the "public censure assemblies." Jasper could never forget the way Kuan San administered slaps. A man of few words, Kuan San always ascended the "stage" at the perfect moment, when the mass's fervor reached a climax. That was when Kuan San would ascend the "stage" with twisted face. Kuan San had a large face teeming with bulging muscles created by teeth-clenching, resembling the rippling muscles on Bruce Lee. It was said that, unlike the muscles of body builders, rippling muscles are best for fighting. They are living rather than dead muscles. The rippling muscles can be as calm as a maiden and as fast as a darting rabbit, while the clumped muscles of body builders are stiff and frozen. I once heard that a foreign coach wanted his student to compete with Bruce Lee. But the minute the latter took his top off, the foreigner immediately changed his mind and said, "Forget it! Just take a look at his muscles—they got there through beating, not exercise!" So you see the superiority of Kuan San's facial muscles. Therefore, although Braggart's face was as swollen as a pumpkin, it couldn't possibly compare with the insidious rippling muscles on Kuan San's face.

The "public censure assemblies" always began with the shouting of slogans. Later, the slogans of Diamond Clan would progress and change with the time. People could not just shout anything; they had to holler whatever Braggart yelled. But since Braggart's mouth was crooked, his slogans came out so indistinctly that the villagers were unable to comprehend them, thus creating a comical scene of everyone hollering inarticulately. After much hollering, Kuan San would shout, "Escort the 'bad lots' to the stage!"

Donning dunce hats, the "bad lots" would ascend the platform with bent backs like a string of skewered grasshoppers. A little over ten of them would show up. If it weren't for the fact that some of them had died of starvation, there would've been at least an entire row of them. Many Diamond Clan men had been captives of Brilliant King Clan. At first they charged most heroically toward Brilliant King Clan, riding on horses and brandishing broadswords, hoping to abduct young women like Snow Feather to screw to their heart's content. They didn't expect, however, that a single horse-tripping lasso would render them all captives. There was nothing Diamond Clan hated more than captives. From its point of view, all captives were members of the "bad lot" that made Diamond Clan lose face completely. Fortunately, starvation sent most of them to the underworld before their time, so they were spared the furious cracking of Kuan San's birch sapling whips.

Few words were spoken at the "public censure assemblies" of Diamond Clan. Braggart would repeat the words that everyone had already memorized by then. And then the "fixing" would begin. Kuan San would bellow, "The time has come to get even with the 'bad lots'!" and then charge up the stage with Cripple Big and the others. Dozens of birch sapling whips would rain down upon the bad lots in haphazard fury. Jasper always remembered the cracking swish and earth-enveloping dust created by the tips of the whips. But no one screamed. As he remembered it, there was only the cracking of whips but no screams. The folks sat around the graveyard and watched the beaters and the beaten in the center. He remembered a few grannies with bound feet who had suffered the same experience Snow Feather's mom did. They were the least resistant when it came to the whips and would topple over like strewn bundles of wheat on the riverbank after just a few cracks with the birch saplings.

Snow Feather's mom didn't fall over so lightly. Being blind, she couldn't see the flashes of birch saplings around her and knew not where to duck. So she bore the beatings with the help of the extra layers of clothing she wore. Kuan San and the others derived immense satisfaction from beating her. The militiamen competed in the lashing, just as the Japanese devils competed in slaughtering the local people after they entered Nanjing. The grannies with bound feet were no fun, as they all toppled over after a few lashes. So they decided to compete in toppling Snow Feather's mom. The person who could topple her with the least number of lashes would win. Snow Feather's mom swayed back and forth like a tilting doll, always standing back up again after almost falling over. She was wrapped and pulled by the tips of the whips. How Jasper wished that she would fall, but she simply would not! Pulling a wooden face streaked with blue and red wounds, she would occasionally trip over the "bad lots" but immediately rose up again. Her stubbornness invited ever more furious cracks of the whip.

A stream brought the cool water from the snowy mountain. Many girls were weeping next to the stream. They were the daughters of the "bad lots." They washed their tears as they wept. They wished they could pretend not to care the way their brothers did, but their tears betrayed them. They didn't want the villagers to notice they were crying, so they scooped up snowy water and washed their faces with it. Just then, the village kids shouted, "What are you crying for? Why cry about the struggle against the 'bad lots'?" Quickly, they would scoop up more water to bury their faces; bubbles formed in the water.

Jasper always remembered them. Many years later, the only items that remained clear in his memory of the scene were the cracking of the birch saplings and the tearful faces of the girls.

Kuan San and his men finally succeeded in toppling Snow Feather's mom. The militiamen cheered, as it represented the ultimate victory over this female "bad lot." Snow Feather's mom rolled in the mud. She hoped she could get back up, but Jasper hoped she couldn't. Then, one day when she really could not get up, he became terrified. Finally, he had to carry the fainted old woman back to the monastery.

Monk Wu's Purgatory

The process of "fixing" Monk Wu is described in detail in *Historical Mirror of Forgotten Events.*

One day, Cripple Big sought out Jasper and whispered to him, "Monk Wu will be 'fixed' tomorrow!" Jasper had treated Cripple Big well. So to Cripple Big, Jasper was his only friend. Back then, Braggart loved to use the word, "fixing." He loved to "fix" others, and all his power derived from "fixing" people.

Jasper immediately relayed the information to Monk Wu.

The following morning, Monk Wu took off all his underwear and only wore a pair of cotton-padded trousers and a sheepskin jacket. He was barely ready when Kuan San arrived with the militiamen to escort him away. The birch sapling whips were duly prepared. As soon as they made it to the graveyard, they heard Braggart shouting, "Escort Bad-Lot Wu up here!"

So Monk Wu was dragged onto the platform. He had barely stopped walking when Kuan San and his men began "cooking their dish of birch sapling fried meat." Jasper heard the splitting noise of swishing whips on the sheepskin jacket. Cripple Big stuck his tongue out at Jasper, who cracked a grateful smile.

The birch saplings resounded with the fury of a splattering storm. It was a bellowing whirlwind. Monk Wu braced his head and let the whips shower upon him. Jasper realized that Monk Wu bracing his head wasn't just for self-protection; more importantly, it signified an attitude. The posture made him appear pitiable and consequently would reduce aggravating the hitters further. Monk Wu had totally lost the composure of a guru. Jasper pinched his own thigh forcefully and felt a numbing pain.

Gradually, Jasper began to distinguish the force of the birch sapling lashes. The loud, crisp lashes were not able to penetrate the sheepskin. Its outer layer would absorb the main force, and the wool inside would reduce it further and diminish the pain. The lashes that landed with a heavy thump were, on the contrary, more penetrating. Jasper could tell that most of the lashes were of the former variety, with an occasional blow of the latter type. Cripple Big's strokes were particularly loud; he obviously didn't intend for Monk Wu to suffer. Although he shouted thunderously, he didn't actually hit hard.

Ajia said Braggart's goal for organizing this "fixing" was to ruin Monk Wu's dignity. The collapse of one's dignity always begins with the trampling of his body. Braggart had accomplished his goal. Diamond Clan folks suddenly realized that the once-dignified monk was only a human being, who would brace his head comically when whipped. If only he would yell and scream, then he would disappear completely from people's hearts. But he only braced his head and without squealing. Monk Wu explained later that he braced his head so they wouldn't blind him since he wanted to continue to read and chant the sutras! Monk Wu's explanation was compelling, and became the theoretical foundation for reestablishing people's reverence for him more than ten years later. According to Monk Wu, to resist by stretching one's arms like a praying mantis when encountering the crushing wheel of history could only be described as stupid. There's no worry for lack of firewood if the mountain is saved—save one's priceless body, and then wait and see. Ajia said the later actions of Jasper and Snow Feather were, to a large extent, influenced by these words of Monk Wu. Bracing himself and tucking in his head at this moment didn't ultimately influence people's belief in him. He still became one of the greatest men in Diamond Clan's history. *Historical Mirror of Forgotten Events* even considers him as great as Grandpa Jiu because often those who remain in the world endure more danger and tribulations than those who transcend the world.

It was hard to tell for how long the birch sapling whips cracked. Jasper had the impression that the sound lasted for at least a kalpa! Based on the theory of relativity, his feeling must have been correct. Sometimes, the practitioners entering deep meditation can experience a kalpa within the flick of the fingers. However, if you are surrounded by fire, a flash of time would be comparable to a hundred years. For many years thereafter, the cracking of birch sapling whips continued to resound in his heart, sometimes even in his dreams. He knew the sound had already penetrated his soul.

A voice halted the lashing. It was Braggart's.

Braggart said, "Look at the old thief—he's wearing armor! He came prepared! Take them off—take off his sheepskin jacket and the padded trousers!"

The militiamen took off Monk Wu's sheepskin jacket immediately. Monk Wu had no underwear. The women screamed. Kuan San laughed and said, "Look at the old thief—how come no underwear?" Monk Wu said, "No underpants either. Shall I take off the trousers?"

Many people exploded in laughter. Jasper realized why Monk Wu took off all his underwear before he left. He also laughed.

"Leave them on!" Cripple Big laughed and said, "I'm disgusted even if you're not. Just an old dick—what's there to look at?" The clansmen laughed and agreed with him, saying, "You're absolutely right—leave them on!"

Thereupon, Monk Wu tightened the string on his pants.

Before the "fixing" of Monk Wu, the female "bad lots" were mostly the ones greeted by the birch whips. Theirs was, in fact, preferential treatment because they participated as a group. The falling of any one of them represented the group. The men, however, were targeted singly.

The folks felt particularly gratified by the "fixing" of Monk Wu because he used to be revered by the people. Oftentimes, one's reverence for something also signifies pressure from the thing. Jasper discovered this through these "fixing" sessions. Back then, those who hit Monk Wu the hardest were frequently those who used to revere him the most.

Monk Wu was a practitioner of Tantric Buddhism. So the main focus of "fixing" him aimed at denigrating the esoteric aspect of this religion. Voluntary offerings, provided in the past, became evidence of his deception. If he hadn't deceived the people, who would've been willing to offer him good food? The stories on karmic retribution he told became the theoretical foundations for his deception. On this point, a tremendous amount of evidence was found as proof for this crime since he was fond of teaching others. During the "fixing" of Monk Wu, folks were particularly interested in teachings related to women. Braggart brought over the statue of a Vajra deity and said, "Look—this is the Buddha he worships! Look—this is a man embracing a woman! This is what he uses when he performs visualization. He visualizes himself as this Vajra god embracing Bright Consort.[2] They fool around with each other to produce what they call delight. This is what he practices."

"How many women have you done?" asked Kuan San.

Braggart's sinister face twitched. He bellowed, "Guess how he chose the women? Hey! He chose the pretty ones, the young ones, the ones who smelled good and looked like peach flowers—the ones with large boobs, narrow waists, long slanted eyes, jet black hair, and pearl white teeth; the ones with tight hot cunts, round asses and the ones who made trembling sounds when fucked."

"How many good women of Diamond Clan have you fucked?" demanded Kuan San. Monk Wu said nothing. He just smiled.

After shouting a few more times, Kuan San commenced the slaps. Kuan San's slaps were renowned for their loudness and force. One whack and the magenta imprint of a palm immediately appeared on Monk Wu's face. People looked at Kuan San in amazement. Monk Wu also stared at Kuan San coldly. Fearing that stare, Kuan San whacked furiously. After whacking more than ten times, Monk Wu collapsed on the platform.

Kuan San's ridicule of Esoteric Buddhism became the main subject of the public censure assemblies. Taking passages out of context, he concentrated on asking questions that couldn't very well be explicated. In order to explain them, Monk Wu would have had to reveal the "orthodox" in order to refute the "heterodox." But the "orthodox" was precisely what one wasn't allowed to reveal in Esoteric Buddhism. Kuan San took advantage of this fact and made a great issue of it.

Kuan San became Jasper's nightmare during those days.

Another Mystery

Tale of the Goddess mentions Snow Feather's mom in the section on the Dakini goddess's "heritage." The book follows the conventions of ancient Indian biographies by listing the many specialties related to Snow Feather, such as her birthplace, her heritage, her guru, the merits of her achievements, the location of her attainment, her career, etc. This was one of the conventions of ancient Indian biographies, which *Tale of the Goddess* followed. Although the Chinese didn't have the

---

2. Bright Consort refers to the partner of Brilliant King (Vidya-raja), one of the Vajras, for the practice of couple-cultivation.

four castes found in India, her heritage would still have included her parents. Nothing was known of her father. Information on her mother was relatively complete, but even then it only noted that she came from a wealthy family and harbored karmic wisdom; although she suffered tribulations, she never betrayed the Tripitaka[3] and invoked the name of the Buddha continuously, etc.

Historical Mirror of Forgotten Events, however, discovered through research that Snow Feather's mom was made captive and eventually sold to a brothel. The tribulations she suffered were linked to this fact. Hiding this fact would've been as impossible as a tiger wishing to consume Heaven, since many of her fellow captives always talked about it. This presented a challenge to Snow Feather's biographer. It would've been easier if he could've gotten away with not including her heritage. Despite the importance of one's heritage, however, one's own behavior ultimately plays the decisive role.

According to Diamond Clan's view at the time, Snow Feather was obviously the "daughter of a whore." To those who took heritage seriously, this wasn't something one would brag about.

Ajia said, this was precisely what made Snow Feather great. What ultimately made her great wasn't her heritage but rather the choices she made herself. In other words, it was her actions and nature that enabled her to become a Wisdom Dakini goddess.

But her previous identity as a whore did ultimately become the main cause for the tribulations suffered by Snow Feather's mom.

The day following the "fixing" of Monk Wu, two broken shoes were found hanging on Diamond Monastery's gate—one on the right, the other on the left. The villagers recognized them immediately as signifying two people—the left indicating maleness, the right indicating femaleness. One of them was a monk, the other a layperson. At the crack of dawn, Jasper heard a scream: "Ah—broken shoes!"

All the folks of Diamond Clan drew close. Jasper came out of the monastery, took down the shoes, and threw them away with force. At first, he thought it was just someone who wanted to ruin Monk Wu's reputation. What he didn't expect was that this was the prelude to a major event—an overture to the fated tribulations in the life of Snow Feather's mom.

---

3. "The Three Baskets" refers to the earliest collection of Buddhist writings.

When Grandpa Sun reached the height of a white poplar tree, Kuan San arrived at the monastery with the militiamen. Monk Wu and Snow Feather's mom were taken to the graveyard by the riverbank, dunce hats on their heads and broken shoes hanging off their necks. Offensive words decorated the dunce hats. Braggart also got people to find two companions for the "execution." Jie Big and Old Daddy-Nine were captives at the same time as Snow Feather's mom and were known to have screwed her under unusual circumstances. Because of this, they stood on the "public censure assembly" platform along with her. It was their duty to unveil Snow Feather's mom's identity as a whore.

Through the narration of Jie Big, we saw a dilapidated room filled with clothes. This was the laundry room of the Brilliant King Clan militiamen. The laundry room was situated in a huge garrison. The garrison was very old; people said it was built during the height of the Tang dynasty. It was encircled by tamped-earth walls more than thirty feet high and was most imposing. Many years later, I used to ride my motorcycle and visit there. I felt an overwhelming sense of oppression whenever I stood under the massive wall. I wondered how Snow Feather's mom felt when she was tossed inside it by fate.

Through Jie Big's exposure, we saw Diamond Clan women who were trapped within the tiger's den. I saw no sign of their having fought to death the tigers and wolves. They looked clean but tired. They were herded into the laundry room and stripped naked. I saw the men enter, guffawing lecherously. Their lecherous guffaws sounded exactly like our lecherous guffaws. I don't know whether we'd have laughed the same way and do what men do under the same circumstances? Jie Big said, "It was the same everywhere back then. That was the custom. The winner got all the gold and silver, and fucked all the beautiful women!"

We saw a pile of soft, squirmy intestines—the result of their owner gouging out a man's eyeball. We also saw whistling whips—one crack of that horsewhip would've made the strongest horse cower. They created streaks of blood in the flesh of some women's bodies, just like those scratched by the women on the men's faces. We also saw some "corn cobs" stabbing into the lower part of the women, pushing and pulling, dragging out scarlet-colored blood. We saw many such scenes. We couldn't bear to hear any more.

Thereupon, we understood why Snow Feather's mom finally succumbed. She lay on the pile of clothes and let the men who were naked from the waist down jab away, huffing and puffing. We saw nothing lascivious; we were inclined to feel anger. Then I really became angry as I heard Cripple Big's voice, "Oh—so Snow Feather was a bastard!"

I could tell Jie Big's intention through his "exposure." He wanted people to realize Snow Feather's mom's situation. He wanted to elicit people's sympathy for her. He almost reached his goal, for I saw many women weep. They rubbed their eyes and sobbed. Their weeping indicated to me that there was still hope for Diamond Clan.

Jie Big emphasized the situation of Snow Feather's mom with all his might. He didn't admit to raping her, not that he thought he was any better than the others. He said after staying at a place like that for a length of time, any man would become crazy upon seeing a woman. Over there, one would even feel a freshness just from thinking about women. He said he also wanted to fuck the women back then, but there was no chance. He was one of the male captives. He had done it with her once, but that was much later, when she was working at the laundry room. He gave her a silver dollar afterward. "You can ask her if you don't believe me!"

The additional information Jie Big gave at the end created an intensely negative effect. It immediately eliminated the sympathy people had for her. The silver dollar effectively turned Snow Feather's mom into a whore. The village women hated nothing more than whores because they feared their men would also spend such a silver dollar. Consequently, the sobbing ceased, and disdain displaced the sympathy.

"How was she?" asked Donkey Two.

The question provoked an explosion of laughter. The same question would, no doubt, have provoked abomination if it had been asked before the "silver dollar."

Jie Big didn't describe how she was. Although his faux pas produced a negative effect, Jasper nevertheless felt he was worthy of respect. And then, after Kuan San shouted at him, he said hesitantly, "Like a bitch." He clenched his teeth and just said "like a bitch" thereafter, no matter who shouted at him.

The meaning of "like a bitch" became a mystery at Diamond Clan. The folks discussed it for decades thereafter, without knowing the real meaning behind it.

In order to understand the meaning of "like a bitch," Braggart had Old Daddy Nine describe his experiences and bid him emphasize the period when she worked in the laundry room. Old Daddy Nine was a meek and scrawny old man. He seemed anxious to use the opportunity to prove himself in order to atone for his sins. He wanted very much to describe how she was, but the taste of it transcended words. Even if he were the best writer, what he could say right now would not accurately describe how it was back then; how much more so when one considers the fact that he was but an inarticulate peasant. Old Daddy Nine mumbled for quite a while, without making any clearer the meaning of Jie Big's "like a bitch."

Later, in order to cover up for her, *Family Instructions of Diamond Clan* explained the "bitch" roughly as a vehement attempt at resistance by Snow Feather's mom—that she bit and tore at the men like a female dog. This was obviously contrary to reality. If it were true, she'd have been long dead. Back then, none of the women who refused to comply got to live. But the book did contain a valuable detail, noting that the laundry room served dual purposes: one, laundry washing; and two, the site for rewarding Brilliant King clansmen. The clan head would tell anyone who had displayed bravery, "Come, Boy, take this reward and have some fun" and hand him a piece of paper. The man could then enter the laundry room by just giving the piece of paper to the guard and playing to his heart's content.

The book also recorded the memories of one of the women who said that there were more "wolves than there was meat." It was a laundry room in name only. The female captives had to receive more than twenty men each per day. While the militiamen could only enter with permission, the clan VIPs could arrive at their convenience. Sweat soaked the women's beds, which reeked with a foul odor.

This detail was the same as what Old Daddy Nine exposed later. So a woman exclaimed, "Aiyo! They were peeing pits!"

Donkey Two's Talent

Diamond Clan's public censure assemblies embarked upon a new stage thereafter. Because of the presence of Snow Feather's mom, the public censure assemblies became more interesting. Association with sex can always induce excitement.

Whenever Snow Feather's mom was being "fixed," not only the entire village but also those tens of leagues away participated. As a consequence, Diamond Clan became even more renowned throughout Liangzhou.

According to *Historical Mirror of Forgotten Events*, Diamond Clan's fame had spread throughout Liangzhou a few previous times. It made news throughout northwestern China when the Liangzhou city police station was smashed, under the leadership of a man named Qi Feiqing.[4] The most recent event was that, during a great famine when everywhere else was reporting problems, Diamond Clan alone was still able to send tax grain to the county government. It was said no one died of starvation there. This statement was proclaimed by none other than the county chief of the time.

But the most conspicuous event was ultimately this one. The "parade for public exposure" of Snow Feather's mom enabled everyone—young and old, big and small—to become acquainted with Diamond Clan.

The "fixing" of Snow Feather's mom began with designating her a "bad lot" and then adding to it "broken shoe," "whore," and other labels. At first, Monk Wu was only a "stage companion," but as assemblies for public censure rose in stature, he gradually developed into a main character.

At first their "fixings" were similar to those performed earlier, which consisted of a dish of birch sapling fried meat. But the clansmen gradually grew. The moment the evil in their hearts encountered a suitable climate, it would sprout and engender all sorts of tricks. Due to the stubbornness of Jie Big and the inarticulateness of Old Daddy Nine, Braggart selected Donkey Two, an incredibly articulate "bad lot," to help with the "struggle" against Snow Feather's mom. A frequent visitor of Hexi Hotel, he had gained fame for whoring. According to him, although he wasn't a Brilliant King Clan member, he had indeed slept with Snow Feather's mom. He had once presented opium as a gift to the Brilliant King Clan head. The head was so pleased that Donkey Two was given an opportunity to have fun. He obviously wanted to establish merit in order to redeem his sins. Knowing fully well what Braggart wanted, he grafted onto Snow Feather's mom all the most memorable sexual experiences he'd ever encountered, making Braggart yell with delight. Braggart said, "Fucking Donkey Two—who'd have thought you'd be so eloquent!" Of course, Donkey Two never thought he would become an instant celebrity in Liangzhou because of this—or that one evening many years later he would die from having his genitals yanked out by a group of furious devotees of Snow Feather.

---

4. Qi Feiqing (1868–1911) led a local rebellion in 1908, after several years of famine.

Donkey Two was extremely good at detecting nuances in people's faces and would adjust his speech's content according to the program host's reaction. If the host showed approval, Donkey Two would wag his tongue and embellish with all his might—so the entire audience would feel they'd been on the spot, feeling what he'd experienced. His confessions became the best course in sex education. They became the entry to knowledge for many boys. At the same time, because bachelors who participated in the public censure assemblies were wont to masturbate, objectively speaking, Diamond Clan's labor productivity declined.

Donkey Two was both detestable and lovable. He provided many dramatic memories of that period but was also a cause of instability within Diamond Clan. It was through his narrations that many women realized females could have something known as sexual climax. Donkey Two's illustrations of sexual climax were the most graphic explanation of Jie Big's "bitch." According to Ajia, the prevalence of adultery by Diamond Clan's women thereafter apparently originated in Donkey Two's encouragements.

Heeding Braggart's hint, Donkey Two dragged Monk Wu in as well. At this point, Donkey Two was transformed from a "John" into an exposer. Naturally, he thought he would expose how Monk Wu and Snow Feather's mom practiced couple-cultivation. Through his exposure, Diamond Clan folks realized that the sweet dew people often talked about was fluid from sexual intercourse, that the "great fragrance" used for making sweet dew pills was actually excrement and that the "small fragrance" was really urine. These and things like human flesh, were the ingredients of the sweet dew pills the villagers frequently consumed. In the past, villagers used to pride themselves on whenever they could obtain sweet dew pills from Monk Wu. Now many of them wanted to throw up. It ruined the last shred of respect the villagers had for Monk Wu. Just like Snow Feather's mom, Monk Wu had become a pile of dogshit, held in contempt by humankind.

Donkey Two's portrayal of the practice of double-cultivating by Monk Wu and Snow Feather's mom was most graphic. His voice and emotions rose; he was one with the characters. The villagers saw a fat naked monk twisting around the scrawny hag. They crooned and moaned. They writhed as they chanted a mantra. Donkey Two couldn't replicate the mantra, but he could tell it was an evil curse. The object of the curse was our glorious clan head. He saw a torrent of lewd fluids surge from the lower parts of the two ugly bodies and flow into a washbasin.

Donkey Two said it was from this basin that Monk Wu scooped out fluids to make the sweet dew pills. He said, "I don't care what you two demons practiced, but you shouldn't have used your foul juices as sweet dew pills to cheat us for offerings! We are the clansmen of Diamond Clan, not religious slaves! It's simply intolerable! Down with the old rogue!"

Thereupon the villagers yelled, "Down with the old rogue!"

"So the two ganged up together. Sometimes, they made out entire nights doing what they called couple-cultivation—but really just fucking! Ah! They even made out in the temple's main hall!" Donkey Two was furious. He spat at Monk Wu and sprayed the latter's face with spittle.

Donkey Two also made gestures to show what the rogues looked like when they practiced double-cultivation, by imitating the statue of the Vajra deities. He said, "The old monk sat on the prayer mat naked. Don't underestimate him because of his age; his thing was huge, as big as a braying donkey's! Yeeah!" He clicked his tongue as if in great admiration. That old hag sat right on it. In no time at all—you hear the sound of a cat lapping lard. The old woman shouted like a bitch. She screamed and screamed, more madly, more amorously, and more disgustingly than any woman he had ever seen before. She was certainly an old expert! Certainly, an old ginger root is spicier than a young one!

"Haha! Haha!"

"Haha! Haha!"

So now, Snow Feather's mom really stank.

Chapter 24

The Wooden Donkeys of Diamond Clan

Some more yellow dust descended from the sky,
You said a sandstorm had arrived.
Is it that terrifying?
Look at you almost calling for Heaven
Without knowing whence it had come,
A river of large and small stones
Rolled and tumbled on the Gobi Desert.

Secret Contests of the Wooden Donkeys

The public censure assemblies, which began with the denunciation of problems related to public morality, gradually escalated in stature and spread to other villages and other locations.

The angry crowd was no longer satisfied with merely having broken shoes hung around the necks of the offenders. Braggart thought it would be best to strip the couple naked and parade them through the streets, tied together the way Donkey Two described couple-cultivation. But some of the elderly in the village opposed the idea. Monk Wu was a monk and erstwhile abbot of Diamond Clan Monastery, after all. Other villages would laugh at them for tormenting a monk like this. This was reason number one. Reason number two was the fact that, even if the old monk practiced couple-cultivation as per Donkey Two's exposure, it wasn't a big deal anyway. They'd heard that the practice of couple-cultivation wasn't considered an infraction against Buddhist vows, once the practitioner had accomplished a certain level of attainment. The ancestors used to say, "Even if a saint does something mundane, his mind remains pure."

According to *Historical Mirror of Forgotten Events*, the fiercest opponents of the idea were people like Cripple Big. Their families had Monk Wu perform the Abhiseka ritual on them soon after birth. Monk Wu had performed the longevity Abhiseka ritual on almost all the children in the village and taught them the Six Word Mantra of Great Brilliance.[1] According to the local custom, Monk Wu would be considered their guru. Betraying one's guru would bring bad luck for the rest of one's life and lead to punishment in Hell. Although they wouldn't voice it, they were subconsciously concerned about the taboo. So Braggart conceded, saying, "Fine, we'll fix the old hag first, and just have the old monk come along!"

And then he added, "Since we can't parade her in the form of couple-cultivation, then let her ride the wooden donkey!"

Family Instructions of Diamond Clan describes the wooden donkey in detail. Many women had ridden the wooden donkey throughout Diamond Clan's history. The wooden donkey was, in fact, a single-wheeled cart. Instead of a seat, there's a round trunk resembling the back of a donkey. Upon the back of this "donkey" was affixed an upright wooden rod about five centimeters long that resembled a phallus. Whenever a lascivious or adulterous woman was discovered in the village, she would be stripped naked, trussed up tightly, and placed on the back of the "donkey" with the rod in her vagina. Someone would be ordered to push the cart and have it toss about on a particularly bumpy road. A man carrying a gong would lead the procession. As he struck 'kuang—' 'kuang—,' he would shout, "Hey—elders! Open your eyes wide and look at what happens to a lewd woman! I urge you, gentlemen, to love yourself and remain clean. Do not transgress sexually; do not rob. Behave yourself, and abide by the law. As the proverb says, gambling engenders robbers and thieves; adultery causes deaths. Bed a wildflower and the family will be ruined. Of the ten thousand evils, sexual transgression is the worst; of the hundred virtues, filial piety is the foremost . . ."

Historical Mirror of Forgotten Events records how a woman who had murdered her husband was placed on a wooden donkey and paraded through the local eight counties and twenty-one villages. They would

---

1. "Om maṇi padme huṃ" in Sanskrit; "om ma ni bai me hum" in Tibetan.

slice off a piece of her flesh whenever they encountered a dog and another piece whenever they saw a cat. She was paraded for four and a half days before they finished slicing her.

So Kuan San and his men brought out the wooden donkey from the Ancestral Hall. The wooden donkey had been placed among the other penal instruments displayed by the ancestors as visual instructional materials. Who'd have thought it would come in handy now? The only defect on this donkey was that its wooden rod had disappeared, through the actions of women who couldn't give birth. It was believed the consumption of water, mixed with ashes of the rod's burnt shavings, guaranteed the births of big fat babies. After many years, the rod had disappeared. Braggart had someone make a new one, which turned out as rough as a corn cob. Knowing what it was used for, Cripple Big spent half a day polishing away the rough bumps, so Snow Feather's mom would suffer less pain.

The parade began. People stripped Snow Feather's mom naked. Her wrinkled skin and flesh were quite ugly. Someone said, "It would be much more fun if Snow Feather weren't in prison—we'd get her to do it instead of her mom." Others sighed in agreement. They all said, "You're so right—Snow Feather got off of the hook too easy!"

Snow Feather's mom pulled a wooden face. One couldn't tell her emotions, but she exhibited a certain calmness one would find in an enlightened person. She let the militiamen manipulate her however they wanted. She took a bath for the struggle parade. She spent half a night washing off all the dirt in the nooks and crannies. Although she wasn't able to tighten her aged skin through the wash, she nevertheless looked clean. Her breasts had become drooping lumps of dried skin. White streaks covered her belly; they were caused by pregnancy. Her legs were so scrawny that they were just skin and bones. The ugliest parts of her were her small feet, which used to be bound, but were then unbound. Their crooked bones were conspicuously disgusting.

Jasper couldn't bear to look at her. He asked Braggart, "Why do you hate her so much? She's never done anything to you people."

Braggart replied, "This isn't personal—this is related to Diamond Clan's fate!"

"What did she do?" Jasper wiped his tears.

Braggart said, "She's a broken shoe, a rogue!"

"Why are you so hard-hearted?" asked Jasper.

A group of youths crowded over and pushed Jasper aside. Their faces burned with an excitement even more exuberant than Braggart's.

Jasper had witnessed them flinging their leather belts and blinding a "bad lot." Jasper was afraid to look at them. He just covered his face and wept. He thought, if Snow Feather knew this, she'd cry her heart out. But then, Snow Feather would never have let her mom suffer this. She'd have saved her mom using martial arts and flown away, high and far. *I shouldn't have brought her back from Old Mountain*, he thought, *but then, she'd have starved to death a long time ago.* Jasper regretted that he didn't have them return to Old Mountain when Snow Feather's legs got slightly better. If so, they wouldn't have had to suffer so much.

A few people lifted Snow Feather's mom and placed her on the wooden donkey. This was the most exciting scene before the inception of the "struggle parade." During the parade, it would be very difficult to see the "spring radiance," if one could consider an old hag's private parts such a thing. Snow Feather's mom was only in her fifties or sixties, but she looked very old. Once the subject was old, the stimulation engendered by this kind of trick diminished considerably. But it attracted a sizable audience, nevertheless. When she was placed onto the wooden donkey, people formed a circle around her, just like when an executioner was ready to chop off a head. The only difference between the two situations was that people craned their necks when they watched a decapitation, but most of them bent their knees to watch the riding of the wooden donkey.

People heard a piercing scream that didn't sound human. Red fluid dyed the back of the wooden donkey.

Cripple Big hollered, "It was too long! It was too long!" He had people lift the woman back up and shaved the rod with a plane, without further ado.

"Have some conscience!" Snow Feather's mom wept.

After working on it for quite a while, Cripple Big shortened the rod by an inch. Jasper knew he really wanted to help Snow Feather's mom. Occupying a lowly position at Diamond Clan, anything Cripple Big would say would've been as useless as a fart. Since he couldn't stop the evil conduct, he tried his best to lessen her pain. Jasper felt grateful to him.

Some people placed the woman on the wooden donkey again. She didn't weep this time. Her eyes were closed, so people couldn't see her emotions. But everyone could see the calmness on her face. It was as if the following words were written on her face: "Go ahead with the slaughtering and slicing. If you can do it, I can take it." Because blood continued to flow from the wooden donkey, most of the faces didn't exhibit a sinister expression.

The single-wheeled cart wobbled forward. The thighs of Snow Feather's mom were dyed red. Four "execution ground companions" followed her. They were of course the "matches" of the broken shoe. Monk Wu walked calmly; Jasper could tell that he was chanting a mantra. He used to have a string of rosary beads, but Kuan San had snatched it during one of the struggle sessions and the beads flew in ten different directions. Although they were but ordinary beads—the moon-star bodhi seeds of the yellow vine—they had turned glossy black from being used for twenty years by Monk Wu and were believed to possess great powers. Once, a demon possessed a woman who became as strong as an ox; even an iron chain as thick as a finger couldn't restrain her. One of her family members came to Monk Wu to beg for assistance, and Monk Wu gave him his string of rosary beads. The family member placed it around the woman's neck, and she immediately fell asleep. Later, the demon came to Monk Wu to beg forgiveness, and Monk Wu made him one of his own dharma protectors. But no matter how much power these beads had, they were not able to save Monk Wu himself, who was dragged around like a donkey. He had to wear a dunce hat and a placard on which was written words like "old rogue, big cheater." He was followed by Jie Big, Old Daddy Nine, and Donkey Two. Jie Big and Old Daddy Nine looked very dejected. Although they had been classified as "bad lots," the reason they were part of this struggle parade was because of their involvement with a broken shoe. They could only blame their problem-causing dicks. If it weren't for relieving their temporary "starvation," they'd be watching on the sideline with the other "bad lots"!

Among the four, only Donkey Two's face beamed with splendor. Aside from Snow Feather's mom, he was definitely the center of attention. Their arrival at each station would invariably be accompanied by his onsite broadcast. This seemed to have been the most glorious period of his entire life. His fame spread throughout the realm for his graphic elucidations taken from personal experience. His speeches enabled people to feel that Snow Feather's mom deserved her punishment, that her sins were odious to the extreme, and that nothing short of death could appease the people's wrath. The later tribulations of Snow Feather's mom were obviously directly linked to the brilliance of his speeches. His behavior would anger many of Snow Feather's believers years later: they would come down on him the way an eagle comes after a chick and yank out his genitals, as well as other meandering, wriggling inner organs.

Cripple Big led the procession, beating on a gong, and hobbled into the hall of shame of Diamond Clan's history. This wasn't a position of his choosing; it was only that none of the other villagers were willing to walk in front of a woman with her belly exposed. According to Liangzhou's local customs, this would bring bad luck—since the folks of Liangzhou considered women's genitals ill-omened. Even accidentally seeing a woman's private parts might bring bad karma. A woman who felt taken advantage of, and at the end of her rope, would weep all the way to the opponent's gate, pull off her pants, pee right there, and wail. This would be equivalent to insulting his ancestors. An older male cousin of mine fell to his death from an electric pole some twenty-four feet high, a day after he was thus "ruined" by a woman. No man would want to parade in front of a woman with her belly exposed. Braggart said, "Cripple Big—you lead!" Cripple Big said, "I'm not good at shouting slogans!" Braggart said, "Just beat the gong—I'll have someone else lead the slogans!" Braggart selected Donkey Two, who had the greatest eloquence, to lead shouting of the slogans. So Donkey Two held dual positions and had his fill of glory.

This strange parade attracted innumerable spectators. Hearing the news, people swarmed in from near and far. A few days went by, although Snow Feather's mom continued to bleed, the amount had lessened discernably; at least there was no fear of her bleeding to death. Because the wooden donkey was bare, the rider's body would frequently lean to the side. The elders suggested that the woman not be trussed. Snow Feather's mom now had the use of her hands to adjust the angle of her body, to lift herself up and hold onto the seat—consequently, it was, comparatively, somewhat more comfortable than the days before.

A few days later, the folks of nearby villages were no longer content with being just spectators. They'd been infected by Diamond Clan's madness. Each village had their own "braggart." Those "braggarts" also felt the need to establish their power and prestige through grandiose excuses, either to fulfill their own private desires or to "fix" those who differed from them. They "drew a tiger by watching the cat," selected some broken shoes, and rushed to construct their own wooden donkeys. However, without a talent like Cripple Big, the rods were so crudely fashioned that a broken shoe hemorrhaged profusely in less than half a day of usage. People rushed her to a nearby clinic immediately. The doctor extracted a splinter five inches long, about the thickness of a chopstick, from her vagina. Phew—just a false alarm! Instead of the rod, they stuck a ball of white thorn, normally used to stop bleeding, into her and continued the parade. Since she was young and better looking than Snow Feather's mom, the throng of spectators was jam packed.

To prevent the occurrence of such incidents in the future, the local government stipulated regulations for the construction of the wooden donkeys. Thereupon, the surrounding villages dispatched members to Diamond Clan to "seek scriptures," Cripple Big suddenly became a popular "hot steamed cake." Although a bachelor, he was extremely perceptive; so that although women's vaginas were of different widths and depths, the rods he made were just the right size for serving the purpose of punishment without causing death through excessive bleeding. He made almost every scripture seeker feel they've "seen the light" and leave satisfied. He told Jasper secretly he had intentionally shortened the rod's length by two sizes and emphasized the importance of polishing it. He asked Jasper, "Would you say I'm performing a good deed?" Jasper smiled wryly without answering.

However, Cripple Big was convinced that he was performing a good deed. In order for his good deed to be practiced, he collected wood from fruit trees and fashioned many strangely shaped rods, which he polished with leather-working implements. He then doused them with oil and buffed them with soft sheepskin until they were glossy black. He would bestow one upon each of the scripture seekers, telling the person to place it directly into the hole in the wooden donkey. He thought surely this would lessen the suffering of the women. Who'd have thought, however, on the day of the collective parade that almost all the wooden donkeys featured rough, shoddy copies. Cripple Big was furious. He questioned the people self-righteously but was castigated by them instead. They said, "What were you trying to do? Do you call what you made punishment? You made them so well that all the women would want to use them!" The idea planted a seed of wisdom in Cripple Big. Many years later, he fashioned many lifelike dildos of different shapes and polished them until they were a hundred times smoother than the real thing, using his skills as an expert leather craftsman. His products were so popular that they were exported to Europe, America, and Southeast Asia, and created many millionaires. Back then, he would brag to children that he'd accumulated tremendous merit during that special era. Donkey Two, who knew the ins and outs of the matter, would taunt him with the line, "Tell them how you fucked the women too!" And Cripple Big would zip his mouth as if choked by boiled yam.

So Cripple Big's kindness wasn't accepted by the people, and the riding of wooden donkeys continued to produce cases of deaths from hemorrhaging due to pierced uteruses. However, cases of chopstick-like splinters definitely decreased. Cripple Big continued to strike the gong in front of the procession. He ventured to shout a slogan occasionally but would always reverse the content and turn it into a counter-revolutionary slogan. Because he lisped, plus the fact that the crowd was clamorous, it was never discovered. But when he saw Jasper staring at him the tenth time he made such a mistake, a cold sweat broke out. He thought, *Let me stop while I'm ahead and not be the mule from Shanxi that pretended to bray like a donkey*; thus ended his glorious slogan-calling career.

Due to the fact that the surrounding villages sported no shortage of beautiful young women who rode wooden donkeys, outsiders ceased to watch Diamond Clan's parades. Braggart appointed several organizing "committee members." Just like with the lunar New Year celebration, the committee members were responsible for maintaining order, ensuring participation, organizing the event, and more. In order to create a respectable crowd, Braggart made participation in the parades mandatory for all clansmen and provided a subsidy from the Ancestral Hall. Absences were penalized by requiring payment of a certain amount of grain. The committee members took attendance each time. Only then did they manage to prevent "brain drain," since their young men would much prefer to go to other villages to watch their young women ride wooden donkeys. They had heard that the riders of wooden donkeys in other villages were not only numerous but also beautiful, with incomparably attractive "spring radiances"—definitely better than looking at Snow Feather's mom! This infuriated Braggart. He said, "When did Diamond Clan ever play second fiddle to anyone?" He thought and thought, and finally came up with a plan. Under his proposal, the villages agreed to hold a united parade. Now, the event promised to be magnificent.

Inquiry

According to *Historical Mirror of Forgotten Events*, the counties and villages used to organize some activities communally back then. They were akin to the temple festivals of the past. For example, all the villages would organize a Chinese New Year celebration during the First Month of the lunar calendar. The villagers would wear opera costumes, hang a drum about their waists, and twist and dance to their hearts' content to the rhythm of the drums. That was the liveliest time of the year.

According to custom, the festival entertainments from the different villages would gather together on the fifteenth of the First Month. This competition was almost the equivalent of the national military parade. It was an exhibition of the "real stuff" of each village. Rivalry was extremely intense when they competed. Each troupe exerted itself to attract more spectators and cheers. The level of intensity was no less than that of a war. Some drummers even secretly wrapped iron rods in red silk and used them instead of their wooden drum mallets. When the festival entertainment groups met, they would stab right through the cowhide of the opponents' drums so those would become "dumb" after they passed each other. The villagers with the "dumb" drummers would feel devastated, as this also signified the loss of a good "origin" for the year. This "origin" is similar to the meaning of "origin" in Buddhism, but it also connoted "omen."

Kuan San used to be renowned through Liangzhou as an expert performer of "waist drums" and became "local hero" of Diamond Clan.

Therefore, the united parade proposed by Braggart could be considered an idea that both conformed with popular sentiment and was current with the times.

The most celebrated figure during that particular month, which outshone even the New Year festival competition, was Donkey Two. His speeches, which combined animated dramatizations with exuberant emotions, were the stock repertoire of all the gatherings. More than anything else, they helped to improve Diamond Clan's reputation since other than being able to claim as originator of the activity, Diamond Clan parades had lost their charm. The folks of other villages notwithstanding, even its own young men would secretly slip away to watch the women riding wooden donkeys elsewhere. If it weren't for the bloody suppressions carried out by the "committee members"—slapping faces until the noses bled—Diamond Clan would've been thoroughly discredited a long time ago. But one could restrain the bodies, not the hearts—their bodies might have been captives of Cao's garrison, yet their hearts still belonged to the Han.[2] Although they stood next to Diamond Clan's procession,

---

2. This reference appears in the novel *Romance of the Three Kingdoms*, and refers to Han generals who were captured by Cao Cao (155–220) but remained loyal to the emperor associated with the Han. Three generals satisfied this proverb in the novel.

their eyes were staring at the voluptuous pale bodies elsewhere. At first, Braggart castigated them vehemently, but later on even he drooled and gazed at the bobbing breasts elsewhere.

This was inevitable. The riders in other villages were not only young but completely varied. There were even a few who were unmarried but had the gall to do broken shoe with young men in their villages. Two of them even became pregnant. One of the pregnant ones gave birth in an outhouse. People said the baby was a fat little boy with a voice that pierced the clouds and was as sonorous as a bronze bell but was stoned to death by his mother with bricks. People also said the bronze bell didn't stop ringing until his mother hurled more than twenty bricks at him—then his voice turned into sobs. This type of goods obviously attracted more popularity than Snow Feather's mom. Above all else, the bobbing and nodding breasts alone presented the indescribable charms of precipitous peaks—enough to snatch one's soul!

Truly, in the territory of Diamond Clan, "the mountains and rivers are ruined, floss wafts in the wind;/ weapons and arms are sparse, one is surrounded by stars."[3]

Braggart stamped his feet and beat his chest.

After the assembly ended, he issued an "edict" to Kuan San ordering him to find an unmarried girl who had been impregnated. Kuan San racked his brain but to no avail. After going down to the village and conducting a lengthy investigation, however, he finally found one. The woman's beauty compared favorably to the unwed mothers of the other villages, but she'd already been sold to a middle-aged cripple in Inner Mongolia ten years ago. There'd been no news concerning her whereabouts.

Braggart said, "This is fart! Investigate some more; see if we have any right now!"

"None," Kuan San said, "the passable ones all starved to death a few years ago. The rest all look sick and scrawny. Some are seventeen or eighteen, but look twelve or thirteen."

Kuan San said, "If only Snow Feather were still around. She'd be the grand finale type for sure!" Braggart's eyes lit up. He told Kuan San to go to the Reform Labor Farm at Wangjing Stockade right away and tell them Diamond Clan insists on having Snow Feather back for public exposure.

---

3. These are lines from a poem composed by Wen Tianxiang (1236–1283) after his army suffered defeat, and he was captured.

Three days later, Kuan San returned. He spread his palms and said the people wouldn't release her.

Braggart's face turned black from anger. He twitched his face for long while and said, "Check out the widows then! Check the cute ones first!"

After a lot of investigation, Kuan San discovered that all the widows looked sickly and scrawny. They all got shriveled up from that calamitous bout of starvation and hadn't had time to recover from it. The only young woman who was sexy was Heavenly Girl, who had "worn Heaven's head." The year she turned sixteen, her dad invited all the significant members of Diamond Clan over and engaged in a ritual known as "wearing Heaven's head" performed for her. This meant she was essentially married to Heaven. She could freely sleep with whomever she desired, and the children born would belong to her family. Kuan San asked, "She can't be considered as a widow, can she?"

Braggart was infuriated, "Do you have more farts?" This was when Kuan San remembered that Heavenly Girl was Braggart's woman. Ever since she started to "befriend" Braggart, she hadn't been known to have fooled around with anyone else. Kuan San said, "Then we have no choice but to mobilize the clansmen's wives." Braggart said, "Sure! Go give it a try. Tell them, the women, that this is like competing for glory with the other troupes during Chinese New Year—we can't possibly allow the might of Diamond Clan to be diminished!"

Kuan San spent nine catties of his saliva in doing the persuasion and received at least eighteen catties in return. Once they heard him, nearly all the clansmen spat at him. They said many unpleasant words, which when compiled, consisted of, "Shit, Kuan San! Is your dick crazy? How could you come up with this? Get your one-eyed mom to ride it! Get your smelly wife to ride it! Ride the donkey yourself with the rod in your mouth! Get your girl to ride it! Your head must've been hit by a fucking hammer—why else run around like a cat or dog, stirring up trouble all over the place! If I were you, I'd have tripped into a shit pit head first a long time ago!" And so on and so forth. Kuan San was so angry that his throat grumbled for a long while, without being able to fart out a single word.

Braggart said, "Are we really going to let the other villages win?"

Kuan San said, "What if I try to ask Heavenly Girl?"

Braggart was quiet for a long while before he said, "You might give it a try. Just don't tell her that I put you up to it."

Thereupon Kuan San went to the home of Heavenly Girl. The woman was chopping firewood with an axe. When she heard what he had to say, she lifted the axe and spat at him. Kuan San's face felt numb. He had been her temporary husband before Braggart monopolized her. He knew the woman was lecherous and wild. It felt like riding on a powerful horse. The woman said, "What! You want this old lady of yours, to ride the wooden donkey? This lady doesn't even feel like riding a donkey like you! You think I itch so much I need to poke myself with a corn cob? Did my 'wearing Heaven's head' make me a 'bad lot' too? Did I make you pay when you slept with me and became a prostitute? Or you found three hundred men under my bed that you couldn't take? Someone didn't mend her pants properly so a trash like you snuck out! Get the hell out of here! Any more fart, don't blame my axe!"

Kuan San returned dejectedly.

"We're done for!" he said.

The Rumbling Wheels

Braggart had no option other than calling a meeting of all the clan members. He shouted himself hoarse, recounting Diamond Clan's glorious past history. He proceeded from the Song, Yuan, Ming, and Qing to the mythical three sovereigns and five emperors—he forgot their order—and made things up as he went along. He carried on from the thirty-six heavenly deities to the seventy-two earthly demons[4]—short of matching the names of the constellations to the characters in *The Water Margin*.[5] He said the four great beauties of Chinese history[6] were all ancestors of Diamond Clan—and included Wu Zetian,[7] Cixi,[8] and

---

4. According to religious Daoism, the thirty-six heavenly deities and seventy-two earthly demons are constellations within the northern dipper; each of the constellations constitutes an individual deity or demon.

5. The 108 (36 plus 72) main characters of the popular late Yuan–early Ming novel, *The Water Margin*, are supposed to have been earthly manifestations of the constellations.

6. Usually recognized as Xishi (born 506 BCE), Wang Zhaojun (born 50 BCE), Diao Chan (may have been fictional; immortalized in *Romance of the Three Kingdoms*), and Yang Guifei (719–756).

7. Empress Wu Zetian (624–705) was the only female emperor in Chinese history.

8. Empress Dowager Cixi (1835–1908) was a regent who essentially controlled the government for forty-seven years toward the end of the Qing dynasty.

Pan Jinlian[9] in this list. He even attributed the four greatest Chinese inventions[10] to Diamond Clan ancestors. According to Braggart, the four inventions were mahjong, poker, water, and fire. He lamented bitterly the degeneration of the human race. He was he first to come up with the theory of the degeneration of the human race about twenty years ahead of most scholars.

"We can't possibly allow Diamond Clan's eminence to be diminished!" Braggart did everything short of plucking out his heart for all to see.

Deeply touched though the clan members were, they also knew the wooden donkey wasn't made for humans to ride on. The blood of Snow Feather's mom on the donkey's back was enough to scare away the souls of many women. The minute they thought of that dripping red color, they shook their heads at Braggart's suggestions that they sacrifice themselves. Although they dared not castigate Braggart as they did Kuan San, they all stared at their own feet, without averting their eyes. Braggart's flowing saliva tumbled down three thousand feet but was as effective as an autumnal wind blowing past the ears of a donkey.

Furthermore, the men glared at their women fiercely—fearing lest their women succumb to Braggart's magic potion and cuckold them with the wooden donkey's rod. Although no one dared to oppose Braggart openly—there had been dissenters in the past, but the dissenters immediately became Diamond Clan's public enemies as soon as they voiced dissent—they stared at their women as if facing a great battle, their hearts throbbing in their throats like a frog on a hot iron plate.

Kuan San said, "How about taking turns? Each riding it once?"

The men talked now. Although Kuan San inspired awe, he was just the chief of the militiamen after all; he was neither the clan head, nor a representative of the entire clan's members. Reckless said, "Kuan San, good idea! Your woman is a kohlrabi that even the pigs won't eat. You toss her into a pile of shit and see no difference. Of course, you won't mind how many times she rides on a wooden donkey, but my woman is different. Mine is so beautiful and delicate that water would drip from a tiny pinch!" All the men roared in laughter because in fact Reckless's woman was even uglier than Kuan San's. Kuan San's

---

9. Pan Jinlian is a minor character in *The Water Margin*, further developed into a major character in the Ming dynasty novel, *Jin Ping Mei*. She is famous for lasciviousness.

10. Usually recognized as: the compass, paper-making, printing, and gunpowder.

woman might've been dark skinned, but she nevertheless had fat on her. Reckless's woman was as withered as a dried carrot. Although Reckless's woman wasn't attractive, his words struck a chord. Many men agreed. One of them said, "Kuan San, so you want our women to be fucked by the rod—are you human or not?" Another said, "Fine, Kuan San! Get your woman to go first. We'll make the rod three feet long—would you be satisfied then?" And then, they all roared, "Down with Kuan San! Down with Kuan San!"

It seemed the mobilization session had now turned into a struggle session!

Kuan San's face turned purple red, "What's with all the bawling? My dick is numb from your howling! So you're all lords of Diamond Clan—am I some donkey of Brilliant King Clan? Too bad I'm not educated. If I'd studied three basketfuls of words, I wouldn't even want to be a magistrate! I was just thinking of Diamond Clan! Look at how the other villages have all those colorful girls and young wives, and we, our Diamond Clan is the only one with an old hag! Don't you feel ashamed? Fine! This is out of my hands! Who wants my job?"

Braggart said, "Who but you? So the potato is too hot for you?[11] They've called my attention to a problem, however. How can I face the ancestors if we really had all our women take turns riding the wooden donkeys? However, though our women can't ride the wooden donkeys, how about the wives of the nonclan members? They should be able to do it. They've benefited from Diamond Clan for many years—it's time they make a contribution. We don't care how they look, as long as they've been fucked by men before, which means other than the unmarried girls—the unmarried ones who'd been made pregnant before should be included—be they old or young, we want them all 'enter the battlefield'! Ours might not be more beautiful than the others, but we'll beat them on variety!"

Much debate ensued, mainly surrounding the fear that the wooden rod would create health hazards. Concerning this, the "committee members" ruled that the wooden rods should be made uniformly by Cripple Big, according to the following specifications. All the wooden rods would be 3.5 inches long and one inch across, regardless of the depths of the riders' vaginas. They would be made using superior fruit tree wood,

---

11. The original says, "So the noodles are too hot for you?"

strictly prohibiting the use of those with cracks. The production process involved shaving with a plane, sanding away roughness with sandpaper, and polishing with implements used by leather workers; finally, the rods would be doused with vegetable oil and subject to an even more refined round of polishing with soft sheepskin. The goal was to make them so smooth to the touch that they would feel better than the real thing. Braggart announced, "If the cripple should skimp on the job or stint on the materials, I will personally yank out his dick!" After this, it was difficult for the clansmen to say more. Nonclan members had no speaking rights; their only other option was to give up their residency and get the hell out of Diamond Clan.

A few carpenters and Cripple Big stayed up the whole night. The carpenters worked on the wooden donkeys while Cripple Big processed the wooden rods. The wooden donkeys were easy to make since all homes had a single-wheeled cart that could be easily outfitted to become a wooden donkey. The processing of the wooden rods was much more complicated, however. Cripple Big had only finished making three by midnight. Those—plus the three he'd made earlier, but were not put to use—meant he was still short by seven or eight. Thereupon, Braggart ordered the carpenters to join in the production. Although the carpenters wanted to do a good job, they were not as professional as Cripple Big. It was said all the women who used rods made by the carpenters bled to different degrees. Because of the great popularity of rods made by Cripple Big, demand superseded supply. Women riding wooden donkeys would visit Cripple Big in the dead of night. Most of them eventually got what they came for. The condition was that they had to try out Cripple Big's flesh rod first before they could obtain a rod that was even smoother than the real thing. So, this old bachelor of Diamond Clan got to experience to the hilt the "spring desires" of the mortal world. Some people accused Cripple Big of being short-sighted. They said he could have taken advantage of the situation and gotten one of the unmarried daughters of those women as his wife. Some of those who rode the wooden donkeys did indeed have charming daughters who might've been persuaded if Cripple Big had asked. But others immediately retorted, saying this was precisely where Cripple Big was crafty. If he had married the daughter of an outsider, he'd have immediately become the son-in-law of an outsider. How could he have the magnificence and karmic rewards he'd obtain later? The views concerning this were varied, and the debates never ceased.

A detail of the greatest historical significance was that several decades later, a few foreign experts who came to Diamond Clan to conduct research were curious about the wooden rods. After discovering the function they had served historically, the foreigners offered to buy them from those who rode the wooden donkeys. At first the offering price was ten U.S. dollars. Few women responded to the offer. So the offering price was gradually raised until it went up to more than several hundred dollars. That was when many women in the village regretted that they hadn't ridden the wooden donkey.

The weather was glorious the following day. The villagers placed the wives of all the nonmembers of the clan on the wooden donkeys. There were so many of them that, although some of them felt embarrassed, they soon put on the feigned expression of not minding the "slaughtering and slicing." This was when Cripple Big's talent became obvious; all the women rushed at the wooden donkeys that featured rods made by him. Cripple Big wore the expression one would only find on Nobel Prize recipients. Verily, heroes are created by circumstances!

Due to the appearance of riders of all shapes and sizes, Kuan San suggested that Snow Feather's mom be retired. But Braggart disagreed because he discovered that the other villages comprised only women. There were no men. The presence of Snow Feather's mom provided an excuse for the four men to accompany her as associates. Also, the participation of an old monk served to spark the imagination and make the parade more interesting. However, since "new blood" was injected, it wouldn't hurt to place Snow Feather's mom at the back of the procession.

Kuan San said, "The clan head is ultimately more brilliant!"

Now, Diamond Clan finally regained the attention of the spectators. The long row of white-skinned bodies alone afforded a magnificent sight; thin ones, fat ones, tall ones, short ones, everything imaginable was there. The site that harbored the wooden rod was obviously of great interest, but it was hidden by the wooden donkey. Hence the breasts became the pivotal spectacle. How one's horizon was greatly expanded! One would never have thought these things, which served basically the same function, would come in so many strange shapes and sizes: some jutted straight up to the azure sky; some drooped boundlessly toward mother earth; some were swollen like large balls; some were empty like leather bags; some were as flat as the Gobi Desert; some were as long as leather pouches; the nipples of some were as large as jujubes; others, as small as mung beans. Complete was the variety of strange sights, bobbing up and down along with the wooden wheels! Cripple Big continued to be striker of the gong. He was so anxious to exert himself he unintentionally struck a hole right through the gong. The gong made an ear-piercing thud. Unexpectedly, this accident turned out to have been a blessing in disguise. The sudden appearance of such a horrible, cringing sound among similar beatings of the gong made all the heads turn in this direction. One look, and all the eyes were glued to the sight. One had heard of "wine pools and meat forests," but who'd ever seen a breast jungle? A row of white-skinned flesh approaching from the distance—talk about magnificence! This procession was ten thousand times livelier than the New Year celebrations!

Now, Diamond Clan had fully regained its reputation. Thunderously, like the crashing of a huge building, the crowd rushed over en masse; the pattering of their footsteps overpowered the rumbling of the single-wheeled carts and resembled the howling of ten thousand wolves in union. A loud voice was heard saying, "Aiya! Has to be Diamond Clan—just look at the style!" This comment did wonders for Braggart. Glowing in spirit and bursting in radiance, he verily exhibited the bearing of a leader. Kuan San "tailgated" him, tending to his every need in the true manner of a military advisor and prime minister. Kuan San's face was forever changing. Before Braggart, it was the image of flattery. But when he faced the people, he was the picture of insufferable arrogance. Later, I saw many of Kuan San's characteristics in a book titled On Inferiority Complex, and I came to think of him as an inferior man. If it weren't for the existence of another event that crashed my prejudice, I'd have nailed the coffin that deemed him an inferior man. Oftentimes, the value of a person is determined by that person's heart.

"The eyes of the masses are discerning and bright!" While they watched the unceasingly bobbing breasts on the wooden donkeys and the various faces that were either shy, or wooden, or beautiful, or wrinkled— they also issued their assessments. They graded all the wooden donkey riders of Diamond Clan. Aside from a young wife who received sixty points—she was caught having an affair with a carpenter—most of the others received forty or fifty points. One of them actually received less than twenty points! Hence, although Diamond Clan sported variety, there was no one who could be considered a "grand finale" type of character. The most disappointing aspect about them was the fact that these naked women lacked talent in performance. They rode the wooden donkeys as if they wore masks, without any sign of liveliness or sexiness. How could they compare with the charming woman from Brilliant King Clan? She swayed on the wooden donkey, face flushing sweetly, producing "spring radiance" just like during orgasm—causing the men to lose their spirit and soul. People said many lads of the younger generation thought of that woman's expression when they masturbated. According to *Historical Mirror of Forgotten Events*, back then seven virgin boys in the village contracted anthomaniac disease. At the sight of women, they'd drool and giggle foolishly. Five of the seven were victims of this woman's behavior.

After perusing the stuff paraded by Diamond Clan, a portion of the crowd began to retreat to Brilliant King Clan. Someone cried, "Let's go! The Brilliant King Clan woman is better!" Braggart suspected he was a spy from Brilliant King Clan. So he got Kuan San to holler, "Diamond Clan's is better! An exhibition of all sorts! Look—you've got old ones, young ones, ugly ones, pretty ones, fat ones and skinny ones. It's got everything you want! What does Brilliant King Clan have? Just a water-dripping hussy!" The person hollered back, "Better take one bite of an immortal peach than eat a basketful of rotten apricots!" "Let's go! Let's go!" a crowd of people hollered and left. Anxious to stop them, Cripple Big grabbed the guy's hair, yanked it with all his might, and pulled him flat onto the ground. Someone called, "A fight! A fight!" Cripple Big did it originally without thinking. The holler now served as a reminder, and he began to swing his fist furiously at the man's face. As he struck, he bawled, "Spoil it for us, will you!" The man's nose became crooked after just a few blows. Blood gushed out of his nose, and two of his front teeth also disappeared. With this, the people who left returned to watch the fight. Braggart heaved a sigh of relief. But fearing lest Cripple Big's behavior would provoke revenge on the part of Brilliant King Clan, he used a revolutionary slogan and hollered, "Come, tie up the villain!" Kuan San and the others came over and gave the "drowning dog" a few more kicks before they tied him up.

The women riding on the wooden donkeys also watched the fighting scene in surprise. More people ran over to that side. Braggart didn't expect the trick pulled by Cripple Big to become such a winner. He was highly pleased. But he feared that if the man were really from Brilliant King Clan, an ensuing fight could produce devastating results. He lifted a woman off one of the wooden donkeys and jumped onto it himself. Holding onto Cripple Big so that he wouldn't fall off, he bawled, "Listen, Brothers! There are people who want to take this opportunity to 'create damage'! Listen, Diamond Clan's militiamen—seize anyone who is 'creating damage'! Shoot anyone who resists! Not at their heads—I want you to shoot their legs but careful not to shoot the main artery. Best to shoot at their balls in the crotch!" Kuan San and his men were very smart. Their rifles were actually all for show and had no bullets! But they all yelled, "Yes! We'll just shoot at their asses!" With this, the clamor quieted down immediately.

Braggart noticed that many people concentrated their eyes on the wooden rod underneath his feet. The rod had a sticky fluid and streaks of blood, which provoked dubious reactions. Having dismounted the wooden donkey, the naked woman became unexpectedly embarrassed. She covered her private parts with her hands, and her face turned scarlet red. Braggart had a mind to deliver an extensive lecture on the superiority of Diamond Clan's wooden donkey riders and its historical and actual significance; but some people told him, "Enough!" So, he descended from the wooden donkey.

The hollering spy was already trussed up by the militiamen and escorted behind Donkey Two. Now that five men participated, the procession was even grander. This was the result of a struggle session. Struggle sessions were always productive.

Braggart was very pleased.

Braggart

According to *Historical Mirror of Forgotten Events*, the fact Diamond Clan had captured the limelight notwithstanding, Braggart perceived the looming danger of an impending crisis. He knew, although Diamond Clan was able to win through numbers and capture attention through the "blooming of the hundred flowers," this was something others could easily copy. Should another village also attempt this, they could easily beat Diamond Clan. Take Brilliant King Clan, as an example; its population was several times that of Diamond Clan. There must have been many strangely shaped breasts there. He had to work on quality, which meant he needed to get an attractive woman to ride the wooden donkey. This would certainly be the most effective. Just as with writers, a prolific writer without a grand finale would soon die out through natural selection. He thought and thought, and finally locked his gaze on his "girlfriend."

So, as soon as he returned from the competition, he headed for his girlfriend's place. As his fame also enhanced her status, she swayed her waist and fixed him a good meal. Braggart also swayed his waist furiously to allow her to reach the highest climax of her life. Finally, the two of them lay on the brick bed, faces flushed and bodies sweating.

Ajia was very imaginative and true to Braggart's character when he related the latter's words. I suspect that he had Ananda's talent. Ananda was able to memorize all the Buddha's teachings like a tape recorder, and then transcribe them into sutras. Sometimes, he was able to relate even the scriptures he didn't personally hear. For example, *Garland Sutra*[12] was what the Buddha taught when he had just attained enlightenment. Ananda hadn't even met the Buddha then! Furthermore, it wasn't until many years later that people made offerings at the site where the Buddha spoke. Monk Wu said, "This is precisely what makes Buddhism inscrutable." Ajia was contentious about this, but I found him no less competent than Ananda.

According to Ajia, Braggart's words poured forth almost like a waterfall. He said, "Don't be scared—it's just riding on a wooden donkey. Plus, I can get Cripple Big to make the rod into the best in the world, a rod ten thousand times more enjoyable than my flesh rod, a rod that no matter what happens in the world, you'll never want man again—one the size of a turtle's head and so smooth people'll cry in shock when they see it! Instead of fruit tree wood, I'll have him use purple sandalwood. You must have seen that kind of wood before. Its texture is so fine it's a hundred times smoother than the smoothest skin in the world! And its fragrance—that pure fragrance makes your soul so calm and peaceful it's like having reached orgasm ten thousand times! Or, even better, I'll have one made for you with ocean agarwood. I just happen to have gotten a piece from the monastery. What a treasure that is! A veritable treasure from the depths of the ocean! If you take just a tiny chip from it and throw it into a bottle of liquor, you'll see a red thread rise up in spirals like a silk filament. Don't underestimate this! It will soon dye the liquor into the most beautiful liquor ever—as beautiful as amber. It will make the liquor into something as wonderful as sweet dew, capable of harmonizing the blood and vital energy, extinguish calamities and bring blessings, aid sleep and calm the spirit, prolong life and add longevity. Of course, you may not know how great agarwood is. Though agarwood is as expensive as gold, it's but a pile of firewood to peasants. But, of course,

---

12. Also known as *Avatamsaka Sutra* of the Huayan School, *Buddhavatamsaka-ma-havaipulya Sutra*, and *Flower Adornment Sutra*.

you are no idiot—you are an intelligent woman. If you are moistened by the rod of agarwood, you will become even more intelligent and even more beautiful!"

Braggart said, "Furthermore, as the proverb says, 'A rich man who doesn't return to his native home is just like someone who wears satin in the dark.' How can he show off? You have the figure of a nymph, the face of a celestial, skin like butter—but how would anyone know if you don't show them off? Wouldn't this be the same as walking in the dark, wearing damask gauze and silk satin? In a few years, your face will become wrinkled, your hair will turn white, your back will hunch and your waist will bend over, your eyesight will fail and your skin will shrivel up. When people get old, three problems emerge: they shit when they fart; their talk becomes meaningless lice; and they wet their shoes when they pee! If you take off your clothes for others to see then—yuck—even if you pay them three silver dollars for it, no one would want to waste their energy to watch you! By then, who'd have known you were once as voluptuous as a fat, skinned jaguar? Ah! What can I say?"

Gradually, the narrating Ajia fully embodied Braggart's personality the way I enter a character when I write. "Of course, you can take a larger perspective. Think of how Diamond Clan never played second fiddle to anyone—aside from the fight for water with Brilliant King Clan! I once organized a rebel/revolutionary troop. Although it wasn't clear if we were soldiers or bandits, I in fact did organize a troop. Who dared to defy me? If it weren't for the fact that my old dick stirred up trouble by getting that chick pregnant, I'd be nothing short of a county magistrate right now! There were so many other things too—you know about them already. There's no need to repeat them. You can't let me lose with the wooden donkeys, can you? Though I'm publicly recognized as a revolutionary spearhead in getting the 'bad lots' to ride the wooden donkeys, I still have to be careful—the tiniest laxity will lead to defeat. Waves from the back will overwhelm those in the front—a generation of newcomers will replace the old! A thousand sails will pass by a sunken ship; a diseased tree will be fronted by ten thousand flourishing saplings! We can't let Diamond Clan lose to the others, particularly not to Brilliant King Clan! I've watched with sharp eyes. I know they don't have anyone as beautiful as you—some have faces that don't compare, some have figures that don't compare, some have complexions that don't compare, some don't have your sexiness. Who can resist the charming glance of your eyes that send people's souls halfway up the sky? Few had them all. Just think of the innumerable bloody battles that our ancestors have had with Brilliant King Clan. They advanced wave after wave, one fell but another moved forward. If their heads were smashed, they tied them together with grass ropes; if their teeth fell, they swallowed them into their tummies; if their legs broke, they walked with sticks; if they were blinded, they became blind men; if their ears were taken off, they went around without ears! The bodies might die or be mutilated, but their spirit endured! Do you know the meaning of the word 'diamond'? Let me tell you, it is something nothing can destroy!"

Ajia's spittle splattered—he was the spitting image of Braggart. "If you listen to me and agree to sacrifice yourself for Diamond Clan, then you will become a hero of Diamond Clan, the Hua Mulan[13] of Diamond Clan, the Mu Guiying[14] of Diamond Clan . . . Actually, no, how could they compare to you? You'd be a splendid, brilliant sun—they were only fireflies like flies and dogs! You'd be an ocean, they were just drops of water! You'd be a great garuda bird, they were just sparrows next to dung pits. You'd be a heavenly dragon capable of creating clouds and rain, they were just churning dung beetles in outhouses. You'd become a veritable clan hero, permanently praised by the descendants of Diamond Clan for generations to come, forever and ever!"

"Furthermore, from a private perspective, I'll give you thirty catties of wheat for each day you ride the wooden donkey. This is because you are different from the others. The others rode because they were 'bad lots' or outsider-devils, but you are a martyr of Diamond Clan. How about it?"

"And, from another, a minor perspective—you see, that sickly wife of mine is getting ready to kick the bucket. If she dies, then I will make you a formal wife right away and you'll become the lady of the head of the clan!"

The woman finally spoke.

She said, "I, this old lady of yours, have no intention of becoming a hero. I couldn't care less for becoming lady of the head of the clan

---

13. Hua Mulan is a legendary fictional woman warrior from the Southern and Northern dynasties (386–589) who was originally described in a ballad known as the "Ballad of Mulan." In the ballad, Hua Mulan takes her aged father's place in the army and surprises her army companions ten years later, after she returns home and reveals to them her gender.

14. Mu Guiying is a legendary fictional woman warrior the Northern Song dynasty (960–1127) and a prominent figure in the Generals of the Yang Family sagas.

either. I have even less craving for praise by descendants for generations to come. But I am willing to ride the wooden donkey. I, this old lady of yours, just want to give it a try and find out what those sisters suffered."

"Are you happy now? Shit!"

Total Victory

Because of Heavenly Girl's participation, Diamond Clan's strength magnified. Although Brilliant King Clan quickly exceeded Diamond Clan in numbers, it truly didn't have the talent of one such as Heavenly Girl. Their wooden donkey riders were true "bad lots." After experiencing numerous bouts of "fixing," the "bad lots" had all turned into "dehydrated veggies." The form was there, but none of the moisture content or spirit remained. Although an exceptional beauty would appear occasionally, she would only be exceptional among the "bad lots." Heavenly Girl, however, was a famous beauty of Liangzhou. To Ajia, who had experienced innumerable great changes, she was one of the four great beauties of the last thousand years. In *Historical Mirror of Forgotten Events*, she was also equated with the Eight Great Sights of Liangzhou. It was precisely because she had too many suitors, and her parents were reluctant to marry off such an exceptional daughter, that they had her "marry Heaven" and go through the ritual of "wearing Heaven's head." This was, of course, a good thing; many men tried to "glue" to her. But this Heavenly Girl was different from the other Heavenly Girls. Although the other Heavenly Girls were also selective, they had many boyfriends concurrently. This Heavenly Girl was relatively faithful. She'd only have one partner during any period of time. When she went steady with one man, others would have no chance. You'd then have no choice but to swallow your drool, seek through dreams, and masturbate by visualizing her beauty with your eyes closed.

What wonderful news—now the woman of men's dreams will also ride the wooden donkey! Many men hailed "long live Diamond Clan" because of this, indicating the efficacy of this measure by Braggart.

Diamond Clan subsequently formed the "imperial domination over all under Heaven!"

Braggart appointed many more committee members, whose duties had now undergone a tremendous change. While in the past they had been charged with preventing Diamond Clan members from encroaching on other villages' territories, they were now responsible for maintaining order. Throngs of charging people blocked the pathway of Diamond Clan's procession. To clear a path, Kuan San deployed more than half of the militiamen. The committee members, for their part, held hands and created two walls between the procession and the spectators. Now and then they would holler, "Damn! Motherfuckers—what are you pushing for?" Later, their hollering became as effective as autumnal wind blowing past a donkey's ears. Thereupon, Kuan San procured many tree branches, which he gave to some committee members. They struck furiously at the heads and faces of any spectators who pushed too forcefully. This was a trick used on livestock that tried to steal crops. It now worked somewhat effectively. The words, "somewhat effectively" were used, explained Ajia, because the trick became useless very quickly with up to a hundred people pushing forward. At first, people were deterred by the brandishing branches, but after a while, the people at the back became infuriated. They shoved hard in unison and pushed Kuan San and his men under the wooden donkeys. The minute the wooden donkey toppled over, the woman sitting on it would fall off. If the woman was vigilant, she got off as it fell. But if she wasn't, then the wooden rod would tear apart her vagina instantly. The first time the women were pushed over, one of them screamed and hemorrhaged continuously. "It's torn! It's torn!"—Kuan San immediately got a committee member to carry her to a doctor. Later, when the congestion got even worse, the vaginas of three women were torn apart and hemorrhaged continuously. To prevent such happenings in the future, Braggart ordered all the women to get off the wooden donkeys. Thereafter, the wooden donkey parade turned into an exhibition of naked women.

The situation was getting ever more difficult to control. No matter how the committee members brandished the branches, they were unable to block the surging crowd. Everyone bawled and pushed furiously with flushed faces. Instead of opening the path, Kuan San and his men now joined the ranks of the committee members. They pushed with their rifles horizontally, which was even less effective than brandishing branches. At least, the flung branches made some of the men temporary allies of the militia, by pushing backward. The rifles, however, actually assisted the resistance. The crowd held on to the rifles and pushed in unison. Fortunately, Braggart had the foresight to order the women to dismount, otherwise all their vaginas would've been torn since all the wooden donkeys were overturned. Gradually, the distinction between spectators and "performers" disappeared. Only vigorously pushing throngs remained.

Braggart cursed in utter exasperation. However, although one saw his mouth open, one couldn't hear any sounds, since the crowd's uproar had swept his voice back into his chest.

"Let's fuck them! Let's fuck them!" a voiced yelled.

This obviously ignited the crowd. The people became even more excited. They roared like beasts with flushed faces. More people charged toward the location of Heavenly Girl—although this designation could only refer to a general vicinity because no one could see any nude women, aside from an occasional glimpse of part of a naked body through a crack among the throng. One could only feel the tremendous force of swirling whirlpools. The crowd had turned into a sea; while the individuals had become leaves. No one had control over their bodies any longer. They all perceived the danger but could do nothing about it. They could only shuffle their feet with great care, knowing that if they were squeezed to the ground, they'd be trampled into mush.

Suddenly, the crowd in one area indeed toppled over. It seemed to have been where Heavenly Girl was. All the people then flowed toward it, the way more than ten thousand rivers converge into the ocean. A woman wailed loudly, screaming, "My boy's trampled to death!" Another cried, "My leg is broken!" Another hollered, "Don't pinch me—I'm not a woman!" And then, with everyone bawling, one couldn't hear what they were yelling anymore.

Ajia said he has never seen such a surging flow of crowd since that period of confusion back in Xixia! However, this situation was a hundred times fiercer than the muddled warfare between the Iron Hawks and Mongol cavalry. Look at how all the faces were flushed, the mouths wide open, the arms waving, and the hearts twisted. People's sweat poured like rain; they roared like wind, wailed like thunder, and then collapsed like a huge building being demolished. *Yeeah*—wonders never cease!

After I can't remember how long, policemen on horses approached from afar. One of them shot three rounds into the sky. It wasn't until they heard the volley of shots that the crowd ceased their violent surge. "Disperse! Disperse!" one of the policemen yelled, "those on the outside, disperse first! The others stay put or I'll shoot! Disperse right away! Don't run anywhere—go back to where you came from!"

Gaps gradually appeared in the airtight crowd; open spaces gradually appeared and showed their true features.

Several children had been trampled into bloody pancakes. An old woman had stopped breathing a long time ago; her eyes were white, and her face was earthen and blue colored. The excrement under her groin created a mess and spread all over the bottom half of her body. Following the gradual evacuation of the crowd, more corpses were found. They were all spectators. Most of those who rode the wooden donkeys suffered injuries from being pinched. People pinched them not out of anger, but as a form of intimacy from emotional arousal. A woman's nipple was bitten by someone. She was wailing. A woman's shoulder was also bitten. Most of them had bleeding vaginas. Judging from the looks of it, most of those injuries were caused by the gouging of men's fingers rather than by the wooden rods.

Heavenly Girl was the last to appear. So many people had pushed against her—they were like walls that prevented her from falling down and being trampled into mush. The pants of a few men next to her were pulled down. They obviously wanted to take advantage of the situation. One wonders if they had succeeded. Heavenly Girl's mouth was bloody and had become a swollen mess from being bitten. Her body was also covered with teeth marks. A piece of flesh had even been chewed off. Her thighs were streaked with blood—some wounds were dry, while others were still dripping! It wasn't clear whether the injuries were caused by the wooden rod or by the violence of men's fingers. No one cared to investigate.

The injury-laden Heavenly Girl looked very ugly. People discovered that beauty couldn't withstand being tampered with. The once beautiful face and body exhibited open wounds. It was only through her eyes that one could vaguely discern her original liveliness.

Unexpectedly, Snow Feather's mom wasn't hurt. The reasons were twofold. Firstly, she was too old to have any sex appeal. Secondly, the old monk got the four men to surround and protect her as soon as he realized that things were going wrong. They were very brave. At first they spat on those who tried to get close; then they used phlegm and mucus; and finally, they did everything—beating, kicking, cussing, and biting. Consequently, Snow Feather's mom wasn't hurt. But she seemed to have suffered a great injury. She stared around her with her lusterless white eyeballs and kept on repeating, "How did humans come to this?"

"How did humans come to this?"

Historical Mirror of Forgotten Events contains a detailed record of this event. According to its data, eight people were trampled to death—five children, and three adults; five women's vaginas were torn apart—those excluded wounds under three inches; fifty single-wheeled carts were ruined. Three of the women who rode wooden donkeys were raped—but their names were not publicized. In order to prevent future occurrences of similar incidents, the local government issued a prohibition of any such parades. Should the citizens feel a strong need for parades, they could organize them as individual clans.

Chapter 25

The Butcher's Heart

Are you not worshipping the moon as well?
    One time after the other,
    One row of tears after another.
Are you really going to visit the Palace of Pervading Cold[1]?
Didn't you hear how Su Shih[2] had advised for a thousand years
That it is too cold up there!

Man Long Geri

Continue with the story, Ajia!

One day, a yogi named Man Long Geri[3] arrived at Liangzhou. He was renowned in Tibet, known to have attained the "iddhi-vidha" and could travel a thousand leagues in an instant. He had enviably traveled through the sacred realms of all twenty-four Dakini goddesses and made records of them in amazing books.

In one of them, he wrote about the girls floating in midair inside Diamond Maiden Cave.

---

1. The Palace of Pervading Cold is the residence of the beautiful immortal, Goddess Chang E, in the moon.

2. Also known as Su Dongpo, Su Shi (1037–1101) was a famous writer, poet, painter, calligrapher, pharmacologist, gastronome, and a statesman of the Song dynasty. His popular lyric, "Shuidiao getou (Water Music Prelude)" includes mention of a desire to fly up to the moon but also fears that it would be too cold there.

3. A Tibetan living Buddha.

According to the original, "In the past, their feet were one *xun* above the ground, now they are one *ka* above the ground. "

The book included a footnote: a *xun* is eight feet; a *ka* is the span between the tips of the middle finger and the thumb.

Man Long Geri also recorded his meeting with Butcher Zhang when he was there.

The plot was very simple. Man Long Geri invited Diamond Maiden to his offering ritual, and Butcher Zhang also came along. After partaking of the offerings, Guru Man Long expressed his desire to speak with Butcher Zhang. However, Diamond Maiden said Butcher Zhang wouldn't know his way back to the Pure Land, so they left together.

That was all.

Butcher Zhang's Heart

Later, Butcher Zhang who struck it "rich" due to his association with Diamond Maiden, also fashionably wrote a memoir. In his fashionable memoir, he fashionably exposed his heart and soul in a stream of consciousness.

We include an excerpt here:

Responding to the invitation of the great saint Man Long Geri, I accompanied Diamond Maiden to the ritual. We flew from the sacred realm of Niguma toward Liangzhou, along a khata-like avenue created by mind-light.

The clouds of my native land floated past us. The wind of my native land rushed toward us, bringing the odor of the earth of my native land. It beckoned me continuously, "Return home! Do return home, oh the wanderer who'd roamed to the ends of the earth!"

It's been a long time, my native land that wandered in my dreams!

I remember that twenty-fifth day of the lunar calendar . . . It seemed so long ago, but always flickered before me . . . Those organs of the animals were so delicious! Hey—so scrumptious that the taste went right into the brain! Diamond Maiden loved to eat them, and of course I loved them too.

I must have liquidated more than a thousand pigs' intestines when I was a butcher in the past!

Although pig intestines were delicious, I could never forget the chopped yam with noodles. Chopped yam with noodles—ah, how you've always been the song of my dreams! "Three days without yam with noodles; the heart feels dry and parched!" But that Man Long Geri grumbled, "I can't bring a big offering for a small deity like you, you idiot!" He thought the most delicious food was roasted barley flour with yak butter. Heck! That stuff reeked of animal odor—how could it compare with yam with noodles? You old Tibetan—you country bumpkin!

He wanted to keep me behind to interview me. I knew he wanted to discover the secrets of the Buddhist realm! Of course, it was a beautiful place with blooming flowers and charming women. An old Tibetan like you couldn't even dream of it. Indeed, it was a kingdom of freedom! Tut! Tut! . . . Oh, or do you want me to leak to you some secrets for cultivation that Diamond Maiden transmitted to me? Sure—it's no more than the two words Milarepa[4] whispered to Gampopa:[5] "Cultivate arduously." Did you want to find a shortcut or take advantage of a trick? Forget it . . . Hahaha! Of course, I know you are an accomplished guru—you can go to any Buddhist realm you so desire . . . I was just teasing you—why be so serious?

Haha, haha! I'm going to be denounced again by that Lu, whatever, Xun[6] in the mortal world. He's going to blame me for making a joke out of the cruelty of butchers! So? Why can't I have some fun with him anyway?

I am a butcher—I fear none!
I'll stay if you want me to!

---

4. Jetsun Milarepa (1052–1135) is generally considered one of Tibet's most famous yogis and poets.

5. Gampopa (1079–1153) is the founder of the Kagyu school of Tibetan Buddhism.

6. Lu Xun (1881–1936) was the penname of Zhou Shuren, a leading figure of modern Chinese literature.

But Diamond Maiden said, "If so, you won't know your way back to the Buddhist realm." I, *sajia*,[7] couldn't help but hesitate on account of this. After all, even a maidservant at the prime minister's residence is as powerful as an official of the seventh rank! I was always up there, at least, eating and drinking whatever Diamond Maiden consumed. Just consider the case of that Marshal Tianpeng.[8] Following that Monkey, he endured nine times nine equaling eighty-one calamities, the soles of his feet acquired eighty-four thousand shining bright blisters. One might conclude that he'd endured tremendous hardship. Even then, all he got was the pretty good job of an altar-purifying emissary!

So, what more do I want? . . . Okay, okay! I will leave well enough alone! Though I might not compare well to some, I do compare favorably with others. When people compare themselves with other people, they end up dead; when donkeys compare themselves with mules, they can't carry loads. Though I don't get to eat yam with noodles during the offerings, I nevertheless got to stuff myself from being with Diamond Maiden. In fact, I was much better off than the common masses who stuff their stomachs with chopped yam and noodles every day . . . Furthermore . . . This . . . Actually, stuff like yam with noodles is fine if you only 'taste' bites of it once in a while. If you eat it all the time, hey, your scalp would tingle from it . . . Just as well I don't have it. No way you'll get me to live in that hovel again! Therefore, I 'triumphantly' returned with Diamond Maid while singing that favorite song of mine, "The sun sets behind the western mountain, red clouds hover; sated with meat, the butcher heads back to camp . . ." I know, in the future, I will descend upon a Chen Village north of the city of Liangzhou to keep a destined appointment, but living for a day is the same as having lived two half-days, why bother with something in the far future? Who worries about the future these days? Really! We'll talk about it when it happens. What's there to worry?

---

7. A boastful, colloquial term men used to refer to themselves during the Song dynasty in northern China.

8. Marshal Tianpeng, a constellation deity within the Northern Dipper, was the original incarnation of Pigsy in the novel *Journey to the West*.

Please remember the famous saying that will enable me to become a celebrity forever:

A butcher I am, I fear no one!
So don't insult me, okay?

Patriotism

During the confused historical era when Butcher Zhang attended the offering banquet, the iron hoofs of Genghis Khan had already trampled the world, like intense rain.

A small city near Diamond Clan by the name of Suzhou was butchered.

Thirty thousand innocent commoners were slaughtered. Adult men were cut in half at their waists; women were raped and then killed. Babies wailed "Mama!" on the tips of waving spears. Territories the Mongols swept through were burned to the ground. The earth of a thousand leagues turned barren—not even a blade of grass grew.

The migrating swallows that returned to the north chirped mournfully. They could no longer find the houses where they'd built their nests the previous year, so they had to repose upon piles of white bones.

According to *Crazy Ramblings of Ajia*, the fighting tactics used by the iron cavalry of Genghis Khan consisted of the following: During the first round of attack, they shot with powerful crossbows; arrows flew like rain and blockers routed. Then, select cavalry gave chase and shot arrows too. Finally, the main troops would begin a murderous charge. Consequently, through righteousness, frugality, loyalty, and finally terror—tens of thousands of commoners became pools of blood.

However, the "mediocre lots" of the Southern Song and other places wagged their either shriveled or bloated heads and waved a dirty dishrag banner marked with a ridiculous word to trick the commoners out of their precious heads.

The hubbub was righteous and forceful, resonating for a thousand years.

"Comrades—charge! This is the moment you can offer your loyalty to our beloved emperor! Don't be afraid of losing your heads! Should you lose it, the venerable emperor would enfeoff you as a great loyal minister and you'll be able to eat cold, raw pig's head at a temple. Charge! Kill! Who was able to escape death since antiquity anyway? Have your loyalty shine in the histories! Slaughter! Kill! Charge!"

So they charged until white bones were strewn all over the wilderness and widows wailed, shattering heaven and earth.

Yet the one wearing the yellow robe, that is, the emperor, was imbibing liquors like Remy Martin and whiskey. He frowned, wrinkled his nose, shook his yellow whiskers, swayed his head, and complained about how off-key the widows' wailings were.

One word snickered sinisterly on the dishrag banner created by the "mediocre lot."

Ajia said, "That word was 'patriotism,' which was as disgusting as 'heroism.'"

The meaning of "patriotism" was most aptly analyzed by Lu Su[9] of the Three Kingdoms:

> If people like Su should surrender to Cao, he'd have Su return to the countryside and bestow upon him nothing less than the prefect's position in a county or province. Should you, the general, surrender to Cao, would you be at peace with that which you will be given? Your position would not exceed that of a marquis; your carriage would be just one, neither would the number of your mounts exceed it; and your entourage would be just a few people. How would that compare to facing the south and addressing yourself as an emperor?

Later, Ajia, who had pretentions to culture, translated the above in this way:

> If 'Old I' surrendered to that fella, I would still have a position and be able to nibble on two pig's feet, gnaw on three pig's tails, and drink four cups of hard liquor. But you, Great Chief, where are you going to be? Who will give you, the venerable one, Remy Martins, whiskies, and those large-breasted, beautiful chicks? At most, they'll give you a vulgar servant maid who looks like an ugly kohlrabi that even pigs won't eat. I'd find her disgusting, even if you won't! Better be decisive, oh Great Chief! At most, it'll just cost more commoners' heads. I don't believe

---

9. Lu Su (172–217) was a politician, diplomat, and military general who served under Sun Quan in the late Eastern Han dynasty (25–220). Sun Quan (182–252), formally known as Emperor Da of Wu, was the founder of the state of Eastern Wu during the Three Kingdoms period (220–280).

that you can't block the wheels of that whatcha-ma-call-it—history!

Thereupon, the one wearing the yellow robe immediately said, "Excellent! Excellent! Brother Lu Su is the one who knows me! Do a good job of it, then! Use however many heads you need, just block the wheels of that carriage. We will bestow upon you the beauty who is slightly cross-eyed—she's not being used in any case. She's almost the beauty of a generation after all! Furthermore, we will hang a plate that says "loyal minister" on your carriage so that you can do anything you want in the future. What do you think?"

"Long live the emperor! Long live the emperor!"

So when all the commoners under heaven were roaming in nature hoes in hand, those wearing yellow robes were worried about having no seats for their butts. What a ludicrous situation it was!

Ajia said the fella wearing the yellow robe smiled sinisterly. Shaking his goatee, he bestowed upon his "mediocre lot" accomplices the title of "loyal minister." Under his direction, the accomplices searched all the nooks and crannies before they found a tattered dirty rag. They wrote a bloody curse on it and turned it into a soul-summoning banner. Look—they waved it while they hollered and swayed. They swayed away humanity, and commoners' heads turned into rolling stones in the wind.

Stones as large as soup bowls filled the riverbed and rolled with the wind.

The rag with the curse was waved for a thousand years and generated numerous bloody poems on heroism. What a spectacular sight!

Two Dogs in Dialogue

One day, Yue Fei[10] of the Song dynasty dreamed about two dogs having a dialogue.

---

10. Yue Fei (1103–1142) was a famous general of the Song dynasty. He was renowned for his loyalty and for insisting on continuing to fight even after the emperor had signed a truce with the Jurchens. The emperor dispatched twelve summonses before he ultimately returned to the court out of loyalty and was subsequently put to death. A later emperor rehabilitated his reputation, and Qin Kuai (1090–1155), the prime minister of the former emperor, was saddled with the responsibility for Yue Fei's death and condemned in Chinese history as the most notorious traitor.

An old monk named Daoyue interpreted his dream as signifying the word "yu," meaning "prison," as the "yu" character consisted of two glyphs for dog flanking a glyph for speech. It was an omen for imprisonment should Yue Fei should return to the court.[11] Later, Ajia, who was an expert in interpreting dreams, said Monk Daoyue's interpretation was erroneous.

Ajia said, "The two dogs in the dreams were actually two aspects of Yue Fei himself."

White Dog said, "Continue to fight—for the enduring glory!"

Black Dog said, "Damn the glory—it's a waste of the commoners' heads! To please the goddamn artist dad and the wastrel son[12] is, in fact, a real sin!"

White Dog Yue Fei therefore thought, *He's so right! Why should I charge at Huanglong? Why should I waste commoners' heads? Whether or not the emperor relinquishes his throne simply means a change at the imperial court—it matters not to the commoners. The commoners have to pay grain taxes no matter which dog sits on the dragon throne. Why please the two ignorant scoundrels? Let me take advantage of the twelve summonses and get the hell out!* Thereupon the accomplices lamented for a thousand years and denounced him for being "stupidly loyal."[13]

In fact, White Dog Yue Fei had made up his mind a long while ago: there was no need to waste commoners' heads for those bastards. He thought, *Better for me to give up my head!* The Buddha had said, "If I don't go to Hell, who would?" Thereupon, he stuck his neck into the "groundless" noose!

So White Dog Yue Fei died for a "groundless" crime. Black Dog Yue Fei became the prime minister and was named Qin Kuai.

---

11. This was an episode from Qian Cai's (a Qing dynasty figure) *Biography of Yue Fei* (*Shuo Yue quanzhuan*), a novel that glorified Yue Fei and vilified Qin Kuai.

12. The father and son refer to Emperor Huizong (1082–1135) and Emperor Qinzong (1100–1156). Emperor Huizong was an expert painter and calligrapher. Emperor Qinzong (1100–1156) was considered an inept weakling, mainly because he lost the territories in the north to the Jurchens. The two emperors became captives of the Jurchens and eventually died in Jurchen territory. The Chinese continued the Song dynasty in southern China by enthroning another of Huizong's sons and named it the Southern Song dynasty (1127–1279).

13. Many felt that he should not have returned to the court as bid by an inept emperor.

Soon after that, a man known as Saban[14] in the histories, led the people of the "snowy region" in surrendering to the Yuan dynasty. Because of this, he became a renowned figure in Tibetan history. The one called Qin Kuai, however, sits in a corner of history, grieving for the past thousand years. To this day, he weeps in a temple in Hangzhou!

One day, he approached Ajia, weeping, to ask about the meaning of "loyalty and treachery." He said grievously, "Loyalty and treachery are basically one and the same. To be 'loyal' to that thing called emperor inevitably entails treachery to the commoners. Manifestation of loyalty to the former, frequently demanded the heads of the latter."

Of course, Qin Kuai, an expert in officialdom and possessor of the most brilliant brain, realized the kind of stuff the ignorant ones—the one who knew how to paint and the one who didn't know how to paint— were made of. He knew even more clearly whether it was worthwhile to exchange the two pieces of garbage (who didn't even know how to hold hoes) for the heads of several hundred thousand robust commoners.

On account of Qin Kuai's "treachery," millions of commoners of the Southern Song got to enjoy their natural lifespans.

So, Ajia said, "Okay! Okay! Stop crying! Long live Qin Kuai! Okay?"

Ajia said there was another admirable "treacherous official" in Chinese history. Betraying a declining court, he surrendered to a vigorous and robust people.

The greatness of his treachery was different from that of Qin Kuai. He prevented barbarous slaughter by the Aisin Gioro clan.[15] It was due to his efforts that there were very few cities whose people had all been slaughtered, like those attacked by Genghis Khan. Through his onerous interventions, events like those in "Record of the Ten Days of Slaughter in Yangzhou"[16] gradually ceased. Taking advantage of his prestige and influence, he wrote letter after letter to persuade the muddle-headed

---

14. Kunga Gyaltsen Bei Sangbu Saban (1310–1358) was a Tibetan imperial preceptor (*Dishi*) at the court of the Mongol Yuan dynasty (1279–1368).

15. Aisin Gioro is the family name of the Manchu imperial family of the Qing dynasty (1644–1911).

16. In 1645, an army of the Manchus encountered staunch resistance when it attacked the city of Yangzhou. When the city fell, the Manchu commander ordered the slaughter of all its residents. The slaughter continued for five days. The atrocities were recorded by Wang Xiuchu in "Yangzhou shiri ji," which was banned by the Manchu Qing dynasty.

people waving their soul-summoning banners to stop their resistance, thereby preventing many women from the misfortune of wearing the laurels of widowhood.

Because of this, his name stank forever, and he was listed among the *Two-Timing Officials*.[17]

His name was Hong Chengchou.[18]

The Hoarse Throat

Ajia said, "Just open up the history books—those shivering in spittle are precisely such figures. Their sole crime was simply not forcing commoners to foolishly offer their heads for a scoundrel."

In the so-called histories, those who are glorified are precisely the criminals and their accomplices.

This so-called patriotism is, in fact, merely the self-righteous cry made by narrow-minded tribes when they brandished knives at its own kind. All the shrieks and explosions, which lasted for a thousand years on this small planet, originated in this.

This was what the literati had praised in song for the past thousand years.

This disgusting type of sneeze began when mankind developed so-called civilization and has resonated to this day.

The soul-summoning banner bewildered generation after generation of mediocre lots. They followed along with the crimes like clamoring sparrows and praised the "emperor's new clothes" like cheerleaders.

One day, the crisp voice of a boy will sound, "The emperor is wearing nothing!"

That was the Jasper of the future.

In order to moisten his hoarse throat, Jasper wept for a long time in a rarely visited Xixia cave.

---

17. The *Erchen zhuan*, which contained biographies of officials who had served both the Ming (1368–1644) and Qing (1644–1911) dynasties, was commissioned by the Qianlong emperor (1711–1799) in 1776, more than a hundred years after the inception of the Qing dynasty. By then, the emperor was more interested in promoting loyalty than acknowledging the contributions made by these officials to the Qing. Inclusion in the list was considered a disgrace.

18. Hong Chengchou (1593–1665).

Chapter 26

The Fifth "Nightmare": The Curse of Ajia

I once shouted ceaselessly,
    The wilderness resonated with my helpless weeping.
My raspy throat was torn,
Yet I still couldn't control the carriage of my soul,
    Like a drowning child,
Unable to struggle out of foolishness.

Doomsday

Nightmares records a fulfillment of Ajia's curse. According to the book, after Ajia's corpse was burned to ashes, he continued to appear in the village now and then and would shout, "Repent! Repent!" After that, a plague would infest the village. People attributed it to Ajia's curse.

The plague arrived quietly.

A father and son went to the southern shoal to herd and picked up a fat marmot. The son said, "I've never seen a marmot as fat as this!" He then grilled it, and the father and son both ate pieces of it together. When they went home, they both had a high fever. The father was physically weak, so he lay in bed. The son, however, roamed the village with flushed face and shouted uncannily, "What have I ever done to you, Ajia?!"

Twirling a hand drum and holding a Vajra bell, Ajia roamed the village and shouted, "Repent! Repent!" Many people saw him.

Ajia still visited Jasper frequently. He looked dignified and showed no injuries. Jasper thought, *Could the fire really cure his injuries? Ajia* said, "I now feel grateful to your uncle. I've discovered that he's a really accomplished guru. Fortunately, he'd transmitted a technique to me, and I'd chanted the mantra a hundred million times. I couldn't have done what I did otherwise. All sorts of people are pulling at me, promising to take me to wonderful places. I told them I'm not going anywhere and I'm not entering any gates. I only want to abide by my own heart."

Jasper said, "This means you believe in yourself."

"Yes," said Ajia, "the power of meditation is believing in yourself. Fate only applies to those who are living. When you are no longer alive, then things like fate have absolutely no meaning. The only thing of significance is your heart. Tell them to repent!"

Thereupon Jasper left the monastery. He wanted to transmit Ajia's message to the world. He also knew that penance could save people. The young man with flushed face had already fallen on the ground at the entrance to the village. A flock of people surrounded him.

"Doomsday has arrived!" cried John, "Heaven has sent down a plague. Look—Heaven's gate is open, the god of plague has descended in his carriage. Only penance will save you!"

Jasper discovered a big problem. He'd wanted to tell all the villagers to repent, but John announced it first. The villagers had always considered John a demon. When the demon cried for them to repent, they would never repent.

Sure enough, the villagers laughed. Kuan San tore a piece of red paper from the couplet, which flanked someone's door, spat some saliva onto it to get the red color out, and smeared it on John's face. John immediately turned into a clown. He waved and danced like a clown.

"After the god of plague, the gods of fire, wind and water will arrive! Only love will save you!" John shouted until he was hoarse.

"Better love a young widow!" Kuan San went up and gave John's butt a hard kick. John flew into the distance with open arms and then flat onto the ground.

At this point, people noticed that the young fellow with flushed face was already dead. They swarmed over to take a look. John also rolled over and hobbled to the scene.

"Hey—your dad is dead. Go home quickly!" A man waved in this direction from the distance.

"Who are you talking about?" hollered Kuan San.

"Flat Head is dead. Where's his son?" The man sounded flustered and exasperated.

"He's also dead." Kuan San pointed to the ground and said, "Strange—the father and son left together!"

The man shouted, "You know they ate a marmot? It was brought over by someone from Brilliant King Clan. I heard that all the marmots there are dead, the rats too. Just like that other year. Remember?"

Jasper remembered. That year the rats also died first in the village, and then the marmots died, and finally the people. He looked up and saw Ajia at the tip of a tree, twirling a hand drum furiously. But the villagers ignored him. Jasper remembered what Ajia had said. He mustered up all his energy and screamed, "Repent!"

Greatly shocked, the villagers scampered over like monkeys. They surrounded him and asked, "Are you mad?"

Lantern

That night, many people saw Ajia. A lantern in hand, Ajia twirled a hand drum and roamed the village. He yelled, "Repent! Repent!" now and then. At first people thought it was Jasper and said, "The kid sounds like Ajia now."

After twirling the drum for a while, he again shouted, "I am Gonpo Ajia. Repent! Repent!"

All the villagers came out and saw Ajia. One of them said, "This Ajia wants to be a Gonpo!" They all laughed. Ajia turned red from embarrassment and rushed away into the distance. His voice wafted from afar, "I am a Gonpo, repent!" At this moment, someone said, "That Ajia was burned to ashes a long time ago, so who is this Ajia?"

Now, the villagers became flustered; they wanted to ask him which Ajia he was, but the lantern had disappeared into the distance. The mud road darkened suddenly. Jasper shivered. He looked around helplessly and discovered himself in an empty wilderness without any villages or people. He could only see an old woman digging into the earth of a new grave.

Jasper asked, "Is this Ajia's grave?"

"I don't know whose it is." The woman answered. It wasn't a familiar voice. Jasper stared hard at her wishing to identify her, but darkness hid her face.

"I don't know whose it is." The woman sounded hollow. "I only know this is a grave. Everyone says that old graves have treasures. Do you believe it?"

Jasper didn't know what to say.

"I've been searching and searching. I want to find a clean corpse." The woman said, "The kind that cultivated for three incarnations, the kind that never transgressed Buddhist precepts, the kind that would enter the Buddhist realm of the Fixed Tathagata. Once I find it, I'll place it on a ritual altar and perform a ritual for three days. After that, it'll stick out its tongue. You have to grab it right away. If you can't snatch it the first time, or the second time, by the third time you can't snatch it—the corpse'll fly away like a bird and slaughter all the living beings of the three realms. Hence, you'll have to use your teeth and snap at the tongue the moment it's stuck out. The tongue will then transform into a precious sword. You can travel through the ten directions and three realms riding on it. This sword will be mine. You can have the corpse—it'll turn into gold. Just think, an entire body made of gold! You'll be rich your entire life. Want to do it?"

Jasper's heart throbbed. The woman had already dug open the grave. Ajia lay there. Jasper thought it was strange since he saw Ajia being burned with his own eyes! When the woman wasn't paying attention, Ajia opened his eyes secretly and made a face at Jasper.

"Are you in?" The woman asked.

Suddenly Jasper felt his hair stand on end, he turned around and ran. The woman chased after him, screaming. "Don't run away, Boy, I'm your mom!"

There was no way that Jasper would believe her, however. He ran with all his might but was unable to run away from the screams of the woman.

The Parrot

A few more people died in the village the same way the father and son died. John said, "It really is the plague. The last plague aimed at the livestock, but this one aims at humans."

Of course no one in the village believed him. They were going to believe him, but then what kind of a person was John? Anyone who believed his words would be considered a demon's companion!

Uncle returned from the holy land. He noticed a difference as soon as he entered the village. He asked Jasper, "What happened? How come the air is filled with grievance in the village?" Jasper told him about Ajia. Uncle said, "They've wronged Ajia. The last plague was caused by people from Brilliant King Clan burying a cursed object in the pastureland. They've wronged Ajia."

Jasper said, "So he was wronged and there's nothing we can do about it?"

"Yes," said Uncle.

A parrot flew over and shouted, "Revenge! Revenge!" It was followed by a flock of little parrots repeating the same word. Jasper laughed and said, "I haven't seen you for quite a while! So you went away to make babies!"

The parrot continued to holler, without any sense of embarrassment.

Uncle said, "The world is already messy enough—what are you joining in for?" The parrot said, "We've got to survive too!" Jasper shot a glance at Uncle and smiled.

Uncle said, "But why do you always scream for revenge? You should scream for people to repent." The parrot said, "John said to repent, so we won't." Having said this, it flew away with its children, screaming continuously, "Revenge! Revenge!"

"Everything's been turned upside down!" said Uncle.

Jasper said, "There's nothing we can do—no one's willing to repent."

"That's why it's called a plague!"

Jasper and Uncle left the wood and saw the butcher squatting on a rock and tearing off his own flesh. Half of his arms had but bones left. Uncle couldn't bear to see it. He returned to the house for some sweet dew pills. He had to chant the Penance Sutra ninety-nine times for making each batch of these pills. He tore off a piece of yellow paper in which he wrapped some pills and handed the package to the butcher, saying, "I've done penance for you since you won't. Eat these, you'll feel better."

The butcher sniggered and said, "What right do you have to repent for me? What is there for me to repent? Don't you know my father is still wailing in Hell? As I've told you, Hell didn't exist for him before. It was your constant talk about Hell and his believing in you that made Hell exist for him. If you didn't talk nonsense, there'd be no Hell! And, that tea pot wasn't yours to begin with. It was an offering. Why do people make offerings to you? They do it because you know how to cheat them!"

Uncle smiled with a grimace as he looked at Jasper and said, "See—this kind of people . . ."

"Get the hell out of here, you hypocrite!" screamed the butcher.

Ajia stared at Uncle jeeringly from the distance. Uncle said, "Don't laugh—some thieves don't get caught because they haven't stolen frequently enough."

Passing Under the Crotch

Several monks died at Diamond Monastery. They didn't die from the plague—they all committed suicide. Their mode of death was the same; they all hung themselves. There was no warning sign ahead of time. They would just suddenly put their heads into a noose.

Four died this way.

The fifth one was discovered as soon as he put his head into the noose and was saved.

He said, "I thought he was a real Gonpo! He was going to put this glittering, golden string of rosary beads around my neck, so I stretched out my neck for him to put it on." That monk was just taken from the noose on the beam, his neck still sported the imprint of the rope.

Another monk explained to Uncle, "We saw him hanging and immediately brought him down. The others died before we could save them." Four corpses lay in the sutra hall, covered with quilts with the dharani mantra[1] on them.

"It's that Ajia again," sighed Uncle.

"It wasn't Ajia." The monk refuted, "It was a real Gonpo in a ceremonial robe. He was so dignified! Those rosary beads were a profusion of colors with a golden glitter that made the entire body and heart feel cool. Who'd have thought I was hanging myself? Maybe they—" he pointed to the corpses and continued, "they all ended up in paradise!"

The manager of the monastery wasn't happy, "Are you saying we did you a disservice?"

"That's not what I said!" replied the monk.

The manager said, "I've been seeing Ajia walking around in the courtyard. He'd shake his string of rosary beads whenever he saw someone and say, 'What does this mean?' But no one knew what it meant."

---

1. A mantra to promote virtue and obstruct evil.

Jasper smiled. He thought, Ajia was saying, "I've chanted the litany a hundred million times already. Who do you think you are?"

The manager said, "I didn't know you were returning. I've sent someone to report to the Gonpo and asked him to send someone over. He should be on his way by now."

Jasper followed Uncle out of the monastery to greet the Buddhist priest dispatched by the Gonpo. There were two mountains outside the gate of the monastery. They were a husband and wife couple and used to be of the same height. But the wife mountain had an affair with a person later, and had her legs broken by her husband; so she ended up shorter. Ajia stood astride the two mountains. More than ten horses and a palanquin were approaching from the distance.

Uncle smiled and said to Jasper, "That Ajia is just like a child." Jasper laughed and hollered, "What are you doing, Ajia?" Ajia lifted a finger to his mouth and hushed him.

Puzzled, the manager looked at Jasper and asked, "Where's Ajia?" Ajia yelled, "Don't tell him!" So Jasper went over to the stairs and sat down there to watch Ajia play his prank.

The men, horses, and palanquin gradually approached. They passed under Ajia's crotch without being aware of his presence above them. Uncle smiled and said, "I'm afraid the person they invited over won't be able to subdue Ajia." Ajia laughed heartily. Jasper also laughed. He thought, *This is someone the Gonpo sent over after all!* Ajia was ever so pleased.

Grandpa Jiu smiled and said, "He's always like this. Whenever he sees the head of the clan or monks approach, he'd stride across the mountains and have him travel under his crotch!" He feigned ignorance, grabbed a handful of white mustard seeds, and drew near. When Ajia was off guard, he waved his hand and threw the seeds at him. Ajia tumbled down the mountain.

"When have I ever provoked you, old lunatic?" cussed Ajia.

Buddhist Priest

The Buddhist priest was very young but stout. Youth does nothing for a person, but stoutness creates a sense of dignity. He had a multi-layered chin with many, many folds. Jasper forced himself not to laugh and thought, *How can you subdue Ajia if you had to pass under his crotch?*

Ajia's voice floated from afar—

I am a Gonpo
Through my own cultivation.
I don't care what others say,
I stick to my own ideas.

He then twirled his hand drum, which resounded like dense splattering of rain. But Ajia's voice was clear—

My greatest expertise
Is to place black curses,
To awaken the world,
But no one heeds me.

Grandpa hollered, "Who says that no one heeds you? Am I not listening?" Jasper thought, *There's probably more than meets the eye with this Grandpa Jiu—he can also see Ajia!* But then he wondered, *Did Ajia become a deity?*

Several people took the Buddhist priest by the arm and assisted him up the stairs. The priest wore dark sunglasses and was very young. It was through people assisting him, by taking him by the arm, that his priestly dignity was manifested. This was a custom that created panache. Without panache, he'd have been a nobody. His followers introduced him, "This is Khenpo."[2] Jasper thought, *Another Khenpo? How can there be so many Khenpos under the Gonpo?* Ajia hollered from a distance, "Of course there are! The Gonpo designates several Khenpos a year. One has no choice if he is designated!"

The Khenpo ascended the stairs and seemed to be panting. Grandpa Jiu slipped over quietly and said to Jasper, "Do you see? This man is an ox. He'll turn into an ox very soon." "Why?" "From taking people's offerings in vain! He's all fat and tubby, without attaining any achievements or merits from cultivation. In his next life, he'll turn into an ox in order to settle the debt."

Grandpa Jiu pulled Jasper to him and whispered, "Did you know I almost turned into an ox? As soon as I entered purgatory, I began to

---

2. A Tibetan Buddhist monk of great learning.

roam around. Suddenly, I saw a palace, a most magnificent palace. I was just going to enter it when my guru pulled me back and tossed a Vajra scepter into it instead. Later, the cow gave birth to a Vajra scepter. Wasn't that the strangest thing?"

Jasper knew he was on a crazy binge again. He freed himself from his hold and went to the sutra hall with Uncle. As Uncle's attendant, Jasper had the right to enter it with him. The Buddhist priest was already seated on the dharma throne. The throne was originally the abbot's seat. No one else dared to sit there. But the Khenpo sat there anyway. He was the Gonpo's man after all!

The manager had already relayed the situation to the Khenpo, whose expressionless face made him appear unfathomable, "I already knew." And then he continued, "The Gonpo said to perform a Yamantaka Fire Ritual. Any ghost, no matter how powerful, will be subdued. However, one must not skimp on the offerings. It's not that the Gonpo is greedy, but—"

"Yes, yes, of course!" the manager said promptly. "Everything will be made of gold. Only gold will suffice when dealing with the Gonpo!" Jasper laughed. He thought, *What a forthright manager!*

"What kind of language is that?" The Khenpo was displeased. "What do you mean by 'dealing with the Gonpo'?"

"I meant 'making an offering,' I mean when 'making an offering.'" The manager corrected himself immediately.

The Offering Ritual

The Subjugation Fire Offering Ritual began at night.

Surprisingly, the mandala was respectably built. Strips of wood formed a pyramid. All the food offerings were black in color and formed into triangles. Jasper had learned all this from Uncle. He wondered why the monastery didn't ask Uncle to perform the ritual. He was a very accomplished guru, after all! So he asked Uncle about it, and Uncle said, "Accomplished priests don't return home. At home, his accomplishment is considered trash. The monk from elsewhere always chants better!"

Unexpectedly, the Khenpo's voice was quite sonorous. Other than mispronouncing a few words, it was generally fine. Many people knew the Vajra Yamantaka ritual, however, so they all noticed where he mispronounced. But concluding that the Gonpo's man couldn't possibly make any mistakes, they decided that they themselves must have had them wrong. So they tried hard to correct their memory and ended up in a sweat.

The ritual was to last for seven days. During those seven days, the Khenpo meditated in the mandala without leaving it. People brought his meals to him. Outsiders were not allowed in there. Because of his stoutness, the resonance of his voice was full bodied. Everyone said, "The Gonpo's man is truly remarkable!"

But Grandpa Jiu whispered to Jasper, "Did you know he was trained by reading outloud struggle session denunciations!" Jasper scolded, "Nonsense!"

The mandala was established inside the main hall with a curtain over its door. People in the monastery could hear but not see him, which created an even more mysterious aura.

Night approached. All the monks returned to their own cells to perform their daily acts of merit and penance. Jasper, however, wasn't sleepy. Suddenly, Grandpa Jiu came over. He dragged Jasper along and said, "Let's go and see how he performs the ritual!" Feeling worried for Ajia at that moment, Jasper followed him to the main hall and peeked through a crack in the door.

Ajia had already been summoned to the mandala. He said, "You hooked me here using a spell, so I had to come. But you can't subdue me!"

"Why?" asked the Khenpo.

Ajia said, "Because I'm your guru! Who's ever heard of a disciple subjugating his guru?"

Khenpo said, "Nonsense!"

Ajia said, "So you've forgotten! I was the one who taught you the *mani* chant and performed the *guiyi* baptism on you, when you were three years old. Remember how you always got the tones wrong when you chanted *ah mi tuo fuo* later, and I was the one who corrected you!"

"So you are Ajia!" said the Khenpo.

"Who else?" Ajia continued, "How you've advanced! You couldn't even pronounce the words correctly when you studied Exoteric Buddhism.[3] But as soon as you joined the Gonpo, hey, you became a Khenpo! That Gonpo certainly has a Midas touch! Can you also perform the Abhiseka ritual?"

---

3. Exoteric Buddhism is in contrast to the Esoteric or Tantric sect of Buddhism.

"Yes, I've gotten permission from the Gonpo to do it." The Khenpo wiped off a profusion of sweat.

"But the Gonpo didn't transmit it to you! Even if he did, how can you perform a ritual technique if you yourself didn't attain accomplishment through cultivation? If people hear about it, they'd laugh until their teeth fall off!"

The Khenpo knelt down and said, "Okay, okay—my dear guru! Please keep your words to yourself. It wouldn't be good should anyone hear them. What if I make offerings to you for seven days? Let me make offerings to you for seven days and you agree to stay away for a few months. You can create havoc after that. I'm your disciple after all! Look—I've kowtowed to you. All the good food here are yours to take!"

Thereupon, Ajia sat in the mandala and relished the offerings from his disciple.

Jasper laughed. Grandpa Jiu stuck his tongue out a few times and said, "Look—this is the dharma priest. But don't gab about it. If you should say that the dharma priest is the disciple of a demon, then people will call you mad again!"

The two stealthily left the main hall. The chanting of the dharma priest resonated again, reverberating through heaven and earth.

Consecration

After subduing the demon for seven days, the Khenpo seemed exhausted. He left the closed room and squinted his eyes. During the seven days, Ajia was quite agreeable and kept his distance. The monastery was calmer, which inspired people's confidence in the Khenpo. They all decided to ask him to perform the Abhiseka ritual on them as soon as he would leave the closed room. So, as soon as the Khenpo came out of the room, he was greeted by a floor full of monks on their knees before him.

Grandpa Jiu asked loudly, "Did you subjugate that Ajia?"

The Khenpo shot a glance at Grandpa Jiu nervously and said, "Almost."

"What almost? Did you almost make enough offerings to him, or did you almost subjugate him?" Grandpa Jiu asked, laughing.

"Almost! Almost!" said the Khenpo.

The monastery manager brought over a Buddhist statue and asked the Khenpo to consecrate it. Grandpa Jiu snatched it and said, "Let me do it!" He put the statue on the ground, squatted over it, and broke a loud fart. "It's consecrated!" screamed Grandpa Jiu.

The manager said angrily, "How can you do this? You've desecrated the statue; I don't want it anymore!"

"You don't want it? Who wants it? Who wants it?" Grandpa waved the statue and hollered.

Uncle said, "I want it." He fished out some money and gave it to the manager.

Jasper saw the statue glitter with golden rays—it was obviously consecrated. Exceedingly pleased, Uncle fished out a khata scarf, wrapped the statue, and handed it to Jasper. It was so hot that it scalded Jasper's hands.

"Transmit a ritual to us, oh great guru!" a monk yelled.

"Yes, transmit a ritual to us!" the others also yelled.

The Khenpo looked around nervously. Noticing the snicker on Grandpa Jiu's face, he was at a loss as to what to do.

"Ask him!" He pointed to Grandpa Jiu. He then grabbed the gold ingot from the manager's hand and slipped away on his palanquin. He didn't notice that Ajia was already standing astride the two mountains, waiting for him to pass under his crotch.

Collective Karma

Ajia's tricks had become ever more vicious. Not only appearing at night now, he also showed up during the day. More and more people died at the village. Corpses were strewn about the riverbank. Half of Braggart's workforce was gone. They were his hardest-working men. The head of the clan was very upset. The monks in the monastery also performed the subjugation ritual daily. At the height of the ritual, Jasper would find Ajia rolling on the river embankment.

"It hurts! It hurts!" he would scream.

Jasper said, "Stop inflicting suffering on people!"

Ajia said, "I'm not inflicting suffering on them! People inflict sufferings upon themselves! Don't you see how all the ones who died are guilty of monstrous crimes and had committed terrible sins? When their karmic process is done, they have no choice but to die! I'm only aiding the process!"

"Can you stop the plague?"

"No, I can't." Ajia spoke as he rubbed his skin that was inflamed by the mantras, "That is collective karma. No one can stop it. When everyone commits evil acts and regards them as normal, or if the evil acts become customs and no longer considered evil, then collective karma comes into being. This collective karma can take the form of a plague, or a war and is inescapable."

"Is there no help?" asked Jasper.

"There is. It's still that word: Repent!" shouted Ajia. But people couldn't hear Ajia's voice. Only a few people could hear his voice, and they practiced penance earnestly.

But people could hear John's voice. John said, "Look! Heaven's gate is wide open, the god of plague has descended. Doomsday has arrived. Only love can save the world!" Many people in the village were baptized by him. A cross was erected on the mountain. Many people prayed and worshipped the cross each day. The strange thing was, none of the people who were baptized by John had the plague.

Grandpa Jiu rubbed the grime off of his skin forcefully, rolled them with his palms, and threw them into the air. Mom told everyone she met, "You won't get the plague if you eat Grandpa Jiu's sweet dew pills!" She called the grime sweet dew pills, but few villagers believed her. Some sought the "black pills" after they had contracted fever. Those who found one would eat it secretly; those who couldn't find any ended up dead.

Mom searched for Grandpa Jiu everywhere and finally located him on a mountain slope. He was playing with the five girls who'd painted his face with a riot of colors. Grandpa Jiu was singing, while the girls danced to its rhythm. The song went thus:

Mortal affairs are by nature impermanent,
Mortals of the world covet material things.
Material things lead to avarice,
Avarice manifests itself as stupidity.
Stupidity eventually leads to anger,
When will anger of the heart subside?
When the heart is calm, calamities will cease,
When the heart is rapacious, fire will blaze.

"Hi, Grandpa Jiu!" cried Mom.

Seeing Mom, Grandpa Jiu pulled her into the dancing procession and danced as he sang:

The mountains, rivers, and plains,
Are joined due to karmic affinity.
Though they manifest themselves in myriad forms,
Their own nature, should you seek, does not exist.
May I offer some advice to mortals of the world,
Look through them and see their true colors!
Live without attachment, and abandon nothing,
Live with neither anger nor consternation.

"Okay! Okay!" Mom said, "You're obviously having fun—see how the corpses are piling up! Why don't you do something about it?"

The lunatic said, "The myriad forms will all revert back to emptiness. People are the same. They are born, but not born. They die, but do not die. Only they themselves can save themselves."

"Everyone says that the plague was brought about by Ajia," said Mom.

"No, it wasn't. The plague can only manifest itself when the heart is plagued. When the heart is calm, then everything will be peaceful. When the wind topples oneself, don't blame Old Heaven for it!" Grandpa Jiu turned to the five girls and said, "Come—let's continue our singing!" He then told Mom, "We are eliminating the plague!" And continued to sing:

Alas, alack—alas alack,
How we exert ourselves!
I advise mortals of the world,
Why be so attached and confused?
In an instant, the myriad realms will be empty,
You can't take the myriad fates with you.
Why not come with me?
Hee, hee, hee—ha, ha, ha!

Suddenly a flock of parrots arrived, repeating what Ajia was always saying.

Mom said, "Get out of here! You good-for-nothings!"

Chapter 27

Another Way Snow Feather
or Her Mother Died

Listen to "Ambush from Ten Sides"[1] once again!
The Hegemon is bidding farewell to his queen,[2]
Large and small pearls splatter on the jade plate.[3]
Were they tears?
Unexpectedly, the old man of history pronounced,
Heaven knows who actually won and who had lost?

Evidence

According to *Historical Mirror of Forgotten Events*, a legend existed that
the flying thief, Snow Feather, was put to death shortly after she stole
the grain. The book claims the villagers hated Snow Feather bitterly.
Although her act of thievery saved their lives, they didn't like being
saved by a thief and considered it the worst shame they'd ever endured.
Snow Feather's whiteness allowed them to see their own blackness.

Ajia gave a knowing smile. I knew he was jeering at me, as I'd
always trodden in Snow Feather's footsteps.

---

1. Title of a famous *pipa* lute solo piece.

2. '*Bawang bieji*' (Hegemon King bids farewell to his queen/concubine) is the title
of a renowned Peking Opera.

3. This line is almost exactly the same as a line in Bai Juyi's (772–846) poem, "Pipa
xing" (Ballad of a lute), which describes an expert performance of the lute.

But *Crazy Ramblings of Ajia* claims that *Historical Mirror of Forgotten Events* mistook Snow Feather's mom for her. Ajia said, "In fact, during that absurd era, the person who got cooked and cannibalized was Snow Feather's mom, and not she."

The time: before Snow Feather was released from prison.

The first time I read *Crazy Ramblings of Ajia*, I considered the event to have been truly nothing but crazy ramblings by Ajia. I didn't believe that the villagers really ate Snow Feather's mom. But later, I discovered a record of the same event in an authoritative work, which used the incident as an example of man's cruelty. The author even specified the dates, location, and names of those involved.

Consequently, I thought maybe it was indeed true!

The Plowshare Sounded Again

According to *Crazy Ramblings of Ajia*, Snow Feather's mom died from having stolen crops after the parade, when starvation had become another inextricable nightmare at Diamond Clan. I've had a poignant, firsthand experience with starvation myself. The most profound experience of my innermost soul during my childhood was starvation. I used to steal crops too when I was a child.

According to Ajia's mysterious narration, the iron plowshare in the Ancestral Hall was struck again, which signaled the impending occurrence of an important event.

The plowshare served as the alarm for the village. Everyone had to rush to the Ancestral Hall as soon as they heard the sound. The head of the clan had the right to "fix" anyone who wasn't present.

The villagers arrived in twos and threes. According to Ajia's ramblings, the kernels on the wheat stalks had already showed white piths. Although the militiamen undertook night shifts, it wasn't possible to fence off all the fields, tie dogs there, and place militiamen everywhere. Hence, guarding crops was a major problem for the village.

Jasper also went to the Ancestral Hall. Because of the poor harvest, offerings to the monastery were drastically reduced. So he and Monk Wu also joined the labor force to earn some food. He practiced dream yoga daily, which diminished for him the boundary between dream and reality; and he came to experience all manifestations as dreams. The myriad things in the world became illusions. He was unable to see the existence of anything independently. Everything was dependent on everything else and changing constantly. He frequently sank into a state of nightmares, which existed in a world of their own; and just like the world before him, it seemed at once tangible and intangible, real and unreal. Oftentimes, he was unable to distinguish a nightmare from reality and felt he was roaming in the world like a shadow. At any moment, nightmare and reality could blend together. He questioned Monk Wu about it. Unexpectedly, Monk Wu told him that this was a good sensation. Through this, he could eliminate many attachments that constituted the root of distress. When you discover that everything before you is illusory, you will be able to recognize the truth and not take falsehood as reality. Continue to practice it! Monk Wu then sighed and said, "Although what's happening these days manifests a stereotypical polluted evil world, it ironically also provides the best opportunity for attaining enlightenment. You know—sometimes, bad karma is in fact the best karma!"

On that afternoon, which was to be so painful for Snow Feather that she'd wish she were dead, Jasper approached the Ancestral Hall in a dream state. The splattering mud made it even more dreamlike. The ashen sun shone on the ashen village and made everything appear illusory and hazy. Jasper saw many shadows enter the Ancestral Hall. He couldn't tell whether they were humans or ghosts. Barbarian Hag was even older than before. A red light continued to glow in her eyes. She continued to stare at him gluttonously, the way an old wolf looked at a young lamb. He always saw Barbarian Hag roaming around the entrance to the village and taking approaching beggars to her home. But the villagers said she had died a long time ago. He didn't know whether he should believe his own eyes or the mouths of the villagers. He wanted to see if Barbarian Hag cast a shadow under sunlight. He'd heard that the main difference between ghosts and humans was that humans cast shadows but ghosts didn't. But he always forgot to check whenever he saw Barbarian Hag. Now that he remembered, Grandpa Sun had, however, hidden himself behind the clouds. Jasper discovered that Grandpa Sun and Barbarian Hag were probably in cahoots with each other.

Jasper was also afraid of walking under the sun himself. He feared nothing worse than discovering someday that he didn't cast a shadow himself. That was due to a story Monk Wu was wont to tell about a murderer who was to be executed in the city of Liangzhou one year. However, this person was a sworn brother of the executioner. The man approached his sworn brother before the execution and said, "My dear brother! Can you save me?" The executioner said, "I do want to save you, but I'm afraid you won't follow my instructions!" The criminal said, "But I will, I will do whatever you say!" The sworn brother then said, "On that day, I will scream 'run' the moment I lift up the knife! That's when you should start running, the further away the better. Under no circumstances should you turn your head back or return. Can you do that?" The criminal said, "Sure!" On the day of the execution, the sworn brother lifted the knife and screamed "run," and the criminal took off without daring to look back. He ran until he reached Hangzhou and was hired as a shop assistant in a store. Having become somewhat well-to-do after a few years, he got himself another wife and had two sons. But he missed his native home and slipped back secretly. As soon as his original wife saw him, she spat at him. This was a common method used by the women of Liangzhou to exorcise ghosts. The woman said, "You were human when you were alive. Now that you are dead, a deity, please leave us alone!" The husband said, "But I didn't die! I was saved by my sworn brother back then. I escaped to Hangzhou and made a lot of money." The woman spat and said, "Why don't you lie to the ghosts? This old lady of yours saw your head drop off! The villagers with tuberculosis even dipped steam buns in your blood and ate them!⁴" The husband didn't believe her. So the woman took him to his grave. When he dug open the grave, the body that had turned into a skeleton was still wearing the bloody top he wore when he was executed! That was when the husband realized he'd already turned into a ghost long ago. He let out a loud howl and melted into a pool of blood. Monk Wu said he had met the man, who was a scrawny fellow. His faith created another body for him. Monk Wu said, "That man was basically the same as a real person. He cast a shadow under sunlight and his voice echoed. The only evidence that he'd died was the top he wore." After hearing that, Jasper feared someday someone would produce evidence that he'd departed from the world long ago. Although he cast a shadow and his voice echoed, these traits didn't prove he was alive.

Was Barbarian Hag the same as that man? Jasper wondered.

Barbarian Hag stared maliciously at Jasper for a while before she smiled and entered the Ancestral Hall. It was very crowded. Jasper saw the faces of many who had already died. They all sat reverently on the

---

4. This is in reference to Lu Xun's (1881–1936) story "Medicine," in which a boy with tuberculosis was given a steam bun soaked in the blood of an executed revolutionary. The "cure" didn't work and serves to expose the superstitious nature of the Chinese.

low stools made especially for the Hall. Maybe they didn't know they were dead, so they rushed over as soon as they heard the plowshare ringing. Jasper kept on seeing new arrivals sit on top of the starving ghosts since they couldn't see the latter. Although Jasper suspected that what he saw were just illusions, they were extremely clear. He then thought of his nightmares—they were distinctly more real than reality too!

The children of the village also swarmed in. The children were the happiest group during such meetings. They were the most easily satisfied animals. So long as they were fed, they would whistle their way over and laugh their way out. Jasper also smiled when he saw how happy they were. The children blended in among the adults. Gradually, however, Jasper noticed something weird. The children could go right through the low stools like swimming goldfish! His heart missed a beat—the children whose hearts had transformed into mutton were also among them! Jasper thought, *Maybe they didn't know they were already dead?* According to Monk Wu, after a person died, they would be in a state of unconsciousness for three days. On the fourth day, they would gradually regain consciousness, see their dead body, and realize they were already dead. Jasper thought, "*These children were turned into 'mutton' within the three days that they were unconscious. So maybe they really didn't know they were already dead?*"

Am I also already dead? wondered Jasper. He was reminded of the many "death karmas" he'd encountered. He might have died from shock the night he dreamed of the ghost. He might have died from the leeches sucking his blood. Maybe he was devoured by the hungry wolf. Or he fell to his death. Even more likely, the jujube red horse might have died during one of the earlier escapades; but not knowing that it had died, it continued to carry Jasper who also didn't know he had died, and the two experienced the absurd fantastical experiences.

Jasper thought some more and wondered if it was Snow Feather's mom that the jujube red horse carried back that afternoon? The moment this occurred to him, he was wrapped in a dense feeling of illusion. He then thought, *The affairs of the world are real when one says they're real, or unreal when one says they're unreal. Why worry about it?*

While he was still feeling the sensation of illusion, the militiamen escorted Snow Feather's mom into the room. The rope that bound her was dripping with blood, which proved she was still alive. However, sometimes the faces of wronged souls could also be covered in blood!

Ajia said, "Snow Feather's mom was bound because she had stolen crops again. She disappeared from the monastery after the parades and was often seen curled into a black mass in the fields." It was said she survived by pulling off wheat kernels. On this particular day, she had just rubbed some wheat kernels between her palms and was putting them into her mouth, when Braggart caught her.

Braggart began to talk. His voice was awe inspiring. He prefaced all of his sentences with a long "um." He said, "Um—what did we stipulate last time we had a meeting? Um—what were we going to do the next time we caught someone stealing crops?" Kuan San answered, "Didn't you say we'd boil and eat the person?" Some people agreed, "Yes! Didn't you say that we'd boil and eat the person?" Thereupon, Barbarian Hag hollered, "Cook her!" Others hollered in unison, "Cook her!" Jasper discovered that most of the ones clamoring to "boil her" were starved ghosts and realized that those who had died were the most avid about not letting others live.

Braggart said, "Okay! We'll cook her and see if anyone else dares to steal again?"

The Roasting Pan

Thereupon, the militiamen set up a large roasting pan in front of the Ancestral Hall. This roasting pan was Diamond Clan's public property and had been used for countless generations. In the past, the villagers would gather to "roast buns" around Chinese New Year. Since a family could only roast so many buns, it wasn't worth the trouble for a family to set up the roasting pan just for themselves. The women would prepare the buns with wheat flour and take them to the home that had agreed to set up the roasting pan. Men would light firewood, place it on top of the roasting pan, and burn hay underneath it. My family had done it a few times. Back then, it was my job to rotate the roasting pan's lid. I'd use sticks to fasten the four hooks on the lid. I'd rotate the lid the distance of one hook at a time. Any more or less than that distance would affect the roasting of the buns. Father was responsible for feeding the fire, which required expertise. Too intense a fire would burn the buns; not enough fire would result in colorless buns. The most delicious type of roasted "buns" was the "roasted pretzels." Women would roll the dough into long sticks and twist them two or three times like decorative Chinese knots. To this day, "roasted pretzels" are a necessity during Chinese New Year for the folks of Liangzhou.

The roasting pan was filled with cold water. Snow Feather's mom's face was dark; her mouth also looked black. Ajia said, "Hunger is the most terrifying thing in the world. No matter how pretty a woman may look, hunger can transform her into a dehydrated vegetable." Ajia loved to talk about the way Snow Feather ate pickled vegetables. The moment she saw them, her mouth would water, and her face would become as moist as her lips. She would then verily become a dewy woman. At the moment, Snow Feather's mom was totally parched, and her face was sallow. A few kids whose hearts had become Monk Wu's "mutton" shrank in a corner and stared at her dolefully.

Monk Wu pulled a gloomy face. Jasper knew what he was thinking. Monk Wu wanted to say what he needed to say. A person has to say what they need to say. Sometimes, to pretend foolhardiness when one ought to speak is also a shame. A preacher by the name of Martin Niemoller[5] wrote a poem that said, "They first came for the Communists/ and I didn't speak up/ because I wasn't a Communist.// Then they came for the Jews,/ and I didn't speak up/ because I wasn't a Jew.// Then they came for the trade unionists,/ and I didn't speak up/ because I wasn't a trade unionist.// Then they came for the Catholics,/ and I didn't speak up/ because I was a Protestant.// Then they came for me,/ and by that time,/ there was no one left to speak up." Monk Wu said, "When you are present at a scene, not speaking also represents the making of a 'statement.'"

Jasper saw Monk Wu approach Braggart and spoke what he ought to have said. Braggart waved his hand as if brushing away a fly and said loudly, "Sure! How about you protect the crops from now on?"

Monk Wu said, "Sure! I'll protect the crops then!"

"If you lose one kernel of wheat, I'll crush one of your fingers, okay?"

"Sure!"

Barbarian Hag continued to clamor, "Cook her! Cook her!"

Jasper remembered how Barbarian Hag used to offer long incense. How come cannibalism changed her nature to this?

Braggart said, "You only have ten fingers—there aren't enough to make up for the difference!"

Monk Wu said, "Then use my flesh as well!"

---

5. Friedrich Gustav Emil Martin Niemöller (1892–1984).

Braggart asked the clansmen thunderously, "He wants us to let go of the wheat-stealing thief and offers to perform night duty—do you agree to it?"

"No!" hollered Barbarian Hag. Several women also screamed, "We want to guard the crops too! We want to guard the crops too! We want to guard the crops too!" Jasper knew they hated Snow Feather's mom on account of her daughter's loveliness. Their screams were really directed at the latter.

So Braggart smiled at Monk Wu and said, "See—the masses don't agree!"

Ajia said Jasper noticed that Braggart had changed his mind on the sly.

"Go ahead!" Several militiamen put Snow Feather's mom into the roasting pan. They wanted to put her flat in the pan. But each time they pushed her down, she sat up again. Braggart waved his hand and said, "Go ahead! We'll let you sit if you can after the fire is lit!" Mom sat in the pan and stared at the world and the villagers with her lusterless eyes. No one knew what she was thinking.

Braggart roared, "Light the fire!"

Kuan San lit a handful of hay and put it under the roasting pan. A waft of black smoke drowned Snow Feather's mom. She stood up and coughed. Jasper yelled at Kuan San, "Are you really going to cook her?"

"Military orders must be obeyed!" replied Kuan San.

Snow Feather's mom continued to cough. She began to switch her feet, which meant the bottom of the pan had become hot. She jumped out of the pot. Braggart roared, "So you know heat when it's hot! How come you didn't know to think of what I'd said, when you were stealing? Throw her back in! If she can't stand up, then have her lie down!" So the militiamen tossed Snow Feather's mom back into the pan. They held hands and surrounded her.

"Feed the fire! Feed the fire!" Braggart added, "I'd have some qualms if you were a good person, but aren't you a 'bad lot' anyway? If I don't 'fix' you, Heaven won't tolerate it! Kuan San, feed the fire! It's your job—add a lot of hay!"

Kuan San stuffed a large bundle of hay, and flames flared up around the pan. The militiamen holding hands around the pan backed up a bit. Snow Feather's mom continued to cough; her body arched as she coughed. The speed with which she switched her feet accelerated. One could tell that the bottom of the pan had become very hot. Her lips shivered; she clenched her teeth, and her face turned pale. Jasper wished that she would cry and beg for mercy. He believed that the villagers would become tender-hearted if only she would beg for mercy. This would also give Braggart an excuse to back down. But she just clenched her teeth and refused to say a word.

Steam rose from the water. The fire underneath the roasting pan burned explosively.

Jasper's body tightened.

The salivating starving ghosts continued to scream, "Cook her! Cook her!"

Jasper realized that they really meant to cook her!

Jasper screamed, threw himself over, and gave her a vigorous shove. In an instant, Snow Feather's mom fell onto the ground. He then pushed the pan over. Water flowed into the fire; a cloud of smoke and mist surged up.

"Are you really going to cook her? Are you human?" screamed Jasper.

A militiaman smiled in embarrassment and said, "Who's not human?"

Braggart roared, "What are you saying? Do you want to be a filial descendant of a 'bad lot'? Tie him up first and then fill it with water again!"

Vote

Ajia said Jasper was strung up into a *zongzi*[6] and hung in the horse stable-shed. Jasper yelled, "There's nothing more precious than human life! How can you do this?"

Braggart's face changed color when he heard this. He said, "It's up to the clansmen. If you want to cook her, I'll cook her. If you don't want to cook her, I'm not wearing the clan-head hat anymore!" Kuan San said, "You are the clan head, we'll do whatever you say!" Barbarian Hag hollered, "Cook her! Cook her!" The starving ghosts also roared, "Cook her!" Jasper could see that although the clansmen were silent, their Adam's apples were surging up and down. They were obviously salivating over Snow Feather's mom's meat.

---

6. Boiled or steamed glutinous rice tightly wrapped in bamboo leaves.

Braggart shouted, "Anyone who agrees thieves should be punished, raise your fist!" Jasper noticed Braggart's sophistication. No one dares to disagree with this statement. So he yelled, "He changed the topic—but Snow Feather's mom is not a thief anyway!"

Braggart said, "Who said so? Anyone who stole unripe crop is a thief. Raise your fist if you agree!"

At first, a couple of fists went up. They were those of Kuan San and Cripple Big. And then three women who had quarreled with Snow Feather's mom raised theirs. Then some others began to look around. Jasper discovered that the fists of the starving ghosts were raised the highest; but Braggart couldn't see them, so they didn't really count. Some other fists began to rise hesitantly above the heads.

"How come your fist is not raised?" Braggart hollered at a person. The person said nervously, "I'm just raising it!"

Jasper asked loudly, "Is this the way to hold a vote?"

Braggart sniggered and said, "Do you also want a taste of the roasting pan too?"

Jasper said, "Of course! Why don't you cook me? I'll consider you a real man then!"

Braggart sneered, "A thief not caught hasn't done it frequently enough. The day you're caught, I'll cook you for sure. Why don't you raise your fist?" he yelled at another person, who tucked his neck in and raised his hand.

Consequently, fists filled the Ancestral Hall.

Braggart turned to Snow Feather's mom and said, "See—when a wall falls, everyone joins in to push it down! Don't you blame me!"

Covered in mud and water and collapsed on the ground, Snow Feather's mom said slowly, "Whatever you want! To kill or to slice, you hold the seal! I didn't mug, I didn't rob. All I did was grab a handful of wheat kernels. Even if Lord Heaven knew, he wouldn't cook me, would he? I can't believe Lord Heaven would be so heartless, he'd want you to do this!"

Braggart said, "Listen to her! The 'bad lot' even dares to curse Lord Heaven! Clansmen, does she deserve to be cooked?"

"Yes!" they all yelled.

Kuan San said, "Of course she deserves to be cooked. The only problem is that the pan is too shallow. We need a larger pot to cook her. How about the pot for scalding pigs?" Barbarian Hag immediately agreed, "Yes! That's a big pot—we should cook her until the meat falls off the bones, so we can really eat!" The starving ghosts all yelled, "Yes! Cook her thoroughly!"

The militiamen carried over the pot used for scalding butchered pigs. The pot was big enough to cook enough rice for half the village. The militiamen propped it up with several large stones and brought over armfuls of dried twigs from someone's pile of firewood. They then filled it with seven or eight buckets of water and lit the fire.

Braggart asked, "Shall we cook her slowly or scald her with boiling water?"

Opinions differed concerning this. Most of the men endorsed scalding her with boiling water, so that she would suffer a bit less. Toss her in after the water boiled, and she would die very quickly. The women, however, endorsed cooking her slowly so that she would suffer more. In the past when there was enough food, their men always compared them negatively to Snow Feather, resenting them for not being as clean nor as handsome as Snow Feather, or not as pretty. They could never forget the coveting gazes their husbands had when they looked at her. They'd wanted to fix her a long time ago—to fix her slowly with a small knife and a fine rope. Since they were unable to fix her, being able to fix her mom was the next best thing. How could they let Snow Feather's mom die so easily?

The fists were raised once again, but the two factions still shared the limelight equally. Finally, Braggart took a count and said one side had an extra vote. So Snow Feather's mom was escorted into the pot. She was first dunked in the water. Her hair came loose and clung to her face; she looked like a veritable ghost. She quivered and took a deep breath. She tried to climb out of the pot. The minute she tried, the pot began to sway. Kuan San and his men steadied the pot as they pushed her hands off of the rim and shoved her down toward the bottom of the pot. As soon as she reached the bottom, a string of bubbles surged to the surface. Braggart yelled, "Don't let her drown! Don't let her drown!" So Kuan San lifted her up with a pitchfork. Emerging out of the water and puffing, Snow Feather's mom burped and vomited. She was, by nature, prone to cleanliness, but the pot was used to scald butchered pigs. The stench of pig excrement and other stinking stuff surged as the water temperature rose. So she threw up a lot of green fluid and polluted the water of the pot into an unbearably horrible spectacle.

The flame flared up to the rim of the pot. Snow Feather's mom clung to the rim and wailed. She twisted her body, indicating that the bottom of the pot was beginning to scald, and wailed loudly like a helpless child. Her weeping trampled Jasper's heart like a rolling stone.

Jasper struggled furiously a few times. He felt the rope digging into his wrists. A few clansmen lowered their heads. Jasper thought those who were able to lower their heads at this juncture, instead of watching the scene with relish, could be considered human!

The fire died down gradually. "Feed the fire!" roared Braggart. The militiaman said, "I can't do it anymore. I've got a cramp in my hand!" Sure enough—his hand was twisted like a chicken claw. So he yelled for Cripple Big to do it. Cripple Big didn't move. Kuan San pushed Cripple Big aside, snatched a handful of hay, and shoved it underneath the pot. He gave it a hefty puff and the amber flared up again.

Jasper could never forgive Kuan San for this. *He will receive karmic retribution for sure!* Jasper thought. So he kept his eyes peeled for the retribution to descend upon Kuan San. Unexpectedly, however, Kuan San lived until the ripe age of eighty-five and was one of the longest-living elders of Diamond Clan. The only karmic retribution he ever received was imagining his wife fooling around with Cripple Big. Starting from when he was seventy-five, he would always be yelling, "Son, Cripple Big was in your mom's bed again! I know she wants me dead so she can go with Cripple Big." His son would yell at him furiously, "We can't wait for you to die either! Why don't you die so we can take your corpse to the riverbed and feed it to the dogs!" Kuan San never suffered any major illnesses, but he was always complaining of hunger. He'd complain of hunger even after downing three large bowls of noodles. He was always roaming the village with the aid of a cane and yelling, "Can someone take me back home on a cart? I can't walk anymore!" Then, the villagers would tell the kids, "Look at that old guy—you'd never know how tough he was when he was young! He was the one who cooked Snow Feather's mom!" People were reminded of his brutality, in feeding the fire under the pot, whenever they saw him.

Snow Feather's mom screamed, "Dear Lord Heaven! Please open your eyes!"

Jasper couldn't forget her screams either. Just like Kuan San's brutality, they reverberated in his heart for many years. I heard that many Jews wavered in their faith after their experiences during World War II because they were gassed by the millions, even though they were God's chosen people. Countless people called out to God, but God remained shamelessly silent. When Snow Feather's mom called out to Lord Heaven, Lord Heaven also remained shamelessly silent.

Ajia said, "If Lord Heaven did indeed exist, but didn't save her when he could, then he had committed a crime and wasn't worthy of worship. If Lord Heaven had wanted to save her but wasn't able to, then he was incapable and was also not worthy of being worshipped."

Therefore, Ajia came to the conclusion that either Lord Heaven was less capable than a dick, or he didn't exist at all.

Kuan San was very good at feeding the fire. He could keep the fire going without creating any smoke and actually prevented Snow Feather's mom from suffocating. He also sped up the rate the water temperature rose. The minute Kuan San began feeding the fire, Snow Feather's mom wasn't simply being boiled—she was also being roasted. The flames that flared up around the pot surrounded her and licked away at her hair when she struggled. She didn't dare grip the rim of the pot anymore. She only plunged in and out of water now and then. Before the water came to a boil, it was apparently better to endure the hot water than to be roasted.

All the women lowered their heads. Women were women after all; their hearts were not as hard as rock. The wailing of Snow Feather's mom raised their temperatures; specks of sweat appeared on the tips of the women's noses. Braggart's face sported two bulging muscles, indicating that he was clenching his teeth. Jasper realized how he hated the woman. He'd heard that Braggart used to knock at Snow Feather's door in the dead of night and was always cursed by the old woman. Many villagers gossiped about this. Braggart may have heard about them, but he never tried to dispel the gossip. He knew any attempt at protesting against this kind of rumor would only add fuel to the fire.

Jasper cried, "Auntie, jump! Jump out of there!"

The militiamen around the pot had disappeared. They'd all left, either because of the heat or whatever else. Ajia said, "If Snow Feather's mom decided to jump out of the pot, no one could stop her. Maybe no one would put her back in once she jumped out." Jasper saw Braggart giving him a furious stare and realized this was Braggart's strategy for warning others against stealing. Now that the string of the bow had been pulled, there was no way he'd take the cocked arrow back.

Snow Feather's mom yelled loudly. One could no longer make out what she was yelling, the yelling had become the goal in and of themselves. Steam rose from the pot.

To show his resolve, Kuan San stared at the fire like a meditating old monk, totally devoid of facial expressions. This seemed to have been the watershed of his life. Soon after this experience, Kuan San also managed the village school and went there frequently to teach the children. He would raise his voice and espouse magnificent garbage. No one could tell that he was totally illiterate. From then on, Kuan San held de facto power at Diamond Clan. He would snatch those he didn't see eye-to-eye with and take them to the village school for public humiliation. No one dared to fart at him thereafter.

As Jasper remembered it, Kuan San was one of the few at the Ancestral Hall who wasn't perturbed by the screams of Snow Feather's mom. Braggart, Kuan San, and Kuan San's wife became the nucleus of power at Diamond Clan. The folks called Kuan San's wife "Sister-in-law San." As tall as a donkey and as large as a horse, she was the only female who stared at Snow Feather's mom—from when she was screaming until she was fully cooked. She was interviewed decades later. The numerous details she provided were recorded in *Historical Mirror of Forgotten Events*.

Sister-in-law San said, "When the steam became very thick, Snow Feather's mom could do nothing but splash around in the water meekly. In fact, there was very little splashing. The bottom of the pot was obviously very hot, and the temperature was very high. Water shot up in waves from the splashes. It flowed over the rim now and then, creating sizzling sounds in the fire. As Snow Feather's mom plopped in and out of the water, most of her clothes came off." Sister-in-law San said, "Just like people who'd drowned." She said, "The corpses in flash floods are always naked. The water demon is very lascivious. It always strips the corpses of young women and flirts with them. The arms of Snow Feather's mom were exposed. The skin was very tough and red; it looked just like a diseased pig's with its hair scraped off. The pores of her skin were large and full of rashes that looked like goosebumps, with barely visible bloody dots. With jutting ribs, her body looked just like a washboard. Although her lips were moistened by water, they still looked blackish. And then she couldn't make any more sounds. She just panted. Her lusterless eyes turned red and became larger. A red light shone from them—just like Barbarian Hag who ate a lot of human flesh."

Sister-in-law San said, "When the water temperature became really high, the biggest change in Snow Feather's mom was that her cheeks suddenly became higher." This indicated that suddenly her eye sockets had sunk, and the skin on her face had tightened. She said, "There was very little flesh left on Snow Feather's mom's face, even less meat than what you see on a sheep's head that had starved to death." Ajia said, "Hearing this, I suddenly felt nauseated. I couldn't eat sheep head thereafter. In the past, the folks of Liangzhou always offered pig heads to the deities. Temples would always accept pig heads. Later, the folks considered pig heads too expensive and offered sheep heads instead. But whenever I saw a sheep head on the offering plate, I would be reminded of Snow Feather's mom, and the sheep head would turn into her face. This is most disgusting, but there's nothing I can do about it. Sister-in-law San had totally destroyed my appetite for sheep head. Thereafter, I always disappointed the folks of Liangzhou who asked for protection by making offerings of sheep heads to me."

According to Sister-in-law San, Snow Feather's mom died before the water came to a boil. This was a realistic detail. Later, I read about an emperor who died from heating himself with a brazier that raised his body temperature too much. According to the book, the minister who carried the imperial dragon chair took leave on a certain day. The emperor ended up sitting next to the brazier for so long that he croaked from the rise in his own body temperature. Ajia said, "In fact, Snow Feather's mom wasn't boiled and roasted to death; she died of high body temperature." I never told the villagers this because I was afraid this knowledge would lessen the sense of guilt in Braggart and the others. In fact, however, Braggart never did repent. Many years later when he was "struggled against" by fighting others, he came to an insightful conclusion concerning his life: *I've fixed others, but I've also been fixed by others.* Later, this was the justification that many famous murderers also used.

Snow Feather's mom was unable to make any sounds before she died. The first thing that turned white was her eyes. You might have seen the eyes of dead sheep. That's right—her eyes were just like them. Her eyes turned white for a while, and then she plopped down into the water. Soon she floated up again. Her collars were the first to float up. Her clothes quivered for a while, and then her white back floated above the surface of the water. Another realistic detail described by Sister-in-law San was that the chests of women who died in hot water always faced downward.

In the Pot

I've always wondered how Snow Feather's mom felt in the pot. I soaked myself in a tub of hot water to experience it. I had the water heated to a bearable temperature and then asked my wife to add hot water to it gradually. To be honest, I didn't feel the water; I only felt as if I was in a hot oven. I discovered I was surrounded by flames that sang jovially as they continuously pierced my pores. They licked at my nerves, sometimes turning into needles of fire, sometimes into flat irons, and sometimes into wild firebirds. They rumbled and trampled like tanks through my veins. They charged in all directions without reservation. They crushed me with iron chains, while they fired cannonballs at me. And now and then, they shot at me with a jet spray of fire.

I saw her corpse floating in that pot like a dead fish, white belly up. Her mouth opened and closed like a fish out of water. Columns of bubbles plopped around her, indicating that she was soaking in boiling water. Although according to Sister-in-law San, Snow Feather's mom was already dead by the time the water came to a boil—I still felt she could sense the heart-stabbing heat. Although her body was dead, her soul was still being cooked. According to the ancestors, one's thought at the brink of death was of utmost importance. The moment your consciousness is about to leave your body, you will go to paradise if you should think of paradise. You can only be a hungry ghost if you are confined by the distress of starvation then. Although starving ghosts have no body, they still suffer from hunger. You may not have known that it was really their souls that felt hunger since the sense of hunger had already seeped through their souls. So also was the case of Snow Feather's mom. She must have suffered from the pain of being boiled before she took her last breath. That pain must have also penetrated her soul. In the midst of the plopping boiling water, she watched her body being cooked, until the flesh fell from the bones. She saw a flock of starving ghosts salivating over her corpse. She could hear the sound of people swallowing their saliva. She must have also seen Jasper strung up in the horse stable shed. She also saw Kuan San's face, which glowed from the flames. She felt snakes of fire wriggle in her body. She must have realized that the sensation of being boiled and roasted would accompany her to the other time and space.

She saw people fishing her out of the pot, stripping off her clothes, and washing her carefully. The people were as intent as when they plucked pig's hair. Through "fermenting" in the boiling water, her body looked fatter. She knew that was due to moisture.

Of course, she now possessed the supernormal power of Ahbinna.

Everyone knew ghosts possessed five supernormal powers;[7] the only power she didn't possess was the power of eliminating worries. This meant she still had worries; she'd have been liberated if it were otherwise. She who now possessed Abhinna would also know, during an evening many years later, a novelist would write about her. She would also see a large flock of people condemning him for concocting this cock-and-bull story. They obviously couldn't believe that such cruelty existed among human beings. They do not understand that, during a specific historical juncture, humankind lost its humanity collectively. A great psychologist by the name of Jung called this phenomenon the "collective unconscious." Therefore, to the novelist of many years later, she said, "Thank you!" sincerely. She knew if it weren't for him, humankind would've forgotten about this mother who was cannibalized by her own kind.

She even heard a discussion by some critics. They took exception to this episode, which they either felt was too unrealistic or too bloody. You wanted to tell them events even crueler than this had occurred! But you were only a newly deceased wronged ghost. Although you possessed insights that transcended time and space, you were unable to endow the wisdom of an enlightened being to those who are confused.

You must have shed tears. Although your tears would've dropped into the boiling water immediately and became the liquid that was cooking you, have no fear. Weren't you already dead after all? You'd never have to worry for your life again. Although the boiling water would continue to cook your soul, and you'd always feel the scalding hot waves the way starving ghosts always feel hunger—have no fear. You know—once dead, you would never die again!

Let the boiling water make your soul transcendent and take a look at the world that cooked you. Although you were cooked by them, they would be cooked by others. The boiling water that cooked you would ultimately cool down. What continued to cook you was actually the distress in your heart. All the hot water would eventually cool off. But the accompanying distress would continue to stay with you unless eliminated by a coolness of the soul. No need to blame the forgetful folks either. Although many fine people like you were cooked, there would always be those who would not believe in its existence. No one wants to

---

7. The five *abhinna* are: divine eye, divine ear, reminiscence of past births, thought-reading, and various psychic powers.

think about such unpleasant things. Life is too tiresome; everyone wants to play mahjong and be merry! There's no need for sporting sophistication either. So you're dead—let it be! Just blame your bad luck that you happened to have lived during that particular era and encountered those particular people.

You might have felt sorry for your skin. You used to enjoy looking in the mirror when you were young. The loveliness was so wonderful. You used to chew almond and smear the pulp on your face to care for it. It had now turned white from being boiled, a whiteness that you'd have died for when you were alive: a whiteness that only postpartum women who got their fill of millet congee would've had. Your eyes were wide open. They were staring at you while you stared at them. You knew the eyeballs were juicy and delicious. Didn't you relish sheep eyeballs the most? It would be the same when the others ate your eyeballs. There'd be a sibilant crunch—only when one bites into the bitter fluid would they taste some bitterness.

You saw Kuan San poke at your flesh with a pair of chopsticks, the way you used to do when you cooked sheep's head. You suddenly realized that in the depth of darkness, you've already complied with the law of nature. Some people call it the law of karma. You cooked mutton innumerable times, without ever thinking you'd be cooked by others the same way. So you thought, "*Maybe I am reaping what I sowed?*" The moment you thought this way, you felt your negativity relieved somewhat.

Kuan San continued to poke at you the way you poked at mutton. You noticed that the part he enjoyed poking the most was your chest. Although only a thin layer of softness remained there, it was still the site that could enable one's imagination to run wild. You even felt the sensation of the chopsticks. You knew it was just a perception, your body had obviously already become a separate entity. You saw many people smacking their lips. Of course you also heard the rumbling in their bellies. You knew they had already turned into starving corpses and crazy lice. Most of them had already had a taste of delicious human flesh. Hadn't you also stir-fried a human heart once? Have you forgotten? You ran out of food in that distant frozen land. You were so hungry your head was dizzy and your eyes blurry. So you scooped out the heart of the companion who'd died in the snow and cut it up. You could feel the heart thumping as you cut it up—your hand slipped, and you cut off half a fingernail. You hadn't forgotten, have you? When you stir-fried it, pieces of the heart jumped around joyously. You didn't know at first that you had to place the lid on the pot when you stir-fry human heart. You heard the pieces of heart jump up and down, slamming furiously against the lid. You knew they wanted to fly away and not become your excrement!

You saw a woman's husband lying on a brick-bed deflating. He was also waiting for your flesh. But you knew he was going to meet up with you soon. Look—water was flowing from a corner of his mouth and dripped right onto his collar. He was breathing his last. He might have felt something. Look how one could almost discern a smile at the corners of his mouth! You realized he was your brother, the one the villagers called Degree Holder Ho. But you didn't feel bad at all. You suddenly discovered he seemed to have nothing to do with you.

You saw many men slicing your flesh. In fact, there was very little meat. You felt sorry that you had so little meat that they couldn't eat their fill. You realized that other than your legs, which had what might've been considered meat, the rest could only be called skin. The skin of some areas was a little thicker than that of others. Seeing them so excited but then getting so little meat, you felt embarrassed about letting them down. You discovered Braggart and Kuan San eating your heart. Your hands were also awaiting them. You knew that aside from the heart, the hands were the best to eat since they had comparatively more meat due to labor. The heels were also good, but they'd already been grabbed by people. You heard the sound of smacking. You wished you could have video-recorded the scene for future readers, lest they accuse Xue Mo of concocting a cock-and-bull tale.

You also observed some scenes that were moving, however. Some folks were actually vomiting because they weren't used to eating human flesh; either that, or they took exception to the fact that your offal wasn't drained first. Whichever it was, you were still moved. The one who moved you the most was the wailing Jasper who was strung up in the stable shed. You noticed a halo around his head, which indicated the brightness of his heart. You also saw him, many years later, practicing cultivation with your daughter and attaining the supernormal power of eliminating worries. You would find him during some moonless night. By then, your lonely soul would've roamed for many years without anyone to rely on. Although you'd wanted to go to the court of Yama, you were unable to find the way. You'd have preferred climbing the mountain of knives, or burning in the sea of fire at Yama's court, than roaming aimlessly forever. But you could only float around in the bleak wind and mournful rain. Years later, you'd be pleasantly surprised to meet the Jasper who, by then, had attained enlightenment, and you wanted to rely on him. Thereafter, you'd become his dharma protector. But you knew this wouldn't happen until many years later. At this moment, he was greatly distraught. You couldn't understand why someone not related to you was wailing over your death.

You saw Kuan San snatching your leg bone. You knew he was going to suck its marrow. He was always doing that whenever the village slaughtered cattle. You've watched him shovel manure into oxcarts with your own eyes. The spade he used was so large that you stuck out your tongue just from looking at it. But he handled it as easily as one would a matchbox and could fill an oxcart using seventeen or eighteen shovelfuls, when others would've needed thirty to forty. You've seen how, when he distributed grain among the clansmen, each of his shovelfuls of grain was more than five pecks. You wondered if his tremendous strength was derived from consuming all that marrow. Whenever the production team slaughtered a cow, he would slurp up the marrow from all four legs. That's why you knew he was going to eat your marrow. You felt a cramp in your legs. Don't worry, this was just a reflex. In fact, you didn't have any marrow anymore. You were just a wisp of wind. Although you've never read the book titled *The Wind-like Soul*, you still should know the soul is like wind and that wind has no marrow. You now saw him smashing your leg bones with a rock. You immediately felt a sharp pain in your legs. He smashed them more than ten times, and you felt the pain more than ten times. Although you screamed, no one was able to hear you. Wind has no vocal cords. In other words, you've lost the right to scream about your pain. In fact, you lost all your rights a long time ago. You lost them the day you were kidnapped by fate.

You heard a slurping sound issuing from the fella's mouth. You felt a leg spasm, and energy drained from your leg like a cramp. You knew that was also just a feeling. You felt disgusted by the fella and could almost smell the stench in his mouth. You could hardly bear the thought of having such beautiful marrow enter that putrid mouth. You thought, *I'd rather have them tossed into a mountain gully to feed the wolves!* You should refrain from having a "heart of distinguishing," however. Whether they were eaten by him or by wolves, they'd end up as feces. There's no fundamental difference between human excrement and wolf excrement. Don't be perturbed!

You should think instead, *Aiya! This fetid leather-bag of a body of mine actually enabled many to relieve their starvation and possibly saved some lives!* For instance, Barbarian Hag might have taken one beggar fewer to her home after she'd had her fill; or someone from whose mouth clear water was just about to flow might've been able to swallow the water after eating your flesh; or—enough, such instances were numerous. If you had gladly bestowed your body to them as alms and saved their lives, you would've become another type of human. Of course, you probably have no idea what I'm talking about.

You also saw a few women who chewed on your legs. That Sister-in-law San was in the process of scooping out your eyeballs! That was one of the most delicious parts of your body, and she obviously knew this. A woman tried to fight for it. But one swing of her arm, and that woman flew more than ten feet away. You felt sorry for the woman and wanted to give her one of your eyeballs, but was it up to you? You couldn't even do anything when you were alive! And now you are nothing but a wronged ghost! Who did you think you were?

You noticed some people actually drinking that soup. You felt like throwing up. Lots of stuff from your bowels ended up in that soup. Of course, you were disgusted. That soup wasn't tasty—it was very much like the soup of an old pigeon. Have you ever cooked an old pigeon? Yes, that was it. It was the kind with just a few drops of fat floating on top—couldn't compare at all to the delicate white soup of a baby pigeon! But it had a bit of meat flavor nevertheless—so stop being fussy!

You noticed that you finally turned into a pile of bones bunched together at the bottom of the pot. They were not as white as you expected them to be. One would've expected your bones to be white since you'd never consumed any poisonous medicines. But you should know the whiteness was already cooked into the soup. There's no need to bicker about the appearance of the bones. Whether they were a bit grayer or a bit whiter didn't alter your intrinsic nature. Only when you offer your flesh and bones to those people, without any rancor, could you become a Buddha. At that point, a monastery might take your bones and have a pagoda built to house them. At that point, your bones wouldn't be called "bones" anymore. By then, people would revere them as relics. Do you understand now? The quality of one's bones is dependent on the nature of the heart of their owner.

You finally realized you are devoid of life and understand the significance of everything that's happened. In other words, you are no longer human. You've already become a ghost. Do you remember how you used to shudder whenever people talked about ghosts? In fact, everyone is also a ghost and human at the same time. You're a ghost the moment that thumping heart stops beating; you're already a ghost. Look—the transformation from being human to ghost is actually quite easy!

But you still felt aggrieved. You suddenly realize that you were devoid of life. Which was to say, you no longer had that which one could only have once. Heaven could age, the earth might endure, but you no longer had life. You'd never ask, "Who gave Braggart the right to deprive others of their life?" because you never knew that you had the right to ask such a question.

In fact what saddened you was not just your death but also disappearance of the event in people's memory. With the death of the generation that consumed you, people won't remember that you were cannibalized. Even the writer who'd record this event will be criticized for fabricating nonsense or describing bloody violence. They should know that sometimes one manifests violence in order to eliminate violence. Only through understanding the symptoms and causes of a disease can a physician find the right cure.

You noticed how people smacked their lips with relish. This was the largest communal meal of the village.

You noticed a flock of starving ghosts arrive in merriment and telling you, "Come! Let's go for a spin in the fresh air!"

But you only wept. You didn't wish to join their ranks. Your crying was filled with such sobs that I thought my chest was going to burst. You must have realized my pain and wanted to help me. You grabbed my hair and yanked me out of the water.

"You wanna die? Drowning yourself for so long!" My wife's voice sounded like a broken gong.

The Taste of Bear Meat

Historical Mirror of Forgotten Events also records interviews with some participants in the event. Most of them partook in the consumption of Snow Feather's mom's flesh. According to them, what they ate was evidently bear meat rather than human meat. The folks who'd undergone the famine had gained an incredible ability for discerning different types of food. They truly could tell the difference between human flesh and bear meat. About 60 percent of them—most of whom had tasted both human and bear meat before—said, the human flesh they ate truly resembled bear meat.

Consequently, *Crazy Ramblings of Ajia* says the "husband" of the bear Snow Feather's mom assisted when it was giving birth, became a spirit from cultivating itself by worshipping the moon. It had completed the practices just when Snow Feather's mom met with the calamity. Therefore, it transformed itself into the likeness of Snow Feather's mom, brought her back to Old Mountain, and took her place in the torture.

This version came to be widely accepted by Snow Feather's worshippers. A dharma protector resembling a bear was added to the Tanka depicting the Dakini Goddess. In Liangzhou, after the bullock, this was the second animal that entered her Tanka.

I like this version, although I've always doubted the veracity of *Crazy Ramblings of Ajia*.

Gaps

What confused me were the many obvious gaps among the manuscripts discovered in the Xixia cave. Professor Chen Sihe of Fudan University studied such gaps extensively. In one of his lectures, he pointed out some gaps in Cao Yu's[8] *Thunder and Rain,* which inspired me to create a new perspective on the concept of "gaps." According to Professor Chen Sihe, gaps reflect things the author may not have noticed. It was through a certain "gap" in *Thunder and Rain* that Chen discovered Zhou Puyuan's great romance.

For instance, according to *Historical Mirror of Forgotten Events*, Snow Feather's mom died from "crop stealing" toward the end of a famine. If that were true, then she couldn't have suffered the series of struggle sessions after that. Based on experience, people wouldn't have had the energy to hold parades during times of famine. It was said there were no real famines at Diamond Clan during the years after the struggle sessions and exhibition parades. So, some of the descriptions concerning the cannibalism of Snow Feather's mom seem to lack veracity.

Family Instructions of Diamond Clan explains this "gap" as follows: "Some claimed the cannibalism only happened in Jasper's nightmare." This was a most ludicrous explanation. Because of this, I couldn't help but laugh at all of the so-called family instructions. "Some claimed Snow Feather's mom died in a 'crop stealing' incident which occurred

---

8. Cao Yu (1910–1996), born as Wan Jiabao, was a renowned Chinese playwright, often regarded as one of China's most important twentieth-century writers.

after the exhibition parades." In other words, starvation had become an inescapable nightmare at Diamond Clan. I have had actual experience with this. Although I was born in 1963, the childhood experience that impressed my soul the deepest was starvation. I used to always "steal crops" when I was little. Back then, I would ride and herd a jujube red horse. Whenever no one was in sight, I would pull off a handful of wheat kernels and burn them. My mouth would turn white from the kernels' juice, and my chin would turn black from the soot. To eliminate the traces of theft, I had no choice but to use my urine to rinse my mouth and wash my chin. I might add that, during my infancy, urine was the fluid dearest to me, except for mother's milk. Mother used to carry me on her back to her production team's field when I was just a baby. Whenever I was thirsty, Mother would catch my urine in a container and feed it to me. Later, my digestive system was so good it could even digest stones. Mother attributed it to the power of child urine. Years later, "urine panacea" took China by storm. It was said urine was derived from blood. Its constitution was similar to blood serum and contained many active ingredients vital to the human body. It was supposedly capable of curing innumerable diseases. Ajia also told me a secret: the "wine" he drank with his beloved, when they exchanged cups of it,[9] consisted of a mixture of urine from both of them. Later, I became convinced that this was one of the most creative activities of his entire life and gasped in wonder whenever it was mentioned. Later, I decided to include this highly imaginative poetic element in this book. Even later, this became my means of testing for true love: I would insist that any woman who declared their love for me drink a mixture of our urines in the form of the "exchange cups of wine." This strategy scared away innumerable beauties obsessed with cleanliness and thus allowed me to remain pure hearted and devoid of lust to this day. So, one can't deny the merit of urine in the achievement of my religious attainments. I digress—this was simply intended to win a laugh from you, dear honorable readers. No more will be said about it.

A third version included in *Family Instructions of Diamond Clan* claimed that the victim of cannibalism was Snow Feather, rather than her mom. It claimed she was cooked and eaten after she stole from the granary. This is the version I loathe the most since it fundamentally shakes the foundation of the second part of this book.

---

9. As a part of the Chinese wedding ceremony, the bride and groom drink cups of wine with their arms interlocked.

A fourth version claimed that the victim of cannibalism was a woman other than Snow Feather's mom. It claimed that the latter got to live until the end of her natural lifespan and didn't close those eyes, which had experienced so many ups and downs, until many years after the incident.

A fifth version had been mentioned earlier—that the male bear transformed into human form, to repay the favor received and entered the pot in place of its benefactress. After that, Snow Feather's mom spent the rest of her life happily under the care of the female bear and baby bears.

The various views above serve to prove my viewpoint that the so-called family instructions consist mostly of obviously blind guesses. You'd turn deaf if you were to believe them.

Furthermore, obvious inconsistencies also manifest themselves concerning Jasper's heritage. The Jasper in *Nightmares* seems to have been Braggart's son, a young man of high rank at Diamond Clan. The Jasper in *Tale of the Goddess* was merely a monk. At the beginning of this book, Jasper was a monk who'd just returned from a pilgrimage to Nepal. But in many other places, he also seemed to have been a monk in Xixia.

Furthermore, characters like Braggart, Kuan San, and others also show numerous self-contradictory traits. All in all, the book is strewn with gaps and inconsistencies.

But I'm too lazy to make them into a wholesome entity, as I've discovered that the various apparent "inconsistencies" are actually the most realistic reflections of life.

Perhaps the existence of numerous inconsistencies and gaps is a trait of this book.

Chapter 28

The Leather for Ritual Implements

The Lady of March—where is she now?
      The autumnal wind blows in gusts,
The autumnal wind is speechless.
The autumnal wind lacks romanticism,
The autumnal wind harbors not your smile,
The autumnal wind has already drowned out the She of March.

The Leather Goods of Diamond Clan

Historical Mirror of Forgotten Events also records the process for producing a set of ritual implements. The manuscript does not note the year. It was said this was a formidable task, assigned by "above." The book does not specify which "above" it was, whether it was religious or secular, or whether it was the province or the county. Ajia said, "This wasn't something one was allowed to ask."

According to *Historical Mirror of Forgotten Events*, leather craftsmanship had a long history in Diamond Clan and could be traced as far back as the Han dynasty. Ever since the Han, Liangzhou and the entire Hexi region were the most prosperous pasturelands in China. Pastureland produces leather. Where leather was abundant, leather craftsmen would proliferate; and where leather craftsmen thrived, the likelihood of producing expert leather craftsmen would also increase. Cripple Big was an expert leather craftsman: not just an ordinary expert but one of the very best in all of northwestern China. This wasn't a self-acclaimed designation but one publicly recognized by craftsmen in the trade. Cripple

Big's father, grandfather, great-grandfather, and great-great-grandfather were all top leather craft experts. According to legend, Zuo Zongtang[1] posted imperial notices recruiting leather craftsmen, when he led an expedition to western China. Several thousand leather craftsmen from all over the country were supposed to have participated in the competition. The top finalist was Cripple Big's ancestor. Under his leadership, the group of leather craftsmen selected by him made heroic contributions to the cavalry that invaded westward. But when at length he was due for his pension, he was sacked due to a minor infraction and returned to Liangzhou dejected. Even a dead horse can impress others with its large bones, so his household was nevertheless considered wealthy in Diamond Clan. However, due to opium addiction of members of Cripple Big's grandfather's generation, the family suffered a reversal in fortune and became as poor as church mice. Furthermore, with the gradual retreat of cavalries from the historical stage, leather craftsmanship became a profession existing solely to serve the livestock's needs in the countryside. Although poor, Cripple Big was a talented leather craftsman by nature. His work tended to be highly refined since he was meticulous, skillful, fond of working with leather, and lacked female distractions.

According to Ajia, the most profitable products made by Cripple Big's ancestors in the past were ritual implements rather than regular leatherwork. When one of his ancestors took his leather wares to Tibet to sell, his expert eyes immediately noticed that many of their ritual implements were shoddily made. Consequently, he decided to take up the profession of making ritual implements. Some ritual implements, such as the hand drum, were actually made of human skin. The difference between ritual implements and regular leather products was that the former involved additional expertise—which was a cinch for members of Cripple Big's family. As a result, the production of ritual implements became another money tree for Cripple Big's family.

Due to the specific requirements for making ritual implements, the party placing the order usually supplied the raw materials. For example, the leg-bone horn was made from a human calf bone. The age and gender of the deceased, and whether the person died violently or peacefully, were all significant, depending on the ritual implement use. The person, for whom the ritual implement was intended, had to supply the raw mate-

---

1. Also known as General Tso, Zuo Zongtang (1812–1885) was a statesman and military leader in the late Qing dynasty.

rials to ascertain their background and thereby prevent being cheated by unscrupulous leather craftsmen who might use any old human bones.

Cripple Big had made numerous ritual implements with his dad. The caliber of his work was supposed to have far exceeded his dad's. This was what his dad told someone, and it was most likely not an overstatement. The last time Cripple Big's dad went to Tibet to deliver some ritual implements, a lama told him to disperse his wealth to avert disaster. He took the advice to heart and got addicted to opium and gambling after he returned home. Within years, the wealthy family became as poor as church mice. Cripple Big ended up even poorer. Although his poverty and his being crippled prevented him from marrying, his expertise in leatherwork made him indispensable to Diamond Clan. All the leatherwork needed for the horse and cattle carts in the village was made by him.

Because of the fame of Cripple Big's family, that "important assignment" naturally came to Diamond Clan.

Cripple Big

Ajia said, "Look—the sky is barely bright and Cripple Big is already out of bed!" Ajia has a lot of literary talent. His descriptions always enabled me to imagine myself at the scene. I thought it was a pity he wasn't a professional writer. However, although he wasn't identified as a writer, *Crazy Ramblings of Ajia* was written under his name. He was a writer with a literary work, but he wasn't a real writer. Many years later, *Crazy Ramblings of Ajia* would become a treasure international Sinologists always dreamed of, except they could never figure out if the book was actually written by Ajia.

Ajia said, "After Cripple Big got up, he called for his mom out of habit; but no one responded." At first he was surprised, but then he remembered that his mom had died violently. He couldn't help but feel a knot in his heart and surge of tears. He shook his head forcefully to shake off the images and emotions from his mind. Ajia said, "How Cripple Big wished he could wail to his heart's content, but he had to go fetch water!"

As mentioned earlier, Cripple Big's main job was fetching water. Diamond Clan was always holding meetings at the Ancestral Hall. Everyone needed to drink water there. A lot of water was needed.

According to Ajia, during that era, Cripple Big wished he could just continue in his original profession of leatherworking, but he had to fetch water. One had to be powerful to retain one's original profession. His leather craftsmanship was superior. None within a hundred leagues could surpass him. If someone wanted a certain pattern, he'd create the desired pattern with one flick of his knife. Drum making, in particular, was his forte. When another craftsman used a piece of leather to make a drum, it would sound muffled. When he made one using the same piece of leather—one beat and the sky would fall! But if Braggart ordered him to fetch water, then he had to fetch water. The guy was the clan head after all! In the past, people from other villages used to ask him to make leather implements for their livestock. He would always get paid for his trouble. But later, Braggart said, "Enough, enough! Why don't you fetch water? Forget about working for them!" So, Cripple Big had no option but to put down his craft tools. Aside from the occasions when his own village needed leather goods—when he could feel spirited—he was resigned to fetching water the rest of the time.

In Ajia's narration, Cripple Big cleared his throat and heaved a long sigh. But the pressure in his chest intensified instead. However, he knew the grief would flow out from his pores after filling a few loads of water.

Holding the camel's rein, Cripple Big loaded the water bags and led the camel down the mountain.

A light mist hid the village. In the east, a splash of red seeped through like watercolors. Ajia said, "Normally, this would be the happiest time for Cripple Big. The air would be as clear as water and Braggart would still be under the quilt," Ajia added, "sometimes under Braggart's own quilt, sometimes under someone else's quilt—and wouldn't yet be able to pierce Cripple Big's back with his eyes." Aside from the camel, Cripple Big was the only one between heaven and earth. Sometimes he would roar furiously. The scream would rush out of his chest and echo ceaselessly around the mountain gully. But he didn't feel like roaring today. The path he used for fetching water was quite narrow—only about two or three feet wide—just enough for one person or an animal. The road for carts was much wider. But it twisted around the mountain so much that the distance was much farther. Aside from carts, few people used it. People preferred this path when they traveled. The person that used this path the most, on any day, was Cripple Big. He had to travel up and down the path all day to carry water. It was boring.

According to Ajia, he could see the village on his way down. Houses scattered throughout the mountain gully. Sometimes, Cripple

Big could see women peeing after they woke up. Their white buttocks glared. As soon as he saw them, flames would flare up in his heart, and he'd force down his saliva. Even before he made the exquisite wooden rods, he'd had a taste of woman. It happened several years ago. Degree Holder Ho's woman asked him to make a pair of short boots for her and promised him two liters of barley in exchange. The woman told him to bring a handful of candies to her home to get the barley. When he got there, the woman tossed the candies upstairs. Her kids cheered and rushed upstairs to look for them. Then the woman slipped her pants off and said, "Come get your barley!" And Cripple Big took it. He remembered the woman being scrawny. Although she was a beauty, age and scrawniness had taken away her charm. Yet Cripple Big still found her unforgettable. He thought of her as soon as nighttime approached. Later, the exquisite wooden rods he made enabled him to get many tastes of this delicacy, but he still always thought of Degree Holder Ho's woman. That was his first time. Ajia said, "Memory of the first time will always stay with the person for the rest of his life!"

After climbing down the mountain, he'd head north on the village path and arrive at the edge of the water. One side of the path was a gully many meters deep. Sometimes, when the mountain god got upset, he would create a flashflood, which would tumble down with mud and sand, deepening the gully even more. This wasn't a problem, however. What the villagers feared most was when the mountains moved. It was fine so long as the mountains were lying down, but when they decided to take a step, then they could bury all sorts of things. I've always suspected Ajia as the culprit behind the mountains' moving—that he would shake his body and cause the mountains to move when he wanted some food as offerings. Ajia, however, said with flushed face, "You think I'm that kind of a person? I'm a protective deity after all!" I said, "So you are a protective deity—but then, how come the mountains move? Look—you should prevent disasters for people once you've received their offerings. If you can't prevent disasters for people, then why should they make offerings to you?" Ajia felt embarrassed. He immediately changed the topic and continued with the tale of Cripple Big.

"Hey, Cripple Big! You made a heroic contribution!" said Donkey Two.

Cripple Big answered him with an incoherent "humph" and hurried away with the camel.

"That Brilliant King Clan never had it so bad before!" Donkey Two added.

Cripple Big didn't respond to him. He pulled hard on the reins. The camel felt the pain from the nose ring and began to gallop with a limp. Cripple Big wanted to say, *Did you eat shit, Donkey Two? What's there to brag about?* He then thought of Kuan San and spat emphatically.

Ajia said, "The water dam was right in front of him. Cripple Big fetched water from here every day. A pile of rocks here pierced his heart every day." Cripple Big wanted to know what his mom looked like under the rocks. What does Mom look like now? But what appeared before his eyes was still Mom's twisted face, as well as her disheveled white hair and messy white brain tissue. The minute he thought of them, he felt a hatred for Kuan San. He said to himself, "Kuan San, you jackass—I'll chop your mom into pieces too!" But he had never seen San Kuan's mom. Ajia said that the day Kuan San was born, a bloody ghost slipped into Kuan San's home; so his mom died of a hemorrhage. Ajia said he could have driven away the bloody ghost, but Kuan San's dad was stingy and had never made offerings to him. Although Ajia didn't care about the offerings, he did care about the attitude. Just think, if no one worshipped him, what's the sense in being a deity? Ajia said, therefore, he pretended not to see and allowed the bloody ghost to commit the murder.

Cripple Big cursed, "Kuan San—I'll fuck your woman!" Although Cripple Big had nothing against Kuan San's woman, his mood was much improved.

Cripple Big tried his best to ignore the pile of rocks. He tied the camel to a large stone, took a small bag, and began filling the large bag on the camel with water. Before Cripple Big took over this job, his predecessors used a wooden bucket to fetch water. The camel would wobble up the slopes and down the gullies with the wooden bucket on its back. By the time it reached the fort, the bucket was less than half full, at most. Cripple Big, however, used a cattle stomach as a bag and fastened a leather mouthpiece to it. He'd plug it up with a wooden plug after filling the bag, and not even a drop of water would escape, no matter how much the bag bounced on the camel's back. Braggart said, "Aiyo! Not bad at all! Who would have thought you'd be so good at this!" Cripple Big said to himself, "I'm good at many, many things! You're using a Ferghana[2] as a donkey!" Yet he pretended to be embarrassed instead.

"Savory Kid!" a voice rang out.

---

2. Ferghana horses were one of China's earliest major imports from central Asia.

Cripple Big's hair stood on end. He feared nothing more than hearing this voice whenever he fetched water. It was Mom's croaky voice. Cripple Big spat on the ground—this was the way his mom taught him to chase away ghosts. Ajia said, "All ghosts, no matter how fierce, fear spit!" Cripple Big didn't want to spit at Mom, but she was always scaring him. Although she wasn't gentle when she was alive, at least she wasn't scary. Once dead, she always frightened him. The image of her disheveled hair, matted with messy white brain tissue, continually surged in his mind. Ever since Braggart had people bury Mom under this pile of rocks, Cripple Big feared nothing more than having to come here to fetch water. At first, he feared the stench. He didn't expect Mom to exude such a horrible stench. She must've been exacting revenge upon the villagers. The horrible stench permeated the village. Later, the villagers burned a lot of mock money. They then tossed the ashes of the mock money, plus those of grain, through the cracks of the rock pile. They also sprinkled lime over the rocks—then the stench was finally gone. But at night, people would hear the sound of weeping from inside the rocks. They were all convinced it was the voice of the deceased hag.

"Savory Kid!" the voice rang out again.

Cripple Big held his breath and filled the water bag quickly. Suddenly, he felt his heart thump and heard the ringing of bells. He turned around and saw Kuan San approach, yelling at his donkey to egg it on. He came to fetch water for himself. Emboldened, Cripple Big shot a glance at the rock pile and saw it sitting there nicely, without any changes. So he complained, "Mom! Please don't scare me! Please don't blame me—I was an arrow in a stretched bow—I had no choice!"

The ringing of the bells came close. Kuan San said, "Cripple Big, have you heard? The folks of Brilliant King Clan lost face totally. Last time I met their head, aiya—so red from embarrassment—his face looked like pig's blood!"

Cripple Big didn't feel like bothering with such information and wondered what Mom looked like now.

"I heard Braggart say you've got your work cut out for you!" added Kuan San. This was actually of interest to Cripple Big, so he asked, "What work?" "Leatherwork. I heard that people above want some leatherwork!" "Really?" Cripple Big was delighted. Ever since Mom moved her residence to that rock pile, he really didn't want to fetch water anymore.

"I heard that they want it in a hurry!" said Kuan San.

After adding a few more bags of water, the container was full. Cripple Big rushed back to the fort with the camel.

Ajia said, "Look—Braggart is waiting for him outside the gate!"

The Dharma Edict

Crazy Ramblings of Ajia doesn't include many descriptions concerning how Cripple Big executed the leatherwork. It emphasizes instead Cripple Big's state of mind. One could say that many of its chapters resemble stream-of-consciousness novels. This might've been the earliest stream-of-consciousness novel in Chinese. Too bad it was buried under the ashes of age and therefore unable to enter Chinese literary history. Oftentimes, books also have their own fate. It couldn't expect to become a bestseller just through authorship of a protective deity.

However, the way I see it, many descriptions in the book were too obvious. I even doubted if Ajia had really attained the "supernormal power of thought-reading." Maybe *Crazy Ramblings of Ajia* was written by someone else. I can't believe that the depth of perception of a deity who had the power of thought-reading, would be equivalent to that of a mediocre writer. I even suspect it was written by a hired hand, which is a common occurrence. Obviously it would be very easy for a protective deity, who'd been in control of a territory for many years, to have a degree-holder ghostwrite a book for him. But Ajia insisted the book was truly his own work. Of course, I pretended to believe him. I'm easily persuaded, you know.

Ajia said, "Cripple Big was going to do leatherwork. But he couldn't feel even a modicum of excitement about it because the 'leatherwork' wasn't normal leatherwork—it should be called 'ritual implement.' The kind Snow Feather would discover in Diamond Maiden Cave."

"So what is a ritual implement?"

"A ritual implement is a ritual implement!"

Ajia mentioned that Braggart said to keep it a secret. He said it was a "dharma edict."

The people "above" dispatched the raw material: five living humans—four males and one female. They were all young.

Ajia said when Cripple Big saw the woman, he was flabbergasted and thought, *Isn't this Snow Feather?* He'd heard she'd been sentenced to life imprisonment—how did she become a "leather"? He didn't know where the others came from, but they certainly weren't from Diamond Clan. Later, he asked one of them and found out they were all selected from a prison. All the men were criminals who had received the death sentence.

The request was for him to make a hand drum, two skull bowls, four large drums, and eight leg-bone horns. Braggart said, "This was an order from above." When asked which above, he didn't answer. There were many levels above Diamond Clan. They could all be referred to as "above." Exactly which "above" it was—the section, region, county, or province—it wasn't specified by the "above."

Ajia never made it clear which "above" it was. This became a mystery in Diamond Clan. *Family Instructions of Diamond Clan* includes many theories concerning this—they all sound reasonable, but all are unverifiable. Therefore, later scholars concluded the incident was probably just another of Jasper's nightmares! Because this was an unsolvable mystery, it provided bread and butter for many scholars. They argued ceaselessly each day, like blind men figuring out different parts of an elephant, and gradually developed numerous streams of thought concerning the event. Many holders of doctorate degrees began their careers by solving this "mystery." One day, Ajia whispered to me, "If you want everlasting fame, then include some unsolvable mysteries in your works."

According to Ajia, the four men stared coldly at Cripple Big without saying a word. They all looked learned and meek. It was hard to tell why they had received death sentences. Snow Feather looked more voluptuous than before; her skin was somewhat darker, however.

Another mystery was whether this woman, who looked like Snow Feather, was, in fact, the real Snow Feather. *Family Instructions of Diamond Clan* also includes many theories concerning this question. One theory is that Snow Feather was one of the prisoners from Diamond Clan who was executed. She never escaped the gunshot bloodshed of that afternoon. Another theory suggests that the woman who was designated as leather wasn't Snow Feather but someone who looked like her. The third version says that Snow Feather was truly designated as leather.

Ajia's narrative chose the third version.

Family Instructions of Diamond Clan also notes that all the "leather" had been selected by experts dispatched by "above," and had to satisfy required specifications. Not just anyone could satisfy those specifications.

It was said the men had to be like the Warrior Gods and the women like the Dakini goddesses. It was said these ritual implements were to be used for performing a very important diplomatic activity. But based on research, *Historical Mirror of Forgotten Events* concludes that these ritual implements were probably ordered by an official in the county to curry favor with a boss in the province, who either collected ritual implements or was a practitioner of this belief system. In order to prove this, the author who wrote a continuation of the above book, for private purposes, even included many examples of people who appropriated prisoners sentenced to death. For instance, a female middle school student had both her kidneys plucked out on her way to the execution ground. In order to prevent negative effects on the kidneys, no anesthetic was administered—only a sharp knife was used to gouge out the throbbing pair, which were immediately rushed to the hospital, where they were transformed into an official's kidneys. This sort of thing happened in Liangzhou all the time. Should the "above" break a fart, the "below" would even dare to cut down Grandpa Sun.

Ajia said, "Stop listening to that nonsense, better listen to my story instead . . . Look—Braggart was talking to Cripple Big, 'Use the materials frugally. If the men are enough, I'll ask the 'above' to give Snow Feather to you as wife.'"

Ajia said although Cripple Big longed for a wife every night, he had trouble feeling happy about this task. His ancestors had used corpses when they made such craftwork. Of course, it would be better to use live people rather than corpses for this kind of ritual implement. For instance, a leg-bone horn would be "alive" when blown if the leg of a living person was used. Also, the horn would remain moist and glossy; while those made of the dried bones of a corpse would always look withered and dry. Ajia said, "One evening, Cripple Big's dad dug up someone's newly deceased young wife, and personally demonstrated for Cripple Big the various techniques for skinning, tanning, and using human leather for making drums, leg-bone horns, etc." Dad said, "Human skin is just like sheepskin. Once the animal has been dead awhile, its skin would become difficult to strip." Dad also taught him many other trade secrets. Cripple Big thought, *Those are four lives after all!* Ajia said, "He'd already excluded Snow Feather from the list." Four people were enough for the items ordered. Cripple Big was a skillful expert and wouldn't waste any materials. Furthermore, the person who selected the materials was knowledgeable. All those he'd picked looked well balanced and had smooth limbs. None of them looked ugly.

Cripple Big said, "You've got to pick someone hard-hearted to be the assistant."

"Would Kuan San do?" asked Braggart.

"Yes!" Cripple Big then added, "Feed them fat mutton for several days, so the leather will be moist."

Braggart said, "Sure! Just tell the cafeteria what to feed them!"

Disappearance

Ajia said, "Night permeated very quickly and drowned the village in no time. The cart stable, Ancestral Hall, and Diamond Monastery used to belong to the fort. The cart stable was located in the outer courtyard of the fort. The Ancestral Hall was in the inner courtyard. Diamond Monastery was originally the family temple of the fort. The clansmen had finished work and returned to the cart stable. The noise of carts and the mooing of cattle filled the entire fort. The sheep had already entered the corral. Old Daddy Nine closed the gate, which creaked heavily and shut out the night. A dim, yellow light shone from the oil lamps under the eaves. In the flickering light, Cripple Big was completely out of his wits."

Ajia continued, "Ever since the arrival of the 'leathers,' Cripple Big no longer fetched water. He felt relieved from what tore his heart since he didn't have to see the rock pile anymore. Now that he had food and clothing, he began to long for a woman. Although his experience with Degree Holder Ho's wife was hurried and not altogether great, its memory provided him with much room for imagination and excitement. Woman is like this—good when one thinks about having one, even better when one can't have any. Once she lies underneath one, however, the taste is not all that great after all; in fact, not even as tasty as a sheep's tail when one is hungry! This is, of course, easily said; but when desire really surges up like a tide, the angst is intolerable!"

Ajia sounded different when he talked about women. He always seemed to be particularly excited. I discovered that was the reason he was never able to achieve transcendence. In other words, although he wanted to attain the "supernormal power of no-worries," he was never able to transcend desire. No matter how highly he regarded himself, he was still just a "broken pot." Therefore, I wonder if the man in the numerous sexual escapades dreamt by the women of Liangzhou was actually Ajia. I've interviewed many women known as female shamans. Without exception, they've all had dream love affairs with men they recognized as deities and received satisfaction that would not have been possible with ordinary men. But I dared not ask Ajia about it. You know—Ajia is a gentleman the minute his pants are pulled up when it comes to this kind of thing. Even if he'd done it, he'd deny it with vehemence.

Ajia said Cripple Big rarely returned to his little house since Mom died, lest she'd laugh unexpectedly or gather up phlegm and create the noise of an *erhu* violin. That night, he got into the large brick-bed in the cart courtyard with the other militiamen and began fiddling around with his leather craft tools. He ground the cow-ear-shaped knife until it was razor sharp and checked to see what was missing from the tanning ingredients. He then reported to Braggart who immediately had the missing items gathered and sent over.

After eating mutton for several days, Snow Feather's face looked more moistened. Her prettiness was such that even Heavenly Girl couldn't compare favorably with her. Cripple Big was worried about no one except for Kuan San, who might take advantage of his proximity to Snow Feather's location and ruin "the nest" for him. As soon as night fell, Cripple Big's heart would throb into his throat. He wanted to keep watch on the prisoners but was afraid of being laughed at. But whenever no one was around, he'd poke his head through the central gate. Only after finding nothing amiss around the little house that held the prisoners, would he heave a sigh of relief.

Jasper appeared again in Ajia's narrative. I could never figure out whether the Jasper in his narrative was the same as the Jasper in real life.

This mystery applies to several other characters in this book, but I don't feel like dealing with this kind of problem. Firstly, I don't feel the need to argue with a slightly crazy narrator; secondly, I've discovered that many things in the world are but illusory games. Why should I treat fiction as truth and consider illusion as reality?

Ajia said Jasper grabbed Cripple Big and led him down a veranda. He squinted his eyes and looked around before he asked Cripple Big, "Are you really going to skin them?" Cripple Big said, "I'm just a cocked arrow in a pulled bow—I have no choice!" Jasper said, "Think of a way—can you use some other skin?" Cripple Big said, "Aiyo! There's no way! Human skin is translucent. Its pattern, quality, and sound when struck are all different. Let alone experts—even nonexperts can tell the difference right away." Jasper thought for a while and then said, "Use my skin then, and release them." Greatly shocked, Cripple Big said, "You've gone mad! I heard that those people were to be beheaded originally." Jasper said, "People were not born to be killed. Even the Buddha was willing to sacrifice his body to feed the tigers. Why can't I?" Then, he turned around and entered the courtyard gate. Cripple Big found it ludicrous. How can there be anyone so stupid?

Seeing no one around, Cripple Big slipped into the courtyard and felt his way toward the little house with the prisoners. Suddenly, he heard the sound of moaning. His heart throbbed faster. It was the sound that Degree Holder Ho's wife made when she lay underneath him. He wet a finger with saliva and poked a hole through the paper windowpane. Although the room was dark, he could see clearly. That Kuan San was naked from the waist down and was pushing! Cripple Big tightened and screamed in a high-pitched voice, "Kuan San! Asshole! How dare you fuck my wife!" His voice was so loud that many people hurried over. Braggart said, "Cripple Big, what are you talking about?" Cripple Big was almost in tears, "That Kuan San is fucking my wife!" Braggart laughed and said, "You must be dreaming! Look—who's this?" Kuan San was standing right next to him. Puzzled, Cripple Big looked at the house. The inside of the house had now turned completely murky.

Kuan San laughed and said, "I'm not taking the blame in vain—I'm going to fuck her sooner or later!"

When the lamps were lit, the militiamen went to the Ancestral Hall. Braggart bid them to be extra alert, lest the "leathers" escape. He also ordered them to keep their lips sealed and maintain absolute secrecy.

In the middle of the night, however, all the "leathers" vanished without a trace!

Ajia's narrative was filled with suspense. He asked, "Guess where they went?"

The Experienced Monk

The divine drum sounded. The dense beats struck at Jasper's heart thunderously. Specks of torchlight surged toward the Ancestral Hall. Ajia said Jasper knew very soon the specks of light would disperse as they searched for the escapees throughout the mountains and fields.

Ajia said, "Jasper obviously knew he'd created a catastrophe." That divine drum was rarely struck. In the past, it would only be struck during major occasions such as worship of the tutelary god, worship of the crop fertility god, fighting the enemy, celebrating a communal festival, and protecting the dam. According to regulations, all the villagers had to gather at the Ancestral Hall and await orders the moment the divine drum sounded. If they were ordered to jump into boiling water, they'd jump into boiling water; if they were ordered to leap into fire, they'd leap into fire. No one dared to show any hesitation.

The pieces of "leather" also discerned the gravity of the situation and became somewhat anxious.

Jasper knew Braggart was an expert tracker. Even fleet-footed wild animals were unable to escape his eyes, how much less of a chance of escape would these few pieces of "leather" have!

The autumnal wind had turned cold. A strong wind gusted. Jasper sneezed and thought, *We'll let fate take over!*

Jasper said, "Look—they've begun the search! Once day breaks, even a hawk won't be able to fly away. Go your separate ways and run for your life! The four of you can go in the four directions—use all the energy you have! If you manage to escape, it will be your good fortune. If you get caught, you'll be skinned alive!" Seeing how the specks of torchlight were spreading, they shook each other's hands and disappeared into the night.

Jasper took Snow Feather's hand and felt his way toward Monk Wu's isolation cell in the mountain. Ever since the exhibition parades, Monk Wu rarely stayed at the monastery. He built a cabin in front of his master's grave to serve as his isolation cell. The darkness congealed into a mass through which eyes couldn't pierce. Snow Feather lost her footing several times and would've fallen into the gully if Jasper hadn't pulled her up.

Jasper's heart throbbed violently. Several years ago, he thought of this woman night and day. Who'd have expected her to show up as "leather"? Weird things happen often in these years. Events even weirder than the transformation of people into "leather" have happened so frequently—nothing shocked Jasper anymore.

The torches were spreading throughout the gullies. Jasper could feel Snow Feather trembling. So he gave her hand an energetic squeeze and pulled her toward Uncle's cabin in the mountain gully. The snakelike pathway was drowned by the night. But ever since Monk Wu went into the mountain, Jasper had traveled this path frequently to bring him food. The holes and bumps were already imprinted in his heart, so he cautioned her of them now and then.

That cabin finally emerged out of the night. Jasper heaved a sigh of relief. He tightened his fist and beat on the door vigorously. "Is it you, Jasper?" Monk Wu opened the door. Jasper was surprised by how Monk Wu knew it was he. Monk Wu closed the door, and the light of the lamp filled the room. Different types of Buddhist statues and ritual implements decorated the room. The hand drum was made with two pieces of bones from a human skull. Its "leather" was also human skin. Snow Feather probably didn't know she and the others were to be made into such ritual implements.

Monk Wu said, "You've created a disaster!" Jasper said, "I tried my best. Heaven will decide whether it will succeed." Monk Wu filled a cup with water and handed it to Snow Feather, and said, "You've lost weight." Snow Feather didn't say anything. She just accepted the water and drank it slowly.

"They'll chase you here very quickly." Monk Wu said. "They know how to track. Besides, we can hide her for awhile, but not for the rest of her life. We've got to think of something." Jasper said, "We'll hide here for the night and then decide. The other four escaped in different directions."

"Don't tell me anything. I know nothing," said Monk Wu.

Ajia said, "You know, although Monk Wu was a guru, he was also an experienced monk. He'd gone through the mortal world for more than sixty years after all!"

The Prayer

According to *Historical Mirror of Forgotten Events*, Jasper prayed to Ajia before he did this. I don't know which Ajia he'd prayed to since there were numerous Ajias in the manuscripts. There was the Ajia in *Tale of the Goddess*, the protective deity Ajia, the Ajia in *Crazy Ramblings of Ajia*, and other Ajias. Although they were represented by the same name, they nevertheless had different faces and were portrayed in different situations. I was also unable to figure out the relationships between all these Ajias.

In the brightness of a dream, Ajia heard Jasper's prayer and said, "Of course you should save them! Saving one life is better than attaining seven levels of Buddhahood. People are not born to be killed!" Jasper said, "I heard they are demons." Ajia laughed and said, "I'm a demon too! So what is a demon? When an expanse of water tumbles eastward as it always does, the occasional spray in a wave would be considered a demon. That demon is also part of the water, except it transcends the other water. There were many demons abroad such as Copernicus, Bruno, and Darwin . . . They were all demons. But it was precisely due to the existence of these demons that the world progressed. The more people consider them to be demonic, the more they should be saved!"

That night, Jasper took action. He knew Braggart had a hobby—it was opium smoking. Every other hour, he'd go to an isolated room and take a few drags. As soon as Braggart turned the corner, Jasper slipped into the house. He jabbed a thong into the lock, gave it a yank, and pulled out the iron lock. Jasper thought it clanged so thunderously that the noise would tear apart the sky. But strangely, it didn't wake up the militiamen. Jasper knew the sound was in his mind.

All the militiamen were drunk. Jasper brought them a jerry can of liquor. They were all drunkards who'd forget their own names the minute they saw liquor. One really shouldn't blame them, since they were not members of a regular armed outfit; they were just militiamen. What were militiamen? Militiamen were a group of peasants who'd recently learned to handle rifles. Those rifles, which resembled burning sticks, were unable to change their nature.

The door opened. Jasper lifted a finger to his mouth to signal silence and whispered, "Snow Feather, I'm Jasper." Jasper thought she'd embrace him, but she just caught hold of his hands and squeezed them very tightly. She asked, "Where's Mom?" Jasper didn't answer.

Withdrawing his hands, Jasper retreated quietly. He forced open another door and made the same gesture with his finger. Jasper said, "You have to flee! They're going to use your skin to make ritual implements!" One of them said, "Didn't they say there's going to be an exhibition parade?" Jasper tried to explain but the men didn't believe him. Snow Feather said, "Whatever it is, let's make our escape first." The men then followed Jasper and felt their way to the gate. In order to prevent damage to the "leathers," the shackles around their ankles were taken off a long time ago. But their footsteps still sounded loud enough to tear one's heart. Jasper was convinced that they would arouse suspicions. Ultimately, however, they didn't provoke any action. Jasper knew it was thanks to the ringing bells on the horses that were chewing hay at night.

His heart throbbed violently. Jasper thought his throbbing heart could be heard throughout the entire fort. If they were discovered, a full beating was the least he could expect. Ajia said, "Jasper was afraid of being beaten. Dad had beaten him when he was very little. His head hummed from the furious slaps. But when he thought of the bloody skinned body, he thought, let them beat me if it should come to that!"

They finally felt their way to the gate. Ajia said, "Jasper was scared the most of Old Daddy Nine who guarded the gate. An old fellow who resembled a scrawny ghost, Old Daddy Nine was dark and gaunt, with a pair of sharp eyes. He'd guarded the gate for ten years without any mishaps. He must've been asleep also. If he were awake, none of these people could have felt their way out of the gate."

Jasper pulled out the latch very slowly. The latch was made of a small pine tree with a trunk as thick as a bowl. The gate was a foot thick and more than thirteen feet high, studded with brass knobs and lions' heads. Most imposing. In the past, he always felt oppressed by the grandeur of the door whenever he looked at it. Jasper didn't like the fort. He much preferred simple things. Oppressive grandeur always made him uncomfortable.

The gate was open. The night wind charged at him violently, and choked his throat. Jasper slid out of the gate sideways, and the others followed him. Because of the high threshold, the loud clang of metal gate pieces was heard several times. Fortunately, they didn't awaken anything in the silence of the night. Jasper told them to join hands, and then they felt their way down the narrow mountain path.

What Jasper didn't know was that a pair of eyes had witnessed the entire process.

"Who was it?" Ajia asked mysteriously.

Escape

Nightmares also mentions the escape made by Jasper and the others. The language is very similar to that in *Crazy Ramblings of Ajia* and also filled with details that were obvious. The writer was apparently imitating the style of *Ramblings*. According to the book, Jasper was terrified when the torches approached them. He felt as if he were in a nightmare. He was always dreaming of not being able to shake off the demon that chased him. Sometimes, he felt it was the god of death. Sometimes, he thought it was the natural way of fate. Both were the same in that neither could bring him peace. He felt he was in a nightmare even when he was awake. This was one of those moments.

Monk Wu's voice sounded weak. He said, "You've got to think of something else. I'm a monk. People would laugh their teeth off if I were to hide a woman here." Jasper wanted to say, "You abided by all the Buddhist vows so strictly in the past—but didn't you end up being paraded in any case?"

Jasper also knew many people couldn't wait for an excuse to get rid of Monk Wu. Some of them didn't get along with Monk Wu. Some were defrocked monks who'd wanted to become abbot but didn't succeed. There was also Braggart. They'd wanted to chase Monk Wu out of the monastery for a long time and replace him with a more obedient abbot. If they were indeed to find a woman in his room, that would really be entertainment for all!

Jasper turned to Snow Feather and said, "Let's go! I'll think of something."

Monk Wu said, "Please don't blame me. They're looking for an excuse right now. I'm not like you."

Jasper led the woman out of the door. Monk Wu puffed at the oil lamp and extinguished it. He said, "Why don't you go to Grandpa Mao Cave and hide there first? Hide there for a few days before you make other plans." Snow Feather heaved a sigh. She shot a glance at the "dragon of fire" that was approaching, grabbed Jasper's hand, and turned onto a narrow path.

Grandpa Mao Cave was located halfway up Reflecting Wall Mountain. It faced the south and was a small cave. Situated in treacherous terrain, it could only be accessed by a narrow path slightly wider than a foot. Although it was called a path, it was barely wide enough for walking. When it rained, flash floods would pour down and clear away all the earth and sand, leaving nothing but treacherous rocks that formed the so-called path. Snow Feather knew they couldn't possibly reach Grandpa Mao Cave in the dark. The mountain was so steep that one misstep, and the person would become a rolling ball of flesh. She thought they should find a place to hide first and climb the mountain after daybreak. Locating them would be no easier than finding a needle in this sea of darkness in any case. Although Braggart was good at tracking, he'd still have to wait until daybreak.

A musty smell encased them. The two of them turned into the forest. Dense and dark, the forest was filled with trees as thick as cart-wheels. Birch saplings and some unnameable bushes grew beneath the trees. Many unnameable worms and insects thrived among the bushes. Jasper cringed the moment he thought of worms and insects. He feared centipedes the most. These hairy things gave him goosebumps. His mother had told him that centipedes loved to crawl into people's ears. As soon as they got in, they would get at the brain matter and eat it. One's brain matter would be drained before he knew it. One day, someone would touch the person's forehead and poke a hole there unexpectedly. Inside the hole, there'd be nothing but centipedes of all sizes. Mom was fond of telling this story. Jasper tried his best not to think about centipedes, or even to make mention of them. He thought maybe Snow Feather was even more scared of centipedes than he was, or maybe she was more afraid of snakes? He'd heard that snakes loved to crawl into the lower part of women. Jasper shuddered.

Snow Feather remembered the existence of a nest made of stones in the depths of the forest. It was made by a bear. During the height of summer, the bear would bring twigs and dried grass to line a cradle, fashioned out of stones, and make a comfortable nest. It would lie inside the nest to get out of the summer heat. Toward the end of autumn, however, it would leave for its cave. The nest had a strong smell, and other animals wouldn't dare to use it. She thought, *Let's hide there for a night first.*

Snow Feather had a bit of a limp. The fame of her martial arts skills had at one time spread throughout Liangzhou—who'd have ever expected her to come to this? Jasper felt his heart ache. The torches had been blocked by the forest. They were enveloped by dampness. Snow Feather's panting sounded lovely—it was a charming pant—unlike the bull-like panting of the other women in the village. Jasper wanted to listen to her panting, but he thought of the torches fanning out through the mountains and fields in search of them and a feeling of gloom set in. He thought, *If people knew I'm escaping with the woman, what would they think?* He couldn't help but feel his face burn.

They finally found the bear's nest after much searching. It was close to the beginning of winter, and the bear had already left for Old Moun-tain. Jasper had seen this nest last time he came here to pick herbs. By then, it had already looked like it hadn't been used for many days. But many dangers lurked around. Snakes, wolves, and other animals must've been watching them from some corner.

Having traveled for quite some time in the darkness, the light in their minds shone, and they were able to distinguish many things in the haze. The wind gusted in the forest, blowing on their sweaty bodies and making them feel as if they'd been splashed by water. Jasper said, "Let's wait here for a night. We can decide the next step tomorrow." The woman intoned softly. Jasper stepped on a rock and jumped into the nest first. The soft twigs immediately made him feel the warmth of a home. He stretched out his hand, took her outstretched hand, and led her into the nest.

Jasper finally heaved a sigh of relief. But he immediately realized he'd made a mistake: he didn't bring a fur jacket. There were two fur jackets of different sizes at Monk Wu's place, either of them would have been fine. After all the traveling, his garments were soaked by sweat. It must've been the same with the woman. Good thing they had this nest, it would've been torture if they'd had to spend the night on wet ground.

"Are you cold?" asked Jasper.

"No." Snow Feather yawned.

"Take a nap!" said Jasper. Sleepiness poured down his body like rain. He became unconscious.

After a while, he felt someone tug at him. He shuddered. His body felt as if it had been splashed with water. Snow Feather pressed closer to him and was shivering. Jasper felt his inner organs had all turned to ice. He wanted to build a fire. He felt his pocket. The matches were still there. He always carried matches with him, as he was always lighting incense for the Buddhist deities. He couldn't leave matches in the sanctuary since the clansmen would take the matches either intentionally or unwittingly. So Jasper carried the matches in his pocket. Jasper said, "Shall we build a fire?" The woman said, "Fire is obviously good, but it could also attract people."

"You're right," said Jasper.

Snow Feather said, "My clothes are soaking wet—they feel icy." Her teeth chattered. She stretched out her hands. Jasper held them in his hands. There wasn't even a hint of warmth in them.

"Come closer, you'll feel warmer." Snow Feather pressed closer to him. Jasper felt thirsty all of a sudden. Coldness immediately fled far away. A firelike sensation permeated his entire body.

Snow Feather said, "Closer—hold me." She put his arms around her, while she herself also embraced him. "We'll freeze to death otherwise." Jasper felt a parching heat fill his entire body. He thought it was strange that Snow Feather would have such strong inner fire.

Waves of heat wafted from the soft flesh of her chest. Jasper heard Snow Feather swallow her saliva. Two things pressed onto his face—he knew she was kissing him. He thought, *Am I transgressing my vows?* And then unexpectedly, he felt Snow Feather stick her tongue into his mouth.

The cold disappeared. He only felt thirst. Jasper thought, *Should people find out, they'll think I saved her for this!*

"Do you want it?" Snow Feather whispered.

Jasper felt a pair of icy hands grope into his collar and slide down his back. The hands were truly cold. He shuddered. But in no time at all, he felt warm. The hands roamed downward and made their way into the waist of his pants. "But I'm a monk!" He wanted to refuse her, but a new kind of intoxicating sensation enveloped everything. Jasper felt like he had entered into a nightmare again. He knew he shouldn't do it, but he couldn't wake himself up.

The hands unfastened his girdle and slipped off his pants slowly, squeezing and releasing his "root." It was already overbearing down there and was becoming unbearably imperious from Snow Feather's kneading. She slipped off her own pants gradually, lay face up on the twigs, and pulled him over to lie on top of her.

Thirst surged at Jasper. His heart throbbed against his chest furiously, its sound echoing throughout the mountain gully. That hand held his "root." Jasper felt as though he'd suddenly melted into volcanic lava. He screamed uncontrollably.

His scream woke him up. So it was a dream! His face burned immediately. He realized that the desire of the flesh didn't vanish with his taking the tonsure.

Nightmares

The description of the dream above was so vivid and detailed in *Nightmares* that I used to wonder if the book's author was Jasper himself. Some of the details would have been difficult to imagine, without having had personal experience. Later, I discovered the fundamental mistake I made in drawing that conclusion. Of course, we can't conclude that Wu Cheng'en,[3] who described Monkey, Sun Wukong, so realistically, must have had the experience of being a monkey himself.

According to *Nightmares*, Jasper woke up in the dead of night from the cold. Snow Feather still held him tightly. One of her legs pressed upon one of his and made it numb. Her thin face could be discerned in the dim light. Unlike the women in the village, whose skin was rough and whose cheeks were red from the wind, Snow Feather's skin was white and refined. Her delicateness had the charm of a white magnolia.

When that strange fire flared, Jasper's face burned. Monk Wu used to tell him that semen was the quintessence of the human body and should not be wasted. He'd heard that relics could be obtained when eminent monks and gurus were cremated, precisely because they'd never leaked their "vital essence." People who frequently practice "the pleasure of leaking" (i.e., doing that thing with women) would never be able to attain ultimate wisdom. But the moment Jasper thought of Snow Feather, flames flared up in his lower belly. There was nothing he could do. Rationality and emotions were always at odds with each other.

Snow Feather woke up. She seemed very tired. Goosebumps appeared on her face. Jasper was very disappointed at his own lack of control. Although he didn't want to think of that thing, the thought would surge by itself. He had no control over it.

The morning wind was as cold as seawater and as sharp as a knife. Although the parts of the body that were in an embrace were warm, his back felt icy. Jasper was afraid of being drowned by the fire in his lower belly, so he avoided Snow Feather's eyes. Unexpectedly, she buried her head in his chest and held him even tighter. Jasper knew she liked him, but as soon as he thought he might become a "broken pot," distress surged at him.

The feeling of coldness intensified and gradually drowned out the heat in his lower belly. Jasper took a look at the sky and knew the fire's light would no longer be conspicuous, so he said to Snow Feather, "Let's build a fire—it's okay now!" Snow Feather released her hand and stared into the distance as if deep in thought. Jasper grabbed a handful of twigs and lit them on one side. He used very little in order to prevent

---

3. Wu Cheng'en (d. 1582) was the author of the renowned Ming dynasty novel, *Journey to the West*.

smoke. They were surrounded by the forest, so light from a fire wouldn't be a problem. The twigs lived up to expectations and transformed into flaring flames.

Fire was so good. As soon as it flared up, warmth rushed toward them. Snow Feather stretched out her hands and placed them on the flames greedily. Jasper did the same. The heat turned into earthworms—which entered his palms first and then went along his arms into his heart until they gradually spread throughout his entire body. When he was completely heated by the fire, he grabbed the bag of roasted barley flour and handed it to Snow Feather.

After warming themselves with the fire for a while and consuming some barley flour, the sensation of coldness disappeared. However, tiredness took the opportunity to invade again.

Although the fire was extinguished, Jasper could still see in the darkness Snow Feather's bright eyes staring at him. He felt the parching heat in his body again. Snow Feather said, "Don't laugh—when I was at Wangjing Stockade, there was a time when I thought of nothing but you. I almost went crazy! So miserable back then! I wanted you to tear me apart. . . . Do you want it now?" Jasper turned red, shook his head nervously and said diffidently, "I . . . I'm still a monk!" Snow Feather smiled and grabbed him as if playing a joke on him. She unbuttoned his jacket, put her head on his chest and kissed his nipples gently. Jasper felt himself drowned by that fire again.

Snow Feather guided his hand for him to unfasten his girdle himself. Jasper didn't want to do it, but his hands trembled and went through the motion. Like many horrible nightmares, his fingers also betrayed him. And that mouth, that dick of a mouth, also reached out on its own and began sucking the tongue Snow Feather stuck out. *I'm betrayed once again!* thought Jasper.

Snow Feather's face was flushed and looked beautiful. Jasper thought, *for such a handsome woman—it's worth it!* Monk Wu used to always tell him that sexual desire was the seed for going to Hell. But he still thought, *Fine if I have to go to Hell!*

Snow Feather grabbed an armful of dried grass and laid it next to the fire. She then lay down on them and took off her underwear. Jasper felt his blood turn into a flood. He thought, *What if I end up in Hell!* He charged at her and found what he wanted, without the guidance of the woman.

"Slower!" the woman pinched his arm lightly.

"Don't rush!" the woman added.

Jasper felt he was ready to collapse. He tried his best not to look at the woman. He breathed hard and looked at the big tree next to him that soared into the clouds. He saw the sky between the leaves—strange, how could he see the sky now?—and the angry tide that surged up gradually subsided before his body shook slowly.

The bizarre feeling of delight invaded him wave after wave. Jasper couldn't help but moan.

Snow Feather pushed him until he woke up. "Are you having a nightmare? Why all the moaning?"

Jasper was embarrassed. *Why do I keep having such dreams?* he wondered.

Chapter 29

The Monk Who Broke His Vow

Who can tell me the truth about life?
Who can reveal the secret of death?
Who can teach me how to escape the wheel of fate?
Who can lead me to the Pure Land for the soul?

Below the Window of His Date

Ajia—Open the book that was found in the cave and continue to seek the tracks of your soul!

Although you were clearly aware that this was a historical nightmare, you were still unable to escape from it.

It was just like the pressure of reality, you know. It will ultimately question you and question this land.

The Diamond Maiden Cave of that period was as busy as boiling water. The emperor of Xixia was always visiting Liangzhou. Its monasteries were therefore most imposing. You needn't describe its appearance. The valleys in Tibetan regions are strewn with such buildings.

You were obviously a monk who had broken your vows. Of course, you could deny it. But since everyone thought so, denying it would have been useless. However, if you'd insisted that your heart was pure, I would believe you. But the practice of cultivation, *xiuxing*, embodies *xing*, which also refers to behavior. No way would others care whether your heart was pure or not! Others only cared that you behaved in a dignified manner.

During that vague moment of history, were you also in Xixia? Don't consider me the director of your story—you're the one who directed your own play. Look—you can obviously envision that era. The Xixia of that era was on its last leg like a setting sun. Genghis Khan had already begun his assault on Xixia. His force was even more ferocious than when Xixia fought the Great Song of China. The world is a strange place, isn't it? Even their fighting styles were ironically similar! You know—it was during that very year that Xixia would become a black hole in history.

Don't give me that scowl—concentrate and enter that space and time!

In the dimness, you saw the moonlit night. There was a snowfall the night before; heaven and earth were boundless. The mountain paths were as clean as a khata scarf. You left the cave, thinking that heaven and earth had fallen asleep. But don't forget that my eyes weren't closed. I've never closed my eyes from 1004 until the present. I wanted to be tired, but there was nothing I could do about it. Just as the Gonpo's wish to be young was to no avail, I was also unable to ignore my mind wisdom.

I could hear your heart throbbing. I knew what you were thinking. I knew you had a date with that woman. You who forgot the pain, once the wound was healed—you should know, although female temptation brings ecstasy, the amount of enjoyment is always equivalent to the amount of trouble. Because of this, Genghis Khan's executioners reduced numerous Xixia state priests to slices of meat. Each time he invaded, he would always capture some bald-headed fellows and slice them the way your mom skinned mountain yams. I don't know why he harbored so much hatred for them. *Was he jealous of the state priests?* Honestly, according to my calculations, the number of women he did was also shocking, quite comparable to that of the state priests. Why did you hate the state priests so? Unless it was alright for you to consume platters of meat but not alright for others to even drink some soup?

I've personally witnessed the slicing of a state priest by an executioner. The state priest was very fat. Strange—state priests tended to be fat, although one might find a thin one occasionally. It was alright to be thin—no one said a thin person couldn't be a state priest.

You scowled again. You were just like the rest of them. The folks of Liangzhou were like dogs—they think everyone was as low as they! You were the fucking same. Sure, I had no money, no power, and I had never been enfeoffed by one wearing a yellow robe. But was I any less than the state priests who were sliced? Look at how the fatso was tied to the pillar by a hemp rope, soaked in water. The rope was so sturdy it cut right into his flesh. Then, the executioner began to slice him. He carved the toes first. Genghis Khan said, "Didn't you enjoy practicing visualization of the skeleton? We'll start with the carving of your big toes!"

With one cut—the knife was very sharp—half of the toe had turned into bones. The state priest screamed. Consequently, you knew he wasn't a real priest. He was also a monk who had broken his vows. A real state priest would have been devoid of self and could have faced the blade as if he were bathing in a spring breeze. Carving his flesh would be like carving the earth in the ground. I thought, what were you screaming for? You would have looked like a respectable state priest without screaming; but once you screamed, you revealed the stuff you were made of.

After the second cut, the entire toe turned into bones. The executioner guffawed as he drank liquor. This didn't seem to have been his regular style. By then, the great army of Genghis Khan had already fought for many years and annihilated almost forty countries. It had beaten Russia until the latter cried like a baby. When the Mongols killed, they either shot people into porcupines or they cut right across people's shoulders. They were always fast and precise. Only in the case of Xixia's priests did they not allow an easy death. Most strange!

The state priest yelled and yelled. His voice was sonorous but hoarse. That voice used to be his working capital. Heaven and earth rumbled when he chanted the scriptures. But now his voice betrayed him. Indeed, his throat picked the most importune time to be hoarse. And then the voice was gone; one could only hear gasps.

Unexpectedly, there was very little blood on the ground. Since the earth was parched, it opened its mouth wide and swallowed the blood before it formed a pool. If you thought the state priest was greedy, the earth was even more so! It was so insatiable even the state priest's voice was swallowed by it.

Just like the way you began with the toes when you practiced visualization of the skeleton, the bones of the state priest emerged one section after the other. Slice after slice of bloody flesh flew into the air and was snatched by ravens before it landed. During the years of fighting between the Song and the Xia, the real winners were the ravens. In their mouths, the flesh of the Song and the Xia tasted the same. Later, they also swallowed the Mongols. I've heard them complain that the skin of the Mongols was too tough and not as tasty. The best was skin of the women of Jiangnan.[1]

You asked them, "Was the state priest's meat tasty?"

They said, "Very tasty—there was a lot of fat! The Mongols were always fighting. They'd spent all their fat. Their meat was too tough. The state priest was tastier!" I said, "Gluttonous ravens, you have no conscience—don't you remember how the state priest gave you food as alms?" The ravens said, "Don't you see? The state priest is giving his body as alms right now. We're helping him with fulfilling his vow!"

That skeleton was hung over Liangzhou's city gate. A throng of flies whirled around it and bred a pile of soft, white maggots.

The state priest was snoring in a cave one snowy night before he was butchered. You figured he was dreaming. Sure enough, the moment you entered his dreams, everything was in pink. No wonder.

The dreams of the other monks in the cave were also very odd. Some wanted to be state priests, some wanted a pretty woman, some roamed in a Buddhist realm, and some had fallen into Hell. On a certain night a thousand years earlier, you also left your room in the midst of a colorful dream. You looked around guiltily. Don't worry, no one saw you. You tiptoed down the mountain slope, which was lined with snow and left a row of your footprints. You weren't worried. You thought it was still snowing heavily and that your footprints would soon be covered. Right?

You went down that steep slope and passed over the river valley. The graveyard was full of shadows. They were the ghosts of the deceased from the Han to the Xixia dynasties. They cried, "Aiyo! The monk will sleep with someone!" One of ghosts came to your defense, "What are you yelling about? If he doesn't sleep with someone, where would little monks come from?" Thereupon they tucked in their necks and disappeared into the night.

You also saw an owl with wide-open green eyes that glowed. It didn't like you. It would've preferred a mouse instead of you. But you were unable to read its mind. You should have brought a piece of meat when you came down the mountain. Wasn't there a sheep on the butcher block? You should have cut off the egglike testicles that always shook

---

1. South of the lower reaches of Yangtze River. It often refers to the area encompassing southern Jiangsu, southern Anhui, and northern Zhejiang. The women of Jiangnan were famous for their beauty.

furiously whenever the ram ran and tossed them to the gluttonous cat-faced thief of an owl, lest it reveal your secret.

You floated in the darkness like a spirit, accompanied by many spirits at your side. But you weren't scared. People who dared to commit sexual offenses aren't afraid of ghosts. One has never heard of an adulterer fearing a ghost. Don't laugh—this is really the case. You saw the door curtain; its flapping looked like a woman patting her own belly.

So, you charged like a dog. In an instant, you were beneath your date's window. You rushed in like a fish. You needn't have worried; Genghis Khan had already eliminated all your rivals in love. It was a Xixia regulation that all males from fifteen to sixty years of age had to be conscripted. Real men were all trampled into mush. Don't worry—she was a piece of land, and you could plow her however you want, be it straight, diagonally, or horizontally.

Holding her hand, her sweaty hand, made the itch in your heart unbearable. She led you into a side room. Although the main room was spacious, it had been the ancestors' territory ever since the time of the Xixia. Look—Diamond Maiden was watching you. You didn't have to be shy. She was only taking a look. There was nothing she could do about shameless people like you.

A pea-sized light was lit in the mutton oil lamp. You took a look at her and found her brighter. Maybe you didn't know she looked very much like the Snow Feather of a thousand years later. Of course, you were just an ignorant deity, unable to see events a thousand years later. Don't get mad at me. My lips are sealed.

Untie your robe. She'd already unfastened her skirt; only her petticoat remained. Don't watch her. Just take off your clothes. She needed your embrace and almost bit you. That's right—take off your coat and then your cassock. I thought it was funny when I saw your purple-red robe. If I had a camera, one flash and people would chuckle a thousand years later. You must have realized your ridiculousness. Red-faced, you tore off your garments. While you were still thinking of getting closer, she'd already charged into your embrace.

You didn't realize it had stopped snowing a long time ago. The row of distinct footprints was in the process of betraying you.

You had no time to bother with extraneous things; you concentrated on embracing her and kissing her awkwardly. You had imagined kissing as something wonderful, but it wasn't so easy in practice. You tried hard to think of the tricks described in a book. You used the book as the reason for your arrival. Although you were obviously transgressing against the vow of chastity, your reason was—the desire to perform couple-cultivation.

Don't look at me! Go ahead and do what you want to do. There's no need to flush from embarrassment. You don't have to worry; I won't envy you. Although I also have desire, I won't envy you unless my body betrays me. Aiya! I'll say no more. Truth be told, I have trouble controlling myself too.

The woman's body was unexpectedly voluptuous and issued seductiveness. This was a thoroughly ripe soft pear. Bite a hole into it, and you'd be able suck out a mouthful of nectar. Your hand caressed her shoulders and then her vertebrae and tailbone. You drew a lotus flower on her back. This was one of the tricks taught by the book, except your touch was too hard—you should be gentler. The touch should be so soft that it's as if you're boneless. That's right—just like this! Look—her nipples are sticking up. Go ahead, suck them like a baby.

Ignore her moaning, just keep on sucking. Don't stop moving your hands. Paint gently according to your heart, like the flowing of roseate clouds in the sky. Don't rush. Take long, continuous breaths like the reeling of silk, slowly and continuously. You might not even feel your own breath. That's right—just like this. Although you obviously see a lively living body, you should treat it like a dream, like an illusion and a dream—a flower in the mirror. Don't regard this as reality. There's nothing real in this world. Even this woman is a result of karma. If you are attached to her, then you've taken the illusory as reality.

You can kiss her back. Don't hurry. Close your eyes. Didn't the book say that's the sweet dew of great delight? You drank and drank. Although your emotions might be aroused, your mind must realize that this is unreal. It's still an illusion and a dream, still as illusory as a flower in the mirror.

You heard her moan. She was still twisting her body. Don't hurry. Spread your fingers and tap on her shoulders. She'll know what you meant. She was still moaning, still twisting, still thrusting her passion to the boiling point.

You now felt a fire raging in your body. That fire is called energy. It's like crashing waves on a shore that will sweep up a thousand piles of snow. Be careful. You have to be very careful at this point. The fire is very dangerous. It's very mischievous. It charges east and west and gallops like a feral horse. But it's only the waves in a sea. Your heart must remain as peaceful as the bottom of the sea. You have to realize that the fire, like all manifestations in the world, is just an illusion. Be sure you don't let it drag you away.

You could feel the madness of the other party now. You even discovered that her blooming lotus flower was shyly dripping with dew and emanating an incredible fragrance. Display yourself gently. Emit a spray, and visit the flower petals! Did you hear? Both heaven and earth resounded. Whistling delight drowned the vast emporium.

At this point, don't rush; it's as if you are treading on ice. Although you clearly hear the summons of antiquity, don't rush. Have you ever drunk tea? That's right—you should relish it meditatively. It should be a gentle breeze, not a raging storm. Of course you feel the joy, but you still need to realize that it's without its own nature. This joy is morning dew and lightning. It dies the moment it comes into being. Just go ahead and transform yourself into a gentle breeze. You may remember the couplet from a poem: "Accompanying the wind, it slips into the night; Moistening everything gently and soundlessly." That's right—just like that.

You finally woke up from the initial sensation of inebriation. You gradually felt the power of concentration. You can open your eyes. Look—she was looking at you! She was very charming indeed. Her body looked so soft it seemed boneless. Her face glowed like a red cloud. She chirped like a small bird. That's her wisdom. Try to gallop among her expansive wisdom. Don't be nervous. Continue to resemble a gentle breeze and fine rain. Although you clearly heard her parched cry, you shouldn't let it draw your soul away. You should realize—that cry was as illusory and vague as her body. Just concentrate on clarifying your mind and let the horse gallop on its own. Relax your heart so it can play that piano and savor its light music.

You finally heard her create the most beautiful music, that heavenly music. It seemed to be a song in a soft, low voice; it seemed to be the howling of a tiger and the intoning of a dragon; it seemed to be a wind blowing across a great desert; it seemed to be gathered water flowing into molten lava. You can muster up the wind of your spirit to melt her passion. But be careful because your heart has already melted into molten lava. Don't let it get excited; let it quiet down for a while. You can use that great joy as an offering for your soul.

You meandered along the small path of wisdom. The paradise of your life was there. All the beings there were without form. So you led your joy up and up the path. You felt it explode, one wave after the other, toward the horizon.

Her crazed voice could be heard. Be careful—don't let your soul boil. She was only an illusory being. She became wild like a feral horse. She was weeping. The fine wine of life was surging in her soul. She was transformed into a jade girdle to wrap around you who were frightened.

Don't covet that joy. Joy is the seed of life and death. You have to scrutinize. Joy is also impermanent and illusory. Illusoriness is joy—joy is illusory. Guard yourself carefully lest the feral horse struggles free of its reins. Look—the snake was spitting out its pistil again, and the storm began to rage too. She rode on the peak of the wave. She was a malicious goddess. What she wanted to destroy wasn't just you. You've been taken!

The unexpected torrent exploded abruptly. You were ultimately unable to escape this calamity.

Eat it up—you glutton!

The Sky That Betrayed

You realized it was the sky that betrayed you. That snow didn't cover your tracks as expected. You felt the ghastly cold wind blow. The day was about to break. Stars had already scattered around the entire valley. The wan moon revealed the wan road. I know you felt remorse. Take this as a lesson. The avaricious will ultimately be swallowed by avarice. No wonder—you were but a warrior who'd never really engaged in battle.

Wrap your robe tightly around you—don't let the cold wind get you sick. The woman also bid you the same. She was already imprinted on your heart. This was fate and a karmic debt. There was no escaping it.

But you still sighed in remorse. You had repeated your vows every day and knew what you should comply with and what you should keep away from. Although women frequently visited the state priest's room, he was the state priest after all. Didn't Kumarajiva also have a wife because he was Kumarajiva? Who did you think you were? Even though you considered yourself a hero among mediocre men, that was only what you thought. I know your fame would ultimately spread all over China, but that would be in the future. Your future fame couldn't save the present you.

In the vagaries of that time, you were just a monk. Didn't you call it the nightmare of history? Genghis Khan was also in that nightmare.

His great army had already invaded Xixia five times and had practically wiped the Iron Hawks out. The fatal sixth invasion was just a matter of time. With that powerful enemy surrounding your people like the arrival of doomsday, yet you betrayed yourself and enacted that romance instead. If the state priest had known about this, it would be a wonder if he didn't skin you alive!

But I knew this wasn't what you regretted. Although your heart was romantic, you had always wanted to see through the illusory nature of things and attain the fruit of permanence. In other words, your body was always fighting with your soul. It had been many years. Ever since you saw the woman, you'd become hopelessly muddled. I knew the intensity of the process. I understood you, but they. . . . So who were they? They were the regulations.

Regulations were snickering in the wind and snow. You weren't scared; you proceeded forward, while listening to the creaking under your feet. You obviously knew female temptation was inimical to cultivation. Although you used couple-cultivation as an excuse, a woman's body was, after all, a woman's body. No matter how you tried to view it as illusory, the reality was an unalterable reality. She had real breasts, a real body, real moans, and real frenzy. But even more real than those was the fact that you'd become a "broken pot." This was a terrible term.

As a result, the palatial hall within your mind collapsed. You realized you were but a mundane person.

The return path meandered interminably toward the black cave. That cave seemed dim in the morning mist. What was distinct were the body and breath of the woman. The breath kept on coming as reality and set the heart aflame. Consequently, you discovered how wonderful the mundane world was. Live women existed in the mundane world. Compared to them, Nirvana was a dull word. Although you knew sexual desire was ultimately impermanent, impermanent sexual desire was still sexual desire. Whenever you thought of it, self-control became impossible.

A lament rose from the bottom of your heart. You were the cat, who'd had a taste of fish! Could you still enter that cave? The state priest's face was always cold. It resembled a rock that had been alone for a thousand years. There were also those protective deities with round, glaring eyes—although you didn't owe them any money! It was their duty to look awe-inspiring. They were in fact very compassionate. They could read your mind. They knew you were human, and as a human you couldn't avoid the temptations, desires, and stupidities of humans.

I also knew this. I also knew you were innocent. You've always wanted to struggle free of the fate of reincarnation through reaching Nirvana. Although you've always failed, you've never faltered from your original aspiration. However, that sexual desire was so overwhelmingly powerful—it was surging waves, while you were but a floating withered leaf. Although I knew you couldn't free yourself from the whirlpool, I nevertheless wanted to comfort you. I almost said, "Let it be!"

Your heavy gait betrayed your anxiety. The huge shadow of the cave began to overwhelm you. You passed through the graveyard and the shrine of the tutelary god. You saw the tutelary deity god snigger. But don't worry, he won't disclose your secret. He was an experienced old man and had also had your experience; except he was old now, so old he'd lost passion. Only memory remained. Memory is a good thing. Didn't I say he understood you?

Although the way up the mountain was strenuous, it was at least an upward trip. Your ascent wasn't just your footsteps—hadn't you begun to feel remorse? Although this remorse was a snowflake, which would vanish without a trace under the splendid sunshine of the woman, remorse is nevertheless better than shamelessness. Shamelessness was the most common tale of the past thousand years. Yet your heart was always nabbed by the poisonous snake of remorse. Your soul was truly rescuable, while shamelessness is completely incurable. Another name for Hell is shamelessness.

The huge cave had appeared. The lamps were already lit. Although the lights were only pea-sized, they glared. Other than these, you didn't see anything else—neither the state priest, nor the monks, nor the furtively observing eyes. But you knew your footprints would undoubtedly reveal the secret that had been hidden for a thousand years.

The Furtively Observing Eyes

As I remembered it, the busy days went by without an inquisition. The chanting of the sutras went on as usual, and the vegetarian meals were normal. We did hear that the iron cavalry of the Mongols was attacking Suzhou, which was only a few days north of the cave by foot. We also heard that General Black of Black Water Kingdom had died. I will write his story in *The Gray Wolf of Xixia*. Before the Mongol army broke the siege, General Black killed his wife and daughter, and he buried several cartloads' worth of gold and silver in a dry well. No one knew where the dry well was. The Mongols couldn't find it either, but they didn't care. They'd already annihilated thirty-nine countries, plundered innumerable treasures, and abducted innumerable beautiful women. Their treasures were piled up higher than Qilian Mountain; and the beauties formed a sea of breasts. They couldn't have cared less about the general's cartloads of treasures. They simply slaughtered. What they cared about was General Black's noble smile—which they found offensive. Therefore, the Mongols roared, "Kill! Kill the fucking bastards!"

Just like this.

As I remember it, none of the monks could concentrate on chanting the sutra. Their voices were obviously still up to standard, but their minds were all distracted. They'd heard that the great Khan hated nothing more than Xixia's monks. Although it was just hearsay, there'd be no waves without wind. The rumor couldn't have been a drunken tittle-tattle or a fart in a dream.

The state priest remained a state priest, who looked like a dead donkey that no longer feared devouring by wolves. You knew his background. He definitely was someone who worked for his living. Without interrogation, he already knew someone had left the mountain in the snowy night. He knew all about you, just by looking at your muddy priest shoes. You knew he was truly irritated. Quite a few annoying events had occurred these past days: an attendant stole one of his ritual implements; another attendant didn't steal anything but grumbled about him behind his back. The details of the grumbling were atrocious. He'd wanted to kill a chicken to warn the monkeys. You, however, were ignorant of those happenings.

But don't you worry! The greatest catastrophe that could happen to anyone would be no worse than losing one's head. Losing one's head means nothing more than having a scar the size of a bowl. So what are you afraid of? You continued to chant the sutras. But I knew you felt perturbed. The deity you used to visualize had disappeared; the distinct image you now envisioned was that of the woman. I knew your "female catastrophe" had arrived. Of all the catastrophes, "female catastrophe" was the most ecstatic but also the most difficult to pull oneself free of. But don't you worry—as I've already said, if you lose your head, the scar will be no larger than a bowl.

You discovered that you had lost your ability to concentrate. Although you chanted the sutras, your mind was distracted. Your energy had been spent by the madness of the night. And that lovesickness—that lovesickness was a poisonous snake that coiled around one's heart, squirming bit by bit, inciting desire. Did you finally realize the horror of female calamity? It destroyed you by destroying your vows, your concentration, and your wisdom. It crackled and burned explosively all the merit you'd accumulated. Did you know that the fire of desire—not anger—was the worst for burning away all your merit?

Actually, I've also gone through it. I've also experienced what you experienced. In fact, which man, other than eunuchs and men afflicted by illnesses, hasn't? The only difference is that they didn't feel the soul-afflicting pain you experienced. So, you are responsible for what you are.

I knew you were enduring torment. You longed for that lively body, the soft moist kisses of the woman, and the joys of "fish in water." You even found it difficult to endure austerity now. In the past, love and warmth filled the cave; but now, a woman's body had shown you how unbearable the place actually was. This was precisely what female calamity meant. Wasn't it horrifying?

You felt uncertain in your swoon of happiness; but Grandpa Sun lingered in the sky lazily. That huge white plate dangled above the snowy wilderness. So vast and white was great Mother Earth. You saw a speck of red at the end of the snowy wilderness. Two furtively observing eyes were also inlaid in that speck of red. Needless to say, it was the woman. Like you, she was also filled with wounds, burned by the flames of lovesickness.

You were both able to see each other's eyes—eyes that spoke volumes. But you couldn't see another pair of eyes, those of the state priest. The state priest had been eying you, without knowing another pair of eyes had also been eying him! Those belonged to the god of death. In no time, he would be strung up by the Mongols. By then, the city of Liangzou would no longer belong to the Xia; the iron cavalries of the Mongols would strut around showing off their military might. The state priest feared their swords, which were sharper than wind. But regardless of how much he feared, he was ultimately unable to change fate.

Yet he didn't know of the pair of eyes behind him. The god of death was eyeing everyone. According to the Buddha, life exists between one's breaths. One less breath, and the person will become the ghost of another world.

You waited with difficulty for the arrival of dusk and termination of the evening lessons. When the sound of light snores filled the entire valley, you left the cave. You felt heaven and earth watching you. It was a realistic feeling. Many living beings were watching you. You must have seen them too. But you couldn't have cared less about them. You continued on your way. Last night's snow had already melted into ice—watch your footsteps!

You descended the mountain slope carefully. You passed through the graveyard and crossed the small bridge to arrive at the main road.

The Beginning of the Exile

You saw a few dim yellow lamps in the state priest's room. They shone on many Buddhist statues. A few Vajras glared at you angrily. But you weren't scared. You knew that was just the revolting way they appeared. They looked furious on the outside but were really compassionate within.

"So they were somewhat like you in this respect!"

However, you would rather have had them rage at you instead. You hoped they would pour their heaven-stirring flames of fury at you and turn your body and soul into ashes to be blown away without a trace by a strong wind. You felt as if you had made a long journey and were thoroughly exhausted.

The state priest was flipping through a book silently. It resembled a sutra, but you didn't believe it was a sutra. You were convinced it contained things, such as pornographic pictures. You could always detect falsehood in the state priest's truths. It was precisely from this that you realized the incurability of your soul. Fortunately, the state priest wasn't your guru, even though he had performed the *abhiseca* ritual for you. He reminded you several times about transmitting to you techniques leading to attaining enlightenment, but you always feigned ignorance and turned a deaf ear to him. If he had indeed become your guru, your present attitude would've led you to the Impenetreble Hell.

You didn't believe in this concept in any case. You didn't even believe in the existence of things like the Impenetrable Hell. The Buddha said everything was created by the mind. A person creates their own Hell. Of course you didn't believe this. Neither did I. Did you know I wasn't happy when I discovered that there was no Hell in the Buddhist realm? Why? Because that's when I finally realized I'd been fooled for many lives.

They knew the truth but readily made up stories to fool me. I became truly angry. Were you like that too? However, one can't say that Hell doesn't exist. It exists for some but not for others. Only when one has my level of attainment would Hell cease to exist. Although it's a good thing for Hell not to exist; for some, however—take the Mongols, for example—the lack of belief in the existence of Hell led to horrendous massacres and slaughtering.

Just like not having God, the lack of Hell can be a terrible thing. The world would be hopeless should Hell really not exist.

Let's leave this nonsensical topic!

But don't worry. The state priest wouldn't have you beaten, lest you leak the secret. It was best you tell no one about this secret concerning Hell. Heaven would punish those who leak its secrets.

The state priest didn't look at you. But you knew he was watching you; you were also watching him. You two had been sneaking glimpses of each other for many years already. The state priest was always using the Gonpo as an excuse to manipulate people. But you knew he hadn't even met the Gonpo. Although one could never be sure. Even if he had, there's no need to worry. During one of your incarnations, the Gonpo had accused you of placing a curse on him, and you admitted to it. So what were you worried about now? The only thing violence could destroy was your body. But you, Ajia, were still Ajia. And Jasper was still Jasper. We were two sides of the same woven brocade. But back then you felt you had aged somewhat. Of course that was just a feeling. But you knew it was a bad omen.

The state priest finally opened his mouth. His voice echoed as if it poured out of a urine chamber pot. He said, "The Gonpo said you are to go to Suzhou to bring salvation to those who deserve it." You knew what was on his mind. "Look," said the state priest as he waved a piece of paper. "There was a request from the people there." You really wanted to read that piece of paper, but you ultimately restrained yourself. There might've been writing on it. You wanted to ask him, "How did the Gonpo tell you?" You thought it was strange how you'd looked for the Gonpo for several lives, without success, but he would always slip out conveniently the moment the state priest wagged his tongue.

But you just swallowed your spittle. You saw three people who looked like Iron Hawks watching you by the door. You also knew what the state priest said was just an excuse to get you to leave the cave. Once you left the cave, you could go to Ganzhou or Suzhou if you'd wished. You just found the pretense of bringing salvation to people rather ridiculous. It was clear that the Mongols had already surrounded Suzhou. You also knew the Mongols couldn't read Xixia writing; but you still went along with the state priest and said, "Sure!"

In fact, whether you wanted to leave or not wasn't up to you. You knew he was saving your face. He only needed to give one command, and the iron-rod lama would've been right there. One strike from that stern-faced monk, and you would've tumbled down the mountain gully like a small chick. However, there really was no need for the excuse about bringing salvation to people. Everyone knew Suzhou was facing imminent catastrophe. The excuse concerning bringing salvation was phony to the extreme.

This was when you realized the state priest's words were actually an edict. You had to go to wherever he decided to exile you. According to my research, this Diamond Maiden Cave controlled all the monks of Liangzhou.

You reverently received with both hands the piece of silk concerning your exile, handed to you by the state priest. You retreated from the room silently, without kowtowing. You entered your own cell, piled up all the sutras, and took only your journal. And then you left the cave. You really wanted to look in on the woman. But you needed to be on your way by night; once the day broke, many eyes would appear and yell, "Look—this is a monk who has broken his vows!"

The cave sighed, but you didn't look back.

Don't you remember? That was the beginning of your exile, which lasted for a thousand years. Regardless of your various outer manifestations, in actual fact, you were nothing but a monk who'd broken his vows and was forced into exile.

Accept your fate—you of bitter fate!

Chapter 30

Cave of the Red Bats

I wept helplessly, in a black cave as large as heaven and earth,
      Where is my final destination?
I can't see the light of dawn;
      I can't glimpse a thread of hope;
      I can't get a wisp of comfort.
I know not where fate will take me;
      I know not who I was when I was born;
      I know not who I will be after I die.
I struggle and struggle with all my might,
      But can never free myself of karma more durable than fishnets.

The Treehouse

Snow Feather and Jasper went to Great Slope Entrance first and dug out from the sand the sheepskins and dagger. These were buried by Snow Feather when she escaped with her mother previously. Because of the sand's dryness, the sheepskins weren't spoiled.

After that, they rested in the large bird's nest in the tree.

The large bird's nest was in the depths of Old Mountain. It was so remote and so full of dangers along the way that they figured it would be very difficult for Braggart and the others to locate it.

Snow Feather thought if they did manage to find their way there, she'd have no choice but to take action. She'd restrained herself for many years and had hoped to allow Mom to spend some time in peace, but nothing good came of it. If they should press her any further, she wouldn't restrain herself again. She tried a few martial arts moves. Although somewhat sluggish compared to before, they were more than adequate for dealing with a few clumsy fellows. The thought of this eliminated for her the terror of running for one's life.

Snow Feather said, "Let's live here first. I can look for a better place later."

What made her happiest was that she found her "treasure bag" in the small bird's nest she'd used for storage earlier. Due to the ventilation up there, many of the items were still usable, despite the fact that many years had passed. Jasper was also very happy as this was a good karmic beginning.

Snow Feather said, "Let me tie a few nooses and trap some wild animals first!"

Each noose was made of horsetail. She had used a lot of them earlier, when she'd tied pine branches together to make the "bird's nest"; but some remained. That hair was so sturdy even a strong person would've trouble breaking a rope made by twisting a few dozen of them together. When one tied the rope into a noose and placed it two feet above the ground between two trees, it would hardly be visible. Should an animal's head get trapped in the noose, it would try to charge forward from fright; but the more it charged forward, the tighter the noose would get. Having a loose connection in its brain, the wild animal wouldn't know it could extricate itself, just by taking a step backward and lowering its head. Of course, if a wild animal knew that the sea would widen and the sky would become vast—just by taking a step backward, then it wouldn't be a wild animal. Oftentimes, even people don't realize this—how much less can one expect of the animals?

There are many other ways of setting traps using nooses. The above is the simplest. The author will not go into detail, lest hunters are thereby created.

Having set some traps in the forest, Snow Feather went back up into the pine tree. The fog in the mountain had become dense, and everything was misty now. The mountains in the distance and the trees nearby had all dissolved into the fog.

A few wolves appeared again not too far in the distance. They were watching with their necks craned. She knew wolves feared people and wouldn't provoke people under normal circumstances, but she hung the dagger on her waist, nevertheless. Quite a few wild animals had met their demise from this dagger in the past. She was always able stab the dagger into an ear of the wild beast after she'd ducked out of its way.

Snow Feather took a slingshot out of the "treasure bag" and shot down a few birds. She then lit some twigs and leaves underneath the pine tree, grilled the birds, and then plucked out their feathers and intestines. The yellow bird meat made her mouth water. She saved two fat, tender ones for Jasper and ate the rest, bones and all, with the exception of the birds' heads and hearts.

Back in the nest, she saw Jasper's lips moving and knew he was chanting a litany. Lined with the sheepskins, the birds' nest now seemed warm and comfortable. She bit into the birds' heads, removed the skull caps, and told Jasper to suck the brains. She then gave him the hearts and the tender meat. Jasper must have been starving. He ate ravenously.

Originally, she'd planned to spend just a night in the tree and look for a cave the next day. But she changed her mind now. She found the birds' nest quite nice—things like wild beasts and snakes couldn't climb up with ease—so it was quite safe. The only defect, if any, would be its size. It would be a perfect abode if it were larger and sturdier. So Snow Feather chopped down a few small pine trees, stripped some palm fiber from palm trees, and built a wooden frame. By noon, a treehouse had begun to take shape.

As soon as Grandpa Sun emerged, the fog dissipated. All sorts of birds appeared and sang merrily as they looked at their new companions. Jasper loved to hear birds chirp. He looked happy and became talkative. One could tell he also loved this place, which had no contentions with the world.

But Snow Feather knew Braggart and those who regarded her as the enemy wouldn't let her go so lightly, unless she were to disappear from the world like a wisp of smoke. She didn't feel like thinking about it, however. One should pick firewood from whichever mountain one happens to climb—no need to be a baby donkey scared by the noise of its own fart.

Once the frame was built, Snow Feather tied pine branches together with palm fiber to line the walls and then tied a large mass of pine branches to form the roof. She almost stripped completely the fiber of two palm trees and "made thinner" more than ten pine trees before the treehouse looked presentable. Once she lined its floor with the feathers, hairs, and twigs of the original birds' nest and covered them with sheepskins, even she was amazed by her own talent as a builder. When Jasper entered the treehouse, he laughed. This was the first time he'd laughed in many months.

The Traps

Snow Feather went to check the traps. Various weeds had sprouted up as if they were playing a prank on her, and she lost her way. Opium poppies furiously sprayed a sinister fragrance, which penetrated until one's bones melted. Irises rioted. Crickets flapped their wings and shrieked—the sounds of which reverberated and harmonized with the gibbons' desolate howls. Bullfrogs glared and spurted a silklike floss, which wove into horse-tripping ropes. Rotten twigs and leaves exuded halolike gases, which wafted up gradually in layers. The marshes blew bubbles that could create a tremendous fire in the presence of a single spark. The fog had dissipated somewhat. Grandpa Sun had become so ugly he resembled a scarred pancake. Snow Feather remembered the area as being quite different when she set the traps in the morning. She suspected a mountain demon had played a trick on her. Mountain demons were evil ghosts, capable of making themselves invisible and shifting shapes. They had supernatural powers and could chase away the mountain god and take its position when their powers surpassed those of the mountain god. According to Grandpa Jiu, when he first arrived at Old Mountain, a mountain demon always played tricks on him until he subdued it. But Old Mountain was full of mountain demons. Although Grandpa Jiu subdued one, a hundred other such "troublemakers" remained!

Somehow, she also had the vague feeling that the place had really looked like this previously. Otherwise, why would it be called Old Mountain? She remembered the pathway as being relatively more level when she came earlier. Although animals abounded, she didn't see the marsh. Of course, it was all due to the fact that she hadn't been interested in observing appearances at the time—her confused mind had only become clear now!

Snow Feather entered the forest, which had paths habitually traveled by animals. Like humans, animals liked to use paths they were accustomed to travel. The traps were set along the path commonly used by mountain goats.

She set three traps and managed to catch a yellow mountain goat and a black mountain goat. The third trap was torn apart by some unidentifiable animal. Back then, mountain goats roamed like clouds in Qilian Mountain. They weren't even afraid of people.

The horsetail trap had already cut into the neck of the black goat. There was a pool of blood on the ground, and the goat stopped struggling, knowing that its fragile neck would break from further struggle. Black mountain goats were very strong. If it were to relax its body and then use force violently, it would've broken the horsetail trap a long time ago. But it just kept on struggling. Of course, if it were to lower its head and take a step backward, then it could have extricated itself from the noose. But animals were ultimately animals.

Knowing they couldn't consume two goats at one time, she knotted the horsetail into a headstall and tied the yellow goat with it. She twisted and broke the neck of the black goat. The black goat wailed a few times. Tears overflowed its porcelain white eyes, and its limbs twitched meekly. Although Snow Feather felt somewhat badly, she wanted to skin it whole to make a bag for carrying water. Such a bag of water would be enough for them to cook and drink for several days.

Snow Feather returned carrying the black goat on one shoulder, while she pulled the yellow goat with the other hand. Seeing its own fate to be that of the black goat, the yellow goat bleated the whole way. It also sank its hoofs into the ground and refused to budge. Snow Feather didn't want to bother with it and just pulled. So the hoofs drew four lines on the ground the entire way.

Although the yellow goat was female, it had no milk since it wasn't lactating. Snow Feather thought, *Wait till I trap one that's lactating and then we'll have fresh milk to drink!*

Snow Feather took the bag, freshly made with the skin of the black goat, to the stream and brought back a bag of water. She had Jasper toss down one of the sheepskins and turned it over to use as a cutting board. She then cut the black goat's meat into fist-sized lumps and cooked them in a pot. The pot was small and couldn't hold much. She used to have a large pot and a small pot in her kitchen. The large pot was used for cooking food, while the small one was used for boiling water. When she carried Mom into the mountain last time, she left the large pot and just took the small one because of the anticipated distance. Even that was due to a reminder by Mom. They'd have had to eat grilled meat otherwise.

She found three stones to prop up the pot, lit a fire, and began to cook the meat. As she added branches to the fire, she couldn't help but feel intoxicated by the atmosphere. This is a really wonderful place, she discovered. Grandpa Sun shone warmly. The birds chirped. In a short while, the meat and water in the pot would issue a bubbling sound, the best music for pacifying the nerves. *This must be what the celestials' lives are like*, she thought.

Suddenly, she heard the sound of romping. It turned out to be the two baby bears rolling on the ground, tangled together. Seeing the innocence of the baby bears, Snow Feather felt the warmth of home in that cave. She also wanted to find a cave to stay in, since caves were definitely superior for keeping warm, particularly during the winter. One couldn't possibly endure winter on a tree. *We'll deal with that when it gets cold*, she thought.

The water boiled. Steam spilled from the lid. Snow Feather ladled off the scum on top as she added firewood. She shot a glance at "home," and saw Jasper craning his neck and looking down. She said, "Don't be anxious—let me cook until the meat is more tender!" Jasper said, "I'm not anxious. I was just thinking that you have to think of—how you're going to climb back up with a pot so hot? Snow Feather said, "I'll go up first and then suspend the pot and pull it up." Jasper said, "Why don't you get a small tree and chop some dents into it—it'll become a ladder then!" Snow Feather said, "I'll make it after the meat is tender."

The pot's aroma spilled out and attracted a pack of wolves. They stuck out their long tongues, and saliva drooled like waterfalls. Some even made smacking sounds. Snow Feather wasn't afraid of wolves. In fact, she liked wolves. She liked the wolf's ability to survive in all sorts of environments. She'd killed many wild animals, but would never kill a wolf lightly; because Grandpa Jiu had said the mountain god was the wolf's protective deity—wolves were the mountain god's dogs. One night more than ten years ago, she had even saved a wolf. A big thorn pierced the wolf's lower jaw, and it wailed at her. So she pulled out the thorn.

Snow Feather scooped out a piece of meat and said, "Dear Mountain God, this is an offering to you!" She then threw it into the distance. The wolves swarmed after it. She scooped out another piece and took a bite. It was still too tough. So she added another handful of pine branches to the fire. The wolves must've been tempted by the meat's aroma; they all drooled and howled. When more than a thousand wolves howled in unison, the sound could be quite frightening. Snow Feather was used to that sound, but Jasper was terrified. He said, "Come up! Come up!" Snow Feather laughed and said, "Don't worry! I don't owe the wolves any lives—they won't eat me! They're begging for the cooked meat!

Hey, wolves—if you want to eat this, you'd better catch one and cook it yourselves!"

Suddenly, the wolves dispersed together. An intense stench accosted her. Snow Feather could tell it was from a python. She turned around; and sure enough, a male python had already dragged half of its body outside the cave. This male python could understand humans. When Snow Feather practiced inner kung fu in the cave in the past, she used to "play" with it. Back then, the python was smaller. Snow Feather would let it wrap itself around her. She would feel surging energy envelop her and tighten in spasms. When the tension reached a certain limit, she would give the python a few scratches, and the python would relax its body instantly. The "brother and sister" would then fall to the ground and roll down the slope together. The skin of the python was so thick it wasn't bothered by the slope's sharp rocks. Snow Feather could never forget the buzzing sound when they rolled down. The python was her greatest joy during those lonely years.

Snow Feather scooped out a piece of meat, walked over, puffed on the meat a few times to cool it off, and placed it in the python's mouth. The meat disappeared without any movement of its mouth. Snow Feather said, "The rest of the meat is for us! If you're hungry, you can eat the yellow goat." She pulled the goat over, but the python wriggled back into the cave without touching it.

"If you want a cooked one, then go find a big pot and I'll cook a nice pot of it for you!" Snow Feather yelled at the cave of the python.

She then cut off the black goat's leg and tossed it into the cave.

The God of Thunder

The treehouse began shaking suddenly during the middle of the night. A strong wind spilled into the house through the thick pine needles. The wind pierced into every single sweat-filled pore and robbed the house of all its warmth.

Snow Feather got up and covered Jasper with a sheepskin. Jasper had been awake for a while already. "I'm not cold," he said, "take good care of yourself." Snow Feather said, "It's safer in a cave—shall we move into the cave?" Jasper said, "That's someone else's home—what are they going to do if you snatch it from them?" Snow Feather said, "I didn't say I'm going to snatch the cave from the bears. I'll find another one."

Jasper said, "Judging from the sound, the God of Thunder is getting ready to strike at something. I wonder what has turned into a spirit."

Sure enough, a huge fireball rolled toward them from the distance. It cavorted like a mischievous child; its tremendous roar obliterated the sounds of the wind and the rain. That thunderous roar didn't seem to be of this world. It came from beyond this world and was accompanied by the self-confidence of destined fate. When it resounded in this world, the myriad beings immediately became silent. A state of panic prevailed over everything—confusion abounded in heaven and earth; nothing could locate its own place. It was as if exterior appearances and interior minds were all swimming in a pool of mud. They swam and swam, but no matter how hard they swam, they were unable to find the shore. A thread of white light emerged through the crack struck by the fireball. It vaguely resembled the sinister face of the moon. But more likely, it was a developing lightning bolt—dodging like a frightened maiden yet continuing to be whipped by the thunderbolt arriving from the distance.

Jasper said, "I hope it's not striking at that python!"

The thunder clapped again—it may have struck down a tree. Soon, the eight directions were choked full of this sound. Snow Feather thought, maybe the soul and body of the python would be struck asunder by the heartless lightning in an instant. Its life had once appeared in the darkness; it would disappear again in the darkness and ultimately melt into infinite darkness. Therefore she screamed, "Hide, quickly!" Although she screamed until she was hoarse, her voice vanished without a trace the way sprays of water splash into a rapid.

Lightning flashed and thunder clapped. Everything in Old Mountain seemed to have been crushed into pieces, which floated and roamed between heaven and earth. The sky had been ripped apart. The crack reached from the horizon to the ground. Heartless roars flooded heaven and earth. Snow Feather discovered that at this juncture, life was at once precious and cheap. Trampled by the continuous flashes of lightning, human dignity and self-confidence were torn apart heartlessly and turned into ashes! But who could stop this nightmare?

Suddenly, heaven and earth became silent. It was a terrifyingly dead silence. It was as if innumerable cloaked wolf-demons had passed through the forest. But neither their voices nor their footsteps could be heard. And then they unleashed all the terror. Thereupon, the animals' horrifying howls shocked heaven and earth, as if doomsday had arrived. In the darkness, innumerable animals seemed to be fleeing in fright. The flashes of lightning became ever more sinister. The myriad beings bared their fangs and brandished their claws. The sky, which covered the earth, shrieked horribly. Everything on earth was shivering. Jasper said, "The sky will collapse! The sky will collapse!" And then he added, "Tell it to come to us!"

The sky truly collapsed!

Snow Feather cried, "Come to us!" Grandpa Jiu had told her that thunderbolts wouldn't readily strike humans. Some animals' lives were preserved, precisely due to the protection of human beings.

In the dimness, a black shadow approached gradually. It looked like an old man wearing a cloak, but the two green lights on its head gave it away. It was the python, wasn't it? It was charging forward with all its might toward the depths of the forest, toward the darkest location and the most mysterious site; but it couldn't escape the pair of eyes watching it from destiny. It charged and charged until it was dashed into innumerable bones. It charged among the bones until it was transformed into a desolate old tree. But one clap of thunder, and the old tree was split apart. A small snake slipped out of the tree's center and dashed to the bottom of a lake. One loud bang of a thunderbolt—and the lake evaporated instantly and became a desiccated pit. At this point, the python reared up and spewed fire into the sky. It gouged out one of its own eyes and tossed it into the sky. The eye transformed into a thunderbolt and shattered the sky into smithereens. Suddenly, a huge noise reverberated through the forest. The python roared angrily, as it soared into the sky where it circled. All the animals cheered in unison to urge it on. An earth-shattering energy surged into the python. The brilliance of its heart-nature was manifested.

But maybe Snow Feather had imagined all this. Due to the proximity of the fireball, Snow Feather heard the tree, on which they stayed, heave a sigh. It must have realized its precarious situation and was preparing to make its escape. Possessing even more legs than a centipede, every single branch was waving. Snow Feather even heard the shuffle of the tree's footsteps, which resembled the advance of thousands of soldiers at night. In fact it sounded even more like the tree had taken flight. Each pine needle had transformed into a wing; the branches waved and danced. The entire sky had become a dance arena. Fearing lest the treehouse would fall apart from the shaking, Snow Feather made waist cords for Jasper and herself and tied themselves to the tree.

A few thornlike flashes of light exploded into the treehouse, followed by claps of thunder. Through the "window" of the treehouse, Snow Feather saw streams of gilded cracks over the mountain range. At some point, a tree next to them had snapped. It looked like a feeble hand stretching toward heaven and was conspicuous in its strangeness. The slit in the tree resembled a woman's miserable shriek. Many unnameable large birds wove back and forth in the night rain, as if they were unable to locate their homes. In the lightning flashes, the mountains in the distance heaved like the backs of furiously running wild beasts, showing a frightening and indescribable furtiveness. The world was a spectacular jumble. Everything was stirred together. Heaven and earth couldn't be distinguished. It was as if a tsunami had arrived. The treehouse creaked. Now and then, the wind extinguished the lightning. Dim shadows of ghosts and spirits emerged vaguely between heaven and earth. The various noises tangled like a mass of hair; the peals of thunder and the bellowing of wind had become indistinguishable. Thousands of wolves howled, causing one's hair to stand on end.

Huge crashes reverberated ceaselessly. They lingered in one's very pores, seeped through them, and then exploded into whirlpools.

One's own safe haven had disappeared—nothing to rely on for survival, except for one's bare body. Large hands of darkness stretched out, trembling. One held one's breath, not daring to scream but at the same time not willing to resign to being drowned by the terrifying forest. Although thunder continued to rumble, it was unable to dissipate the loneliness and darkness that enveloped everything.

The Python

Later, Ajia told me that the first major event involving Jasper and Snow Feather on Old Mountain was saving the python. The python spirit, which escaped being struck by the thunderbolt, attained transcendence. Years later, it became one of the Eight Categories of Protective Deities and was known as the Mahanaga, meaning the Great Snake or python god. The other seven categories were: the brave and fleet-footed Yakshas; the Gandharvas who could perform music in midair and sustain themselves by consuming aromas; the large and warlike Asuras; the Garudas, the golden-winged bird deities with wingspans of more than three million kilometers; the singing-god Kinnara of human form, but with horns; and the numerous devas and nagas.

I've always been skeptical about the above. You know I'm a cynical person. Often, I even doubt whether I'm alive. Of course, this refers to when I've entered a dream state.

Then one day, I suddenly believed what Ajia had said because simply by chance the python became my friend and had its photo taken with my family. Friends with karmic affinity will be able to see the photo. Back then, Indra[1] had ordered the python to protect Diamond Maiden Cave. It was in that cave that I met and befriended the python. I've recorded the story of our meeting and how it joined in a photo with my family in *Mahamudra: Essence and Practice*.

Ajia said that the day after the storm, Snow Feather discovered that the python had wrapped itself around the trunk of her tree. That's how it escaped being struck by the thunderbolt. I've heard that the God of Thunder doesn't dare to strike unjustifiably. It could only strike what the Jade Emperor of the Heavens ordered it to strike. If the God of Thunder killed indiscriminately, then it wouldn't have been any different from the demons, right? Jade Emperor wouldn't want to be considered a murderer either.

Ajia's reasoning seemed very sound.

The most popular versions of the tale in Liangzhou claim that Jasper and Snow Feather saved the python. The litanies Jasper chanted unceasingly possessed incomparable power and issued a holy light, which shielded the old pine tree like a metal bell. It was an "other-worldly" holy light to which the "this-worldly" deity, the God of Thunder, couldn't possibly get near. Ajia said not only could it not get close, but it was even afraid to look directly at the light!

However, the folks of Liangzhou were convinced the python was saved by Snow Feather's sanitary napkin, marked with menstruation blood. You must know, the folks of Liangzhou were most imaginative. They were able to forecast the following day's weather through a louse's sneezing, and predict the forthcoming plague the following year from the way mosquitoes hum. According to them, Snow Feather held up the bloody napkin when the Thunder of God pressed close. The napkin exuded an incomparably powerful blood-light, capable of causing all the world's ghosts and spirits to vanish without a trace. You may not know, but the women of Liangzhou weren't allowed to enter the main hall of the households during menstruation lest they drive away the various ancestors and the gods of happiness and wealth worshipped at the offering table there. Remember the story found in *Historical Mirror of Forgotten Events* I told earlier? Someone from a wealthy household in Liangzhou took advantage of a widow. Thereupon, the widow cried

1. Leader of the devas.

all the way to that household. She sat on the threshold of its gate and howled like a she-wolf. It just so happened she was menstruating that day. The blood flowed out with her wailing, broke the lines of blockade that prevented the entry of evil influences, and imprinted itself on the threshold. Thereafter, the wealthy household met with misfortunes. Mules and horses died; fire and flood raged; and their riches drained away like water through a sieve. Within a year, they became so poor they didn't even have pants to wear.

Look—such was the power of blood! Stories about it could fill an entire mule cart!

Regardless of the legend's different versions, however, the ending was the same—the python escaped its destined calamity. It was said that for such spiritually attained beings, whether human or animal, Jade Emperor would only dispatch the God of Thunder to make one attempt at striking it down. If the attempt was unsuccessful, then it signified the being wasn't destined to die. Jade Emperor would then have to eventually offer it amnesty and bestow upon it a position. All those enfeoffed by Jade Emperor were entitled to enjoy offerings. The people could then build shrines and worship them.

It was said there was another route for spirits that didn't receive amnesty and a position from Jade Emperor. They could be awarded honors by eminent priests, gurus, and emperors. Lord Guan's[2] soul wouldn't dissipate after his head had been chopped off by the Kingdom of Eastern Wu. It roamed throughout the four directions, screaming, "Give me back my head!" A wise monk of the Buddhist Tiantai Sect asked him, "You ask for your head, but from whom should Wen Chou and Yan Liang[3] ask for their heads?" Thereupon, Lord Guan was enlightened and became a follower of the Tiantai Sect's wise guru, and ultimately a Buddhist protective deity. It wasn't until Lord Guan was awarded titles by various emperors later that he became the "Eminent Holy Emperor Guan."

It was further said that even sages asked for entitlements. Even Confucius wouldn't have had so many temples of literature built for him if emperors of the mortal world hadn't granted him titles.

The python, which escaped the calamity of being struck down by the thunderbolt, would continue to practice cultivation in Qilian Moun-

---

2. Named Guan Yu (160–219), he was a great general who served under Liu Bei (161–223) of the Shu Kingdom during the Three Kingdoms Period (208–280).

3. Generals slain by Guan Yu in the novel, *Romance of the Three Kingdoms*.

tain before it became a member of the Eight Categories of Protective Deities many years later. This meant it would spend some time with the protagonists of this book. Of course, this would lead to other events.

The Ancient Cave

After the sky had cleared, Snow Feather came out of the treehouse "door." She found the python wrapped around the treehouse. Snow Feather understood then that the python was protecting the house. The elongated body of the python, which resembled the rope the elderly of Liangzhou used as a girdle, secured the treehouse to the pine tree. This was probably the main reason the treehouse hadn't shattered in that terrifying storm. Of course, the treehouse residents had also saved the python's life at the same time.

Often you are also helping yourself when you help others. This was the greatest insight Snow Feather gained from that unforgettable stormy night.

The python slid down the tree slowly after the sun came out. It shot a glance at Snow Feather before it proceeded quietly toward its own cave. The grass outside the cave had already been scorched by lightning. A strong smell of sulphur permeated the air. The python didn't like this odor, so it coiled itself outside the cave and stared at Grandpa Sun in a daze.

The following morning Snow Feather boiled a pot of black mountain goat meat and brought up the entire pot, soup and all, to Jasper. Having eaten some hapharzardly herself, she took a dagger, a cloth bag, and a nine-segmented whip to search for a cave of their own. It was autumn already. Some yellow leaves had begun to fall in Qilian Mountain, but the weeds and bushes were still quite luxurious. Iris grass grew riotously. It was good for twisting into ropes, which were used to tie wheat into bundles during Diamond Clan's autumn harvest. Snow Feather cut some iris grass and twisted it between her palms into a long rope. Ropes are indispensable for staying in a cave; the longer the rope, the better. And then she took advantage of the presence of some mushrooms and tender dandelion greens and picked some of them as well. She'd intended to look for a cave but had unexpectedly acquired quite a bit of good food.

Although there were caves nearby, most of them weren't usable. The better ones were already occupied by wild animals. Their entrances were strewn with animal footprints. Since Jasper had already shown his disapproval of snatching caves occupied by animals, she had to do her best to find one not already occupied. To Snow Feather, Jasper's words were imperial edicts.

Consequently, Snow Feather cast her sights upon the caves higher up. She remembered seeing caves on some cliffs. Animals couldn't go there due to their steepness. The only disadvantage would be the inconvenience of obtaining food and water. However, given their present situation, such a cave could be the best choice. Snow Feather recalled a cave not far away. Back then, she had always seen a black eagle standing outside the cave. She wondered if the eagle still occupied the cave. As she remembered it, the cave's entrance was nicely chiseled and showed signs of human intervention. Maybe it had been used by a Buddhist practitioner.

Weeds covered the entire pathway—the most aggressive being wheatgrass, which grew everywhere in riotous disarray. Wheatgrass was also good for making ropes. These would've been slashed a long time ago if they'd been closer to a village. Due to the prevalence of wolves on Old Mountain, villagers didn't dare to visit individually. Occasionally, however, more than a hundred people would form a group and enter Old Mountain together. When grass was scarce during drought, they would also herd their livestock here. Now and then, people would eat beef from cattle that had either tumbled down a gully or had their intestines plucked by jackals. But Snow Feather was always considered an alien by the villagers. They always dodged her the way they dodged a leper and never invited her to events such as weddings and funerals. There was nothing she could do about it—although the tiger didn't bite, its foul notoriety had spread! During some odd moments, however, Snow Feather couldn't help but feel being wronged and lonely.

The cave in the cliff wasn't far. Snow Feather saw it very soon. But because of the amount of time she'd spent gathering mushrooms and wild greens, and making rope, Grandpa Sun was already setting. Mist was also beginning to spill out of the deep valley and was spreading toward her gradually. Snow Feather wanted to go back because, once the sky turned dark, she wouldn't be able to feel her way back home. "Road" on Old Mountain referred to any place the feet could tread. Once night fell and heaven and earth merged into blackness, then "road" could be everywhere and nowhere. But she only wanted to take a look at the cave. She thought, *I'll just take a look and see if it's viable; if not, then there's no need to return here!*

Snow Feather climbed up the cliff. Someone had chiseled holes into it, which made the climb unexpectedly easy. Snow Feather was happy since this type of cave was the most suitable for humans. It would invariably be comparatively flat and spacious within. Sometimes, there would even be a location for placing an oil lamp on its wall. She had forgotten to bring the oil lamp from home last time she entered the mountain. Once she found a suitable cave, she planned to gouge a hole in its wall and use the yellow-colored goat's fat for light. With the arrival of autumn, all the animals had become fat. Fat would even line their intestines in lumps. She'd already torn off a pile of fat from the black goat. Unfortunately, she did not have a bowl she could use as a lamp.

The entrance to the cave was also overgrown with weeds. Nothing one could do about it—this was Old Mountain after all! Old people's faces get hairy; old mountains get weedy. Snow Feather pulled up some dried grass, rolled it between her palms into a torch, and lit it. Flint steel, and tinder were necessities on Old Mountain. Carrying them had almost become a rule.

Snow Feather noticed a horrible stench, even before she entered the cave. It was a moldy smell. She frowned. She didn't like this odor. While it was normal for caves to smell moldy—moist caves inevitably smelled of mildew—the stench in this cave was terrible. She wondered if the cave had dead animals in it.

Puffing at the rope-torch so that it flared, Snow Feather entered the cave. Piles of black stuff were strewn about the ground. She twirled some between her fingers and realized that they were bird droppings. Proceeding further, she unexpectedly found a human skeleton. It rested against the cave wall and looked as if it were meditating. Next to that person was a leather bag, also covered with bird droppings and dust. Snow Feather gave it a kick and heard the unexpected clanging of metal. She shook the bag, which still retained elasticity. This was the advantage of leather. If this were a cloth bag, it would've disintegrated into ashes a long time ago. Shaking out its contents, metal clanged, and a pile of stuff poured out. Unexpectedly, there was a pure-water bowl among them—perfect to use as an oil lamp. There were also a Vajra bell, a Vajra scepter, and other ritual implements, as well as a few books made of sheepskin parchment. She used to see such books at Grandpa Jiu's place but was never interested in them. She thought Jasper would like them, however, so she tucked them into her bosom. The bell and scepter were unexpectedly fine. They were obviously antiques and could probably fetch some money from someone who knew the items' worth. Having lived by herself in a graveyard before, Snow Feather wasn't scared of corpses. There really was nothing frightening about them if one thought about it. Weren't all living humans nothing but corpses being dragged around? Wasn't that which one smeared with cream and powder, and treasured a hundred different ways, nothing but a skeleton?

Snow Feather picked up the leather bag, puffed at the rope-torch again to make it brighter, and proceeded into the cave. She unexpectedly discovered several other skeletons, all leaning this way and that, and showing signs of having suffered a violent death. Now, Snow Feather began to feel scared. She wasn't surprised by the skeleton of someone who was obviously meditating. She used to see many such practitioners who spent their entire lives on Old Mountain. There seemed to have been no difference between when they were dead and when they were alive. They were loners and no one knew whether they had attained enlightenment through their practices. Aside from those who promulgated Buddhist teachings after they'd achieved enlightenment, only they themselves knew whether they'd attained enlightenment. It was just like drinking water: only the drinker knew whether the water was cold or warm. Aside from the guru who confirmed him, others were all clueless, like those feeling for the attic window in the dark. Snow Feather didn't want to spend her entire life practicing cultivation like Grandpa Jiu—precisely because she didn't want to be a loner. Who'd have known that she who didn't want to be a loner, was in fact nothing but a loner?

Hoping to find some rare objects, Snow Feather gave the skeletons a few kicks but was disappointed. The moment her foot touched them, all their clothes turned into dust. The skeletons clattered together happily.

Suddenly, Snow Feather discovered a sickle and spade of the kind commonly used at Diamond Clan. They indicated at least one of the deceased was from Diamond Clan. The person must have died when he or she came to Old Mountain to cut wheatgrass. When the rains were scarce and most grass had already been grazed by livestock, the villagers would enter the mountain to cut wheatgrass to make ropes. That person must have died then. The spade was probably brought along for digging up badgers or marmots. Each year, a few people would vanish from the village inexplicably. Some were killed by Brilliant King Clan as enemies. Who was this deceased? Snow Feather wasn't able to verify at this point.

Although the sickle and spade were rusty, Snow Feather intended to take them. Everything was useful on Old Mountain. The cave was deep, but she didn't feel like advancing further. She thought, *Let me come back to pick up a few more things tomorrow or the day after. If Jasper was willing, they could stay at Old Mountain.*

Little did she expect the sky to have become as dark as the bottom of a wok by the time she returned to the cave's entrance.

Let me stay here for the night then, she thought. Although she felt somewhat anxious, she knew it was easy to get lost on Old Mountain at night.

She yanked up some dry grass, twisted it into rope-torches, and entered the cave. After picking a spot, she crouched down. And just as she was dozing off, she surprisingly felt a waft of cold wind blowing toward her.

Red Bats

The cold wind attacked her quietly. It was merely a sensation. It was as if a large invisible hand had touched her and withdrew as soon as she woke up. Although it was only an instant, Snow Feather knew danger surely lurked nearby. She blew at the rope-torch so that it flared brightly. The rope-torch had the advantage of smoldering when it wasn't in use and flaring up when needed. Just a few puffs were needed to brighten the world before one.

Snow Feather searched the cave with the torch in one hand and the dagger in the other. The piles of bones under her feet clattered eerily. Because of the cave's vastness, the strange sound spread some distance before it echoed back, and then the cave was filled with strange echoes. Fortunately, Snow Feather had learned Machig Labdron Dakini Goddess's technique for "attaining calmness" from Grandpa Jiu and had practiced it in the past. She'd have been scared stiff otherwise. Machig Labdron Dakini Goddess was one of the few people revered by Grandpa Jiu. Regarding himself highly, Grandpa Jiu held few in high esteem and was in the habit of denouncing those generally regarded as divine masters. Machig Labdron Dakini Goddess was the only exception. Machig was the founder of the Zichey Chod Sect and had taught a series of techniques for cultivation. Snow Feather had only learned Machig's technique of meditation and had meditated in 108 malevolent sites. Snow Feather had spent seven days and seven nights at each site and underwent legendary experiences at almost all those locations. Most of the malevolent sites were located in corpse-forests, where people dumped corpses. Ferocious beasts and all sorts of weird things roamed there. They all made deep imprints in Snow Feather's mind; which meant she'd been frightened by all of them. Fortunately, Grandpa Jiu had taught her the technique of dissolving the outer world into the inner world of wisdom, so she was able to gradually subdue them all. Originally, she was supposed to also meditate at 108 springs and 108 holy lands, among others. But because Snow Feather was more interested in learning Grandpa Jiu's martial arts, he said, "Enough! Girls meditate to gain concentration, so they won't scream whenever they see corpses in the future." Fortunately, the meditations in the 108 malevolent sites enabled Snow Feather to be courageous anywhere. Even if she were scared, she could deal with that—by dissolving the various manifestations into illusions. The experiences from those two-plus years enabled her to understand that what scared one in this world was actually one's inability to control one's own mind.

Grandpa Jiu had taught her the technique of using terror and fright to experience the illusory nature of things, so she could feel that special sensation instantly. This would benefit Snow Feather for the rest of her life. She consequently saw through the illusory nature of many things. She frequently transformed herself into a dream state and gradually came to realize that this world is merely a dream.

Ajia said, "This was the essential difference between Snow Feather and a common flying thief." Ajia told me about the miraculous events that happened when Snow Feather practiced cultivation at the 108 malevolent sites. Due to their length, I will leave them for another book.

Ajia's narrative was intensely subjective, this being one of the characteristics of his descriptions. He deliberately mystified and always exaggerated what Snow Feather herself may have ignored or neglected at the time. I knew he was either trying to show off his supposed literary talents, or hoping to make me tremble in fear, and thereby gain my reverence.

For example, he described Snow Feather's search in the cave as follows.

Snow Feather held up the torch and waded through the thick air toward the unknown. The sound of terror, which resembled the ringing of a bell, permeated the air. Suddenly, weeds a foot high surged from the ground. The white bones clattered against each other with a sinister laugh. They used to be men; so they used men's guffaws to tease Snow Feather. The suggestiveness of their guffaws would've been obvious to anyone. Even skeletons could be lascivious! *Hahaha!* However, the most unbridled were the walls, which tugged at her impudently. Snow Feather must've been frightened. Although she'd gone through the 108 malevolent sites, she was still frightened. What she feared wasn't the skeletons—even if they were to attain flesh in an instant and could rape a woman—that wouldn't frighten her. She was full of tricks for dealing with this type of man. What she feared was the source of the murderous atmosphere. She who had endured strict cultivation knew this murderous atmosphere was no mere wind in a cavern.

The rope-torch exuded a dark glow as mysterious as Ajia's narrative. Snow Feather's face turned pale. In the legends of Liangzhou, Snow Feather was always pale like that. She was the archetypal beauty of ice and snow.

That dark cave seemed interminable. Skeletons were strewn about its floor. Their corpses had all died the same way and seemed both incomparably miserable and joyous. The dripping of water on the cave ceiling sounded like the trickling of blood. The stench in the air was no less than that found in Sitavana, which was strewn with rotten corpses. Sitavana was one of the eight most famous corpse-forests of India. The secret Pure Land of the guru Niguma, who had attained the Rainbow Body, was in the heaven above it. This was the permanent Pure Land Grandpa Jiu always mentioned and that which Snow Feather longed for.

The evil demons bared their fangs and charged at Snow Feather's jade-white face. But they were smashed into smithereens by her face's holy light and transformed into wavering foul wisps. The source of the murderous atmosphere, however, gave a sinister smile. I said, "Okay, Ajia! Stop mystifying! If you have a fart, break it! So what happened next?"

Ajia laughed and said, "Nothing! If there's nothing weird in the mind, the weirdness will vanish!" He then bellowed, "What's the rush? Listen patiently!"

Snow Feather puffed at the rope-torch a few times. She searched the cave thoroughly and discovered that what seemed to have been an unfathomably deep cave was actually not very deep at all. Many things are like that. They can only fool people when the truth was unknown. Once the truth behind the trick was known, then people would say, "Aiyo! So that's all it was!" And hey! There'd be no more mystery about it!

I saw Snow Feather wipe off the sweat on her forehead. Her handsome face showed a sense of relief. And then she yawned, picked a dry spot, kicked away the bones leaning whichever way, crouched down, and entered into the state Grandpa Jiu had taught her. Later, Grandpa Jiu also transmitted the technique to me. I call it merging the outer world with the inner world.

It was at this moment that the red bat came charging at Snow Feather.

Ajia said, the very moment the red bat charged, the scabby monk who'd stolen the golden top of Luoshen Monastery and a red-robed lama with expertise in the Technique of Killing were performing a Fire Offering Killing Technique. The cloth bearing the request sported the picture of a black triangle. Inside the triangle were the words, "Snow Feather."

Scarlet red flames engulfed the yellow cloth that denoted the request.

The technique performed by the lama was a curse that had originated in Xixia.

It was said that all the calamities suffered by Snow Feather arose from this Xixia curse.

The Poeticism of Terror

Snow Feather swished the dagger in her hand. The cold wind vanished as if it had been cut down. Snow Feather saw a pair of eerie blue eyes. She puffed at the rope-torch and discovered a huge bat on the cave ceiling. It was staring coldly at her.

Her scalp tingled and her mind drew a blank. She'd even forgotten to visualize what Grandpa Jiu had taught her to counter this condition. Later, she realized her concentration wasn't yet sufficient. She had no fear of skeletons, since she knew they could do nothing to her; she had no fear of wild animals because she knew the animals couldn't deal with her either. But like all girls, she was afraid of grotesquely shaped monsters—such as this bat.

The red bat stared at her coldly, as if it were watching a pile of food it had no interest in. Snow Feather's mind hummed loudly. Should the bat attack her at that moment, she might react instinctively; but she wasn't confident she could strike her opponent to death. This was related to one of her subconscious fears. One year, several monks died at a monastery at the foot of the mountain. Investigations led to no clues, so people asked Grandpa Jiu about it. Grandpa Jiu said the deaths had been caused by red bats. He said red bats could suck out people's brains and take their lives before they knew it. This made a deep impression on Snow Feather.

The red bat stretched its wings a few times. Its wingspan was at least three feet across. She had never seen a bat that large before! And in the dark recesses of the cave ceiling she suddenly discovered a few smaller bats, all hanging upside down and staring at her. She broke out in a cold sweat. She wondered if these were the vampire bats Grandpa Jiu had mentioned. She puffed at the rope-torch and worried that there wouldn't be enough torches to last the entire night. She was truly afraid she wouldn't be able to withstand her fear in total darkness.

She gathered the torn cloths and dried weeds from under her feet and lit them. The fire gradually became brighter. The ground was covered with shreds of cloth. They were the loincloths and clothing that provided warmth for the skeletons' former bodies. They then became tattered scraps that now provided illumination for Snow Feather. The fire brightened the cave warmly. The skeletons became conspicuously offensive again. She suspected they'd been victims of the red bats. Even the practitioner might've been their victim. If she had slept soundly just now, she might've been in a different world already.

Come to think of it, the person named "Snow Feather" could have vanished very easily. If she'd dozed off for just a moment—the waiting red bat would've charged at her and sucked out her brain. Then, Snow Feather would've vanished. Like the skeletons under her feet, she'd have become something that would trip the next person entering the cave.

Snow Feather also thought of Grandpa Jiu. The last time she left him, he said, "Girl—go experience the mortal world! Experience and taste everything. Perform acts of filial piety that we should all perform. Just don't forget to look for what I've told you to search for. When you've found that permanent thing, then come back to me. Offer it to me and I'll transmit to you the technique for attaining the Rainbow Body." Snow Feather had searched for something of permanence ever since. She was convinced nothing was impossible in this world. One would always find the path if one kept on going. One night, she was convinced she'd found it—it was her love for her mother. She thought although life had a limit, her love for her mother was everlasting. But ever since the appearance of the red bat, she discovered that even if Mother were still alive, Snow Feather's intense love could have become a vanished emotion through merely taking a careless snooze.

The red bat stretched its wings a few times. Snow Feather thought it was going to charge at her, but it just looked like it was perched to attack. Since she had never seen how red bats attacked, Snow Feather didn't know whether she could deal with it. Those eyes, which issued an eerie light, made her shudder. She was reminded of an owl she saw on the mountain one night that had the same eyes. It was a moonlit night. Many mice were romping around under the tree. Now and then, the owl would swoop down and grab a mouse. The other mice were totally oblivious to what was happening; and so the owl grabbed the mice, one by one, without dampening the liveliness and clamor of the mice kingdom. Observing this scene, Grandpa Jiu laughed heartily. His laughter was loaded, just like the eyes of the owl.

Suddenly, one of the bats shrieked. Its shriek was conspicuously piercing. The shrill of a tsunami reverberated immediately. Waves surged throughout the ceiling of the cave from the flapping of the bat wings. Snow Feather discovered that all sorts of bats, big and small, hid in the dark—awaiting an opportunity to stab her with their pointed mouths. She couldn't help but be frightened that this small space harbored so many things that could instantly kill her. She realized they were protesting the gusts of smoke and thought, *So, is this what you fear?* But the shrieks were unbearable, and the grotesquely shaped wings also created wafts of sinister wind. So this must've been their strategy. They must've been waiting secretly in the dark for a long while, intending to take her off guard. But seeing their conspiracy discovered, they now created wafts of sinister wind to destroy her willpower. Ajia said that the emotion known as terror drowned Snow Feather. She knew she should remain calm but was still unable to control herself completely.

Snow Feather took off her coat to deal with these "gods of death." It was more effective than knives and swords. She really didn't want to stay in the cave any longer. She thought, *No matter how horrible the darkness outside, it can't be worse than this, can it?* So she took the bag of things left by the skeleton and retreated backward slowly. She was afraid the bats would take the opportunity to ambush her. But they just shrieked. The noise reverberated like a whirlwind, and a powerful sound wave pushed her out of the cave.

The darkness outside the cave was even more all-encompassing, with possibly countless dark secrets that could kill her. This was when she realized how insignificant she was. No matter how skillful she was at martial arts, how feather light she could be—she seemed insignificant and helpless when facing an immense unknown.

She retreated outside of the cave but dared not climb down the cliff. She was frightened that the vampire bats would take this opportunity to ambush her. She remembered the slope was extremely steep. The gully hugged the mountain and was irregular. A fall would cause permanent injury, if not death. She used the rope-torch to burn grass. Fortunately, she had the sickle, which could cut a lot of yellow and green grass very easily. She used the grass as frugally as possible until she saw light on the horizon.

However, the red bat's eyes continued to shine in the depths of her soul and made her shudder. She was even convinced that terror was the thing of permanence she was seeking. She believed terror was that which no one could be free from. But at the same time, she also realized that even terror was impermanent. With the change of environment, terrors could even transform into poetic memories.

The Mind of Discrimination

Light gradually appeared on the horizon. The morning wind was very sharp. Without the protection of a sheepskin, the wind stabbed at her piercingly. She added grass to the fire and felt somewhat disgusted since she suspected there were bat droppings on the grass. After many years of cultivation, she had gotten rid of many problems—except for her obsession with cleanliness, which continued to accompany her as the shadow follows one's body. Grandpa Jiu called it the mind of discrimination and said it was one of the obstacles to attaining enlightenment. Grandpa Jiu had a guru who willingly gave up a king's throne and practiced cultivation as a beggar. He succeeded in his practices with everything, except for his attachment to cleanliness. One day, a Dakini goddess handed him a jar of sweet dew. He could attain instant enlightenment by drinking it. However, it had the exterior appearance of something covered with green mold. The guru frowned and refused it. Greatly incensed, the Dakini goddess scolded him, "What have you been practicing if you haven't even gotten rid of the mind of discrimination!" Then she added, "All the blockages in your chakras have been cleared, except for some pollution in your heart chakra caused by the mind of discrimination." The guru was very embarrassed. In order to rid himself of the mind of discrimination, he refused all the world's delicacies and ate only fish intestines discarded by people on the streets. He attained great achievement twelve years later. People called him Luipa, which meant "eater of fish intestines." The intention behind Grandpa Jiu's narration of this tale was obviously to cure Snow Feather of her mind of discrimination. Snow Feather understood it and had been trying, but her obsession with cleanliness persisted as if it had taken root. To a large extent, her unwillingness to marry was also related to her inability to endure men's dirtiness.

Once the fire flared up, warmth rushed at her face. After an entire night of tenseness, she felt exhausted. The sensation of warmth seeped into her heart and swallowed her alertness, so sleepiness took advantage of the opportunity to attack. She shook her head emphatically, but her eyelids were stuck nevertheless. Subsequently, she saw Jasper walking toward her as a beggar. She vaguely understood he'd been a monk in Nepal in his past life. Grandpa Jiu had also learned his techniques from Nepal. For practitioners, Nepal was a holy site. Just as she was wondering, she felt a cold wind charge at her. She swished her dagger, and something dropped into the fire. The sparks it created burned her feet. She opened her eyes and gasped. A red bat—cut into halves—was squirming in the fire.

She dared not sit there any longer. She waited for a while to make sure other bats weren't going to continue the attack. Then, seeing the sky turn bright enough for her to see her way, she tied the bag to her waist, clenched the dagger between her teeth, and felt her way down the mountain. The path was very complicated indeed. Although Snow Feather could see the big pine tree with the treehouse from a distance, it took her a long time to get close. She'd have lost her way for sure if she'd attempted it at night. She thought, "*I'll try not to travel again at night. If necessary, I'll get Jasper to come along with a lamp.*" What made her happiest was having found the pure-water bowl. Its presence meant that they would have light.

Jasper craned his neck and was watching from the tree. She called and thought Jasper would complain, but he didn't.

Snow Feather climbed up the tree and poured out the pile of things. She played down her frightening experience, which was typical of her. Jasper said, "Thank goodness you're okay. I was worried the whole night." Jasper felt the sheepskin parchment books and the Vajra bell. He was very happy. Jasper had always been partial to the ringing of Vajra bells, but he liked the books even more.

Chapter 31

Cripple Big Walking the Leather

They herded for several hundred years,
And made the entire wilderness withered.
Where are the sheep—the dream-seeking sheep?
Have you ever noticed
The desolateness of the string music?

Cheers That Resembled the Howls of Animals

According to *Historical Mirror of Forgotten Events*, the most important event at Diamond Clan, after Snow Feather and Jasper had disappeared, was the walking of "leather" by Cripple Big. It was a major event in Diamond Clan's history and has been ruminated on by its elderly residents for many years. I call it a major event because it provided unusual excitement for Diamond Clan. You know—everything enters the realm of legend, after the conclusion of reality. The line between major and minor events is very fuzzy in the realm of legend. Sometimes, the excitement about an illicit love affair can exceed excitement about a war.

The walking of "leather" by Cripple Big brought to Diamond Clan an enduring excitement. People always discussed it enthusiastically. Like "riding wooden donkeys," it was one of the "illustrious" events that gave Diamond Clan notoriety.

According to *Historical Mirror of Forgotten Events*, five pieces of "leather" escaped that night, but only two were recaptured. Braggart stamped his feet with fury and cursed others' mothers. Cripple Big stuck to his view that Jasper was responsible. Jasper's disappearance provided proof. But Braggart said, "Maybe Jasper was abducted by them!" Once he said that, all the villagers believed him and said, "Jasper was abducted by the 'pieces of leather'!"

Braggart gave Old Daddy Nine, the gatekeeper, a full whipping. Old Daddy Nine's oxlike bawls resounded throughout the front courtyard.

Monk Wu said, "Why beat him? Everything is preordained. There's no way you can kill a person destined to live, or save a person destined to die."

Braggart, however, complained, "You people have ruined the tracks by running all over the place! Otherwise, how the fuck could they escape?" He then blamed Cripple Big for not starting the work sooner. All the prisoners could have become leather by now!

Cripple Big, for his own part, was weeping beyond himself! The woman he'd just acquired had flown away, without his even getting a taste of her! He roamed the courtyard as if he were dream-walking and complained to everyone he encountered. After a few days, people ducked whenever they saw him. Braggart said, "Enough! Okay—can't you see we're looking for her? If we find her, she's still yours. If we can't find her, I'll get you another one!"

A clear track indicated that one of the "pieces of leather" went toward Brilliant King Clan. Braggart sent Kuan San and others there to ask for "it," but Brilliant King Clan said they hadn't seen "it." Another track passed through a forest, went up a mountain, and then disappeared after crossing some rivers.

The problem was serious. Now there weren't enough materials to make the ritual implements. Four people were required for completing the order. The hand drum stand required the tops of two skulls placed back to back. Two additional skulls were needed for the two skull bowls. The eight leg-bone horns required eight legs. The large drums required the skin of the chest and abdominal areas. Without wasting any of it, the skin of one person was only enough for covering one large drum. Should there be any blemishes on the "leather," such as a scrape, scar, or bruising, then it couldn't be used. Given all the potential problems, how would they justify themselves to the "above" should anything go awry?

Braggart bid Cripple Big not to tarry and to get started anyway with the two "pieces of leather" right away. He would think of something for the others. Knowing that any bruising, scraping, illness, or fright would affect the caliber of the "leather," Cripple Big dared not "break another fart" concerning the loss of the woman he'd just obtained. He wiped away his tears, grit his teeth, and "entered the battlefield." The misfortune made Cripple Big into a different person. He blamed the two pieces of "leather" for the loss of the woman he'd just obtained and no longer felt any sympathy. He only harbored hatred now. Having selected an auspicious date, he burned incense and presented an announcement through prayer, imploring his deity, his ancestors as well as the ancestral masters of the leather craft profession, to help ensure the success of this endeavor.

Cripple Big picked the well-behaved jujube-red horse—he was scared of the ferocious ones—saddled it, and tied a rope to the saddle. He then got a "leather" and tied his wrists to the rope, which dragged him behind the horse. All the villagers of Diamond Clan swarmed over and waited by the mountain path, wanting to see Cripple Big walk the "leather"!

As soon as he mounted the horse, Cripple Big felt himself a changed man. He felt most imposing. All the upturned faces looked surprised as if saying, "Ah! *Who'd have thought Cripple Big could be so impressive?*" Even Braggart guffawed and said, "Hey Cripple—I've underestimated you in the past!"

Cripple Big began chanting a song, only sung when a live person was used as leather. People couldn't make out the words, and the tune also sounded bizarre and unfamiliar. However, in the eyes of the villagers, the weirder something was the more venerable it seemed. They all looked at each other in utter shock. The look of awe on their faces was even more intense than when they listened to an old monk chant a sutra.

The "leather" could sense something was wrong. His face was full of sweat, and he looked around nervously. He was actually just a boy! Sister-in-law San wiped her tears and sobbed, "He still stinks of mother's milk!" Kuan San, however, guffawed. All the clansmen were also very excited.

Cripple Big performed energetically with exaggeration. He had truly embraced the role he was performing. Invoking ancestral masters to come down and unite with him so he'd possess supernatural abilities, Cripple Big felt he had become an ancestral master himself. It was said the first-generation master of leather craft could skin a man without damaging even a hairsbreadth of skin. The Gonpo owned a piece of human leather skinned by him. It was supposed to have been the skin of a great guru. One could become invisible, fly, and shift shapes by draping it over the shoulders. One could also hang it upon the beams of sunlight.

"Giddy up!" Cripple Big hollered. He drew a circle with the whip over his head, and the jujube-red horse began to move its hoofs. At first, it trotted. A few specks of dust rose and scattered slowly. "Giddy up!" Cripple Big hollered again. A flock of red-beaked ravens flew over and quacked in midair. The fun-loving flock made a ruckus.

Braggart laughed, "The empowered cat has become a happy tiger! Look at this Cripple Big—he looks grander than the county magistrate!"

The "leather" was dragged by a rope tied to the saddle and hobbled in the dust. According to the rules, the walk had to be carefully controlled so the "leather" would sweat—but not fall and scrape its skin. The jujube-red horse raised its head as it trotted. It wanted to gallop, but Cripple Big restrained it with the reins. It trotted along the mountain path and won resounding cheers.

"Bravo!" The cheers resembled shouts of beasts.

"Bravo!" The flock of ravens also shrieked. They knew the remains of the skinned man would be a delicious meal for them.

Dust enveloped the "leather" as "it" went down the winding mountain path created by cattle carts, leaving behind the crowd who came to watch the spectacle. Many people had only heard of this "trick": it had been many years since it had been performed. This Cripple Big had truly had his share of the limelight. Within a limited period, he'd actually been in the limelight three different times. The first was when he carried Mom on his back to be drowned. The second was when he made the wooden rods. And now with walking the "leather," he was almost a celebrity! His fame was only short of Braggart's and Snow Feather's. Obviously aware of this, Cripple Big sneezed with excitement—the way a horny mule would, when chased by a braying donkey.

"Hey—Cripple Big!" someone yelled.

"Hey—Cripple Big!" others responded.

The first person yelled again, "Mount it and run!"

It wasn't until they'd reached the bottom of the slope and come to the village's main road that Cripple Big mounted the horse. Wanting to appear savvy, he threw his legs wide apart. Unfortunately, however, the crotch of his pants failed to live up to expectations and split with a resounding rip!

"Hahahaha—" the crowd roared with laughter.

Cripple Big was greatly embarrassed. Nothing one could do—when one's down on one's luck, even a fart will rip the crotch! Old Mom had mended his pants many times, but there'd been no one to maintain them since Old Mom's death. Any wide movement would cause them to "laugh with a gaping mouth"! He squeezed the horse with his legs emphatically, and the horse bolted. He felt the rope tighten suddenly and rub against his thigh. Turning around, he saw the "leather" flush and sway from the rope's sudden yank. Fortunately, "it" didn't fall.

Cripple Big drew in the reins to get the horse to slow down. Although he felt better when the horse galloped, the risk was too high. It would be disastrous should the front or back of the "leather" be damaged from a fall if the horse was galloping too fast. Those parts were needed for covering the large drums. The leather for the hand drums was easier to deal with. Any piece from the thighs, shoulders, or buttocks would suffice. Of course, the skin of the right arm would make the best hand drum. According to the Eight Trigrams, this location was associated with *zhen*, vibration; it symbolized thunder and was consequently the best material for making drums.

"Whoa!" hollered Cripple Big.

Having been oppressed for years, Cripple Big had never before felt so thrilled. In the past, he was like a rope made by people trampling on grass, twisting it together. He was as impoverished as a penniless ghost. But today, so many eyes were on him. He doubted if even Braggart had ever commanded so much attention. He thought, *If only Mom could see me so glorious!*

"Mom!" screamed the "leather."

Cripple Big was missing his mom, but the "leather" called out before he did. Cripple Big thought it strange that a "leather" would also call for his mom. He'd almost forgotten that the "leather" was also human. The cry hit Cripple Big's heart like a stone.

The Stench of Blood

Historical Mirror of Forgotten Events describes Cripple Big's sentiments after he'd skinned the "leather." Highly detailed, the information was derived from interviews, the most thorough of which was about the skinning process. Different ways of cutting were used on different parts of the body. There were the Thirty-Six Heavenly Deity and Seventy-Two Earthly Fiend methods of cutting, each being different and exceedingly meticulous. The method selected was based on the specific type of skin found on the differently shaped bones.

What amazed me most was that the leather craftsman had to chant a different corresponding mantra whenever he used a different cutting method. For example, the most challenging aspect of skinning a live person was to stop the bleeding. If the bleeding couldn't be stopped, the surging blood would distract the craftsman. A well-trained craftsman wouldn't need to use a hemostatic drug since he could chant a mantra transmitted by his ancestors. The mantra to stop bleeding went thus, "Dark Mountain blood, Dark Mountain blood, I wield a knife sharp as iron. Let me see if the knife is sharp enough to cut through the sinews without drawing blood. Should I see a drop of blood, I will face the sun and kick three times. The wind is fresh today, I will hand the knife five times to Supreme Laojun." It was believed that, for this type of mantra to be effective, one had to chant it at least a million times in a calm state of mind.

The process of skinning described in the book was so bloody I've decided to shorten it, lest it ruin the readers' appetites.

According to *Historical Mirror of Forgotten Events*, Cripple Big felt nauseated until the dead of night after he had skinned the "leather." After the joy of being in the spotlight, he hadn't expected the work to be so sickening. He endured the nausea until he finished the final cut, when the queasiness became impossible to withstand. He ran to the side and vomited at length and continued to barf even after there was nothing more to puke. His mouth was bitter. He felt he'd thrown up all his bile fluids.

The work proceeded quite smoothly. People recalled that after walking the "leather" for a couple of hours, Cripple Big directed the horse back to the fort. The "leather" was hot and totally drenched by the time they reached the courtyard. Cripple Big had someone strip the "leather" and douse it with a bucket of cold water. Thereupon, the "leather" sneezed a few times. Such was the purpose of walking the "leather." The combination of intense heat and sudden cold quickly loosened the skin from the body. Cripple Big struck a vertebra forcefully above the pelvis with a leather craft hammer, and the "leather" collapsed instantly. For this, Braggart voiced his utmost admiration.

After the skin was separated from the body, Cripple Big took up his knife. "Mom!" screamed the "leather." Cripple Big suddenly felt weak and said, "I can't do it!" Braggart said, "It'll be easy after the first cut! The guy may look young, but he might have fucked that wife of yours a few hundred times already!"

This instantly gave Cripple Big courage. "How could he have fucked that wonderful, lovely wife of mine?" He gathered up his courage and executed the first cut.

Cripple Big didn't feel like recalling the rest of the procedure. He only felt nausea churning within. The terrifying screams of the "leather" resounded like rolling stones in the gully. Even Braggart was unnerved by the screams and had to stuff the man's mouth with cotton. Although it would have been easier to skin a live person than a dead one, Cripple Big nevertheless stabbed right through the man's heart.

The sooner dead, the sooner he escapes suffering! Cripple Big thought.

An hour later, Cripple Big had stripped the skin he needed. He placed it in a vat, with saltpeter and rice water. Although the man had turned into a bloody lump, he continued to scream in Cripple Big's heart. Cripple Big shuddered as he vomited. Kuan San led other men in obtaining the calf bones and skull. The rest was tossed onto the back of the mountain slope and drew a flock of clamoring ravens.

"Mom!" the "leather" kept screaming in Cripple Big's heart. The image of the bloody lump also kept invading his heart. Cripple Big shuddered and protested, "Please don't blame me! I was just a bridled horse that had to move when struck by the whip! If you want revenge, go after the 'above'!" But the delicate, terrified face of the "leather" continued to waver before him. It was most unpleasant!

Even more horrifying was that Cripple Big could never escape the stench of blood, which would invade his senses at any time. But when he tried to smell it intentionally, he couldn't. The smell constantly peered at him from a dark corner like a demon. The minute he became absent-minded, it would attack and bite him. Cripple Big would then vomit. Even if he'd only drunk water, he'd vomit out a bitter fluid.

"Mom!" he cried.

He remembered the "leather" yelling for mom too. He was, in fact, just a child—barely twenty-something years of age. If he were a child at Diamond Clan, he'd be resting under his parents' big tree right now! How did he become a demon? What exactly is a demon? Cripple Big had no idea. Judging from what Braggart was saying, demons are even worse than Brilliant King Clan. While Brilliant King Clan would do no more than robbing our water and killing us as enemies, demons can make us go to Hell! He'd heard they also plundered and snatched women. They'd strip the women, push them to the ground, and gang rape them. The moment he thought of how his "wife" had been screwed by the "leather," his anger surged. Immediately thereafter, he'd stop smelling the stench of blood and feel inspired to strip some more "leather."

Hatred would be ready to sprout in his heart.

But the effects of anger didn't last long. The moaning, terrifying screams, and stench of blood would reclaim his heart once again; and Cripple Big's soul would feel tormented once more. He thought of how the "leather" also had a mom. And no matter how hard he tried, its mom looked exactly like his own mom. So he became consumed with remorse and felt he had committed murder. How he wished he hadn't taken a life! Although he enjoyed being in the spotlight when he walked the "leather," he really didn't want to kill anyone!

The Abduction

According to *Historical Mirror of Forgotten Events*, an incident recognized as a terrible tragedy in the local gazetteer ultimately escalated into large-scale military strife. Although the history of military strife between the two clans went way back, the ignitor of this particular incident was Diamond Clan's abduction of "leather" from Brilliant King Clan. Of course, this was just the theory of some scholars. You know—often the so-called scholars are simply those good at making obvious blind guesses. If your guesses are shocking to all, you'd become a scientist like Stephen Hawking.

Of course, as a novelist, I wouldn't be interested in scholars' points of view. But I know, without their blind guesses, they'd have trouble maintaining their jobs. I am, rather, more interested in the feelings toward the incident by people like Cripple Big. Fortunately, the book contains copious details about human nature.

According to the book, during that period, the stench of blood would always attack Cripple Big unawares—it was most disconcerting. He wondered where the smell hid and then realized that it had already resided within the depth of his soul. Not only that, now and then, he'd see an expanse of scarlet red. It was blood. Heaven and earth, mountain and valley, everything could be covered in blood. "Mom, ah!" Most disconcerting! Cripple Big tugged at his own hair. *That kind of work wasn't meant to be done by human beings,* he thought.

The skin was placed in the vat with saltpeter. It wouldn't be tanned for a few days. However, there was still no news regarding his "wife," which was also most disconcerting. It was fine for him when he hadn't had a wife all those years; but to lose her, after he thought he had her, was most disturbing. Strangely, however, Snow Feather had the face of Degree Holder Ho's wife, and it kept on smiling at him.

Whenever he thought of women, Cripple Big smacked his lips loudly. Ever since he walked the "leather," his position had obviously risen in people's eyes. The awe-inspiring might he'd displayed would have been unthinkable for others. But strangely, no one made mention of his skinning the "leather." Cripple Big didn't feel like mentioning it either. He knew everyone must have felt stabbed by the scream for "mom" by the "leather." Everyone had a mother after all! Putting themselves in his shoes, no one wanted to be skinned alive.

Cripple Big slipped out of his room to talk to Braggart. After a long while, Braggart made a decision. "We'll have to nab the needed 'leather' from Brilliant King Clan tonight. Otherwise, we won't be able to make the goods ordered by the 'above.' According to the tracks' direction, one piece of 'leather' went to Brilliant King Clan—even though they wouldn't admit to it. Well, if you won't admit to it, we'll nab a couple of your 'bad lot' and use them as 'leather.' We'll nab whoever is down on their luck!"

Kuan San was ready with his rifle and gun. He called for a camel and took along a large bag. After they got hold of the "leather," they'd tie up its hands and feet, stuff its mouth, place it on the camel back, and rush back. Kuan San used to do this all the time. Back then, it was known as "kidnapping."

The three of them slipped out of the stockade and went along the river toward Brilliant King Clan. Night gradually approached. During that time, the nights had become strangely dark. The sky seemed to have been cloudless, but no stars were visible. It was as pitch black as a pot's bottom. There was nothing one could do about it. It was the sky after all and could be however dark it wanted to be!

Actually, Kuan San alone would have been adequate for the job. But Braggart insisted on taking part. It was a hobby of his. Whenever he felt bored, he would play with dogs and hawks for excitement. Nabbing "leather" would be so exciting—he wasn't going to miss this opportunity, of course!

The night was so dark they could hardly see the road. So they had Kuan San lead the way. This Kuan San had night vision and could see at night as if it were daytime. He held the camel's reins. Braggart rode the camel and Cripple Big held on to its tail. Thus, they proceeded without falling.

They arrived at Brilliant King Clan after a couple of hours. Brilliant King Clan was large and spread out. It was as if God had scattered a set of mahjong tiles into the valley haphazardly and dotted it with innumerable little square tiles, each being a household.

It was very quiet. People in the mountains went to bed early. The village had become as silent as a graveyard shortly after nightfall. One could only hear wind whistling through the valley—plus the sound of water, the most enticing sound in the world. It was so absolutely cool and refreshing it could purify the most anxious heart. The sound of the water reminded Cripple Big of Mom who died over the fight for water. No matter how one looked at it, she died at the hands of Brilliant King Clan; if the latter hadn't fought for the water, then Mom wouldn't have died. Cripple Big was overcome by a murderous sensation. He wanted to nab someone from Brilliant King Clan and skin him to unleash his hatred.

Kuan San stopped the camel as soon as they reached the village's entrance. Braggart jumped off before the camel lowered itself. Kuan San asked, "What to do? Should we wait here or enter a house?" Braggart said, "Let's go to the old landlord's and nab him at home!" Kuan San handed the reins to Cripple Big and said, "Wait here while we catch him!" And the two vanished into the night before Cripple Big could say anything.

The camel sneezed very loudly, which gave Cripple Big a fright. He pulled at its reins ferociously. Since the reins were tied to the camel's nose, the pull must have hurt a lot.

Within an hour, Kuan San and Braggart brought back a hemp bag.

Cripple Big had no idea the nabbing of this "leather" would cause blood to flow into a river in their village!

Chapter 32

The Sunshine of Early Winter

I knew I shouldn't say "until the sea has dried up and the rocks
   have rotted";
I knew—the mountains already have additional wrinkles—the sea
   has become a desert.
So what about heaven? What about the earth?
      We'll say "until heaven and earth have aged and become
      deserted" then!
By then—we'll let the intense flames incinerate you, the fox;
So that you and the practitioner you call the beloved
   Will turn into powdered dust of the dharma realm.

The Bloody Light of Fate

According to Ajia, Snow Feather always talked about her mom during
those days. I didn't understand why she was always talking about her
mom. She'd endured so many misfortunes herself, but why couldn't she
let go of Mom? Although her mom died tragically, Mom was nevertheless
already dead. Why punish herself with Mom's tragic death? Each memory
of her mother was a steel blade that stabbed her heart, you know!

When Snow Feather talked about the story of her mom that afternoon, I didn't see her as a Dakini goddess. I saw her only as a woman—a
lovable, pitiable woman. On that day, the evening sun shone through
their south-facing door and turned the treehouse interior a golden yellow.
It was through that golden yellow light that Snow Feather entered my

view. At that time, I had no idea that she would become the everlasting, unforgettable totem of my life.

During the years that followed, I'd always feel a tremendous poetic sensation emanating from her toward me. Although my personal deity is Diamond Maiden, ever since that golden afternoon, Snow Feather's image displaced that of the deity and became the totem for my visualizations when I practiced meditation.

It was during that instant that Snow Feather told me, "Come! Enter my time and space!" And I rushed into it unconsciously. As I remember it, that was when I felt the sensation of enlightenment.

However, I have always only half-believed Ajia's words.

According to Ajia, to Snow Feather, Mom's story was a veritable nightmare. The nightmare lingered on Snow Feather's lips. She said, "The nightmare followed Mom shortly after she crossed the Yellow River. Mom's name was Ping, the same *ping* as that in *fuping*, floating duckweed. Mom had said maybe her nightmare was caused by her name since she indeed became a floating duckweed that first crossed a county and then a province. After that, like a stone rolling down a mountain, she rolled into a huge mud pool despite her efforts."

The mud pool was unfathomably deep! No one knew how deep it was—and it was filled with indescribable horror. At first, Heaven was the problem—one's situation isn't encouraging when Heaven is one's opponent. Snow Feather said, "Ever since Mom was old enough to understand what was going on, Heaven had shown her a cruel face. It had the gloom of a flatiron, a cruelty etched with cold frost, and an unchallengeable despotism that surrounded them like a whistling blizzard. Mom said that was only the beginning of the nightmare! After that, her fate became overwhelmed by horse hoofs as numerous as dense raindrops, snowflake-like flashes of swords, and the sinister gaffaws of the god of death."

Snow Feather shuddered. She squinted her eyes and looked at the mountains, cramped together into folds. Fortunately, there were forests with birds, which injected some vitality into the desolation. The tree-house appeared homey during late autumn, with the sun shining warmly and imprinting a patch of its shimmer onto the treehouse. Snow Feather shivered, however, as she described the cruel flatiron-like face of Heaven.

"Why did they come here?" asked Jasper.

Snow Feather shook her head. She had no idea why Mom came here. Mom was one of the beans on a churning stone mill; she circled with the mill unwittingly. Torn bodies and crushed bones were the natural end result of such a situation. Mom was somewhat romantic about it. She claimed she was swept along by fate, which was an apt description. Snow Feather said, "It was fate that swept her along."

Concerning fate, Snow Feather smiled bitterly and said, "Mom had her fortune divined when she was very little." Hers was a bitter fate—the fate of a wanderer destined to suffer humiliations. The blind fortune teller smiled mysteriously as if he had penetrated a heavenly secret. Grandma's face turned pale, but Mom laughed and said, "Really? I don't believe it." She really didn't believe in it. She had feet and believed she could eventually walk out of that fate: if she'd just kept on walking. So she walked and walked. She experienced the perils of thousands of mountains and rivers until she finally walked into that evening of horror.

Mom said that the blood light had dyed the sky red. The cavalry of the opponent was a whirlwind that swept up everything. The cavalry feared nothing more than cannons. Cannon shots startled the horses, and when cannons were fired, the horses would disregard the will of their masters and charge haphazardly. Mom very much wished there would be cannon shots! But cannons were only an occasionally conjured-up word amidst the terror. The instant she thought of it, the swords' flashes were already visible and would continue to flash in her dreams. Even in her dreams, she wouldn't be able to escape these flashes.

Jasper said, "Why do people massacre each other? Why not treat each other nicely? We're only around for a few scores of years. Fighting and competing are so meaningless!"

Snow Feather said, "Mom said sometimes it is righteous to fight." Jasper said, "Righteous or not, people will die. Death is not a good thing. People have no right to kill others. Being human is an aim in and of itself. Humans are not instruments or materials." Snow Feather said, "Mom was hoping to save others!" Jasper said, "In fact, that which needed to be saved the most was her own heart."

Snow Feather said nothing more. She squinted her eyes and looked into the distance, without sighing for a long while. Jasper knew her mind was filled with strange thoughts. Ajia's mind was also like that. Although the strangeness of the two differed, they were nevertheless both strange. Jasper then thought, *Is saving mankind the same as bringing salvation to the multitude?*

Snow Feather said, "Back then, Mom had no idea that the real nightmare was yet to come!"

Sunshine

According to *Tale of the Goddess*, the sunshine was very bright that day. The roasted barley flour Monk Wu gave them was finished. Snow Feather went to Monk Wu's meditation cell secretly, but it was locked. She wondered if he'd returned to the monastery, or if he'd been nabbed to once again be struggled against?

Snow Feather seemed very tired. Her face was pale, and she looked as if she'd just recovered from an illness. Sometimes she would scream in the dead of night. Based on the content of her screams, Jasper heard heaven-stirring cannon shots, furiously splattering blood and the rolling of heads. Jasper knew Snow Feather always talked about her Mom because she missed her; so, at night she would enter Mom's nightmares. He couldn't understand why people couldn't coexist peacefully, given their limited time on earth. Why do they have to massacre each other instead? We are all people, after all! Since we are all people, we should be able to get along—there's no need to wield weapons.

Snow Feather didn't feel like arguing with him. She knew Jasper and Mom were from two different worlds. Jasper knew she was the same as he, in that they could integrate themselves into the mysterious dream state. What Jasper found most shocking was that this woman, who was as tough as floods and wild beasts in the daytime, would make him so ecstatic in dreams at night. He wasn't sure whether it was a blessing or the beginning of his downfall. He wasn't sure about anything. In those mysterious dreams, he would charge toward the woman like a parched traveler toward water. The woman would respond to him with the same kind of urgency. At that uninhabited mysterious site, they bit and tore at each other and then rolled and swallowed each other. He always felt remorse for his depravity when he woke up. He even avoided looking directly at Snow Feather, in case she had discovered his secret.

The sunshine was truly brilliant. It seemed to have been many days since they'd seen it. Their impression of the sky was that it was a gloomy flatiron, which rarely exhibited the brilliant smile of the day. It smiled gently and dispatched waves of warm contentment into Jasper's heart.

But Jasper knew all this was temporary. Neither Braggart nor the impending winter would allow them to prolong this dream. Of course, there was also fate. Jasper knew everything before him would ultimately pass away. Ever since he was little, his guru had told him everything in this world was impermanent, and he must see through its illusoriness.

Jasper thought, *All this truly feels like a dream.* He looked at Snow Feather in tattered clothes. She shut her eyes and enjoyed the sunshine for a moment. Although they had a fire going at night, a cold draft still continued to lick their backs. The day's sunshine now poured warmth and comfort into each and every pore of their bodies, like a warm iron. He remembered what Monk Wu had said, "Good fortune comes in large and small packages. The good fortune of a lifetime is good fortune; that of an instant is also good fortune. One has to learn to appreciate them both!"

Animal cries were heard from afar. Snow Feather jumped up and said, "Let's see if we've trapped something!" Jasper said, "We've trapped something for sure!" The two got up and went toward the base of the mountain.

The mountains far and near glittered in the sunlight. All the trees on this mountain were evergreens such as spruce, pine, and cypress, with different intensities of color. The water was still "alive." One could hear its splashes now and then. The water would "die" after a while; that's when the mountain would also die, and the birds would hide out in the caves for the winter. The valley would become dead silent then!

"We've trapped something!" shouted Snow Feather.

Grass Ropes

After cooking and eating their meat, Jasper and Snow Feather's bodies gradually felt warmer. The meat was delicious and so was the soup. Coldness was completely chased out of their bodies. The glittering white sunshine sported leaves, which had been tossed about by frosted wind. With the same color as sunlight and swept up by the wind, they flew all over the sky for some time before floating down and coating Mother Earth with a layer of color. Jasper descended from the treehouse and lay down in a pit. The two baby bears looked at him naively. *It's better to be an animal,* thought Jasper, *animals are peaceful and devoid of humans' conflicts.* Although animals also fight each other, they're never as cruel as what he'd witnessed earlier with humans.

Snow Feather still gazed into the distance with her eyes mostly closed. She was always looking into the distance. However, that distance was beyond her eyes—she was thinking of something beyond the mountains. Jasper didn't know what she was thinking about. I don't know what she was thinking about at that moment either. You know, although I'm something of a deity, I can only see through those deities below me or of similar status as myself. I couldn't see into Snow Feather's mind. Similarly, while a chopstick can detect the depth of a glass of water, it's not able to fathom the depth of an ocean. Snow Feather was an ocean; at least she was to me. I did, however, try to peer into her heart, and I thought I saw it. What I saw was a clear sky and a sea without any waves or ripples. You know what I meant, Jasper. Maybe you'd say what Snow Feather attained was the Bright Mahamudra. But no, don't say something like that! It was only a manifestation. She had merely integrated herself into illusory nature. Let me give you an example. Her heart was a drop of water, which had integrated with the sea during that instant. Do you understand now?

The two of them continued to perform religious practices, through meditation and visualizing their own deities. Jasper felt somewhat disturbed. He hated those dreams he had no control over. So he repented. He knew feeling lust in his heart was the same as violating his vow against lustfulness. *This is something terrible!* he thought.

The weather gradually became colder. The mountain wind was intense at night. Wind leaked through the treehouse from all four directions. They needed to find a comfortable home if they were to stay in Old Mountain. Although the bear cave under the tree was good, they couldn't very well nab it from the bears. The bears had treated Snow Feather very well, and their presence effectively prevented animals such as wolves from approaching. So the bears were essentially their protective deities. Although Jasper was aware of the viciousness of bear paws, he didn't fear those bears. Their innocent appearance was truly cute. He was, however, afraid of the python. He had goosebumps the moment Snow Feather talked about it. As soon as day broke, he craned his neck to look outside; but he didn't see any trace of the python. He didn't see the python when he was here last time to fetch Snow Feather's mom. He regretted having fetched Mom and caused her so much suffering. But if he hadn't fetched her, she might have died from starvation. This thought made him feel somewhat better.

Snow Feather said, "It's become very cold! The treehouse is not warm enough. We've got to find a good cave." Jasper said, "The bears' cave is quite good, but I wonder if they'll spend the winter there?" Snow Feather said, "Hard to say. Usually, bears like to move to a remote cave when they hibernate. But maybe this cave is considered remote if we weren't here. We can't very well kick them out." She told Jasper about the cave halfway up the mountain. The only problem was the red bats—they were terrifying.

Jasper said, "That's actually far better than this place. People are even less likely to go there."

Snow Feather took out the sickle she'd found, and got ready to cut the rustling grass, which had turned yellow from frost and wind. Singing a happy song, the grasses welcomed Brother Sickle's manifestation of affection. Swaying to and fro, backward and forward and affecting bashfulness, they cried in unison, "Please cut me first!" They swayed about like an orgasmic floozy and twisted their waists flirtatiously. The autumn insects living on the autumn grass made unusual noises. Jasper could tell they were singing their own funerary songs. They knew they'd become the same kind of refuse as grasshoppers after fall ended. They could only chirp for as long as the grasshoppers could jump. Therefore, they raised their voices and shrilled furiously. They were as desperate as a poet who'd contracted cancer and as aggrieved as a jilted lover. Their voices formed a huge orchestral melody, which filled heaven and earth. Jasper's blood vessels and urinary tract were also bombarded by this noise. So he also felt their rueful laments. He believed that sensation must have been as lonely and solitary as when Chen Zi'ang[1] wrote the lines, "Before me, I can't see the ancients; behind me, I can't see those to come."

Snow Feather cut the yellow grass, which emitted sounds of desiccation. Accustomed to fieldwork, her posture when she slashed the grass looked very harmonious. Both her deportment and movement displayed the essence of Snow Feather. There were many women in the village, but only Snow Feather radiated the essence of Snow Feather. Something like hot water stirred in Jasper's heart. He knew what this hot sensation was. He didn't want this sensation, but it surged into his heart by itself. There was nothing he could do about it. Just as he was unable to control his mother's giving birth to him, he also couldn't control this sensation's arrival. He desperately wanted to control his heart, but his heart wouldn't let him—no matter what. Often he could make use of the power of mantras to calm his heart a bit. But like a balloon that had been pushed underwater, it would pop up as soon as the power of the mantras relaxed a bit, and create a hideous noise.

Snow Feather wiped her forehead and asked, "Do you know how to make grass ropes?"

---

1. Chen Zi'ang (661–702) was a Tang poet famous for the short poem titled "Song of Climbing the Platform of Youzhou." The complete poem reads, "Before me, I do not see the ancients; behind me, I do not see those to come. Ruminating upon the expansiveness of heaven and earth; all alone, I weep grievously."

"Yes," answered Jasper.

"Go ahead and make one then. That cave has no door, you know."

Jasper immediately began to make ropes by rubbing the grass between his palms. This was a simple task everyone in Liangzhou knew how to do. They would all sit on the ground after harvest and twist grass between their palms; and a long rope resembling a rabbit's tail would appear from their hands. Snow Feather told Jasper to make the ropes as long as possible. She said, "The cave has many bats. We have to tie a net with the ropes to seal the cave after they've been chased out, otherwise they'll come back in. They maybe vampire bats." Crystal beads of sweat emerged on the tip of Snow Feather's nose as patches of tiny dots; her face had also become flushed. Its paleness had disappeared. It was good the paleness was gone since it made her look cold and distant and gave one a chill when looking at her! Jasper glanced at Snow Feather and emphatically restrained his heart. He went over and said, "Here—let me cut for a while." He took over the sickle and began slashing.

The grass had realized its fate by now; so it shoved their bodies and tried furiously to grow taller, like burgeoning sprouts. Mosquitoes flew before him like large birds; their wings vibrated and whistled like a gale. A marmot slipped out of its hole. At first, it raised its palms and chirped; then it looked at Jasper furtively and made faces at him. Jasper understood its concern. It was afraid he would cut the grass around its hole. The grass acted as its protective screen. Jasper thought, *What are you scared of? You've at least got your hole and no one is chasing after you! So what are you scared of?* He swerved to one side nevertheless. He thought, *Since I can't bring salvation to the multitude, let me at least satisfy its pitiable wish!*

Snow Feather was very good at twisting ropes. In a short while, she'd already made a large coil. The yellow rope exuded the smell of a cow's cud and was smiling at Jasper.

Snow Feather said, "Cut some more—we'll need it when we get there!"

Bats

The two walked toward the cave, carrying dried grass on their backs. Grandpa Sun had already begun to veer westward. They'd decided to smoke the terrible bats and anything else out of the cave first and clean it up before moving their household goods from the treehouse. Fortunately, Jasper didn't take the sheepskins, cooking pot, and other items with them when he fetched Snow Feather's Mom to the monastery because Mom said, "Let's leave them here just in case! Should anything happen, we can still come back here."

Jasper noticed the female bear, following them at a distance. Snow Feather had told him about how Mom helped it give birth and realized it was worried about them. He felt touched and thought, *Who would have expected animals to have better consciences than humans?* He gave the pile of grass on his back a few shakes. The grass had become light from drying out. It didn't feel heavy, although he'd spent a lot of time cutting it. Snow Feather wrapped the rope around herself and broke off dead tree saplings along the way. Gradually, an additional bundle of twigs appeared on her back.

When they came closer to the cave, Jasper noticed it wasn't very high, although the slope was very steep. Since there were grooves on the cliff for climbing, he didn't think it would be too difficult to scale. Snow Feather unloaded the grass and twigs and climbed up first with the rope. She lowered the rope and then raised the twigs and grass. She then got Jasper to wrap the rope around his waist a few times—just in case, before he climbed up. Jasper thought it would be an easy climb initially. But halfway up, he realized he'd had to use all his strength. However, he did manage to get up there ultimately.

Looking down, Jasper noticed the bear, which appeared shrunken into a black dot. He felt a warmth in his heart. He thought, *This is the difference between animals and humans. If the black dot were a human, then they'd have to look for another home—since humans would betray them; but bears wouldn't. One would just feel warmth upon seeing the bear now; there was no need to guard against it. Animals make the best friends. They will remember every bit of favor you did for them.*

Snow Feather took Jasper into the cave. It was dark, but the inside was still barely visible. He smelled a horrible stench resembling that of corpses; it was a most unbearable smell. When he saw the skeletons, he realized the cause of the stench. He thought, *People are so strange. They treasure their bodies ten thousand different ways when they're alive, not knowing that what they treasure will become the source of the worst stench.* If it weren't for the cold weather, he really had no desire to stay at such a stinking hole. But there was nothing he could do—one has to gather firewood from whichever mountain one happens to be at.

Jasper said, "Let's not go any further! Let's build a bonfire and smoke the cave for a while first!"

Snow Feather said, "Good idea!" She brought in an armful of withered grass, lit it, and placed some bat droppings on top so the fire would only issue smoke. White smoke soon engulfed the cave.

Adding some more grass and bat droppings to the fire, they retreated from the cave. Snow Feather said, "Duck to the side—be careful of the bats!" Jasper took off his jacket. He'd been wearing secular clothing and had packed his cassock away at the bottom of the trunk. He remembered feeling very sad when he'd had to take off his cassock. But Monk Wu said, "When the rock is too large, one has to walk around it! Endure it for now! I'm sure no matter how thick the dark cloud is, it can't shield the sun forever." Sure enough, he heard a squeaking noise, and some black dots shot out of the cave. If it hadn't been for Snow Feather's warning, the dots would have rammed into his eyes and poked out his eyeballs' bitter fluid, for sure! As soon as the dots stopped, a black mass stormed out noisily. The wind created by their wings splashed at him like water. Snow Feather said, "Be careful!" Jasper immediately waved his cloak furiously and felt it hit something. Sure enough, a few bats were writhing on the ground and emitting ear-piercing sounds of anger. They were obviously protesting the trampling of their sovereignty by humans. Jasper felt ashamed. But he heard Snow Feather scream, "Wave faster!" So Jasper waved his jacket until it became a windmill. In between the swinging jacket, he saw a swarm of bats as dense as the mosquitoes on a lake coming at them. Although he wasn't sure if they were vampire bats, the scene was still quite scary. Who'd have thought such small bats could be so daunting when they became united? Fortunately, although their wings appeared large when spread out, they actually had very little strength. As a result, they were easily brought down by the fluttering garment and reduced to writhing and shrieking miserably on the ground.

The ruckus increased in volume until the shrieks became a whistling whirlwind, which masked the garment's sound. Jasper felt his heart thump; he'd never encountered such a situation before. In fact, he was really frightened by such dark monsters. If he'd known about this, he probably wouldn't have "waded this muddy water." Other factors aside, the very thought that this cave had been occupied by such horrible creatures was enough to make him ill at ease. Suddenly, something slapped his face furiously, and a sticky fluid flowed down from it. It became rather itchy. He realized all the bats had left—except the large ones, which were charging at them! Cold, sinister lights flickered—Jasper sensed they were green. They were chanting life-threatening litanies, just like witches who hid in dark caves when performing a Killing Technique. Jasper also felt they had long hooked noses, the shape and characteristics of which resembled creatures in the forests of Russian fairytales. Fluid flowed from their long hooked noses and sprayed his face like splattering rain. With his furled cloak, he assailed the sinister, laughing bats—the way a ferocious bird attacked small birds.

Snow Feather, on the other hand, was very calm. She didn't flutter her garment aimlessly like Jasper. Using stillness to deal with movement, the minute she moved—a black glob would be writhing on the ground. Many bats collapsed among the grass at the cave entrance; some shrieking, some moaning, some staring silently at Snow Feather with cold eyes that emitted green light. Jasper could read their minds. They must've been saying, *What are you so proud of? I'll turn into a man in twenty years, and get even with you then!* Jasper thought he and Snow Feather would, no doubt, have a group of karmic creditors twenty years from now. If he should leave the mountain then, the folks reincarnated from these bats would certainly make life difficult for him. They'd seize his home and beat him. And then he suddenly wondered, *Were those who were against Snow Feather's mom her karmic foes?*

This thought seemed to explain to him the reason people fought each other.

The number of bats gradually decreased. Thick smoke continued to issue from the cave, but it no longer contained any bats. Snow Feather struck down the last black dot. Jasper heaved a sigh of relief. He found some of the bats dead. He had again violated his vows. In his dreams, he had violated his vow of chastity, and now during broad daylight he had infringed upon his vow against killing. He was again overwhelmed by frustration. *I am totally hopeless*, he thought.

Snow Feather knew what he was thinking. She said, "Don't feel badly. I'll perform a ritual to bring them salvation."

Revenge of the Snake

Just as they were getting ready to enter the cave, many snakes wriggled out of it. They were the kind with red bodies and round heads. Obviously not poisonous, they'd also been chased out by the smoke. Who'd have thought the power of smoke was that immense? There were both large and small ones, but they seemed to be of the same kind. Maybe they were from one family? The mountain harbored many families of snakes like this. Snakes were not considered snakes by the folks of Liangzhou. To them, snakes were little dragons. The presence of a little dragon in the home was a good omen and augured prosperity. Just like the fox, the snake is intelligent and will exact revenge upon those who have injured it. Of course, you can cut it into halves, but you might not know the magpie is the snake's uncle. The magpie would watch until you leave. Then, it will fly quietly to the severed snake, tie its parts together, and the snake will come back to life. The snake would then slip into your house in the dead of night, through the cat hole or some other place. It would slither toward you quietly, while you're in a deep slumber, and inject poison into your body. Of course, you won't realize this. But the next morning, when your mom uncovers your quilt, she would scream, "Heavens! How come my child is dead!"

This is only one of the ways snakes can exact revenge.

There are even more vicious ways! Have you ever heard of this other story? One year, a family planned to renovate its house. That night, an elderly man visited the owner through a dream. He said his entire family lived there, and asked the owner to delay dismantling the old building for a few days. The owner agreed to it. But thinking it was just a dream, the following day, he reneged on his promise and the work started before the agreed-upon date. They dug out several hundred snakes and killed them. That night, the owner dreamt of seeing the elderly man weeping and saying, "You've done harm to my family—I will also destroy yours." Having said this, the elderly man entered the womb of the owner's daughter-in-law. Later, a child was born to the family with a congenital skin disease and had scaly skin. He became a high official after he grew up. But because he was exceedingly stubborn, the new emperor who'd usurped the throne ordered the "extermination of ten degrees of his kinship." I'm sure you've heard the story. You can find it in the history of the Ming dynasty. That's right, he was the famous Fang Xiaoru.[2]

---

2. Fang Xiaoru (1357–1402) was an orthodox Confucian scholar-bureaucrat of the Ming dynasty, famous for his loyalty to his former pupil, the Jianwen Emperor, whose throne was usurped by the Yongle Emperor in 1402. While historically, the worst punishment given to ministers was "extermination of nine degrees of kinship" (massacre of the victim's entire clan and others related to it), Fang Xiaoru's stubbornness resulted in the only recorded case of "extermination of *ten* degrees of kinship."

Do you now understand what snakes are about?

Of course, Jasper didn't dare to attack the snakes. The snakes, on their part, didn't ambush them like the bats. They just lined up and proceeded forward, hissing; their skins rubbed against each other and rumbled like tumbling water. Sometimes they lowered their heads diffidently; sometimes they reared their heads and took large strides; sometimes they danced with their own shadows; and sometimes they strolled leisurely. They were smoked until they sneezed, but they continued to sing the song of the snake-kind silently. Jasper could hear its melody distinctly. It was as moving and tragic, as the songs of Cossacks in retreat. Jasper could hardly bear the thought of it. He thought, *According to Monk Wu, all living beings are our parents. So the snakes are also our parents! How can children rob the parents of their home?*

Snow Feather also watched the flood of snakes grievously. She might've had the same thoughts as Jasper, or she might've been thinking of something else. I wasn't able to peer into her mind most of the time, you know. But I could feel the waves of compassion from her heart, which indicated her heart wasn't as cold as her face.

When the last snake went around the corner and disappeared, all was quiet. The smoke in the cave also became thinner. The two of them entered the cave. Snow Feather found a rusty spade, with which she pushed the skeletons together and buried them outside the cave. The skeletons were naturally very happy. The folks of Liangzhou believed that burial provided security. Those with unburied bones were roaming ghosts. The folks of Liangzhou called them "wild ghosts with cracked heads." Jasper heard the skeletons sing cheerful songs of gratitude. He recognized a female voice among them and was quite surprised that a woman had come here. He didn't know a pair of lovers was here many years ago. They were paternal cousins—who were, of course, not allowed to marry—yet they stayed together and produced a lively kicking thing in the belly. Apprehended and taken to the Ancestral Hall, they were going to be clubbed to death by the clansmen the following day. But someone released them that very night. Guess who released them? Of course, you wouldn't know. It was the very same person who used the chicken feather notices to save the entire village but caused three deaths. You would never have guessed who it was. Don't ask now, I'll tell you later.

Jasper heard the woman singing a lively song. She must've been celebrating her entry into the earth. But the voice of the man was very sad. His melody was as mournful as the "Troika."[3] He knew the moment they were buried that he and his lover would have no choice but to be reincarnated. He didn't want to gain security through burial; he wanted to be a free-roaming ghost so the two ghost lovers could wander leisurely until the world turned to dust. But Snow Feather buried them anyway. She obviously didn't want piles of skeletons affecting her emotions. Jasper said, "Go! Reincarnate in good homes!" He also felt a responsibility to tell them not to reincarnate into Diamond Clan. You have to find a place where no one will "fix" you, harm you, or starve you. Jasper wished that he could tell them a specific location, but he didn't know of such a place. So he said, "Go abroad and look for such a place!" He saw the souls smile and float away.

Snow Feather buried the bones, and then scooped the bat droppings together and shoveled them outside. Women are truly talented when it comes to organizing a home. The messy cave looked presentable after Snow Feather's tidying up. She built a fire, pulled some mugwort, and added it to the fire. As soon as the pungent smoke rose, many bacteria screamed and died. The stench of the corpses also rushed away like mad dogs. The cave gradually became cleaner and even well organized.

She added more mugwort to the fire, and the smoke thickened. The two of them climbed down the cliff and brought over the sheepskins and other things from the treehouse. Snow Feather built a large bonfire in the cave for both heat and light, and the two of them tied the ropes into a net so dense that even the smallest bat wouldn't be able to fly through. They then sealed the cave's entrance with the net. The cave immediately felt homey.

Jasper gathered a lot of dead tree saplings and dried grass. He placed the grass on the ground and put the sheepskins on top of it. It was very warm. He broke the tree saplings into short sticks, laid them against the cave wall, and added some to the fire now and then. Having had no human habitation for a long time, the cave seemed chilly and was still cold even after the fire had burned for a while. Jasper surrounded the fire with twigs and grass. He then brought in some stones, pushed the fire into a pile, and circled it with the stones. It was like a fireplace.[4]

---

3. "Santaoche" is the Chinese translation of a Russian folk song about the miserable life of a coachman.

4. In Tibet and nearby mountainous regions, the "huotang," hearth, is in the center of the living room of every home.

This way, the fire wouldn't spread to the twigs and grass. But just in case, Jasper retied the "latch" of the net door, so it could be opened with a tug. This way, even if the fire should spread to the twigs, the two of them would be able to make their escape quickly.

Snow Feather curled up next to the fire and fell asleep. Jasper covered her with two sheepskins: one for her upper body and one for her lower body. Snow Feather breathed evenly and almost imperceptibly. Everything about her seemed soft; she spoke softly, and her movements were also soft. Snow Feather often seemed to be a corpus of fresh air, without any mass, when Jasper thought of her.

Jasper added some twigs to the fire and closed his eyes for a while. Although he felt tired, he was afraid of falling asleep because of his nightmares. That world was as colorful as this one. Often he couldn't distinguish between wakefulness and the dream state, just as Zhuangzi[5] was unable to tell whether he was Zhuangzi who had dreamed he was a butterfly, or he was a butterfly who was now dreaming he was Zhuangzi.

Dimly, Jasper saw an avenger approaching them.

---

5. Zhuang Zi (370 BCE–287 BCE) was one of the most famous philosophers of Daoism.

Chapter 33

The Bodhisattva

You said this is the road to Hell!
    I've always suspected
That you should have said Heaven.
Where you exist—the mortal world is Heaven,
Without you—Heaven will become Hell.
See—the minute you crack a smile,
    Celestial music resounds.

In Exile

Ajia, continue to tell us your own story!

In a vague moment of history, you were rushing toward Suzhou.

There was no need for you to prattle about the difficulties of traveling at night. I knew the melted snow had turned into ice and stabbed you whenever you fell, but then it would claim to be helping you eliminate bad karma. You heard its crass guffaws.

Although this road was fraught with danger, it didn't occur to you to go anywhere else. You knew what was called danger had no nature of its own. Beds are not dangerous, but people always die in beds. Because Suzhou was but an egg under a rock, it really wasn't that important. If one was fated to be pushed down, then they should stretch their neck and wait for it. Since the word "death" was already in your fate, then you should have simply accepted it with equanimity.

You must have thought of that woman. You definitely must have. I was also always thinking about her. Women are a good thing, although they are awfully troublesome. But you were right. Some things should be put aside when the time is right. Although things like fame, profit, and women clamor furiously in one's life, they'll all vanish without a trace in a few winks. It's better to take care of your soul! Guard your nobleness, hold fast to your solitude, and walk your path.

Haven't you walked that path for a thousand years already?

You walked toward your unknown fate, along the small path resembling a wandering snake. This path was known as the Hexi Corridor. For an indeterminable time and space in your life, you walked it more than a thousand times, leading camels carrying silks on their backs. One day a thousand years later, you'd leave Xikou along this road and sing a different song:

> In front of me is the Gobi Desert,
> Behind me is the Pass of Jiayu.
> On my sides are two mountains,
> Above are the skeins of the sky.

Did you know what the two mountains were? Let me tell you—they were the dark nights of antiquity. Humans were the occasional flashes of light in that darkness. But don't worry about it, just keep on walking. The road may be far, but it wouldn't exceed the length of your feet. So you traveled and traveled. Although you couldn't walk out of your fate, the process of traveling was the best part of it! Furthermore, you also had dreams!

I could discern the shame in your heart. It was the same as with all monks who'd broken their vows. No matter what your appearance, you were but a monk who had violated your vows. This you knew clearly. The outer appearance couldn't alter your inner nature. I could discern your feeling of shame; you had no idea that the punishment of the soul would be so harsh. But why be so serious? You were a man, after all. It was but natural for a man to pursue woman. She would have been there in any case.

You didn't believe that the "joy of fish in water" was sinful. That joy of the body and mind, and the ecstasy of two lovers—had never caused harm to anyone. So why should it be sinful? Why grieve and lament over it? However, I wouldn't use these facts to console you, as I appreciate remorse. It was the brightest light of the heart. The most shameful in this world was the shameless; I liked the fact that you were ashamed.

You kept on going along Qilian Mountain and the desert! You might have encountered many refugees along the way. They had lost their souls a long time ago. Those who had lost their souls were true refugees. The great tide of their bodies tumbled along, wave after wave, for a thousand years. Arriving from antiquity and moving toward the unknown, it was an unchangeable scene on earth! You must have felt pity for them. They were once your parents and must have nursed you during the great calamities of innumerable reincarnations. You discerned their look of contentment—they thought they'd escaped the butcher knife! Little did they know the wings of the god of death had already engulfed them! They spread their feet and went east, west, south, and north; but they could never walk out of death's palm.

You heard that Shazhou was occupied and that Suzhou was in a state of emergency. The monastery was under siege. You could neither go forward nor backward. But you'd better proceed forward in any case because walking was your fate. Beseiged or not, just go toward your destination.

Everyone's destination was certain—everyone was going toward his or her tombstone the moment they were born. It was an unalterable conclusion. Your case was the same. So keep on walking!

You only wished the process of your death could possess more brightness. About that, you were quite determined. I knew you really wanted to bring salvation to that butcher. That was a good idea—the world needed such good ideas. The workability of the idea would depend on karma; but the desire to do something depended on you. Because of this desire, your soul shone brightly. Only then did the dark shadow of the woman leave you and recede into the distance.

You might have been thinking for quite a while already. I always saw you frown and in deep thought during those years. You were always asking, "Why do people kill others?" I knew you were thinking about this topic. Just keep on thinking—you had nothing better to do in any case.

When you reached Suzhou, the siege had already broken. Heads spun like rolling sand; blood formed vast oceans. The swallows were chirping, as they could never find their way home again. The city of Suzhou had turned into a gust of foul-smelling wind. Three hundred thousand people had become bloody rain.

It was said that you practiced cultivation on that scorched land for twelve years. You cursed the crime and made a vow that you would become a protective deity after your death.

Ultimately, you accomplished your goal through the power of your vow.

The Truth

Stop asking questions, Ajia!

You are not a philosopher with a command of jargon. Maybe people would forget about you in no time. You don't believe me? Well, just take a look at how that desert was already licking around it. There was no cure for that big ringworm. In no time at all, even the word "Liangzhou" will be licked out of existence.[1] During the past thousand years, I've seen too many instances of impermanence. The world would change suddenly from red to black, without warning.

The hurricane of time would also blow you out of existence. With the passing of this group of people, no one would know of the erstwhile existence of Ajia. No one would know he'd been watching the expansive land of Liangzhou for the past thousand years, with compassionate eyes!

There'd no longer be space in people's hearts for you. A godlike but filthy stain would take over the territory you had once occupied, although you didn't deserve death. In fact, that era direly needed a deity from Xixia.

But you knew you had to leave. Don't ask where you went—those who were born came and those who died left. Coming and going were simply informed by the discriminating mind of the mortals.

Do you remember how, on a certain day of a particular year, a mad philosopher proclaimed, "God is dead!" That was when you realized that you would die, although you didn't deserve death.

You belonged to Liangzhou, which existed in the past. When Liangzhou ceased to exist, so did you! You might enter into history through my writings, but you will never be able to enter permanence. There is no permanence in this world. Of course, you've said one's "spirit" is permanent. But I don't know whether, by "spirit," you are referring to "benefitting the masses," which you've often mentioned.

So, what does "benefitting the masses" mean?

---

1. Liangzhou is now known as Wuwei.

Superficially speaking, it meant that Yuanhao did a fairly good job of "benefitting the masses" and sincerely meant to help Xixia. He wasn't a vegetarian and wasn't into drugs. Although Yuanhao was somewhat easily seduced by female charms, that wasn't a significant problem. What man wasn't, after all? In short, Yuanhao had numerous admirable characteristics. Yet, you still considered him a sinner. You judged the greatness of a person, irrespective of one's community or nation. Although you hailed from Xixia, your frame of reference was mankind and history, and things common among all sentient beings and the universe. Some people and ideologies had great starting points. But if they ultimately led to atrocities and violence, caused blood to flow in rivers, and brought disasters to mankind, then they were sinful.

Wasn't it true? Take for example Xixia's concept of "valuing dying through war and despising dying through illness." They considered dying on the battlefield glorious, while living to the end of one's natural lifespan was shameful. They brandished foxtails and wrapped them around the necks of those who treasured their lives. Did you know wearing the foxtail was the worst humiliation for the folks of Xixia? They'd rather die than suffer such a humiliation! So, they spurred on their horses and began killing and maiming as if playing a game, until they provoked the onset of even more atrocious broadswords.

My experiences of the past thousand years told me that those who brandished their swords would inevitably meet with more swords.

Ajia—do you know why I'm smiling? Yes, it's because I've seen too much ludicrousness. For the past thousand years, those with the eyes of mice unable to see beyond a few inches were always yelling, "Come to me—I have thousand-league-eyes!" They were known as either philosophers or thinkers. They clamored and created false truths. They knew the louder they clamored, the more they resembled someone with thousand-league eyes. Thereupon, the world would become crazy and enveloped in a plaguelike mist. Masses of men, who were infected and became nearsighted, brandished their swords with flushed faces, guarding the truths of those thinkers until they were buried by the sin.

They forgot the fact that "he who wishes to rule all under Heaven, will invariably be ruled!"

What a ferocious plague it was, Ajia! Just as you described, "Heads spun like rolling sand; blood formed vast oceans." Listen—you can still hear their screams!

Don't listen to the clamor, Ajia! Just zoom in on whether the truth was beneficial to all of humanity, regardless of ethnicity, nation, or race. Use mankind as your frame of reference. Truth should at least contain one word—benevolence.

The antithesis of which would be sin.

This truth even applies to those beyond mankind. Should this truth die, then the world is hopeless!

Ajia's Blood

Thereupon, Jasper began the writing of his inopportune essay. Having read many histories in the sheepskin parchment books in that Xixia cave, he felt inordinately moved and subsequently poured his emotions into writing. From a certain literary perspective, these jottings by Jasper could be eliminated from this novel since they were only tangentially related to the advancement of the plot. But they were vital to his characterization. It was through such writing that Jasper manifested his transcendence and surpassed his role as a common monk to become a humane figure of wisdom.

According to Jasper, around 1226, when the butcher had drunk and eaten his fill and was writing his memoir while burping, three hundred thousand living beings in Suzhou, a famous small city in western China, turned into pools of blood overnight.

All the cities in the west were swaying in a rain of blood.

Liangzhou, however, escaped the butcher knife of the Mongol soldiers because of an official's surrender. It was also due to this surrender that the ancient architecture of Liangzhou escaped incineration by the fires of battle—indicating that the surrender brought more to the city than mere humiliation.

The arm-waving of a praying mantis, against the irresistible force of an approaching hefty wheel, could only be termed stupidity. Why not move sideways and let it pass? Wait until transience destroys the cart before you push it away from the road. The heads of the commoners are by far more important, by far, than the honor of an emperor!

On this particular day, a man arrived at a Xixia cave named Diamond Maiden Cave.

He was none other than 'Saban.' His complete name was "Sakya Gungga Gyacan," and he was the fourth ancestor of the Sakya Sect.

Because of his expertise in the Pancavidya,[2] he was renowned throughout Tibet and was honored as "Sakya Pandita," meaning 'Scholar Sakya.'

By that time, Ogedei[3] had succeeded Genghis Khan as the Khan of the Mongol empire. His son Godan[4] occupied Liangzhou and was known as the Prince of Xiliang. Godan's general, Doorda Darkhan, led the Mongol forces into Tibet. They occupied Rezhen Monastery, massacred several hundred monks, and burned down Jielakang Monastery.

Sakya Pandita was sixty-three years of age that year. After receiving an aggressive letter of invitation, he made the trip of a thousand leagues to Liangzhou, despite his advanced age. In 1247, he and Godan, the Mongol Prince of Xiliang, reached an agreement, which was known historically as the "Liangzhou Meeting."

At that time, Mongol cavalries had already spread all over the earth like dense rain.

This was a famous meeting historically. Before this, Tibet roamed "far and wide"; after this, Tibet became part of China for the first time. In other words, Sakya Pandita led his people to surrender to the Yuan dynasty. However, this was undoubtedly an admirable surrender. Back then, the various territories of the west were vast pools of polluted blood; as those who resisted the butchering knife of the Mongols were annihilated. Heads spun like rolling sand; blood formed vast oceans.

Even the sun wailed when the Mongol iron cavalries kicked up dust, as they charged madly at all the weaker multitude of the world. Grief-stricken clouds covered the sky, and showers of blood splattered. Aside from the pulp of flesh into which the horses' hoofs sank, nothing else in the world could deter the speed of the iron cavalries' advancement.

At this moment, a Daoist priest was willing to be trampled into pulp. He left his quiet meditation room, walked against the whistling,

---

2. Pañcavidyā are the five categories of knowledge (Vidyā) of ancient India. The five sciences are: the science of language (śabda vidyā), the science of logic (hetu vidyā), the science of medicine (cikitsā vidyā), the science of fine arts and crafts (śilpa-karma-sthāna vidyā), and the science of spirituality (adhyātma vidyā). In the Buddhist context, a recognized master of all five sciences was afforded the title "pandita."

3. Ögedei Khan (1186–1241) was the third son of Genghis Khan.

4. Godan Khan (1206–1251), also romanized as Koden Khan and Khodan Khan, was a grandson of Genghis Khan, and administrator over much of China before Kublai Khan came to power.

foul wind, and entered Genghis Khan's tent, asking, "What crime had the multitude committed? Please stop the massacre!"

Genghis Khan, who must have been shocked by the man's courage, stared coldly at him at length. Heaven and earth stopped moving . . . finally, Genghis yawned and said, "Okay! I'll take it more easily from now on."

This "taking it more easily" meant the survival of more than ten thousand people.

Later, Kublai Khan[5] of the Yuan dynasty bestowed upon him the title of Changchun, the Dao-Manifesting Religious Head and Perfected One.

It was said this man held a contest of magical power with a Tibetan monk by the name of Phagpa[6] later. He was supposed to have entered into a bottle the size of a finger and gained the title of "The Old Celestial" because of this. The monk, on the other hand, used a knife to disembowel himself first. He then cut off his own limbs and transformed the five parts of his bloody body into five different Buddhist realms.

These details were very realistic. As the former was a Daoist, and the latter was a Buddhist, the magical powers they manifested reflected their respective philosophies.

But the Daoist was grander than the philosophy he espoused.

What he was respected for, during the last thousand years, was neither his title nor his magical abilities.

His name was Qiu Chuji.[7]

A literati by the name of Lu You[8] died on a certain day, when it was still the Song dynasty.

A figure famous in Chinese history for having written many superior "patriotic" poems, he was praised as a "patriotic" poet.

As early as twenty years of age, he sported the ambition of, "Mounting a horse, I strike the crazy barbarians;/ Dismounting the horse,

---

5. Kublai Khan (1215–1294) was the fifth Khagan of the Mongol Empire, reigning from 1260 to 1294, although it was only nominal due to the division of the empire. He ruled mainly China and established the Yuan dynasty.

6. Drogön Chögyal Phagpa (1235–1280) was the fifth leader of the Sakya school of Tibetan Buddhism. He was also the first imperial preceptor of Kublai Khan's Yuan dynasty.

7. Qiu Chuji (1148–1227), also known by his Daoist name Changchun Zi. He was the most famous among the Seven True Daoists of the North.

8. Lu You (1125–1210) was a prominent poet of China's Southern Song dynasty.

I draft a military document." At forty-two, he was dismissed from his official position for "consorting with remonstrators to rabble rouse and advocate vehemently for the use of military force." At eighty-two, he still displayed the heroism of "Greatly aroused the instant I hear the rumble of war drums;/ I am still able to pacify the Yan and the Zhao[9] for the state!" The melody of 'patriotism' ran through his entire life. How could Chinese literati not look up to him with admiration for the past thousand years?

One day, after he had touched the "pink creamy hands," viewed the "willows by the palace walls," realized that the "east wind was hateful," recognized that the "joys of love were scarce," and that the "years of separation" caused "a heart full of sad thoughts,"[10] Lu You was lying on his deathbed. He was able to let go and say "no more, no more, no more'[11] to everything; but the grief of not seeing China united, prevented him from exhaling his last breath with ease.

On that very day, the Southern Song capital celebrated peace with songs and dance, pearls filled the markets, mist and willows adorned painted bridges, curtains and kingfisher screens decorated the throng of one hundred thousand households. Look—the multitudes were all listening to the Tang poet Du Mu's[12] song! Two of the lines have resonated for a thousand years since then: "The women of Shang knew not the grief of a vanquished nation,/ Across the river, they continued to sing 'Flowers in the Courtyard.'"

The throngs were restless, the crowded audiences formed walls. Intoxicated, they listened to flutes and drums; chanting, they admired the mist and roseate clouds. It was truly the manifestation of great peace.

Because of a "traitor" named Qin Kuai, the heads of the people of the Southern Song remained safely glued to their necks, so they could

---

9. Territories around Hebei and Shanxi to the north, which had been occupied by the Jurchens.

10. These are allusions to Lu You's lyrics to the tune of "Phoenix Hairpin," titled "Pink Creamy Hands," the first refrain of which goes, "Pink creamy hands,/ Yellow-labeled wine,/ Spring colors filling the city, willows by the palace walls./ East wind hateful,/Joys of love scarce,/ One heart full of sad thoughts,/ How many years of separation!/ Wrong, wrong, wrong!" (Translated by James, J.Y. Liu in Wu-chi Liu and Irving Yucheng Lo eds., *Sunflower Splendor: Three Thousand Years of Chinese Poetry*. New York: Anchor, 1975), 384.

11. The last line of the second refrain of the above lyric.

12. Du Mu (803–852) was a poet of the late Tang dynasty.

listen to the famous "Flowers in the Courtyard" by the legendary female singer! Everyone swayed their heads, squinted their eyes, and hummed along in infatuation.

Among them was the mother of a martyred general surnamed Yue. She had just liberated herself from the grief of losing her son. She thought, *If that son of mine were still alive, he might have found a wife like this star singer!*

In her eyes, that cold martyr's plaque could never be as pleasing as the baby face of her son. An intense feeling of sorrow enveloped her once again. She thought, *If only wars didn't exist! My grandsons would've been quite big by now, and the land my son bought would've still been there. This business of suddenly being "Jin" and suddenly being "Song"—who knew what next? It's all so senseless . . . Dear Goddess of Mercy! Please help us to not fight anymore! Anymore fighting, I'll probably lose my younger son too!*

She must've heard of the two ignorant, narrow-minded, yellow-robed old ones who were wont to "view the sky from the bottom of a well"—the two so-called Xinzong and Huizong emperors. But since even Huizong's son ignored them,[13] what need was there for us commoners to worry about them? Better not "interfere with the internal politics of the others"! You be great emperors and just let puny me live out the rest of my insignificant life!

Ah mi tuo fo!

After hearing the prattling of that old mom, Lu You, who was gasping his last breath, retorted, "No way! How can a man die from women and wine? A corpse on the battlefield is better than one in bed!"[14]

The old mom wept again upon hearing the words "women and wine." Feeling she owed her deceased son particularly on this matter, she wailed, "My dear Doggie Number Two! My bitter-fated treasure! Your mom had wronged you in the past. I didn't want you to drink and go whoring because I was worried for your health. Who'd have known that you'd vanish after joining the army! My dear Doggie Number Two! If only you could come back to life—I'll let you drink all the liquor you want, chase

---

13. Gaozong (1107–1187) was a son of Huizong. He fled when the Jurchens overran northern China during the Jin–Song wars and became the first emperor of the Southern Song dynasty. He was apparently not interested in freeing the original emperors (his father and brother, known as Huizong and Xinzong), from the Jurchens and returning the throne to his brother.

14. These are lines from one of Lu You's poems.

after all the hussies you desire, and be a "groupie" type if you so desire. This old mom of yours would never nag at you again! So long as you come back to life, Old Mom will agree to everything! Just remember to take care of your health and not drink too much! This mom of yours will think of some way to save money to get you a wife, so you can have a son and eventually a grandson . . . What more does one want out of life anyway?

Such sentiments of the commoners had been despised, for a thousand years, by the war-mongering Lu Yous. They've even come up with a descriptive term for this point of view: "seeking ease without attending to responsibilities."

So, an even stronger emotion surged in Lu You's heart.

"Bring me my writing implements!" he struggled up and shouted.

Consequently, the poem "For My Sons," which was to be sung for a thousand years, came to be preserved on paper.

Although I knew all is empty after death,
I grieve that the Nine Provinces are not united.
The day that the imperial army pacifies the north,
Do not forget to notify me during the family sacrifice.

Lu You knew "all is empty after death"; the commoners must have felt the same way. Religious practitioners aside, ordinary people have always had doubts about an afterlife. But they all knew that their heads were securely placed on their necks when they could see and feel them, that each person had only one head, and that when it was gone, no amount of welding could prevent the "emptiness."

Unexpectedly, China, known as the Nine Provinces, actually stayed "solid" for a thousand years, separating and joining in turn. The green mountains remained, no matter how many times the setting sun turned red. The surging Yangtze River vanished in the east, its sprays having cleansed away all heroism. Whoever sat on the dragon throne would don that yellow robe and issue edits decreeing "corvée labor" and "military service." The commoners would continue to sing the song proclaiming that "one does not fear officials once the imperial grain taxes are collected." What right did one have to force a group of commoners, who were listening to "Flowers in the Courtyard," to raise butcher knives to kill another group also listening to "Flowers in the Courtyard"?

Whether that which Master Lu wanted to strike and subjugate were "crazy barbarians," or "the Zhao and the Yan," they were basically commoners. The "north pacifying imperial army" doomed for bloodshed, was also composed of the descendants of individual commoners.

It might have even included the younger son of that old mom!

The "patriotic" poet who, at his deathbed, wanted the heads of millions of commoners as the offering for his deceased spirit—didn't seem to love the commoners.

So, what, in fact, is "country?"

Is it based on territory?

If so, then how come there is no country in Antarctica where no one resides?

Is it based on a monarch?

If so, then why, when the State of Chu was annihilated, did its people remain?

Apparently, the people defined the country's existence.

So, what was the "country" Lu You so loved—the country that belonged to the muddle-headed monarchs of the Zhao family, for which Lu You, at his deathbed, wanted to use the lives of the people to snatch territories? Did it ever occur to him whether it was the "Southern Song" or the "Northern Song"—the state would ultimately be replaced by another dynasty? Even if he had piled the commoners' heads into a mountain, he wouldn't have been able to resist the rotations of the wheel of history. Those who'd suffer during military successes were the commoners; those who'd suffer during defeat were also the commoners. The most important thing was to allow living commoners to live happily.

Fortunately, the "Goddess of Mercy" ultimately protected that old mom. The "factions" that advocated peace eventually won. Although they were denounced for a thousand years, by what was called "history," the old mom was delighted. Her younger son escaped being snatched for military service—although she'd spent many sleepless nights worrying!

And then?

And then, just like the end of children's favorite fairytales:

"And then, he and the old mom lived happily ever after."

There was another person who had held positions successively through the Five Dynasties.[15] He served eight rulers, eleven emperors, thrice at the legislative bureau, and as a chancellor for more than twenty years. He lived through the Later Tang, the Later Jin, the Khitan, the Later Han, and the Later Zhou dynasties in the capacities of a general,

---

15. The Five Dynasties refers to the period from 907–960 when a series of short dynasties succeeded each other.

a chancellor, one of the Three Dukes, and one of the Three Excellencies. Since he was never perturbed by the vanquishing and annihilation of states, the histories castigated him as a treacherous court official; he named himself, however, the Old Man of Perpetual Joy.

His name was Feng Dao.[16]

This man who was "never perturbed by the vanquishing and annihilation of states" did care about one thing: the commoners.

One day, Feng Dao obtained a reprieve from his official post to return home to mourn his father's death. It happened to have been a time of warfare and famine. The people of his native home wailed far and wide. Thereupon, Master Feng Dao "donated everything he had in order to save his countrymen." After bankrupting the wealthiest household in the region, he "retreated to the wilderness to plough the land and carried twigs for firewood on his own back." And wielding a hoe and an axe, he began living the life of a commoner. Moreover, he secretly farmed at night for those who were unable to work and obtained joy from it.

His first boss was a cruel and ferocious warlord who executed his followers at the drop of a hat. Once, when the warlord wanted to invade Yizhou and Dingzhou, Feng Dao tried to dissuade him; he was subsequently imprisoned and almost lost his life.

Later, when Mingzong[17] of Later Jin[18] ruled as emperor, Feng Dao served as his chancellor for seven of the eight years Mingzong ruled. His "bible" was still "the people."

One day, Mingzong asked him, "We had a good harvest everywhere under Heaven—how do you think the people are doing?"

Feng Dao remonstrated, "Cheap grain hurts the farmers; expensive grain starves the farmers. Please remember Nie Yizhong's poem, 'Lament of the Farmers!' 'Selling new silk during the Second Month,/ And autumn grain during the Fifth Month;/ We get to cure the immediate sores,/ By gouging out the flesh of our hearts./ I only hope that the heart of the emperor/ Will transform into a bright candle,/ Which shines not upon the banquets with brocades,/ But rather upon the homes of the fugitives.'"

---

16. Feng Dao's dates are 881–954.

17. Mingzong (867–933) was, in fact, an emperor of Later Tang (923–936) of the Five Dynasties.

18. 936–947.

Mingzong said, "Okay! I'll remember it!" He then had it copied down and recited to him frequently.

Because of this, the commoners received unbounded beneficence.

On a different day, another emperor by the name of Yelü Deguang[19] asked him, "How can we save the people from all their sufferings?" Feng Dao answered, "At this point in time and place, even a reborn Buddha would have trouble saving them. Only you, the emperor, can save them now!"

Thereupon Master Yelü laughed and said, "Okay! Then I'll save them!"

Feng Dao's painstaking beneficial words were later condemned by historians as an act of fawning.

Such examples were legion.

An uncorrupt official, Feng was magnanimous, broad-minded, humorous, and wise. He drifted with the waves and preserved himself in order to care for the people. He was wont to remonstrate boldly with the intention of preventing war. Yet, he was criticized by the likes of Sima Guang[20] and Ouyang Xiu[21] as a man of "minor goodness" and a "treacherous court official": "An enemy in the morning could become his monarch in the evening. Shifting loyalties and varying words, yet not once did he ever show shame."

Treating the people as permanent and the rulers as fleeting, and slighting change for enduring benefit, what did Master Feng Dao have to be ashamed of?

Therefore, the Old Man Feng happily wrote, "I am filial in my home, loyal to my country; I serve my sons, my younger brothers, my subjects, my superiors, Heaven, and my father; I have sons and grandsons. Sometimes, I open a book; sometimes I drink a cup. I savor when I eat, I listen to music and I feel alive. I'm at peace with the era, and

---

19. Also known as Emperor Taizong of Liao (907–1127), Yelü Deguang (902–947) was the second emperor of the Khitan Empire.

20. Sima Guang (1019–1086) was a historian, scholar, and high chancellor of the Song dynasty. He wrote the renowned history, *Historical Mirror to Aid Government* (Zizhi tongjian).

21. Ouyang Xiu (1007–1072) was a statesman, historian, essayist, calligrapher, and poet of the Song dynasty. He wrote a new version of the dynastic histories of the Tang and the Five Dynasties.

know how to entertain myself in my old age. Do you know how joyful it is? Hence I name myself 'Old Man of Perpetual Joy.'"

"State" to Feng Dao was obviously not the Later Tang, the Later Jin, the Khitan, the Later Han, or the Later Zhou dynasties; neither was it the monarchs, or a specific piece of land.

"State" referred to the people.

They constituted the real "country."

Let the master of the capital change. One could even tear down the names of the various states and reigns. But what was important was the people.

Throughout the bloody rains and foul winds caused by the successive changes of dynasties, Feng Dao used wisdom and humor to repulse—for the people—the numerous butcher knives pointed at them, and thereby transformed the butchers' cruelty into laughter.

"I only hope that the heart of the emperor/ Will transform into a bright candle,/ Which shines not upon the banquets with brocades,/ But rather upon the homes of the fugitives."

This was a worldly interpretation of "Buddhahood."

Feng Dao was effectively saying, "If I don't go to Hell, who would?"

"What are you so proud of?" Ajia wrinkled his nose but couldn't hide his contentment. He knew it was his blood that flowed under Jasper's writing brush.

Technique of a "Xixia Curse"

Jasper saw an avenging curse-issuer building a mandala in a valley. The shape of the mandala was triangular; and the offerings included black flowers, black beans, and black sesame seeds. That evening, the practitioner performed a "Xixia Curse." He incinerated in the altar fire a prayer on a piece of paper, which contained such words as "Diamond Clan" and "Snow Feather."

Jasper was next to the altar fire when he saw everything. It felt like an unconscious flash. He wondered if it were a dream but was surprised by its clarity. It was as if he were right there. Jasper saw a plume of black smoke rise out of the gully and ascend the sky like a black dragon, a thick and strong dragon writhing furiously and roaring like a tsunami. Jasper knew the person was performing a killing technique and beseeching a protective deity's assistance. A huge grotesque demon appeared in the black smoke, but Jasper didn't recognize it. Years later, many deities were recorded in a book titled, *The Demons and Deities of Tibet*, but it didn't include this deity. Later, Grandpa Jiu told Jasper it was a type of demon that hailed from Xixia. It was incomparably powerful but wasn't an orthodox deity.

Both orthodox and aberrant spirits were deities with magical powers. What distinguished them was their hearts. Those with good hearts were orthodox deities, while those with evil hearts were demons. I'm sure you understand this. It's just like, after being trained in literary studies, what distinguishes a significant writer from an insignificant one is determined by the writer's heart. A significant writer has a big heart, while the insignificant one has a small heart. That which determines whether a spirit is a deity or a demon is the quality of its soul.

Jasper saw the angry, glaring eyes of the demon in the black smoke. Light shone from them the way it does from Grandpa Sun. The scene resembled a burning cloud, or a disastrous fire, or even more—the chamber of a steel furnace you'd see later. It was just like that. Imagine it issuing many mysterious lights. The deity opened its mouth wide—imagine too the horror of this huge mouth. Black smoke gushed out of this horrible orifice and swallowed the sky by the mouthful. It went toward Diamond Clan and swallowed Snow Feather.

Jasper screamed and woke Snow Feather up.

He told her about the dream. Snow Feather said, "I had the same dream. It was exactly like yours. It wasn't a dream. It was an avenger curse-issuer performing a killing technique." And she told him what had transpired at Luoshen Monastery.

Beads of sweat oozed out of Jasper's forehead.

He told her to visualize a fire curtain. "Let the shining star of your consciousness transform into flying Vajra scepters, to form a thick protective layer that envelopes you like an eggshell. You can also visualize fire on this wall of Vajra scepters. This is no ordinary fire. This fire is a hundred times as intense as the sun and even hotter then a kalpa disaster fire. Yes, that's what it's like. That's the fire of wisdom. It's capable of destroying the demonic evil. Do you believe me?"

Snow Feather said, "I've been visualizing that fire since a long time ago." Grandpa Jiu taught it to her many years ago. She was only worried that the curse would affect Diamond Clan.

"The curse issuer might've been more than just the monk I offended." she said.

It might have been the protective deity of Brilliant King Clan, or it might have been Diamond Clan itself.

In Jasper's visualizations thereafter, he included Diamond Clan in his protective fire curtain.

Chapter 34

Issuer of the Curse

The zither of my soul
Has begun to play,
The most famous tune, "Melody of Guangling."[1]
Although it knew dispersal[2] was impossible,
It hummed and sang as if weeping blood.

The Furious Retaliation

According to *Historical Mirror of Forgotten Events*, after Snow Feather coerced Jasper—it wasn't clear why the book used the term "coerced"—and made her escape, Braggart took his followers to Brilliant King Clan and got hold of a couple more pieces of "leather" from there. Cripple Big "walked" and skinned the "leather," carved out the bones and skulls, and began to make the ritual implements. Little did they suspect that they were seen and followed by an old bachelor who was guarding the forest; even worse, that the act would invite furious retaliation from Brilliant King Clan.

Historical Mirror of Forgotten Events recorded an interview with that old fellow whose narration was quite vivacious. He said, "Aiya! That

---

1. "Melody of Guangling" (*Guangling san*) is one of the ten most famous pieces of ancient zither music.

2. The *san* in *Guangling san* referred to noncourt music during the Han dynasty (206 BCE–220). The word *san* also means to "disperse." Here the author intimates the dispersal of anything that ails one through listening to the music.

Diamond Clan was so incredible! They tied up our men and put them behind a horse. And then the cripple mounted the horse as happily as a donkey in heat. He cried, "Deqiu!—that was his way of communicating with the horse—and the horse began to trot. The rope tugged, and Baldy Third Lord and Hoary Third Dad stumbled immediately. The pull of the rope on their wrists drew blood right away. I saw the two oldies frown, but they were toughies and never lost any of our Brilliant King Clan's face! Baldy Third Lord even roared and said, 'Hey—Cripple Big! You're just someone who eats lice eggs on dick hair—a sparrow on a trellis thinking you're grand!' I thought they were doing a demonstration parade. Who'd have thought, after the damned cripple paraded them around, he'd pour cold water on the two old lords and skin them alive!"

"Are you for real?" everyone at Brilliant King Clan asked. The old fellow said, "Of course! Actually one of my old girlfriends told me about it. She saw with her own eyes how the damned cripple took a knife and skinned them alive! She heard it was for making some sort of ritual implements! I heard screams worse than butchered pigs pour out of Diamond Clan's Ancestral Hall. I almost couldn't hold back my pee! I heard the skin was for making drums, the leg bones were for horns, and the skulls for making bowls!"

The head of Brilliant King Clan asked, "How dare they kill people?" The old fellow said, "I heard it was an assignment from 'above.' Some people said it was the regional government, some said the county mayor, some people said the provincial government, some said foreigners wanted them. No one knew, no one really knew! When the celestials fuck, what do mortals know? I also heard that the 'above' picked the material from prisoners, but they weren't careful and some ran away. They abducted from Brilliant King Clan because they didn't have enough raw materials."

The head of the clan said, "Enough! The bastards were obviously putting maggots into our eyes! So they have their 'above,' don't we have our 'above'? So they abducted us—are we to let them chop us? An eye for an eye!"

Many years later, a newspaper reported the results of the 'an eye for an eye.' Selections of the report were recorded in *True Records of the Curses*:

Selection No. 1: On X day, X month, during X year, the heads of more than a hundred slaughtered monkeys were discovered at the entrance to X Bay. The local police rushed there to investigate the crime on the spot, as soon as the report was received. They investigated the scene of crime immediately and continued through the night . . . At the forestry station of an ancient city, the more than one hundred monkey heads which had been transported back by the police were lined up for further sorting. Many of the staff members frowned while they looked at the monkey heads. This was the most serious and unusual case they had ever heard of or seen. The tops of all the heads were sawed off evenly. The monkey heads were ghastly; the scene was immensely oppressive.

Selection No. 2: The biology institute of X University proceeded with identification. Professor Liu of the institute came to the conclusion, soon after careful examination of the objects, that the heads did not belong to monkeys. They were in fact human heads. According to Professor Liu, "None of the heads belonged to monkeys, they were all human heads. There were those of the elderly and those of the young, those of males and those of females. In the young ones, the bones around the noses hadn't grown together yet; and in the old ones, the teeth were severely worn down." He then pointed to the teeth of one skull and said, "This was a man in his prime. He was so fond of cracking melon seeds that they created a small groove in his front tooth."

Selection No. 3: While tidying up the heads, the police noticed that all the tops of the skulls were sawed off straight across the bone behind the brows. The cut was smooth and even . . . The heads retained the painful expressions of their owners before death, with deep frowns and terrified looks. Some opened their mouths widely, others stuck their tongues out. Some members of the staff conjectured that some of the victims had probably been murdered—people dying normal deaths would not have had such strange expressions . . . In terms of the age of the heads, some were from many years ago, while others were quite recent. But judging from the saw marks which were quite fresh, the tops of the skulls were most likely all sawed off fairly recently. The fact that there were new heads among them indicates that this crime was still being perpetuated . . .

According to validated research, *Family Instructions of Diamond Clan* records that the skull caps that had been sawed off were made into "skull bowls." The other parts of the bodies were also made into various ritual implements.

Brilliant King Clan's Cellar

True Records of the Curses contains a record of that disaster at Diamond Clan.

According to the book, mutual massacring had existed ever since humankind came into existence. This crime was an inescapable nightmare that transcended state, region, race, culture, and so on. An expert proposed that the significance of studying what had happened during a specific period was limited—since such occurrences always happened.

The compilers of the above book interviewed numerous people. Various views emerged, but they all agreed Brilliant King Clan had carried out a bloody retaliation against Diamond Clan. The details of this incident will be the subject of another book that readers with karmic affinities for it will be able to read.

It was said more than a hundred people vanished from Diamond Clan. As it was noted earlier, the location where their heads were discarded wasn't discovered until years later in a mountain gully, when it became an explosive news item.

In the middle of a certain night, Cripple Big was also abducted by Brilliant King Clan. He vanished from Diamond Clan for more than three months, as if he'd evaporated from the face of the earth. He eventually escaped and came back to Diamond Clan on a dark night some one hundred days later. But his lips were sealed concerning what he'd done during those three months. It wasn't until thirty-one years and seven months later, a month before he breathed his last, that he revealed to one of the compilers of *True Records of the Curses* his experiences at Brilliant King Clan.

According to Cripple Big, he stayed for three months in a cellar at Brilliant King Clan where he personally taught ten young men the techniques for making human-skinned drums, leg-bone horns, skull bowls, and other ritual implements. Brilliant King Clan continuously brought the raw materials (i.e., members of Diamond Clan) to the cellar. To avoid publicity, they didn't let Cripple Big "walk the leather" the way he did at Diamond Clan. They came up with an even more creative method. They crafted a huge iron board, which was hung so there was space beneath. After putting the "leather" on the board, they lit a small fire underneath. At first the fire was barely visible, but then the temperature rose gradually. The "leather" would begin to sweat as "it" switched from skipping to running on the board. When at length "it" was panting furiously and "its" sweat was pouring like rain, a waterfall of cold water would crash down all of a sudden. According to Cripple Big, skinning this kind of leather was as easy as skinning a sheep that had just been slaughtered!

Under the threat of death, Cripple Big trained ten successors with superior skills, capable of skinning humans as effortlessly as grabbing one's dick in one's own pants. Later, they transmitted that expertise to their descendants. Therefore, skull bowls and other ritual implements became export items from Brilliant King Clan many years later. The only fly in the ointment, however, was the fact that the raw materials became rarer as time passed. Consequently, grave robbers appeared in Brilliant King Clan. They would slip into the wilderness, in the dead of night, to cut off heads and legs. When the body was from someone newly deceased, they would carry the corpse back to skin it. But since it was difficult to skin dead bodies, they eventually used sheepskin instead. The skulls, however, continued to be provided by grave robbers. They were the first group of entrepreneurs at Brilliant King Clan—who exported their products as far as Nepal and India and eventually to the West. Should you visit Southeast Asia someday, you might see one of the skull bowls of Brilliant King Clan at one of their markets. It would be gilded in silver and studded with pearls. You ask for its price, yikes—it'll shock you to death!

According to Cripple Big, he was abducted by Brilliant King Clan when he was in the toilet. It was a dark night—as pitch black as a pot's bottom. An ancient book said that murders are carried out on moonless days, while arsons are performed on windy days. How true! His voice sounded as jaded as that of Blind Immortal Jia. He had a constant stream of phlegm in his throat that made his voice somewhat indistinct. His feet were already swollen. Women worry when they have to wear headgear; men worry when they have to wear boots. He knew his days were numbered. Sure enough, a month later he became a lonely ghost on the road to the underworld. Humming a mournful tune, he roamed like a balloon on the road to Hell. Since he had no descendants to burn mock money for him to use as bribery, he had to endure all sorts of bullying by the horse-faced and ox-headed escort demons. Although he had no body, he could still feel burning pain on his back from the demons' whips. According to Ajia, he'd have to endure the evil flames of Hell for three kalpas for the excessive "killing karma" he'd accumulated when he was alive.

At that point, the experiences he'd undergone at Brilliant King Clan manifested themselves through his *alaya-vijnana*.[3] The first thing he remembered was the discomfort in the seat of his pants when he was first abducted. The sticky stuff there made him extremely uncomfortable. He knew there must've been a yellow mass there and felt somewhat disgusted. Like all bachelors, he hated washing clothes. But he was afraid of asking anyone else to wash them for him. During his most glorious moment, when he was making the wooden donkey rods, many women vied to wash his clothes, but he turned them all down. He was embarrassed that they would see the yellow stuff in the seat of his pants, which informed the most inerasable memory of his life.

Reminded by his *alaya-vijnana*, Cripple Big entered Brilliant King Clan once again. It was a huge cellar. He could tell it had originally been a tunnel. In those days, they dug tunnels everywhere. He saw many men in the tunnel and recognized some of them. They were the vanguard warriors in the past fights for water and the more recent armed confrontations. Their voices resonated "as magnificently as the mountains and rivers." Cripple Big wasn't sure how "as magnificently as the mountains and rivers" should sound, but he could feel it. He remembered collapsing immediately and two streams of hot, sticky fluid flowing down his thighs. This dulled the discomfort he previously felt from not being able to wipe his buttocks before he was abducted. He heard someone say, "Another coward!" Someone else hollered, "Get out, get out! Take him outside to wash off the shit, and give him a change of pants!" Then someone yanked him away to put the order into effect.

Cripple Big remembered being extremely miserable. Of course, it was an emotional misery. How he wished he could be "as magnificent

---

3. Alaya-vijnana refers to the eighth consciousness, the storehouse consciousness that was the deepest subconscious.

as the mountains and rivers"! He thought of all his past splendors, which glorified his ancestors—such as crafting of the wooden donkey rods and his "walking the leathers." Of course, carrying his mother on his back and tossing her into the river was also impressive, but it was done begrudgingly. In any case, he shouldn't very well shit and pee and become a laughingstock the minute he came to Brilliant King Clan! He straightened his back emphatically and cleared his throat. He really wanted to face death with equanimity, the way historical heroes had done; but the moment he saw the sharp shining spears, shit and pee were ready to gush forth! He had to use every bit of his strength to restrain them within their "cradle."

Cripple Big saw pieces of flesh and bones scattered about. He found out later that they were materials that had gone to waste from Brilliant King Clan's previous attempts at making ritual implements. On a head with yellow whiskers, he noted the trace of someone from Diamond Clan. It was none other than Old Daddy Nine! Before Old Daddy Nine became the guard for the Ancestral Hall, he'd been in charge of watching the clan fruit orchard. Cripple Big was always stealing fruit when he was a boy. Sometimes, he was able to fill his stomach nicely when Old Daddy Nine didn't see him. But more often than not, Old Daddy Nine would hide in the wheat field and tiptoe like a cat behind Cripple Big, who was throwing clods of earth at the fruit. Stretching out a clawlike hand, he would grab Cripple Big's neck or hair. At that point, Cripple Big would start to scream furiously. But no matter how hard he screamed, he couldn't stop Old Daddy Nine's other hand from taking off one of his shoes. And then, Old Daddy Nine would yell at him while he slapped Cripple Big's buttocks feverishly with the bottom of his shoe. Of course you've never experienced that sensation—let me tell you, when the bottom of a shoe hits the flesh, it feels just like a red-hot branding iron! Back then, Cripple Big would always yell, "Wait a minute, Lordy Daddy Nine! Be careful of my pants! Be careful of my pants!" Of course, Old Daddy Nine knew what he meant. He'd pull off Cripple Big's pants in no time and proceed to violently slap the bony buttocks with the bottom of his shoe. After the beating, Cripple Big would snatch his pants, run into the distance, and holler as he made his escape, "Yellow Beard, smoking a pipe weird!" Old Daddy Nine was fond of cracking melon seeds, which created a groove in his front tooth. This allowed Cripple Big to verify his identity as a member of Diamond Clan; this fact was also noted in a report many years later.

When Cripple Big saw the head of Old Daddy Nine, he thought, "Aiya—Yellow Beard! Who'd have thought you'd come to this? Did you ever think someone would cut your head? When you slapped my buttocks, did you know you'd end up like this?" It suddenly occurred to him that this might be his own fate, too, and he immediately became scared out of his mind. He thought, "I'm finished! And here I don't even have a son yet! There's been no excitement in my life yet, and I'm going to die a lonely ghost!" He really believed he was going to become a roaming ghost, which could only harass people now and then to get them to burn a bit of mock money for him to spend. Thereupon, Cripple Big began to wail loudly. Of course, he didn't want to cry, but he couldn't help his wails from surging forth. There was nothing he could do—it was just like his inability to restrain shit from gushing forth from his anus!

Someone hollered, "What the fuck are you crying for? Any more crying, and I'll skin you alive!"

Having skinned numerous people, Cripple Big knew being skinned was no fun; so he shut up. He thought, Better not try to be "as magnificent as rivers and mountains"! It's more important to think of a way to stay alive first!

In order to save his life, Cripple Big began to skin the first piece of "leather" from Diamond Clan.

Ajia said although Jasper and Snow Feather included Diamond Clan in the protective fire-curtain they visualized, they weren't able to change Diamond Clan's fate—no matter how they tried to protect it.

All fates are created by individuals. One's heart determines one's fate. The actions of Diamond Clan informed its fate.

Even if the compassion and power of Jasper and Snow Feather were as great as Heaven, they wouldn't have been able to transform a pile of potatoes into mangoes.

Chapter 35

Searching for One's Origin, or a Prophecy

I am no longer lonely,
Because my heart has reached Nirvana;
The heart of Nirvana is a silent pond.
The insensitive autumnal wind
Can't cause a single ripple,
     But the frog's croak was particularly loud
As if saying—
Go! Think of it as going for a ride in the wind.

In the Dim Evening

Ajia said, "During a certain moment of time in the future, Diamond Clan and Brilliant King Clan will both perish in an unexpected flood."

He said, "Jasper, stop searching for your origin! Face the future, okay?

Diamond Clan had many pasts, which one do you want to know about? Was it the Qin and the Han dynasties?[1] Was it the period of the Five Liangs?[2]

I don't know what happened after the Xixia; I was napping then. I just know a little bit about it, would that do?"

---

1. Qin dynasty (221 BCE–206 BCE); Han dynasty (206 BCE–220 CE).

2. The term Five Liangs refers to five local governments that lasted from 301 CE to 439 CE in the Hexi Corridor, consisting of different ethnic groups: including the Han, the Di, the Xianbei, and the Xiongnu peoples.

Back then, the desert wasn't called a desert. It was called a lake shoal. The camel pastureland on the lake shoal supported many tens of thousands of camels! Earlier than that, even that famous desert was the imperial court's pastureland. Read my book *Hunting Ground* if you don't believe me.

During a vague moment of the Xixia dynasty, I dozed off. You know my only weakness was fear of blood. The overwhelming bloodiness of the period scared me, so my mind became tired. I wished I didn't have a mind, but there was nothing I could do about it. Those who had no mind had to first attain the "nonego." But you know I'm a deity with an overwhelming attachment to the ego. Don't call me a spirit, I don't like that word. Although they are basically the same, please refer to me as a deity! Although the folks of Liangzhou also worshipped spirits and called the mediums for ghosts and spirits "shaman priestesses," I still prefer the word "deity." Sometimes, the folks of Liangzhou are so snobbish that one is nothing without a good title, you know!

Waking up from my nap one evening, I suddenly lost track of time. In other words, I had no idea where I was in historical time. I kept asking people thereafter, but no one could tell me. I consulted the pages of a history book but couldn't find the words I needed. Often I would doze off, even for an entire era, you know! But don't worry about it. The folks of Diamond Clan had no sense of history. They have lived the same way for the past thousand years. The only change was: no to pigtails during the Great Ming, yes to pigtails during the Great Qing, and off with the pigtails during the Republican Period;[3] that was all. Their hearts stayed with the Xixia and were "freeze framed" by the blankness produced by butcher knives.

I woke up from the twilight of that timeless evening. The sensation was hazy. It was like the layers of yellowed watermarks on an old painting. The people in the watermarks were fighting. Of course, the population was smaller then. But their appalling expressions were exactly the same! Many events were "freeze framed."

I like the phrase, "freeze frame." I'd been looking for an appropriate phrase for the past thousand years, until the film industry provided it for me. Even deities can't transcend their own period, you know. So don't laugh at me!

---

3. The Great Ming refers to the Ming dynasty (1368–1644); the Great Qing refers to the Qing dynasty (1644–1911); and the Republican Period was from 1911–1949.

In the watermarked "freeze frame" of that evening, they were fighting. In fact, they could be your ancestors! But one never knows because as you will find out, they were without descendants. They had no descendants. Don't interrupt and ask questions. They were without descendants, in any case.

The camel pastureland was very prosperous at the time and had as many as a hundred thousand camels! It was during the mating season. The male camels were chasing after the female camels—their paws kicking up yellow dust like a sandstorm. Camel mating rituals are described in *Hunting Ground*. You can read it if you're interested. I myself am too embarrassed to go into details. There were also workers who were doing you know what. They've been doing the same fucking work for the past thousand years.

Hey—don't stare at me! You know I'm crass!

As I remember it, that was when the calamity descended upon them.

Although I didn't know everything about Diamond Clan's past, I knew their future since their fate was determined by their hearts. No matter how hard they tried, they wouldn't be able to escape their fate.

Pay attention and continue to listen!

The Eyesore Long Mane

Go up along Big Sandy River, and then up some more until you reach the entrance to Big Slope; then you'll come to Small South Sea, which was connected to South Sea where the Goddess of Mercy resided. If we throw a female camel into the sea here, a flock of baby camels will emerge on the other side. Of course this sea was a wide expanse of water. I'm incapable of describing it better. The water there flowed down swiftly and nourished Liangzhou.

There were four treasures in Liangzhou at the time: the mountain-clutching bird, the gold-settling stone, the tiger-beating horse, and the black-cloud dog. You've already heard about the mountain-clutching bird and the black-cloud dog, so I'll just talk about the gold-settling stone, which I've seen. It looked very black—like a lump of dried cow dung. Don't laugh—treasures are all like that. Aren't you ordinary too? You look ordinary and wear ordinary clothes. What is extraordinary about you is your heart. Of course, the folks of Liangzhou, who don't know about hearts, would despise you. Who told you not to be an official instead?

If you were to wear the black gauze hat of an official, hey, you'd never need toilet paper again! Look at all those tongues—all waiting in line to lick your ass!

Let's change the subject. You know I'm no gossiping woman! Although I love to talk and my words filled the sky of Liangzhou, you were the only person who has understood me during the past thousand years.

You're right. They're nothing but drunken words and fart in a dream.

There was a dent on that stone—an ordinary dent, just like the dimples on Snow Feather's face. Okay, I won't talk about her. You can be so petty—don't glare at me! I understand. There was always some golden sand in the dimplelike dent. According to what you call science, this was possible, you know. We don't know where the gold came from, but it had been flowing down Big Sandy River for thousands of years. The river didn't dry up until much later.

The village became wealthy from the pinch of gold in the dent each day. The gold belonged to the public. The word "communism" didn't exist back then, but everything was "shared according to need" . . . Don't laugh at me—even deities must progress with the times! Later, the rich men thought, that dent was too small. If they could chisel into the dent and make it larger and deeper, then the village would be wealthier! So they bore into it and turned the dimple into a huge mouth. From then on, they never saw gold in the hole again!

As I remembered it, that was when Diamond Clan became poor.

The golden sand was only a legend thereafter.

Avarice always leads to the karma it deserves.

Let's talk about the tiger-beating horse next. I have seen that horse. It looked mangy but was able to battle tigers. There were many wolves back then. So many that their dens surrounded the village. Did you know there were many tigers around here too? Scientists didn't think there were tigers in this region, but they were wrong! There are tigers here—I've seen them with my own eyes. The tigers were numerous too and they were always attacking the livestock in the village. They also ate people. And then, the tiger-beating horse was born to rise to the occasion. It was very strange that this tiger-beating horse would emerge from among the feeble livestock—most incredible! That horse was as wild as you. Sporting a long mane, it was as fierce as a blazing fire. The tiger's roar would send the leaves whirling, and then it would attack like a tornado. Aiya! My scalp tingles from the thought of it! But the horse wasn't scared. It would give a resounding neigh, and its mane would explode like blazing fire. Each hair of its mane was an arrow, aiming to pierce the eyes of the tiger. So, the tiger was defeated, as well as the wolves and the jackals. All the wild animals that could harm humans were subsequently defeated by the horse. Accordingly, the village became incomparably peaceful.

What happened later was that the villagers considered the horse's long mane an eyesore. All the other horses had short manes, why should you alone have a long mane? The folks of Diamond Clan were like that, you know. One day in the future, they'll even try to cut your mane—just be careful! Therefore, the elders held a meeting at the Ancestral Hall to discuss whether they should cut the tiger-beating horse's mane. It was a heated discussion, but they all ultimately agreed its long mane was an eyesore. When all the horses of Liangzhou had short manes, what right had you to sport a long mane? Was it just because you could beat the tigers? Then the discussion session turned into a denunciation forum and the decision was one-sided. Aside from the opposition voiced by a few outsiders, the majority approved the decision to cut the long mane. They all claimed the long mane was such an eyesore that it was offensive! So, the mane was cut. Later, when the avenging tiger returned, the tiger-beating horse became its meal.

Don't deride me for being mouthy—who knows if the calamity that would befall them later had something to do with this? People harboring this kind of heart are fated to be short-lived.

So a voice would begin to call, "Is it open yet? Is it open yet?"

Look—calamity was smiling at them!

The Flood

According to Ajia, on a day in the future, the day before the calamity occurred, a shepherd boy from the village, who herded sheep on a river shoal, heard a strange voice. It asked, "Is it open yet? Is it open yet?"

I've heard that voice in the past. While it was barely audible, it was also extremely distinct. I smiled. I knew what the voice signified, but I said nothing. You know I'm not a mouthy deity.

The shepherd boy must've been surprised by the voice. He looked around and must have thought it was from a ghost. He remained silent because his mom told him to remain quiet whenever he heard any strange voices—because the ghost would follow a person's voice and snatch his soul. A person without soul would become confused and transform into a walking corpse. Haven't you also met a lot of people without souls? Don't laugh—I don't mean them! Sometimes one can't speak the truth. They are my worshippers—I need to eat too! How dare I speak the truth? Besides, I am, after all, Liangzhou's protective deity!

Of course, the boy dared not respond to the voice. This lasted for three days in a row. I was also feverishly busy during those three days, looking fervently for "unspoiled" people to become "seeds" for the future Liangzhou. I finally found them. They were some babies who were smiling at their mothers. Their brilliant smiles wavered continuously in my heart. I knew they represented "great beneficence." Evil hasn't had the opportunity to implant itself into their hearts before the arrival of the flood!

I told the ravens to carry them to their nests with their beaks when the calamity arrived. The ravens flapped their wings and said, "Sure! Sure!" Didn't I tell you they were the dependents of Mahakhala? Of course, they'd call me boss too should I decide to feed them! This is a secret of the Buddhist realm—don't you tell scoundrels about it!

One day, Mom baked a "pan helmet"—you can also call it a baked bun—and told the shepherd boy, "When the voice asks again today, you should break the bun into halves and say, 'Yes, it's open!' One has to let open what is fated to open." "Nothing can stop fate!" she added.

You've always claimed fate depends on the heart and that if the heart changes, then fate will change. You're right about that. But whether someone understands this is also dependent on fate. Billions of people have heard this, but only scores of them believe it. And only a few of them will try to change their fate by changing their hearts. As a result, these few are regarded as the wise ones by mankind.

This mother was also a wise one! Although she knew what was fated would ultimately arrive, when she saw her son waving his whip and herding the sheep toward the shoal, she still felt as if her heart had been stabbed by a knife.

I remembered it being a clear, bright day. Good stories tend to transpire on such days. Thereupon, the shepherd boy sang—it was the popular Liangzhou folk song, "Elder Brother Wang Herds the Sheep"—he sang it the same way you did. He held the baked bun to his bosom—he'd never seen anything made with such fine white flour before! And then he heard that voice.

"Is it open yet? Is it open yet?"

The child who was ready, broke the baked bun into halves, and hollered, "Yes, it's open!"

Thereupon, heaven collapsed, and the earth split asunder; water shot straight up into the sky like millions of wild horses. The flood shrieked thunderously. One push by the water, and the shepherd hit a cliff and became history.

The flood tumbled down and engulfed everything, carrying away first the men who fought and then the village, the camel pastureland, and everything else in the world. So you ask about their remains? Well, their dirty white bones will be found beneath the rolling yellow sand of the desert a thousand years later.

The babies who were smiling so splendidly were snatched up by the ravens and placed into their nests on the trees. Their brilliant smiles were the sole "great beneficence" in the world. Because of them, another kind of human got to thrive thereafter. Some claimed that the children were raised by ravens, which consumed human corpses and then nourished mankind. Others claimed that the children were raised by the shepherd's mother who was the only surviving adult.

It was said the earth that buried the corpses was exceedingly fertile. Plant a toe in the soil, and a fellow could grow from it! As the generations multiplied, a different kind of human would flourish.

What are you saying?

Yes—the flood swept away all the dust and dirt.

According to *Historical Mirror of Forgotten Events*, it was the dam across Diamond Clan's river that accumulated the water that destroyed that region's population.

Family Instructions of Diamond Clan, however, believed the flood was caused by an earthquake, which triggered the collapse of Big Buddha Mountain and dammed the mountain gorge. There was also another version that claimed the flood happened in the past rather than in the future.

Be it a legend or prophecy, the verdict was the same: Diamond Clan would be destroyed by an unexpected flood.

A Benevolent Thought

According to *Family Instructions of Diamond Clan*, a wise man was born to Brilliant King Clan due to a benevolent thought. Those who followed the wise man's revelation moved to a high spot the day before the prophesized flood.

It was said that the benevolent thought was recorded in *Nightmares*.

When Ajia was about to be executed, an old man appeared. He had white hair but sparkling black eyes. He said, "I am from Brilliant King Clan. I heard that you are going to execute someone who knows how to place a curse. The head of our clan sent me here to tell you that we'll take what you don't want. We need someone who can place curses to prevent everyone from being muddle-headed and falling asleep!"

It was said the wise child born from this wish was an incarnation of either Jasper or Ajia.

According to a record in *Historical Mirror of Forgotten Events*, one day an old female beggar—people said she was a manifestation of Niguma, who was also Grandpa Jiu's guru—went to beg for food at Brilliant King Clan. None of the villagers gave her any, except for the wise child. Thereupon she smiled and said, "For this baked bun you gave me, I will save your village. She then told the child to take off for the mountain as soon as the eyes of Brilliant King's statue at the monastery turned red, and not to return until the flood was gone. The child believed her and began to watch the eyes of Brilliant King every day. After several days, the monk there became curious and learned why the child was there. Amused by its ludicrousness, the monk decided to tease the child and colored Brilliant King's eyes red. As soon as the child saw the red eyes, he ran up the mountain screaming, "A flood is coming! Go up the mountain right away!" Some people believed him and went up the mountain with him. Those who didn't believe him drowned in the flood that night.

I heard that this was a prophecy.

I also heard that this was probably a fable.

Chapter 36

The Destined Illusory Bliss

Although I knew you were a yellow crane, already in the distance,
    Although I knew from now on,
Nothing would be left, but for the leisurely thousand-year white clouds.
    Yet I need to ask:
    When dusk falls,
Where is my destined native home?

Illusory Nature

Ajia became animated whenever he spoke of Snow Feather. Based on this alone, I knew he hadn't attained enlightenment. Of course, this should have been obvious. If he'd attained enlightenment, he should've been liberated a long time ago and wouldn't have been holding the minor post of a protective deity for the past thousand years. Many years later, after experiencing the most challenging moment of my life, I suddenly realized the illusory nature of things. I spent more than ten years after that to maintain it before I was able to become one with the realization. Through accumulation of my experiences, which progressed from "changes in quantity" to "changes in quality," I realized that many masters who were considered gurus hadn't attained true liberation—since most of their biographies record their leaving for a Pure Land after death. At the moment I attained illusory nature, I suddenly realized that all paradises are attachments. The attachment to an otherworldly realm enables the believer's consciousness to reach the time and space he or she yearned for. However, the real meaning of liberation is nonattachment.

A wisdom, which exploded while I was in a state of extreme calmness, told me: liberation is not possible when there is attachment.

I don't know what made Ajia so attached for a thousand years. What was the ultimate significance of all the cultivation he'd been practicing?

Look at how one can still detect deep affection through the tone of Ajia's voice. He said, "Snow Feather finally woke up from her dream. She also saw the sinister glares of those issuing the curse, but she couldn't tell whether the monk who'd stolen the golden rooftop was among them. Two people executed the curse; one performed the fire-offering, while the other served as his assistant. They were just two dim, dark shadows. The blurriness made them even more mysterious. It was from this blur that the green glares flared. They were executing a black curse, which originated in Xixia. Snow Feather knew that the karma-destroying fire-offering was just the beginning. They'd release an additional string of evil curses subsequently to alleviate their hatred."

Snow Feather cracked a faint smile. After all her experiences, she had learned not to take matters seriously. Naturally, they included life and death. She developed a rational understanding of illusory nature early; in other words, she understood what "clarifying the mind and seeing one's nature" meant early on. But her ability to apply the understanding to worldly affairs didn't mature until she was at Wangjing Stockade. According to experts, "enlightenment" refers to "understanding," *jianxing*. Real religious cultivation can only occur after one has attained enlightenment. All the cultivation practiced before enlightenment is to eventually realize the illusory nature of things.

During the years she herded sheep at Wangjing Stockade, Snow Feather merged various manifestations into her own nature and realized that the myriad entities in the world all resulted from karma. People meet because of karmic affinities and disperse due to the end of karmic affinities. The myriad entities emerged because of karma and disappeared due to karma. She'd transcended life and death a long time ago. But she also realized that the body was a great treasure for cultivation. It was indispensable for attaining Buddhahood, for becoming a grand master, and of course, for perpetrating outrages. Although it was but a "putrid leather bag" filled with various filths not to be clung to, it was still vital for attaining religious achievements!

Fire dissipated the sinister aura of the cave. A homey warmth unfurled gradually. They ate some meat. They always chanted the following litany before they ate: *weng-a-bei-la-hong-kang-cha-la-suo-ha*. After chanting it seven times, they'd blow air on the meat. The animal's consciousness would then receive salvation and be sent to Pure Land. But Jasper would still feel guilty whenever he thought of how the Buddha had sacrificed himself in order to feed starving tiger cubs. There was nothing he could do. Just like the monks in Tibet, who had to consume meat, they had to trap the food they needed for survival.

This Diamond Maiden Cave was truly a perfect place for practicing cultivation. One could hardly hear anything other than the chirping of birds, the wind, and the flowing water. The bats didn't bother them again; the cave seemed very quiet. Jasper had brought a sutra and a Tanka with him. Although the Tanka was only the size of one's palm, the painting was vivid and distinct. Jasper cultivated the Kundalini Fire, while Snow Feather cultivated the Mahamudra. They each performed their own practices, which gradually obscured for them the bloodiness of the mortal world.

After many days of practicing cultivation, Jasper's sexual dreams disappeared. Jasper discovered that sexual attraction was frequently created by strangeness. Once they became familiar with each other, sexual attraction turned into affection. When he first escaped with Snow Feather, even her light breathing would induce the burning of his blood, and an unintentional brush with her hand would create a furious thunderclap in his heart. But now, after many days of practicing cultivation, that feeling was no longer intense. Jasper noticed that Snow Feather possessed remarkable powers of concentration for meditation and frequently entered into the immense meditative state of a cloudless sky. Jasper could feel the peace her state brought to the cave. Monk Wu would have said the cave was empowered by her.

It was getting cold. The downhill mountain wind bellowed incessantly once night fell. It would have been extremely challenging without the cave. The cave was a south-facing, natural haven. There was no need to create a door; covering the entrance with the rope netting sufficed. Snow Feather sewed several sheepskins into a cover and used wolf fur as a mattress. Because wolf fur retained heat well, the side of the body nearest it always felt warm. Jasper began to feel somewhat intoxicated by the cave's peacefulness. *Paradise was probably no better than this*, he thought. But he also knew this peacefulness was temporary. There was no way Braggart and the others would let them go so easily. Even if Braggart failed to find them, they wouldn't be able to escape their other enemy: the god of death. The god of death is truly formidable. One can never escape its claws, no matter where one escapes to.

Snow Feather never forgot Grandpa Jiu's behest that she finds permanence; so she searched for it. It was always on her mind, but she could never find it. Everything before her kept changing—things were constantly being born and constantly dying. During a vague moment one night, everything that had transpired during the past few years appeared before her like a big dream! Despite herself, she'd always been coerced, by some force, to do what she might not have wished to do. She was always thrown by fate into difficult places and situations and coerced to and fro by an uncontrollable force. Yet, the permanence she was searching for never appeared.

She was always thinking about death after Mom passed away. Whenever she thought of her own eventual death, her heart would feel empty and numb; but there was also a sense of transcending the self and all things. However, an almost imperceptible unwillingness to reconcile with the concept of death nagged her. She couldn't help but wish she'd lived a better life. If she could live her life over again, she'd live the life of an ordinary female practitioner. She'd live like Grandpa Jiu—in her own space—and quietly practice the visualization of her own deity. She wouldn't learn martial arts, since many girls who didn't know martial arts seemed to live better lives than she did. She'd live her entire life away from the world and just fill it with mantras. She discovered that real permanence existed within one's yearning while practicing meditative visualizations.

And now, she finally had her own space. Here no one reviled her; no one "struggled against" her. She was away from all altercations. However, the flood of transience nevertheless steadily flowed eastward like a flood!

Jasper breathed lightly and only snored occasionally when he lay on his back. He usually slept on his right side, supposedly (from a scientific point of view) the best position for sleeping. It was also known as the "auspicious sleeping position." Snow Feather heard the sound of water flowing in the distance outside the cave. It was a beautiful sound, reminding one of the unceasing passage of time. She frequently meditated in the midst of the sound of water and entered the Flowing Water Samadhi.[1] Sometimes, she would think of her mother and, by association,

---

1. Samadhi is a state of intense concentration, achieved through meditation. Through practicing the Flowing Water Samadhi, the meditator eventually becomes unmoved by the constantly moving world.

think of the multitudes who'd been her mother. She shed silent tears whenever she thought of all the sufferings bore by these mothers. This was another visualization technique Grandpa Jiu had taught her in order to foster compassion. She remembered having a cold heart in the past. No matter how hard she tried to use thought associations, she was unable to melt the coldness within herself. But lately, her heart had strangely softened. She could regard all living beings as her mother without trying.

From Grandpa Jiu's perspective, she showed progress.

Couple-Cultivation

Crazy Ramblings of Ajia significantly recorded an important detail that transpired between Jasper and Snow Feather in the cave—their practice of the couple-cultivation. In other words, Diamond Maiden Cave was a key location for their attainment of transcendence. This practice was an exalted form of meditation, through what would have been considered sexual activity in the ordinary world. According to Ajia, it was through this form of yogic meditation that Jasper was able to cultivate Kundalini Fire.

Crazy Ramblings of Ajia is not clear about the essence of their couple-cultivation. It only notes that it was mysterious and profound. *Tale of the Goddess*, on the other hand, contains very detailed descriptions concerning the process of their couple-cultivation, the content of their visualizations, the requirements for the practice, and so on. This portion of the manuscript was written in Xixia script, using cryptic language. Even if I, the writer of this novel, were able to decipher the meaning of each word, I would still be hard pressed to fathom the content they symbolize.

According to Ajia, not all religious practitioners could perform couple-cultivation. The practitioners must satisfy certain requirements, such as having completed the *utpattikrama*, a yogic meditation of great wisdom during which the practitioners visualize having become a deity, and then they recite its mantras. There was also the requirement of being able to produce Kundalini Fire. Ajia liked to mystify people, you know, so I didn't know if what he said was correct. But I was able to meet Jasper through meditation later. And according to Jasper, the basic requirement for couple-cultivation was that one of them must have already attained an illusory nature. Because couple-cultivation was also known as the illusory bliss, only people who had attained the state of realizing the illusory nature of things could comprehend the meaning of "non-duality of the illusory bliss."

In the stillness of the dead of a certain night, Ajia vivaciously, while deliberately flaunting mysteriousness, showed me the contents of the Xixia writings. Since he hailed from Xixia, its writing was his strength; so I wasn't inclined to argue with him. His tone of voice was as enigmatic as the sound of a witch peeing. He stretched out his fingers and drew a weird symbol in the air, lest ghosts and spirits overhear our conversation. Although he claimed the manuscript's contents were exceptionally esoteric, I found them very ordinary. But I was nevertheless affected by the ominous atmosphere he created and even shuddered at certain moments. I couldn't help but feel embarrassed about my behavior later.

I finally entered Diamond Maiden Cave through the guidance of Ajia's words. Ajia claimed I entered that time and space through his help, but I had some doubts about that. However, those were just some doubts. I harbored those doubts because I was convinced my own powers of meditation and wisdom allowed me to enter that time and space, rather than the puny powers of Ajia—who called himself a deity. Later, I learned that Ajia's lack of clarity concerning Jasper and Snow Feather's couple-cultivation wasn't due to his modesty or desire for secrecy but rather to his total inability to enter that time and space. I was able to enter that time and space because I had attained the Mahamudra, which enabled me to enter any time and space. But Ajia could only see blazing fire and Vajra scepters around the cave. The brilliance of the dharma realm almost blinded him. He had to be "unclear" concerning their couple-cultivation since he was unable to enter the cave.

We know from *Tale of the Goddess* that the blazing fire surrounding the cave was known as the Diamond Fire-Curtain. Yogis could produce a fire-curtain for self-protection through meditative visualization. When I went to Tibet to visit my guru Grandpa Jiu one year, he told me about two ghosts in his village. Both ghosts had been practitioners when they were alive, and both were experts in meditation and the use of spells. But they didn't cultivate the Buddha mind; consequently, after death they became malicious ghosts who haunted the villagers. For lack of a better option, the villagers asked an accomplished guru to perform a ritual to subjugate the ghosts. Thereupon, the ghost who used to visualize fire-curtains when it was alive hid behind a fire-curtain. Fire blazed throughout the mountain—even the spell of the accomplished guru was useless on him. The ghost who could only use spells but didn't know how to visualize a fire-curtain, however, became exhausted from dodging the spell. No wonder Ajia could never cross the fire-curtain when Jasper and Snow Feather were practicing couple-cultivation.

When I exposed him, Ajia laughed in embarrassment like someone with an ulterior motive.

I've never practiced visualizing fire-curtain myself, since to me, all demons are also mothers. If they need my life, I will offer it to them as alms. Indeed, as a result, demons disappeared from my life. Whenever I feel perturbed, innumerable mothers would come to assist me. They treat me the way a mother would treat her own son—the way a girl would treat her beloved. This verified the truth of what Grandpa Jiu had said: compassion is the supreme armor. It was also because of this Ajia was willing to serve me the way a servant serves their master.

Tale of the Goddess records almost the entire process of Jasper and Snow Feather's couple-cultivation. I even suspect that the author of the manuscript was Jasper himself. According to Ajia, Jasper enjoyed writing even before he took the tonsure. After he became a monk, he was able to put aside myriad karmic affinities—except for writing. He always kept a journal. According to Jasper, the wisdom of words was the best assistant for propagating Buddhism. His point of view had been validated by the writings of eminent Buddhist priests such as Yin'guang, Hongyi, Hanshan, Fenggan, Hanshan, and Shide,[2] among others. But writing could also be a double-edged sword; it could damage as well as help. Too much indulgence in writing could also affect the attainment of liberation. Because of this, Monk Wu was none too pleased with Jasper's obsession with literature; but he taught him Xixia writing nevertheless. Monk Wu was convinced a tremendous number of artifacts were buried in Diamond Maiden Cave, many being sutras with contents that had been lost in Tibet and China proper. Should the opportunity present itself, Monk Wu wanted him to translate them into Chinese.

Tale of the Goddess explains the process of couple-cultivation in great detail. But I had to study it for several years before I cleared the mystifying fog. Although I had penetrated its essence, I'm not able to

---

2. Yin'guang (1861–1940) and Hongyi (1880–1942) were modern eminent Buddhist priests. Hanshan (1546–1623) was an eminent priest of the Ming dynasty (1368–1644). Fenggan, Hanshan, and Shide were Zen monk poets of uncertain dates during the Tang dynasty (618–907) and famed as the Tiantai Trio. The characters for the two Hanshan from the Ming and Tang dynasties are different.

explicate it to the public. I have no option but to declare that like a chopstick, I am unable to measure the depth of an ocean.

One night, in utmost stillness, I met Jasper.

He looked gaunt. His face was somewhat pale, and his eyes resembled the sky—a cloudless sky. I followed a path therein and saw a sea—a sea so calm that there wasn't even a ripple on it. Jasper looked at me silently. I knew, by then, he'd already attained enlightenment and become what we'd call a guru of great accomplishment. When I saw him, I also realized that he couldn't possibly have been the madman lying on a Liangzhou street since he was so pure and clean it seemed as though there wasn't a speck of mortal dust on him. He smiled at me and was most approachable. I felt he was my bosom friend from the moment I saw him. Ajia said, "Of course, you'd feel close to him—you were, in fact, he!" Fortunately I knew Ajia was a deity who always spoke without thinking. I never took him seriously.

I saw Jasper walking toward the cave quietly. The cave was hidden by greenery back then. It's scorched yellow now, since all the trees on the mountain had died due to the lack of water. That cave, which had once blossomed with life, had become a temporary abode for sparrows a long time ago. I used the word temporary because even the sparrows would be heading toward Xinjiang very soon. Liangzhou, which I called my native home, no longer had drinking water for them. Once, when I was traveling on a westbound train, a friend caught a sack of sparrows by waving a jacket. But the cave Jasper entered looked the way it did many years ago. The time and space of my soul was finally able to transcend the scorched yellow earth and maintained itself in that cool resting place. Vines wrapped themselves near the cave. They grew furiously while humming a swinging tune. I recognized morning glory, four-o'clock,[3] and ivy. Later on, ivy also covered the patio of my home. This hopelessly tangled plant always reminded me of the cave in which Jasper and Snow Feather practiced couple-cultivation.

Jasper entered Diamond Maiden Cave. Consequently, I too saw what it was like inside. Honestly, I was very envious of them—what a comfortable haven it was! The wolf, sheep, and goat skins produced a warm ambiance. The only disadvantage was the worms that squirmed on the mountain goat skins! I knew Jasper and Snow Feather lacked salt

---

3. *Dileihua.* Its Latin name is *Mirabilis jalapa* L.

when they trapped the goats; consequently, the skins couldn't be properly tanned, and worms proliferated on them right away. Snow Feather noticed them a long time ago. She could have salvaged the goat skins if she'd taken them outside and exposed them to the sun for a while. But then the worms would've died. Snow Feather was reminded of the story of the Eminent Priest Asanga.[4] She remembered that the guru practiced arduously for more than ten years, without success. When he left the mountain in despair, he met an old dog covered with worm-infested wounds. He wanted to save the old dog, but didn't want to hurt the worms by removing them with his fingers; so he licked them off with his tongue. Suddenly, golden lights flashed, and he saw Maitreya[5] glittering before him. *Let it be!* thought Snow Feather. *We'll let the worms make their home on the skins!* *Tale of the Goddess* records the prediction of a highly accomplished master that because of this karmic affinity, those worms would become Snow Feather's dependents after she became a deity.

Tale of the Goddess also contains several other inferences concerning the above. It said originally it would take fourteen generations for worms to reincarnate into human beings. Of course, each generation of the short-lived worms might only last a few days. After becoming human, they still needed to accumulate wisdom, good fortune, and virtue—which could take innumerable generations. However, because those worms were born in the cave due to a special karmic circumstance, and happened to have been able to bathe in the light from the performance of couple-cultivation by Jasper and Snow Feather; the worms accumulated wisdom, good fortune, and virtue instantly. They left their worm bodies straightaway and were reborn as humans in the mortal world. According to Ajia, many of the people who were born at Diamond Clan later were reincarnations of these worms. They were firm believers of Snow Feather and vowed to build a Niguma Sublime Abode. They firmly believed Snow Feather was an incarnation of Niguma and that she possessed the latter's benevolence. Ajia said her powers were so immense—after cultivation through seclusion, those with "superior root" (with innate ability for meditation), could fly to the Dakini Pure Land in the flesh; those of "mediocre root" could attain instant enlightenment; and those

---

4. Asaga (300–370) was a major exponent of the Yogacara tradition in India, also called Vijñānavāda. Traditionally, he and his half-brother Vasubandhu are regarded as the founders of this school.

5. Buddha of the future.

of "inferior root" wouldn't go down any evil paths. Although Ajia's words were confusing, I still believed them. Later, many others with karmic affinities also believed them and recited the Blessing and Empowerment of Niguma daily. They live peacefully and happily because their souls' Pure Land is in their hearts. Readers with karmic affinities will have the opportunity to meet them.

Permanence and Prodigious Bliss

I practiced a special technique for "corresponding" with Jasper for the writing of this book. During that period, I meditated and visualized his appearance and chanted his mantra. During one of our encounters, which was both dim and clear, he told me his mantra and agreed to be my "nonsharing protective deity." The "nonsharing" here meant that he alone would be my protective deity. Unlike Ajia who was the protective deity responsible for guarding all of Liangzhou (and later became a protective deity of Shangpa Kagyu), Jasper was my personal protector. Jasper's mantra was easy to remember, and he agreed to my recording it in this book. It is the Blessings and Empowerment of Niguma. He wanted me to propagate it throughout the world. All those who recite this mantra will receive great benefits and be able to see Snow Feather at Niguma's Pure Land. You may have encountered the following situation in the biographies of many eminent priests. A mountain god offered its mantra to an accomplished guru and promised to be his protective deity. That mantra was equivalent to the lifeblood of the deity. Hence, when Jasper transmitted his mantra to me, he basically offered his lifeblood to me.

Because of this karmic affinity, I was able to truly understand the meaning of the couple-cultivation by Jasper and Snow Feather.

It was an exceptionally quiet night. The cave was so quiet, you know; everything was swallowed by the night the moment it arrived. They used to be able to hear the barely audible sound of flowing water, but it was already winter by then; so the mountain became "fatter," and the water became "thinner" until the latter gradually died. All the clear water in Liangzhou originated in the snows of Qilian Mountain. Shortly into winter, the mountain would turn white. The animals would hibernate, and the birds would become sparse. Although one could hear the occasional cry of an eagle, these sounds had become quite rare. Jasper entered into "pure brightness" in the ultimate quietness. He was bathed in the mysterious light of wisdom.

This was when a young woman approached him. She didn't tell him her name, but he knew she was none other than Niguma. She led him out of the cave to a miraculous place. Jasper remembered it being a cave as well. He found out later that it was the Sitavana Pure Land. It was said there were twenty-four such sacred places.

Jasper floated toward permanence in the "dense" brightness. Although he knew permanence didn't exist in the world, he still considered that location to be permanent. He was unable to accept the truth regarding permanence. Just like Snow Feather, Jasper was also searching for permanence. So he regarded that cave as permanent. Later, my guru told me that even the Sitavana Pure Land was impermanent; it was just a "transfer station." Those who enter the holy land could practice esoteric techniques under the guidance of Niguma and attain Nirvana very quickly.

"Consequently," I asked, "is Nirvana permanent?"

I remembered Ajia asking the same question. Ajia had said, "If Nirvana is permanent, then what the Buddha said about all actions having no permanence and all dharmas having no ego wouldn't be the absolute truth. But if Nirvana is also impermanent, then what does one practice cultivation for?"

The guru didn't answer my question. The Buddha did not answer this question either, which had been posed by a nonbeliever more than two thousand years ago. It was one of the questions that the Buddha chose to ignore.

Jasper chose permanence, nevertheless. The Jasper of this moment was merely a vehicle for me, a representation of myself. I needed permanence. Mankind needs permanence. The greatest perplexity of my life was the irreconcilable contradiction between the permanence I was seeking and the illusory transience of the world. As a consequence, I'd toss away writing now and then because in the face of the ephemerality of existence, I failed to find the ultimate meaning of writing.

I walked toward permanence. I followed the young woman and approached ever closer to permanence with each step. I discovered that the cave of permanence in my heart didn't look gorgeous. It was just an earthly cave, far from the beauty of the paradise described by the ancestors. It was so ordinary that it didn't seem to be a sacred space.

But I knew it was precisely this type of place that was probably a holy site. A real holy land does not need a false appearance.

I saw a group of people walking toward a young woman. I couldn't tell what they were doing. I felt they were waiting for empowerment by Niguma. All those who were empowered turned into a bright light. It was said they would reach the Heaven of the Buddhist Realm populated by Bodhisattvas who had attained the eighth *bhumi*[6] and above. In other words, all those who turned into light became Bodhisattvas of the eighth *bhumi*. Everything felt like a dream. My consciousness wasn't distinct, but I still approached the silvery-white young woman gradually.

I clearly knew she was Niguma, who was also Diamond Maiden. The two of them were two sides of the same brocade.

Niguma turned around. I thought she would smile, but she didn't. She just looked at me, and I could feel her smile. She spoke volumes but not through her mouth. The words flowed directly from her mind to mine. I felt she was even more like a mother. Look—she truly turned into a mother. I dashed toward her like a child who'd been lost for many years.

I was immediately swept up by a mysterious illusory bliss. It was one of the transformative experiences of my life. That illusory bliss became my breath for the rest of my life. Later, my guru told me what I had entered was the brightness of the Mahamudra. I recorded the sensation in my *Mahamudra: Essence and Practice.*

> Devoid of avarice and desire, my entire body was swept up
> by a warm joy, wavering in illusory-brightness. All my pores
> were dissolved by the mysterious illusory bliss. The sensation
> was the most intense in my abdomen. It felt like a burning
> fire, but without the sensation of being scorched. The fire
> surged comfortably, one wave after the other, like angry
> billows. It was as if a mysterious force was untying all the
> knots in my chakras. I never thought such a sensation could
> have existed in this world. This could never be described in
> human language . . . Gradually, it was as if a great fire of bliss
> also filled the entire universe. The fire burned away all outer

---

6. The Sanskrit term *bhūmi* literally means "ground" or "foundation." Each stage represents a level of attainment and serves as a basis for the next one. Each level marks a definite advancement in one's training that is accompanied by progressively greater power and wisdom.

manifestations. Even I disappeared without a trace from the burning. Everything between heaven and earth evaporated except for great illusion, prodigious bliss, and brightness. I immersed myself in the surging illusory bliss; devoid of joy, devoid of sorrow, without taking, without giving . . .

The Great Exchange of the Nuptial Wine

Crazy Ramblings of Ajia depicts most poetically the process of couple-cultivation between Snow Feather and Jasper. However, the process resembled conventional secular sexual bliss the way he described it. There was nothing anyone could do about it. Just as one can't transform a monkey into a human being, you can't expect a worldly deity to possess the enlightened wisdom from beyond this world. However, Ajia's depictions do nevertheless provide a trace of information concerning that other world.

According to Ajia, the first actual contact in the flesh of Jasper and Snow Feather occurred on a brilliantly sunny afternoon. By then, they had already satisfied the prerequisites for practicing couple's meditation. I've always doubted Ajia's words, however, as he'd after all never attained enlightenment. His ability to verify Snow Feather's level of attainment was an unknown factor. As I've said, one can't use a chopstick to fathom the depth of an ocean.

The writer of the biography of Yeshe Tsogyal[7] was the Vajra Warrior who practiced couple-cultivation with her. Hailing from Nepal, he was a Vajra Warrior whose attainment of Buddhahood was predicted by Yeshe Tsogyal, also known as Guru Rinpoche. Yeshe Tsogyal bought his freedom from his master, using an amount of gold equivalent to his own weight. Because of their closeness, he was often even insolent toward her. After Yeshe Tsogyal merged into the dharma realm, the Vajra Warrior survived for a long time in the mortal world and eventually recorded her wisdom-filled life. Consequently, I suspect the person who wrote the essay about Snow Feather was Jasper—because many of the details

7. Yeshe Tsogyal (757–817) whose name meant "Victorious Ocean of Wisdom" was also known as Guru Rinpoche and Guru Lotus Born. Founder of the Nyingma tradition of Tibetan Buddhism, she was an incarnation of Diamond Maiden and Saraswati Goddess.

described therein couldn't have been imagined by someone who hadn't actually experienced them.

Time is always freeze-framed in many memories. Hence, Ajia always considered himself a god of memory, full of memories of that land. Ajia was the one who told me many of Jasper's thoughts. But I knew the Jasper Ajia spoke of—was the Jasper of Ajia's mind. Whether he was the real Jasper would remain unknown.

According to Ajia, Jasper and Snow Feather came to the entrance of the cave on a bright, sunny day. The warm Grandpa Sun looked at them. I believe in the truthfulness of this detail, since only during this moment could Ajia have glimpsed Snow Feather. As I've mentioned, their locality of meditation would have been blocked by a curtain of fire from Ajia. He could try to edge closer to prevent being blinded by the glare, but then he'd risk the danger of being incinerated; this is because other than holy persons who possessed adequate enlightened wisdom, no gods or spirits of the mortal world could penetrate the fire-curtain created by the fire of wisdom.

According to Ajia, Snow Feather was still talking about her mother that day. She wept. I expressed doubt that enlightened beings would still shed tears, but Ajia said, "Of course, they would!" He gave many examples of enlightened gurus who shed tears now and then. He said they not only shed tears, but they also wailed. The intense compassion which filled their hearts would draw out the tears that represented their emotions. Ajia said, "True cultivation of wisdom would only make the heart more and more tender. That which makes the heart harder has to be heterodox curses."

Jasper told Snow Feather that he was a practitioner during the time of the Xixia, and she was a girl who used to bring food to him then. It was through her continuous bringing of food and water that he gradually distanced himself from stupidity, avarice, and hatred, and became closer and closer to coolness.

When Snow Feather heard this, tears poured down her face.

You might not have ever seen Snow Feather crying. She was truly a pear flower dotted with raindrops and a West Lake immersed in mist. Of course, such an illustration is rather bland. In any case, Jasper was immediately swept up by an extremely intense emotion and wished to hug the weeping girl. So he said, "I want to hug you."

Snow Feather went over, and they embraced each other.

And then Snow Feather said, "Jasper, you've ignited a volcano."

Through some of the details described by Ajia, that segment of Jasper and Snow Feather's existence came to life in my mind.

Ajia mentioned the exchange of nuptial wine by Jasper and Snow Feather. I don't believe they did such a ritual because that was only common at the wedding ceremonies of secular couples. I doubt Jasper and Snow Feather would have cared about that ritual, but I was nevertheless moved by Ajia's portrayal.

Their action was shocking even to me, my vivid imagination notwithstanding.

According to Ajia, they used urine instead of wine and drank a mixture of each other's urine as fine wine. After they drank the "nuptial wine" while embracing, the way a secular bride and groom would, Snow Feather's face turned scarlet red. She said, "This wine really doesn't taste like much!" But immense happiness permeated her face.

I believe in the veracity of this detail. It wasn't possible for the muddled soul of a worldly deity like Ajia to create such a vivid detail. Besides, one of the five "sweet dews" they offered daily was urine. The other offerings included excrement, sperm, bone marrow, and blood. The purpose of making these types of offerings was to help the believer destroy the heart of distinction between filth and cleanliness. I heard later that Jasper even washed wild fruits in urine and had Snow Feather bite into them, and then she fed those chunks to him. It was precisely such details that added another dimension to the love between them.

Ajia said with excitement, "Back then, Jasper was struck into a swoon by a huge sensation of happiness. Snow Feather was so gentle and soft that she seemed boneless." He said her softness could only be found in those who had reached the pinnacle of their practice of inner cultivation. Jasper felt a tenderness surging in him the way a snowflake melted into a hot spring. He kissed Snow Feather's earlobes and heard her moaning, which resembled heavenly music. Snow Feather's eyes looked intoxicated; maybe her heart was also inebriated. Ajia said, "No matter how holy the practice of this cultivation was, its outer manifestations resembled love-making."

The Commencement of Couple-Cultivation

Jasper ignited some pine branches. Snow Feather's eyes were watery, resembling black grapes. This was a vulgar comparison, but very appropriate for this moment. Snow Feather stared at Jasper silently. Later, according to Ajia, Snow Feather had a dream in which she was also led to the Sitavana Pure Land and experienced prodigious bliss, which resembled a raging fire. I knew Ajia had gone overboard with his depictions. One must know that strictly speaking, he was a spirit who was still very much attached to his ego.

Jasper held Snow Feather's hands and stared at her silently. He felt no desire; he just sensed the warm illusory bliss. He was surprised that when he experienced the bliss of disaster-fire at the holy land in his dream, he felt no actual desire. He only sensed pureness, illusoriness, brightness (wisdom), and warmth. He remembered clearly what the young woman had told him. Jasper realized that Snow Feather was destined to be the Dakini goddess of his life. Sweat seeped from the pores of her palms and her nose quivered. Jasper smelled an intoxicating fragrance. Snow Feather had always exuded that fragrance that Monk Wu referred to as "vow-keeping fragrance." According to *Tale of the Goddess*, it was a fragrance specific to practitioners with pure hearts, who abided with utmost strictness to the Buddhist precepts. One's vow-keeping fragrance in fact derived from heavenly deities, rather than the person's human body. Many protective heavenly deities surrounded Snow Feather because of her strict adherence to Buddhist prohibitions. Her fragrance originated in those celestial beings. This view was later criticized by some scholars who felt inclusion of this concept would diminish the scholarly value of this book. But Ajia believed this concept was probably closer to the truth.

Jasper added some pine branches to the fire. The cave became brighter. Snow Feather's face turned red. Maybe it was from the heat of the fire; maybe it was from reflecting the fire. It turned red in any case. Normally, Snow Feather's face was very pale. The red color was very becoming; Jasper liked that reddish color very much. He wanted to kiss her red lips. But what he had in mind wasn't the ordinary concept of kissing. According to the teaching he'd received from the realm of brightness, he regarded Snow Feather's mouth as a bowl for sweet dew. For a long time, Jasper used to visualize a bowl for sweet dew during his meditative practices. It was held by the hands of a female Buddha and filled with the sweet dew of great bliss. Jasper heard Snow Feather's emotional moaning, a sound that resembled heavenly music. Jasper never expected her to make such a sound. Normally, Snow Feather was just a shadow, which floated like a cool breeze. It wasn't just Jasper, even the readers considered her a shadowy figure. It wasn't the author's inability to create her character but rather that Snow Feather was like this.

Snow Feather moaned. Jasper held her face, and she held him in a tight embrace. Jasper felt a fire rise within his body. He couldn't tell whether it was the fire of desire. He felt there must have been some desire since a part of him had surged up overbearingly. As he remembered it, he wasn't like this in the realm of wisdom. Back then, he just dissolved into great bliss, great illusoriness, and great wisdom. He had no corporeal body back then, and his "ego" vanished the way a drop of water vanishes in an ocean. However, at this moment, not only the "ego" but "that thing" also existed. It was dancing, carousing, and screaming—desiring to tumble down three thousand meters like a waterfall. He knew this was truly the fire of earthly desire!

Jasper did all he could to visualize the fire into an illusion. He thought, *All fires are created because of karma affinities and all are without their own nature. According to* Diamond Sutra, *they are all as illusory as dreams and bubbles, dew and lightning.* Although Jasper understood this, the surging fire still continued to charge at him and threatened to sweep him away. Jasper mustered all his might to visualize himself into the likeness of his own deity. *Woman is the most powerful force in the world after all!* he thought. His body apparently couldn't refuse woman, even though he had taken the tonsure.

Jasper knew this was the most dangerous moment. If he relaxed even slightly, all would be lost. He mustered up all his energy to merge himself into the meditative state of bright illusory nature—when his mind would become the sky, the kind of blue sky without a single cloud—to achieve the sensation he had after he'd attained illusory nature. According to *Historical Mirror of Forgotten Events*, Jasper had experienced this sensation several times before. The first time was when he was slapped by his father when meditating. His father's ferocious slap pierced right through his eardrum. It felt like he'd been struck by thunder; he was dumb for three days. The last time he had the experience was after he'd entered the Dakini Pure Land and received empowerment. Although the former gave him the sensation of illusory nature, he missed the opportunity—because he didn't realize it was a karmic occasion for him to attain illusory nature. But he caught the opportunity during the latter occasion because of its mysteriousness. Snow Feather said, the sensations of bright illusory nature and great bliss were none other than the Bright

Mahamudra. This was what Grandpa Jiu had told her. It was the wisdom attained after reaching Buddhahood. According to the renowned book by Tsongkhaba titled, *Brilliant Illumination of the Lamp of the Five Stages*, that "bright wisdom" was equivalent to the eleventh *bhmi*!

Ajia laughed and said, "Aiyo! So you've lent your experiences in attaining enlightenment to Jasper!"

Thus, Jasper merged himself into illusory nature. Thereupon heaven, earth, the cave, his ego and even the illusory brightness vanished. But if he'd continued to sink into this state, he'd have made the mistake of entering into "illusory nature without wisdom," a meditative state without the realization of truth. In such a state, even if he were to meditate for ten thousand years, he would never attain enlightenment. This was what Grandpa Jiu had told Snow Feather. So she taught it to Jasper. She was more advanced than he in terms of cultivation. Jasper had read many sutras and was profoundly learned and literary, but this had little to do with attaining enlightenment. Snow Feather was a woman of few words. She would frequently enter the meditative state of Mahamudra without wishing for it or attempting it. Just like me, she had practiced Mahamudra for many years before she knew its name. But this is a boring topic, so I'd better leave it.

Jasper didn't want to enter that state of "illusory nature without wisdom," which was a terrible trap. A guru named Tabor Raj,[8] who'd entered into that state, was able to eliminate thoughts for thirteen days. One day he told his guru about the experience. His guru said, "How could you eliminate thoughts completely? You were actually suppressing yourself. Why don't you practice visualizing fire in the navel with me instead?" Some of the readers may remember another story. An elderly woman made offerings to a Zen monk for more than ten years. One day she had the girl who brought food to him embrace him and ask him how he felt. The monk said, "Like a withered trunk against a cold cliff; not a hint of warmth for three winters." The servant girl reported it to the elderly woman. The woman said, "Who'd have thought I'd maintained a vulgar fellow for more than ten years?" Thereupon, she chased the monk out with an indiscriminate beating of the rod. The above stories are the best explanations for "illusory nature without wisdom."

Jasper knew "illusory nature without wisdom" was also a sort of attachment. Any kind of attachment is inimical to liberation. Jasper

---

8. Tabor Raj (1079–1153) was a disciple of Milarepa (1052–1135), a major figure in the history of the Kagyu school of Tibetan Buddhism.

thought of the technique the Dakini Goddess taught him and visualized Snow Feather as the sky and his hands as scattered clouds on her body. He heard Snow Feather's moaning but also merged it with illusory nature.

As Jasper remembered it, that night was the beginning of their couple-cultivation.

The Wisdom from Antiquity

I wanted to describe as realistically as possible the process of the couple-cultivation between Jasper and Snow Feather. This obviously could become a most valuable research resource. But whenever I began, Ajia would jump out and holler, "Don't write about it!" He knew what I'd write would be different from what the liars wrote. In order to prevent my describing the details of the process, Ajia created many "karmic oppositions." So, for an exceedingly long month and more, I was stuck attempting to write about their couple-cultivation. Ajia was always shouting and screaming next to my ears, making me so agitated I couldn't write. Of course, as an unenlightened worldly deity, his powers couldn't match mine. But he was also capable of creating "karmic oppositions." For example, he could get my son to cause trouble for me, so that I couldn't write in peace. He could also get people, who normally had nothing to do with me, to visit and prevent me from working. He could even cause malfunctions in my computer. By the time I got rid of the disturbances, my inspiration had vanished. So, thanks to his troublemaking, I couldn't even write a thousand characters in a month when normally penning ten thousand characters a day would have been a cinch. This was when one realizes the value of having a protective deity. Such a deity could be able to keep many interfering people and events from one's time and space.

It wasn't until I agreed not to write about what Ajia considered to be top secret related to couple-cultivation, that he and his underlings stopped harassing me. See how Liangzhou's writers have to sweat much more than those elsewhere with a protective deity like this!

Ajia, however, just laughed mischievously and said, "Hey! I did it for your own good? Have you forgotten the story about dividing the piece of yak butter, the one you wrote about in your *Jianggong Living Buddha and Shangpa Kagyu*[9]?"

---

9. This is the translated title of the book. The literal translation would have been *The Reliance for My Soul*.

A *gexe*[10] named Luosang, at one of the three great monasteries of Lhasa, divulged in one of his books what should have remained secret concerning the Dharma Generation Stage and the Dharma Completion Stage. The Dakini goddesses were displeased. One day, four girls arrived with a piece of yak butter and asked him to help divide it. Gexe Luosang took a piece of red thread, and used it to divide the butter into quarters. After the girls left, one of his disciples suddenly cried, "What happened, guru?" Apparently, two red lines in the form of a cross, the way the red thread divided the butter, had appeared on top his head. Luosang sighed and said, "I've angered the Dakini goddesses. I'm going to pass away." Thereupon, he took a bath and passed on.

Ajia said, "If it weren't for my stopping you, the top of your head might have already been split by the Dakini goddesses! Let me tell you—whenever you wrote about it, Dakini goddesses were glaring at you. It was only the purity of your motive and your proliferate use of figurative language that prevented stupid people from discerning the real meaning: that the goddesses turned their anger into delight." Ajia began to develop "anger" as he continued. The fire of rage incinerated his "forest of virtue" and his true self showed. "Look—so I gave you a bit of color, and you thought you had the dye factory? You became as greedy as a snake swallowing an elephant! Of course, I had to create "karmic oppositions!" That was my responsibility! What kind of protective god would I have been otherwise?"

The more Ajia continued, the more enraged he became. He prattled on in complaint, "Aren't you just a writer? Who do you think you are? Your offerings to me are but some liquor, dried fruits, and regular fruits. How can they compare with the delicacies of the mountains and oceans offered by the big shots? Who do you think you are, anyway? Not even enough money to build me a temple! Although I'm a protective god, I can only live wherever and receive just a few incense offerings. However, if you agree to rebuild for me my temple and have a statue erected for me, I'll ask the Dakini goddesses to accommodate you."

I retorted sarcastically, "Who do you think you are? You're just a ghost with strength! If I worship you, you're a protective god; if I don't,

---

10. Holder of the equivalent of a doctorate degree in Buddhism in Tibet.

I'd call you a puny ghost-spirit and you'd have to take it lying down! Okay, okay! I won't write its details, and you can stop your bickering and nagging!"

This was the first time I had a falling out with Ajia. His face turned scarlet from embarrassment. You see, I'd continued to make offerings to him despite all the "karmic oppositions" he'd created for me! If I didn't put him in his place, he'd think he was the God of Wealth or the God of Literature!

So, I could only write indirectly about Jasper and Snow Feather's couple-cultivation.

Then, I saw a light that radiated from the cave. It was an indescribable light—as bright and expansive as the firmament and as clear and blue as the sea. It resembled a lotus flower spreading through the sky, with the whistle of spiritual bliss flowing from each of its petals. Sometimes it resembled burning clouds, which splashed an aura that penetrated heaven and earth. Sometimes it resembled a kalpa conflagration from which waves of the blissful fire surged, incinerating avarice, dissolving anger, and eliminating foolishness.

It was a wisdom from antiquity.

Chapter 37

The Soul's Progress

I meditate amidst the light of dawn;
      I meditate amidst the quietude of night.
The voice and image of my guru always waver before me;
The mantra of my soul always resounds through my mind.
        Yes—it's bitter hard,
But I still want to meditate until I wear out a thousand prayer mats.

Mozuizi[1]

Jasper—so you left the cave and saw the desert mountain spill into the unknown. There was a renowned site below the mountain named Mozuizi. Artifact aficionados all knew about this famous graveyard. At the beginning, people of the Han dynasty were buried at the initial layer. Later, the peoples of the Jin dynasty, the Former Liang dynasty, the Later Liang dynasty, the Sui dynasty, and the Tang dynasty died, were also buried in this valley beneath the Xixia cave. The gully opened its mouth widely and said, "I will continue to bury them. I will continue until I become a wilderness of antiquity."

Sunlight shone into the cave. Was this the sun of a thousand years ago? The cave was very old. The mountain had already collapsed once. The earthquake of an unknown year and month shook the mountain; it toppled over, and the cave collapsed. A falling rock toppled over the pile of earth that buried the butcher's corpse. Amazingly, however, the

---

1. This place name literally means "argue pointlessly."

statue of Diamond Maiden remained intact. Naked and voluptuous, the girl's lower belly bulged, and the slit between her legs bespoke of the legacy of warmth left behind a thousand years earlier.

Diamond Maiden Cave is situated on that desert mountain. Resembling a reclining Buddha, the mountain is red in color and a wilderness without a single plant. But it is a holy land. It is said more than ten thousand streams of light connect this place to the twenty-four holy sites of the Dakini goddesses. One day, a guru came to the cave and transmitted the Bright Mahamudra to me. This dharma technique had already been transmitted for a thousand years. Because of this karmic occasion, the fame of Diamond Maiden Cave resounded throughout heaven and earth.

Several hundred monks, as well as a state priest, resided in this cave during the time of the Xixia. According to some records, Ajia was also a Xixia monk. Strangely, more than half of the manuscripts in the cellulose sack were signed by Ajia.

You said, "So, you actually snuck out of Xixia!"

Ajia giggled like a woman and said, "Wasn't it so!"

You also noticed Jasper on the pages of some odd papers. Strangely, it was through these that Jasper read about the Jasper of the manuscripts. Ajia said, "What's so strange about this? Although Anan didn't take the tonsure until the Buddha was middle-aged, he was able to repeat *The Garland Sutra*, narrated by the Buddha, when the Buddha first attained enlightenment. Such was the inscrutability of Buddhism." Jasper looked gloomy and remained silent. You ruminated over the strange writing for many days but weren't able to cheer up Jasper.

Ajia said, "Leave him! Don't you know he's crazy?"

"A madman?"

"Yes, a madman. When you realize this, you'll understand those incoherent writings!"

You looked at Jasper, who was still covered in gloom.

Ajia whispered, "Let me teach you a way. Calm your mind, empty your body, make heaven and earth vanish, and make all outer manifestations and yourself disappear. After a long while, you'll see a big hole. Enter, and go down and down into it. You'll eventually reach the world you want to reach."

"What place is that?"

"That is the abode of the soul. If you want to understand him, there's only one way—you'll have to turn into him." "Is that possible?" "Why not? You and he were but one and the same."

"Really? Let me give it try then!"

The Path

Close your eyes, concentrate, and listen to my narration.

Don't forget, that was the progression of your soul. No one cares about the soul anymore in this world; and it's likely that no one can understand it. However, history doesn't care about those who don't care about their souls. They will vanish in the hurricane of time.

You left the village and saw a fireball burning in the sky. It resembled the sun. The weeds around you were very dense. A marmot was crunching loudly while chomping on grass. You heard this sound when you and Dad slept in the horse stable. Yes, that was the sound of the horse chomping on straw at night. It was a strange noise and sounded as if someone were scraping sandpaper against the sky. Although the marmot didn't wear a horse bell, the noise it made was no less loud than that of a horse. The weeds surged furiously; soon you lost your way. You turned around but couldn't see the road you were on. You looked forward and saw nothing. The noise of the horse chomping on straw at night resounded throughout the sky.

You thought, *This was a path—but how come there are no footprints? Thousands of people must have walked this path, but there's not one footprint.* There was nothing you could do. *If there were footprints*, you thought, *then the trip wouldn't have felt so lonely.* But there were no footprints. Moreover, you didn't leave any footprints either. This was quite scary. You wanted to go back but didn't know how.

"Are there any other paths like this in this world?" you sighed.

All the paths are like this in this world. This was what you expected Ajia to say. But aside from the crunching on straw at night by the horse, you heard nothing else. *That Ajia obviously didn't follow me here*, you thought.

The weeds surged furiously and covered the fireball. The sky was bright but not blue. It was a grayish-white color, like a corpse's wrapping. Some insects flapped their wings and flittered around. You wondered if there was a path through their eyes.

You walked a long, long way as if in a trance—the length of several generations. You remembered a sea here before. The hillock you stood on was the bottom of the sea. Later, the bottom of the sea turned into a mountain. And then the top of the mountain was lopped off by a heavenly wind and became this prairie. A clamshell jumped into view in order to prove the truth of your dim memory. You picked it up and thought there should be a pearl inside the shell. But there was nothing in it.

"It had nothing!" you complained.

The discovery was most disappointing for you. You wished you hadn't opened the shell and had just assumed it harbored a pearl. But now, there was nothing in it.

You plopped yourself onto the ground. Night descended rapidly. It was as if someone pulled close a curtain and blocked the light after a few tugs. The noise of a horse chomping on straw also disappeared; so did the insects and the wind. A sound struck at your eardrums furiously. You knew it was your heartbeat!

Somebody should be around! you thought, but then realized: *those who were here before had already gone afar; those who will arrive are not yet here. There's nothing one can do about it, not even Ajia.* You want to weep. There's nothing more terrifying in this world than loneliness.

Night wept and released a blackness darker than ravens. You felt "pickled" by the darkness. You looked up at the sky and then remembered the sky was already dead. A black cloth larger than the sky covered its corpse. The goal of your quest was to save the dead sky.

You said, "I'm scared." But you were unable to find me.

You were moved to tears by yourself. You'd never been immersed in such dark loneliness before. So be it—you've already lost the way, in any case. The result of having no road and having a road drowned by darkness was the same. You thought, *Such is the fate of being human!*

You crawled up and shuffled along step by step. You knew that an even darker animal followed close by. It was panting heavily; you tried hard not to look at it.

You just yelled loudly, "Devour me if you want, I'm not scared!"

The Naked Practitioner

Dawn accompanied the appearance of the village. You didn't know whether it was a mirage or an actual manifestation. You didn't feel like investigating it either—it made no difference anyway. *Did I arrive at the holy land?* You wondered. You'd always yearned for the holy land, but it remained a puzzle.

A naked practitioner approached you and said, "How are you? I know you've traveled a long way. Do you know where the holy land is?" You asked, "Isn't this the holy land?" The practitioner said, "I don't know. Many people came here, one wave after another; they were all looking for the holy land. Some of them said this was the holy land. But many also left here in search of the holy land. Even my older brother left several years ago to look for the holy land." "Did he find it?" you asked. "I don't know. Many people left to seek the holy land. None of them came back. But outsiders who came here all claim this is the holy land. Do you think this is the holy land? We have a brilliant sun and white pigs, and women and wine. These should qualify our land as a holy land—what do you think?"

You said, "I don't know. I've been looking for the holy land as well. I've crossed thousands of mountains and rivers, and traveled for I don't know how many incarnations without finding it. I don't know where the holy land is. However, I think many places have the sun, women, wine, and white pigs; but holy lands are very rare." The person asked, "So, where is the holy land?" You said, "I don't know. I knew someone called Ajia—he said the holy land is the soul's resting place."

The practitioner laughed and said, "Is there such a place in this world?"

"Maybe," you said, "if people say it exists, then it should."

"What is the soul?"

"The soul is the soul."

The practitioner smiled and revealed very white teeth. His skin peeled from sunburn and had cracks. You were afraid to look at his crotch.

Suddenly, a group of women rushed at the practitioner, cheering like a flock of ravens. He immediately pulled a wooden face. The women prostrated before the practitioner and kissed his reproductive organ. Your body stiffened and you yelled, "Be careful—don't let them bite it!" Thereupon, the practitioner smiled. The moment he smiled, his "bird" began to grow. The women scattered away in fright.

"You shouldn't have been aroused!" a man hollered.

"That's right—hypocrite!"

A group of men with cudgels surrounded him and flung the cudgel at him. You yelled, "This is not fair. It was from their teasing!"

One of the men said, "Let's be fair—was that teasing? They were worshipping him!"

The practitioner turned to you and said, "Don't say anything—they'll beat you up! Leave! Send me a message when you find the holy land!"

"But I don't know your address," you said.

The practitioner was already struck down on the ground. You suddenly understood and cried, "Are you Ajia?"

"Who is Ajia?" The practitioner poked his head out from among the cudgels. His blood-stained face showed even more resemblance to Ajia. You yelled, "Why do you ask who Ajia is when you are obviously Ajia?"

"You are the one who is Ajia!" said the practitioner.

You were confused. Yes, many people say I'm Ajia. But if I'm Ajia, then who are you? You still hollered at the practitioner and said, "Ajia—I'll send you a message after I find the holy land!"

"You *are* Ajia!" said the practitioner.

The Holy Land

You followed along the mud pathway. Many practitioners populated the forest near the path. Some were gazing at the sky; some staring at the sun; some swallowing cattle dung; some worshipping fire altars; and some lying on beds of thorns. You shouted, "This must be the holy land! That Ajia was misled! Hey—is this the holy land?"

"Yes—it is!" they yelled.

"Where is the holy land?" you asked.

A Fire-Worshipper pointed to a fire altar and said, "Here!" A person lying on a bed of thorns pointed to the thorns and said, "Here!" You asked a Sun-Gazer, "To you, the sun must be the holy land!" The person retorted angrily, "Why ask if you already knew?" You turned around to a Dung-Eater and asked, "What do you say?" The person tossed a cow pie at you and said, "Eat it and you'll be in the holy land!"

Seeing the group of Dung-Eaters stop eating and proceeding to pick out the largest pieces, you knew they intended to stuff them into your mouth—so you took off.

"Don't run away—we'll send you to the holy land!" hollered the group.

You turned your head and said, "I know the way—I'll go there myself!" Before he finished speaking, it occurred to him that this was the first time he'd come here. He thought, I *should've asked them where the path was.*

"There is no path anywhere," said an old man.

He must know, you thought, *those who claim there's no path know where the paths are.* So he asked him, "Reverent One—where's the path?" Highly displeased, the man retorted, "What a stupid question! The path is where you're going!"

"What about the holy land?" you asked.

"It's where you want to be!" The man was already impatient.

You thought, *another madman,* and continued, "Do you know Ajia?" The man laughed and said, "You're Ajia's friend." You said, "I don't know if I'm his friend. Some people think I'm Ajia. But in fact, I'm not!"

"Why not? He is you—you are he!" The man's face flushed scarlet and looked angry.

You said, "But Ajia's already dead."

"Is he a Gonpo?"

"No."

The man spat and said, "Why mention him if he's not a Gonpo? But some people think Ajia is a Gonpo."

You smiled and thought, *I'm lowering myself by speaking to him.* Unexpectedly, however, the man grabbed you and pulled him[2] into a large hall. The hall was crowded. People were all hollering, "Gonpo! Gonpo!"

"Look—they're making an offering!" said the man.

Then, you saw a large altar with a naked young woman lying on top of it. Dagger in hand, a ritual priest was carving her body. The woman's face was giddily flushed and beaming with happiness.

"Gonpo! Gonpo!"

Red flesh fell onto the altar fire and sizzled. An aroma specific to human flesh pervaded the hall. People's noses flared to smell the aroma as they screamed for the Gonpo.

"Where is the Gonpo?" you asked. He really wanted to meet the Gonpo. He'd also made offerings to the Gonpo but never knew what the Gonpo looked like.

"The Gonpo is in your mind!" the man yelled.

You frowned and kept your distance from him. You'd heard such clichés too many times. But the man followed and said, "I know you don't like to hear this. I don't like it either. To date, I have no idea what 'mind' is!" You said, "I thought and thought and finally realized it is the holy land. Do you agree?"

You thought this idea made some sense.

---

2. The translator follows the original in changing the pronoun from "you" to "him" in the same sentence.

"Doesn't the Gonpo live in the holy land?" asked the man.

You immediately retorted in anger, "You are a madman!" Not admitting to it, he ran away repeating clichés. Judging from his gait, he was obviously a madman.

The ritual priest continued to slice the young woman's flesh and toss the pieces into the fire as an offering to the Gonpo.

But the Gonpo was nowhere to be found among the crowd.

Chapter 38

A Ritual from Antiquity

That ordinary summer day was not ordinary;
        The pure wind wafted gently—Green shadows swayed.
A Buddha-light wafted off a lotus seed of wisdom,
        And planted a lotus flower in my heart.
        I've searched for a thousand years
Wearing out five hundred pairs of iron shoes
Before I was able to obtain—that short but permanent meeting.

The Xixia Cave

Look—time flew away like a bird!

To Jasper, the boundary between him and Ajia had become blurry.

Are you still thinking about that story, the one situated in Xixia? It was said a practitioner meditated for a thousand years in a cave deep within the great desert of Tenggeli. He had the appearance of a piece of dead wood and was supposed to have been waiting for a woman: a woman who'd been worshipping the moon arduously for the past thousand years but who was still unable to rid herself of her fox body. It was said the fox did not know the location of the practitioner and searched for him every night. This fox, always lively, had become your totem. Frequently, you would unconsciously remember this fox, which had been searching for you painstakingly just to keep a promise from a previous life.

It was said that after performing arduous practices for many kalpas, the white fox transformed into the girl who brought him his meals.

According to the pile of manuscripts, Jasper was the practitioner after a thousand years. The moon-worshipping fox was Snow Feather's previous incarnation. The books were jam-packed with ludicrous stuff like this.

You've congealed into a piece of rock in Diamond Cave. You were meditating in isolation. The fire of wisdom had risen within you. Its red flames turned into a vivacious fox's fur, which began to lick at your veins.

Yet didn't you continue to hear her weeping chants on moonlit nights?

Look—here she comes again! She's entering into this book from the distant Xixia. Her garment was sometimes of Han dynasty style, sometimes Tang dynasty style—always indistinct at first glance.

You kept on thinking of her appearance. You were under the impression that she had a voluptuous figure, just like the statue of Diamond Maiden, with plump arms and a round lower belly. And her smile—it was the kind that exuded the insight of the soul. Later, a foreign artist named Da Vinci would capture it in a painting.

She must have exhibited other characteristics that made her stand out from the common crowd, but you were unable to imagine them no matter how hard you tried. You cried, "Please come out, Snow Feather! Let me take a look at you!" But the person who responded to your call turned out to be Ajia. He said, "What are you yelling for? Although the lady left Xixia, she'd been trampled into mush by the Iron Cavalry!" You knew he was lying, but you were unable to summon Snow Feather. In the mistlike curtain of rain, you could only espy her indistinct shadow.

The cloud and mist, which had flown into the distance, already concealed many a truth.

Only you, the arduous ascetic, remained distinct. Your shadow accompanied your form; your body resembled a rock. You tried your utmost to pursue spiritual transcendence yet you were "dragging your tail in mud." Ajia knew well that image had been around for a thousand years. You are still yourself; but the woman who had accompanied you is no more.

You wanted to trace the trajectory of her soul, but to no avail. Ajia said, "Stop wasting your energy. If you want to understand others, you have to understand yourself first. Don't you know? You are the others; the others are you. That peach-sized heart of yours contains all the secrets of the dharma realm!"

"Look! The colorful-cloud filled sky is her skirt. The brisk winds across the valley are her sighs. That smile, that desert, that gorge filled with iron chains are all just her limbs. Her soul, however, had already crept into a special book and turned into a bright candle. You, ah you! Why seek for a firefly when you've already discovered the sun?"

Thus Ajia nagged. He was always like that—most annoying! You understood his argument a long time ago, but you wanted to travel. It was easier to talk than to travel. You took a few hobbled steps and clearly heard Ajia sigh.

You finally saw Snow Feather. She entered the cave. Her features were blurry, but her youthful figure was lively and distinct. She put down an earthen pot and wiped her forehead. Her chest heaved and her face flushed. She looked at you smilingly. You'd finished reciting the merit-giving mantras and were lying there with your eyes closed. You were afraid of looking into her eyes.

The wind was screeching in the gulley like the whistle of Iron Hawks's arrows. You knew the wind was embarrassed and was trying to cover up the throbbing of your heart.

You understood "you." Many years later, there'd be a Thai monk named Chah Phothivan.[1] Living in desolate villages and graveyards, he cultivated himself arduously for many years until his mind was like dead ash. He thought he'd attained a firm Buddhist mind. But one day, he accidentally raised his head and felt as if he'd been struck by thunder. Because he saw a woman. He said, there's no animal in this world more beautiful than woman; there's no temptation in the world greater than woman.

Did you think so too?

I'm sure you thought so. Many years later, you would write, "I understood the terrifying magical power of woman. She can annihilate completely your Buddhist mind." During a fated chance encounter, you would meet the Snow Feather who'd returned.

But during this moment, the cave was filled with her gentle breathing. It was a roaming snake searching in all directions, spitting its tongue. You could feel it distinctly. Oftentimes, her aroma permeates my study. She could actually traverse through the time and space of a thousand years and locate me hidden in my secluded home. Ah you! I know exactly what you were up against!

You chanted the heart mantra to suppress the sensation of desire; but temptation bared its teeth constantly. Temptation had formidable support, which was the flesh. When the flesh surged with mountain-like

---

1. 1918–1992.

desire, it could smash to smithereens the mantras. Your flesh and soul were always at odds with each other!

"Wasn't that so, Ajia?"

"Don't ask me," screeched Ajia as he hopped into the distance. You knew you'd scratched where it hurt. Do spirits also have desire?

Ajia hid in the distance and cowered in a corner. He said grievously, "I would've been liberated a long time ago if it weren't for desire. Do you think I'd be waiting till now?" You laughed heartily, "That woman was not a wolf—what were you afraid of?"

Suppressing your increasingly heavy breathing, you ate silently. You saw it was a bowl of noodles. "The folks of Liangzhou are like this. They do whatever they'd done a thousand years ago. They are the incarnations of laziness. You're the only exception. Only you changed. As a result, spit hurled at you like a storm. But who told you to stick out anyway?" Ajia's voice sounded like the humming of a mosquito.

You finished eating. You wiped your mouth and handed the earthen pot to the woman. She looked at you without taking it. Only then did I see her face clearly. What a true beauty she was! A sort of wave undulated from her body—an enchanting type of wave. You obviously felt the wave. Beads of sweat seeped from the tip of your nose. Men with beads of sweat on their noses look funny, but Ajia didn't laugh. You thought, *Ajia must have been sweating too*. You couldn't see Ajia—he'd already escaped to a remote location.

"Go ahead!" you said.

Snow Feather bit her lip and turned away. This was often the way she left. You felt she'd said volumes. She was a wordless heavenly book.

A peal of thunder exploded in the sky.

Broken Pot

You felt the python deities were causing mischief. It must have been them—they were always entwined together with tails interlaced and causing the sky to be filled with rain. The villagers always saw them, and knew they were the dharma protectors of Diamond Cave. On a certain day during the twentieth century, you captured them with the click of an instamatic camera. You developed their image from film and presented it to your guru. You thought he'd praise you, but he said nothing.

When did the python deities arrive? When did the cave come into being? No one knew. You only remember that this used to be the bottom of a sea. And then the earth buckled up and became what it looks like now. "Did the python deities already exist when it was still a sea?" I asked Ajia, but he said nothing. He is the sort that's snotty to the weak but stoops to the strong!

You dimly felt the python deities might have escaped pursuit by thunder in Qilian Mountain. Emerging victorious from their fated disaster and greed, they gradually gained transcendence.

You know, that thunderclap was generated by those python deities!

Snow Feather left the cave. The sky was as black as the bottom of a wok. The wind was whistling, creating hemplike rain. Just like dragons, making rain was easier for a python than breaking a fart. Ajia hid behind the cave and made faces stealthily. He knew what the pythons were up to.

The python deities scooped up ladlefuls of water from the stream and splashed them into the mountain valley. Thereupon heaven and earth joined, with rain as threads attempting to sew them together. It was just as well they got sewn together. Too high a sky induces indulgence in inappropriate fantasies. I wanted to get a taste of trampling the sky under my feet. Ajia—have you ever had a taste of that? Ajia snickered. He always acts guilty, you know.

Snow Feather retreated into the cave, biting her lip and looking charmingly helpless. The crafty girl was sniggering, wasn't she, Ajia? Her face was awash with a red flush. She dared not look at you. You were obviously aware of it but acted as dumb as a wooden rooster.

As you remembered it, night followed rapidly as soon as the rain sewed heaven and earth together. You lit the lamp, the mountain goat oil lamp. The congealed oil melted gradually and formed a pool of cool freshness. A white wick trembled and bent over, holding in its mouth a pea-sized light. This was not the only light in the cave. The brightest light was in the heart and was in the process of accumulating power!

Snow Feather sighed as if she were totally helpless. Knowing what she was thinking, you said, "What awful weather!" Ajia could not help but crack a grimace. Snow Feather flushed from embarrassment.

So the two of them sat there, while the pattering of rain outside brought peacefulness and nervousness. Their breaths transported affection. Who would be the first to voice it? Ajia—any ideas?

It was the dead of night. You lay on your side on the three-foot circular prayer mat. You pointed to the "bed" on the floor and said, "You must be tired—go ahead and sleep."

You knew it was the fingertip that betrayed Snow Feather. The pea-sized light was extinguished. The fingertip roamed like a snake. It was parched with thirst but moved slowly. The throbbing of hearts filled the cave. Ajia had long vanished. You knew he always slunk away at crucial moments.

The fingertip touched your collar and spoke—so loudly that it reverberated to this day! At first the nails sang, and then the fingers danced. You felt the looming of a great disaster; you cried over and over again, "Gonpo! Gonpo!" You knew, however, the word "Gonpo" was useless at this moment.

Your pores began to quiver. Your blood rumbled. The sound of crashing waves shook your collar. You little demon! Ajia's dejection was inane. You shivered like a leaf in the wind. You wanted to escape to someplace but knew that locality did not exist.

The hands mutinied—the sweaty hands held each other. And then the bodies—the sweaty bodies embraced each other. And then the mouths. One day, a poetess would express the sensation: "It was like pouring water into water."

Snow Feather cried. You knew what she meant. She ripped off her garments—they furled like butterflies and filled the firmament of history.

You didn't know how you became naked. Your clothes also betrayed you with impatience. Your bodies twisted together. She moaned hysterically, with the wild abandon found only among Xixia people. You were breathless. "I'm going to Hell!" you screamed voicelessly. "I've taken vows!" Your voice became lower and lower. You felt something sweaty leading it along. It was a demon and an angel. It led your impatient body toward the unknown, inch by inch.

"Heavens!" Ajia's moans were hardly perceptible.

You heard a loud *boom*. You remembered that was when your body was set aflame. The cave whistled with the flames of great bliss. The fire rose, expanded, and filled heaven and earth. The ground shook within a sensation of delight. No—actually the ground had vanished—the ego had vanished—only bliss remained. What an ecstatic bliss! "Mommy—I will die!"

"Be careful!" yelled Ajia.

You knew what Ajia was referring to, but Snow Feather's moans rose feverishly. "Take me!" she screamed. You thought, "*Let me go to Hell if I must!*" You might as well charge forward—yes, charge forward!

"Ah—!" The woman seemed to have died after a loud wail.

The cave became completely silent—an empty void.

After a long while, a pair of hands groped and lit the pea-sized lamp. Snow Feather saw you sitting there quietly, ashen faced. She knew what it meant. Ajia said, "Of course she knew. Would you have loved her if she hadn't?"

Snow Feather wanted to tell you to weep out loud and wipe away the woodenness, but you just sat there like a piece of dead wood. You felt that once something was broken, everything had lost its meaning. According to the guru, you'd become a broken pot.

What is a broken pot?

A broken pot is a broken pot.

The Holy Land in the Dream

Continue to portray the trajectory of your soul!

Never mind whether anyone understands it. I don't think everyone was nearsighted during the past thousand years!

As you remembered it, the silvery-gray woman appeared in a dream. It must have been a dream. But one can never be sure. You racked your brain but were ultimately unable to distinguish the boundary between dream and nondream. Smilingly, she pushed you into a cave. What kind of place was that? You knew this was the holy land. It vaguely resembled the Xixia cave.

The holy land in the dream looked very ordinary, with mountains, valleys, and caves. You didn't know whether it was in Xixia. You didn't know. In the dream, you didn't know anything. You only knew that you were keeping a promise. You and she had a promised date in a vast wilderness during antiquity.

There were many others at the holy site. You didn't know their names, nor whether they were humans or nonhumans. You were also unable to distinguish the boundary between you and them. But there was nothing spectacular about the place. Nothing at all. The cave was very ordinary; indeed, so ordinary it looked just like a cave.

The woman said, "Come! I'll show you!"

You knew what she wanted to show you, but you felt calm. Although the words, "Buddhist vows" flashed through your mind, they gradually disappeared into the distance and became but an imprint of the evening. Mine is a clean soul, so clean that it's just a colorless and odorless puff of pure air.

"Do you believe me, Jasper?"

She pulled out a piece of paper, which featured the bizarre-looking script. "Do you remember this? I transmitted it to you that morning." You finally realized who she was.

Jasper—don't give away her name!

Snow Feather's Wisdom

You cried, "Dear Niguma! Please empower me and give me wisdom!" She smiled. She was obviously Snow Feather but Diamond Maiden even more so. Her trembling nostrils and translucent pores—every single soft hair on her glittered! Waves of temptation poured forth from her pores. That temptation was Snow Feather's wisdom, you know.

You felt the expansion of an energy within you. There's no need for explanation; I know what it was. It also came from Xixia. It roared and clamored like the tide at Qiantang. You knew you were trapped in a snare that you believed was attacking every single word in your soul.

You edged close to the woman. You saw her flushed breathing. Her roselike lips exuded waves. "Don't laugh! I know who you are, Snow Feather!" But this name was jarring. Forget it then! Everything was gone—heaven and earth, you and me, antiquity and present. You knew that the butcher knife of time would eventually lop off all names.

Come closer—even closer—so that I can see your pupils! Your pupils were filled with compassion. "Compassion" is a malicious word. The myriad roses bloomed in your eyes. Aiya! I don't know if anything more beautiful than this existed in this world! You looked at me shyly. I saw through your trick. I said, "Come closer!" You were always inciting me, but I'm not afraid of anything.

Your jadelike face turned red. Let's call it warm jade—warm jades are good! I stretched out my hand, traversed the changes of time, and placed it around your shoulders, which had been waiting for the past thousand years. I could feel the shoulders trembling lightly. There's no need for confessions; I know what you're saying. Best not to say any-thing—nothing can express what you want to say.

I took your hand and embraced your shoulders. The rumble of ocean tide also cuddled me. Dear Diamond Maiden! Be my witness and see how I took her to that remote locality, roaming toward life's unknown—by riding on a canoelike camelback across sand dunes, which seemed to keep getting higher and higher. In that other time and space, she will embrace you and sing another kind of song:

> Whoever wants to become a Buddha—go ahead!
> The truth of my attainment is Lady Yu
> Next to the piebald horse of the Hegemon King,
> And asking the world, who the real hero was?[2]

Now, don't say anything else. Just enjoy your solitude. Let the solitude ferment for a thousand or ten thousand years. I'm sure it will eventually obliterate the ecstasy.

I climbed up your mountain—it was trembling lightly. That was the breeze panting. That ultimate softness—was it your heart or the wind? Don't moan, love sickness is a loaded word. Just hold your breath and let the mountain fall silently under my palm. If you can't control it, then let it dance! Dancing is its nature—too much restraint, in fact, profanes it. Don't worry about saying the word "love" in the softest tone possible to melt me and the red dust of the mortal world—just go ahead and exhibit all your charms with abandon! But instead I said to stay quiet for a while. I only made an imprint upon your shoulder with the hand that held my pen. I was afraid you'd fly away. Heaven and earth are so expansive I wouldn't be able to catch up with your windblown skirt. I have no choice but to bare my protruding fangs to seek the treasured sweet dew. Lightly, lightly—don't startle you who are in a drunken slumber! In fact, however, there's nothing wrong with startling you! You had already been startled. I've wanted to be your wild boyfriend for a long time already—you seductive, foxy slut!

Thereupon, I scooped up the "charms of spring" forcefully and began to drink it. It's been three hundred years since I was moistened

---

2. Xiang Yu (232–202 BCE), self-proclaimed Hegemon King, was famous as a beloved hero in Chinese opera. Both his horse and his consort (Lady Yu) committed suicide to show loyalty to him.

by such a spring breeze. A sudden rise of the gale wrinkled a pool of spring water. Surging spring water pushed me up against the precipice of a dike. So I transformed myself into a vine to follow the path of your fate in search of the unknown. Do I see an immortal peach—the kind that ripens once every three thousand years? A quick glance—everything is carved out of jade. The peach is carved from jade; you are carved from jade. I can't tell what is real.

I inquired and inquired along the endless camel route, filled with imprints of your hapless name. My search was knitted into a net, which sought inch by inch, continuous and dense like the silken threads of a broken lotus root. Your calls echoed. In the echoes, plum blossoms filled a mountain slope. Spring water splattered, divulging an irresistible life force.

"Dear Diamond Maiden! Please accept this ritual, which hails from antiquity! And you too, Ajia, protective deity of Liangzhou! Open up your sealed bosoms to embrace the hurricanes of time!"

Wind blew from the ancient cave. Was that wind, or was it, in fact, water? Say what you will—anything would do. I will simply get ecstatically drunk and dissolve into you, the Xixia cave.

However, a sound approached quietly. It was imposing but ill-timed. She was always like that, always sounding during the midst of intoxication. Although I knew intoxication was a venomous poison, I also knew it was the best medicine. I was willing to swallow this medicine in order to discover the unknown, to interpret fate, and to transcend life and death. I understand you, Snow Feather!

I did my best to merge myself with the wilderness. The wilderness was as clear as a cloudless sky. There was also the seawater that accompanied us, keeping us afloat and tossing in great bliss. Please don't scream ecstatically—don't arouse my madness and infatuation!

Look, a fire raged! Some people called it the wildfire of genesis. But never mind! Let the souls dance in the fire! Let the heavenly breeze blow at me; let the billows cleanse me, and let the ceaselessly quaking earth rub me into a piece of white paper from a piece of uncultivated land.

You finally found the pathway in the fire. That pathway was as narrow as a horse's tail and as wide as the universe. You don't need to say its name—all names are but phony words. Was the bliss reality? No—nothing is absolute in this world.

A group of girls responded and arrived, singing and dancing. I shouted, "Are you Dakini goddesses?" A girl giggled and said, "You've mistaken the false for the real again!" You still thought she looked like

Snow Feather. Waving her wide sleeves slowly, she began to dance. You thought that the fire would burn her sleeves! Ajia said, "Let them burn then! You are too narrow-minded and attached to things!"

The pathway to great bliss wound forward endlessly, like a roaming snake. The universe also shook like a sieve sifting chaff. The universe was huge—it was a floating mustard seed in the cave.

You finally saw a palace. It was dancing like a rainbow. A voice cried, "Come here—my son!" So you forged ahead without thinking. You know, there were five palaces in your fate. Every day, they'd shout in unison, "Come keep your promise—you who's lost!"

You left yourself behind and charged forward, like a sperm rushing to the womb of a loving mother. The fire of great bliss chased after you and blocked the side roads. Thereupon, you also transformed into fire. Whistle and rage—the son of Niguma! The fire swallowed up heaven; it swallowed up earth; it swallowed up the wind; it swallowed up the rain; it swallowed up the bricks of the Qin and the tiles of the Han; and it swallowed up the traveling caravans of the past thousand years. You'd be the last to be swallowed up.

A voice shouted, "Wake up! You who's lost!"

The Heart of Bright Wisdom

As you remembered it, her eyes were tightly closed. She was afraid to look at you. You knew she was shy. Her naked body was studded with beads of sweat. She was voluptuous. Her upward tilting breasts refrained from breathing, but the nipples danced wantonly. They screamed ceaselessly, "Swallow us—you coward!"

You pushed apart her voluptuous legs—the "scenery" invaded your eyes. The flames of temptation surged at you once again. You held your breath and patted her jadelike thighs. She barely opened her eyes and cracked a smile. Red tide flew at her gradually and landed on her cheeks. "Save me—my woman!"

Using the brush of my soul, I painted on your bare back the shape of plum blossoms, just as you filled the wilderness with imprints of your life's steps. But why did you keep on moaning shyly? I distinctly heard the rising tide in your heart! I also knew a voice was singing in your palace, "Return home! Return home, ah, the traveler who'd roamed far and wide!"

I took the seal of my soul and stamped it on your craving heart, as well as over your flawless jade body. I heard people bestowing blessings smilingly. I knew who they were without looking. Their bodies were also stamped with Xixia writing, but they came from an even earlier era—so distant that it was beyond the mind. There's no need to trace its origin, all origin-tracing is but hapless sighs.

I swam and swam toward you. Did you hear my heart pound? No need to restrain it; it was but a ball of fire, no matter how it pounded. The fire raged in the mountain gully. There was also a drum—many people danced to it.

Come—let me embrace you, so we can taste the sweet dew! You were always crazy about shyness. My dear Fox, entwine and twist with me, like the pair of python deities! They are still entwined—the water in the mountain streams is rising. The waves crash as usual!

Embrace me tightly so that I can press closer to you. We'll merge with each other and dissolve into each other's lives. Mouth joins mouth, tongue wrestles with tongue; transform your pliant limbs into ropes, and abduct the soul and flesh once more! Let the manic wind bring the manic rain; and the manic wind and rain wash the manic you and me. Let us turn into rocks, merged and together until the leveled earth becomes wrinkled and then rolled into ten thousand leagues of yellow sand!

Lightly, my dear Fox—don't let the fire incinerate you! Right now you should follow the style of a gentle celestial—no gusts of wind nor bursts of rain. Just let your long flowing breath merge with the depths of my soul. A treasure resides there. Enter it! Happiness is but an ordinary word.

Be gentle—even gentler, ah my dear Fox! Melt away the fortress in my heart; melt away the quivers, and melt away you and me! Do you see? The soul is but a ball of expanding air, and the flesh is but dregs of dust in it.

Don't fly away! The sky doesn't exist anymore—it's jam-packed with your moans. Moaning is the mantra for fermentation—why don't you both scream! The world of this moment is but an intoxicating bubble. Come closer—be even closer. Don't evade me! I am the blaze of great bliss dancing wildly towards you. Why don't you transform into fire butterflies? Tens of thousands of fire butterflies are carousing in the blaze, singing a song from the Xixia. How familiar the melody is! It relates an elevated and rare tale of love.

Don't become intoxicated—stare into my eyes! Intoxication is a dizzy dark night that will engulf the clarity of your wisdom. Look at me quietly. Stare at the depth of my eyes for an impregnated shadow. Yes, it is Niguma, the Diamond Maiden. Merge yourself with it! You were she; she was you. You, she, and I came from the same source of life.

It was as if everything happened in the distant past. Their breaths became ever more distinct. Draped in wind and thunder and piercing through time and space, they swallowed up the world and filled the void. Like Ali Baba, I shouted, "Open sesame! Open sesame!"

You smiled, my dear Fox! You knew well that my shouts would not awaken it, but I will continue to shout until the day a full stop is placed on the world. Do you believe me? I know my throat has become hoarse. So I will shout with my soul. My dear Niguma—please endow me with more courage!

Embrace tightly my solitude! Embrace me tightly and turn me into a fish, so that I can swim in your sea of permanence! But Ajia is snickering. "Does permanence exist?" he asks. I wave away his image without answering. I'm just a fish—this topic is too heavy a topic for me. But I will answer it. I believe there is something permanent. "You're right—it is one's spirituality."

The spirituality also turned into a happily swimming fish. Can you feel it? There's no need to close your eyes—stare at me fixedly. Don't be afraid of those peeping Toms. They are time robbers who'd snatch away a piece of flesh now and then and put an end to many a permanent thing. But don't be scared—just fix your gaze upon my pupils. There's a smiling, red-robed woman there with a curved dagger in one hand and a blood-filled skull bowl in the other.

Take the sweet dew of great bliss and inject it into her body. Don't be scared of the dagger. Although its light flashes in ten directions and has butchered innumerable sins, you have not sinned—you are just a woman. Women are mirrors that reflect those who look within. In fact, sin is also something that can't exist on its own.

Contract your four great regions: the Shengshen region of the east, the Zhanbu region of the south, the Niuhe region of the west, and the Julu region of the north—they are but your four limbs. Everyone knows this secret, but no one wants to say it. Contract them, lest they leave you. And then absorb the rays of the sun and the moon and go with me to visit our celestial palace. The celestial palace is also filled with great bliss. They are all screaming, "Come to us—you moon-worshipping fox!"

Tell the earth to rise and exchange its position with the sky! Don't fear for the stars—they won't fall off! They are the radiances of souls.

The stars won't be extinguished if the minds aren't. Let them shuttle back and forth, from the east to the west, from spring to winter; shattering change into smithereens and forging objects you want to forge.

The rain continued to pour while the python deities danced. They dared not peek since a ray of light seeped from the cave. Such brightness! At first it was just a roaming thread, and then with a flash, the sky turned completely bright.

Ajia, could that be what you referred to as the heart of brightness?

Tides of Change

The two of you woke up.

You lay there naked, without wanting to dress. The sky was your cave, and the cave had become your garments. You only felt hunger. You opened the lid of the earthen pot. The once-delicious meal had turned black with mold. What mischief have you been up to, Ajia? How can an instant of ecstasy induce such change? Ajia refused to answer, however. You came out of the cave and noticed many more wrinkles on the mountains.

In the dimness of history, Ajia was weeping somewhere in the mountain range! He told you that the Xixia and the Song had fought several battles. That Yuanhao flung his arms and reduced the Great Song to wailing. A man named Han Qi[3] was traveling in the mountains then. When he arrived, he led a vigorous and lively cavalry of ten thousand. But now, they were filler for the cliffs of Xixia. Han Qi traveled alone, and his military flag had become a soul-summoning banner. Thousands of commoners wailed, "Sons! When you left, you were the shadows of Han Zhaotao. But now he came back alone. Where are your souls?" Flushing from shame, Han Qi said not a word.

Wronged souls also existed among the folks of Xixia. Those who brandish knives always attract knives. Back then, the entire population of Xixia was conscripted. Each time they embarked on a military expedition, they'd herd their cattle and sheep, bring along their households, and scream and swarm at the enemy, regardless of their age. Should they win, they would divide up all the looted riches on the spot. Should they

---

3. Han Qi (1008–1075), also known as Han Zhaotao, was a prime minister and poet of the Northern Song dynasty.

lose, they'd lose even their "capital"—their people and livestock. The households became the wind at the tips of waving swords, and were decimated without a trace.

Ajia said, "What belongs to someone else is someone else's. Why covet it?"

Snow Feather took the earthen pot and left the cave. She left hurriedly and was afraid of looking at you. You, however, worried that she might not be able to find her way back after that war.

The singing of children could be heard in the distance:

Under Helan Mountain, in the land of Hexi,
An eighteen-year-old girl wears a high coiffure.
Her fennel-root-dyed dress glistens like roseate cloud,
Yet, for lord and husband she takes a monk!

Ajia asked, "Anything else?"
Grandpa Jiu's voice arrived from the distance, "What else?"

Chapter 39

Coda

Clutching rosary beads in hand,
The wooden fish[1] pounds in my heart.
The black robe is the cassock of my present life,
The tall building is the cave of my past life.
Aren't you also worshipping the moon?
      You prayed to it over and over again,
      Tears flowed one stream after another.
Did they really enter the Pure Land?
Haven't you heard Su Shi proclaiming for a thousand years
That it is extremely cold up there?[2]

The Dakini Goddess

Grandpa Jiu told me about what happened the night before Butcher
Zhang found "release through salvation."

He'd heard it was a snowy day. The wind gusted. The wind is
always strong in the mountain villages of western China. So the snow
turned into arrows as vile as those shot by Genghis Khan!

---

1. The *wooden fish, also known as the Chinese temple block,* is a percussion instrument
used by monks and laity in the Mahayana *Buddhist* tradition. It is hollow and often
beaten during rituals.

2. This line derives from Su Shi's (1037–1107) lyric, "Prelude to Water Music,"
in which the poet intended to ride on the wind to the moon but then decided it
would be too cold up there.

At that very moment, an old granny entered into history. Wearing tattered clothes and hobbling unsteadily, she resembled a relief carving.

She looked like the Barbarian Hag Jasper had met.

You'd encounter this type of old granny in any of the small cities in western China. Carrying on her back a faded, tattered bag filled with shapeless garbage, she'd left her native home to roam far and wide. The sky is her home; the earth is her bed. She is a "beggar."

The person who arrived that day was an elderly person like this.

People covered their noses and avoided her.

There was also someone like this on the streets of Liangzhou several hundred years later. Whenever she slept, she'd be surrounded by several scabby dogs. People also covered their noses. Grandpa Jiu told me, "Don't underestimate her. She's a Dakini goddess." At that very moment, the woman suddenly vanished.

I heard that a young monk saw her at another remote location. The woman gave him some extremely dirty food and liquor. The young monk ate the food but did not dare to drink the liquor so as not to violate his vows. As soon he returned, Grandpa Jiu, who already knew about this, frowned and said, "You should have drunk the sweet dew . . . So be it! You won't succeed in your practices this life—you can always wait till your next life!"

"You missed an opportunity given by the Dakini!" said Grandpa Jiu ruefully.

The person who arrived at the small mountain village that day was also a Dakini goddess.

I heard she was a manifestation of the Wisdom Dakini Goddess Niguma, the founding ancestress of the Bright Mahamudra.

It was said that she came from a Pure Land named Sitavana.

Esoteric Technique

Grandpa Jiu told another story that day.

One day, a monk acquired an esoteric technique that would enable him to attain Buddhahood, that is if he practiced it for three years in isolation. So he hid in the depths of a remote mountain to practice it assiduously. On the last night of the third year, he had clearly attained observable wisdom. At that moment, he heard the inopportune wailing of a woman.

That day was also a snowy and windy day. The scene resembled the time when the "Dakini goddess" entered the village.

Grandpa Jiu said, the monk was no longer able to meditate. The wailing pierced through his ears incessantly and disturbed his soul. Although the monk knew the woman would undoubtedly freeze into an icicle in the snowy night of the remote mountain, he persevered in hardening his heart as firmly as a rock. He was as ridiculous as Tripitaka in *Journey to the West*.

He knelt on his bed and covered his head with a blanket. With his buttocks sticking out of the blanket, he held his breath and waited for the wailing to "freeze to death."

It was said that, at this very moment, a monk who'd been practicing for just three days also heard the wailing in the snow. He thought, *Well, I might as well forget about attaining Buddhahood—saving a life is more important.*

The next day, to the surprise of the monk who'd been practicing arduously for three years yet remained a mortal, he came face to face with a Buddha covered in glittering golden rays. He discovered later that the individual had only practiced cultivation for three days.

This story will accompany me for the rest of my life.

Although the bones of the impressive-looking Butcher Zhang and those of the poor eight-year-old girl remained in the same cave, people referred to the former as "skeleton" but revered the latter as Buddhist relics. The former was nothing more than that which polluted a bit of space, while the latter was cherished as a valuable treasure. Their difference lay in the disparity in their owners' hearts.

Those who understand this story, understand me: I, who had left the cave.

Karma

The wind blew ever fiercer the night before Diamond Maiden flew away. The snow flurries wove into a dense carpet. At that moment, the old granny in tattered clothes entered a small mountain village in the blizzard.

She didn't desire much—a place to stay for the night would do, lest those old bones of hers end up being tossed into the snow!

The old granny knocked at one gate after the other and received one berating worse than the previous one. The majority of them were practitioners who were chanting "*ah mi tuo fuo*," the name of the Buddha. They hated nothing worse than having their invocations interrupted by the inopportune old hag.

It was said that the angriest was Goodie Wang, who had attained the highest level of meditative practices. He was already able to see the long-awaited Buddha. How it shone and glittered! The Buddha held a golden dais in his hand, indicating that he would enter a high level in the Buddhist realm after death. It was during this very moment that the old hag banged on his gate! The golden dais disintegrated into twinkles before his eyes.

"Get lost!" roared Goodie Wang. He wanted to add something vicious, but stopped short of voicing it, for fear of creating bad karma.

He saw the woman smile. *Why did the old hag have such bright eyes?* he wondered.

That snowy night, the poor elderly woman experienced the entire mortal world smilingly. She seemed disappointed. The gates of all the good people ultimately remained tightly shut. They had good hearts but were unable to endure her dirtiness. They would even rather she died dirtily in the snow.

That was when Butcher Zhang, the one laden with the sin of killing, said, "Ah well! You might as well stay at my place! I'm not so clean myself anyway!"

Karma is based on just such a thought!

So the old woman told him not to let go of that girl the following day . . .

So, Butcher Zhang followed the girls and entered Niguma's Pure Land.

His putting down the butcher knife and attaining instant Buddhahood was caused by nothing more than the one good deed.

The Last Rumor

The reader may still remember the "Chicken Feather Notices."

It was said Kuan San confessed on his deathbed that he was responsible for the "Chicken Feather Notices" that led to the grain robbery incident. He only wanted to let the villagers eat a full meal and not starve to death, not expecting that some ended up "eating iron pellets."

According to *Historical Mirror of Forgotten Events*, a careful tally shows that the deed Kuan San committed was ultimately a good one; since aside from the few who stuffed themselves to death, there were no more deaths by starvation in the village after the Chicken Feather Notices. To exchange the lives of the few who were shot for the ultimate survival of Diamond Clan—this was a winning trade, no matter how one tallied it.

Kuan San's final confession changed the villagers' impression of him.

I also heard that Barbarian Hag's son finally returned. However, since she'd become a habitual cannibal, it wasn't until she carved up the corpse she'd clubbed to death that she recognized the familiar birthmark on its leg. Thereafter Barbarian Hag wailed nightly—her voice resembled crashing waves. She remained in the world forever as a wailing Yaksha. Heaven endures, earth endures, but both will eventually end; this unending wailing, however, will go on forever without an ending date.[3] If you listen carefully at midnight, you can still hear her unrelenting wailing!

There were many other unverifiable rumors.

A Vivid Totem

On a certain day during the twenty-first century, a giant locust tree in a shabby old courtyard covered the ground with its fragrant blossoms. Grandpa Jiu related Niguma's tale unhurriedly, the way one slurped down rice soup. He became my enlightenment guru. The setting sun shone on me, as well as on a hairy donkey. The donkey and I savored what he'd said quietly and smiled knowingly.

He was an earthy, simple, elderly man.

He was also as mysterious as a Dakini goddess.

Unfortunately, mortals were all misled by outer appearances.

Grandpa Jiu fixed his gaze and stared at me. But what was reflected in his experienced eyes was my own world. In it, I saw clarity like the sky and great bliss like kalpa fire.

Grandpa Jiu said he'd gazed in despair for a thousand years. He'd kept the most valuable treasure between heaven and earth and had been waiting for the arrival of an important moment ordained by fate.

---

3. This sentence parodies the last lines of Bai Juyi's (772–846) ballad, "Song of the Everlasting Sorrow."

Those guarding the treasure were none other than the two pythons. This merit entitled them to join the ranks of one of the eight "heavenly dragons," the Mahanagas. Having endured parching thirst, loneliness, and frequent itchiness of the skin during the past thousand years, they examined the immense void with the "heavenly eyes" they'd attained through practicing cultivation. One day during the twentieth century, they finally discovered the person. He left a corner of the desert and sought an unknown fate. After experiencing refinement of the soul, he became an expert of a mysterious writing. Among the mortal world within the expanse of heaven and earth, only a handful of people have mastered this writing. It was said the writing originated from the brightness of a clear mind.

I've already written the story of that man in *The Gray Wolves of Xixia*.

On a windy day laden with whirling yellow dust, many years later, Grandpa Jiu solemnly handed the treasure that had been hidden for the past thousand years in a Xixia cave to a man named Xue Mo.

Back then, although the sky of Diamond Clan remained the same, the appearance of the land had changed drastically. Sand was overflowing, and trees had withered and died. The good and honest folks were also showing their true colors. With glaring greedy eyes, they wanted to smash bones and suck up their marrow!

As for Snow Feather, she left the cave on a moonless night. She finally found permanence—it was the truth about permanence. It told her: nothing is permanent in this world. Years later, after she had endured many similar refinement ordeals for the soul, she'd merge into the dharma realm, amidst praise as well as condemnation. Her once exceptionally exquisite features would be embroidered into Tankas and become a totem for worship and adoration. The skull that held her thoughts was bought by me for a huge sum and made into a specimen to serve as a warning. Just like the cuckoo bird that chirped for the past thousand years, she'd cry, "Wake up! Wake up!" whenever I was deluded. Each mouthful of the cuckoo's blood[4] came from her enlightened heart.

In the melody of the tides of change, the moon-worshipping fox became a vivid totem—

---

4. The cuckoo bird, *dujuan*, which chirped until it spat blood was a popular literary trope.

Frosted wind made hoary your black hair
  But it cannot make old your search.
  Petals of plum blossoms
Shoot toward the horizon every night.
  The road to the end of the world leads not to your beloved,
Your beloved is the snow and rain of the tides of change.
  They always arrive quietly
  And leave quietly. . . .

First draft completed September, 2002
Second draft completed May, 2003
Third draft completed April, 2007
Edited at the Bright Mahamudra Studio in Liangzhou, March, 2009
Revised at the Bright Mahamudra Studio in Liangzhou, September, 2009
Edited at the Mahamudra Studio at Zhangmutou in Dongguan, January,
  2010

Postface

"Shattering" and "Transcendence"

I've always wanted to write about people who reside in another "time and space." They have their own unique mode of existence beyond the mundane world. Seeking tranquility of the soul, they abandon the ruckus of the ordinary world. They have their own dreams, their own reasons for living, their own value systems, and their own spiritual pursuits. It is impossible to understand them without entering their world.

Although all the characters in *Curses of the Kingdom of Xixia* have their prototypes in real life, just as Cao Xueqin[1] says of his novel, "Filled with preposterous words and heart-rendering tears, everyone deems the author crazy; who understands its real meaning?" One should know that these seemingly insane ramblings are the truest life experiences of another people. We might term them "metaphysical beings." However, their existence is not meaningless. They represent the spiritual searches of a group of people. When I wrote about them, I always burned incense, bathed, cleansed, and purified my mind and extended utmost sincerity. It was not until the draft was completed that I discovered the manuscript had taken the shape of something I'd never have imagined. I have no idea why it turned out the way it did.

It was beyond my control. All my books had their own karma or trajectory of fate.

Real writers are but mothers. They can provide nutrients to the fetus within but are unable to design its appearance and personality according to their own preferences. But they must respect its rights.

---

1. Cao Xueqin's (1715–1763) *Dream of the Red Chamber*, also known as *Story of the Stone*, is considered to be the greatest romance of traditional China.

They and their child should be two sovereign nations that can talk to each other, communicate with each other, and help each other—but not invade each other.

Similarly, I do not wish to invade my child.

I only want to clarify one point. Like my other works, I nurtured this book with my life, without any frivolousness. It represents my unique understanding of that unique world. I'd like to stress that the seemingly absurd world of *Curses of the Kingdom of Xixia* also lives within our hearts.

Life is an immense dream; at the same time, it also has real existence. Between existence and dream, there must be that which cannot be clarified. It's probably futile for a writer to attempt to clarify it, but I still immersed it into the babbling ravings of the novel. You might not burn incense and cleanse your heart before reading this novel, but you must believe I wrote it with utmost sincerity.

Before his demise, Yang Zhiguang, assistant editor of *Chinese Writers*, wrote a letter to Mr. He Jianming of the Writers' Publishing Co. that said, "*Curses of the Kingdom of Xixia* is a truly important work by Xue Mo. . . . From a literary point of view, this is a very unique and valuable work. . . . The writer poured into this book utmost sincerity, and his heart and soul."

If in writing *Sacrifice in the Vast Desert; Hunting Ground;* and *White Tiger Fortress*, I threw my life into them; then the creation of *Curses of the Kingdom of Xixia* was imbued with my soul. I was constantly in a state of intense excitement when I composed it.

It originated in the earnestness of my soul, without any intention of mystifying it purposefully. It was as if the work should have been like this and was not to be changed through human will. All my writings are completed in between meditations. Indeed, they are a form of meditation for me. Between writing and practicing cultivation, I value the latter more.

So although on the surface they underwent several iterations, the revisions were but artistic polishes resulting from awaited karmic opportunities. I dared not submit this novel to be considered for publication lightly, fearing lest an unappreciative editor might not give it the credit it deserved and ruin its "karmic inception."

I would like to thank Mr. He Jianming at the Writers Publishing Co. and the reviewers for their appreciation and tolerance, which afforded this novel the opportunity to see the light of day.

Observant friends can tell that this novel seems to differ from other contemporary novels. At the least, it announces Xue Mo's departure from his past. In one sense, I've "shattered" myself once again.

∾

During the first half of my life, I experienced the "shattering" of myself three times.

The first thing I shattered was my delusion toward life.

I discussed this in the preface to *Calamity of the Wolves*:

The greatest advantage to living in a village in western China was the opportunity to experience death. The clamor of large cities frequently drowns out people's hearts. The sound of death always seems faint, making it difficult for death to awaken the either happy or depressed city folks.

Where I lived was so quiet that the desire for material things became weak; consequently, the sound of death exceeded heaven and earth and filled the empty void. The sound of funeral dirges, Chinese oboes, and wailing would seek one out, without the need to pay special attention. One always saw flower wreaths and funerary garments flutter in the desert wind; one always heard news of deaths, and saw friends turning into ghosts at the drop of a hat; one always heard sighs lamenting someone's death and then the person who sighed would also become the object of sighs . . .

I noticed death when I was very young, and always felt it was a terrifying huge hole next to me, attempting to pull me in. I trembled day and night, terrified by the existence of such a thing in the world. Gradually, I realized not only would humans die, but the moon, the sun, and this earth would all die someday. So, a question arose in my mind: since everything will die, what is the significance of being alive?[2]

---

2. Xue Mo, "Tan zuojia de renge xiulian (preface)" in *Langhuo* (Beijing: Zhongguo wenlian chubanshe, 2004), 4.

Although in "theory" my attachment to life was shattered quite early, in "actuality" my real experience with death originated with the passing of my beloved younger brother, Chen Kailu.

My brother had always wanted to be a government worker; hence he was named Kailu, meaning "starting government emolument." Yet, he struggled until death and was nothing more than a migrant worker. Seeking government emolument but to no avail, his cherished aspiration was smashed to smithereens by fate.

In the postface of *Sacrifice to the Vast Desert*, I wrote:

My younger brother's death, to a large degree, rectified my view of life and improved the quality of my existence. Not long after I buried my brother, my study harbored a human skull which served as warning for me. It constantly cried, "Death! Death!" to remind me that death could always visit me the way it visited my brother. So, I evaluated my daily schedule in terms of hours. I always took into consideration whether certain things were worth wasting the time of my priceless life. Consequently, I conducted research concerning various aspects of the culture of western China and was able to write books that advance my own ideas, informed by my own style.

Aside from a two-year-old daughter and a two-month-old son, my brother left only a few pages of his diary. After his death, his house, furniture, clothes . . . his everything, including his wife, ended up belonging to others. But those pages of his diary remained his own. They recorded the struggles of his soul. This made me realize the temporary nature of life, versus the relative permanence of writing.

In order to pay for my schooling, my brother left school early and worked as a laborer. His death crushed me. I remained in a daze for a long time, unable to accept the reality. Whenever I saw a raven or something like it, I'd consider it my brother's reincarnation, and talk to it like the old woman in Lu Xun's short story, "Medicine." Back then, the only time I could be happy was in my dreams, because there my brother was still alive. Although he pulled a gloomy face and didn't say anything, I nevertheless longed for such dreams. Agonizingly, such dreams were rare, and then they eventually vanished![3]

Back then,

I tragically discovered that everything was meaningless. When death arrives, one's studies become meaningless, one's house becomes meaningless, and one's writings also become meaningless. Even if one writes a work that will be passed down through the generations—since even the universe has limited life, then even passing down through the generations is but a huge illusion. The date the earth ends, even Tolstoy is meaningless. Consequently, I was completely disheartened for a long time. . . . The change in my disillusionment occurred after I made contact with Buddhism. When I saw the Buddha sacrificing himself to feed a tiger and slicing his own flesh to feed an eagle, I suddenly discovered the meaning of life. The meaning of life is informed by one's spirit. Although the tiger, eagle and flesh have all been reduced to dust, Buddha's spirit was transmitted among people who'd lived for thousands of years through the form of stories. His spirit brightens souls and enables many to leave suffering and gain happiness. This was their significance. . . . The significance of literature is the same. It isn't about fame or profit; it is rather about the spirit that literature should possess. While fame and profit are like passing cloud and mist, the spirit is relatively permanent. . . . I believe good literature should satisfy the following: the world is better because of its existence; one is better for reading it; and its existence makes the world better. Good literature should satisfy these criteria."[4]

~

---

3. Xue Mo, "Didi, fumu ji qita (postface)" in *Damo ji* (Beijing: Zhongguo dabaike quanshu chubanshe. 2017), 501.

4. Xue Mo, "Tan zuojia de renge xiulian (preface)" in *Langhuo* (Beijing: Zhongguo Wenlian chubanshe. 2004), 1–2.

The second item I shattered was my delusions concerning the "literary circle." When I realized that the literary circle—which I've yearned to belong to for many years and into which I finally "ascended" after more than ten years of effort—wasn't as lofty as I'd thought, I was unable to write a single word for two years.

I also wrote about this in my preface to *Calamities of the Wolves*:

> People outside of the circle were always asking me: What is the literary circle really like? I replied: Some members are good and some evil. The good ones are comparable to Bodhisattvas; the evil ones deceive the world and steal others' fame.
>
> They would then ask: What percentages are the good and the evil? How would you assess them as a whole?
>
> I was silent.
>
> But privately, I do have an evaluation of the literary circle. My standard of evaluation was based on one of the songs of *Thirty-seven Songs on the Ways of Buddhists*:

> > If accompanying them causes the three poisons
> > to grow,
> > And ruins what one hears, thinks, and practices
> > ritually,
> > If they can change compassion and cause it to be
> > forfeited—
> > Distancing oneself from such bad friends is the
> > way of Buddhists.

> So, 'evil friends' are revealed by their engendering growth of the three poisons (greed, anger and stupidity), and one's loss of compassion when in contact with them.
>
> I entered the literary circle through serendipity. Soon afterward, I realized, with surprise, that I had unwittingly become corrupted. I became greedy and began to care about my ranking within the literary circle. I became angry when my works were maliciously denigrated. I also became stupid and lost myself day after day. When I returned to my small city in the west, I had unexpectedly lost the sense of calm and transcendence I used to have.

According to *The Way of Buddhists*, I had apparently met 'evil friends.' But none of the familiar faces looked evil. At a glance, none of the individuals were bad; in fact, some were clearly good people. Strangely, however, when I re-entered the literary circle, I unconsciously slid downward once again.

This was a bizarre phenomenon. There's definitely a problem when, instead of engendering high-mindedness among those in contact with it, the group fosters growth of the 'three poisons' of greed, anger, and stupidity.

Thirty-seven Songs on the Ways of Buddhists also mentions the 'good knowledge' one should be in contact with:

> If accompanying them causes the gradual termi-
> nation of evil
> And the growth of merit and virtue like a waxing
> moon,
> Making evident particularly love and respect for
> oneself,
> Abiding by such good knowledge is the way of
> Buddhists.

The literary circle doesn't lack members with this type of 'good knowledge.' But they undoubtedly aren't the majority; the literary circle couldn't have been able to foster people's 'greed, anger and stupidity' otherwise.

I urged myself to distinguish clear-headedly those with good knowledge from evil friends. But to my great disappointment, while I could discover sparkling elements in the individual members, the literary circle as a whole was imbued with a thick malaise which fostered an increase of the 'three poisons.' In other words, the Chinese literary circle at present lacks the soil and climate for healthy growth. Many 'good' people unconsciously become 'marinated' by its trends, and produce a sort of 'evil.' Even more terrifying is the fact that those who've been 'marinated' don't even realize they've been transformed. Instead, they tirelessly enjoy scrambling to it, as if it were a treasure.

When such a corrupt atmosphere prevails, unwritten rules develop to assist the trend. Only two options are available to any outsider encountering those rules: if you remain clear headed and independent, and keep your distance from the rules, then the rules will disregard your existence. The Shanghai writer Li Chaozheng, who'd written three million character words, is a case in point. Until his death, he was ignored by literary reviewers. Or you can become covertly coopted through the influence of 'evil friends' and ultimately become a source of 'evil' yourself.

At one time, I had sincerely wished to enter the literary circle and worked for it laboriously. But once I entered it, I resolutely wanted to beat a retreat. My beliefs and wisdom told me: all external matters and circumstances that foster 'greed, anger and stupidity' are 'evil,' and must be kept at a distance. The urgency of my escape was similar to that of a young deer that, having fled from the muzzle of a gun, wanted nothing more than finding a recess in the depth of a dense forest and lick its wound quietly.[5]

The so-called deep recess in a dense forest was my meditation room, used specifically for isolating myself from the rest of the world. During the past twenty years, I always had a meditation room, the whereabouts of which no one—including my family members—knew. I frequently lived away from people and practiced cultivation on my own.

During the many years after the two occasions I "shattered" myself, I even stopped writing completely and entered wholeheartedly into religion. Back then, for many years and months, I frequently entered into deep meditation in isolation. Greatly worried, my wife often shouted at me, "Why don't you write? What's the point of meditating your entire life? If Shakyamuni hadn't composed the Tripitaka Scriptures, would he still be the Buddha?" It was only through her intervention that I took up writing again.

---

5. Xue Mo, "Tan zuojia de renge xiulian (preface)" in *Langhuo* (Beijing: Zhongguo dabaike quanshu chubanshe. 2017), 2–4.

I spent almost my entire life practicing what I felt was truth. In a strict sense, the twenty years during which I wrote *Sacrifice in the Vast Desert, Hunting Ground,* and *White Tiger Fortress* were also the years when I embarked upon the cultivation of my personal character and search for wisdom. During those years, I wrote during the gaps between meditations. I often practiced four sets of three hours each of meditation per day. During isolation, I even meditated for more than twenty hours a day.

I practiced eight years of Theravada meditation and twelve years of Tantric Mahamudra meditation—and I received confirmation from expert gurus.

Perhaps, without such intense personal training and wisdom cultivation, I'd just be another ordinary citizen of Liangzhou. Many folks around me were satisfied with getting by with what they had in Liangzhou. I was surrounded by the shouts of drinking matches and the rumbling of mahjong. Aside from my own introspection and desire for character building, I could hardly discern any karmic assistance for success.

I would like to clarify, however—as I found out later—although the literary circle wasn't as sacred as I'd expected it to be, it also wasn't always full of the despair I felt when I was "shattering" it. It had a definite threshold after all, and did not lack the brightness I longed for. Indeed, I met many kind people there who helped me, even though I came from a destitute and remote place. I received many awards, without knowing any members of the judges. It was essentially due to the assistance of various karmic "honorable ones"[6] in my fate that I, son of a peasant family in western China, was able to attain my present achievements.

I would like to take this opportunity to thank all the "honorable ones" in my life!

∽

The third item I shattered was the shackles of religion.

I have written about my religious travels in the "postface" of *White Tiger Fortress:*

---

6. *Guiren* refers to someone who is not directly related to one but who nevertheless helps make a great difference in one's life.

For many years, I made pilgrimages, but never cared about the monasteries I visited. One year, I worshipped at almost all the monasteries at Mount Wutai, but did not remember any of their names. All I recalled was the process of making the pilgrimage and trekking peacefully during scores of days. Obviously, to me, making a pilgrimage was not to visit specific buildings or admire geographical scenery; it was rather a kind of spiritual yearning and awe. All my pilgrimages were merely for purifying my soul—to immerse myself in the immense energy and thereby dissolve my tiny self.

More often than not, I chose remote and desolate locations for my pilgrimage; for only when you reject the clamorous world and dissolve into peacefulness can you get close to the spirituality that is worthy of reverence and awe. Many times, I would approach the site of my pilgrimage, but then choose to contemplate from a distance, and then turn around; what I sought was not the buildings and statues. No—what I yearned for was a sort of spirituality and self-purification. Maybe those were real pilgrimages. To me, the sacred sites were no longer specific locations. They became instead a symbol—sites in one's fate which one must not profane or demolish. They were merely conveyors of my longings and yearnings—from whence originated the surging excitements of my life.[7]

For many years, I studied the more than ten renowned religions of the world, including Christianity, Islam, Hinduism, Jainism, and almost all the schools of Buddhism. I even examined in depth their branches. I was not merely studying them; I was in fact putting into practice confirmation of what I'd learned. The aim of "action" and "learning" was to assimilate nourishment for the soul. Once religion is institutionalized, it becomes an entity based on doctrines distanced from truth and without its original spirit; it becomes, in a sense, fetters and shackles. Of course, the same applies to institutionalized literature. The true spirit of religion is the pursuit of absolute freedom. That is, no outer appearance or existence can interfere with a subject's sense of independence,

---

7. Xue Mo, "Xiezuo de liyou ji qita (postface)" in *Baihuguan* (Beijing: Zhongguo dabaike quanshu chubanshe. 2017), 570–572.

peacefulness, and unrestrained ease—which is true liberation. However, once religion is institutionalized, it distances itself from such thoughts. The complex religious rules make religion into shackles of the soul, and secular greed also makes religion into a type of "business." The goal of hundreds of millions of believers was merely to exchange the pittance of their belief-cash for fortunes resembling gold mountains. Even more terrifying is the fact that institutionalized religion takes advantage of precisely this fact, and makes "belief" into another type of "incentive" for greed. As we know, almost all the desire-inducing incentives for greed are sinful. As a consequence, I have written in the "Inscription" for my *Jianggong Living Buddha and Shangpa Kagyu,* "True belief is unconditional. It consists merely of reverence and yearning for spirituality. Belief is not a strategy for seeking a reward. Belief is a goal in and of itself."

So is the writers' freedom to create. Only when all the systems, rules, appearances, and existences are nourishment for creation, and not cangues and manacles—that is, when no exterior appearance can interfere with the independent soul of the creative subject—only then, can freedom be produced. Freedom is a product of an independent soul; it is a genuine manifestation of the "absence of worries."

Therefore, strictly speaking, I am just a believer. I have never been and never will be the follower of a religion. I merely hold in reverence and awe of, and yearn for a type of spirituality; I've never wanted to prostrate myself under the feet of a "god" and be a "god-slave." I most dislike listening to religious jargon that is devoid of the topic of "wisdom."

When, as a "practitioner and learner," I acquired a type of spirituality beyond religion and reached an indescribable state, writing became my belief. After having observed the institutionalization of philosophies, the systematization of religions, and the utilitarianism of literature, I searched for something new. Something that could draw nourishment from religion, philosophy, literature, and art, but also transcend them. It would eliminate the problem of institutionalized religions, abandon the detail-mired complexities of philosophies and the superficiality of literature, to become something that could "dive straight to the heart." It would be simple, clear, clean, and artless; it would transcend names and appearances, and be capable of providing nourishment for the soul, the way spring rain moistens the earth.

People say that we live in an era without gods. Religious followers continue to worship, but the gods they adore are no longer there.

As mentioned above, I finally entered the core of religion after more than twenty years of studying and practice. Unexpectedly, however, I discovered that institutionalized religion was also a breeding ground for sin. Although religion overflows with the light of truth, it is also flooded with mostly blindly following multitudes, and isn't lacking in sinful "cells."

I also encountered some absurd experiences from my contact with institutionalized religion. I wrote the two books, *Jianggong Living Buddha and Shangpa Kagyu*[8] and *Mahamudra: Essence and Practice*[9], using several years of my life—which to a novelist, is something that cannot be bought with gold. They were immediately translated into English. The world of religion held two entirely different attitudes toward them. Mr. Ji Tiancai, biographer of Guru Gong Tangcang, scholar of Tibetan studies, and past editor of *Southern Gansu Daily*, praised them for revealing many secrets not stated explicitly in Buddhism during the past thousand years and considered them timely products of Buddhist culture that will invariably leave a heavy imprint in the literary history of Buddhism. According to Dr. Sun Wanpeng, a Canadian scholar of Buddhism, the two books carried out the rescue, excavation, systemization, and study of the nearly extinct Shangpa Kagyu Mahamudra tradition and possess epoch-marking cultural and far-reaching historical significance. Dr. Sun wrote,

> Shangpa Kagyu has always emphasized practice without pursuing false reputation. Transmitted for a thousand years until the present, it has preserved the most systematic, the most complete and the most quintessential heritage of the Mahamudra. Xue Mo was both its beneficiary and an important link for its transmission. Deeply versed in both Chinese and western cultures, he has assimilated the essence of many of mankind's outstanding traditions. Along with more than ten years of persistent practical cultivation for confirmation,

8. Xue Mo, *Wode linghun yihu* (Chengdu: Chengdu Foyuange Zuoming Fomu shang-mao youxian gongsi, 2006).

9. Xue Mo, *Dashouyin shixiu xinsui* (Lanzhou: Gansu minzu chubanshe, 2008).

his 'teaching,' 'confirmation,' the scope of his outlook, his viewpoints, and his learning, all surpass by far those of the traditional religious practitioners.[10]

Some gurus also awarded the author affirmation, confirmation, and authority. Many readers even cherished the books and considered them treasures. Some—such as Gu Zhicao of Shangdong—even wrote up to a thousand essays on them. After the books were translated into English, foreign scholars also came specifically to western China to meet with the author to ask him questions.

At the same time, however, those who wanted to profit from religion regarded them as poisonous snakes and fierce beasts. Acquiring the books at high prices (to keep them off the market), some buried them, some made paper pulp out of them, and some tossed them into the sea. This was because the books conveyed truths—views of Mahamudra—that differed from their own religious ideas. Mahamudra aims at eliminating names and appearances. It is a truth that opposes believing uncritically and endorses distancing oneself from believing and obeying blindly. Buddhism is atheistic. It has always opposed believing blindly and advocated belief in wisdom. The aberrant religions that aim at "thought control," on the other hand, achieve their own hidden motives by taking advantage of people's gullibility. Based on the "seal of Buddhist teachings," many of those labeled as "Buddhism" are, in fact, heterodox teachings. They steal the "names and appearances" of Buddhism, but the stuff they sell is actually heterodoxy.

Even worse, the main reason for their slandering and vilifying the author's work was because these books could induce their readers to have great faith in the author's teachings. Consequently, to the books' detractors, Xue Mo became an opponent in a fight over their "rice-bowl" (i.e., their source of income) and absolutely had to be eliminated. As a result, those who appreciated the books bought them at high prices as collector's items, while those who despised or feared the books also acquired them at high prices in order to destroy them. Consequently, the first edition of these books originally priced at forty-eight *yuan*, ended up selling for more than five thousand *yuan*!

---

10. Sun Wanpeng, "Dashouyin shixiu xinsui: yiben hua shidai de juzhu" in Vol. 2 of Xue Mo, *Guangming dashouyin: shixiu xinsui*, Appendix 2 (Beijing: Zhongyang bianyi chubanshe. 2011, 320–325).

This scenario is so amazingly similar to what was found in *The Platform Sutra of the Sixth Patriarch*,[11] that it is obvious that many corrupt practices in religion have deep roots.

A similarly absurd situation was also found concerning my scribbling "brushwork." Although I never claimed to be a calligrapher, those who love my "calligraphy" would travel great distances to ask for it and regarded it as a treasure once given. On the other hand, those who hated my "calligraphy" belittled it in every possible way—they hated Xue Mo's brushwork so much that even incinerating it and tossing away its ashes wouldn't adequately vent their immense ire. In cities, such as Chengdu and Shenzhen, there were even those who organized conferences to brainwash attendees and called for mass denunciation of my brushwork that rivaled book burning and the burial of words.[12] I couldn't help but laugh at the events' ridiculousness. After the clamor of all the praise and denunciation, my scribbling "brushwork" also unexpectedly became a collector's item in great demand. A friend in Guangzhou even offered me a huge sum for the exclusive rights to my "Mahamudra" brushwork. When I asked him the reason, he said someone with "divine eyes" claimed that those humble words gave off a "light," and had an aura of ingenuousness and spirituality found in "consecrated" objects. He also said things that gave off "light" can convey humaneness and bring peacefulness, freshness, and auspiciousness. But I had to refuse his offer because his "buying" the "exclusive rights" to them was for promoting business and would also have deprived me of the right to present them to those with whom I have a karmic affinity.

As for talk of them being "consecrated" objects, I just smiled. Repulsed by such concepts, I've never deemed miracles beyond the mind to have been more important than a humble "true mind." But a friend, a monk who'd comprehended the essence of religion, laughed and said, "Those Daoist priests who chant spells and draw talismans—aren't they also seekers of the 'true mind'? Once they find the 'true mind,' their wondrous brushwork in vermilion ink would find correspondence to the powers of creation. Herein lies the secret of talismans. The crooked, aberrant brushwork in red and black ink isn't really important."

---

11. *The Platform Sutra of the Sixth Patriarch* is a Chan (Zen) Buddhist scripture composed during the eighth to thirteenth centuries. The "platform" refers to the podium from which a Buddhist teacher speaks.

12. In 212 BCE, Qin Shihuang (259–210 BCE), the first emperor of China, ordered the burning of books and live burial of Confucian scholars.

All this became the nourishment for *Curses of the Kingdom of Xixia*. The fates of Jasper, Ajia, and Snow Feather reflect my pursuits and experiences.

Indeed, all religions possess light, and all light creates shadows. Light and shadow are inseparable. Many immensely moving stories have also taken place among other believers. Many gurus also withstood various pressures and confirmed my enlightenment in Mahamudra.

After I entered the Mahamudra, I spent twelve years maintaining this state of wisdom, before I was able to convert it into an inseparable light for my life. That was when I began a reassessment of religion. Mahamudra keeps one away from blind beliefs and foolishness; it instead reveres the subjectivity of the enlightened. When institutionalized religion charged at me, brandishing weapons such as "spiritual control" and "religious terrorism," I shattered it without the slightest hesitation. I broke the shackles of all the names and appearances of religion and assimilated only its beneficial nourishment and wisdom.

When something can become shackles rather than nourishment, then one has to sweep it out of one's mind—without the slightest hesitation.

Such is the real spirit of Mahamudra.

∽

Observant readers can tell that all my works benefitted from the Maha-mudra tradition's nourishment.

Even more so is the case of *Curses of the Kingdom of Xixia*.

"Mahamudra" contains some of the most brilliant wisdom in human civilization. It originated in the glorious civilization of ancient India. Hailing from India, the "Western Paradise," it took root in western China; and was a fruit of the coalescence of the Indian and the Chinese civilizations.

Although the culture of western China is as vast as mist and sea, its breadth can be manifested through two elements: its ballads and its Mahamudra tradition. While the ballads emphasize the emotional, the Mahamudra tradition accentuates the rational. The ballads are all-encompassing, while the Mahamudra tradition aims directly at the soul. The ballads are the wave sprays on the ocean, while the Mahamudra tradition is the sky above the ocean. However, the sky also exists within the ocean, and the ocean exists below the sky. The roseate clouds of the setting sun and the lone duck fly in unison; the autumnal water and the expansive sky share the same color. The ballads are the tales of the commoners, while the Mahamudra tradition contains the smiles of sages. The ballads represent outpourings of the soul; the Mahamudra tradition recasts the soul. The ballads employ great beauty to embody great benevolence, while the Mahamudra tradition manifests great beauty through great benevolence. The ballads win over the world with their distinctive local flavor; the Mahamudra tradition nourishes the world via its permanent universality. Complementing and serving each other, the two represent the breadth and depth of western China's culture.

The nourishment the ballads provided me is reflected primarily in my *Sacrifice in the Vast Desert*; *Hunting Ground*; and *White Tiger Fortress*. *Curses of the Kingdom of Xixia* clearly reflects the influence of the Mahamudra tradition on me.

Mahamudra emphasizes both concern for the moment and ultimate transcendence; it stresses both the building of culture and personal action.

Simply put, the implicit meaning of Mahamudra—literally, "Great Hand Seal/Imprint" in Chinese—consists of three main points:

The "Great" signifies vast realms, broad mindedness, and deep compassion.

The "Hand" signifies action, contributing to society.

The "Seal/Imprint" signifies the wisdom of comprehending illusoriness and possessing ultimate caring for others.

The most representative figure for the spirit of the Mahamudra tradition was Lama Thangtong Gyalpo, who was active in western China during the fourteenth and fifteenth centuries. As the founder of Tibetan drama, he was a prominent figure in the cultural history of China. He was also a landmark figure of the Shangpa Kagyu Mahamudra tradition.

In October 2009, the Xinhua News Agency announced the following: "The Autonomous Region of Tibet had successfully applied to the United Nations Educational, Scientific and Cultural Organization (UNESCO) to name Tibetan Drama as an Intangible Cultural Heritage. This constituted a high degree of acknowledgement by UNESCO and the international community of our nation's work in the preservation of Intangible Cultural Heritage. It will contribute to the self-esteem of the Chinese people, improve the ability of all humans in recognizing the value of its cultures, ensure the continuation of Tibetan drama in the Tibetan regions, and thereby advance the transmission and development of this cultural heritage."

Occupying a unique position in world theater, Tibetan drama wasn't created by literary giants. It was founded, instead, by a practitioner of Mahamudra. This phenomenon deserves consideration. It illustrates at least one point: only the great water of the wisdom of benevolence can keep afloat the great ship of art. The immortality of Tolstoy is a case in point.

I devoted a chapter to introducing Thangtong Gyalpo in my *Mahamudra: Practice and Essence*. I include here a rough reproduction of the chapter.

Thangtong Gyalpo is a historically recognized great guru, with merit rivaling the sun and moon, and fame lasting through the ages. He was an achiever of the wisdom of Bright Mahamudra. He sought to learn from renowned Buddhist masters, practiced cultivation arduously, and his fame spread far and wide. There's a song about him:

> Boundless was his illusory nature,
> A yogi who had attained enlightenment.
> He was just like a Fearless God,[13]
> His name was Thangtong Gyalpo.

People honored him with the title of "God Thangtong Who'd Attained Freedom."

After Thangtong Gyalpo attained the wisdom of Mahamudra, he left his cave, having gotten rid of the attachment to "names and appearances." Daringly breaking ingrained practices of religious institutions, he proposed that monks should leave monasteries, wander as errant priests, and help the people through relieving their sufferings; that is, manifesting benevolence through actual action. His conduct earned the love and respect of the people, but like a thorn it pierced the monks who were the beneficiaries of the traditional monastic system. They mobilized their own followers to oppose and isolate him. They used contacts to create obstacles for him and concocted rumors to slander and vilify him. Unmoved, Thangtong Gyalpo stood his ground and resisted the profiteers of religion. He opposed the so-called eminent priests who espoused the dharma but took no practical action. He said, "In benefitting the people, loathing, sorrow and sloth

---

13. The title of *wang*, which I have translated as "god" can also refer to "king" and "prince."

are all disasters. Eminent priests explicate the scriptures and expound on the dharma like singing songs, but disregard the sufferings of the people. Monks live in the mountains like wild beasts, and burrow into caves like mice in order to meditate; but they do not solve real problems for the people. Those who are willing to follow me must not fuss over their food and clothing. We have to use physical action to benefit the people."

Such was the spirit advocated by the Mahamudra.

So we see that the earliest advocate for "worldly Buddhism" was not Dharma Master Taixu. It was instead Thangtong Gyalpo, born in 1385, more than five hundred years before Dharma Master Taixu.

Thangtong Gyalpo's tracks spread throughout Tibet. Seeing how people frequently drowned in turbulent rivers due to the lack of bridges, he vowed to build bridges for the people. Back then iron and steel were almost as rare as gold, but Thangtong Gyalpo exerted himself and ultimately built more than a hundred bridges. More than fifty of them were iron-chain bridges, while more than seventy were wooden bridges; thereby he benefitted innumerable people. Luding Bridge, which the Red Army crossed during the Long March, was one of them. Thangtong Gyalpo worked as a blacksmith when he built the bridges, wielding a hammer and pulling the bellows personally like a coolie. One should know that, back then, blacksmithing was considered a lowly profession.

In order to solicit funds for building the bridges, Thangtong Gyalpo established a Tibetan Drama troupe for which he personally wrote play scripts and toured the region with the chief of Beina's seven daughters. For this, Thangtong Gyalpo was later honored as the founder of Tibetan drama.

Aside from his benevolence in bridge building, Thangtong Gyalpo also built numerous meditation places and temples. Among his disciples, hundreds attained Mahamudra's wisdom. Thereby Thangtong Gyalpo also manifested two other characteristics of the Mahamudra: ultimate transcendence and ultimate caring.

Thangtong Gyalpo's life was the stuff of legend. Concerning beyond-the-world dharma, his attainment of wisdom was unrivaled throughout the ages; concerning within-the-world dharma, his merit for building bridges and temples rivaled the sun and the moon; concerning culture, he was the founding master of Tibetan drama.

There is a memorial ballad in praise of Thangtong Gyalpo. It is profound and amusing. I record it below:

On a river with crashing and raging waves,
Stone-piled bridge-supports resemble hills,
Hills comparable to Mount Sumeru!
Iron rings link to form a chain,
How neat, beautiful and imposing they are!
Be they of high or low status, people
Cross the bridges smoothly and safely.
The poor are even more appreciative of his benevolence!
Ah! How Thantong Gyalpo of incomparable compassion
Has done a tremendous good deed for the populace!
Among other practitioners in the past,
There was no lack of those with exceptional powers
Who also wanted to benefit the various multitude.
But who among them could rival Thangtong Gyalpo,
In his caring for them like a wet nurse?
All the practitioners attained Buddhahood and left;
Was it due to shame that they hid from the people?

I have frequently said that what "Bodhisattva" refers to in Buddhism is not a personified deity. It should more appropriately refer to something spiritual—the spirit of benevolence. The spirit of benevolence, which emphasizes compassion, is called "Guanyin"; the spirit that emphasizes wisdom is called "Manjusri," and the one emphasizing courage and strength is called "Vajrapani." Buddhism represents such a spirituality. What it has illuminated throughout the ages is also this spirituality.

The Mahamudra tradition, for which Thangtong Gyalpo is a representative, transmits precisely such a spirituality.

I have frequently thought about the significance of life. I was deeply aware of the non-ego nature of dharma and the illusory nature of all things but was perplexed about the following conundrum: since "ego" does not exist, then what needs to be liberated? Since none of the myriad beings can avoid "creation, being, injury, and dissolution"—the world will eventually perish; then good deeds will also not be permanent—they too are devoid of existence and are as illusory as dreams. Consequently, what is the use of self-cultivation? I eventually realized that, although human existence is also an illusory phenomenon, so long as the person sublimates his or her character—or recasts his or her soul—relative spiritual permanence can be attained.

The meaning of many things has transcended those things themselves. The fleshly bodies of people like Lei Feng and Kong Fansen have, by now, disappeared into the dust of an unknown place. But their spirits are transmitted through oral stories and written accounts that provide everlasting nourishment for the soul. Herein lies the significance of the Mahamudra tradition.

We can't help but be moved by Thangtong Gyalpo's undertakings and try our best to distance ourselves from sin to become nobler. The significance of this transcends even that of his bridge building.

Similarly, Snow Feather's significance in *Curses of the Kingdom of Xixia*, has exceeded that of her own life.

~

The three Chinese words, "Great Hand Seal" representing Mahamudra, encompass all the mind-and-matter phenomena of human wisdom found in the sacred and secular realms. The "Great" is the root, the "Hand" is the way, and the "Seal" is the fruit. All three must be present: without the state of "Greatness," the "Seal" of recognizing illusoriness alone can exist on its own but wouldn't be able to exert great influence. Without the practice of benevolence in the secular world through action (i.e., the "Hand") the "Seal" would easily turn into "mad wisdom"; then the broad-mindedness of the "Great" would degenerate into empty discourse without a means for manifestation. Without the "Seal" and its wisdom of realizing illusoriness, "Great" and "Hand" would be merely secular techniques, making fruition difficult.

Only when the "Great" and the "Seal" are manifested through action by the "Hand" would it become meaningful. The "Mahamudra," without benevolence, is not the genuine "Mahamudra."

I am an inheritor and beneficiary of the Mahamudra tradition. *Mahamudra: Practice and Essence* (Gansu Ethnic People's Press) contains a detailed record of my experiences. Much of *Curses of the Kingdom of Xixia* benefited from my putting into practice the Mahamudra teachings. The richness of *Curses* owes itself to the rich experiences I underwent.

I've often said I'm only a believer. I will never be the follower of a religion and will never confine my soul to a "small" sect, the "large" religious institution of Buddhism, or the "numerous" religions. I hope to draw upon the nourishment of wisdom derived from all of humanity to enable myself to become a torch: one that can dispel darkness and bring light. Of course, the first thing this torch will shine upon is myself.

All my choices and practices are essentially but ways to transform myself.

When we want to change the world, we have to change ourselves first.

I wrote a poem once:

A gale blows at the white moon,
Pure light fills the empty void.
Sweeping away things and cognizance,
That would be the Mahamudra.

The difference between myself and those who make a living from religion is that I'm always shattering what they cling to. To me, true freedom can be obtained only after one is nurtured by all human cultures, rather than letting them be one's shackles. Those in the know claim that only when one has attained ultimate brightness and practiced the final sweeping away of the attachment to "things and cognizance," could nonattachment truly manifest itself. Only then would it be the true Bright Mahamudra. In other words, the final "sweeping away of the traces of attachment to cognizance"—that is, attachment to the dharma and to the barely perceptible nonbrightness—could one attain true freedom.

I wrote two poems, which recorded my feelings toward life after I shattered my attachments. One of them read as follows:

Once a person not involved in anything,
Into the mortal world I fell, serendipidously.
Having created havoc in the three realms
And a ruckus among the six sects,
On this day I realize the nature of being—
Which was non-death and non-birth.
Leisurely I retreat into the forest,
To be once again involved in nothing.

The second one said,

The common girl is also the pure girl,
Kicking up dust on a mundane path.
The delightful moon of the three pools,
Such is not what I seek.
As an immensely ordinary man,

I sincerely love the pure girl.
Cleansing away thoughts of awakening,
She picks lotus seeds on the West Lake.

Not long ago, I had a conversation with a Guangzhou writer named Mingzi. The topic of our conversation was "transcendence and shattering." I said, "I don't know what success is, what the state of existence is. Sometimes I feel like I was at that familiar place and found an old set of furniture I'd once possessed. The difference between myself and so-called successful people is that they won't let go of the rubbishy furniture, whereas I'd just smash the stuff." It's like that—I'm always shattering myself. When there's nothing more to shatter, then that would be the "No Meditation Yoga."[14] When I have shattered the highest state of existence, then it would be what I consider the "ultimate transcendence." Once I've shattered that highest state of existence, then existence would cease to exist, and duality would be no more. What is the state of existence? The state of existence is the discriminatory mind. Those who feel the state of existence still possess the discriminatory mind. A guru once said, "To shatter rubbish that others cling to obstinately, herein lies the 'charm' of Xue Mo." In fact, the first to be shattered was always myself. Take, for example, *Curses of the Kingdom of Xixia*—what it shattered first was the familiar Xue Mo.

During that conversation, I concocted a so-called Daoist-style song to manifest my feelings after I shattered my affiliation with religious institutions.

Without defamation, without acclaim, I arrived in nakedness;
With defamation, with acclaim, I leave in nakedness.
The defamation and acclaim have turned into cloud and mist;
Facing the sky, I turn my face up and heave a sigh.
Clearly and lucidly, I am awake within a dream;
Free and unfettered, I smile as I weep.
Facing heaven, I laugh without hearing any echoes;
Lowering my head, a shadow recognized by no one.
I seek for neither liberation nor truth;

---

14. This is the ultimate stage of the four stages of yoga in Tantric Buddhism, which consists of Concentration Yoga, Leaving Drama Yoga, One Entity Yoga, and No Meditation Yoga.

Without dharma, without ego, without a body in the flesh.
The hundred weeds cannot hide the way I came;
The disorderly clouds cannot distract me from my course.
Remembering that year, after I'd heard the dharma,
Shattering and establishing, seem like a lifetime ago.
The devotion of ten years, where it is now?
The vows of three lives, let it go wherever.
The demons from wherever are sniggering at me right now,
But it is heavenly music to my ears, as I live in contentment.
Yeeya! Dandelion flosses flow in the wind,
Floating and drifting, where will they land?
I send a letter to the Mingzis of Shangpa Kagyu,
Whirling wind and timely snow are a good match.
My mind is now devoid of perturbing clouds,
Moonlight shines like daylight upon the road.
Borne by a thousand-league swift wind beneath my feet,
And a bit of expansive energy in the midst of my bosom.
Cutting off my fetters, I've soared into the emporium,
To the ten directions and three realms, freely I roam.

It is heartening to me that those parts of my soul's journey and my personal understanding of life have not only been reflected in my two philosophical books but also integrated into *Curses of the Kingdom of Xixia*.

Allow me to add that all the poems at the beginning of the chapters—readers may not have noticed those celestial-like words—were selected from my unpublished poems. I've written several hundred poems, none of which have been submitted for publication. The writing of poems, just like my beliefs, is an end in itself and not a means for something else.